XANTH
BY TWO

TOR BOOKS by PIERS ANTHONY

THE XANTH SERIES
Vale of the Vole
Heaven Cent
Man from Mundania
Demons Don't Dream
Harpy Thyme
Geis of the Gargoyle
Roc and a Hard Place
Yon Ill Wind
Faun & Games
Zombie Lover
Xone of Contention
The Dastard
Swell Foop
Up in a Heaval
Cube Route
Currant Events
Pet Peeve
Stork Naked
Air Apparent
Two to the Fifth

THE GEODYSSEY SERIES
Isle of Woman
Shame of Man
Hope of Earth
Muse of Art

ANTHOLOGIES
Alien Plot
Anthonology

NONFICTION
How Precious Was That While
Letters to Jenny

But What of Earth?
Ghost
Hasan
Prostho Plus
Race Against Time
Shade of the Tree
Steppe
Triple Detente

WITH ROBERT E. MARGROFF
The Dragon's Gold Series
Dragon's Gold
Serpent's Silver
Chimaera's Copper
Orc's Opal
Mouvar's Magic

The E.S.P. Worm
The Ring

WITH FRANCES HALL
Pretender

WITH RICHARD GILLIAM
Tales from the Great Turtle
(anthology)

WITH ALFRED TELLA
The Willing Spirit

WITH CLIFFORD A. PICKOVER
Spider Legs

WITH JAMES RICHEY AND ALAN RIGGS
Quest for the Fallen Star

WITH JULIE BRADY
Dream a Little Dream

WITH JO ANNE TAEUSCH
The Secret of Spring

WITH RON LEMING
The Gutbucket Quest

PIERS ANTHONY

XANTH BY TWO

DEMONS DON'T DREAM
AND HARPY THYME

x

A TOM DOHERTY ASSOCIATES BOOK

NEW YORK

XANTH BY TWO: DEMONS DON'T DREAM AND HARPY THYME

Copyright © 2010 by Piers Anthony

Demons Don't Dream copyright © 1993 by Piers Anthony
Harpy Thyme copyright © 1994 by Piers Anthony

Map by Jael

A Tor Book
Published by Tom Doherty Associates, LLC
175 Fifth Avenue
New York, NY 10010

www.tor-forge.com

Tor® is a registered trademark of Tom Doherty Associates, LLC.

ISBN 978-0-7653-2415-3

First Edition: February 2010

Printed in the United States of America

0 9 8 7 6 5 4 3 2 1

XANTH

Contents

DEMONS DON'T DREAM

1.	Companion	11
2.	Ogre Fen	23
3.	Isthmus	35
4.	Water	53
5.	Pewter	66
6.	Hydrogen	81
7.	Black Wave	94
8.	Bubbles	109
9.	Germ	122
10.	Chasm	135
11.	Dragon	150
12.	Merci	163
13.	Virus	177
14.	Foundry	191
15.	Talents	206
16.	Gourd	221
17.	Ass	235
18.	Prize	247
	Author's Note	265

HARPY THYME

1.	Gloha	271
2.	Second Son	287
3.	Reconciliations	306
4.	Escape	325
5.	Xxxxxxx	349
6.	Marrow	373
7.	Madness	394
8.	Play	413
9.	Nympho	435
10.	Graeboe	453
11.	Metria	475
12.	Love	498
	Author's Note	526

DEMONS
DON'T DREAM

1
COMPANION

Dug was exasperated. "Forget it, Ed! I'm not interested in any silly computer game. They all claim to be so easy to play and so exciting, and every one of them has a squintillion stupid things you have to do just to get started, and then the games are just awkward figures on painted backdrops, and you have the May-I syndrome."

"The what?"

"You know. No matter what you do, you get an error message and you have to start over, because you forgot to say 'May I?' or something just as idiotic before you did it. Computers are great at that. They figure you're supposed to know everything before you start, and they're going to make you do it over and over until you finally figure out what they want, by which time you're sick of it all. I don't want to waste my time."

But his friend Edsel had the annoying fault of being too persistent. "I'll bet I can find you a game you'll really like. No May-I syndrome. No dull backdrops. Real adventure. Something you'll get into easy and never want to leave."

"And I'll bet you can't. There is no such game, because real people don't program them, just computer scientists who lost touch with reality decades ago."

"It's a bet," Ed said immediately. "What're the stakes?"

Dug refused to take it seriously. "My girlfriend against your motorcycle."

"Done! I always liked your girlfriend anyway. Give me a week to get the game in, and you can kiss her goodbye meanwhile."

"Hey, I wasn't really—" Dug protested. But Edsel was gone. Oh, well. It wasn't as if there was any real risk. Dug wouldn't take his friend's motorcycle anyway.

Now it was time to get into his homework. So he called Pia instead. "Hey, I just made a bet with Ed. The stakes are you against his motorcycle."

She laughed. "You better hope you lose, because that cycle needs work."

"I know. I won't really take it."

"But he'll really take me if you lose. He likes me."

Suddenly Dug was nervous. "You mean, if—you'd—?"

"A bet's a bet, Dug. You have to make good on it. You know that." She hung up.

Shaken, he stared at his unopened books. She had hardly seemed surprised, and not at all annoyed. Had he been set up?

It didn't take a week; Edsel had the game Saturday morning. "You crank this into your computer, and call me when you're sick of it. If you don't call in an hour, I'm calling Pia for a date, because I'll know I won."

"Aren't you going to stay and help me get the thing loaded? You know it's going to take time just to—"

"Nah. The bet is that you can do it yourself, with no hassle, and you'll really like it. So if I'm right, you won't need me at all, or care that I'm not around. If I'm wrong, you'll be on the phone within an hour to let me know."

"Half hour, more likely," Dug said grimly.

"Whatever. So try it and find out." Ed departed.

He seemed so sure of himself! But Dug had never met a computer program he liked, other than the one that blanked the screen after five minutes, and he seriously doubted that he would like this one. But if it was easy-loading, he'd give it a fair try, and still be on time with the phone call.

He looked at the package as he went upstairs to his room. COMPANIONS OF XANTH. This appeared to be a silly fantasy setting, exactly the kind Dug didn't much like. How could Ed think he'd go for this, even if it wasn't too hard to get going? Then he looked again. There was a picture of a young woman of truly comely face and figure, in an outfit resembling the sinuous contours of a serpent. Wouldn't it be something to meet a creature like that! Maybe she was the inducement; they figured that some poor sap like him would buy the game in the hope that she was in it. If she was, it would be only as an animated flat picture. A ripoff in spirit if not in technicality.

He settled himself by his computer table and turned the system on. While it warmed up and went through its ritual initial checks and balances, he opened the package. There were no instructions, just a disk. There wasn't even the usual warning note forbidding anyone to copy it. Just the words INSERT DISK—TYPE A:\XANTH—TOUCH ENTER. He had to admit that was simple.

He inserted the disk, typed the mysterious word, and touched ENTER. There was a momentary swirl on the screen. Then a little man appeared, almost a cartoon figure. The figure looked at Dug and spoke. His words appeared in type in a speech balloon above his head. "Hi! I'm Grundy Golem. I'm from the Land of Xanth, and I speak your language. I'm your temporary Companion. If you don't like me you can get rid of me in just a minute. But first listen a bit, okay? Because I'm here to take your hand and lead you through the preliminaries without confusion. Any questions you have, you just ask me. You do that by touching the Q key, or clicking the right side on your mouse. So go ahead—ask."

Why not? Dug touched Q.

There was a ding. A huge human finger appeared and nudged Grundy on the shoulder so hard that he stumbled to the side. "Hey, not so hard!" Dug had to smile. "Okay, so you have a question. You have one of those primitive Mundane keyboards, right? So you have two ways to do it. You can type the question so I can see it, or you can touch ENTER and it will bring up the list of the ten most common questions at this stage. Then you can use your arrow keys to highlight the question you want, and touch ENTER again, or just shortcut it by typing the number of the question you want. I'll wait while you decide. If you want me to resume without waiting, touch ESCAPE." Grundy took a step back, twiddling his tiny thumbs.

Dug found himself intrigued despite his cynicism. He touched ENTER.

Grundy reached down and caught hold of a bit of string at the bottom of the screen. He pulled it up, and a scroll of print unrolled. There were numbered questions.

1. HOW DO I GET OUT OF THIS CRAZY GAME?
2. HOW CAN I SHORTCUT TO THE ACTION?
3. WHO IS THAT CREATURE ON THE COVER?
4. CAN I GET MY MONEY BACK IF I QUIT NOW?
5. HOW DO I GET A BETTER COMPANION?
6. HOW DO I SAVE MY PLACE SO I CAN TAKE A PEE BREAK AND PICK UP WHERE I LEFT OFF?
7. WHAT MAKES YOU THINK THIS GAME IS SO GREAT?
8. CAN A FRIEND PLAY TOO?

9. WHAT'S THE PRIZE FOR WINNING?
0. HOW MANY PRINTED QUESTIONS ARE THERE, AND CAN
   I CALL THEM UP ANYTIME?

Dug smiled. It seemed they had had some player input. He touched 0, which he took to be 10; he realized that it couldn't be listed as 10 because when a player touched the 1 it would take him to 1 without giving him a chance to complete the number. That was one of the things computers did: pretending not to know what the player really wanted.

The question highlighted. Grundy came to life. "There are a hundred questions in this edition of the Companions of Xanth Game, and there may be more in future editions as we get more player feedback. You can call up the list anytime by touching HELP and paging down. For two-digit numbers you can hold down the first number while you touch the second, and both digits will register. But it's probably easier just to ask me."

It probably was. But Dug decided to play with the list a bit more. The questions were still on the scroll. So he touched 1.

Grundy animated again. "To quit this game, touch ALT ESCAPE and turn off the set. But I hope you don't quit yet; you haven't given us a fair chance. We hardly know you."

They hardly knew him? As if they were real and he was a mocked-up player! That seemed arrogant. But also intriguing. Dug touched 2. "To shortcut directly to the action, touch SHIFT ESCAPE. But I strongly advise against this, because there's more you have to do, like checking in, and you'll be stuck with me as your Companion. Once you know the ropes, you can skip this whole scene, but please don't do it this time."

Fair enough. So far there had been no confusion, and he had not yet gotten into the game proper. He could skip ahead and look at it, but it made sense to give the Golem his chance. He touched 3.

"That creature on the cover is Nada Naga, Xanth's most luscious eligible princess. She is one of the available Companions." Grundy cocked an eye at him. "Maybe it's time you asked about Companions, if that isn't clear yet."

So Dug typed WHAT ABOUT COMPANIONS?

"I'm so glad you asked about Companions!" Grundy said. "That is of course the name of this game, and the main thing that distinguishes it from others. In this game you are never left to flounder helplessly, guessing at the procedures. You have a Companion to guide you through. Anything you need to know, you can ask your Companion, and if he (or she, if you select a female) doesn't know the answer, he'll give you a responsive guess. He will also warn you when you are going wrong, and in general be a true friend to you. You can trust your Companion absolutely—except for one thing. Touch Y or ENTER if you want to know about that one thing."

Dug was tempted to touch the ESCAPE key instead, but was hooked. So he touched ENTER.

"That is smart of you," Grundy said. "You see, your Companion is your truest friend, ordinarily. But there is one chance in seven that he will be a False Companion. That one will pretend to be your friend, but will lead you into mischief and doom. So if you get that one, you must be wary, and not take his bad advice. Unfortunately, there is no obvious way to tell a Fair Companion from a False Companion, because they look and act the same—until some key point in the game, when the False Companion will betray you. You must judge only by assessing the quality of the advice you are given, and recognizing bad advice. If you are able to identify your False Companion, you can not exchange him for another; once you choose your Companion, you are stuck with him throughout the game. You can ask him to go away, but then you will be alone in the game without guidance and are likely to get eaten by a dragon, or suffer some worse fate. It is better to keep him with you, but to be wary of him. It is possible to win the game with a False Companion, just a lot more difficult."

The Golem paused, so Dug typed in a related query. SUPPOSE I JUST QUIT THE GAME, AND COME BACK NEW?

"If you try to leave the game and return, so as to get a new Companion, you will find that the layout of the game has changed, so that not only are you not certain whether your new Companion is True or False, you are not sure whether paths which were safe before remain so. If you are well along in the game, it is better just to continue. But it is your choice, of course."

This warning, rather than turning Dug off, intrigued him. So he could never quite trust his Companion. That promised a special thrill of excitement that would not have been there otherwise. He looked at the listed questions, and touched 9.

"The prize for winning the game, which is not easy to do, is to receive a magic talent, which will be yours in any future games you play. We do not know what that talent is, but it will surely be a good one, that will be a great advantage for you."

Sort of like getting a free pass to another game. Dug shrugged. He didn't care much about fantasy anyway, so this wasn't much of an inducement. He was beginning to get bored with this, so he touched 5.

Grundy frowned. "I was hoping you would decide to stay with me. I can speak the languages of animals and plants, and learn things that others can not." Then he smiled. "But maybe you still will choose me. Here are the six other Companions from which to choose." He pulled up another scroll.

This contained six names: Goody Goblin, Horace Centaur, Jenny Elf, Marrow Bones, Metria Demoness, and Nada Naga. Dug recognized the last name: the luscious creature of the cover. He didn't need to check the others. He highlighted Nada Naga, and her description and a picture appeared.

NADA NAGA, PRINCESS OF THE NAGA FOLK OF XANTH, WHICH ARE HUMAN/SERPENT CROSSBREEDS, CAPABLE OF ASSUMING EITHER FORM OR ONE IN BETWEEN. AGE 21, UNMARRIED, INTELLIGENT, NICE, BEAUTIFUL. ASSETS: MATURITY AND ABILITY TO ASSUME FIGHTING FORM. LIABILITIES: PRINCESSLY LIMITATIONS.

Being a princess was a liability? Dug had to laugh. He was prepared to cope with it. What fun it would be to have such a woman as his Companion! Without hesitation, he touched RETURN.

The picture expanded, and Nada Naga stepped out onto the main screen. "Thank you, Grundy," she said in a dulcet voice. Actually it was print in a speech balloon, but Dug could almost hear it. "I shall take it from here."

Grundy sighed and walked off-screen. Nada turned to Dug. "Please introduce yourself," she said appealingly. "Just type your name and description, so that I can relate to you."

Eagerly he typed. DUG. MALE. AGE 16. So she was five years older; who cared? This was only a game.

"Why, hello, Doug," she said. "I am sure we shall get along very well."

Oops. DUG, he typed. NO O. IT'S NOT SHORT FOR DOUGLAS, EITHER. IT'S JUST DUG.

She lifted one dainty hand to her mouth, blushing prettily. "Oh, I apologize, Dug! Please forgive me."

Actually, if she wanted to call him Doug or Douglas, let her do it. From her it would sound just great.

NO NEED, he typed quickly. I NEVER MET A PRINCESS BEFORE. It was a game, but it had become an interesting game, and he wanted to play it for what it was worth. He realized that he was losing his bet with Edsel, but he no longer cared. He just wanted to continue playing.

"It is a liability, being a princess," she said. "It was nice of you to select me anyway. I shall try to be an effective Companion for you."

I'M SURE YOU WILL BE PERFECT, he typed, speaking the words at the same time, really getting into it.

"Dug, may I give you some advice?" she asked prettily.

"Anything you want," he said, his fingers flying to keep the pace.

"It will be easier if you get into the scene with me. So that we can relate to each other more readily. Do you know how to do that?"

"I'd love to get into the scene with you," he agreed. "But you're on the computer screen, and I'm out here in real life." So maybe it was a foolish business, getting emotionally involved like this, treating her as if she were a real person, but it was fun. He was amazed at how responsive she was.

"This is true. But though I can not come out to join you, you can in effect come in to join me. You have to suspend your disbelief a bit, and refocus your eyes."

"I'll try." He wished he could forget this was a fantasy game, and just live the fantasy: himself with this lovely woman.

"You see, the screen looks flat to you because you are focusing flat. But if you will try to focus your eyes on something behind the screen, as if it were a window to another world, you will find that it becomes rounded. See if you can do it."

Rounded. She was already so nicely rounded that he hardly cared about the rest. But he obligingly tried to focus his eyes beyond the screen. The image of Nada fuzzed somewhat; that was all. "I don't seem to be getting it," he said.

"See the two dots at the top?" she asked, pointing. Now he saw them, hovering just above her speech balloon. "Try to make them become three dots. Then you will be in the right range. It may not happen right away, but once it does, you will know it."

"Okay," he typed. He was glad that he could do it by touch, so that he could answer her without taking his eyes from the screen. He refocused his eyes, trying to make the two dots into three. He didn't really believe that anything would come of this, but he wanted to give his best try to whatever she asked him to do.

The picture blurred, refocused, and blurred again. The two dots became four, then bobbed a bit and fused into three. And then, quietly, the third dimension came.

Dug stared. Literally. The picture was now 3-D! He wasn't wearing colored glasses or using one of those two-picture stereo dinguses; it was just the computer screen. But now the screen had become like a pane of glass, a window opening to a scene beyond. Nada Naga stood in the foreground, with the grass of the glade behind her, and the fantasy jungle in the background. It was all so real he was stunned.

"That's better," Nada said smiling. "I see you in rounded form now, Dug."

She saw *him* as rounded? She was the most delightfully rounded woman he could imagine! But he did not type that in. Instead he made a safer statement. "It's amazing! How did it happen?"

She frowned prettily. "I don't suppose you would believe me if I told you there's some magic involved?"

He shook his head. "I don't believe in magic."

"That's too bad. That is the second, and greater step. When you manage to do that, you will truly be in the game."

"Suspension of disbelief," he agreed. "I really wish I could! But I'm a skeptic from way back. As they say, I'm from Missouri."

She looked blank. "I thought you were from Mundania."

Mundania. Cute notion. "I think Missouri is a state in Mundania. The people there always have to be shown something before they believe it. So if you show me magic, I'll believe it. Otherwise—"

She smiled. She made a sinuous ripple, and suddenly she was a snake with her human head. "This is my naga form, which is natural to me. My magic enables me to assume human form, or full serpent form." She became a coiled python, whose reptilian eyes fixed on him as it slithered from the fallen garments. But he was not revolted. He could take snakes or leave them; he knew they were beneficial creatures, so he just left them alone. This one did not dismay him at all. He knew it was Nada, in the context of the fantasy game. It would be useful to have such a reptile on his side, if some game threat materialized, as was sure to happen when he really got into it.

"I realize there is magic in a fantasy game," he said carefully. "Things happen all the time in movie cartoons and such. People get flattened by steamrollers, and then pumped back into round with a shot of air, and they are normal again. So you might say that I believe in magic in such a context. But never in real life."

The snake slithered behind a screen, carrying the woman's piled clothing in its mouth. In a moment the human form reappeared from behind the screen, decorously dressed. "But if you come into Xanth, then magic will work. If I went to Mundania, I would not be able to change form; I'd be just a little helpless snake." She frowned. "I know; it happened once. But here we follow *our* rules. So when you can manage to believe, then you will experience magic."

"When I believe that, I'll be crazy," he said sourly.

"No, you will just be in another realm. But you don't have to believe, to play the game. Just remember that our rules govern here."

"I'll do that," Dug said, surprised by her responsiveness. It really seemed as if she were a real person, communicating through the barrier of his disbelief. "How do I play this game?"

She smiled again. The glade lighted when she did that; it really did become brighter, as if a slow flashbulb had gone off. So it was a foolish technical effect; he still liked it. She was just such a beautiful woman that he could bask all day in her smiles.

"Take my hand," Nada said, "and I will lead you into it." She extended her lovely hand to him.

Dug reached for the screen, then caught himself. He typed I TAKE YOUR HAND.

The scene expanded. Now he seemed to be *in* the glade, and Nada stood beside him, about half a head shorter than he. She turned to him, her bosom gently heaving, her brown-gray eyes complementing her gray-brown tresses. Suddenly brown-gray was Dug's favorite color. "Thank you, Dug; it is so nice to have you here."

"It's so nice to be here," he said, discovering that disbelief was getting easier to suspend, at least in this context. He knew he would never get close to a woman like this in real life, so he might as well do it this way. Certainly the way the scene had come to life was amazing.

"Now, this glade is a safe haven," Nada said. "But the moment we go out of it, we're playing the game proper, and there will be challenge and trouble. So while I don't want to bore you with too many explanations—"

"You aren't boring me," Dug said quickly. She could have been delivering the world's dullest lecture on Shakespeare's most boring historical play (which was a fair description of a normal English class session), and still have fascinated him. He was satisfied just to remain in this glade and watch her talk. Because she seemed to be genuinely interested in him. That was surely the fakery of the game programming, but it was excellent fakery. He remembered a challenge that was ongoing: companies were trying to build a computer that could maintain a dialogue with a person so effectively that the person would not know it was a computer. The computer would be in a sealed-off room, so the person couldn't see, and would have to guess whether there was a computer or a person in there. So far no computer had fooled the experts, but it was getting close. Nada Naga, as an animated projection for such a computer program, was awfully close. She seemed so alive, and not just because of her appearance.

She smiled again, as he had hoped she would. "Thank you, Dug. I need to be sure you understand what is happening, because it is my job to take you as far through the game as possible, and if you fail to win the prize, it won't be through any fault of mine. But my ability is limited, and in any event the decisions are yours; I can only answer your questions and advise you. I myself don't know the winning course. But I do know Xanth, and so I will be able to guide you away from most of its dangers." She paused, glancing at him. "Are you familiar with Xanth?"

"Never heard of it," he said cheerfully. "I'm not a fantasy reader. I gather it's a hoked-up fantasy setting, with beautiful princesses, ugly goblins, walking skeletons, and smoky demonesses." He had picked that up from the list of alternate Companions. "I presume I'll have to cross mountains and chasms and raging rivers, and fight off fire-breathing dragons, and find special magic amulets to enable me to get into magically sealed vaults where the treasure lies. And that there are so many threats lined up that the chances are I'll be wiped out early, and then I'll have to start over, knowing a little more about what to avoid. Frankly, I'd rather just stay here and talk with you." His glance fell to her bosom, and bounced away, because when he was standing this close to her he could see right down inside. He loved the sight, but didn't want her to catch him staring. She might put on a jacket, ruining the view.

"You do seem to have a good notion of the game," she agreed. She inhaled, and he almost bit his tongue. "But you can't win it by staying here. So soon we shall have to start the trek. Normally the best first step is to go to ask the Good Magician Humfrey for advice. Unfortunately he charges a year's service for a single Answer to a Question. Since that isn't feasible for you—"

"Right. No point in going there. Let's talk. Do you ever date Mundanes?"

"Date? Do you mean one of the Seeds of Thyme? We might find one of those if we go to the right garden."

He laughed. "I mean, do you ever go out with Mundanes?"

"I am about to go out into Xanth with you, to show you the best route to—"

"I mean like doing something together. Seeing a show, having a meal, talking. Having fun."

Her lovely brow almost furrowed. "We shall be pursuing the quest together, and we shall see what Xanth has to show along the way. We shall talk as much as we need. I hope this is not unpleasant for you."

She just wasn't getting it. So he tried once more. "Like maybe dancing together, and kissing."

Nada gazed at him, a peculiar expression crossing her face. She was finally getting it! "I think not. I am here to be your Companion. I am not your romance. Please do not try to kiss me."

Dug laughed again, but it was to cover up embarrassment. She had told him no plainly enough. If he tried to kiss her, she would turn into a serpent and chomp him. "I was just asking. So what else do I need to know about the game?" Because if he had to play the game to keep her with him, it was worth it.

Then he had to laugh at himself. Nada was a game figure on his computer screen! He couldn't kiss her anyway. Yet here he had gotten all interested, in the faint hope that she might agree to do it. He really was getting into this.

But wouldn't it be great, if it were possible, and she were willing! She was so much better than the girlfriend he had just lost to his friend. So foolish as it was, he was going to try to please her, in the hope that eventually she would agree to kiss him, even if it could be in name only.

Nada got down to business. "It is almost impossible to win the prize directly, because we don't even know where to look for it. So we shall have to go see the Good Magician, and hope that you can make some kind of deal with him for his advice. I know the way there, so will guide you. However, the path is dangerous in places, and we don't know what might happen, so we shall have to be very careful. There are enchanted paths, but those are for the regular folk of Xanth. We shall have to go cross-country." She glanced up, smiling briefly. "That means we will encounter those mountains, chasms, rivers, and dragons you described, and may not even get as far as the Good Magician's castle."

"If we don't, and I'm out of the game, may I ask for you again, the next time I play?"

"You may do so, but I will not be able to help you any better than the first time, because the threats will be changed. So you may be better off choosing another Companion, who may work better for you."

"Will you remember me, in the next game?"

"Yes. But it may be difficult for me, because I may have seen you get eaten by a dragon. That would be traumatic for me."

"Then I'll try not to get eaten," he said gallantly. "Is there any good way to discourage dragons?"

"That depends on the dragon. I will be able to back off a small one. But a large one—it is better simply to hide."

"Aren't there any repellents, or weapons, or whatever? So I could travel prepared?"

"There may be, if you are clever enough to find them. This is one of my liabilities: I do not know very much about human weapons, or how to use them. If you wish to exchange me for a Companion who does, such as Horace Centaur—"

"No thanks. I'll try to make do on my own." Dug looked around. "Is there a town nearby, where we might get weapons or supplies? That might be our first stop."

"There is Isthmus Village. I could take you there. But the people are not friendly to strangers. It might be better to avoid it. There are fruit and nut trees, and egg rolls, and pie plants, so food will be no problem, and perhaps you could prepare a staff or cudgel for your defense."

But Dug was feeling ornery. "No, let's try Isthmus Village first. That's a funny name; why is it called that?"

Nada bent down to sketch a map in the dirt in the center of the glade. Dug caught a compelling glimpse down her front, and wisely gave no sign, though he feared his eyeballs were about to bulge out of their sockets. Talk of three-dimensional effects! "This is the general outline of Xanth," she said. "This is where we are, at the edge of the isthmus. Here is the village a little farther along. It derives its name from its location."

Dug tore his errant eyes away from her décolletage long enough to glance at the map. "Why, that's the state of Florida!" he said, surprised. "You mean we're in the Florida panhandle?"

"If that is what you call it. It is the main route to and from Mundania, which is why we meet Mundanes here. But this is not your Mundane state. This is Xanth, and you must remember that, because there are things here you are unlikely to find in Mundania."

He had been glimpsing some of them, but of course he couldn't admit it. "Good enough. Let's get moving."

She straightened up, nodding. She started to walk to the edge of the glade, and it was evident that he was walking with her, because the scene shifted with his motion. This should be interesting, if only because of its realism. He didn't care about the prize; he just wanted to stay in the scene.

2
OGRE FEN

J enny Elf waited nervously in the chamber reserved for the prospective Companions. Sammy Cat, unconcerned, snoozed in her lap. She had to serve a year for the Good Magician Humfrey, because she had asked him a Question and gotten an Answer. But he had sent her to the Demon Professor Grossclout instead, and now she was part of this weird game for Mundanes. Why the demons wanted to run a game for Mundanes only the demons knew, but she was obliged to play her part.

Nada Naga had just left, being chosen as a Companion by a Mundane Player. That left the Demoness Metria, the skeleton Marrow Bones, the zombie Horace Centaur, and the polite Goody Goblin. In a moment a new person arrived, to fill the vacated space in the roster. She was a woman just about as beautiful and well endowed as Nada. She wore a gown as brown as the bark of a tree, and her hair was as green as foliage.

"Hello," the woman said. "Is this the Companions' den?"

The others sent glances around, but none of them connected. Jenny realized that it was up to her to answer. "Yes it is. Come and join us. I'm Jenny Elf, here to serve out my service for the Good Magician."

The woman stepped inside. "I am Vida Vila, a nature nymph. I owed Professor Grossclout a favor." She took a seat.

"Vida Vila," the skeleton exclaimed. "We have met before. I am Marrow Bones. I brought Prince Dolph through your region several years ago."

Vida nodded. "I thought you looked familiar. But I am not good with skeletons; they all look alike to me. That prince must be about grown by now."

"Yes. He married Electra, and they have twins."

"Oh, pooh!" Vida said, dispirited. That was impressive, because for that instant she became a growly bear. But she quickly reverted. "I hoped to marry him myself, when he got old enough. Princes don't grow on trees, you know, or I would have grown my own."

NOW HEAR THIS, a disembodied voice blared. IT IS TIME FOR THE SELECTION OF THE FALSE COMPANION.

"But we already had that selection," Jenny protested. She had been relieved when the lot had not fallen on her, because she did not want to be false to any person.

TRY NOT TO LET THE MUSH IN YOUR HEAD SHOW, the voice said sternly. It was Professor Grossclout, of course, the demon in charge. A NEW FALSE COMPANION MUST BE SELECTED BEFORE EACH PLAYER CHOOSES HIS COMPANION, SO AS TO PRESERVE THE ODDS. REMEMBER: ONLY THE CHOSEN ONE WILL RECEIVE THE INDICATION. THAT ONE MUST CONCEAL THE STATUS FROM ALL OTHERS. NO ONE MUST KNOW, UNTIL IT IS REVEALED IN THE COURSE OF THE GAME.

"Oh, get on with it, Clout," Metria muttered.

DID I HEAR A MUTTER? the voice demanded dangerously.

Metria's mouth zipped shut. In fact, a zipper appeared across it. She was a demoness, but she knew whom not to aggravate. The Professor was said to be a creature who had been wheeled from Hell, or something.

THE SELECTION IS—NOW.

Jenny kept herself perfectly still. No indication came. She had escaped selection, again. What a relief!

After a moment, she looked around at the others—and found them looking around too. Each was trying to discover who had been selected, but none of them could tell. It could be any of the seven of them, because Grundy Golem was also a potential Companion. Maybe the lot had fallen on him.

"Look out—here comes a Player," Metria said, peering out the window.

Immediately they all sat still in their seats, so that their images would be ready when the Player asked to see the prospective Companions. They could see the Player in the one-way window, but he could not see them until he asked to.

He? She. It was a girl. She looked sort of ordinary, but that was typical of all Mundanes. Her hands hovered over the keyboard, which was the clumsy way Mundanes had to access magic, and her eyes were fastened to her side of the window.

Grundy Golem was the master of ceremonies, and he was good at it. "Hi! I'm Grundy Golem. I'm from the Land of—"

"Why, hello, Grundy!" the girl exclaimed. "I'm so glad to see you. How is Rapunzel?"

That set even the loud-mouthed golem back. "She's fine. She's home because she's expecting a delivery by the—" He paused. "Do you mind telling me how old you are?"

"Sixteen," the girl said brightly. "I know all about the Adult Conspiracy. I attend a progressive school."

"Uh, yes," Grundy said, still somewhat at a loss. "So you have come to play our Companions of Xanth Game, Miss—"

"Kim. I won a talent contest, and this was the prize. To get the first copy of the new Xanth computer game. I love Xanth. So here I am."

"Um, there may have been a mistake. You're actually the second to play."

"The second? Oh, darn! Who's first?"

"A boy named Dug. We didn't realize that the first had been promised to you."

"Well, it wasn't exactly promised. But the game's not officially on the market yet, so I figured—well, never mind. I'm used to being second." She looked sad.

Jenny was getting to like this girl, for some reason. Maybe it was because she looked so ordinary, but had so much personality. The boy, Dug, had been handsome, but more like a blank in character, and Jenny was glad he hadn't chosen her to be his Companion. Of course he had chosen Nada; any male human being would. But this girl Kim was different, in a number of ways.

"So you know about Xanth," Grundy said, trying to get reorganized, now that this introductory spiel had been broken up. "But do you know about this game?"

"Oh, sure. All I need to, anyway. I have to choose a Companion, and she'll tell me everything else."

"You can choose a male Companion, if you wish," Grundy said. "I happen to be available."

"Gee, Grundy, you'd be great! You can talk to anything. But maybe I'd better at least check the others, just in case."

The window became two-way. Now Kim could see the six available Companions.

"Oh, there's Jenny Elf!" Kim exclaimed, delighted. "And Sammy Cat! Hey, Jenny, I wrote you a letter!" Jenny felt a thrill of pleasure at the recognition. "But I didn't get an answer." Jenny squirmed. "But I know how it is. You have a whole lot of other stuff to do, like getting better. The Mundane Jenny, I mean; of course I couldn't get a letter from Xanth."

Kim turned to Grundy. "I'm sorry, Grundy. I like you, really I do. But Jenny Elf's my favorite, and Sammy can find anything except home. I've got to go with her."

"That's all right," Grundy said graciously. There was nothing else he could do. He walked out of the glade.

Jenny stood and stepped through the window, into the main scene, carrying Sammy. She was really glad to be chosen, because Kim seemed like a nice girl, who already knew about Xanth. Jenny was also doubly glad now that she was not the False Companion. It no longer mattered who else had been selected, because the Player had chosen, and would deal only with Jenny.

"Hello, Kim," Jenny said. "Thank you for choosing me. I will try to be a good Companion for you."

"Oh, I know you will!" Kim said enthusiastically. "I wish this could be real, instead of just an old game. But I don't guess you can't tell me how to step into the real Xanth."

"Well, not quite," Jenny said apologetically. "But I can tell you two steps that will bring you a lot closer. First you have to refocus your eyes. Do you see those two dots?"

"I see them." In a moment, following Jenny's instruction, the girl had succeeded in bringing the third dimension. Instead of being a flat image beyond the screen, she became a rounded one, and the screen seemed more like a window. It was almost as if they were in the glade together. "Oh, this is wonderful!" Kim exclaimed.

"The other thing is harder. You have to suspend your disbelief. If you can do that, then you will seem to be right here in Xanth, because you'll believe it."

"Oh, I want to believe it!" Kim exclaimed. "I'd give anything to be in Xanth for real! But deep down inside, I'll always know this is a game, and not real."

Jenny was saddened to hear that. How could she convince the girl that it was Mundania that wasn't quite real? But that was why this was the harder challenge; people just couldn't make themselves believe what they didn't believe.

"Well, we can play the game anyway," Jenny said. "At least the visual magic is working. Now, I don't know what the prize is, or where to find it, so I think you will have to go to ask the Good Magician Humfrey, if you don't mind."

"Mind? I'd love to meet the Good Magician! Will I get to fight my way into his castle, too?"

"Yes, I'm afraid you will."

"Wonderful! Oh, this is so thrilling! I can't wait to get started."

Jenny was somewhat taken aback by this enthusiasm. She herself had had some trouble adjusting to the Land of Xanth, which was so different from the

World of Two Moons where she had lived before. But of course Kim was Mundane, so she had to be thrilled to be anywhere else. "We can start now, if you wish. Sammy can find us a safe path past the Ogre Fen." For each Player started from a different place in Xanth, so they wouldn't interfere with each other. Dug had started from the isthmus, but this was farther to the east. The demons moved the site back and forth each time.

"Oh, are we near the Ogre fen Ogre Fen? Will we get to see an ogre?"

"We don't *want* to see an ogre!" Jenny protested. "Ogres are dangerous. If we get near any of them, they are liable to squeeze us into pulp and plop us into a cook pot, or worse, if they're in a bad mood."

Kim looked disappointed. "Well, could we maybe just sneak by where they can't see us, so we can just catch a little glimpse? It would mean so much to me."

Jenny saw that they had a problem. "Look, Kim, maybe you are used to reading about Xanth, where nothing really bad happens to major characters. They just get scared, but it always turns out okay in the end. But you're not a Xanth character; you are a Player, and if an ogre catches you, he'll do something mean to you, like biting off your head, and you'll be out of the game. Furthermore, if you should come back in the game, not only will you have to start from scratch with a scrambled set of threats, that ogre will remember you, and come after you faster next time. It doesn't get easier to start over, it gets harder. So you don't want to run afoul of any ogres; they'll ruin your chances, even if you don't really die when they pull you apart and use your legbones as toothpicks. I'm sure Sammy can find a way through the Ogre Fen without encountering any ogres, and that's what we should do."

"But I don't want to get caught by the ogres," Kim protested. "I just want to see them. So when I go home I can say I saw a real live game ogre. What's the sense in playing, if I can't see what I want to see?"

"Well, I sort of thought you might want to win, and get the prize."

"Well, of course I want to win the prize! But the fun is also in the playing. I want to experience every part of Xanth, and enjoy it to the utmost. It's great already, just seeing it in three-dee and talking with you just as if you're real."

It was worse than Jenny had feared. Underneath all her knowledge of Xanth, Kim really didn't believe at all. So she wasn't taking it seriously enough. She had an Attitude Problem. This was sure to lead to mischief. But Kim was the Player, and she was the one who made the decisions. All Jenny could do was help and advise her.

"Well, if you insist on seeing an ogre, we'll go see an ogre," Jenny said. "I'll have Sammy try to find a path that leads to a place where we can see without being seen. But I still think it's a bad idea."

"It's a terrible idea," Kim agreed. "But fun, too. Adventure is the spice of life. Let's go!"

So Jenny set Sammy down. "Find a path that leads to a place where we can see an ogre, without any ogres seeing us," she told him. "Don't run ahead; just find where it starts." She had learned how to manage the cat, so that she didn't have to chase madly after him when he went to find something. She had first come to Xanth when Sammy had dashed off to find a feather, and she had followed him so he wouldn't get lost, but gotten lost herself. Since then she had been stuck in Xanth, but soon enough she had come to like it, though she did miss her family back on the World of Two Moons. The last thing she wanted to do was have Sammy run into some other world, so that they wouldn't be able to find their way back to Xanth.

Sammy headed off. Jenny held on to the invisible leash the demons had given her, so that she could tell by its tug where the cat was. Sammy couldn't feel the leash; in fact, he didn't know she had it. It stretched just as far as it needed to, invisibly long, but contracted as she caught up, until it was invisibly short. So she no longer had to dash pell-mell after the cat, trying to keep him in sight; he was always within the feel of her hand.

However, this did not make things perfect, because the cat took the most direct cat-route to whatever he was finding. If this was along a path, fine. But it could as readily be under a thorn bush, or up along a tree branch, or through a river. Or under the nose of a sleeping dragon. Sammy would zip by before the dragon woke, but Jenny was slower, larger, and smelled of elf, and all those things made a difference to a dragon. So care was still required.

In this case the cat merely zipped through the thickest tangle of a cornfield. The corn popped madly as she forged through it. "Oooh, firecrackers!" Kim exclaimed, delighted.

"No, just popping corn," Jenny said. "Oh, I hope the sound of it doesn't alert the ogres!"

Then she felt something sticking to her. She looked, and discovered kernels of caramel corn. They were overripe and gooey, so they made a real mess. She tried to pull them off her clothing, but they had melted in and wouldn't come out. Well, this was the kind of nuisance that happened, when she chased after Sammy.

Soon they came to the cat, who was sitting at the end of a path, licking the caramel from his fur. This was the one.

Jenny glanced at Kim. Kim was not really here; instead there was the square window to Mundania, showing her as she sat at her keyboard. The window was always right in sight, so that the Player could see the game scene; it moved along with Jenny. So it was easy to forget that Jenny was traveling alone, physically. Kim would not really be in the scene until she achieved the second act of belief, and believed in magic. But that would happen as the game progressed. Some things just took time to believe.

Jenny picked up the cat. They followed the path through the deepening reaches of the dread Ogre Fen. Jenny would be glad when they got out of here, because it was the kind of place only an ogre could like. The trees were warped, the victims of ogre pranks; some had been tied in knots, and others looked like pretzels. Some were in tatters, showing that once an ogre in a bad mood had passed. The ground was no better; it was grudgingly shifting from a swamp to a bog, and thence to a marsh; soon it would become a full fen. Fortunately the path itself was dry. This was because the ogres preferred awful paths, so didn't use this one; thus Sammy had found the one safe from ogres. Or at least less dangerous; no path was truly safe from an ogre.

They passed some cords hanging down from branches extending over the path. Jenny's elbow brushed one. It twanged loudly. Immediately several other cords twanged, forming a quartet of notes, as if several people were singing.

"What's that?" Kim inquired, startled.

"A vocal cord," Jenny said. "I hope it doesn't attract the ogres."

But when she tried to move on, she brushed another cord, and there was another group of simultaneous notes. She shuddered; the ogres were sure to hear this music!

They were lucky; no ogres came. Jenny breathed a sigh of relief. But she knew that the danger wasn't over. They needed to get out of ogre country.

They came to a hugely spreading tree whose trunk looked like thick rubber and whose branches had rubber rings spaced along them. The tips of the branches touched thin wires, which in turn swung away through the branches of other trees. There was a faint humming coming from the wires, and now and then a crackling sound.

"What kind of tree is that?" Kim asked. "It's grotesque!"

Jenny studied it. She had had to take a cram course in the flora of Xanth, so that she could be a good Companion and identify anything that might be either helpful or dangerous. "It's an electrici-tree," she said. "It has a lot of power, I think."

Kim laughed. "I'm sure it has! Maybe this is where our electric power comes from. I see the wires headed away. We better not stay here too long; the electric field might be bad for us."

Jenny looked. Sure enough, the tree's roots extended down into a shimmering field. There was water below, but the wire grass grew up thickly. She hadn't run into this in her studies; maybe she had snoozed through that particular lecture. "An electric field is harmful?" she asked.

"Well, we don't know, for sure. But folk don't like to live too close to power lines, just in case."

Then they heard an ominous thudding, and the ground trembled. "The ogres are coming!" Jenny said, alarmed. They must have heard the vocal cords after all. "We'd better hide in the tree."

So she scrambled up, with Sammy scampering up ahead of her, and the screen view that connected them to Kim angling along. Just in time; the first monster was already heaving into awful sight. Of course there was no such thing as a good sight, near an ogre, except the sight of a fast way out of sight.

"Oooo, an ogre!" Kim exclaimed.

"Quiet!" Jenny hissed, horribly alarmed. Ogres had adequate hearing: adequate to locate whatever they wanted to squish flat or pound into oblivion or chomp into quivering fragments.

"What are they doing?" Kim asked, in a lower tone.

Jenny studied the scene. It was a whole tribe of ogres, males and females, and they seemed to be looking for something. Then they spied it: a glowing ball nestled in the electric field. One ogre lumbered into the field and grabbed the ball—and burned his hands. He dropped it, with a small curse that set fire to the nearby grass. Or maybe it was the fiery ball that did that. "I think they're collecting a ball of lightning to heat their cook pot," Jenny whispered. "Ogres aren't smart enough to make their own fire, so they must have to take it where they find it."

"A lightning ball!" Kim exclaimed. "How Xanthly!"

"Not so loud!" Jenny warned.

But it was too late. An ogre perked an ear. "Me hear thing near," he said. Jenny felt deepest dread. Then he cocked an eye. "Me see a she!"

Disaster! "We have to flee!" Jenny said.

But the only route out was the one they had come in on, and the ogres were standing too close to it. The big male ogre was already stomping toward the electrici-tree. They were trapped.

The ogre reached up and whammed the branch they were on with his ham-fist. The whole tree shuddered, and the branch vibrated violently. Jenny was jarred right out of her perch. She screamed as she fell.

But the ogre swept his hamhand across and caught her by the scruff of her collar. "See she!" he exulted, waving her around for the others to inspect.

"Leave her alone!" Kim cried. "She's with me."

The ogre peered at the sound of her voice. There was the window-screen, showing Kim beyond. "Fox in box," he grunted, and grabbed the screen. He hauled it up to snout level, upside down.

"Eeeek!" Kim cried as the picture jolted around. Her hair fell away from her body as the screen was inverted. Then the ogre got it turned over, and her hair flopped back into place. "Let go of that screen!" she said, shaken. "Imagination in the game is fine, but this is ridiculous!"

The ogre laughed. "Me dump in sump," he said, shoving the screen down into the water of the marsh.

"Oh!" Kim cried as her picture emerged. "Blub!" Now her hair was soaking wet. "Stop that!"

"Just look—me cook," the ogre said, carrying both Jenny and the screen toward a huge pot an ogress was setting up. The lightning ball was already under it, and the muddy swamp water was beginning to bubble.

Jenny tried to think of something to do, but couldn't. They had fallen right into the worst possible situation: captives of the ogres. She had tried to warn Kim to be careful and quiet, but the girl hadn't paid enough attention.

But now Kim regrouped her composure. "You can't do this," she said angrily.

The ogre paused, evidently perplexed. He was trying to figure out how to ask why not, but couldn't make it rhyme, so he just stood there stupidly. Ogres were good at that. But then he put it together. "Not got?"

Jenny still couldn't think of an answer. She was really washing out as a Companion! She should have thought of some way to stop Kim from insisting on coming here.

But Kim was now defending herself. "You can't cook us just like that. We're people. You have to win us in a contest."

All the ogres looked at each other, confused. They had never heard of this. That meant that they couldn't be quite sure it was wrong. But Jenny was confused too. What kind of contest? An ogre could win just about any physical contest, especially if it required strength. Ogres were justifiably proud of their strength and ugliness. "How, now?" the ogre who held them inquired.

"We must have a stupid contest," Kim said. "To see who is most stupid."

The ogres liked that. They were most proud, with most justification, of their stupidity. They were bound to win such a contest. "Rules, tools," the main ogre said in what in a smarter person would have passed for bad rhyme and worse logic.

"It's like a game," Kim said. "You must be the Ver and I'll be the Pid. Those are our names. But we have to find the rest of our names. When we do, we'll know who is smarter, and so who loses."

The ogres were confused. That wasn't surprising; so was Jenny. What did Kim have on her mind? She obviously wasn't stupider than any ogre, and would be hard put to it to prove it, especially to an ogre.

"Me Ver," the ogre said. "She Pid." He was so confused that he wasn't rhyming.

"First put us down," Kim said. "You can't play with your hands full."

The ogre set the screen down next to the bubbling pot. He set Jenny down beside the screen. The other ogres settled on their haunches, waiting to see what to make of this.

Kim brushed back her hair, which was drying. "Now we will take turns naming us, until we find names that fit."

"How know?" the ogre asked, in another sloppy attempt at rhyme.

"Why, the other ogres will know," Kim said brightly. "When they hear a name that makes sense, they'll exclaim with recognition."

The other ogres looked doubtful. Their doubt was well taken; they were hardly smart enough to recognize any sense in anything even if they understood the game, which they didn't.

"I'll start," Kim said. "Sil. That's the name. Can you match it to our names?"

The ogre pondered hard. Fleas jumped off his head, annoyed by the heat. But it was no good; he did not know what to do.

"Like this," Kim said. "You are Sil-Ver. I am Sil-Pid. Are those good names?"

The ogre pondered harder. A wisp of steam rose from his head as a thought tried to forge through heavy resistance. He was unable to form a conclusion. Neither could the other ogres.

Jenny saw that the ogre's name made a word: silver. That could be considered a name. But it didn't seem to be very unintelligent. That might be why the ogres couldn't recognize it. What *was* Kim trying to do?

"Well, then," Kim said. "They must be bad names. You try one now."

Jenny was afraid the ogre's hair was going to catch on fire as he tried to think. But just as the first curl of smoke appeared, he got it: "Bop."

"Very well," Kim agreed. "You have challenged me to make good names with that. You are Bop-Ver and I am Bop-Pid. Are those good names?"

The ogres remained doubtful. So did Jenny. They were nonsensical names.

Kim looked disappointed. "I guess I couldn't make any good names with your suggestion. So I'll make another for you. Riv. Can you make good names from that?"

The ogre was finally catching on. "Me Riv-Ver," he said. "She Riv-pid."

There was a stir among the other ogres. "Riv-Ver," an ogress said. "River! Good name."

"Oh, my," Kim said, looking unhappy. "You did make a good name! It's probably a really stinky river, too."

The ogres clapped their hamhands, pleased. They were getting into it now. But Jenny wasn't; she didn't see how this was going to keep Kim's screen out of the boiling pot. She knew that if Kim's picture got boiled, it would be just as if *she* got boiled: she would be out of the game.

Then Kim frowned. "But is it a really obtuse name?" Then, seeing the ogres' confusion, she clarified her reference: "witless."

The ogres considered the matter, and slowly concluded that it was not ogrishly witless.

Now it was the ogre's turn to offer a name. "Chomp," he said.

Kim concentrated. "Now, let me see. You are Chomp-Ver. I am Chomp-Pid. Are those good names?"

It turned out that they were not. She had lost her chance, again.

But now it was her turn to supply a name. "Stu," she said. "Can you make a good name with that?"

The ogre tried. "Me Stu-Ver," he said. "She Stu-Pid."

There was a pause. Then an exclamation. They had recognized a name! "She Stu-Pid!" an ogress exclaimed. "She Stu-pid! Stupid!"

Then they were all chorusing it. "Stupid! Stupid! Stupid!"

Jenny began to get a glimmer where this might be headed.

Kim sighed. "I guess you have done it. You have found a good name for me. I'm Stupid."

The ogres were quick to agree.

"But we still haven't found a good name for him," Kim said after a moment. "Do you have another one to try?"

The ogres were unable to change mental gears so swiftly, and could not come up with a name.

"Well, then, let's try Cle," Kim said. "Does that work?"

The ogre managed to put it together. "She Cle-Pid. Me Cle-Ver."

There was another slow reaction. The ogres recognized a word! "Cle-Ver! Clever! He Clever!"

"Why, so he is," Kim agreed. "That must be his name. Clever."

"Clever! Clever! Clever!" the ogres chorused.

Kim frowned. "Now we both have names. He is Clever. I am Stupid. So which one of us is more stupid?"

"She stupid!" the ogre said, nailing it down.

"So he is Clever, and I am Stupid," Kim said. "So I am more stupid than he is."

They chorused agreement.

Suddenly Jenny saw the point. "So she wins! Because she is the most stupid!"

The ogres stared at each other. How had this happened? Kim had won the stupid contest! They had to let her go.

But when Jenny started to walk away, the ogre stopped her. "Elf no stupid," he said. "Elf go potty." He picked her up by the scruff and swung her toward the hot pot. Sammy Cat, perched on her shoulder, seemed about ready to jump off.

Oops. Kim had won her own freedom, but not Jenny's. Without Jenny as her Companion, she would not fare well in the game. She would not actually die if they dumped her in the pot; the demons would conjure her back to the character storage bunker. But she would be through for this session.

"Then we shall have to have a contest for the elf," Kim said. "But we'll need new names." She pondered briefly. "Let's see, you're male, so you must be called Gent. She is female, so let's call her Belle. Can we find good names?"

The ogre couldn't think of one, so Kim suggested one. "Co."

"Me Co-Gent," the ogre said. "She Co-Belle."

Cogent? Jenny saw that Kim had this set up for another win. But it didn't work, because the ogres didn't recognize the word.

Then the ogre suggested a name, trying to force a win for his side: "Dum."

Kim considered carefully. "Then you are Dum-Gent, and the elf is Dum-Belle."

Again the slow reaction. "Dum-Belle! Dumbell! Dumbbell! She Dumbbell!"

Kim's mouth opened in seeming dismay. "Oh, you have named her! She's a real dumbbell, all right!"

But Jenny remained smart enough to keep her mouth shut.

The ogres agreed. But the game wasn't over, because the ogre still had to be named. Kim suggested Intelli. And to the amazement of all, they got a good name out of that: not Intelli-Belle, but Intelli-Gent. Intelligent!

After some further consideration, the ogres realized that they had been had again. They had to let Jenny Elf go, too.

The two hastened to depart. Kim had evidently seen more than enough of real live ogres for the day. But Jenny had to admit that she had done a very nice job of getting them out of their picklement. She might make a good Player after all.

However, there was a lot more of the game to go, and not all the other creatures they encountered would be stupid.

3
ISTHMUS

Nada hoped for the best, but expected to settle for less. She had indeed been chosen to be the Companion of a teenage Mundane male, which was her worst-case scenario. He had already tried to get fresh, and male freshness was really stale for her. Almost as bad, he knew nothing about Xanth, and did not believe in magic. This was bound to be a real chore.

It had seemed considerably more romantic when the Demon Professor Grossclout had first broached the notion. He had explained that Clio, the Muse of History, was getting ready to write up another volume in her ongoing *History of Xanth*. She had assigned the production chore to the demons. They expected it to be a good story, and there were openings for major characters therein. "Provided their heads are not full of mush," he said.

Nada wasn't interested. She had little concern for the business of the Muses, and less for demons, and none for the role of a major character. "I just barely escaped having to marry a child, last time I was a major character," she reminded him. Now she hoped to remain comfortably retired, and let others carry the burden of notoriety.

"Ah, yes," the Professor said knowledgeably. "You needed to marry a prince, and only two were convenient. One was underage, and the other was your brother Naldo Naga. Now both are securely married, and you are Xanth's most eligible princess." He gazed at her through his impressive spectacles. "Have you considered that such an episode may be excellent for introducing you to new prospects?"

Nada's sleeping interest began to stir. "Prospects?"

"If a new eligible prince of sufficient age is to show up anywhere, it will be in such a volume. I should think you would want to be on hand for the occasion."

The demon was beginning to get to her. Nada was now in her thoroughly marriageable decade, and time was passing. It would be disheartening if a suitable prospect escaped because she wasn't keeping an eye on the scene.

"But why are the demons involved in this?" she inquired. "Demons are never major characters. They care nothing about human events, unless they wish to interfere with them."

"Will you make a princessly oath of secrecy?" the Professor asked. "The question has an answer, but it is not given for mere humans to know."

"I am only half human," Nada said. "No one ever called me mere." She inhaled. It was an action that normally had a peculiar effect on any adult human males in the vicinity, making them become more reasonable and attentive, especially if she happened to be leaning forward at the time.

"Precisely," Grossclout said, yawning. In this manner he demonstrated his immunity to this particular magic.

Now her female curiosity was stirring too. Something phenomenally significant might be in the works. "Very well. So oathed."

"It is truly demon business," Grossclout confided. "The Demon E(A/R)th is attempting to take over Xanth. Naturally the Demon X(A/N)th objects to this. So the two are settling it in the Demon Way: by a contest of innocents in a dream."

"But demons don't dream," Nada protested.

"Because they don't sleep," he agreed. "Except for confused ones such as Metria. They merely go into stasis and think. However, mortals do sleep, and do dream, which is what keeps the realm of the gourd in business. Mortals also have waking dreams. Thus they will dream for the demons. The Game of the Companions of Xanth is intended to be an animation of such a dream, wherein mortals can participate as if it is reality. One of them will win the prize, and one will not. This entire volume of the Muse's history is to be devoted to this decision. Thus it falls to the lesser demons to make the arrangements, and to the mortal folk to play it out. We do not know what will constitute a win for the Demon X(A/N)th, but we are certain that this matter affects us most intimately."

Nada was horrified. "If the Demon X(A/N)th loses, magic will disappear from Xanth!"

"This, too. So it does behoove us all to cooperate, hoping that our efforts will facilitate his success."

"But suppose we unwittingly make him lose?"

The Professor grimaced. He was very good at it, having terrified generations of hapless students at the Demon University of Magic. "That would be unfortunate," he remarked, his tone making Nada feel exactly like a student.

She did not dare question the matter further. She agreed to participate in the volume. Thereafter she attended rehearsals diligently, because the Professor assured her that she would be chosen to be the Companion to a Mundane Player.

"A Mundane!" she shrieked, horrified. "I don't want to associate with any Mundane!"

The Professor could be amazingly reasonable when he tried. "Grey Murphy was a Mundane."

And Grey Murphy was Good Magician Humfrey's assistant, and a Magician in his own right. If Nada didn't marry a prince, she could marry a Magician; they were of similar status. Princess Ivy had already sewn up Grey Murphy, of course, but it did illustrate the point. It was theoretically possible for a Mundane to be worthwhile.

"Particularly if the Demon $X(A/N)^{th}$ should lose," Grossclout said, as if reading her thought. He had had generations of practice in that sort of thing too, reading the guilty faces of students. "Mundania would then be much more important, and you would do well to have an association with a Mundane."

So Nada acceded to the notion of being a Companion to a Mundane. "But I won't let him touch me in any Adult Conspirational way," she said firmly.

The demon glanced at her torso, which was among the firmest in Xanth. "Naturally not," he agreed. "He will probably be underage anyway."

"Underage!" she shrieked, echoing her horror of two moments before. "I have *had* it with underage males!"

"This is simply the nature of Mundanes who are interested in fantasy games," he explained soothingly. "They are all rebellious teenagers. It is in the *Big Book of Rules*."

She allowed herself to be soothed. "But how do you know that I will be selected to be a Companion? Aren't there any other prospects?"

"Certainly. There will be six or seven. But suppose one of them were your brother Naldo, and the Mundane Player were female? Whom would she choose, regardless?"

"Naldo," she said immediately. "He is Xanth's handsomest and most accomplished prince, until recently Xanth's most eligible bachelor."

"And if the Mundane is male?"

Nada opened her mouth, and closed it again. He had made his point, in his irrefutable professorish manner.

Thus the rehearsals, which included male demons playing the parts of uncouth teenage Mundane males with grabby hands. Nada had to learn how to discourage these without biting their heads off. Because in her large serpent form she could readily do that, and the Professor made clear that this was a no-no. Players were not to be harmed in any way by their Companions. In fact, it was the Companion's task to ensure that their Players were not hurt at all, and to help them proceed through the game and win the prize.

"But suppose he's really obnoxious?" Nada demanded. "*Then* may I chomp him?"

"No. You must find some innocuous way to avoid his unwarranted attentions."

"But Mundane males are famous for their oafish persistence in the face of polite demurrals."

"True. Consider it a challenge."

"I shall do no such thing! I resign my position in this stupid game!"

The Professor looked pained. "Please do not force me to exert disciplinary persuasion."

"Forget it! I'm not one of your demon students! I'm a princess! I am departing these premises forthwith."

"I can not allow you to do that."

"Who cares what you allow! You have no authority over me."

"Unfortunately for you, I do have authority."

"Oh? Give me one indifferent reason why I should remain here against my princessly preference."

Grossclout sighed a small cloud of smoke. "Do you remember when you and Electra toured the realm of the gourd? You tasted some red whine."

"So I tasted some red whine!" she agreed. "I wanted to identify it. So what?"

"So any creature who partakes of the food of the realm of the gourd thereafter remains bound to the gourd. Had you forgotten that?"

Nada's hands flew to her face to cover up her unprincessly gape of horror. "Oh, my! I had forgotten."

"Therefore you have an obligation to the realm of the gourd. The demons have acquired the option on that obligation. You must participate in our project. That will acquit you."

Nada realized that she was stuck for it. The Demon Professor was notorious for leaving nothing to chance. Wearily she returned to the rehearsal.

Now she was glad of those tedious rehearsals, because she was well versed in turning aside obnoxious male moves without in any way diminishing her princessly status or maidenly appeal. She could handle herself. That of course did not make the situation fun, but at least it was tolerable.

This Dug promised to be exactly the type she had rehearsed against. He was tall, handsome, halfway smart, and oafishly ignorant of magic. Furthermore, his hands were just twitching to put a move on her. He had spied her in the lineup, and his orbs had spun into twin WOW position. What a job this was going to be!

But once it was done, she would be free of her obligation to the gourd. Possibly it might even be worth it.

They came to Isthmus Village. Because Dug had exercised his prerogative to Make Decisions, and naturally had made a bad one. He was from Mundania, where food evidently did not grow on trees. He thought they had to get supplies. Even weapons. How could he use a weapon from the other side of his screen? He needed neither food nor weapon here, as long as he refused to believe in magic. As long as he thought it was just a game.

At least that gave her some respite. As long as he did not believe, he could not truly enter the scene, and thus could not annoy her with anything other than verbal harassment. Of course she would have to handle the reaction of the villagers when they saw the screen traipsing about.

It did not take long for the villagers to notice them. A gruff village headman approached. "What are a beautiful Nada princess and a weird magic screen doing in our desolate village?" he demanded. Gruffly, of course.

"We wish to obtain supplies and weapons," Nada said dutifully. "We are traveling to see the Good Magician, and fear privation along the way."

"Why don't you just use the magic path?"

"We can't. It's supposed to be a challenge, so the protection of the enchanted paths are denied us."

"Well, you won't get any help here. We are angry folk who don't like outsiders. Were you not so beautiful, we would be inclined to chastise you."

"Listen, twerp, you can't talk to her like that!" Dug exclaimed from the screen.

Sure enough, he was getting them into trouble. "It's all right, Dug," Nada murmured. "They can't hurt us."

"Yeah, I'd like to see them try," he said aggressively.

The headman grimaced. "We may oblige you, apparition. Come out of that wandering screen and we shall enjoy giving you a decent thumping."

"Boy, I'd sure see about that, you old goat."

Nada moved to cover the screen as well as she could with her body, blocking Dug off from the scene. "We shall be going immediately, thank you kindly, sir," she said to the headman.

"Oh no we won't!" Dug cried, as the screen circled around to recover its view of the proceedings. "Much as I like the sight of your backside." There was a slight fuzziness about the last word that indicated that the magical translation had had a problem; evidently he had used a different word that might or might not mean the same thing. Nada had the distinct impression that had it been possible for him to reach through the screen, he would have done something that required her to wham him across his insolent face.

"Oh, do you think so, you seclusive wretch," the headman said, as other villagers closed in around them, each looking more surly than the others. "Just because you can hide behind a lovely woman, you think you can insult us."

"No, no!" Nada said desperately. "He's not trying to insult you. He just doesn't understand." She tried to cover the screen again, this time being careful not to show her backside to it. Unfortunately this was worse. Not only did she have the impression that Dug was peering down the front of her dress, the village men were inspecting her posterior. What a mess!

"The bleep I don't understand!" Dug shouted. The word "bleep" was strongly fuzzed, showing that the Adult Conspiracy had blocked out the original word. Which was odd; she had never heard of it operating that way before. For one thing, there were no children close by, and Dug, at sixteen, was eligible to join the Conspiracy. There should have been no suppression of speech. "Much as I like looking at your bleeps up close."

Angry herself, Nada stepped away from the screen, folding her arms across her bosom. She would let Dug and the villagers exchange their own words; she had done all she could to avert trouble, but since both parties seemed to want it, that was that.

"Get out of the village!" the headman shouted back. "We don't want your kind here! We have trouble enough already."

"Not without our supplies," Dug said.

A canny look crossed the headman's face. "And how will you pay for supplies?"

That evidently made Dug pause. He didn't have anything he could pass through the screen. But in a moment he bounced back. "With information, you bleep. What would you like to know? How ugly your puss is? How big your feet are?"

"We don't need information, we need to be rid of the censorship," the headman said. "What can you do about that?"

"Censorship!" Dug exclaimed. "You mean you have that here?"

"We certainly do! And it's a horror. Its power is increasing all the time, too.

Soon it will totally enslave us, making us wholly miserable instead of merely frustrated."

This was new to Nada. But perhaps it offered an avenue for resolution of the crisis. "What is a censor-ship?" she asked.

"It's a ship, of course. It sails into our port every day, and its censers send their incense smoke through our village, ruining our dialogue and incensing us. That is why we are so angry all the time."

"Censorship!" Dug exclaimed, laughing. "So that's what it is! I had thought it was something more serious."

"We find nothing humorous about it," the headman said. "We just wish to be rid of it."

"But it's just a pun. Where I come from, it's a serious matter. They take books out of the libraries, and they stop the people from knowing the truth about government, and next thing, in countries where it's really strong, they get into thought control."

"Exactly. At first it seemed mild, even beneficial. To protect our children. But it kept protecting more things and more people, until now we are almost slaves to it. But we are powerless to throw it off."

Dug reconsidered. "Okay, I guess maybe you do have a real problem. I don't like censorship; I want to make up my own mind what I should read or hear. I guess you do too."

"That is the truth," the headman said dourly.

Nada still found this confusing. "Why don't you just ask the ship to go away?"

"We should have done that at the outset," the man agreed. "But we were seduced by what it seemed to offer. It promised us advantage, indeed, dominance over all others. Sheer folly, we now know to our cost. There are a number of ships, and some will depart when asked. But this one, though it masqueraded as a nice one, is actually the worst of them all, and once it establishes control it never lets go by choice."

"Does this particular censor-ship have a name?" Dug asked.

"It is the dread vessel *Bigotry*. If only we had fallen victim to some other ship, such as *Politics* or *Literary* or *Prudish* or *Social*, we might have escaped. I understand that some ships really do have the welfare of their victims in mind. But not this one. This one closes out all other views, being absolutely intolerant of differing belief. We deeply regret ever being lulled by its seeming care for our welfare; it cares for no welfare but its own."

Dug nodded with agreement. "You got that right! Okay, this must be a game challenge. Something I have to handle before I move on. So we'll help you get rid of it. Will that be a fair exchange for our supplies?"

The headman forgot to be angry. "We would give anything we have, to be rid of that ship and its insidious fumes."

"Deal!" Dug said. Then: "Exactly how does it work? I mean, does the smoke smell bad, or something?"

"No, it has only a faint perfume. But wherever it circulates, it suppresses anything it deems to be offensive. It is a puritanical vessel that will not allow any bleep, bleep, or bleep thoughts to be expressed." The man turned his head and spat, disgusted by his inability to say the words. "This of course ruins our fishing, building, social lives, and even our entertainment, because it is impossible to perform tough manual chores without venting an occasional bleep, or to woo a maid without telling her bleep, or to play a game of dice without saying bleep."

"Wow!" Dug said. "You mean it really does stop you from saying bleep?" He looked surprised as he heard his own word. "Yeah, I guess it does. Boy, I don't blame you for getting mad! Nobody likes getting censored and incensed."

"To be sure," the headman agreed gruffly, looking less angry. "Many ships do that, and originally this had appeal. We thought to improve our speech. But we assumed that our wishes for speech would govern. We discovered that *its* rules governed instead. And not merely for speech; that is merely the first stage. Soon it will begin controlling our actions, and finally our thoughts. But we have been unable to escape the devious incense fumes from the censers of the ship. Worse, the definitions are expanding. Originally it was only cursing it stopped, but now we can not even say bleep."

Dug nodded. "I think I have it. I read about it in civics class. What do you call a female dog?"

"A bleep."

"I thought so. Pretty soon it will be running your entire lives, because censorship feeds on its own power to enforce its rules. They don't have to make sense; that's not the point. They just have to be followed, or else. Eventually you won't even be able to breathe without choking on the fumes, and life won't be worth living."

"Exactly. We are already somewhat short of breath." The other folk nodded agreement, and some coughed.

Nada was amazed. Dug was actually getting along with the villagers. He understood their problem. Maybe she had misjudged him.

"Okay. What do I have to do to get rid of this ship?"

"It is very hard. That is why we can not do it for ourselves. But perhaps an outsider, not yet fully suppressed by the fumes, could manage it. You have to get the solution."

"That's what I want, the solution," Dug agreed. "What is it?"

"It is a magical fluid that can put out the censers, so that the incense no longer burns. Only that special solution can do it. When the incense no longer burns, there will be no more smoke and no more fumes. Then the ship will be unable to harm us, and will have to go away."

Dug's mouth quirked. Nada realized that he still was not taking this quite seriously, but she decided to stay clear as long as the dialogue was making progress.

"And where may I find this magical solution?"

"It is beyond the pail."

"Beyond the pale," Dug said. "Of course."

"You must take the pail and bring the solution back in it. That is the only way."

"I shall try to do that. But just how far beyond the pale, uh pail, is this solution?"

"We do not know. We know only that it is in the possession of the Fairy Nuff."

"Fair enough?"

"Yes. If you can convince her to give you the solution, all will be well."

"I'll do that. Which direction is the pail?"

"That way," the headman said, pointing to the side.

"Well, let's go," Dug said briskly. "I shall return."

Nada had no idea whether they would be able to find the pail, let alone the Fairy Nuff, or get the solution, but at least this was better than quarreling with the villagers. She walked in the indicated direction, and the screen walked with her.

Soon they saw the pail. It was colored daylight blue, and looked very bright and nice. But as they walked toward it, it receded, staying out of reach.

"I begin to see why the villagers didn't get it," Dug said. "But we'll have to prove we're smarter. Can you get around beyond it, so I can herd it in to you?"

For answer, Nada changed into small serpent form and slithered out of her clothes. Then she realized that she shouldn't have done that; how was she going to get back into them, without Dug seeing her body? A princess could not allow a mere man to see her torso or her panties. Especially not a Mundane man. But she would have to worry about that later; she had already changed.

She slithered rapidly around to the side, and through the underbrush. She circled around until she was well beyond the pail. Then she started to change—and realized that she didn't have her clothes here. She couldn't grab the pail unless she had hands. So she slithered back under the brush near a blanket bush, changed back to human form, wrapped a blanket around her, and walked back out to intercept the pail. She lay down, hiding, then changed back to serpent form, keeping the blanket more or less in place so that it would be there when she changed again.

. Now Dug's screen advanced on the pail. The pail retreated, teasing him. But when it crossed the place where Nada lay, she abruptly changed back to human form, grabbed its handle with one hand, and her blanket with the other. "Gotcha!" she exclaimed with unprincessly vernacular.

The pail flung itself about, but could not get free. After a moment it hung quiescent, defeated.

"Great!" Dug called, his screen hurrying across the terrain. "Now we can go on beyond the pail."

"In a moment," Nada said. "Stay here; I will be right back." She hurried back to where her clothing was. She picked it up, went behind a very elegant and even symme-tree, and hastily got back into her formal human garb. She was careful not to let go of the pail, because if it got away from her, she knew they would not catch it in the same way again. Then she walked out to rejoin Dug. She had managed to get by this incidental personal crisis, but she would have to be more careful next time she needed to change.

They moved on—and discovered snow. It covered the path and extended into the forest to the sides. "This can't be right," Nada said. "Xanth is warm. There is snow only on the mountaintops, and sometimes in unusual storms. There hasn't been any storm here, and it's not cold."

"Maybe it only looks like snow," Dug said.

She squatted and touched a finger to it. It was cold and somewhat gooey. She licked her finger. "Eye scream!" she exclaimed, surprised.

"Ice cream?"

"Eye scream," she clarified, pointing to her eye and mouth.

"You scream? Oh 'I scream.' What's it doing here?"

"I don't know. It must be coming from somewhere. See, it seems to be flowing and melting."

"Then let's find out where it's coming from. Maybe we can get around it."

"Or at least across it," she said. Her slippers were already thoroughly gummed up. "It seems to be flowing from somewhere ahead of us."

As they went, the ice cream (as Dug called it) became colder and harder, so that her feet were no longer gummy. Now they were cold. Dug, within his screen, had no problem; he just floated over it.

Fortunately she spied a shoe tree. She plucked a warm pair of boots from it and put them on. Now her feet were all right, and the blanket over her dress helped keep the rest of her warm. But she hoped they found a way out of the eye scream soon, because she knew she would get cold again as soon as she stopped moving.

They came to a castle formed of packed sugary snow. It wasn't a big castle, but that was because there was not an awful lot of eye scream available to make it. It had nice windows formed of thin sheets of ice. "Maybe whoever lives here knows what this is all about," Nada said. She went up to the frozen chocolate door to knock. She discovered that there was a screen door before it.

There was a large eye set in the screen. "Who are you?" the eye screamed.

"I am Nada Naga, Companion to Dug Mundane, who is a Player in the game. We are trying to find the Fairy Nuff. I don't suppose she lives here?"

The eye screen blinked. "No, she lives on down the fairway, of course. But you can't reach her unless you settle with my mistress of the castle first."

Nada was getting cold standing there. "Who is the mistress of the castle?"

"The Ice Queen, of course." The eye was still screaming; that seemed to be its only mode of dialogue.

"Then may we talk to the Ice Queen?" Nada asked, trying not to shiver with the chill.

"Actually the mistress isn't here right now," the eye confided with a conspiratorial wink. "Her clone is here. She looks just like the Queen, though."

"Then may we talk with the Ice Queen Clone?"

"The Ice Queen Clone!" Dug chortled.

The eye eyed him. "You find something funny about that?"

Dug, perhaps remembering how sensitive the villagers had been, decided to back off. "No, I'm an I-Screen-Clone myself."

This kid was quick on his mental feet, Nada realized.

The eye was mollified. "Sure." The eye twisted in its socket so as to look back beyond the door. "Hey, mistress!" the eye screamed. "There's a luscious eyeful of a maiden to see you."

"Have you eye-screened her?" a voice called back.

"Yes, I screened," the eye screamed. "There's an I screen with her."

"Are they appropriately awed?"

"The maiden is shaking and her teeth are chattering."

Nada was shivering cold, but decided not to clarify the matter.

"Then send them into the cone room, and have a scone for yourself."

The door opened. "Follow my glance," the eye screamed, looking into the hall. There was a dotted line marking its glance.

Nada entered, with the screen close behind. When she looked back, she saw the eye screen scone rolling up.

The cone room turned out to be shaped like a giant cone, unsurprisingly. In its center was an old woman wearing a snowy shroud. "I am the Ice Queen Crone," she said.

Nada realized that of course the clone would not admit to being a copy; she was pretending to be the real crone. "I am Nada Naga, and—"

"Yes, yes, I heard the eye scream," she said impatiently. "You want to reach the Fairy Nuff. But first you have to do something for me, or I will turn you to luscious slush, or maybe slushious mush."

"Yeah?" Dug said. "I'd like to see you—" He hesitated as the Ice Queen Clone lifted a cold finger, preparing to implement her spell. "I mean, that won't be necessary. What do you want of us?"

"I want a new flavor of eye scream, of course. One no one ever heard of before. What have you got?"

Nada was blank. But Dug came to the rescue. "No problem. How about Spinach Soufflé ice cream, for the child who won't eat his vegetables?"

"Wonderful!" the Ice Queen Clone cried. "I love to make children suffer! I will make up a potful right away."

"Just so long as I don't have to eat it," Dug said. "Now will you let us go on to see the Fairy Nuff?"

"Of course. Just go right down the fairway there." She indicated a door in the side of the cone.

They went out the door, and found themselves on a sunny green expanse. There was no snow. "Why, this is a golf course," Dug said, surprised.

"It looks like a finely clipped lawn to me," Nada said, as surprised.

"The fairway, of course. That is where the fair enough would be, in this crazy place."

"What would a fairy want with a lawn?"

Dug glanced at her through the screen, then shrugged. "I suppose there is a pun there. You know, this place—what do you call it, Zanth—might be okay if it wasn't for all the stupid puns."

"They are there for the cri-tics," Nada explained. "Because the cri-tics can't handle the intelligent puns, and they hate to think they're missing anything."

"Critics are like that," he agreed.

Nada grew warm as she walked, and had to take off the blanket, and then the boots. But this was certainly preferable to the snow.

In the center of the fairway they found a kind of exhibit or marketplace, with things set out for inspection. "This is a fair," Nada said. "We must be getting close."

"It's some affair," he agreed, looking around. "A fairground on a fairway."

In the center of the fair, with flair, was the booth of the Fairy. She was very fair, even beautiful, with scintillating wings. But she looked sad.

As they approached, Nada discovered that the Fairy was not female, but male. He was so delicate that he seemed feminine from a distance. His booth was set out with decanters of all shapes and sizes, containing fluids of many colors.

"Are you the Fairy Nuff?" Nada inquired hesitantly.

"What's it to you, snaketail?" he snapped. "Can't you read it on the ledger?" He pointed to the words FAIRY NUFF.

"Listen, you winged freak, don't talk to her like that!" Dug said.

"Why not, screenbrain?" the Fairy demanded.

"Because she's a lovely and good person, and she's trying to do her job, that's why, you androgynous creep."

Nada couldn't help it; she was getting to like aspects of Dug Mundane. She kept her mouth shut.

"Well, you aren't any of those things, you midget-brained Mundane," the Fairy retorted. "So what did you come here for?"

"We need a solution," Dug said. "Just give us a bucket of it, and we'll get out of your face."

"And what will you give me for that solution, you fugitive from dreariness?"

Dug paused. "Tit for tat, eh?"

"No. That's the next booth over."

They looked at the next booth, where several bare-breasted nymphs perched. A man was approaching it, hauling along a bag marked TAT. Nada decided not to inquire further.

Dug seemed quite intrigued by the nymphs, however. His eyes seemed eager to zip over there, hauling his head along after them. "Don't forget what you're here for," Nada murmured.

He forced himself to remember, without perfect success. "What are those creatures?"

"They are nymphs, of course. Females almost without minds, existing only for the sport of the moment."

"But what a sport!" he breathed.

"If you want to have brainless fun," she agreed.

"Yeah." He seemed oblivious to her tone.

"That is evidently just about your velocity," the Fairy remarked.

That got Dug's attention. "What's it to you, Nuff? You never heard of play?"

"Fair play, of course," the Fairy said.

"Ouch! I walked into that one. Okay, what do you want for your solution?"

"I want not to be the object of misrepresentation."

"You don't have a solution for that?"

"My solutions apply only to others."

Dug considered. "Exactly what kind of misrepresentation are you the object of?"

"Folk insist on calling me gay, when as you can plainly see, I am nothing of the kind. I want recognition as the sour individual I am."

"Let me see if I have this straight. You are a fairy, therefore folk call you gay?"

"Exactly, I have no idea why they think all fairies are gay."

Dug pursed his lips, seeming to think of something obscure. "Maybe this is a problem it's better to avoid," he said. "Exactly how is your name spelled?" Dug could have read it on the ledger, but for some reason his eyes were straying back to the nymphs.

"Eff Aay Eye Are Why. Enn You Eff Eff."

"Try spelling it FAERIE."

"That will change things?"

"It just might."

Nuff looked extremely dubious, which was the way Nada felt. How could such an irrelevant change affect the attitudes of others?

"Very well." He touched the ledger, and the letters shifted. Now it read FAERIE NUFF.

Another person approached the booth. "What are you spelling, Nuff?" he asked seriously.

"Nothing to interest you, clodbrain," Faerie Nuff snapped.

"What a grouch!" the man said, moving away.

Nuff stared after him. "It's magic!" he breathed.

"Right," Dug agreed. "Now they know you're not gay. How about our solution?"

Nuff made a negligent gesture.

"Take any bottle," Dug told Nada.

"But who said to?" she asked.

"Nuff said."

So it seemed. She lifted a nice decanter of purple elixir, pulled off the stopper, and poured it into the pail. When she set it back on the table, it refilled of its own volition. She replaced the stopper. "Thank you, Nuff," she said.

"You earned it," the Faerie said sourly.

But when she looked in the pail, it was empty. Had Nuff cheated them? She started to speak, but Dug beat her to it. "Did we misunderstand the nature of the deal?" he inquired in what was, for him, a remarkably peaceable tone.

"Fair well," Nuff said, waving.

Nada looked around—and saw several wells she hadn't noticed before. "I think it's in a well," she said.

So they went to the wells. There were five of them, labeled A B C D and E. One of them must have the solution they could haul away.

Dug's face lighted. "Fair-E-Nuff!" he exclaimed. "Well-E-Nuff. We want E-Nuff."

"We want enough, yes," she agreed, perplexed.

They went to Well E, which was somewhat isolated from the others. "Well E Nuff Alone," Dug said with satisfaction. "It makes weird sense."

There was a bucket on a rope. Nada let the bucket down into the well until it splashed in the water below. She drew it up. The fluid was purple, matching that of the bottle they had chosen. Nada poured it into the pail, and this time it stayed there. "Good," she said, relieved.

"Good E Nuff," Dug agreed cheerfully.

They returned the way they had come. When they reached the castle of the Ice Queen Clone, they walked around it—and found themselves immediately in a snowstorm. Nada had forgotten to bring along her boots and blanket, and was suddenly cold again.

"Try a drop of solution," Dug suggested.

Nada dipped her finger in the pail and flicked a drop of fluid out into the snow. Immediately the storm calmed, and a clear path opened before them. The solution was working.

"You are really coming to understand how things work here, Dug," she said, impressed.

"Well, I always was a quick study," he said. "Once I caught on to the rules of nonsense, I just had to apply them."

So it seemed. He was young, arrogant, and a Mundane, but he did have his points.

They returned to Isthmus Village. "We have the solution," Dug announced. "Where's the ship?"

The headman led the way south to the port. There was the sinister ship, with its great awful censers hanging fore and aft. On its hull was its name: BIGOTRY. Nada felt a tingle of horror as she beheld it. This ship was made from the disgusting wood of the bigotree! No wonder it smelled so bad. It was

surrounded by an aura of suppression; it was impossible for there to be any joy
or freedom near it.

There seemed to be no sailors on that dread vessel. It was a ghost craft,
bearing no living creature. What person could stand to be near it?

"Looks good," Dug said. "Let's get aboard her and douse those censers."

That meant that Nada would have to do it, because Dug wasn't really in
this scene. He was protected by his screen.

She sighed silently and got into the dingy little dinghy boat the headman
showed them. She set the pail between her knees and took the oars. She hauled
on them. They were heavy, but she heaved hard and made them move. The headman watched as the dinghy moved out. She was alone, except for the screen.

"Boy, you sure look great when you're moving like that," Dug said, staring
at her front.

As if things weren't bad enough! "Why don't you take an oar?" she gasped.
Because she was a maiden she did not speak the rest of her thought: *And shove
it somewhere loathsome*. In fact, because she was a princess, she could not
even think of it in greater detail, frustrating as it was. She suffered the same
sort of repression the censor-ship brought to the isthmus, only hers could not
be doused by any solution. She wished that just once she could step out of her
role and do something fiendishly unprincessly.

Meanwhile the awful mood of the ship intensified. There was an ambience
of gloom, hatred, and loathing. The ship was here on a mission of destruction,
seeking to extirpate not only all pleasure in life, but ultimately life itself. Total
repression, so that it would no longer be possible even to breathe, and all the
victims could do was expire and rot away. What a cargo of malice! Her breath
was getting short, and not just from her effort of rowing; it was as if a depress-
ing weight were bearing down on her, squashing out her strength and will.
How much longer could she continue?

The dinghy touched the somber hull. "Okay, tie the boat close, and carry the
solution up there," Dug said. "This isn't nearly as hard as I thought it would be."

Nada tried to make an angry remark, but the overpowering fumes of the
censers left her barely able to breathe. So she took the pail in one hand, and
grabbed a rope ladder with the other. She hauled herself up, rung by rung, until she made it to the deck.

"Great!" Dug said. "What an antique this is! I wish I had a model of it."

Nada just wished he could be physically here, to suffer the effects of this
ship of doom. She dragged herself across the dark planking toward the nearest
censer. It was as if she were climbing a mountain, and the slope got steeper with
each step. She had to drag each leg forward through a seeming miasma that

clung like rotten goo. Every breath seemed to bring in a thick sludge of vapor that soiled her tenderest innermost recesses. She closed her eyes and plowed on.

"Come on, Nada, you're real close," Dug said encouragingly. "Just a couple more steps, then heave the pail up and slop some in."

Two more steps? It might as well have been two more worlds! Nada couldn't even keep her feet any longer. The stench from the looming censer was overpowering her last resolve, and she was falling. The pail was tilting, its precious solution about to spill out across the deck, wasted.

Hands caught her and the pail. "Come *on*, we've got to get this done," Dug said. "We can't give up now." He coughed. "Phew! What a stench!"

He lifted the pail from her slackening grasp and lurched forward. His breath wheezed. His body trembled. He seemed to be swept back by a sickly wind. But he fought forward just a little more, closing the grudging gap between the pail and the censer. He heaved the pail up, tilted it, and splashed some solution into the censer.

There was a pouff! and a hideous cloud of vapor spread up and out. It soiled the air, then thinned, and faded away. The incense had been extinguished. For the first time she saw the lettering on the censer: HATRED.

A breath of clean air swept in. Nada, sprawled on the deck, inhaled. How sweet it was!

They had done it! They had overcome the censor-ship. The isthmus would be free!

Then another whiff of awfulness came. Nada looked—and saw the far censer. They had extinguished only one of the two. The job was only half done.

She dragged herself up. She had no idea how she would ever make it the length of the ship and to the other censer. She would just have to try.

"Oh, brother, the other one," Dug said, staring across at it. "I don't think I can make it."

As her mind cleared, Nada realized something. "Dug! You're in the scene!"

He looked around, startled. "I guess I am. How did that happen?"

"It means you believe," she said.

"I don't believe! I just couldn't stand to see you struggling like that, when I'm the one who got us into this thing. It wasn't fair."

"You must believe I'm real, or you wouldn't care."

He stared at her. "I guess maybe I do, then." He shook his head, not really believing his own belief. "Maybe it's just that when I realized this was serious, I had to believe. I couldn't let censorship win, even in a joke land like this." He smiled. "Well, maybe we can make it to the other censer together."

"Maybe we can," she agreed. "Take my hand."

He took her hand. Then they walked together across the deck. It was much easier now. There was far more strength in unity that she had imagined. Also, she now knew that the solution worked, and that gave her more courage. What they were doing wasn't pointless; all they had to do was do it right, and the censorship would be finally defeated.

The fumes intensified, but their effect was no longer overpowering. The two of them forged onward, not even slowing. They reached the grim censer, and Dug lifted up the pail and poured out more of the solution.

The fumes stopped. A glow came from the censer, but not of burning incense. It was the glow of clean daylight. The gloomy cloud surrounding the ship was dissipating, and the deck was brightening. They had defeated the second censor censer more readily than the first.

Nada looked at it. Its letters said IGNORANCE.

"Hatred and ignorance," Dug murmured, awed. "The two pillars of bigotry. And I'll bet this is the ship of fools, too. Because only fools would let such bad things govern them."

"And only fools would try to stop all others from saying or even thinking what they wanted to," Nada said. "Fortunately we don't have a lot of that in Xanth."

"We have plenty in Mundania, though," he said. "I guess that's what makes it such a dreary place." He looked around. "Damn! I'm glad to be here!" Then he laughed. "Hey, I swore! It didn't get bleeped out. The censorship really has been beaten."

"It really has been," she agreed. "For now. But it will surely be back, once it returns to its source and gets its censers restored."

"I guess so. Too bad. But let's get off it and get back to Isthmus Village. We have a whole adventure to get through."

So they did. This was only the beginning.

4
WATER

Kim was glad to get out of the Ogre fen Ogre Fen. She knew herself to be a smart, and therefore unattractive, girl, but it had taken all her ingenuity to outsmart those stupid ogres. She wanted no more such encounters. This was after all supposed to be a fun game, wasn't it?

"So which is the fastest way to the Good Magician's castle?" she asked Jenny Elf.

"Well, it's south, but we shouldn't go that way."

"What do you mean, shouldn't go that way? Why not?" Kim remembered how Jenny had warned her against messing with the ogres, and in retrospect she appreciated that advice more than she had in futurespect. Henceforth she would pay more heed to the advice of her Companion.

"Because of the elements."

Kim remembered. "Oh, yes! Those five regions in north-central Xanth. Air, Fire, Water, Earth, and the Void, going from south to north."

"What?" Jenny asked, seeming confused.

"What's the problem?"

"That's not the order."

"Of course it is! I read it in the *Visual Guide*. There's a map."

"Well, the guide is wrong. Is it a Mundane book?"

"Of course."

"That explains it. Mundanes don't know about magic."

"Well, I'd have to see it to believe it. We should be closest to the Void, and south of that is Earth."

"You're right about the Void, but the next one down is Water. The Water Wing, in the shape of—"

"I get it. It has little waves on it, too. And Fire is in the shape of flames, and Air is like a puffy cloud. Everything's punnish, in Xanth. Okay, let's circle the Void and go see the Water Wing."

"You don't really believe me," Jenny said.

"I didn't say that." But it was true. Kim didn't believe that the map was wrong. It was in print, after all.

"Maybe we should go east to the Sane Jaunts River," Jenny said. "The birds are there, but they won't bother us if we don't do anything to annoy them."

"Why should birds bother us anyway? We can just shoo them away."

"Some of them are big birds."

"Big birds? Is that another pun?"

"I don't think so. I mean rocs."

"Rocks?—oh, *rocs*! The hugest of birds! Like Roxanne Roc, in the Nameless Castle."

"Yes. We don't want to bother any rocs. They know we're in the game, but still, we shouldn't take chances."

They had taken chances in the Ogre Fen, and almost gotten wiped out. Kim could have sworn that her hair got wet when the brute dunked her screen. That was her imagination, of course, but it had been uncomfortable at the time. She didn't want anyone turning her screen upside down again, either; she had felt giddy as the whole landscape inverted and swung around. Just how an ogre could grab her screen she didn't know; it was just the picture of Xanth she saw. But funny things always did happen in Xanth.

"Okay, let's go by the birds," Kim agreed. "I'd like to see a roc, anyway, as long as I'm on this tour. From a distance." She no longer wanted to see any monsters up close, because now she was afraid that one of them would smash her screen, or eat it, and it would go dark and exclude her from the game. She wasn't yet ready to quit the game, by a long shot.

They found a path that went east. These were not enchanted paths, Kim understood, because those were reserved for regular Xanth folk. It was just the game's excuse to force the Players into out-of-the-way places where they could get into trouble. If Players were allowed to use the enchanted paths, there wouldn't be much challenge. Anyway, it was surely more interesting along the bypaths.

In due course they came to the bank of the river. Kim was disappointed; she had hoped that it would be a real fantasy spectacle, but it was just a meandering stream, similar to any in her own realm. However, the plants along its banks were interesting; she recognized a pillow bush and a pie tree. If only she could eat a meal here, and stay the night, so she could use these things! But it was her fate as a mere Player never to actually be *in* the Land of Xanth. She hated that limitation.

Some plants were unfamiliar. They looked like hollow straws sticking up from the foliage. "What are those?" she asked.

Jenny looked. "Oh—straw-berries. We use them to drink tsoda pop."

Strawberries. She should have known.

Farther along there was an odd stick on the ground. Jenny picked it up, holding it so that Kim could see it. She discovered a red pair of lips on its surface. "Don't tell me, let me guess," she said. "Lipstick!"

"Of course," Jenny agreed. "Some girls use them to make their lips stick to things more firmly. I've never been quite sure why, unless they're afraid their kisses are too short."

The ground shuddered. Something large and solid was coming. Jenny hid behind a tree, and Kim peeked past her shoulder.

It was an animal with a bovine body, horns, and a weird wide-mouthed head. It sniffed the air, smelled Jenny, and looked at her with its bulging eye. "Croak!" it bellowed.

"Croak?" Kim asked.

"Well, it's a bull-frog," Jenny explained.

The creature leaped into the river, made an enormous splash, and disappeared under the surface. It was a bull-frog all right.

They walked on along the river. Kim half hoped she would see a water dragon, but she didn't. It was like Mundania: the creatures were there, but seldom to be seen. Maybe it was just as well.

"Are we south of the Void yet?" she asked after a bit. "Maybe we should cut back west now."

"I don't think so," Jenny said cautiously.

"Oh, come on; let's go see." Kim found a path and forged along it.

"No, no!" Jenny cried. "It's not safe!"

But Kim was being willful again. She knew it, but also knew that she was tired of walking down the river. She wanted to see the Water Wing—or the Earth region, to verify that her map was correct.

She came abruptly to a line of demarcation. The trees of the forest were reasonably normal—and then there just didn't seem to be anything much. It wasn't exactly a wall or precipice; she just didn't seem to be able to focus on it. How odd!

"Stop!" Jenny cried from behind. "Don't take one step farther!"

"Oh, don't be silly," Kim retorted. "I can't take a step here anyway; I'm just looking at it through the screen." Except that she wasn't exactly looking, she was just, well, *trying* to look.

So she moved forward. Suddenly there was a scene ahead: a gently sloping valley, with lush green turf and pretty little flowers of several colors sprinkled throughout. Pleasant puffy clouds drifted above, delicate columns of mist hovered over a lake, and the air was sweet. "Oh, this is nice!" she breathed.

Then the view jerked and turned sideways. The terrain spun horrendously. "Hey!" Kim cried. "What's happening?"

There was a change of scene. Suddenly there was Jenny Elf, her arms spread wide, hands clenching on something. The lovely landscape was gone.

"What are you doing?" Kim demanded. "I saw a really beautiful place, and I want to go back there."

"I'm hauling you out of the Void," Jenny said. "You're lucky I managed to catch hold of the back of your screen. Otherwise you would have been gone. Because nothing can cross out of the Void, once it is past that boundary."

"But I was just looking!" Kim protested. "I'm immune to getting caught, because it's just a picture, to me."

"Well, your screen was getting caught!" Jenny retorted. "And what happens to your role as a Player if you fall into the Void?"

That sobered her. "I lose," she admitted. "And I have to start over again, with the hazards at least as bad. That's no good. Even if I do lose, the first time, I want to get just as far as I can, so I know what to look out for next time. Thank you, Jenny; you did the right thing."

"That's all right," Jenny said. But she looked shaken, and Kim knew why: it was now twice that Kim had willfully gotten them into trouble.

"I'll try to behave better, really I will," Kim said contritely. But Jenny still looked wary.

They returned to the river and moved on south. Suddenly a huge bird took off ahead of them, perhaps startled by their approach. "That must be a roc!" Kim exclaimed. But then she saw that it had four legs with hooves, and the head of a horse. "No—it's a winged horse!"

"An alicorn," Jenny said. "I never saw one of those before!"

"A what?"

"An alicorn. A winged unicorn. There aren't many, but sometimes a griffin and a unicorn will meet at a love spring—well, I don't know what happens, but then we have alicorns."

"What do you mean, you don't know what happens?" Kim said sharply. "I read about how you were inducted into the Adult Conspiracy at age fourteen, and you must be fifteen now. Only a year younger than me—and *I* know what happens."

"You're Mundane," Jenny said. "Mundanes have funny ideas about things. But for the purpose of this game, I'm still a child, with the limits of a child. Professor Grossclout decreed it. So I can't know anything that's in the Adult Conspiracy, even if I might know out in real Xanth."

"Why should you be defined as a child?" Kim asked, surprised.

"So I will have the innocence of a child. That's an advantage, in some situations. I may be able to help you get somewhere, or do something, that an adult couldn't."

"That would be interesting," Kim said. "Very well: we won't discuss how alicorns come to be. They get delivered by the stork, or whatever."

"Yes."

They moved on. Kim never did get to see a water dragon, but she realized that there was plenty of Xanth to go yet.

It was clouding up. A storm was building in the sky. "Oops," Jenny said. "Try to stay out of sight. That looks like Fracto."

"Who?"

"Cumulo Fracto Nimbus, the meanest of clouds. He always blows an ill wind. If there's anything interesting happening, he comes and wets on it."

"Oh, pooh," Kim said, intrigued. Now she remembered Fracto, with contempt. "I'm not afraid of any ol' cloud!"

A vague face formed on the cloud. "I heeeard thaaaht!" Fracto puffed.

"So what? You're just a bag of wind."

"Ixnay," Jenny was murmuring. "Don't work him up."

But it was too late. The angry cloud was swelling up like a toad with gas, looming over them. Already the first cold gusts of wind were coming, bearing the first fat drops of water. Fracto's mouth pursed and blew out a much fiercer wind, containing flecks of sleet. They were in for it.

"I'm sorry," Kim said, realizing that this could indeed be mischief. "I guess my big mouth has gotten us into another."

"It's all right," Jenny said without overwhelming enthusiasm. "Let's see if we can maybe get up in a tree, so we don't get flooded out."

"It's *not* all right," Kim said. "You've been trying to do your job. But I'm just—well, I know I'm no beauty, so I try to make up by being smart with my mouth. It's a defensive mechanism. Only sometimes I'm doing it when I shouldn't. Like right now. And making it tough for you. So I'll try to watch it. Okay?"

"Okay," Jenny agreed, with an appreciative smile.

Meanwhile, they had Fracto's rage to deal with. Jenny cast about for a suitable tree to climb, but all the trees in view were wrong in separate ways. Some had tall, featureless trunks not easy to climb, some had thorns, and many were too small. "Sammy, find us a close tree to climb," Jenny said to the little cat.

Sammy bounded off. "Wait for me!" Jenny cried, chasing after him. Kim followed. Her screen just seemed to go wherever she looked, exactly as if she were really in the scene, and much of the time she forgot that she wasn't.

Kim heard a faint, eerie music. It was enchanting, but too distant to be intelligible.

They crossed an open area. Kim saw a giant spreading acorn tree beyond, easy to climb and sit in. The cat knew exactly where to go. But Fracto chose this moment to strike with all his fell force. A solid—well, liquid—sheet of rain came down to smite them. The water smacked into her screen, blurring it; she wished she had windshield wipers.

"Sammy!" Jenny cried, diving down. The cat had gotten swept into a sudden gullywasher which was taking advantage of a gully, and he was getting washed away to the side. Jenny grabbed him, but then fell into the gully herself.

More rain poured down, sluicing across the scene. Kim grabbed a handkerchief and tried to wipe her screen, but her hand just passed through it without effect. How silly, to think she could affect a scene within the computer game!

"Oh!" Jenny cried, being carried along by the rushing water. She was flailing, but couldn't get free, because she was holding the cat with one hand and water was coursing in from all around.

There was a rumble of satisfaction from Fracto. He was succeeding in messing them up.

Kim followed along, unable to do anything to help. She felt really guilty, because she was the one who had set off the irascible cloud, while Jenny was the one paying the consequence. "Jenny!" she called, knowing it was pointless.

But maybe she could help. She could go ahead and see if there were any good places to get free of the gullywash. Then she could tell Jenny, and she could get out of there.

But the storm just seemed to get worse, and she just couldn't see anything other than bits of overhanging branches and more water flowing in. All the world seemed to be water!

Again she heard that eerie music. It was as if someone were singing, and playing a stringed instrument. It was ethereally lovely, but still too faint to understand.

The gullywash became a stream, and the stream a river. Kim tried to find a shore, or even a shallow place, but the trees had retreated, leaving a broad expanse of water, with still more rain pelting down to trouble the surface. Jenny was being carried into a veritable sea!

Then she heard a sinister rushing sound. That sounded like—like a waterfall! Right ahead.

She hurried back to find Jenny, who was doing her best to stay afloat with the cat. Her hair and clothing were matted, and her spectacles were thoroughly fogged. "You have to get out!" Kim cried. "There's a waterfall!"

Sammy perked an ear. He meowed. Jenny smiled. "He says it's only a cataract," she reported.

A cat-aract. Naturally the cat wouldn't worry about that. But it remained a serious matter for a person. "You don't want to go through that," Kim said. "Who knows where it leads!"

"I don't have much choice," Jenny said sadly. "I'm sorry I wasn't a better Companion for you. But if you move on south, maybe you can still find the Good Magician and go on with the game."

"Don't be silly," Kim said. "I'm not going to leave you here." But how could she do anything useful?

The sound of the cataract swelled. Within it seemed to be that eerie melody, not quite drowned out, tantalizingly familiar. As if there were a damsel with a dulcimer somewhere beyond. But between her and them was the crashing water. Kim floated along, trying desperately to think of something, and failing. The rain was still pouring, and a stiff wind was boosting Jenny right on toward the disaster.

Maybe it wasn't so bad. Maybe it was just a little bit of rapids, and then the water would drain off to the side and Jenny could scramble out onshore. Kim went ahead to take one more look.

It was much worse than she had had any right to fear. There was a misty veil, and beyond it a plunge into a dark ocean. That seemed hopeless.

She turned back to find Jenny—and the elf was already there, being carried right into the plunge. Jenny shrieked as she floated over the brink.

Kim dived for her. Her hands caught hold of something. Then she, too, was hauled over the brink. Instead of saving Jenny, she had just gotten herself into trouble.

They fell, seemingly endlessly. Water was all around, in columns. Below was a frightening whirlpool.

They plunged into it, Jenny was swirled away. Kim inhaled to try to scream, but breathed water. She choked.

Then something was hauling her. She struggled feebly, to no avail. Whatever it was would have its way with her.

She landed on a warm grassy bank. She blinked, seeing the head and shoulders of a man. She had been rescued!

"Jenny!" she gasped. "Jenny Elf! She's in there—"

The man dived under the water. A fluke showed as he disappeared.

A fluke?

Kim sat up, coughing out pockets of water. She was utterly bedraggled, but safe, and the rain had stopped. But where was she?

Then Jenny Elf appeared, still holding Sammy. She seemed to be swimming rapidly, but without effort, just halfway sliding across the water. Kim blinked, then realized that Jenny was being carried by the man, who seemed not to need his arms for swimming. How strange!

The man set Jenny on the bank beside Kim. She was smaller than Kim had realized, being only about two-thirds her own height. But of course she was an elf. Other elves of Xanth were even smaller.

The man started to haul himself out of the water. "Eeeek!" Jenny cried. "You can't change here! I'm not in the Adult Conspiracy!"

"Oops," the man said. "Then I remain in merform for the nonce." He flipped up his nether section, and lo, it was a green tail. He was a triton! A man with the tail of a fish.

"Thank you for saving us," Jenny said. "I am Jenny Elf, and this is Kim, a Player in the game. I'm her Companion. If I may ask—"

"I am Cyrus Merman," the man said. "Son of Morris Merman and the Siren. My mother makes beautiful music, but she no longer makes it for strangers."

"That music!" Kim exclaimed. "That was the Siren's song!"

Cyrus looked chagrined. "Oh, you heard it! We thought no one was near. My mother's music always leads strangers to trouble, so she never—"

"She didn't know," Jenny said. "We were just passing, and then we ran afoul of Fracto, and he blew up a tempest and washed us into the Water Wing."

"The Water Wing!" Kim cried with recognition. "That's where we were heading."

"You picked a treacherous route," Cyrus remarked. "It was fortunate I happened to be near. Of course I was near because I was listening to my mother's music. I don't have a wife to keep me distracted, you see."

"I thought the Siren stopped her music," Kim said, perplexed. "I read how Chester Centaur destroyed her instrument, where the magic was."

"For a long time she wouldn't sing or play at all," Cyrus agreed. "But there are so few people in the Water Wing that it seemed safe, so she remade her magic dulcimer, and now my father and I love to listen. The music doesn't hurt anyone, it is just incredibly fascinating to men, who must come and listen to it. The problem is that they tend to forget what they are doing, and crash their ships into rocks or do other foolish things. But my father and I are used to it, and anyway, we are unlikely to drown. So we just listen and enjoy it."

"Oh, I would like to hear some more of it, before we go," Kim said. "All I heard was so faint, but I loved it."

"My aunt the Gorgon's talent affected only men, when she was young," Cyrus said. "But when she matured, so did her power, until it affected everyone, even animals. I think the same is true for my mother's talent."

"Then we should listen, before we go," Jenny said. "Because Kim wants to experience all the things of Xanth as she goes along."

Cyrus turned his handsome gaze on Kim. "What is this game you are playing?" he inquired. "You look like an attractive but otherwise ordinary young woman to me."

Kim opened her mouth, but stalled out before speaking. Attractive?

"She's Mundane," Jenny explained. "She won a talent contest, and the prize was to be the first to play the demon's Xanth Game of Companions. Somebody else sneaked in and was first, so she's actually the second, but still, she's playing the game. We're going down to ask the Good Magician how to proceed, since we don't know where the prize is, or even what it is. I mean, it's a magic talent, but we didn't know what talent."

Cyrus considered. "I suspect it is a good talent, so as to provide a strong incentive for the Players. I suppose it would be especially strong for Mundanes, who otherwise can never have magic."

Kim finally found her voice. "It hardly matters, since I can never actually be in Xanth. All I can do is play a role from the other side of the screen."

"The screen?" he asked blankly.

"This one." Kim put her hand out to touch it. And froze, astonished.

"Your screen is gone!" Jenny exclaimed. "Now I remember: you grabbed my hand. Trying to stop me from going over the waterfall. But instead I pulled you down. I must have pulled you through the screen!"

"But you couldn't have!" Kim protested. "There's no direct contact."

Cyrus smiled. "Are you saying that I merely imagined hauling you to shore? It certainly seemed like contact to me."

Kim reached down to touch the ground. It was solid. She touched Jenny's shoulder. It was there. She reached for Cyrus, then hesitated.

"By all means touch me," the merman invited. "In fact, lean over the water, and I will kiss you. That should be contact enough."

Was he daring her? Or teasing her? Kim decided to take him up on it. After all, she would never have another chance to kiss a merman.

"Uh, I don't think—" Jenny started, worried.

Kim leaned forward, and Cyrus leaned forward, and their two faces met. They kissed. It was wonderful.

"You are an effective kisser," Cyrus remarked, smiling.

"I must be here," Kim said dreamily.

"You must have taken the second step," Jenny said. "Now you believe in magic."

"So it seems all the way real," Kim agreed. "But I know it isn't."

"But in Xanth, illusion is part of our reality," Cyrus said. "So if you have the illusion that you are here, that is good enough for me. You must come and meet my parents."

Jenny looked alarmed. "I'm not sure—"

"But I want to hear the Siren sing," Kim said. "I'd love to meet your folks, Cyrus."

"Excellent. Allow me to go change. When my mother changes, she can form a sequined dress at the same time, but I have never mastered that ability. I shall return." He swam away.

"Changes?" Kim asked.

"They can turn their tails into legs," Jenny explained. "But then they are bare. As a juvenile, I'm not allowed to see a bare man. That is why I had to stop him from changing before."

"Oh. Changing from merform to manform," Kim said. Then she thought of something else. "Why were you alarmed when he offered to introduce us to his parents?"

"In Xanth, people mostly meet people just as they are," Jenny explained. "But if they bring their parents in, it means they may be getting serious."

"Serious?"

"Like maybe getting married."

"Married!" Kim exclaimed, astonished.

"He likes you. He's not married. So—"

"But I'm only sixteen!"

"So maybe he would have to meet your parents, too. Prince Dolph was still fifteen when he married Electra." Jenny smiled. "I understand they had a time trying to figure out how to signal the stork, because neither knew. But they did manage to do it."

"This is ridiculous. I'm not about to get married. Certainly not to signal any stork! This is only a game."

"Maybe it's not a game to him. Remember, you did kiss him. That's a pretty strong sign." Jenny shrugged. "Of course I'm not party to the Adult Conspiracy, so maybe I'm all wrong."

Kim was nonplussed. She was not at all sure the elf was wrong. She liked the merman, but this was getting ridiculous. "Maybe we had better get on out of here, then."

"Maybe we had better," Jenny agreed.

They stood, and Kim became aware of two things: her clothing was sodden and chafing because of the dunking, and Jenny was not only smaller than she was, she had pointed ears and four-fingered hands. She was different not only from Kim, but from other Xanth folk.

But already Cyrus was returning. Now he was with legs, and he wore a shirt and trousers. He looked twice as handsome as before. It was too late to get away, and it would have been impolite to go without waiting. Anyway, Kim realized that she wasn't eager to separate from him quite yet. For all the mischief it might portend, that kiss had been fun. Back home, no boy had kissed her and complimented her the way the merman had.

"Right this way, ladies," Cyrus said grandly. "My folks are expecting you."

Kim wasn't quite sure how she felt about that. But she did want to meet the Siren, about whom she had read.

They followed Cyrus along a pleasant path. Soon they came to a nice little house. It seemed to be made of glass. But the glass shimmered, as if not quite solid.

Cyrus saw her looking. "Water bricks," he explained. "Lacuna's son Ryver made them for us."

Water bricks? "May I touch one?" she asked timidly.

"Certainly; they are tough. It's just his magic; he's good with water. That's a talent we respect, here in the Water Wing."

Kim gingerly touched a brick. It was soft but resilient, giving way only a small amount before resisting. Like a velvet-covered block of stone. Ryver was indeed good with water.

The door opened, and a lovely older woman stepped out. This was the Siren. "Come in, come in!" she said. "We have set the table for you."

Set the table? But Kim knew she couldn't eat, because she wasn't really here. Or could she? About all she could do was try it and see what happened.

Then the Siren got a closer look. "But you're soaking wet, both of you. Come inside; we'll have you dry and changed in no time."

Inside it was pleasantly warm. A fire was burning in the hearth. The sticks there were translucent and colorless: waterlogs, of course. Ryver wasn't the only one who was good with water.

The Siren bustled them into a lavatory whose walls were fortunately lined with opaque water bricks, and helped them out of their sodden clothing, and put them into nice fresh dresses. Jenny looked much improved; her regular trousers and jacket had made her look like a child, while now she looked more like a young woman. A very petite one, by human standards, but still ladylike.

"You look wonderful, Kim!" Jenny said.

Which was what Kim should have said to Jenny first. "You too," she said belatedly. But she sneaked a peek at the ice mirror on the wall, and saw that she did look rather nice, in contrast to her usual. Maybe the magic of Xanth was enhancing her. Too bad she didn't have that magic in Mundania!

They went out to join the family. Kim tried to remind herself that this was all just a game setting. But it did indeed seem like a friendly backwoods family, and she liked it. Maybe Fracto had done them a favor, blowing them here so that Cyrus had had to rescue them.

Morris Merman was a handsome older man, also wearing legs and clothing for the occasion. "So you're Cyrus' young woman," he said affably.

Kim knew she should demur, but she didn't quite know how. She looked desperately at Jenny.

Jenny tried. "Kim is just passing through. This is a game to her—"

"A game!" Morris exclaimed. "That was a serious kiss!"

Kim's emotions were getting so mixed it was as if someone were stirring a big wooden spoon in them. She loved being complimented, but knew she couldn't afford to be taken seriously.

"I mean, she's a Mundane, just visiting Xanth, and—"

"A Mundane!" the Siren said.

It was sounding worse and worse. "Maybe we can talk later," Kim said uncomfortably.

But underneath her embarrassment was the wild excitement of recent developments. She had made the giant second step, and now seemed to be right in Xanth—and a handsome magical man had kissed her and called her attractive. Who needed to win the prize? This was fun enough.

The Siren served water cress, water chestnuts, water lemon, water rice, and water fowl, served on water lily leaves. For a beverage there was seltzer water. This was, after all, the Water Wing.

Somewhat dubiously, Kim tried her first mouthful—and it seemed real. So her belief was strong enough now to make it work. Relieved, she went ahead and enjoyed her meal.

Then they sat before the fire, and the Siren played and sang for them. It was absolutely beautiful and wonderful, and it evoked emotions Kim could not define. She wanted to be here always!

"Now we must talk," Cyrus said. "There is something I would like to ask you, Kim Mundane."

"Oh? I really don't know very much about things here." Kim had thought she knew a lot, but she had made so many mistakes that she realized she was an ignoramus.

He was unfazed. "As you know, I am unmarried. I am twenty-eight years old, and it is past time. But until now I have not had much opportunity to find a suitable woman. Now I think I see that opportunity."

Oh, no! Kim had almost forgotten about that. She loved this adventure, but she knew she couldn't stay, and she knew she couldn't marry anyone here. She didn't want to hurt anyone's feelings. Especially not anyone as handsome and nice as Cyrus.

She looked at Jenny, but it was evident that the elf didn't know what to say either. Kim had once again overridden Jenny's cautions about kissing Cyrus and meeting his parents, and thus sent signals she had not properly understood.

How was she going to get out of this?

5
PEWTER

Dug was glad to be on the way again, with a knapsack of supplies and some weapons. That business with the censor-ship had seemed like a joke, but had turned deadly serious. Maybe that was because it was all too easy to joke about serious things, avoiding really coming to terms with them. He had never much liked censorship, mainly because it always seemed to cut out the fun parts of anything he wanted to read or watch. But he hadn't taken it seriously. Until he had seen Nada Naga struggling across the deck of the ship, trying to do the job that he, Dug, had undertaken to do. That just wasn't right. Suddenly he had come to believe in the importance of the mission, and with that belief, it seemed, had come acceptance of the larger situation. The realization that some genuine values underlay all the funny fantasy stuff he was seeing. Maybe he didn't really believe in magic, but he did believe in those values, and was willing to sacrifice in order to support them. Maybe most people went through life without ever discovering such values, maybe even poking fun at them, but those were empty people who didn't count.

Of course he also happened to be with a beautiful woman, and wanted to impress her. That had to figure in. She had let him know early on that she was not about to go on a date with a mere Player, but maybe if he did something really worthy she would change her mind. So he had had that other reason to get into it. She might be a mere fantasy character in her fantasy setting, able to do a type of magic nobody in his right mind would believe, but she was the loveliest creature he ever expected to see. Even if he never got to first base with her—in fact, even if he never came up to bat with her—he wanted her faint favor. He wanted her to remember him as more than a teenage jerk from Mundania. That potential memory had become very important to him.

They were walking east, proceeding along the isthmus toward central Xanth. Because this was a game, there was bound to be another challenge soon. Things never just carried along smoothly, in games. That was why he had wanted supplies and weapons, though Nada had claimed that they were unnecessary. She had said that there were many things to eat along the way, and that it was her job to protect him from harm, so he would not have to defend himself. But he didn't want to depend on the largess of the land for food; a good game would see that they wound up hungry at some point. And he certainly didn't want to depend for protection on the woman he wanted to impress. So maybe she thought he was being foolish, but he was playing it smart. He hoped.

Actually he sort of hoped for a bit of trouble to come, because he wanted an excuse to try out his new weapon. It was a magic sword the grateful Isthmus Village headman had given him. It was supposed to be infinitely light for the user, and infinitely heavy for the opponent. What that meant was that he would never get tired swinging it, but if he used it to fend off an opponent's blow, it would be as solid as a boulder. So nobody would brush his sword aside to get at him. He was no expert swordsman, but this should give him a great head start in using his weapon. If only he could find a pretext to try it out.

They came to a river. It wasn't broad or savage, but it was big enough so that it was clear that they could neither jump over it nor wade through it. The path went up to the bank, and resumed on the far side.

"Maybe there's a boat," Dug said, looking along the bank.

"I fear not," Nada said.

"Why, are there alligators in the water, so we can't swim?"

"I see no allegations. But I think there is normally a bridge, that must have been removed before we arrived."

"To make the river a challenge to cross," he said. "Well, it doesn't seem like much of one. If it is safe to swim, we can do that."

"I am not sure we can. You see, this is my liability."

He glanced at her. "If you have any liabilities, I sure can't see them."

"I have princessly limitations."

Oh, yes; there had been a mention of that. "Like what?"

"I may not show my human body to a man who is not my husband."

"Oh, you can't go naked? Because you're a princess?"

"Yes. An ordinary woman could do so if she chose, provided that the one who saw her was not underage. You are not quite underage, though there are those who would argue the case. But as a princess, I must set a perfect example of propriety. So human nudity is impossible for me in this instance, and allowing a man to see my, uh, undergarments would be worse."

"Worse? You mean that bra and panties are worse than—"

She blushed. "Please don't use such terms in mixed company. They are integral to the Adult Conspiracy."

Dug sighed inwardly. He had sort of hoped to get a look at her body, coincidentally. Pretending not to notice. But the game makers had scotched that. "What about using your snake form? That doesn't count as naked, does it?"

"No. Serpents have no concerns about nudity. Neither my full serpent form nor my natural naga form presents any problem. But if you wish me to accompany you in my human form, there is a difficulty."

He did prefer her in human form. She might be the world's most beautiful serpent, but he was no judge of serpent beauty. He had more of a notion of human beauty, and she had that in overflowing measure. "Okay—suppose you cross in serpent form, and then change back to clothed human form when you're dry?"

"I must resume human form in order to don my clothes. I can leave them behind when I change to serpent form, but I can not don them in serpent form."

So she had to be a naked woman before she could be a clothed woman. It figured. "So I'll turn my back while you change. Will that do it?"

"It may. But I fear trouble, and I must try to protect you from it."

"You mean something will maybe attack us when my eyes are closed? But your eyes will be open, won't they? So we won't be unprotected."

She looked doubtful, but nodded.

"Then let's do it," he said briskly. "This hazard is a lot easier to handle than a dragon."

She still looked dubious, but did not argue.

"But it's okay for you to see me?" he asked. "No impropriety there?"

"If you do not object," she agreed.

Actually he would not ordinarily care to have a woman see him naked. But this was different in several ways. First, it was only a game, so wasn't really happening. Second, if he couldn't see her body, maybe he could get a little bit of the feeling by letting her see his body. This gave him just a flicker of comprehension how a flasher might feel. Third, he wanted to show that nakedness was no big thing, in the faint hope that eventually she might agree. But mainly, he wanted to get across that river, and he didn't want to get his clothes or supplies wet. So he just had to do what had to be done.

He went ahead and stripped, not letting himself think about it too much. It was a funny thing, disrobing in a game that seemed so real. But sort of exhilarating, too. It made him feel free, as if civilized hang-ups were being dumped along with the clothing. Could this be the way nudists felt? He was getting an education in feelings from the oddest situations!

Naked, he didn't look at Nada. In fact, he didn't face her, either. He just jammed his things into the top of his knapsack and closed it tight. Then he waded into the water, holding the knapsack up. When he was deep enough to swim, he went into modified sidestroke, so he could keep the knapsack clear of the water. It was easy enough, and he hoped Nada was impressed.

Soon he was across, as it really wasn't very far. He found his footing and walked on out. He set down the knapsack and shook himself dry, still facing away from the princess. "Okay, you come on across," he said. "I won't look."

"No, you must watch," she said. "Because there could be some other danger, such as a harpy, attacking while I am defenseless. I watched you, and you must watch me."

"Okay," he said, surprised. He got into his underpants and turned. His body was not yet dry enough for the rest of his clothing.

Nada was in her naga form: a serpent with her human head. Her clothing was neatly bundled. She must have done it while in her human form, then changed before he turned. But how was she going to carry her bundle?

Then she assumed full serpent form. The snake's mouth opened wide and bit down on the bundle. The serpent slithered smoothly into the water. She was carrying her bundle as readily as he had carried his.

But now he understood her point: if something attacked her right now, she would be unable to fight back, because her jaws were taken by the clothing. If she dropped the clothing to fight, then she would be unable to dress when she resumed human form later. It would be quite awkward. So he had to protect her, in this moment of her vulnerability. That made him feel obscurely good.

Fortunately nothing attacked. The serpent completed the crossing, dropped the bundle, and became the naga. "Finish dressing," the human head said.

Dug hastily did so. Then he turned to face away, so that Nada could change: first to human form, then to human clothing. He picked up the knapsack, to close it up again and put it on. Then he noticed the shiny buckle on it.

Shiny buckle. Reflective. If he held it up, just so, could he possibly manage to see—?

He fought with himself. Could it be so bad to catch just a distorted glimpse, if she didn't know? How could a creature invented as a game character know or care? Especially when she thought the real crime was showing panties? It wasn't her panties he wanted to see!

He lifted the knapsack, angling it so that the buckle turned. The reflection showed the tops of trees, then the river, then—

Suddenly the screen was blank. Dug was back in his room, staring at a dead computer screen. A system malfunction? No way! He had done it! He had broken a rule, and the game had kicked him out. Bleep!

He looked around. Everything seemed so infernally *mundane*! Not like the pretty colors and magical contours of the game. He had never realized before exactly how dreary ordinary life was.

Why had he done it? He had known he wasn't allowed to look at the body of the princess. He hadn't known that the game had this way of enforcing its rules, but that didn't matter. The point was that he had tried to do wrong, and had been punished for it.

"Oh, Nada Naga, I'm sorry," he breathed, experiencing cutting remorse.

Then he seemed to hear something. He cupped an ear, listening. He didn't hear anything, but faint words appeared in the screen: DUG! DUG! WHERE ARE YOU?

It was Nada's speech! Very faint, but definite. The lockout wasn't complete!

"I'm out in Mundania!" he answered. Then, remembering, he typed it on the keyboard.

There was a pause. Was he getting through? The screen remained dark, except for the faint glow where a speech balloon might be.

DUG! IS THAT YOU? I CAN'T SEE YOU.

"My screen went blank," he said as he typed it.

WHAT HAPPENED?

There was no point in trying to conceal it. "I tried to see you," he typed. "In the buckle on the knapsack. I'm really sorry, and I apologize. I deserved my punishment."

The screen brightened. Now he could see Nada, clothed, standing beside the river. Near her was his fallen knapsack.

She turned to face the screen. "But did you actually see me?" her speech balloon asked.

"No. But it didn't matter. I tried, after I promised not to. I'm disgusted with myself."

"If you didn't see me, then I have not been compromised," she said. "I can still be your Companion."

"Except that I'm out of the game," he typed. "I'll have to start over." Somehow that seemed dreadful.

"No! It is just a warning. You can return, to this scene, if you are careful."

Dug was abruptly excited. "I can! Great! I'll be really careful!"

He refocused his eyes, and in a moment the scene became three-dimensional. But the screen remained; he was seeing the scene, without being *in* it.

Nada peered through the screen at him. "What is the matter?"

"I'm seeing it, but I can't seem to get back into the scene," he said. "Maybe that's my remaining punishment for—"

"No, your belief must have been damaged," she said. "Can you get it back?"

How could he patch up a damaged belief? The game had punished him doubly: first by kicking him out, and second by reminding him that he was just a figure behind a screen, unable ever to be really part of the scene. He was never going to go against a game rule again! He had gotten into the scene the first time by suffering a realization that there was something of importance underneath the punny façade. He had come at it obliquely, not quite believing in magic, but believing in *something.* So what did he believe in this time?

Dug closed his eyes, searching within himself. What was the nature of his belief?

Suddenly he knew what it was: he believed in the game. Because it had had the power to boot him out when he tried to cheat. It was a real world, there beyond the screen. The computer was merely his limited access to it. Maybe his being in the scene was an illusion, but it was a real scene he seemed to be in. He might have doubted before, but now he believed.

"Oh, Dug—you're back!" Nada exclaimed, hugging him.

Hugging him? He opened his eyes.

Immediately she drew back. "Oh, I have done something unprincessly!" she cried, appalled.

"I'll never tell," he said gallantly. But he would never forget, either; that was the best hug he had ever felt, and maybe the best he ever would feel.

"Oh thank you! For a moment I feared I had disqualified myself."

"No, I was the one who almost did that." Dug looked around. All of it was there. He was definitely back in the scene. He intended to do his utmost to remain in it. Because, fantasy or reality, this was the greatest experience of his life.

They were across the river, which had in its fashion proven to be a much greater challenge than it had seemed.

Nada looked around. "I see a pie tree," she said. "I feel like doing something wicked, after that scare, such as eating something fattening."

"I can hardly imagine you being fat," Dug said, trying not to look too closely at her body.

"Well, it certainly wouldn't be princessly. But I don't splurge often." She walked to the tree and plucked a rich lemon meringue pie. "Would you like some, Dug?" she inquired prettily.

Could he eat here? There was one way to find out. "Yes. Thank you."

She drew a knife from somewhere in her clothing and cut across the pie.

Dug was startled; there had seemed to be no place in her costume to conceal such a knife. But of course she was a magical creature; she might have a magic pocket. The rules were different here, as he had just been so forcefully reminded.

She handed him a slice of pie. He took it and tried a bite. It was delicious. It probably wouldn't have been, if he hadn't believed, but that was no problem now.

"I should explain that Companions represent another kind of challenge," Nada said as they ate. "We may be approached, but only in appropriate manner."

"Oh, I've learned my lesson!" he reassured her hastily.

"Yes. You were penitent and you apologized. Therefore you were allowed to re-enter the game. You could not have hugged me, but I was able to hug you. Because you had moved me to do so, even if it was unprincessly."

"It was one great hug."

"Were I other than a princess, it would be easier for you to relate to me."

Dug realized that she was telling him something significant. Not outright, but obliquely. That if he wanted, for example, to kiss her, he might be able to do so, if he impressed her enough to make her kiss him. So the proscriptions weren't absolute; he just had to learn to play the game right. It was good to know.

They finished the pie in short order. Then they resumed their walk.

After a time, a flying dragon spotted them. It veered toward them, blowing out anticipatory puffs of smoke.

Dug drew his sword, but Nada stopped him. "A sword won't work against a firebreather," she pointed out. "It would toast you before you could use your weapon."

Dug had to agree. "I guess we'd better hide behind a tree, then."

"No, I will simply scare it away." Suddenly she was a small snake, slithering out of her fallen clothing.

That was supposed to scare a dragon?

But once she was free of the clothing, she changed into a large serpent. In fact, it was huge. Three times the size of the dragon. Then she lifted up her giant head, opened her enormous mouth to show a terrible array of fangs, and sent a ferocious hiss at the dragon.

The dragon didn't argue. It made a U-turn in air and fled.

The serpent slithered back to Nada's clothes. Dug didn't need to be asked; as he had said, he had learned his lesson. He also had a glimmer how she could stop him from kissing her: by biting his head off. He turned and put his face to the trunk of the nearest tree, and closed his eyes. He waited until Nada told him it was all right to look.

When he did look, she was back in her normal, lovely human form. "You are impressive," he said. He was not referring to her human form.

"Thank you." She knew what he meant.

They resumed their trek. Dug was happy; not only had he returned to the game, he was now experiencing its full adventure. What more could he ask?

The day was declining. "We shall have to make camp for the night soon," Nada said. "Because I am not competent to protect you well against the predators of the night."

"Night? Already? It seems like only an hour!"

She shook her head. "Perhaps time is different in Mundania. It may be that only an hour has passed there. But here much of a day has passed. I suppose if you prefer to leave the game, and return in the morning—"

"Nuh-*uh*! I don't want to get out of the game at all, if I can help it. I might not manage to get back in."

She considered that seriously. "I think you should be able to return, if you obey the rules and maintain your belief. Certainly you should be safer there."

"But shouldn't I be exposed to the danger, instead of copping out? I mean, is that fair play?"

"I don't know. I think that is your option. I understand that it is possible for a Player to depart, and to return to the game another day without any time having elapsed in the game. This is marvelous magic I do not understand, but surely convenient for you."

Dug recognized her description of a saved game; of course it wouldn't change when not being played. "Well, I didn't think I would like this game, when I heard about it. But I do. I want to play it right. That means day and night. If I win, I win; if I lose, I lose."

"You do not object to sharing a tent with me?"

Dug managed to keep his face sober. "I do not object. I will keep my eyes away, if you just tell me when."

She smiled, and he realized that he had scored another minor point. "Then we must seek a suitable campsite."

Soon they found one. It was marked CAMPSITE—ENCHANTED. It looked very nice.

"But just what exactly does it mean, enchanted?" he asked.

"It means that bad creatures can not attack here. So we may sleep without fear."

"But I thought we couldn't use the enchanted paths."

"This is not a path. It is a safe area. Players are allowed to use these."

"That's a relief." Because Dug had learned to take the fantasy threats seriously. He knew that if he got chomped by something that went bump in the night, or bumped by something with teeth, he would be out of the game. He could appreciate how dangerous it could be to sleep unprotected.

There was a big fabric plant growing nearby. They harvested some blankets and canvas, and soon had used available ironwood poles to fashion a framework. There was a box of magic tent pegs that gripped the edges of the fabric and held them firm. Nada knew what she was doing a good deal better than he did, so he followed her lead. The resulting tent did not look professional, but neither did it look incompetent. They spread pillows from pillow bushes on the ground, and the blankets over them.

Then they harvested potluck pies from the pie trees, and some milkweed pods. Dug was getting used to the way puns became real here; this was just the way it was, in Xanth.

There was a pleasant stream crossing a corner of the protected site. Nada went there to wash. "Please do not look," she said politely.

Dug went to the tent, lay down, put his head in the pillow, and closed his eyes tightly. He had always been a quick study, and the game had taught him well. Absolutely no peeking!

Soon she came to the tent. "Your turn," she said.

He got up and went to the river. He was not surprised to find it cool and pleasant on his skin; he had been reminded that this was a game, from which he could be excluded, but also that while he was in the game, it was increasingly real. So he no longer questioned that reality; he reveled in it. Whatever the rules of this fantasy land were, he would follow them literally, from now on.

Nada was sitting up on her pillow-bed when he returned. She was in a stunning nightdress which actually was far more discreet than it seemed, showing no extra flesh. "Dug, I must ask you something," she said hesitantly.

"All the rules!" he exclaimed. "I'm not breaking any one of them!"

She smiled. "Of course. My concern is this: I normally sleep in my natural form, but if you would prefer that I retain human form, I will. I understand that some people are uncomfortable in the presence of reptiles."

He needed no thought at all before answering. "Make yourself comfortable, Nada. I know who and what you are, I've seen you change to snake form, and if I wake and find a serpent beside me, I'll understand." Because much as he liked her human form, he now knew that it was completely off bounds, and he didn't even want to be tempted. Only if he behaved himself absolutely could he ever hope to be allowed *not* to behave himself. So he was going to do all he could to keep her happy. She might be his Companion, but he was going to be a perfect escort for her, too.

"Thank you, Dug." Her face did not change, but her body melted into serpent form, the nightdress sagging around it. She slithered out of the apparel, formed a loose coil, and laid her human head on the pillow.

There would have been a time, Dug reflected, when such a sight would have amazed him. But that was history, as of a few hours ago. He changed into the pajamas she had laid out for him and lay down on his own bed.

Sleep was magically swift and restful. Dug could not be sure whether he slept eight hours, or one, or one second. Because this was a game, it could be just a fade-out, fade-in leading to the next scene. But it seemed like slumber.

Next day they came to a sign: SHORTCUT TO SUCCESS. There was an arrow pointing down a side path.

"Does this make sense?" Dug inquired.

"I have not been told about this," Nada said, frowning. "I don't believe that such a sign is normally here. That suggests that it has been set up for the game."

"Does that mean we have to go that route?"

"By no means! A challenge set up for the game is as likely to be troublesome as rewarding. It may be safer to avoid it and make our own way south."

Dug considered. "About how much farther is the Good Magician's castle?"

"Several days, at our present pace. We shall also have to cross the Gap Chasm, which is formidable."

"And the shortcut might take us there sooner?"

"A magical route could take us there in one moment," she said. "Two moments at the most. But it could also lead us into mischief. I suspect it is a gamble which can either help us greatly, or complicate things greatly, depending on how we manage to handle it."

"What do you recommend?"

Now she considered a good half-moment. "Do you like traveling with me?"

Dug forced himself to be subdued. "Yes."

"You would not mind taking several extra days?"

"I would not." He would not mind taking several extra years with her, even if he never got to look at her body.

"Then I recommend avoiding this shortcut, because I can convey you to the Good Magician by the slow route, while I am not sure what will happen on the shortcut."

But Dug was becoming canny about his real objectives. "Which do *you* prefer, Nada?"

She was surprised. "My preference does not count. You are the Player. I am here to be your Companion, to help you accomplish your desire in the game."

Except if his desire was to grab her and kiss her. Failing that, his desire was to please her. He didn't care about winning the game; he just wanted to stay a while longer in this magical land, and be with her, and make her smile on occasion.

"I would love to be with you extra time," he said carefully. "But I realize that for you this is just a job, and I don't want to make it more burdensome than it has to be. I can go either the safe slow route or the mysterious adventure route. Which would you prefer it to be?"

"I have to confess that I am femininely curious about that shortcut," she confessed femininely. "But I seriously question whether it is wise, so—"

"I'm curious too," he said. One thing this game had done: it had made him figure out his true desire. Pleasing her was more important than being with her for a longer time. "So shortcut it is. The foolish Mundane has made another foolish decision."

She shot him an appreciative glance that made it all worthwhile, regardless of the outcome. "Perhaps not entirely foolish," she murmured.

They followed the shortcut. It led to a marshy glade with odd-shaped depressions near a sharply rising mountain. Nada looked uneasy, but didn't comment.

Dug sniffed the air. "What is that smell? Did a whale die here after eating a mountain of cabbage?"

Nada sniffed. "Oh, I don't like this!"

"Neither do I. If that's the Good Magician's castle ahead, he needs to catch up on a century's worth of baths."

"I fear it is an invisible giant," Nada said faintly.

"Oh, is he going to step on us? Then we'd better get onto the shadow of that mountain."

"Worse. Because—"

The ground shook. The very trees seemed to jump. In fact, some *did* jump, as if kicked by an invisible foot. Then a swatch of nearby forest was abruptly flattened, as if the foot had landed on it. The smell intensified.

Dug stared. "That invisible giant—you weren't joking?"

"A princess seldom jokes."

Another swatch of forest flattened. "It's coming toward us!" Dug cried. "Run for the mountain!"

"I fear we have no choice," she agreed, running with him. Even distracted as he was by the overpowering stench and the threat of being stepped on, Dug couldn't help but notice how she looked when she ran. He wished he could watch that when not distracted. But he would never tell her that, of course. It wouldn't be Mundanely.

They reached the mountain. There was a cave opening, leading into a dimly lighted tunnel.

Another invisible foot landed, squishing more forest. It was alarmingly close. "We'd better hide in there!" Dug said.

"Not if we can help it," Nada said.

He hesitated. "Why not? It can't be worse than here."

"Oh, it can," she said. "I fear this is Pewter's cave. It shouldn't be here; it's south of the Gap Chasm. But the shortcut must have conveyed us there."

"A pewter cave? You mean it is used to store metal carvings?"

"No. It—"

Another invisible footprint was forming. This one was right before them, and the ground was rapidly indenting toward them, as if a huge boot had landed heel-first and the sole and toe were coming down. The smell had become an intolerable stink.

They launched themselves into the cave, where the boot couldn't reach. Just in time, for the whole region shook, and dust stirred everywhere except where the footprint was.

"Oh, nuisance!" Nada swore. "We have been driven into Pewter's lair. The shortcut is a Pewter Plot."

"What's so bad about pewter? It's just tin and lead, an alloy they use to make pretty figurines and things."

"This is Com Pewter, Xanth's evilest machine," she explained. "He was turned into a nice machine recently, but for the purpose of the game he is defined as he used to be. He changes reality in his vicinity, so as to have everything his way. Now we're really in trouble, and it's all my fault, because I told you to try the shortcut."

Com Pewter. Another stupid pun. "No, I told you we would try it. Obviously this is a special game challenge. So I'll just handle it and go on, no sweat."

"You can't just handle Pewter!" she protested. "He handles you."

"Well, we'll see about that." Dug marched on into the cave, having concluded that foolish boldness would impress her more than ineffective caution.

They came into a larger cave, where there was a collection of junk. A screen stood up in the center of that pile. WELCOME, MUNDANE PLAYER, it printed.

So this was the dread machine! But Dug had learned not to dismiss magic things contemptuously; they could indeed fight back, here in this Land of Xanth. "Hello, Com Pewter. What can I do for you?"

YOU CAN SERVE ME FOREVER, the magic screen responded.

"Apart from that."

YOU CAN FORFEIT YOUR GAME.

"No choices in between?"

NONE.

"Well, I don't care for those options," Dug said firmly. "So I'll just be departing now. It's been nice meeting you."

MUNDANE PLAYER CHANGES HIS MIND.

Oops. "Then again, maybe I'll stay and chat with you awhile," Dug said, discovering that his mind had indeed been changed. He was beginning to understand what Nada had meant about the evil machine changing reality. This could be worse trouble than he had figured on.

"Now wait, you evil machine," Nada protested. "You aren't allowed to give him a no-win either-or! You have to give him a chance to beat you."

WHO SAYS? the screen demanded irritably.

"The Demon Professor Grossclout," she retorted. "He set up the rules for the game, and if you don't obey—"

PRINCESS COMPANION CHOKES AND IS UNABLE TO COMPLETE HER SENTENCE, the screen printed.

Nada choked and coughed, not finishing her sentence.

But this was enough to give Dug the hint. "So it's this Demon Big Cloth who runs the game, not you! And he says you have to give me a fair chance. Which means you have to give my Companion a chance to advise me. Otherwise—"

OTHERWISE WHAT, IGNORANT MUNDANE?

Dug did not like being called ignorant, but since that accurately described him in this situation, he let it pass. He made a flying guess. "Otherwise you forfeit, screen-for-brains, and I win. Now let Nada go."

GIRL COMPLETES HER IRRELEVANT REMARK, the screen printed grudgingly.

"Grossclout will make mush of your crockery brain," Nada finished.

I WOULD LIKE TO SEE HIM TRY.

Nada rose to the challenge. "If I snap my fingers, he will appear," she said. "Because that's my signal for game interference." She held up her hand, fingers cocked.

DAMSEL'S HAND GOES NUMB.

Nada's fingers sagged. She could not snap them.

"But I can snap mine," Dug said. "Want to bet he won't respond to somebody's finger snap from this area?"

IGNORANT MUNDANE'S HAND GOES NUMB.

Dug lost sensation in his hand. This computer was sharp!

But now Nada was free. "My hand has recovered," she said. "You can't control both of us at the same time. So now *I'll* snap."

NO NEED, the screen printed quickly. IT WAS ONLY A JOKE. HAVE YOU NO HUMOR? THE MUNDANE WILL BE GIVEN AN EVEN CHANCE.

Dug had seen that kind before: bullies who claimed it was only a joke, when they had to back off. He had never liked that kind. At least they had backed the ornery machine off a bit. "So I'll have an even chance," he said, getting it officially stated, because it was apparent that statements had the force of reality here.

I SHALL GIVE YOU THREE TASKS TO PERFORM, AND—

"Nuh-*uh*!" Dug interrupted. "I'll define the rules." Again, he hoped to prevail by getting his definitive statement in first. He knew that any tasks the evil machine set would be almost impossible to accomplish. "We'll have a pun riddle contest. First one who can't guess the other's riddle loses." Because he was pretty good at riddles.

NUH-*UH*, the screen printed. ONE MUST ANSWER AND THE OTHER FAIL. IF BOTH ANSWER OR BOTH FAIL, THE ROUND IS NULL.

Dug had to admit that was fair. At least he had defined the nature of the contest. "Okay. I'll go first." He paused, but the machine did not object. So he dredged up a punnish not-too-dirty joke he had heard, hoping Nada wouldn't object: "What is spelled with a hymen?"

MAIDEN-HEAD, the screen printed.

Ouch! Pewter had heard the joke! Now he was down one, and if the machine floored him, he'd be lost.

HOW DID THE DEMONS PULL THE KISS-MEE RIVER STRAIGHT?

"What river?" Dug asked blankly.

"He's Mundane," Nada said. "He doesn't know our landmarks. You have to tell him before using them."

THE KISS-MEE RIVER FLOWS SOUTHWARD ALONG EASTERN XANTH, CONNECTING THE KISS-MEE LAKE TO LAKE OGRE-CHOBEE. THE DEMONS PULLED IT STRAIGHT, RUINING IT. BY WHAT MAGIC DID THEY ACCOMPLISH THIS?

Now something clicked. "There was a river somewhere—Florida, I think—the Kissimmee—that the Corps of Engineers channelized. You mean this is a pun on that?"

ANSWER THE QUESTION.

Dug looked at Nada. "It is true," she said. "The demons did do that. You must answer."

In the real world, the demons had simply dug a straight channel and routed the river through it, eliminating the meanders. It had been reckoned an environmental disaster. No magic there, and no puns; it had been one seriously unfunny business. How was he supposed to make a joke of it?

"I guess they used a pushmi-pullyou spell on it," he said without much hope.

ERROR! the screen printed. HEE-HEE!

But he wasn't quite lost yet. "You have to show that you have a good answer," Dug said. "Because if you don't, it doesn't count."

"That is true," Nada said, relieved.

The evil machine wasn't fazed. THEY PULLED THE S'S STRAIGHT, MAKING THEM L'S. THUS KISS-MEE BECAME KILL-MEE, WITH NO MORE CURVES.

And when the S's went straight, making them small L's, the river became straight too. It did make punnish magical sense. Dug knew he had lost.

"Okay, Pewter, you beat me," he said. "What now?"

YOU ARE IN A DREAM WHICH IS OUR REALITY. YOUR REALITY IS OUR DREAM. RETURN TO IT.

Com Pewter's screen showed a picture: Dug's room, with his messy bed in the background and used socks on the floor. Mundania—suddenly the dreariest possible place.

He looked at Nada. "I'm sorry. I lost. I really wanted to stay with you, but I have to go."

"Yes," she said sadly. "I have failed you."

"No, I failed myself. I didn't make the grade." He was determined to be a good loser; it was all that was left.

He faced the screen. "How do I—?"

STEP THROUGH.

So Dug lifted a foot and put it to the screen, which seemed to grow larger. His foot passed through without resistance and landed on his chair. In a moment he was through, and back in his room.

He turned, and saw Nada on the screen. "But you can play again, Dug," her speech balloon said. "If you ask for me—"

SILENCE! the screen printed. Then it went dark. Dug was definitely out of the game.

6
HYDROGEN

Cyrus Merman was about to pose his question to Kim. Jenny quailed, fearing that the pleasant evening was about to become extremely awkward. Even without much knowledge of the things hidden by the Adult Conspiracy, she could tell that this was an extremely serious matter. She had failed to protect Kim from this, and so had not been a good Companion.

"Dear, perhaps you should give her the background," the Siren said to her son. "Remember, Kim is not from Xanth, and she may not understand, otherwise."

"Certainly," Cyrus agreed. "If it is not too boring."

Jenny knew that Kim would not be bored by any postponement of the dread question. "We're sure it will be most interesting," she said quickly.

He smiled. "It is nice of you to say that, Jenny Elf. Certainly it interests *us*, but we are natives of this region."

"Oh, we want very much to know," Kim said with all the faint heartiness she seemed able to muster. The irony was that she really did look very nice in the dress the Siren had provided, and had she been a regular denizen of Xanth, such a union would have been entirely appropriate. So Cyrus was twenty-eight; he was still a handsome, vigorous man, surely nicely experienced, who could be good for a girl of sixteen. There were many such girls in Xanth who would jump at the chance.

"Then we must do it in appropriate style," Morris said. "For this history has become a play, and we like to reenact it on significant occasions."

Jenny and Kim exchanged another glance of doubt. Significant occasion?

But what could they do, except agree, hoping that some diplomatic way would turn up to get out of this misunderstanding?

"We must assume roles," Cyrus said. "For this narrative concerns the Curse Fiends, and their concern is acting. Indeed, it was from one of their traveling troupes that we learned it. Of course we can not hope to do it as well as they do, but it is more fun being in it ourselves."

Kim found a bit of her voice. "A play? I was interested in acting, but—" She broke off, looking troubled.

"Oh, you were?" the Siren asked solicitously. "What happened to prevent it?"

"I—I guess I wasn't right for the part," Kim said reluctantly.

"The part?" Cyrus inquired. "Couldn't you have any part you wished?"

Kim laughed. "Hardly! People have to try out for parts, and only a few get the good ones. I didn't want to be a person lost in a crowd scene, so I tried out for the ingenue. The more fool, I! After that disaster I stayed away from acting."

"Ingenue?" the Siren asked.

"The role of the lovely, quiet, innocent girl."

"But surely that was perfect for you!" Cyrus exclaimed.

"A perfect disaster. I'm a talkative, pushy, unlovely girl."

"Surely this is not so," Morris said. "You have seemed, if anything, somewhat reticent."

Jenny knew why: because of this embarrassing question of marriage. But she didn't dare try to clarify that.

"And you have not seemed at all forward," the Siren said. "You have been, if I may say so, extremely well behaved."

"And you are lovely," Cyrus said. "Even when you were bedraggled, I saw the beauty marks on your face."

"Beauty marks!" Kim exclaimed. "Those are zits!"

Cyrus' brow furrowed. "Do they not serve the same purpose, in Mundania? Just as Jenny Elf's freckles add luster to her face?"

Jenny jumped. She did have freckles, as did Electra, who was now a princess, but she had never been sure they were an enhancement. Now she saw that Kim was trying to suppress a flush. This was evidently an embarrassing subject for her. Perhaps she thought the merfolk were teasing her. Yet if they were not, it was no better, because it meant they believed she was suitable for marriage. Somehow this predicament just got worse as the mer people got nicer.

"It is obvious that Mundanes know little of character or beauty," Morris said. "But as it happens, this is a violent narrative, with no important female players. Would you prefer to assume the role of a prominent male?"

Kim was taken aback. "Oh, I couldn't!"

But Jenny saw a possible avenue of escape here. An unfeminine role might be just the thing to divert the notion of marriage. "You should try it, Kim," she said. "It could help."

Kim looked at her, gradually comprehending. "A pushy male," she said. "Yes, that could be good." Then she glanced at the others. "I mean, a real challenge. To portray someone that—that different."

"That is the heart of acting," Morris said. "To assume a role that is quite different from one's own nature, and do it effectively. This should test your skill."

"Well, I'm really not a good actress. Actor. I never got the chance to be in a play."

"Until now," Morris said. "Here are the roles: Loudspeaker, who is the villain. He is a powerful Magician."

"Well," Kim said dubiously. Jenny could appreciate why. It would be a challenge to play the part of a male, and another to be a villain, and another to be a Magician, when she knew so little of the true ways of such folk.

"I shall be happy to be Loudspeaker, this time," Cyrus said. "It is certainly a challenging role, quite unlike my nature."

Morris nodded. "And there is Hydrogen, a beneficial Magician."

"Aren't there any, well, just ordinary parts?" Kim asked plaintively.

"There are some," Morris said. "But I understood that you wished a leading part. This one seems good."

Jenny saw how tempted Kim was, despite her uncertainty. So she gave her a nudge. "Why not try it, Kim? The worst you can do is make an awkward mess of it."

Kim paused, assessing the prospect in the manner Jenny had. If she made an awkward mess, she might become unattractive to the merman, and he would not ask her to marry him. It might be embarrassing, but for the best. So, guided by this nudge, she agreed. "I will be Hydrogen."

"Excellent," Morris said. "Now, Loudspeaker, being evil, has no friends, but Hydrogen, being good, does. One of these is the young woman Bec, who is always on call to help. So if Jenny wishes to be his loyal companion and adviser—"

"Yes!" Jenny exclaimed. "I will be Bec on call."

"And there is an assortment of other men, lesser characters, ranging from lowly to Magicians, with their wives and families. My wife and I will fill those roles, and she will make the background music, so as to generate the realism. With a little bit of cooperation and imagination, we shall see the scenery form."

Jenny wondered how that could be, since the merfolk did not have the magic of illusion. But it didn't matter. She just hoped that the story would divert Cyrus' attention from Kim, so that the play would not be followed by an uncomfortable scene. But she wasn't at all sure this would happen.

"Now, I must explain that in this narration, we do not actually move about," Morris said. "We only speak our parts. It may facilitate the effect if you close your eyes, at first, until the mood takes hold."

Jenny was glad to oblige. She did not fancy herself much of an actor anyway, and this made it easier. Then she realized that she could contribute in another way: by humming. Because it was her magic talent to form a dream when she hummed, that anybody who wasn't paying attention could enter. Maybe she could form a dream of what the merman described, and they could all seem to be in it.

"But where is the script?" Kim asked.

"Script?" Morris seemed perplexed.

"To read our lines from. So we know what to say."

"Oh, nothing like that is needed. I will narrate the background, and each role will speak as appropriate. It is never quite the same twice. This gives it renewed vigor."

"Oh, improvisation," Kim said. "I suppose I can try that." She seemed less than certain, however.

"Now we commence," Morris said. They sat back in their comfortable water chairs and closed their eyes.

The Siren played her dulcimer. It was beautiful, as before, but eerie. Jenny felt a lukewarm shiver ripple through her spine. That music really was magic! It was doing things to her imagination, so that she began to see a landscape. In fact, it was the map of Xanth, as seen by a flying roc, with all its little trees and lakes and the Gap Chasm jaggedly crossing its center.

Jenny hummed faintly, forming her dream from that description. It was easy to do, working along with the Siren's music.

Morris spoke gravely, setting the scene.

In the year 378 following the First Wave of successful human colonization of Xanth, there came the Seventh Wave. The Human King Roogna had died almost a century before, in battle with the invading Sixth Wave, and there had been a time of distress. But now things were relatively quiet. The Seventh Wave, unlike some others, was peaceful. Its members had fled their own land to escape harassment by more powerful groups, and did not wish to inflict their ways on anyone else, or to do harm to either people or animals. They remained together, rather than mixing with the human folk already here, and married among themselves. Consequently the magic talents of their children were relatively weak, being mostly what is termed the spot-on-the-wall variety: a person could make a spot of color appear magically on a wall, but of what real use was it?

This lack of significant magic made the Seventh Wavers feel inferior, which tended to isolate them even more. They were poorly equipped to defend themselves against the depredations of dragons, who liked to tease them by snatching them up, toasting them with fire, and feeding smoked pieces to their offspring. Often the more talented other Wavers were as bad, abducting them for slaves. They retreated to the deepest wilderness in the most unexplored region of Xanth, but there were violent ogres there who harassed them by twisting them into pretzel shapes, hurling them into orbit around the moon, and other nuisances. So they built a castle under Lake Ogre, around the vortex that was the gateway to the underworld, and there they were able to hide—until the demons came up from below to interfere with them by molesting their women and twisting their men's heads around to face backward on their bodies.

"We have to have more magic!" they concluded at last. So in the year 400 they set up a research group to discover the secret of magic talents. It was an ambitious undertaking. They did not want to wait another generation for stronger magic to develop in their offspring; they wanted actually to learn to manipulate the talents they already had, to make them more effective immediately. It was called the Talent Research Group, headed by the good man Hydrogen, whose talent was to make dirty water become clean. This was considered to be the best talent the Seventh Wave had produced, which was why he was put in charge. Even so, it was not phenomenal, because anyone could duplicate his feat by pouring water through a bag of sand, and changing the sand every so often.

Morris paused in the narrative, and there was a silence. Jenny had found herself seeing the group of people, beset by dragons, hostile folk, and ogres, finally hiding in the great Ogre Lake and trying to find magic. Now she realized that this was only the background. It was time for the players to play.

"Oh, Hydrogen," she said. "How are you going to find the secret of magic talents?"

Kim realized that it was her turn. "Why, er, we'll just have to study the matter and see what we can come up with." Then, realizing that that was inadequate, she added: "Bec, go call the others together. We'll have a brainstorming session."

"A storm on a brain?"

Kim laughed. "Who knows? That might be good magic! But what I meant was that we should have a good talk about it, and see what ideas we can come up with. We can't do anything if we don't have a good plan of action."

So Bec called the others: "Hey, others! Come together! Hydrogen wants to storm your brains."

There was a shuffle of feet, and when Jenny closed her eyes again she seemed to see a number of people coming to join them. Soon her dream took better hold, and she saw them clearly. "We are here," one of them said. His voice didn't even sound too much like Morris'.

"I want you all to make suggestions," Hydrogen said. "Any suggestions, no matter how silly they might sound. Because the good idea we need may be the one that seems too silly for anyone else to consider. No negative comments are allowed."

"I have heard it said that there is unity in strength," someone said. "I have noticed that our weak talents are sort of similar. Is it possible that we could get together and reinforce each other's talents, making one big strong talent?"

"It's an idea," Hydrogen agreed.

"But it has never been done before," someone objected. "In Xanth, talents never repeat." Then, receiving the stares of the others: "Oops! That was negative, wasn't it! I take it back."

"Could we change our talents by mimicking others?" another asked. "All orienting on the same talent?"

"That's another idea, in harmony with the first," Hydrogen said.

"How about a talent that will set the ogres back?" another asked. "Like maybe a powerful curse?"

It seemed good to Hydrogen. So they got together and tried to emulate the one who had a faint power of cursing. And it worked. At first all they could do was produce a floating voice saying $$$$! But in time that unified curse became strong enough to wilt nearby foliage.

After a year they took their group curse out into the field for field testing. A brute of an ogre stood in the field. "Me see he flea!" he exclaimed as he advanced on the group, ready to squish the flea with one swat of a hamfist.

"One," Hydrogen said, counting. "Two. Three!"

They all threw their pieces of the curse together, directly at the ogre. It detonated in front of his face. **$$$$!** It scorched his eyebrows and burned the fur of his nose.

Temporarily blinded, the ogre stumbled away, swiping at the air. He wasn't retreating, because ogres didn't know how to do that. He was merely advancing in the wrong direction.

"It worked!" Bec cried jubilantly. "The curse foiled the ogre!"

But it wasn't strong enough to foil a group of ogres. So they returned to their laboratory and labored for another year. In that time they developed the curse to such a strength that it could blow an ogre into the next scene. In fact, they were now able to drive the ogres away from Lake Ogre, forcing them to start their long trek across the length of Xanth to the Ogre fen Ogre Fen. The Talent Research Group was a success.

"But it is not enough to handle dragons," Hydrogen said grimly. "We must keep working." So they had another brainstorming session, and looked for something even more potent. They also set to work training the rest of the Seventh Wavers to unify their talents, because though each person's magic was small, the accretive effect was large. They began to call themselves the Curse Friends, but those on the receiving end of the curses preferred to call them the Curse Fiends. That was all right; their neighbors were learning respect, thanks to Hydrogen's Talent Research Group.

In three more years they had their second breakthrough: they discovered how to expand their talents. Now Hydrogen focused on his original ability to clean water, and learned how to tap the basic elemental forces so that he could permanently enhance the properties of any substance. Loudspeaker, a member of the group, was now able to expand his talent of amplifying his voice, and could use it to create Words of Power. Other group members enhanced their own simple talents. In the course of the next several years, eight of them managed to build up their talents enough to enable them to qualify as Magicians. What a change from their former puniness!

But now came unforeseen consequences of power. Each person, having tasted more of it than he had ever believed possible, wanted yet more. Resentments flared. Others wondered openly why Hydrogen should be the leader, when there were now many excellent talents. Hydrogen tried to maintain peace, but people who had been nice and mild and powerless now were grasping and savage. Power had corrupted them in direct proportion to its increase.

Then Loudspeaker did the unspeakable: he used his Words against his own people. He used an especially potent Word to turn the other members of the research group into green chobees, who promptly fled to Lake Ogre, where they were lost. They remembered none of their manlike lives, and wanted only to

chomp men. They had very long mouths full of sharp teeth, so it was dangerous to get close enough to try to reason with them. So there was no alternative
except to rename the lake Ogre-Chobee and let them be. At least others would
be warned of the danger by the name. Actually, there was a bright side: now no
strangers could wander across the lake and find Gateway Castle beneath it, because the chobees would chomp any who tried.

Only Hydrogen escaped, because he had been away at the time of the
sneak attack. He realized that Loudspeaker had to be stopped before he caused
even more trouble. The only one who could stop the evil Magician was Hydrogen, because he was the only other surviving Magician among the Curse
Friends. "Loudspeaker, you have done a bad thing," he said grimly. "But I will
stop you." It didn't seem like much of an oath, but the people applauded.

Bec went to call other curse-wielding actors. Hydrogen formed them into a
new group, whose joint curse could be charged with his own elemental energy.
Now they had a weapon capable of destroying Loudspeaker.

The evil Magician meanwhile had gone to a region north of the Gap Chasm
in central Xanth. He had set up a palace formed of spliced Words, and used other
Words to enslave the resident fairies, harpies, and other creatures of the air so
that they had to do his bidding. There was a chain of linked Words around the
whole estate, and each Word was barbed. No one could get close without receiving a terrible tongue-lashing. He had what seemed to be an impregnable bastion.

But Hydrogen assembled his team, and they stood on a mountain opposite
the palace. Hydrogen stood at the pinnacle and called across to the evil Magician. "Loudspeaker, I demand that you surrender, and practice evil no more.
Otherwise we shall blast you out of your fortress."

Their only answer was a barrage of sharp Words. They flew like daggers,
and slammed into the wooden shield the heroes hastily erected. For Hydrogen
had expected more treachery, and had prepared for it.

"Okay, you asked for it!" Hydrogen cried with noble righteous ire. "One—
two—three!"

His loyal group hurled their joint curse, modified to contain plenty of Hydrogen's magic. It was an air attack. It struck the palace and blew it away. It
whirled around, searching for Loudspeaker, but he was not there. He had
sneaked out during the night, leaving only his sharp Words to guard the palace.

The curse, its target undestroyed, was unfulfilled. It continued to search the
area, blowing wildly. Hydrogen had not thought to put dissipation into it, in
case of failure. So it just continued to rush around, never relaxing. There was
nothing to be done except to let it be. Hydrogen and his band had won the battle but not yet won the war. "Oh, fudge!" Hydrogen swore.

Thus there came to be the Region of Air, where the wind eternally whirled and searched, seeking what wasn't there.

Loudspeaker retreated north and set up another small evil empire, this time using his Words to dominate trolls, goblins, and other denizens of the earth. Battalions of mean creatures marched around the central earthworks, shouting awful insults at any who were foolish enough to come into range. It seemed to be another implacable retreat.

Hydrogen sent Bec to scout out the territory. Bec reported that it was an ugly place, almost as drear as Mundania.

"Mundania!" Hydrogen exclaimed. "What do you have against Mundania?" Then, reconsidering, he said, "Oh. I forgot. Yes, it sounds pretty bad."

So he gathered his force on the ground near the empire, and called again to the enemy. "Loudspeaker, give it up! Or we shall bury you!"

The only answer he received was a barrage of thrown spears, tipped with the sharpest Words yet. These plunked into the hasty shield with expressions that caused the group's ears to burn. Loudspeaker certainly had an evil way with Words!

"Sticks and stones will break my bones, but names will never hurt me!" Hydrogen called. Several of his group were startled; they had never heard that particular expression before, and it did not seem to make a lot of sense here in Xanth where names could be devastating.

Then they launched a massive adapted curse. It looped up across the land, and came down directly on the earthworks. Boom! The earth flew up and out, with rocks spewing across the landscape, and melted rock flowed across the scenery. Some bits of stone coalesced in the air to form tiny glass teardrops which would have seemed highly significant to Mundanes, but were merely fragments here.

But the curse couldn't find its target, because Loudspeaker had again cravenly fled. The curse searched diligently, refusing to quit until it had accomplished its mission. Hydrogen had forgotten to put a dissipation into it, again. There had just been too much on his mind, and that detail slipped through the cracks, as it were.

Thus came to be the Region of Earth, where the ground continually moved and mountains spewed their intestinal lava out randomly. It was not exactly Xanth's nicest place.

Hydrogen shook his head. "I'm having some trouble getting the hang of this heavy magic," he confessed.

Meanwhile Loudspeaker had moved north again, and used more Words to dominate fire-breathing dragons, salamanders, and other hot creatures. He fashioned a castle of burning Words, and surrounded it with a ring of fiery language. Once more, he seemed to be securely ensconced.

But Hydrogen refused to quit. He brought his group up to the edge of the territory. "Loudspeaker!" he called. "Now, you quit destroying the environment like this, or I'll blast you out!"

His only answer was a fiery Word from a dragon. The tongue of flame licked against the hasty shield and heated it until it melted. The men had to drop it before their fingers got burned.

"So that's the way it is!" Hydrogen said, annoyed. "Well, I'll just fight fire with fire!"

Then his group fired a curse so hot it set the neighboring air on fire and blazed across the sky until it seared into the castle and blasted it to flaming fragments. The very sky caught on fire, and it flickered forever after, called the aurora. A forest on the ground burst into a flame so fierce that it was never possible to put it out.

But once more the target was missing. Loudspeaker, in cravenly anti-hero fashion, had sneaked out, leaving his unfortunate assistants to bear the brunt of the fire curse. The fire looked and looked, burning everything it encountered, but the evil Magician just wasn't there. So why hadn't Hydrogen put a time limit on the curse: "I really thought we had him, this time," he said sheepishly.

In this manner came to exist the Region of Fire, where flames were eternal and only creatures of flame could survive for any length of time. Fireflies and spitfires loved it, but few ordinary people or creatures resided there.

"I guess I'm just not much of a hero," Hydrogen confessed woefully.

Meanwhile Loudspeaker had moved north again, into the veriest heart of Unknown Xanth, thinking no one would find him there. He settled by a nice lake, and compelled the poor fish to serve him, and water nymphs had to disport themselves for his satisfaction. Around his water works a monstrous water dragon curled, ready to chomp anyone who intruded. Water fowl kept sharp eyes out for the approach of any hostile forces. It seemed that no one could bother Loudspeaker here.

But Hydrogen had not learned how to quit. He brought his group to the verge of the lake and sent loyal Bec to investigate. Bec was always on call, and always finished her task before starting another. She swam quietly through the lake and observed its formidable array of defenses. "This will be a very wet undertaking," she reported.

So Hydrogen came up to the lake and called, "Loudspeaker, now you get out of here and become a nice model citizen, or I'll wash you out!"

His only answer was a great splat of bilge water that almost drowned his group. Then the water dragon and water fowl oriented on him and massed for an attack.

"Well, then, it will be a water war," Hydrogen said wetly. His group pumped out a curse so wet that it would have drowned the sun if it had struck that orb. Fortunately the sun had the sense to stay well away from it. The curse went splat on the water works, and washed everything into the lake. It filled the lake to heaping, and then piled up into a mountain whose crest foamed angrily, looking for its target.

But Loudspeaker was gone again. The water searched all over, washing a deep depression into the land, but could not find him. So it made a liquid shrug and settled into flatness, overflowing into the west where it formed the Half-Baked Bog, and into the east where it drained off into the Sane Jaunts River, and it was done. Because—surprise!—this time Hydrogen had remembered to put a time limit on the curse.

Thus came to be the Water Wing, a passive region where men and creatures could reside and interbreed. It was a rather pleasant place, overall, and soon developed a nice community of merfolk who had consideration for the local environment and always welcomed visitors.

Meanwhile Loudspeaker had set up operations to the north. This was a desolate region where no one cared to go, and the truth was that Loudspeaker wasn't too keen on it either, but he was running out of options. Since Hydrogen had pursued him to all the nice regions, he had to try a nasty one. Maybe then he would be left alone long enough to build up his army and magic and conquer Xanth in style. Because this was his fell ambition: to make all the land slave to his merest whim. Even if his whim wasn't nice. He was collecting a band of whims who would do whatever he wished, and whatever no one else wished. He had even found a cute female whimsy to entertain his off-hours.

Hydrogen was a slow learner, as was shown by the time it took him to learn to put limits on his curses. But in time he did get there. So this time, considering that Loudspeaker always retreated before the solid (or liquid) curse could score, he put Bec on the job of cutting off the escape. In fact, this time she would even make the challenging call. Hydrogen had a secret reason for this.

So Bec went around to the north, then stood at the edge of the ugly place and called out the challenge. "Loudspeaker, quit this funny business and give up your bad magic, or I will curse you into irrelevance!"

Her only answer was a whimsical blob of garbage that went splat against her shield. So Bec called Hydrogen and told him about it, and he swore a medium oath that he would this time blow the enemy into sheer nothingness. He readied his group's worst curse, an awful Nothing bomb.

Loudspeaker, thinking that the charge would be from the north, tried to sneak back south to hide in the nice lake of the Water Wing. But this was where Hydrogen was. Now Hydrogen bombed him. The Nothing curse exploded, forming a tremendous dome of chaos that destroyed everything in its range, then sank down through the ground in a singular fashion, and was never heard from again. In fact, nothing else that entered that singularity ever returned, because Nothing had made its ultimate home here.

Thus came to be the Void, the home of nothing. Around its edge was an event horizon, where normal events stopped and became nothing. Only largely imaginary creatures like the night mares could enter the Void and return.

This time Loudspeaker had not escaped. Even his memory was gone, so that only a few storytellers knew he had ever existed. He was now nothing, and Hydrogen's job was done.

Now Hydrogen considered. He realized that a great deal of damage had been done by this momentous campaign against evil. All of the battles had done damage to central Xanth. He wanted to see that never again would there be havoc wrought by an air attack, earth encounter, fire fight, water war, or void violation. It would be better if the secret of modifying magic talents were lost, so that no other person could make himself into an evil Magician.

As it happened, Hydrogen was now the last of the original Modified Magicians. So he sent the other members of his group back to Gateway Castle, except for Bec on Call, then settled in the Water Wing, and devoted the rest of his life to developing the talent of keeping a secret. Finally he perfected it, and invoked it, and forever after no one in Xanth was able to rediscover the secret of modifying talents. Hydrogen's last great enchantment had made it impossible.

Hydrogen married Bec, of course, and their descendants became the merfolk of the Water Wing. They had to marry humans and fish in alternate generations, to maintain their status as mer people. The Curse Friends remained a close-knit group with weak individual talents, all of them related to cursing, and became great actors. The villages around Lake Ogre-Chobee were always glad when one of their troupes arrived, because their plays were always superb. Thus it was a regular circuit of the lake. In time no one remembered that the Talent Research Group had even existed, or that for fifteen years there had been havoc in central Xanth while things were being put to rights. For more than two and a half centuries Xanth was reasonably quiet, until the onset of the Eighth Wave.

"But that is another story," Morris concluded.

Jenny opened her eyes. The ancient scenery of Xanth faded away with its heroic deeds and misdeeds. She was back in the present, with the nice mer family. She was no longer Bec on Call, but Jenny Elf. However, she now knew a good deal more about Xanth than she had.

"Now we know the background," Cyrus said. "It was a stroke of fortune for my father when the Siren arrived here, because then he could marry her instead of a fish. Now I would like to do something similar."

Jenny saw Kim freeze. As Hydrogen, Kim had become a reasonably bold if error-prone hero. Now she was just a girl who remained error-prone, or perhaps error-supine. What was she going to do?

"Which brings me to my question for you, Kim," Cyrus said. "This is something which perhaps only you can do for me, but which is supremely important to me. It concerns my marriage."

"I—I—" Kim managed to say, before her voice freaked out and fled. Jenny's voice had already done so. Morris and the Siren looked on benignly.

"Therefore I must ask you, Kim," Cyrus continued grandly, "whether you will allow me to travel with you until I find a suitable mermaid elsewhere in Xanth to marry? For you see I am not used to traveling beyond the Water Wing, and fear I would encounter mischief if I did so alone. You are the first human traveler to pass this way in some time. As my father says, you seem to be the right young woman for this purpose, because you are not of Xanth and so there is no impropriety in our keeping company for a time. We merfolk are highly conscious of the proprieties, perhaps because we derive from the play-acting Curse Friends. With a man there would have been no problem, of course, but it may be a long time before a traveling man passes this way."

Kim looked as if about to faint with relief, perhaps tinged with a dab of disappointment. Jenny emulated Bec on Call and stepped into the breach. She found her voice, where it had been cowering under her chair. "Kim will be happy to have you travel with us," she said. "Until you find a suitable mermaid to marry."

Kim scrambled to find her own voice, but it was just out of reach. So she nodded her head vigorously, smiling. There were tears in her eyes.

"Excellent!" Cyrus said heartily. "This is a great relief to me."

At last Kim recovered her voice. "Me too!" she squeaked.

"We are so glad this has worked out," the Siren said. "Now you must rest here for the night, so as to be fresh for the morrow."

Kim and Jenny were glad to agree.

7
BLACK WAVE

Nada glared at Com Pewter. "Aren't you proud of yourself," she said severely. "You tricked my Player into coming here with that shortcut, and herded him into your cave, and used your superior knowledge of Xanth to defeat him in the riddle contest, so now he's out."

EXACTLY, the screen printed smugly.

"Thereby making me a failure as a Companion. I hope you're satisfied."

I AM.

"Oh, you're impossible!"

I AM AN EVIL MACHINE. HO HO HO!

"I liked you better when you were a nice machine."

I WAS NICE ONLY BECAUSE LACUNA TRICKED ME INTO RE-COMPILING. NOW IN THE GAME I GET TO BE EVIL AGAIN. BUT YOU ARE WELCOME TO ASSUME YOUR LUSCIOUS SERPENTINE FORM AND CURL AROUND MY HARDWARE ANYTIME, NAGA CREATURE.

"Well, Dug will come back into the game, despite you, you crock of capacitors."

THEN HE WILL HAVE TO MEET ME AGAIN AND DEFEAT ME IN A HARDER GAME THAN BEFORE. I WILL HAVE THE SINISTER PLEASURE OF DUMPING HIM AGAIN. SO YOU HAD BETTER SHOW HIM YOUR PANTIES WHILE YOU HAVE THE CHANCE, PRINCESS.

"You unspeakable cad!" she cried, outraged.

YOU'RE LOVELY WHEN ANGRY.

Nada snapped her fingers. Professor Grossclout appeared. He was an imposing old demon, complete with fangs and tail. "This annoying machine is insulting me!" she said.

Grossclout frowned. This made his natural grimace even more formidable. "You come to this position with a head full of mush, and you complain because your charge washed out?"

Nada suffered an instant of absolute unholy fury. Then she realized that the Professor was baiting her, as he did with those he hoped might someday improve. It was actually almost a compliment. "I hope to do better next time," she said bravely.

A peculiar expression fought to cross the demon's face, but lost. Nada realized that it was a smile, which would have been in alien territory had it emerged. "Maybe, just maybe, *if* you succeed, you will become a creature worth knowing," he grudged. Then, to Pewter: "Carry on, evil machine."

THANK YOU, Pewter replied, obviously thrilled with the compliment.

Grossclout twitched a little finger negligently. Suddenly Nada was back in the Companions dugout, with Grundy Golem, the Demoness Metria, Goody Goblin, Horace Centaur, Marrow Bones, and a new one, Vida Vila.

"What happened to Jenny Elf?" Nada asked.

"She was chosen to be Kim Mundane's Companion," Grundy said.

"Oh. So Vida came in to replace her in the roster."

"No. Vida replaced *you.*"

"But I'm still here," Nada protested, confused.

Vida laughed. "I replaced you, then Jenny was taken, now you have returned, so maybe now I'm replacing Jenny. Do you mind?"

Nada had to laugh too. "No, of course not. I was just surprised by the change. I shouldn't have been."

"How was it?" Goody asked politely.

"It was awkward, at first, because Dug was trying to express crude male interest in me."

Vida smiled. "It comes with the territory," she said, inhaling. She was of course one of Xanth's loveliest creatures. Nada realized that had she been in the lineup, Dug well might have chosen her instead of Nada.

NOW HEAR THIS, Professor Grossclout's voice blared. IT IS TIME FOR THE SELECTION OF THE FALSE COMPANION.

Oh, that. She had forgotten. She sat up straight, so as not to betray any reaction, along with the others.

THE SELECTION IS—NOW.

YOU.

Nada was too petrified to jump. The lot had fallen on her! She was now the False Companion. Oh, disaster.

But she had to play it out, because part of her role was to conceal it from others. That way no other participant in the game could tell her Player to beware of her. She had to keep it secret, acting exactly like a Fair Companion— until she found the perfect chance to send him into ignominious loss.

She gazed around, pretending not to know who it was, and saw the others doing the same. Except with them it was not pretense. Then she shrugged, as if realizing she would never know. The others did the same, looking relieved. So she made herself look relieved too. Oh, how she hated this! A role of ultimate deception—it just wasn't princessly.

"Look out—here comes a Player," Metria said, peering out the window, exactly as before. Nada wondered whether she had been the False Companion last time; she would have enjoyed it, being forever mischievous.

They sat straight in their seats, ready for consideration. Nada gazed out the one-way screen.

And froze. It was Dug, of course—re-entering the game. And she knew exactly whom he would choose. Because he knew her, and liked her, and trusted her.

This time she was required to betray his trust. Oh, woe!

Another voice sounded in her head. *You will receive further instructions. You will obey them implicitly, without imposing your own judgment on their merit.*

Yes, she responded unhappily. Could she possibly hide behind one of the others, so that Dug would think she wasn't available this time?

"Hi! I'm Grundy Golem. I'm from—"

"Sure thing, Grundy," Dug said amicably. "Let's cut it short, okay? I'm a retread."

Maybe, just for variety, he would choose one of the others. Such as Vida, who was even lovelier than Nada, because she could change her form to match her mood. Maybe Metria, who would take him exactly as far as her mischievous impulse went, possibly even flashing a naughty glimpse of her panties at him before vanishing in smoke. Maybe even a male, so he wouldn't have any problem crossing the river.

"I'll take Nada," Dug said, as she had really known he would. He had sealed his fate, the innocent fool! He had forgotten that a new game meant a new False Companion, who could even be the last game's Fair Companion.

She stood and stepped through the window. "Hello, Dug," she said, according to the formula. "I will try to be a good Companion for you." It was a lie; she would pretend to be a Fair Companion, awaiting the chance to mess him up worse. The False Companion was not supposed to do any ill early, because she might only betray her nature without washing out her Player, giving him the clue how to handle her. She had to wait until late in the game, when he had his best chance to win—and make him lose instead. So that it would be much more difficult for him to re-enter the game and win. Because the hazards grew more formidable as progress was made, and any hazard that defeated a Player had to be overcome in the next game, when it would be worse. That was to discourage Players from deliberately washing out, so as to get a better layout next time.

"It's great to be back with you," he said gladly. "I've already refocused my eyes, and in a moment I should be all the way back inside the game." Indeed, as he spoke he was becoming more sharply defined, and his screen was fading. He had caught on well, and wanted to believe in the magic, so was doing it.

"I am glad to be your Companion again," she lied. Oh, how she wished he had not chosen her this time! But she was stuck with her revised role. If he asked her whether anything had changed, she would have to lie. If she gave herself away, or tried to wash him out early so as to get out of the False assignment with minimal damage, she would be in trouble herself. Professor Grossclout would know, and disallow it. So she couldn't arrange to accidentally show him her panties or anything like that. Not that she would, of course; it wasn't princessly.

"Well, let's go!" he said happily. "This time I'm going to do things better, and not goof up the way I did before."

Nada concealed her sigh. Little did he know!

They set out along the path. "Now, it's okay to go get supplies and all at the Isthmus Village," Dug said. "That turned out satisfactorily. I mean, we did them some good, right? And we abolished the censor-ship. So I won't avoid that, I'll just do it more efficiently this time."

"But the game layout will be different," she reminded him. "And you will be unable to avoid your nemesis Com Pewter, no matter what you do, because he will remember, just as I do." She was now a False Companion, but she had to play the part of a Fair Companion, and this was exactly what a Fair Companion would say. In fact, she would have to act exactly the same as she would have, until after he got by Pewter, because it was pointless to wash him out when it might occur naturally. Her job was not merely to wash him out, but to wash him out just when he was on the verge of a significant breakthrough or victory. To make it as painful as possible for him. So she had to be the perfect Fair Companion, until that dastardly chance came to be the perfect False one.

"That's okay," he said in his Mundanish idiom. "I want to settle with Pewter anyway. He was just lucky, beating me in that riddle contest. I just didn't know enough about Xanth."

She saw that he was in danger of hurting himself through overconfidence.

She should warn him—but the Fair Companion would not have the heart to hurt his feelings, and the False Companion noted that his attitude would make him an easier patsy. So she allowed her silence to be taken as agreement.

The path led to a strange village. Its layout was different, and the houses were dissimilar, and the people—Nada had never seen folk exactly like these. They were just like regular humans, but they were black. Or at least dark brown.

"What's this?" Dug asked, startled as he made a similar observation.

"The layout has changed," Nada said. "I didn't realize that it would be this drastic. This is an entirely different village."

"You said it! Those are blacks."

"You recognize them?"

"Well, not as individuals. But they are—I think the dictionary word is Negroes. People from Africa. We had—I mean, in Mundania there was an ugly—they were brought over as slaves, and then after a war they were freed, but the white folk never did really accept them. It's supposed to be all equal now, no discrimination, but—well, it's like that censor-ship. One of those bad things that exist."

Nada found this confusing. "White people brought black people to their land—and then would not accept them?"

"Not as free people. Not as equals. Not to live next to. There was a whole lot of trouble about integrating the schools, because—" He saw her blank look. "Just take my word: I'm white, and I'm not proud of what my people did. But it's not all that easy to set things right. I mean, once there was this black girl in my math class, and I sort of liked the look of her, she was almost as pretty as you, in her way, and smart too, but I knew if I even said boo to her, I'd lose most of my friends, and her brothers would maybe beat me up. So I just had to ignore her, and I guess she thought I was pretty snotty, but I mean it just wasn't worth the hassle. Probably she thought I was a jerk anyway. So there never was anything there, but I wish—well, I don't know what I wish, but I feel sort of bad about it."

Nada was perplexed and relieved. Perplexed because it was apparent that the social attitudes of Mundanes were stranger than she had known, and relieved because this had nothing to do with her role as a False Companion, and she could just put that aside for now and not think about it. "You wanted to associate with her, but others would not allow it?"

"Yeah, I guess. Her name was Princilla, not Priscilla, and I thought it was a really neat name, you know?"

"Princilla—like Princess," Nada said, appreciating it.

"Yeah. Like you. But whites just don't date blacks, in my town, not if they want to stay healthy. It's even worse if a black man wants to date a white girl.

We're all in classes together, and we play ball together, and we ride the bus together, but there's a line—" He shrugged. "But that's there. Now we're here. I'm sure Xanth doesn't put up with that bleep. What do we do?"

"There is no need to visit this village," she reminded him. "We don't need weapons, and food grows on trees. So the only reason to stop here is if there may be something you can learn or acquire that will help you farther along in the game, which is doubtful." This was the truth.

"You know, in other games, you have to go fetch a magic key, or something, before you can get through a locked door to get something else. This isn't that sort of game?"

"I don't think so. I suppose there could be a key, but I don't know where a locked door would be. I really don't know how you can get where you have to go; that's why we need to see the Good Magician."

"Yeah. Well, maybe there is something I can learn here, that will help me. So let's go talk with these people."

"As you wish." It was amazing: so far her status as False Companion had made no difference at all. At the rate Dug was going, he very well might wash himself out despite anything she could do, leaving her clear both with respect to the game and her conscience. It was, ironically, a somewhat endearing quality in him.

"Hi there," Dug called as they approached the nearest man. This was a carpenter, or at least a man doing some sawing of wood. He seemed to be building a house, slowly.

The black man paused, staring at them. He did not speak.

"Look, I mean no harm," Dug said. "Last time I passed this way, there was a whole different village here. I'm amazed how it changed so suddenly. If you don't want to talk to me, okay, I'll just move on. I'm not looking for any trouble. But I sure am curious what happened."

The man turned his gaze on Nada. She smiled, cautiously. There was a subdued glow when she did that, brightening the man's face. That happened, sometimes. He had to smile back. "You got one pretty woman there," he said.

"She's not my woman," Dug said quickly. "She's just my Companion." Evidently realizing that this lacked clarity, he made a more formal introduction. "This is Princess Nada Naga. She's just showing me around the game."

The man nodded. "That must be some game."

"This is Dug Mundane," Nada said. "He has to find his way to a prize, we think. I am a native of Xanth, so I am guiding him. But it is clear that there are some parts of Xanth I don't know very well myself. I never saw folk like you before."

"You're a magic woman?" the man asked.

"Yes. I can show you, if you wish." She wasn't eager to do this, because then there would be the complication of returning to her human form without allowing her body or underclothing to be seen. But it was her job to help Dug get through the game, for now, and if showing her magic was required, then she would do it.

"Show me," the man said.

So she assumed serpent form and slithered out of her clothes. Then she assumed Naga form. "We are serpent folk," she explained. "This is my natural form."

Other black folk were walking toward them. Nada hoped they were friendly. She did not want to have to assume large serpent form and fight them to protect Dug, but the game required that she do so if necessary.

"You really are magic," the first man said. "Okay, change back, and we'll talk."

Now Dug interceded. "She can't just change back, because then people would see her bare body. She needs a private place."

The man nodded. "Body like that, I can see why." He turned and shouted at the half-built house. "Hey, Mari, someone to see you."

"All right, Jaff," a black woman called from the house.

Dug picked up Nada's clothing, wadded it into a bundle, and proffered it to her. "Go ahead, Nada," he said. "I'll be all right."

She returned to full serpent form, took the bundle in her mouth, and slithered toward the house. She did seem to have broken the ice.

Mari opened the door, and Nada slithered in. Then she set down her bundle, assumed naga form, and explained: "I'm a naga—a serpent woman. I need a private place to resume my human form and get dressed."

The woman hesitated. "This is the only room in the house. We're still building it."

"Oh, it's all right for you to remain," Nada said. "Just so long as there are no men or children."

"My man's outside. No children."

So Nada resumed human form, and quickly got into her clothing.

"You've got some human form!" the woman said.

"Well, I'm supposed to. I'm a princess."

"There are others like you?"

"Yes. We naga folk live mostly in the mountains, underground. We fight goblins when they try to intrude."

"Goblins!"

"No offense intended," Nada said quickly. "Some goblins are nice. I have friends who are goblins. But—"

The woman burst out laughing. "Did I say something funny?" Nada inquired, nettled.

"Goblins raid our stores," Mari said. "We don't like them either. It's just that what you said sounded so much like what we've heard when white folk talk about *us*. About how we're okay, as long as we stay in our place."

Nada was mindful of what Dug had just told her, about the strained relations between the white and black folk of Mundania. "Are you by any chance from Mundania?"

"That's what you call it, yes. We left, because—"

"Because they wouldn't let you be equal, or intermarry."

The woman nodded. "Something like that. But we don't know that it's different here. This is one weird place, but the folk are white."

"Actually there are other colored folk in some places," Nada said. "Green, purple, gray—"

"Maybe we should try to meet them."

"I suppose you could. I don't know where they live now, but there used to be some around Castle Roogna."

Nada was all the way dressed now. They went out. Dug was talking with a group of men. It seemed to be friendly.

Dug saw her. "Hey, I think we can make a deal," he said. "These good folk will give me supplies, if one of them can travel along with us, to see if there's a place in Xanth they will be welcomed. If it's okay with you."

"It is your decision to make," she reminded him. "But perhaps we should learn more of these folk before deciding."

The black men glanced at each other, and glanced at bit longer at Nada. "Sure, let's talk," Jaff agreed.

They walked into the village, where there was a larger, more finished house. They settled on crude wooden chairs. Jaff seemed to be the spokesman, since they had talked with him first. "We're from what you call Mundania," he said. "We crossed only a couple of years ago. We were having a bad time, no good jobs, things were tight, and then somehow we found this path to this magic land and we said, hell, it can't be worse than what we face at home! So we moved here, with our families. But there were some strange things here, like pies growing on trees, and real live dragons, and goblins. So we found a place to camp and sort of hunkered down, and now we're trying to decide whether to settle here or look around some more. We've seen some of the people here, and they're white.

We're not sure how they'll be. We don't want trouble, we just want decent jobs and lives. But things just seem to get weirder, the farther we go in this land, so we aren't sure yet what to do."

"You must be a Wave!" Nada exclaimed.

"A wave?"

"A Wave of Colonization. There have been ten or so, and each Wave usually brings a lot of violence, but not all of them. So you must be the Black Wave. If you don't want to fight, I know the folk here don't want to fight you. We always need more human folk in Xanth, and there are plenty of places to live."

"This sounds pretty good," Jaff said. "Still, we'd like to check it out before we do anything much."

"Look," Dug said. "I'm just a visitor here myself, as I told you. When my game finishes, I'll have to go back to Mundania. But I don't think there's anything in the rules that says I can't take someone else along. I should get a good tour of the region, because I have to find whatever it is I have to find, and anyway, I can make side trips if I want to. So I think it's a fair deal. You fix me up with some supplies, and a weapon to defend myself, and I'll take along one of you, and he can ask all the questions he wants, and maybe find the place you're looking for. Then he can return and tell the rest of you about it."

Nada was uneasy about this, and not just because of her ugly mission. "I don't know."

Dug turned to her. "You have a problem with that?" he asked, half smiling.

"Yes. You are a Player, and I am here to guide you and protect you, to the best of my ability." That was now a half-truth, and she hated it, but she was bound by the rules of the game. "But it is not my job to guide or protect any other person. I might save you from mischief, but the other would suffer it, when he wouldn't have if he had not come with us."

Jaff looked at her. "You are protecting him?" He was obviously dubious.

"You saw me change forms," she replied evenly. "I can become a big serpent if I choose."

"She sure can," Dug said enthusiastically. "She backed off a flying dragon once! And she knows Xanth, so she can keep me out of trouble, if I don't insist on blundering into it anyway."

Jaff looked at his wife. Mari spoke. "She's a good person, Jaff. She's a princess of her kind. Her folk fight goblins."

Jaff turned back to Dug. "We're ready to risk it if you are."

"Then let's do it," Dug said. "Who is coming?"

There was a pause. Then a man who seemed to be in his thirties spoke. "I think I can handle it."

The others nodded agreement. "Sherlock can handle it," Jaff said.

"I'll have to get things from Smith," Sherlock said.

"By all means," Jaff agreed. Sherlock went to another part of the village.

So they got together supplies, and gave Dug a good solid club for a weapon, and Sherlock joined the small party. He was neither large nor handsome, but seemed alert. Nada wondered whether he was a plant by the game, representing some additional challenge. After all, the Isthmus Village had led them into a considerable challenge, and Black Village was where it had been, so it must have been arranged by the game. Dug had chosen to get along rather than antagonize the folk of the Black Wave, but the challenge might not yet be over. Should she warn him about this, or keep silent?

She was now a False Companion. She kept silent.

The three of them were soon on their way along the path. But evening was approaching, just as when they had passed this way before. Was the time fixed by their location, or was it coincidence? She had thought it was still morning when Dug lost the riddle contest and left the game, but perhaps it had been afternoon. So this might be evening of another day. It really didn't seem to matter. All she had to be concerned about was getting him safely through to Com Pewter, and if he didn't lose to the infernal machine again, she would find something worse to make him lose. Then she would be free of her uncomfortable obligation, and if he came back a third time, and chose her again, she might be a Fair Companion.

"We shall have to make camp for the night, soon," Nada said.

"Right," Dug said. "And we know where. Let's get on to it."

"You know where?" Sherlock asked. "I thought this region was just wilderness. We have explored it, and found no safe havens."

Nada nodded. "That must be right," she agreed. "This is our second effort in the game; Dug got eliminated by Com Pewter, the evil machine, and had to start over. The geography got changed, so probably the enchanted campsite we found before is no longer there."

"The geography changed? When did you pass this way before?"

"Yesterday," Dug said. "There was a different village here then."

Sherlock shook his head. "We have been here for a year."

"Well, you would say that. You're part of the game."

"No, you are part of the game. We came to Xanth on our own, and I assure you, it is no game to us."

Dug looked at Nada. "Can you figure this out? Which is real: what we saw, or what they saw?"

"That's easy to resolve," she said, realizing what the key had to be. "The path is enchanted, not to protect us, but to direct us to the challenges of the game. So Isthmus Village must be in one place, and Black Village in another, and the path took us to each in turn, making it seem that they were in the same region."

"Isthmus Village," Sherlock said. "We know of that. It is about a day's walk from here. The people are taciturn and unfriendly, and they refuse to use any expressive words." .

"That's changed," Dug said. "They were being oppressed by a censor-ship, but we managed to douse its censers, and now the folk are expressive and happy again."

"I wish there were a ship we could abolish, to make us welcome," Sherlock said.

Nada realized that though she was doomed to betray Dug, she did not have to do the same for Sherlock, whether or not he was part of the game. "I do not think you are unwelcome here," she said. "Mundania is a dreary, awful place, but this is Xanth."

"It may be Xanth, and it may be magic, but we have encountered unfriendly animals and people," Sherlock said. "The Isthmus Villagers, the dragons, the goblins—"

Nada laughed. "Those don't count! The Isthmus folk we explained about; they were unfriendly to us too, at first. Dragons always attack people; they see us as prey. And goblins are mean to everybody, unless they are taught respect. That is improving now, since Gwenny became their first lady chief, but that's only one tribe; the others are still bad. You don't seem to have met the regular human folk of Xanth yet."

"It's true. You are the first travelers to pass who accepted us. The others either shied away without coming into the village, or were polite but refused to associate with us. That's why we were cautious about you."

"The others were probably cautious because they didn't know you," she said. "Strangers can be dangerous. Even strange trees can be dangerous."

He laughed. "Yes, so we discovered. There's the one full of tentacles—"

"Tangle trees," she agreed. "There are many dangers in Xanth. That's one reason the visitors in the game are given Companions to guide them. I don't know everything about Xanth, but I can spot the obvious threats." She paused. "For example, there's one now. Don't touch that object." She pointed to something lying in the path ahead of them.

"That's just an old horn," Sherlock said.

"That is a stink horn," she said. "If you touch it, it will make a foul-smelling noise."

Dug laughed. "Say—that sounds like fun!" He bent to touch the horn.

"No!" Nada cried, but she was too late.

BBBRRRRRRUMMPPPOOPOOHH! It sounded like the worst imagina-ble odor as it blew back Dug's hair and smirched his face. He stumbled away, but it was no good; the stench had gotten on him.

"Oh, now we'll have to clean you up," she said, dismayed. "Otherwise you won't be fit to be near."

"That's for sure," Sherlock agreed, holding his nose. "She did try to warn you."

Fortunately there was a small stream not far away. They went to it—but Nada hesitated. "I don't think that's a normal stream," she said.

"I don't care what it is, I just want to get clean," Dug said. He dipped his hand and scooped out water to splash on his face. "Uh-oh."

"You'll have to wash your clothes, too," Sherlock said. "Maybe you better just change to new ones. I see a trouser tree nearby; I'll see what else I can find."

Dug just squatted there, staring into space.

"Come on, get out of those things," Nada said briskly.

"No, I can't do that," he said. "You would see me, and I am very sensitive to that, because you are a beautiful princess I would like to know better, and I don't want to make a bad impression on you, and I would make a bad impres-sion if I appeared naked before you, and anyway I don't know if there really is anything else to wear, so I had better stick with what I have on, and in any event I have to wait to see what Sherlock comes up with, and wasn't I a fool to touch that horn, it really stunk me up, and I wish I had listened to you, but naturally I had to just barge ahead and get in trouble, as I always do, because that's my na-ture, and I see the disgust on your face, and that hurts me because that's not the way I want you to see me, because I'd rather be kissing you, you lovely crea-ture, in fact if I had my druthers I'd do more than kiss you, but in this weird land I can't even look at your panties without getting booted from the game, and that's a real pain, so I just have to keep quiet about it and try not to make a fuss, but you must really be disgusted right now, I know I sure would be if I were in your shoes, and"

"That's a stream of consciousness!" Nada cried, appalled.

"they are very pretty shoes too," he continued without interruption. "I must say, more like slippers, really, making your feet look nice, and of course your legs look nice too, and I'd really like to run my hands over—hey, why am I talk-ing like this?" he demanded, dismayed. "I can't stop myself, I'm saying every-thing that's on my mind, no privacy whatever, and every time I look at you it gets really embarrassing, because"

"The water of the stream of consciousness made you have to say everything that's on your mind," she said loudly, using her own voice to drown out his voice, in an effort to prevent him from embarrassing them both any more.

"all I can think of is how luscious you are, and I don't care if you are a princess, and are several years older than me, I just want to grab you and"

"I will go fetch Sherlock!" she screamed, and fled before hearing any more. What a disaster this was!

She found Sherlock, who was returning with shirt, trousers, and shoes. "Did you get him clean?" Sherlock asked. "Or do you want me to scrub him, you being a woman?"

"That's a stream of consciousness!" she cried. "He's speaking everything on his mind!"

His eyes traveled up and down her torso. "That's bound to be trouble," he said. "Is there an antidote?"

"I don't know! I don't know what to do!"

"Then we'll just have to gag him until we figure something better out," Sherlock said. "Here, I found a scarf, too; it should do the trick."

Dug saw them coming. "I don't want to be saying all this!" he said, looking desperate. "It's just coming out. Anything that triggers a thought, out my mouth it comes! Now I'm bound to say something about race relations, because Sherlock is black, and I want to keep my mouth shut, and I can't, and I'm bound to insult somebody even though I don't want to, and what are you planning to do with that scarf? You're not going to choke me, are you? I really don't mean to be like this, I can't help it if my crowd never let me play with black children, and my friends called them ni—" He stifled himself by clapping his hands to his mouth.

"This is a gag," Sherlock said. "Let me put it on you." He did so, and Dug did not resist. He had at last been silenced.

Nada concluded that Sherlock knew what to do. "I will go look for a campsite," she said, and walked away.

She was in luck. There was an enchanted campsite in a different place from the prior one. They would be able to spend a safe night. She set about gathering fruit and pies for supper, and canvas for a tent.

After a while the two men joined her. Dug was clean, in the new clothing, and still gagged. He looked grateful rather than miserable. Sherlock, instead of being a burden to have along, had turned out to be a great help.

What a disaster it would have been had she been the one to touch that stream of consciousness! She would have blabbed out her False Companion nature. She hoped the effect did not last long with Dug; this job was difficult enough without that.

Sherlock looked around. "I don't remember this place, and I've been through here. I'm sure it was just plain old forest before."

"It must have been set up for the game," Nada explained. "The game is super-imposed on Xanth, and interacts with Xanth, but we don't want to bother too many regular Xanth folk who know nothing about it."

"But your path led you right to our village," he pointed out.

"Either you are game folk, or the demons decided you were a legitimate challenge," she said.

"Maybe it doesn't matter. Just so long as we find a good place to settle. We don't want to remain where we are, but we don't want to walk into trouble either."

"If you are the Black Wave, you will find a place to settle. Every other Wave has. Maybe Dug's challenge here is to help you find that place. From what he says, I gather that some Mundanes would not even try to help you."

"That's for sure!" He hesitated. "If this is where we spend the night—separate tents?"

"If you prefer. I change into my natural form to sleep. If you don't mind being in the company of a human-headed serpent, it would be easier to set up just one tent."

"For sure. If Dug doesn't mind."

Dug, gagged, shook his head no. He didn't mind.

"Then let's see what we have here." Sherlock opened his pack and brought out a coil of wire. "We can tie this between two trees, to support the canvas. And I have metal tent pegs too; they hold better than the scrounged ones, usually."

"You have metal things?" she asked, surprised. "How did you get them?"

"Smith makes them. Anything we need, from swords to plowshares. He really knows how to work metal."

"He has magic? He can change the form of metal? Usually, those from Mundania lack magic."

"No magic. He's trained, is all."

Dug laughed through his gag. They looked at him, so he pulled it down. "Black Smith!" he said. "It does make sense." Then he pulled the gag back up before he could say too much more.

Sherlock smiled. "He's a blacksmith, certainly. But what would be the point of magic, since he can do it all with fire and tongs?"

"Well, a magical blacksmith would shape oars from ores, getting an iron oar, or silver oar," she explained. "Something like that. Maybe not silver, as that isn't black. It sounds as if your Mundane Black Smith is more versatile."

"Maybe so," he agreed.

They put up the tent and settled down to supper. But another problem appeared: how was Dug to eat with the gag on?

"I wonder," Sherlock murmured. "The way things work here, maybe it would do."

"What would do?"

"I saw some humble pie growing near the river," he said, rising.

"Humble pie!" she exclaimed. "Maybe it would!"

So Sherlock fetched a humble pie, and they fed Dug a piece. In a moment Dug's endless monologue faded out. He was now too humble to bore the others with all his thoughts.

"How did you ever think of that?" Nada asked, impressed.

Sherlock shrugged. "Elementary," he said. He had not eaten any humble pie.

Nevertheless, Nada was sure they were going to get along.

8
BUBBLES

K im had been enjoying the game. Now she was enjoying it
more. She liked having the handsome merman along, being
satisfied that he was not trying to marry her. For one thing, he
knew this Water Wing well, so they would surely make excellent progress
through it, without running afoul of whatever threats it offered. For another, he
was excellent company. He was mature, clever, polite, and generally nice. What
more could a girl ask?

They started at the eastern fringe of the Water Wing, and floated west in a
water boat that sought and followed the various currents going their way. It
was slow but comfortable. Each of them had packs with supplies, provided by
the mer family. Cyrus showed them how to fish, not for food but to attract ex-
otic specimens to the lure. There were rainbow trout, their semicircular bands
of color making the surrounding water beautiful. There were the tiny white
specks of light that were starfish, and one that was too bright to look at: a sun-
fish. A swordfish playfully feinted at the boat, and a sawfish made bulging eyes
at them: it *saw* them.

But after a time this palled. They were on a seemingly endless expanse of
water, going somewhere but not fast. Kim was getting bored; this wasn't exactly her idea of adventure.

Then she saw a glimmer in the air. It wasn't a bird, it was a bubble. A shimmering soap bubble, perhaps, just floating innocently by, the light glinting iridescently from its surface. Where had it come from? Where was it going?
Who had blown this pretty little bubble? Kim didn't know, and didn't much
care; it was just interesting to watch.

It was followed by another bubble, a bit larger and shinier. Then a third. In fact, there was a chain of bubbles, drifting along on a vagrant eddy of wind, passing the boat and moving on. Each was larger and brighter than the one before it, as if the bubble blower were growing and gaining experience.

Then a bubble seemed to have something in it. Kim strained to see, but could not make it out; just a reflection, maybe. Yet a peculiar one.

The next bubble was empty, but the one following that definitely had something in it. Kim peered closely, but still couldn't quite make it out. So she reached out and caught the bubble.

It popped the moment she touched it, and the object fell into her hand. It was a twisted paper clip, not readily usable. How had it gotten inside the bubble? How had the bubble managed to remain floating, with this weight inside it? This was such a curious matter. She hadn't realized that paper clips even existed in Xanth; they were Mundane.

She tried to bend the paper clip back into shape, but it was beyond redemption. She considered dropping it into the water, but she didn't want to be a litterbug. Finally she hooked it into a buttonhole as an impromptu decoration.

Meanwhile the bubbles were still drifting by, and still getting larger. There seemed to be a loose chain of them crossing the lake, coming from who knew where and going to who knew where else. When she looked behind, she saw the diminishing line of them disappearing in smallness. When she looked ahead, she saw the line maintaining its size, but realized that was because the bubbles were still growing, so that their size balanced perspective. There must be some pretty large bubbles at the end of that line!

She peered at each passing bubble. Now a number of them definitely had objects inside them. They were all different, but there was something similar about them too. What was it?

One bubble carried a worn clothespin. Another had a chipped cup. Another had an empty bottle. And so on: a torn picture, a worn shoe, a stopped clock, a book with the cover torn off, a pair of socks with holes in the toes. Everything was in some way defective or useless. These were all throwaways! Things Mundane people no longer wanted. That explained the twisted paper clip.

She worked it out as the bubbles moved on by. This was a magic land, so it had magic problems and magic solutions. Maybe even punnishly literal, she thought with a smile: somewhere there would be a solution that was a magic solution: a drink or elixir. These bubbles were like trash bags: just put your junk in them and let it float away. A disposal network. The bubbles were probably going to a central dump, where they would pop and deposit their refuse. No fuss, no muss, no bother. Wouldn't it be nice to have something like that at home! Somehow this stuff must have strayed into Xanth, so was being conveyed away.

The bubbles continued, still growing larger. One had a broken bicycle. Another had a stuffed chair with the stuffing leaking. A kiddy car with the steering wheel gone. A large, old, worn dog. A—

Wait a minute! Kim snapped back to the dog bubble. What was a living creature doing in the trash? Because the dog *was* alive; it was lying there with its nose on its paws, breathing slowly and gazing out without much interest. It was nondescript, mostly shades of brown with some white around the edges. A mongrel, undistinguished.

And that was why, of course. With no special pedigree, and well beyond the fun of puppyhood, she was no longer a desirable pet. Maybe she was ill. So she had been thrown away. Kim had heard of this sort of thing. Sometimes people would just dump their pets off on country roads and drive away, hoping someone else would take care of them. Of course usually that didn't happen; instead the poor pets expired of starvation and exposure, never understanding how they got lost. That just made Kim so mad! But she had never had a pet, so maybe she didn't know how it was. Maybe she would have a different attitude, if she had had the experience of keeping an aging or sick pet. But she doubted it.

The bubble was drifting on behind. The dog lifted its head and gazed at her. It gave its tail half a wag, then sank back into hopelessness. It knew it was doomed.

Kim reached for the bubble, but it was now too far away. And what would she do anyway, with a tired old dog? It probably had fleas. It was better just to let it go. It would soon be dead anyway. No one would care.

"No!" she cried. She stood up and then leaped for the bubble. Her hands touched the shimmering surface, and it popped, and her arms closed around the dog. But she was falling, because she had leaped from the boat. Splash! They fell together into the water.

"Help!" she cried. She could swim, but not while holding a large dog in her arms. And she was not about to let go of the dog, because she didn't know if *it* could swim.

Then Cyrus was there, swimming extremely efficiently with his tail. He caught her and the dog and heaved them back into the boat, where Jenny Elf helped them get untangled. "What happened?" Jenny asked, amazed. "Did you fall out of the boat?"

"No, I leaped out of the boat," Kim explained. "To catch the bubble."

"The bubble?"

"Didn't you see the line of bubbles floating by?"

Jenny shook her head. "No."

Cyrus heaved himself back into the boat, keeping his tail. "There were no bubbles," he said. "It must have been a daydream. I think I caught a glimpse of Mare Imbri. She must have brought you that nice dream."

"No bubbles?" Kim asked. "Then what about this?" She let go of the dog, who was now sitting in front of her.

"A dog!" Jenny cried. "It's been so long since I've seen one of those!"

"A bitch," Cyrus agreed. "You found her in the water?"

"What do you mean, a bitch!" Kim retorted. "She's a perfectly nice dog!" Then she remembered that this was what a female dog was called: a bitch. Just as a female horse was called a mare, and a female pig a sow.

"Oh, I'm sure she's nice," Jenny agreed, extending her hand. But the dog shied away fearfully.

"It's all right," Kim said, stroking the dog's damp back. "Jenny's my Companion." The dog relaxed, accepting Jenny's touch.

Then Sammy Cat stepped forward. Kim was worried, but then realized that the little cat would not step into danger, and he knew how to find what he wanted. Sure enough, the two animals sniffed noses. Then Sammy walked away, satisfied. He was Jenny's cat, and Jenny had been accepted, so Sammy was accepted too.

Cyrus extended his hand, but the dog retreated from him too. She didn't growl, she just grew nervous. "She's your dog," Cyrus said. "I never heard of a daydream turning real like that, but it must have happened."

Kim looked around. There were no longer any bubbles in sight. They had vanished. They couldn't all have drifted away so quickly. So maybe it had been a daydream. But the dog was real. As real as anything in this game. Had it been a challenge, to rescue the animal?

"What do you call her?" Jenny asked.

"My bubble dog? I don't know." Kim turned to the dog. She noticed that the dog's mouth was marked with black and white so that she seemed to be smiling, though it was merely a color pattern and not true emotion. "I think someone was—was throwing her away. Because she's old. All the bubbles had old, worn, or broken things. But when I saw a living animal, I—I just couldn't let it happen."

"Perhaps you should check to be sure she is healthy," Cyrus said diplomatically. He knew that the chances were that the dog was not.

Kim seized the opportunity. "Bubble dog, let me see if there is a tag on you, or something," Kim said. There wasn't; probably such identification was unknown in Xanth. "Let me get you dry, while I'm at it." She brought out a towel and rubbed the dog's fur, at the same time checking for mange, fleas, or broken bones.

But the bubble dog turned out to be surprisingly healthy. She was solid—perhaps seventy pounds—but not fat, and her fur was so thick it was like dense carpeting. She was very quiet, not growling, whining, or barking, and did not try to get away. Her teeth were clean, and there were no signs of infestation. She was healthy, just old.

"Maybe she's magic," Jenny suggested. "There are very few straight dogs in Xanth. She might be a werewolf, or something."

"Are you magic?" Kim asked the dog. The dog just looked at her, not seeming to understand.

"Perhaps she was dumped because she was not magic," Cyrus suggested.

"Well, *I* won't dump her!" Kim said firmly. "She's a nice dog, and I like her, and I don't care if she is nonmagical, so am I." But then a nasty thought occurred. "But I'm only visiting here. What happens to her when I go home?"

"I would try to take care of her," Jenny said. "But I don't think she likes me."

"Nonsense," Kim said. "She just doesn't know you." Yet Kim herself was almost as new to the dog as the other two were. Why should the dog accept her?

She knew the answer: she was the one who had rescued the dog from the bubble. Thus she had earned a special place in the dog's affection. That was all right, as long as the dog did not attack the others.

She couldn't just keep thinking of her as "the dog." There had to be a name. "All right, you're officially the bubble dog," Kim said. "Bubbles for short. Okay?"

The dog did not object. She lay down in the bottom of the boat and went to sleep.

"Bubbles it is," Cyrus said. "I wonder if I could daydream of floating bubbles, and find one with a thrown-away young beautiful mermaid?"

Kim laughed. "Who would throw away a young beautiful mermaid?"

"Unless she had a terrible temper," Jenny said, smiling.

"Mermaids do not have hot tempers," Cyrus said somewhat stiffly. "The water keeps them cool and calm."

"Except when there's a storm?" Kim asked mischievously.

"Merfolk dive below when there are storms."

"Maybe she's hungry," Jenny said.

"How can she be hungry, when we haven't found her yet?" he asked. Then he shifted streams of thought. "Oh, you mean the dog. Perhaps so."

They did not have any dogfood in their supplies, but they did have water crackers. Kim took one and offered it to Bubbles. The dog sniffed it, considered, and finally accepted it. She settled down to eat it, slowly.

The boat moved on. The slow progress soon became boring. Jenny and Cyrus slumped, snoozing, and so did Kim.

Until a sharp bark woke them all up. Kim's eyes popped open—and there was a head looking over the boat. She stifled a scream, afraid that it would merely provoke the monster.

Jenny was doing the same. "It's a water dragon!" she whispered, frightened. "And we're way far from land!"

But Cyrus did not seem to be worried. "That's just Plesio," he said. "He's friendly."

"That's a plesiosaurus!" Kim exclaimed. "From the Age of Dinosaurs." For she had at one time been fascinated by the dinosaurs, and had learned a number of the forms of the age of reptiles. This extremely long-necked, flippered creature fit the description.

"Yes, he really likes to please people," Cyrus said. "He must have seen us poking along, and decided to help speed up our journey." He unshipped some rope, tossed out the end, and the creature caught it in its mouth. Then it swam briskly ahead, pulling the boat swiftly along.

"But Bubbles couldn't have known it was all right," Kim said, stroking the dog's head. "She tried to warn us of danger."

"Yes she did," Jenny agreed. "We can sleep safer with her along."

Now their progress was rapid. The surface of the lake fairly whizzed by. A shore appeared ahead, and soon they reached it. Plesio halted and dropped his end of the rope. "Thank you," Cyrus called as he coiled the rope.

They took out water paddles and moved the boat into shallow water, and then into a broad marsh. "But I thought we were going to a river," Kim said.

"The With-A-Cookee River," Jenny agreed. "It flows from the Half-Baked Bog. So first we have to get through the bog."

Oh. Now she remembered the map. "Why is it called Half-Baked?" Kim inquired.

"Because half of it is next to the Fire Region," Cyrus said. "That's not my favorite place, but the best channel passes close by there, so we'll have to use it."

All too soon Kim saw what he meant. There was smoke on the horizon, billowing up from what looked like a wall of fire, and the channel through the marsh led toward it. The green plants along the bank turned white with the increasing heat, and then brown. "Why, that looks almost like marshmallow!" Kim exclaimed.

"Yes, this is the Mallow Marsh," Cyrus agreed. "If you are hungry, you can eat the toasted mallow plants."

Kim reached out and pulled off a mallow. It was crinkly brown on the outside, but gooey white inside. She tasted it. Toasted marshmallow, sure enough.

Jenny ate some too. Then Jenny offered a mallow to Bubbles, but the dog would not take it. So she handed it to Kim, and Kim offered it, and this time Bubbles took it. This was a one-girl dog, without doubt.

The wall of fire loomed closer. Kim realized that the reason the channel was so close to the fire was that this was the only place too hot for water plants to clog.

"We shall have to move rapidly," Cyrus said. "I shall enter the water and pull the boat, as Plesio did. That will protect me from the heat and speed our travel. If the two of you are able to paddle—"

"We'll try," Kim said bravely. That firewall was now impressively high and hot. Her clothing had long since dried out. She dipped her hands in the lukewarm water and splashed herself wet again. The water itself was warm, but did help cool her. Jenny, understanding, did the same. It would help them survive the fire. As an afterthought, she splashed some water on Bubbles, who glanced at her but did not protest.

Jenny paddled near the front of the boat, and Kim paddled near the back, on the other side, trying to time her strokes to match the elf's. Cyrus pulled by holding a short length of rope between his teeth and swimming vigorously. The boat moved well, but still the high flames were ferocious. Both girls had to pause frequently to splash more water on themselves and on the dog. Near the wall of fire the water was boiling, but it seemed to be cooler below the surface.

Now the source of the flames was apparent: a row of burning trees. Somehow they seemed to maintain their height and mass and foliage, despite burning up. How could that be?

"That's firewood," Cyrus explained.

Well, that made sense, in this magic land. Kim had always known how punnish Xanth was; she just tended to forget when under stress.

Kim heard growling. It wasn't Bubbles; indeed, the dog heard it too. Her floppy ears perked up. It was coming from the firewall! But how could there be any living thing there?

"Firedogs," Cyrus gasped. "Pay them no heed. They live in the hot steel and iron section, and harass passersby, but they can't leave the Fire Region."

Kim's fevered mind wondered whether there was a pun buried there: steel and iron. Steel andiron—same as a firedog back home. She kept paddling, though she feared that her hands were blistering.

The growling faded, but was replaced by a heated hissing. "Firedrakes," Cyrus explained. "Very fierce birds."

But the drakes, too, were confined to the fire. Then there came a hot buzzing. "Don't tell me," Kim gasped. "Let me guess: firebugs."

"Right."

The channel began to veer away from the firewall, to Kim's great relief. Then there was a fiery neigh. That would be a firehorse. Sparkling insects flew out and danced above the water: fireflies.

Bubbles barked. Kim started to reassure the dog, then realized that the dog might have smelled something. She looked around—and spied a serpentine form writhing across the surface of the water toward them. Suddenly she knew what it was. "Firehose!" she screamed.

Cyrus lifted his head and stared. "That will burn through the boat!" he said, alarmed.

"Then we'd better hurry!" Kim gasped, doubling her effort. The boat went faster, but she saw that the firehose was going to touch it.

Jenny saw the danger. She stood up and whirled her paddle. She brought it down across the firehose, making a great splash of water and fire. The hose, startled, pulled back for a moment—and the boat slid by, untouched.

There was an angry cry. Kim looked, and saw the flaming outline of a man, standing before his firehose, shaking his fist at them. "Sorry, fireman, you can't burn us this time!" she called as the boat put distance between them.

A flaming human female form appeared. She held some kind of firestick. She pointed it at the boat. Bubbles barked.

"Duck!" Kim cried, throwing herself down.

A bolt of fire shot over the boat, just missing her.

"That was no duck," Cyrus said. "That was Miss Fire."

"So silly of me to confuse her," Kim said.

Away from the firewall at last, they relaxed, catching their breaths. "They were surprisingly determined, this time," Cyrus said. "Usually they don't really try. I wonder what got them all fired up?"

"It's probably a game challenge," Kim said, realizing. "It was getting too easy for me to make progress, so they heated it up."

"That must be it," Jenny agreed. "You have a loyal Companion to help you, but the challenges do get harder as they go. Few Players are supposed to make it through to the prize."

Cyrus nodded. "I see this will be an interesting excursion. I must say you rose to the occasion, Kim."

"No, that was Jenny who rose," Kim said to cover her pleasure at the compliment. "She stood up so she could bash the firehose, so we could pass."

"True. But you gave the alarm."

"No, that was Bubbles. She barked." Kim stroked the dog's head.

He shrugged. "Your modesty becomes you."

"I'm not modest. I'm pushy. I just did my part, the same way the rest of you did."

"Of course," he agreed. But he did not sound quite convinced.

The dog was getting restless, so they paddled to the bank, and let her scramble onto land, where she did her canine business. Evidently she was a house-trained canine, which was fine. Kim liked her very well. It was fun having a pet, even if it was only in the game.

They resumed motion through the Half-Baked Bog. It was extensive, but by paddling and poling they made good progress.

"It is getting late, but we must reach the headwaters of the With-A-Cookee River by nightfall," Cyrus said.

"Why?" Kim asked. "Can't we camp here?" She was so tired that she hardly wanted to push on farther than she needed to.

"No. There is no solid land here, just marshy islands. And it would be uncomfortable for you to sleep in the boat. But mainly, there are the allegations."

"The what?" Jenny asked. "Allegory?"

"A related species, perhaps. The allegories are found in the ever glades, while the allegations are here. We don't dare relax until we are out of their range."

Kim realized that these puns might have unpleasant representations. "Okay; on we go. I hope we don't meet any." But she suspected that the game would not let her get by without tackling this next challenge.

She was right. Bubbles barked as a large aquatic reptile swam toward them, with a ribbed greenish hide, solid threshing tail, and a mouth stuffed with more gleaming teeth than she cared to try to count. "Keep moving," she murmured to Cyrus and Jenny.

"You are intruding on my territory!" the allegation said, with some justice. "I shall have to chomp you."

Cyrus was silent, and Kim knew it was because he could not refute the charge. It was up to her.

"We are traveling an established route," she said. "You don't have authority to interfere."

The allegation pondered. Evidently she had managed to refute it. Meanwhile the boat was moving. Then the creature made another accusation. "You are transporting an illicit animal. I shall have to chomp it."

"Oh no you don't!" Kim cried, putting her arms around the dog. "This is my pet, and nobody chomps her without first chomping me."

The allegation paused again. It seemed she had refuted it again. The boat was still quietly moving. But the thing hadn't given up. "You are a Mundane! You have no rights in Xanth. I shall have to chomp you."

Oops! She was indeed Mundane, so she couldn't refute that. What was she to do? While she considered, the creature was nudging up closer, ready to snap at her. Even if it missed her, it would surely catch the boat, and rip out a chunk, causing the whole thing to dissolve.

But she knew there had to be a way through. So she made what she hoped was a good refutation. "I am a Mundane Player in the game. I have the right to tour Xanth as long as I play the game. You can't chomp me unless I make a mistake—and I haven't made one here."

"Curses," the allegation muttered, turning aside. She had foiled it!

The boat slid on through the bog. Soon the land on either side firmed up, and pretty plants appeared. "The With-A-Cookee!" Jenny exclaimed. "See— there're the cookees growing."

"The cookies," Kim agreed. "So now at last we can camp."

"Yes," Cyrus agreed. "You handled that allegation very well, Kim."

"Thank you," she replied, feeling more justifiably flattered. After all, there were only so many compliments a girl could take from a handsome man before they started getting to her.

"That's odd," Cyrus said. "That wasn't here the last time I passed this way."

And there ahead was what looked like an enchanted campsite. "Does the game provide safe havens for Players?" Kim asked Jenny.

"Yes. But you have to find them yourself."

"It seems I did." Kim turned to Cyrus. "This must be about the edge of your range."

"It is. I travel the Water Wing freely, but seldom venture far into the neighboring regions. Nevertheless, I'm sure this was mere jungle before."

"It surely was," Kim agreed. "But the proprietors of the game must have set up rest stops in out-of-the-way places, and this is one of them. I'm certainly glad to have it." Which was perhaps her understatement of the day. She had used her wit and gotten through just fine, but she had been lucky too. She was willing to bet that luck wouldn't hold much longer.

They tied the boat and walked into the campsite. Cookee plants grew all around, as well as fruit and nut trees, and assorted material bushes. She knew this would do just fine for the night.

Cyrus went to a private spot, changed into legs, and went to work collecting materials and pitching two tents, while Kim and Jenny picked fruits and nuts, pies and milkweed pods and piled them on the picnic table. There was even a dogwood tree bearing dogfood; Kim put some of that in a wooden dish for Bubbles, and the dog liked it. "Ah, this is living!" Kim remarked as they ate.

Both Cyrus and Jenny looked surprised. "This is routine," he said.

"Not for me. Where I live, pies don't grow on trees, and milk doesn't come in pods. This really is the land of milk and honey." She picked up a honey-soaked comb she had found and began licking the tines clean. She would be able to use it on her hair when all the honey was gone.

"Well, they don't where I come from, either," Jenny said. "But it's the way it is in Xanth. There's nothing special about it."

Kim shook her head. "You folk don't know when you're well off. You have such wonderful lives, compared to the pollution and parsimony and poverty we have. That's why everyone who knows about Xanth wants to come here. Even if only for a few hours, in a stupid game."

Cyrus was interested. "What are the mermaids like, in your world?"

Kim laughed. "There are no mermaids! Well, maybe some faked-up ones, in tourist shows, but those are just regular women with their legs bound into tail-costumes. Nothing you'd be interested in."

He was surprised. "There are no crossbreedings with fish?"

"None. That sort of thing just doesn't happen in Mundania. In fact, there can be trouble when different races or cultures marry. It happens, but not often. People stick mostly to their own kind."

He shook his head. "Truly has it been said: Mundania is dreary."

"Truly," Kim agreed.

Kim and Jenny settled down for the night in one tent, and Bubbles lay down at the entrance, satisfied to be a guard dog. Cyrus, always the model of decorum, slept in his own tent.

In the morning they took turns washing, then ate and disassembled their tents so as to leave the camping area pristine for the next travelers. They got in the boat and set off down the With-A-Cookee River. They didn't need to paddle; the gentle current carried them slowly along toward the west and north.

"But don't we want to bear south?" Kim asked.

"We do," Jenny said. "But the river will take us to the sea, and then we can paddle on along the shore, bypassing the Gap Chasm and other menaces such as Com Pewter. We can land south of it and find a path going inland. We can pass Castle Roogna and go on to the Good Magician's castle. It's not a straight route, but it's a fairly easy one."

"Com Pewter!" Kim said. "The evil machine! I'd like to meet—"

"You don't want to meet Pewter!" Jenny said, alarmed.

Kim sighed. Jenny's advice had been good so far, as she had found out when she didn't follow it. "No evil machine," she agreed regretfully.

The cookies growing along the banks became fancier. There were clusters of ginger, chocolate chip, banana, walnut, raisin, and molasses cookies, growing out of beds of sandies. Pinwheels spun around on their stems. Kim reached out to pick one.

"No!" Jenny cried as Kim was about to take a bite. But she was too late, as usual. Kim's mouth was already in motion. She bit off a piece, and it tasted very good.

"Why did you try to tell me no?" she asked. "There's nothing wrong with this pinwheel cookie."

"That's not a pinwheel, it's a punwheel," Jenny said.

"Oh? What will it do to me? Make me a pundit? It can't make me a pungent, because I'm not a man, I'm a girl. Still, I suppose I could go around telling jokes, the way a pun-gent would. I could be his pun-girl, maybe." She paused. "What's the matter?"

"You're punning in circles," Jenny said.

Kim looked at the cookie. She had taken a bite, and it had affected her speech. "I'll try to watch my punctuation, so as not to pun-ish you any more," she said punctually.

"Maybe we'll find an antidote soon," Cyrus muttered. Even Bubbles hid her head under the seat, as if trying to shield her ears from the sound.

Kim decided to keep her mouth shut until the effects wore off. She just kept acting impulsively, then regretting it.

They saw things swimming. They looked like more allegations. There were also small shoes in the water. Kim knew what those were: water moccasins. She was glad they were secure in their boat, because this was not the best place to wade or swim.

Later in the day the river widened, and there were marshes to the left. The marsh water bubbled effervescently.

"Lake Tsoda Popka!" Jenny exclaimed. "Oh, I remember when Che and Gwenny and I had our first popka-squirting fight! Of course Gwenny won't do anything like that now; she's a chief. And Che's her Companion, so he has to behave too." She took an empty water bottle and dipped it into the lake. "But

I'm not a chief, and not a Companion to a chief. I'm just an innocent elf girl who doesn't know any better. So I can do it." And she held her thumb over the top, shook the bottle violently, and squirted tsoda water all over the boat.

"I know about that game!" Kim said, managing not to pun. She grabbed another water bottle and dipped it in the lake. "I'll puncture your balloon!" Soon they had a full-scale squirt fight going, while Cyrus, too decorous to participate, retreated to the farthest part of the boat, and Bubbles hid under the seat.

Then something horrendous loomed ahead. It made a bubbly roar. They paused to stare at it. The thing was like a swirling mass of gelatin, with colored bubbles throughout. "What's that pun-k in the pun-ch?" Kim asked.

"That's the Tsoda Popka monster!" Cyrus said. "It must have been attracted by the commotion."

"Well, tell it to pun-t on out of here," Kim said.

But the monster, perhaps aggravated by the puns, reached out a bubbly tentacle to strike the boat. The tentacle hissed effervescently—and where it touched the boat, the boat began to hiss and sparkle too.

"What's happening?" Kim asked, alarmed.

"I think the Popka monster turned the water boat into tsoda water," Cyrus said, alarmed. "It is dissolving away!"

The monster sank out of sight, but that did not end the problem. The boat was now bubbling at a great rate, and becoming jellylike. They had to scramble out of it before it dissolved away.

There they stood, on a somewhat spongy bank. They were all right, and they had saved their supplies, but they had lost their boat. They would have to walk the rest of the way.

Unfortunately they seemed to be on a squishy island. Around it swam the allegations, moccasins, and other things with projecting fins.

Kim opened her mouth. No pun came out. She wasn't surprised. Their situation did not seem at all funny.

9
GERM

Dug was better in the morning, being neither consciously streaming nor humble. For sure, he was going to watch what he ate
and drank, after this!

The path was just beginning to veer south when they came to a grove of
very tall trees. "I am not sure about this," Nada said. "I think these are hassle
trees. If so, we should avoid them."

"We don't need any tall hassle," Dug agreed.

"I have not been this far," Sherlock said. "I hope you folk know how to deal
with the dangers of this region."

"The best strategy is simply to go around this grove," Nada said.

But there was only one path, and that one proceeded through into the tall
hassle grove. Nada could leave the path and travel in serpent form, but the two
others could not. "Guess we'll just have to chance it," Dug said. "The game
doesn't give us much choice."

"It may be a game to you," Sherlock said. "But it's pretty serious to me. I
mean, if you lose, you're suddenly back home in Mundania, right? But if I lose,
I'm food for a dragon, or worse."

"You're right," Dug said. "I think I got the better deal, getting supplies
from your village. If you want to break the deal, I'll give you back the stuff."

"But you're going on?"

"I have to. I've got a game to play."

"Then I'm going on too. Just let's be careful, okay?"

"Super careful," Dug agreed. "I don't want to wash out again."

They walked on into the tall hassle grove. Dug was afraid that the trees would sprout arms and attack, but they seemed stable. They were so tall that they shut out the direct light of the sun, putting the path into gloom. There were no animals in sight.

Then they heard something. At first it was faint, but it became louder as they moved toward it. It was a sort of thumping and swishing, as of something very large jumping around and breathing hard. The ground shuddered.

Dug exchanged a glance with Sherlock. The black man shrugged. The path led only two ways: forward and back.

By the time they reached the center of the tall hassle grove, the whole forest seemed to be shaking as if an earthquake were practicing its moves. It was hard to keep their feet on the bouncing ground. But there were no roars or other indications of a hungry monster. Maybe it was something impersonal, like a boulder bouncing up and down inside a volcano. They moved forward almost on tiptoe, though it was hard to tell how they could have made any sound loud enough to be heard over the deafening reverberations.

At last they spied a large glade. Sunlight streamed down in a region like an amphitheater. In the center was a flock of birds.

"Birds?" Dug asked, surprised. He had to yell to make himself heard over the noise.

"Rocs," Nada yelled back. "By their color, I'd say female rocs. But whatever can they be doing?"

For the birds were standing in a line, flapping their wings, and kicking their feet up. That was the source of the swishing and thumping. They were so solid that when they set down their feet, the ground shuddered. For the rocs were *large* birds. Each was big enough to carry away an elephant, if it chose, if it could find an elephant.

It was Sherlock who caught on. "They're rockettes!" he exclaimed. "Practicing their routines!"

"Roc-ettes," Nada agreed. "Female rocs. But what do you mean by routine?"

"Dancing. A chorus line. High kicks."

"They do seem to be doing that," she agreed. "But to what point?"

Sherlock exchanged a glance with Dug. "Well, they like it in Mundania," Dug yelled.

Just then the rocs halted, in perfect unison, resting their feet and closing their wings. It was the end of their act. Silence fell like a sudden curtain. Just in time to catch Dug at the top of his voice. His words carried right through the glade with loud and perfect clarity.

Every huge bird head turned toward him.

"Uh-oh," Sherlock murmured.

"They can't fly through the forest," Nada said. "We can escape along the next path. Follow me!" She shifted to large serpent form and slithered rapidly forward.

Dug paused only long enough to snatch up her clothing and jam it into his pack. Then he and Sherlock galloped after her.

The rocs, evidently annoyed by the intrusion, launched in a mass into the air. They bore down on the fugitives. But the circle of trees ringing the glade was too close; the birds had to land before they crashed. So some dropped down to pursue afoot, while others winged on up over the forest to peer down at the path from on high.

This was one tall hassle, for sure, Dug thought.

Nada Serpent slithered out of the glade, down the next path through the forest. Dug and Sherlock followed. The nearest roc screeched as she made a grab for them with her claws and beak. The sound was deafening. But she overbalanced, not being accustomed to hunting on her feet, and fell beak-first on the ground. Dug felt the great whomp just behind him, and kept going.

Then he realized that Sherlock wasn't beside him. He snatched a look back—and saw that one outstretched talon had snagged Sherlock's pack. The man was trying to get loose, but the talon had plunged right into the ground, anchoring him.

Dug stopped, turned, and hauled out the club they had provided. He ran back toward Sherlock.

"Watch it, you fool!" the man cried. "She's watching you!"

Indeed, the huge head was lifting, and the huge near eye was orienting. Even stretched flat on the ground, the bird could readily snap him up, because the foot was close to her head. What could he do? If he fled, Sherlock would be done for; if he didn't, both of them could be done for. Because his club was a puny thing compared to that monstrous beak. If he had gotten another magic sword, this time around—

But he did have a knife. That would have to do. He put away the club and got the knife.

The roc's head swung toward him. The beak opened.

Then he saw a stink horn growing almost in front of him. He jammed the point of the knife through it.

BBBRRRRRRUMMPPOOPOOHH! The foul-smelling sound ripped through the glade, staining everything. But Dug paid no heed. He held his breath, squinted his eyes, and lifted the thing up toward the roc's gaping mouth. He whipped the point about, so that the stuck stink horn flew off—into that mouth.

The roc snapped at it reflexively. Then her eye assumed a somewhat startled, somewhat disgusted look, as if something tasted monumentally bad. A wisp of putrid stench leaked out from the corner of her beak.

Dug didn't wait to watch. He already had a pretty good notion how the big bird felt. Instead he ran up to Sherlock and the claw and wielded his blade. It bit into the claw as if it were so much tough wood. This was like hacking down a tree, except that his meager blade lacked the heft to do much damage.

The roc screeched. It seemed he had struck a nerve. She yanked her talon out of the ground, hauling Sherlock into the air. He slid off the talon, landing neatly on his feet. "Go, man!" he shouted.

Dug realized that he was just standing there watching. He put his legs in gear and ran as fast as he could for the path. He almost expected to have a talon skewer him on the way, but he made it intact.

He joined Sherlock behind a hassle tree. They looked back at the roc. She was dancing in a much fancier pattern than before, trying to get the stink horn smell out of her beak. "That was one smart ploy," Sherlock said appreciatively. "Nothing else could've distracted her. You saved my life."

"I was lucky," Dug said. It wasn't false modesty, it was an exact description.

"Well, it looked good from here," Sherlock said. "Come on—we've lost the serpent lady."

They resumed motion down the path. Nada was waiting, in her naga form. "What happened?" she asked. "I thought you were right behind me."

"Bit of a problem," Dug said. "Let's move on before that roc realizes that this path is wide enough for her to run along if she keeps her wings closed."

Indeed, the roc was already drawing that conclusion. She was blowing out the last of the stench and advancing on the path. She was not nearly as fast on her feet as she would have been in the air, but she was a mighty big bird, and could surely move as rapidly as they could.

Nada resumed her slither, and they followed, running. They heard the thumping as the roc's big feet hit the ground. Her footsteps seemed slow, but that was deceptive; they were far apart. Dug snatched another glance back, and saw that she was gaining on them.

Fortunately the path was winding, which slowed the big bird, because she could not maneuver her bulk in this confined space as readily as they could. Then they came to a fork. They dashed right, because that bore south, and had the luck to hear her take the left fork, losing the way.

But they had hardly begun to relax before a roc wheeling in the sky squawked loudly. There was an answering squawk from the ground, followed by the screech of claws skidding to a halt. The other rocs were correcting her course!

"How are we going to escape, with those spy eyes up there?" Dug demanded. "There might as well be a satellite video unit!"

Nada's pretty face on her serpent body looked perplexed. "Who sat light? What did he do on it?"

"Never mind. I was speaking in Mundane. We can't get away as long as those rocs are watching from the sky."

"Unless we hide between the trees of the forest, until they go away," she said.

Sherlock glanced to the side. "Forget it. I never saw such impenetrable underbrush."

Dug looked too. He saw a solid mass of thorns, brambles, and what looked like poison ivy. No hiding place there. "We'll just have to keep moving, and hope things improve," he said. He realized that this was a rather anemic excuse for leadership, but it was the best he could do for now.

They ran on. It took the roc a while to reverse her course and get on the correct path, so they had a bit of leeway. Maybe the game was giving them a chance.

Then they came to a small, swift river. It was too wide to jump over, and way too strong to wade through. However, there was a footbridge over it.

And a sign: STOP. PAY TROLL.

Sure enough, from under the bridge was coming a tall, thin, brutishly ugly manlike creature with a warty countenance. The troll blocked the access to the bridge.

Dug realized that this was another game challenge. He had to get across that bridge before the roc caught up. So he approached it forthrightly: "What's the toll, troll?"

"All your wealth," the troll rasped.

"Wealth? I don't have any wealth! I'm just a poor Player, strutting and fretting my hour upon this stage."

"Too bad." The troll crossed his ugly but all too serviceable arms, still blocking the way. At that point the sound of the pursuing roc became louder.

"Suppose we just push you out of the way and cross without paying?" Dug demanded.

"Then my friend the diggle will push the bridge out of the way, and you too, if you're on it."

"Diggle?"

From the ground beside them a formidable snout appeared. It had to be the hugest worm anybody ever dreamed of.

"The diggle is the largest of the voles," Nada explained. "It travels through rock, and works only for a song. Maybe the troll sings to it."

"But a vole is a mammal," Dug protested. "This is a worm."

"Uh, friend," Sherlock said. "In Mundania, there are mammals and worms. Here in Xanth it's different."

Dug realized that it was true. The old familiar rules just didn't apply here. He had seen that when Nada first turned from woman to serpent.

"Okay. The diggle works for a song. That lets me out; they tell me that I couldn't carry a tune if I had two others to hold up the ends of it."

"The diggle is not too choosy," she said. "But please don't try to sing; I'm sure it would offend my princessly sensitivities."

That made sense. He had no intention of embarrassing himself that way anyway. He would have to settle with the troll. "Okay. Here's my money," he said, digging into a pocket. He found a handful of coins.

The troll peered at the coins. "What manner of wealth are you?" he inquired.

"I'm a measly dime," the ten-cent piece replied. "I'm a plugged nickel," the five-cent piece said. "We're cheap pennies," the one-cent pieces chorused.

Dug almost dropped the coins. They were speaking!

"Money talks," Sherlock said, smiling.

"Are you solid and true wealth?" the troll asked.

The coins laughed. "Us? We're strictly small change! We aren't even the pure metals we're supposed to be. The pennies aren't pure copper, and the nickel isn't really nickel, and the dime doesn't have any silver at all!"

Dug saw that the coins wouldn't do it. He brought out his wallet and offered a dollar bill.

"Are you solid and true wealth?" the troll asked. Apparently he had a bit of magic, and could make money talk.

"Me? I'm not worth the paper I'm printed on! I'm just one buck, the least of the folding money denominations. This cheap Mundane is trying to foist off zilch on you. Where would you spend me, anyway? Xanth doesn't use money."

"How did mere paper ever get confused with wealth?" the troll asked.

"Well, originally I was backed by gold or silver," the paper dollar said. "But once they got the paper established, they quietly removed the backing, so now I'm only worth what folk think I'm worth, and that's less every year. They keep printing more of us, and that makes us worth less."

"Worthless," the troll agreed.

The sounds of the roc were drawing closer. Dug knew he had to find some way to pay the troll. "What else will you accept?" he asked desperately.

The creature looked around. "Does your black servant work well?"

Sherlock began to get angry.

"He's not my servant!" Dug snapped. "He's a friend, traveling with me. He's not for sale."

"Then your naga princess."

Nada hissed, outraged.

"She's not a servant either! She's my Companion!"

"Precisely. Is she soft at night?"

"She's guiding me through Xanth," Dug said quickly. "No deal on either of them."

The troll shrugged. "Then you can't pay the toll. Go away."

Now the ground was shaking as the roc came closer. They did not have much time left.

Dug looked desperately around. He saw the bridge, and the river coursing through its deep channel. Part of the long body of the diggle was in that channel; it must have drilled through the river along with the ground. Beside that torso was a bit of fluff.

Something percolated through his mind. This was the game. There always had to be a way through. But it wasn't necessarily obvious. Anything odd might be a clue. And that bit of fluff was odd. There was no other fluff, and no pillow bushes in the vicinity; it wasn't from a leaking pillow. It was almost as if it had been carried along with the diggle, as it magically tunneled through the ground. What kind of a hint could it be?

Well, he could ask. "Nada, do you see that bit of fluff? What do you think it is?"

Nada looked. "Why, that looks like a germ," she said.

"A germ? You mean the diggle's infected?"

"It looks healthy to me."

Her lack of a more complete answer just might suggest that there was more to this that she was not supposed to tell him. He had to figure it out for himself. "Germs don't infect things in Xanth?"

"Not exactly," she said evasively.

Suddenly he had a faint nagging thought. Which side was she on? Was it possible that she could be a False Companion? He had almost forgotten about that chance. No, she couldn't be; she had been too loyal. She simply wasn't allowed to tell him some things that were supposed to be game challenges.

The troll, meanwhile, was simply standing there, like a cartoon character who was no longer active. His job was evidently not to attack, but to be a barrier, reacting only when approached. Another game aspect. Xanth had turned real, but the game aspects were slightly flawed, perhaps deliberately.

He got down and reached for the fluff. He held it in his hand—and began to get another idea. Suddenly the pun registered: "This is the Germ of an Idea!" he exclaimed.

"Yes," she agreed. "I wasn't supposed to tell you, but now I can, because you figured it out yourself. The one who has it becomes smarter in thinking up new ideas. It must have been carried along with the diggle after it passed the Brain Coral's pool."

"This is the game-approved explanation for its presence?" he asked, knowing that it was. He had found the key. Now all he needed to do was figure out how to use it.

The roc burst into view. Perfect timing—of course. He realized now that this threat had been carefully choreographed, to give him just enough leeway while keeping him scared. It was indeed part of the game. But he still had to make the right move, or he would be booted out of it again.

He lifted the fluff to his forehead. "Let's have it, Germ. What's the Idea?"

It came to him. *Use the diggle.*

Use this giant worm thing? Here was where his Companion should have useful advice. "How can we use the diggle to escape the roc?" he asked her.

"Why, I suppose we could ask it to carry us along," she said, as if surprised by the question. She was a fair actress, but not perfect in that respect. "But you would have to sing to it."

"You surely have a better voice than I do," he said.

"I surely do. But this is something you must do for yourself, as the Player."

Dug looked at Sherlock. "You heard the lady," the black man said. "It probably won't pay attention to me."

Desperate, Dug turned back to Nada. "But what about your princessly sensitivities?"

She glanced over his shoulder at the onrushing roc. "Perhaps I can stand it, for a while."

"Then let's go!" he said. He tucked the Germ into a pocket. "Diggle, that roc is about to smear us into messy pieces, getting your nice hide all icky. Carry us away from here. I'll sing to you."

The diggle, who had been as quiet as the troll, came to life. More of its long body drew out of the ground. The thing was so big that the torso was as thick through as that of a horse. The three of them jumped on, bestriding it. Actually Nada remained in naga form, so just lay close.

Dug opened his mouth and forced himself to sing. "I dream of Jeannie with the light brown hair!" he sang, badly off-key. He saw both Nada and Sherlock wince.

The diggle began to move. Just as the roc's beak came down, the diggle plunged under the ground—and carried them along with it. There was no impact; they just went under as if the ground didn't exist, or as if it were no more than water, or even air. It was dark, with veins of rock showing. The diggle's magic was at work.

Then it stopped. "Sing, before the ground congeals!" Nada cried, alarmed.

Oh. He had forgotten to sing. "I dream of Brownie in the light blue jeans!" he sang, with even worse melody.

The diggle resumed motion, and the ground did not congeal. So Dug kept singing, and the diggle kept traveling. Since they were underground, the rocs couldn't follow. He had found the way to escape that prior challenge.

He realized that the diggle was making pretty good time. This was a fast way to travel south!

Then the diggle stopped again. "But I was still singing!" he protested.

"You started to repeat yourself," Sherlock said. "The thing may not have much taste in music, but it must get bored with old stuff."

"But I only know so many songs," Dug said. "And parodies of singing commercials."

The ground was starting to congeal. He could feel it thickening around them, becoming viscous. He didn't want it to turn all the way rock solid. "Choka Cola, stinky drink!" he sang. "Pour it down the kitchen sink! Smells like vinegar, tastes like ink!"

The diggle resumed motion, and the ground turned thin again.

But eventually Dug was out of parodies too. The ride would have to end. "Diggle, take us up to the surface," he said. "I'm about to run out of music."

"Music!" Sherlock muttered, pained. Nada murmured agreement. She sounded somewhat ill, and Dug doubted that it was from motion sickness. The two of them had made a great sacrifice, listening to him sing for so long.

The diggle wended upward as Dug sang his last ditty. It reached the surface as he finished.

They dismounted. "Thank you, diggle," Dug said a bit hoarsely. "You were a great help."

The diggle dived back under the earth, leaving no trace of its passage. The ground was solid. "Ain't magic wonderful," Dug remarked, gazing at the undisturbed ground.

"I think that was a diseased germ," Sherlock muttered, rubbing his ears.

"I still have it," Dug said. "It may be useful again."

"Where are we?" Sherlock asked.

"This must be the With-A-Cookee River," Nada said.

"What kind of a name is that for a river?" Dug asked.

"A descriptive one. I have to go change," Nada said. She assumed full serpent form, took her bundle of clothes in her mouth, and slithered off.

Dug looked around. They were not far from the river. This one was too wide for a little troll bridge, and indeed they saw no bridge on it. There were, however, all manner of cookies growing along its banks. That explained the name. The water was calm, but he suspected it would not be wise to try to swim across this one, because it was large enough to contain monsters.

Sure enough, soon he saw a long low snout followed by a faint ripple. Then he saw a single fin projecting from the water. Then a small puff of vapor, as of a water dragon quietly exhaling steam, waiting for some fool to swim by.

How were they to cross? He brought out the Germ and put it to his forehead again. "Got any more Ideas?" he inquired.

Use the cold cream.

Cold cream? Surely it didn't mean the stuff women used to remove makeup!

"Do you see any cold cream around here?" he asked Sherlock.

Sherlock looked around. "All I see is a cream puff—which I think I'll eat." He went to pick it up. It seemed to be growing from the ground, like a puffball. "Hey—this is still hot!"

"How can it be hot, if it's growing? It hasn't been baked in an oven."

"Well, it might as well have been! It's piping hot." Sherlock blew on his fingers, cooling them. The cream puff remained on the ground.

Nada returned, in human form, suitably garbed. "What's happening?" she inquired.

"I'm looking for cold cream," Dug said. "So far all we've found is a hot cream puff."

She looked. "I never heard of a hot cream puff. They're always cool. And cold cream is always cold."

"This puff is hot," Sherlock said.

She went to it. "That's cold cream. I know it when I see it, because on occasion I use it." She bent to touch it. "Hoo. It *is* hot! What can be the matter with it?"

"Look at this," Sherlock said. "There's a hot potato beside it."

"Potatoes don't grow hot either," she said. But in a moment she had verified this too. "This is most perplexing."

Dug saw the outline of a box formed from metallic rods, enclosing the two objects. "Could this be a hot box?" he asked. "With hot rods for the sides?" By this time he knew that he could not trust the Mundane uses of such words.

"A hot box!" she exclaimed. "That explains it! The plants are being cruelly heated by the hot box. We can eat the potato, and rescue the cream puff, which I might as well have for cosmetic. But they are both too hot to touch."

"You don't need any cosmetic," Dug said. "You're already perfect." Then, lest she misconstrue his attitude, he added: "No offense."

She smiled, almost blinding him. "No offense."

Sherlock delved in his pack. "I just happen to have heavy heat-resistant gloves here," he said. "Just in case I had to handle a small fiery dragon or something." He donned them, then lifted up the potato. It was nicely baked.

But when he lifted the cream puff, something odd happened. "This is turning cold!"

"It must be compensating for all that heat," Dug said. "It is naturally a cold substance, so it must have been really struggling to stay cold in that hot box. Now that we have removed it, all the effort is making it too cold."

"I'll say!" Sherlock said. "The thing's trying to freeze my hands."

Then the full meaning of his Germ of an Idea burst on Dug. "Take it to the water! Let it freeze the water!"

Sherlock hurried to the river and dunked the cold cream. Immediately ice formed and spread outward. "Mind if I ask why?" he asked.

"So we can freeze our way across," Dug said. "I got that idea from the Germ."

Sherlock shook his head. "This is almost worse than the idea you had to sing," he said.

"Yet that did get us away from the rocs," Nada said. "And a good distance down the length of Xanth."

"But this time we don't have an angry roc bird chasing us," Sherlock pointed out.

As if on cue, there was a mean sound to the north. *As if?* Dug realized that it was probably choreographed by the game. And it would probably be a worse threat than the last, in the nature of a game.

"That sounds like werewolves," Nada said, looking alarmed.

"Why not garden-variety wolves?" Dug asked as he headed for the water.

"Xanth has very few ordinary wolves or dogs," she said. "There once were some, but they bred themselves out of existence, the same way man once did."

"Now, that doesn't make a lot of sense," Dug said. "Species can fade out by not breeding, but they can only get stronger by breeding a lot."

"Not in Xanth. If a species interbreeds with other species, the crossbreeds are their descendants. That's not bad, but it does mean that the original species diminish. My naga kind arose when human folk bred with serpent folk, and the centaurs were crossbreeds between humans and horses, and the mer folk derive from humans and fish, and the harpies from humans and birds. There are many such mixed species, and few original species. They were foolishly free in their breeding; it's a wonder the storks didn't balk at all those mixed deliveries. Only the fact that humans kept coming in new Waves enabled them to maintain their pure population." She looked at Sherlock. "Which is why your Black Wave should be welcome; your difference from other humans here is trivial."

Sherlock nodded. "That's about the first time I've liked having a white person call me trivial. But considering how different you are, I can't argue."

"Let's get on with the freezing," Dug said.

"For sure." Sherlock pried the ball of cold cream out of its socket in the ice and dunked it in the nearest liquid water beyond. In an instant that too was frozen.

The pack of werewolves appeared. Sure enough, some were in canine form, and some in shaggy human form, and some in between. All were howling villainously. "Let's move it," Dug said.

"I'll try." Sherlock squatted, sliding the cold cream forward. The water froze around it. He moved out onto the new ice, freezing steadily ahead.

"Get on it, Nada," Dug said. "I'll defend the rear." He drew his knife.

"You are becoming more like a hero," she remarked approvingly.

"I just don't want any of us to get chomped!" He stepped on the ice after her. The ice now formed a Xanth-like peninsula extending into the river. He chopped at it with the knife, trying to separate them from the land. He hoped the resulting ice island would stay afloat.

The werewolves arrived. The first beast landed on the narrow neck of ice—and broke through it, splashing into the water. The ice the three of them stood on floated free.

There was a ripple in the water. A green snout was moving smoothly toward the werewolf. But the wolf scrambled out before the long green jaws parted to chomp him. The other wolves milled on the bank, knowing better than to set paw to water. Dug and his friends were on their way.

However, they were now at the mercy of the slow current of the With-A-Cookee River. Where would it take them? He also saw brightly colored fins. "What are those?" he asked, fearing the answer.

"Loan sharks," Nada said. "Everyone knows they'll take an arm and a leg, if you let them."

"Then we'll just have to stay out of the water," Dug said. He should have known that something egregiously punnish would turn up to make things worse.

"We should have brought a paddle," Sherlock said as he continued to add to their ice island. "Now we're up the crick without one."

"That's the way the cookee crumbles," Dug said.

"You can use your club to paddle," Nada said.

Dug tried it, but it was remarkably inefficient and the island started to rotate. "Maybe I can freeze a keel, so it won't spin," Sherlock said. He maneuvered the cold cream so that a spike formed, projecting like a tail. He dipped the cream, so that the freezing went deep. Soon the ice floe stabilized, and Dug was able to start it nudging across the river.

Then he heard a voice. It sounded like a girl. "Hey, Nada Naga!" it called.

There beyond the far bank of the river was a small party of people, waving their hands. "Who are they?" Dug asked, surprised.

"Jenny Elf—and the other Mundane Player," Nada said. "And someone else. A strange man. This should get interesting."

The other Player? Dug hadn't realized that there was one. This should indeed get interesting!

"Uh-oh," Sherlock said.

Dug glanced at him. "What's the matter?"

"The cold cream's giving out. It's no longer freezing the water."

Dug realized that the game was hitting him with another challenge. Their little ice floe would soon melt, dumping them in the river. He saw the predators circling hungrily.

"This is getting *too* interesting," he muttered.

10
CHASM

K im saw the peculiar party crossing the river. She had been alerted by the woof of Bubbles Dog. A pack of werewolves was baying, hunting down something, and it seemed to be a group of people. But the people had a raft or something, because they were out on the water where the wolves couldn't reach them.

Then one of the people turned, so that Kim saw her profile. "That's Nada Naga!" she cried.

"Who?" Cyrus asked. He was stuck in human form, because of the mean creatures in the river and the lake. They would quickly chomp him if he tried to change form and swim.

"Nada Naga. She's the Companion for the other Player. So that must be the other party. Your competition, Kim."

"Well, sure, I'd like to win the prize," Kim said. "But I like playing the game, too. In fact, I just like being in Xanth. Let's see if they're as curious about us as we are about them."

So Jenny cupped her mouth with her hands. "Hey, Nada Naga!" she called.

In a moment Nada answered. "Jenny Elf! Is that you?"

"Yes! We're stuck. On a squishy island. And sinking. Can you help?"

"We're free-floating. On an ice floe. And melting. Can you help?"

Were they destined to watch each other pass, being unable to get together? To separate and never see each other again, after coming so close? Or to watch each other sink into the water and bog, victim of the predators? Kim didn't like either notion. "This is another game challenge," she declared. "There has to be a way for us to help each other, if we want to. If we can just figure it out in time."

They considered. "I could pull their ice floe to shore," Cyrus said. "If someone protected my flank from allegations, moccasins, and loan sharks."

"Nada could do that," Jenny said. "If someone protected *her* flank."

Cyrus peered across at the other party. "How could that luscious girl protect anyone else?"

"She's a serpent woman," Jenny explained. "She changes into a serpent, the same way you change into a fish tail."

He nodded, seeing the possibilities. "They are drifting toward us. But I see that they are precariously perched."

"What can we do about that?" Jenny asked, concerned.

Sammy jumped from her shoulder to Cyrus' pack. He put his paw in. The end of the rope showed.

"Can you throw your rope that far?" Kim asked, catching on. Sammy had found what they could do.

"No. It is light rope, and must be weighted if it is to carry."

Sammy jumped to Kim's pack. "I think—" Jenny started.

Kim delved into her pack. She brought out a spare pair of shoes. "Here is your weight."

He knotted the end of the rope around the shoes, then hurled it toward the diminishing ice floe. A black man there caught it and held it. Then Jenny and Kim braced Cyrus while he hauled on the rope, drawing the other party closer.

Then the melting ice floe capsized, dumping the three into the water.

For an instant they were stunned by the calamity. Then Sammy jumped up on Kim's head and batted at her forehead, as if coaxing out a thought. Kim cried out directions—and because she was the Player, the others followed them immediately. "Jenny, hold the rope. Cyrus, take a weapon and dive for them." Kim herself delved in her pack, finding a knife. Then, before Jenny could protest, she dived into the river herself. Sammy jumped from her head to the back of Bubbles, who looked a bit startled but did not protest. The cat was much smaller than the dog, so his weight was not a problem.

Meanwhile the other Player was reacting similarly. "Loop the rope around us all!" he shouted. "Face out. We'll defend ourselves while they haul us in."

In two and a half moments, Cyrus reached the other party, and in two more so had Kim. They joined the others, roped together, facing out. The sharks and allegations were circling, but the party now bristled with knives and a spear, and one of its number was a serpent with horrendous fangs. Another had a powerful tail, and evidently knew how to swim very well, to intercept any hostile creature.

Jenny pulled on the rope. Her feet were sinking into the marshy hammock, braced by the dog and cat, but she was able to haul the mass of people slowly toward her. They finally reached the island, but did not try to scramble onto it. "We need to find solid land instead!" Kim cried from the water.

Sammy stood on Bubbles' back and said something in cat talk. The dog moved reluctantly into the water and swam toward another hammock, the cat on her back. Bubbles understood what Sammy was saying!

"They are showing the way!" Jenny cried. "Follow them!" Then she scrambled into the water herself, still holding the rope. The water here was not deep; she was able to wade far enough to catch up to the group. She got inside the loop, next to the serpent, so that she too could defend herself from the creatures outside.

It was a clumsy, messy business, but they pushed with their feet and stroked with their free hands, and nudged in the direction shown by the animals. Soon the ground under the water became firmer, and they were able to walk on it, chest-deep, then waist-deep, then knee-deep. At last they stood on solid land again—and saw a path ahead. They were on their way!

But what a motley crew they were! Dog, serpent, merman, three humans, and one elf were soaked through and spattered with mud. Only the cat was pristine.

"Let's get clean before we make our introductions," Kim suggested. The others were glad to agree.

"Sammy, where is there a good place to—" Jenny started.

The cat bounded off down the path. They followed, forming a ragged line. Soon they came to a larger, clearer lake, evidently one of the sections of Lake Tsoda Popka. It sparkled effervescently. But the cat was dipping a paw, daintily cleaning an imagined speck.

Kim squatted and dipped out a handful. "This is champagne!" she exclaimed. "We're supposed to wash in this?"

"Well, we know just how to do it," Jenny said. She fetched out an empty bottle and dipped it in the lake.

In three quarters of a moment everyone had bottles, and they were in the midst of Xanth's most uproarious fizz fight. Lake Champagne might never be the same, but they were getting clean!

Then Nada Naga, who had assumed human form underwater rather than miss the fight, went off in one direction to find a clothing tree, and Cyrus and Sherlock went off in another to find their own tree, leaving Jenny and Kim and Dug to hold the fort, as it were. They had more or less exchanged names during the cleanup. Bubbles and Sammy settled down to snooze beside each other in the sun, seeming to get along fine.

"So you're the other Player," Kim said boldly. "Are you enjoying it so far?"

"I sure am," Dug agreed. "And I'm only here on a dare."

"A dare? You didn't want to play?"

"I don't go for computer games or silly fantasy. But my friend Ed dared me to try one. I bet him my girlfriend against his motorcycle that I wouldn't like it." He smiled sheepishly. "I lost."

"You bet your girlfriend?" Kim asked, uncertain how to take that.

"Yes. Pia. She's Ed's girlfriend now. I think maybe I was set up. But I couldn't even be mad, after I saw Nada."

"You go for that type?" Kim was being guarded, for some reason she didn't care to analyze. It might be mere coincidence that Dug was a handsome young Mundane man.

"Who wouldn't? She's a knockout!"

"But she's a naga princess," Jenny said. "And she doesn't go for younger men."

"So I learned." He spread his hands. "Don't look at me that way! She's the world's most beautiful woman, and I'm just a sixteen-year-old jerk. I'm just saying that anything I might have lost back home no longer mattered, after I saw what was here." He focused on Kim. "That handsome merman—he's not interested in you, either, I'll bet. Same reason."

"He's looking for a mermaid," Kim agreed. "He's just traveling with us until he finds her."

"Same way Sherlock's traveling with us until he finds a place for his people to settle." He paused. "Look, Kim, I guess we're supposed to be in competition, but I want you to know I don't care about the prize. I just like being in the game."

"Me too," she said, discovering that she was losing interest in the prize.

"You too? I got into this on a dare, but I figured you really wanted to play."

"I do want to play. Just to be in Xanth. I love Xanth. It's so much more interesting than Mundania."

"Yes, it is. I don't know anything about it, but I haven't been bored since I got in, and not just because of Nada. It's some place!"

She nodded. "So do you want to travel on together for a while, if the rules allow it?"

"Sure. We may have nothing in common except Mundania, but that's enough of a cross for us both to bear." He glanced at Jenny. "You're her Companion? Do you know if it's okay?"

"I don't know any reason why not," Jenny said. "I don't think there are any rules, really, except about things like not looking at a girl's panties."

He laughed. "I learned about that the hard way! I tried to sneak a peek at Nada's, and I got blotted out of the game. I mean, my screen went blank, and I had to scramble to get back in. I'll never do that again!" He looked around. "Which reminds me: we need to get changed too. These clothes won't be worth much after this workout."

"We can change after the others find clothing," Jenny said. "We're just keeping an eye out now, in case anything else threatens. But as long as Bubbles doesn't bark and Sammy doesn't wake, it's safe."

"Bubbles?"

Kim explained about the way she had found the dog. "She's really very good," she concluded. "It's a shame that someone was throwing her away. I'm sorry I can't take her with me, when I return to Mundania."

"She can stay with me and Sammy," Jenny said quickly. "We won't let her be thrown away again. I'm sure Professor Grossclout will allow it."

"Who?" Dug asked.

"He's the demon in charge of the game. Compared to him, every other person's head is full of mush. But he's not too bad, if you ever manage to get to know him."

"Demons in charge of the game! Why?"

"Well, I think it's because of the Demon $X(A/N)^{th}$. He's the source of all the magic of Xanth. He wanted the game to be played. So the demons are handling it. That's all I know."

"What kind of a demon?"

So they had to explain to him about that. By the time they had done so, the others had returned.

That was a surprise. Kim eyed one party, then the other. Nada was in trousers and a male shirt; Cyrus and Sherlock were in dresses. "All we could find," the black man said, embarrassed.

"Same here," Nada confessed.

"But now we can go in the opposite directions and change," Cyrus said, relieved.

This time Jenny and Kim went with Nada, while Dug went with Cyrus and Sherlock. The girls found the tree, and picked out nice dresses. "Suddenly I feel very feminine," Kim said. "I like it."

But Nada reconsidered. "I believe I will remain in trousers," she said.

"You get tired of getting stared at?" Kim inquired. "It isn't a problem I've had."

"Well, you're not a princess."

Kim nodded ruefully. "That must be it."

They returned to the central camp. They saw the three males coming back from the other direction, all appropriately garbed. They settled down to eat, and to get to know each other better. Kim noticed that Cyrus and Nada seemed to find each other interesting. Well, both were crossbreeds, and he was almost as handsome as she was beautiful. Wouldn't it be something, if—but no, it wasn't her business to speculate.

They organized their party and set off south. It was more interesting, Kim thought, having a larger group. Also safer, perhaps, if they didn't encounter anything truly formidable. It was getting late, and they would have to find a campsite before too long.

They came to a centaur range. Kim could tell, because the path widened and was beaten down by hooves. Soon a male centaur galloped up. He was an impressive figure of horse and man, with a large bow and a quiver of arrows. Centaurs were notorious for their marksmanship; they could score on anything they fired at. "Who are you to intrude on our range?" he demanded. He seemed to have a slight speech defect.

There was something familiar about him. Then she identified it: he was Horace, the zombie centaur. One of the prospective Companions. Since he hadn't been chosen, he was now on backup duty, as Jenny and Nada would have been had they not been chosen. So he was in costume, his zombie nature concealed. She was sure it was him, regardless.

Kim looked at Dug. "He's male; you take it," she murmured. Because of course a Player had to handle it; this could be another challenge.

Dug stepped forward. "We are travelers playing a special game," he said. "We aren't looking for trouble, we're looking for a place to spend the night in peace."

"If you come in peace, you are welcome to spend the night in our village," Horace said.

Dug glanced at Nada, and Kim glanced at Jenny. Nada and Jenny both nodded: centaurs could be trusted. Apparently Dug had handled the challenge appropriately, by expressing their desire for peace. Kim was relieved; centaurs were bad enemies and good friends, and there would be no need to fear any dangers of the night here.

So Horace led them to the village. This appeared to be a group of stalls, but there were human-type houses too, evidently for those who served the centaurs. Several other centaurs came out to greet them, among them two mares.

Kim saw Dug and Sherlock blink at the sight of the bare-breasted lady centaurs. Those were the fullest breasts she had ever seen, and she suspected that the sight had far more impact on the men. But both had the wit to mask their reactions. She managed to mask her smile. Actually she would love to have an upper torso like that, to make male eyes pop.

There were passing introductions. Then the centaurs showed them to their stalls, which turned out to be fairly nice little houses with nice beds of straw inside. The three women shared one, and the three men another. Bubbles and Sammy found comfortable places of their own in the straw and were instantly asnooze. It took a while longer for the others to eat and settle down, but in due course they too were asleep.

So this had turned out to be no challenge, Kim thought. But she knew that if Dug had given the wrong answer, the party could have been in desperate trouble. Was Dug a naturally diplomatic person, or had he been lucky, this time? It was important for her to know, because he was her competition. Even if she no longer cared about the prize.

In the morning, refreshed, they resumed their journey. "Would you like a ride as far as the Gap Chasm?" Horace Centaur inquired.

Kim exchanged another glance with Dug. A ride? Was this another challenge? Yet centaurs were trustworthy. Maybe this was just the game's way of moving them along rapidly to the next challenge. In some other variant there could be a real row with the centaurs, or a dragon waiting along the path. But in this one it was at the Gap Chasm, so the sensible thing to do was to get on down there without wasting time. It was as if the game got impatient with delay, and wanted to get on with the action.

"Why not?" Dug said after a pause. "As long as our friends can ride too."

"Your friends are welcome," Horace said.

"If I may inquire," Sherlock said, "is there a place here where a new community could settle?"

Horace was surprised. "What kind of community?"

"A human Black Wave community."

Horace looked at the other centaurs. "We could use more servants," he said. "For the menial chores."

Sherlock frowned. "We'll keep it in mind," he said, evidently intending to do no such thing. Why should his folk settle for more of the same kind of treatment they had in Mundania?

So six centaurs carried the party rapidly southward. Kim carried Bubbles Dog with her, and Jenny carried Sammy Cat on the back of another centaur. The scenery fairly whizzed by. Kim would have preferred to go slower, because she was a bit afraid of the next challenge. Getting across the Gap Chasm was bound to be no easy matter. She knew there was an invisible bridge, but how could they find it? If they tried to go down into the chasm, the Gap Dragon would get them. Nobody crossed the Gap with impunity.

All too soon they arrived. There was the huge chasm, with its base shrouded in fog and the sheer brink of it taunting them. There was no bridge in sight, of course.

They dismounted and the centaurs galloped away. What next?

Dug, heedless of the scary depth, explored the verge. He walked east. Soon the nature of the chasm changed. The land did not drop straight down, but descended in a series of half-loops, so that it was possible to go down without falling. "We can handle this!" he said enthusiastically.

"But there is a dragon below," Nada warned him.

"You can be a big serpent and scare it off," he said.

"I can't scare *that* dragon. Not the Gap Dragon. The only safe way to handle him is to avoid him."

"Well, we can have Sammy Cat show us a way down and across that will avoid the dragon." He was so confident that it was annoying.

"Perhaps," Nada said guardedly.

Kim could see that the naga princess had her hands full, trying to keep Dug out of trouble. She couldn't even change forms both ways in his presence, because of the problem of clothing. It probably wasn't much fun for her, being his Companion. But it might not be much fun for Jenny Elf, either, being Kim's Companion, because Kim was impulsive too.

"This could be trouble," Cyrus said, glancing up.

Kim followed his gaze. An ugly little dark cloud was scudding from the north. "Is that who I fear it is?" she asked.

"Cumulo Fracto Nimbus," he agreed. "You encountered him before."

"I sure did! He always rains on the party."

There was a rumble of thunder. The others looked up. They shared glances of dismay.

"Hey, what's the big deal?" Dug asked. "So a little cloud passes. So it rains a bit. That won't stop us."

"That's Fracto," Nada said.

"Fractal?"

"Fracto, Xanth's worst cloud. We had better get under cover."

"What's all the fuss about one tiny cloud?" he demanded. "It'll be gone soon enough."

"If you do not care to heed my advice, perhaps you should exchange me for Kim's Companion," Nada said somewhat stiffly.

Dug looked surprised. Then he glanced at Jenny Elf, thoughtfully. "I guess maybe there's something I'm not picking up on here," he said. "But as I see it, we can wait until an actual storm threatens."

But the others knew better. They were already hurrying to find the makings of a tent. Kim went to a pie tree she had spied, to gather a good meal to eat while they waited for the cloud's fury to expire. Jenny was going for pillows. There was no telling how long they would have to wait.

"I can't believe this," Dug said. "One stupid little cloud! You'd think it was a hurricane or something."

There was another rumble. The cloud was expanding, puffing itself up voluminously. A puffy face was forming on its surface. A chill gust of wind came down.

"What an ugly puss," Dug remarked, staring up at it.

Sammy meowed. Dug looked around. "I didn't mean you," he said, flashing a smile. The cat relaxed.

"We could use some help on this tent," Sherlock called.

Dug finally realized that this was serious. He went to help pitch the tent.

The first fat drops of rain spattered down. Then their nature changed. "Hey, that's sleet!" Cyrus exclaimed.

Kim held out her hand. Hard pellets bounced off it. "Sleet? That's hail!" she said.

They got the tent finished, and piled unceremoniously into it as the hailstorm intensified. Bubbles and Sammy joined them, not wanting any part of the storm. The dog huddled close to Kim, nervous about the closeness of so many relative strangers, but not making any fuss. Kim was also highly conscious of Dug wedged on her other side.

Now the hail had become snow, piling down in turbulent flurries. They were safe under the canvas, and they had blankets too, so they were comfortable. Kim just couldn't keep her awareness off her closeness to Dug, under a shared blanket. If only something like this could be real, as in a date!

"That's more of a cloud than I figured," Dug said, paying her no attention. "Snow—on a warm day!"

"Not only that," Sherlock said. "It's colored, if you'll excuse the term."

Kim peered out. She saw pastel hues. The snow was all the colors of the rainbow! "It's pretty," she said.

"Nothing Fracto does is pretty," Nada said darkly.

They ate the pies while the storm continued. "I wonder why Fracto came here right now," Jenny said. "How could he know we were here?"

"The game!" Kim exclaimed. "He was sent by the game! It's another challenge."

"A cloud sent to mess us up?" Dug asked. "But all we have to do is wait for it to peter out."

Sherlock shook his head. "I don't know much about clouds or magic, but I'll bet this is going to make a difference. For one thing, this chasm's going to be twice as hard to cross, covered in snow."

Dug nodded. "You're right. After the storm passes, that funny snow will remain. It'll slow us down."

"Slow us down?" Kim asked. "Maybe it will speed us up!"

The others looked at her. "We don't want to jump into that blind," Nada said. "The smaller crevices will be covered up, and the slopes will be treacherously slippery. We should wait until it melts."

"But that could take days," Kim protested. "No, I'm thinking of skiing down on that snow. That would make a tedious trip easy."

"Skiing!" Dug said. "I tried to ski once, and almost broke my leg. That was just a little slope. This canyon's a mile deep. Even a skilled skier could get himself killed."

He had a point. Kim had skied, but she was no expert, and this would be no easy course. "Well, we could sled down it, maybe."

"Where'd we get sleds?"

Sammy stirred. He was about to head out into the storm when Jenny caught him. "Not yet, Sammy!" she said. "Wait till it stops snowing!"

Dug pursed his lips. "He can find sleds?"

"Sammy can find anything," Jenny said proudly. "Except home. So there must be sleds nearby."

"Can you be sure they are near?" Nada asked.

"Actually, I can't," Jenny admitted. "Sometimes things are way far away. But I know he'll find the closest sled there is."

"Okay, so we can get sleds," Dug said. "But sleds can be dangerous too, on an uncharted slope. I was ready to walk it, but I don't know about this."

"Maybe Sammy can also find a safe route down," Kim suggested. "Then we could follow on sleds."

"I wouldn't let him go alone," Jenny said. "But maybe he could ride on a sled with me, and sort of indicate whether it was safe to go on. I think that might work."

Finally the storm eased. Fracto's rages were severe, but seldom endured long. But what damage they could do in a short time!

Kim and the others climbed out of the tent. The snow was several feet deep, almost burying the tent; they had almost to tunnel to the surface.

It was a changed world. Colored snow lay everywhere, changing the landscape. The nearby trees had piles of blue snow on their foliage, while bushes were buried under yellow snow. The level land was covered in brown, while the descending slopes of the Gap Chasm were clothed in black. But it was definitely snow; Kim dipped a finger and tasted it. Black icy flakes.

They foraged for heavier clothing. There were yellow jackets growing nearby, and the cold had frozen their stingers, so that it was possible to wear them. There was also a boot tree with a fine selection ranging from bootees to jack boots. Before long they were all suitably bundled up, looking like so many stuffed dolls.

Kim realized that all this was unlikely to be coincidence. The game had set up its challenge, with supplies in place, and moved in the storm when they arrived. They were not going to go hungry or cold. They merely had to make it down into the Gap Chasm.

"Now, Sammy," Jenny said. The cat bounded away, leaving pawprints in the snow. The dog, less adventurous, remained in the tent.

Jenny followed the cat, and Kim followed Jenny. Soon they came to a sled shed. Kim knew it was that, because there was a sign on the door saying so. The cat bounded up to the door and waited until Jenny opened it. They went inside.

There were two big rounded devices. One was labeled ROBERT and the other ROBERTA. "But these aren't sleds," Jenny said. "At least, not like any I've seen."

Sherlock arrived. "Those are bobsleds!" he exclaimed, amazed.

"They have nicknames?" Jenny inquired.

Now Kim recognized the type. She had seen them race in the Winter Olympics on TV. Horribly swift three- or four-man sleds. They were supposed to careen down into the chasm in these? "But we don't know the first thing about handling a—a Robert sled," she protested weakly.

"Oh, I wouldn't say that," Sherlock said. "I rode on one once. Course it wasn't far or fast, just a little demo hill. I was the steersman. I probably couldn't have steered it wrong if I'd tried, on that track, but I did sort of get the great feel of it. That's the king of sleds, for sure."

Kim felt a sinking sensation. They were going to do it! Go down into that dread chasm on bobsleds!

They hauled the sleds back to camp. "Look what we found," Nada said, pointing.

Kim looked. There were two clearly shaped trails down into the chasm, with square signs posted where each divided.

"How did those signs get there?" Kim asked. "I don't see any tracks in the snow, and they weren't there before it snowed."

"Must be game magic," Dug said. "We really have to sled down those trails."

"But how will we know which way to go?"

"I see the signs say RIGHT and LEFT," he said. "So all we have to do is follow those road signs."

"What kind of challenge is that?" she demanded. "I don't trust this."

"Ah, you're just chicken to take the ride."

"You bet I'm chicken," she retorted, nettled. "Why would they go to all this trouble to set up a challenge, then tell us how to get through it?"

"To get us quickly down to the bottom, where we'll have to figure out how to avoid the dragon."

It did make morbid sense. But still she didn't trust it. This whole business was just too elaborate.

"Well, let's do it," Dug said. "Sherlock and Nada and I can take Robert, and Cyrus and Jenny and Kim take Roberta. We'll race each other down to the dragon."

"Who will then eat the first arrival, so the second can get through," Kim said acidly.

That finally made him pause. But he recovered. "We'll tackle that problem when we get there."

He was hopeless. And she was hopeless, to be so intrigued by him. But she reminded herself that it was only a game. The worst that could happen was that they would wash out and be back in Mundania.

Or was it? What would happen to the others, if the Players disappeared? The Companions would be all right, probably, but the others—Cyrus, Sherlock, and Bubbles—could be stranded in the snow, in the Gap, with a deadly dragon coming.

The game was no longer the fun it had been. But what could she do? Skip out on a challenge? She was stuck for it.

They hauled the bobsleds up to the ends of the two trails. Sherlock showed Cyrus how to steer. "It's mostly leaning, actually," he said. "But you have to time it right, and pull on these handles, here." Then Sherlock went to the other sled and got in. Nada got in behind him, and Dug was ready to push and jump in at the back.

Their own sled had Cyrus, Jenny with Bubbles and Sammy, and Kim as the push-off rider. They got set. "Do we really have to race?" Kim asked. "Maybe it would be better to have one sled try it first."

"It is set up like a race," Jenny said. "Probably it's better to race."

There was just no getting out of this. Kim got set to push off. She looked across at Dug.

"On your mark," he called. "Get set. GO!"

Kim pushed. The sled tipped over the rim and started down. She leaped onto the back and hung on. It felt exactly like falling.

In half a moment they were zooming toward the fork. The sign said LEFT. "Sammy says go right!" Jenny screamed. Indeed the little cat was almost scrambling out of the sled on the right side.

So Cyrus steered it right. They entered a slanting ledge overlooking a sheer drop into the chasm, then threaded past an outcropping into a kind of narrow valley. There was another fork, with another sign: LEFT.

"Go left!" Jenny cried, as the cat scrambled left.

They went left. Kim looked back, and saw that the path of the right fork turned and went directly down the face of the chasm, an impossible drop.

They came to a third fork and sign. This one said LEFT again. "Right!" Jenny cried, and they went right. The trail looped around, found a channel, and debouched on a large level ledge. The sled slid to a halt. They got out.

Kim's heart was thudding. "Two of those signs were wrong!" she said, outraged. "One of them would have dumped us into the chasm!"

Cyrus and Jenny looked back up the trail. "You're right," Cyrus said. He looked shaken. "We can't trust the signs. All of them said LEFT, but we had to go right twice. We couldn't just do the opposite of what they said, because one of them was correct. So there's no consistent pattern."

"Where is the other sled?" Jenny asked.

Sammy jumped from her arms and bounded along the ledge. They followed. Soon they spied it: jammed in a dead end about halfway between the ledge and the top. Its occupants seemed to be all right, though disheveled and annoyed.

"The middle sign was wrong?" Kim called.

"It sure was!" Dug called back. "You're lucky yours were right."

"Ours weren't. We ignored them. Sammy knew the way."

"That's some cat," he said. Then Dug and Sherlock and Nada made their way down the slope to the ledge. Their sled was hopelessly jammed and unusable. Sherlock paused to look carefully at the signs, and then went to check the signs on Kim's trail.

They consulted. With only one sled, only one party could continue. In fact, there was only one trail leading down from the ledge. "I think this challenge can have only one winner," Dug said ruefully.

"Well, you can have it," Kim said. "This sledding scares me, and so does the dragon below. I'd rather find some other way."

"It is possible to go around the Gap Chasm," Nada said. "But it's a long way, and there are dangers."

"I don't care! I've had all of the Gap I care to."

Dug pondered. "I'd as soon go on down and get it over with. But not with wrong signs. You could make it, with your cat, but we'd probably get skunked again."

"Say, I think I have it figured," Sherlock said, returning. "It's not what they say, it's where they are. When you have to go right, the sign's on the right. When you have to go left, it's on the left."

Kim looked. "You're right! It's like the game of Scissors!"

"Scissors?" Sherlock asked, and the others looked similarly blank.

"It's a game. Most of the players have played it before, so they know the rules, but there are a few newcomers who don't. They sit in chairs in a circle and pass a pair of scissors around. Each one says, 'I receive these scissors crossed,' and passes them on uncrossed, or whatever, and changes the scissors to match. It's different for each one, depending on the scissors. But when a newcomer does it, chances are he's wrong, and everybody knows it. They keep playing until he catches on: it's not the scissors, it's the legs. So maybe someone has his legs crossed, and he passes the scissors on uncrossed, saying they're crossed, and everyone agrees but the poor innocent who's looking at the scissors."

"The signs!" Dug said. "They're the scissors—and you have to look at where they are instead of what they are. That's the challenge—to figure out the key before you get creamed."

"And this was just the practice run, to give us a chance before we blow it for real," Kim agreed. "Though one of those wrong paths sure looked final to me."

"It isn't," Sherlock said. "I saw where it has a leveling slope after the drop, like a ski jump. *Then* it dead-ends. It looks worse than it is."

"So now we know," Cyrus said. "But we have only one sled. I for one would rather not use it."

"So let's go find some other way," Kim said gratefully. "Let *them* have our sled, if they want it."

"I'm not eager to ride down," Nada protested.

Dug pursed his lips. "How do you feel about it, Jenny?"

"I don't mind which way, as long as I have Sammy to guide me."

Dug looked at Kim. "Want to exchange Companions?"

Kim was astonished. "Can we do that?" She had thought Nada's suggestion to that effect was sarcastic.

"We can try it and see what happens. I never saw any rule saying no."

Kim considered this amazing proposal. Jenny was good, and Sammy was useful, but Nada could become a serpent and a formidable bodyguard. Dug would need the cat's ability to sneak through the chasm valley without blundering into the dragon. It seemed a fair exchange. "Let's do it," she decided.

So Nada Naga joined Kim and Cyrus, while Jenny joined Dug and Sherlock. Sammy Cat remained with Jenny, and Bubbles Dog remained with Kim. It all seemed even.

Then Nada assumed large serpent form and slithered up the snowy slope. She could handle it better in that form than in the human form; the snow gave her sinuous body purchase. She reached a small tree, clamped her teeth on it, and let Cyrus and Kim use her body like a rope to climb up more readily. When they reached the sapling, Nada went on up again. After several such stages they reached the top, cold but safe. Then Kim held out Nada's jacket, while Cyrus faced away, so Nada could return to human form and get quickly dressed.

"We're up," Kim called down to the others, who were now out of sight on the ledge.

"Okay," Dug called back from below. "Been nice knowing you! We're going down." There was the sound of the sled moving.

"And now we have to start our long walk around the Gap Chasm," Kim said. "But I'm relieved not to have to ride down any farther."

The others nodded agreement. So, it almost seemed, did Bubbles.

11
DRAGON

Dug watched the other party scale the slope, leaving the Gap Chasm. His feelings were mixed. He was sorry to see Nada Naga go, because she was the most luscious female creature he could imagine. But she had also been a distraction. He had been more or less blundering through the challenges, and that was no good; he needed to focus clearly on what he was doing. He wasn't interested in winning the prize, just in extending his time in the game. But he realized that he had to keep winning challenges, and following the general course of the game, or he would soon enough be dumped out of it. So Nada had probably been a net liability, not because of her, but because of him.

Jenny Elf, in contrast, was not a romantic figure. He had no hankering to see her panties or body. And her cat was one supremely useful creature. The way he had found the bobsleds, and the correct path down the slope—that was a tremendous asset in this game. So Jenny made all the sense Nada didn't, for him. He should be able to do much better now.

But why had Kim agreed to the exchange? She hadn't wanted to sled down into the depths and meet the dragon. He could appreciate why. But Jenny would have gone out of the chasm with her. Nada hadn't wanted to sled on down, but would have, because she had to follow the route her Player decided on. So they hadn't had to switch for that reason. What did Nada offer that Kim wanted?

Well, protection, of course. Nobody much messed with Nada in her huge serpent form. Nobody, it seemed, except the Gap Dragon. She had been quick to point out that she couldn't back off that particular monster, and he had been quick to pick up on that fact. So despite what he had said, he was worried;

there was a real threat down there, and he had better have a notion how to handle it before he got there. So now Kim had that serpent protection. Was that what she wanted?

He turned to look down into the chasm. Cold fog shrouded the depths, so he could not see more than the beginning of the trail. They should be able to navigate it successfully, now that they had the key to the signs. If that went wrong, Sammy Cat would let them know. So the trip down shouldn't be a problem. But the dragon would be more than enough to make up for it.

"What are we going to do about that dragon?" he asked the others.

"That's bothering you?" Sherlock asked in mock surprise. "Me, too. If it eats me, I'm gone. If it eats you, I'm stuck down there with no game Player to lead the way. The Companion doesn't have to help me, you know."

"If Dug gets eaten, he'll disappear from Xanth," Jenny said. "Then I'll call Professor Grossclout, and he'll take me out. I'll ask him to take you too."

"Why should he bother?"

"Because the game isn't supposed to interfere with regular people of Xanth. You're a regular person. So the Professor will have to put you back where we found you." She hesitated. "If I may ask, why did you come with Dug and Nada?"

"I am a member of the Black Wave. I'm trying to find a place for us to stay where folk will be glad to have us, or where there are no other folk to be concerned."

"Oh, like the Curse Fiends!" she said.

"The what?"

"They were folk of the Seventh Wave who settled in Lake Ogre-Chobee and became the Curse Friends, only others call them the Curse Fiends. They remained sort of isolated, and never really mixed with the other folk of Xanth. So I guess you're the Fifteenth Wave. You want to be separate like them?"

"No, not really. But we're prepared to be, if that's the way of it. These Curse Friends—they're not really fiends, then?"

"No, they're just people. They act in plays, and go on tours, entertaining others. I think maybe they would have mixed, but nobody invited them to."

"Exactly. Maybe I should talk with the Curse Fiends."

"After we get by the dragon," Dug said firmly. "Nobody's talking with anybody, if he gets eaten first."

Sherlock and Jenny exchanged half a glance. "Man's got a point," Sherlock said.

"I can ask Sammy how to get away from the dragon," Jenny said. "But I don't think—"

Sure enough, the cat started running up the slope, in the same direction Kim's party had gone. Jenny had to chase after him, cancelling her statement, so he wouldn't keep looking for the way away from the dragon.

Then Dug had a notion. "That evil cloud, what's-his-name, Fractal—he still around?"

There was a warning rumble from the depths. The mist was part of the cloud, and he was still there.

"Maybe better not to aggravate him by mispronouncing his name," Sherlock murmured. "Fracto."

"Fracto," Dug said contritely. "Sorry about that. Of course we don't want to aggravate him. He could blow up a storm again, and bury us."

Sherlock looked at him as if suspecting Dug of some devious purpose, but did not comment. Sherlock was right: Dug now knew how to get by the dragon.

Kim called down from above: they had made it out of the chasm. "Okay!" Dug called.

They were ready to get into the Roberta sled, but Sherlock hesitated. "What's the matter?" Dug asked.

"I've got long legs. That's not enough footroom in this sled for me."

"Isn't it the same as the other sled?"

"No. Take a look." Sherlock climbed in—and his rear came back into the second person's place. It looked uncomfortable for him, and it would push the other two back, so that there wouldn't be enough room for the third person at the end.

"We'll have to change the order," Dug said. "Jenny, you try it."

Jenny got in, but her legs were much shorter, not reaching far into the front. Dug and Sherlock's longer legs couldn't fit in the remaining space, so again there wasn't room for the third man.

"Then I'll have to do it," Dug said. He got in, and Jenny took the middle, with Sammy Cat in her lap, and Sherlock took the end. Now they fit perfectly.

Sherlock showed him how to steer. It was not hard, the man assured him; the other sled had been magically responsive, so that it seemed that even a thought directed it. All Dug really had to do was hold the handles and focus on where he wanted to go, and it would go there.

Belatedly he wondered: had the game arranged it this way? Because he was the Player, who should handle his challenges himself. The prior run had been for practice, so it didn't matter who steered the sled, but this one was for the money. How could the demon proprietors have known that Dug's sled would be lost, and that he would change to the other one? They must have had magical information.

They got settled in the Roberta sled and started down. Dug knew this was going to be one harrowing ride, but he reminded himself that it was after all only a game. There was always a way through, and they had found the way through for the sled. He hoped.

The sled started with a frightening plunge. It gathered such velocity that Dug abruptly doubted that he had a true path down. This could only end in a splat! He felt Jenny tense; a glance back showed her frozen with half a scream in her mouth, and the cat was hiding his head under her knees.

Then the ground curved up and the sled's runners took a better grip on reality. But before Jenny could get her scream the rest of the way out, the trail made a savage turn and ended in a square drop-off. There was space at either side, so that he could steer off the trail, avoiding the disaster. But the trail was clear, and there was no sign. So it should be right, despite the appearance. What should he do?

Dug had only seconds to decide. He froze. That meant that he did nothing. The sled rushed on down the trail. And off the drop-off. Dug heard a muttered "Sheesh!" from the rear.

Then out of the fog loomed a wall, and in the wall was a crevice, and the sled slammed into that crevice and zoomed on. The trail had jumped a gap in the slope; had the sled been moving slower, it would have crashed into the wall beneath the gap, flattening them and dropping them into whatever lay below. Had he steered it off the trail, he might have brought it to a stop, but they would have been stuck partway down the wall of the chasm. So he had made the right decision, by default.

They came to a fork. The sign said RIGHT, and it was on the right side, so Dug steered it that way. This path dropped, so that they sped up again, and again there was a bit of nervous choice. There seemed to be several tracks, all converging farther down, so it made no difference which one he followed. But some were more ragged than others. The sled struck a bump, and sailed into the air, and he almost lost control. It did make a difference, because they could capsize—or whatever it was that a bobsled did—if he managed it wrong. So he steered for the smoothest path, and corrected course as they bounced around, gaining proficiency. He managed to keep them upright and pointed forward.

The tracks converged. Then the main track suddenly curved up so sharply that it looped. "What is this, a roller-coaster ride?" Dug demanded rhetorically.

"No, a flume ride," Sherlock said, as the loop exited into a bank of snow that shook loose and slid down the slope. They were carried along in the flowing current of white powder; the snow had given up being Technicolor and was now plain vanilla white. Again they were falling, part of an avalanche. But it was not an easy ride; Dug had to keep steering by focusing, lest they turn over or turn sideways. This was like one of those purely mechanical computer games, requiring constant finger dexterity and spot judgment to avoid being dumped. Fortunately he had played a number of such games before getting bored with their intellectual simplicity, and had a fairly steady hand.

"If this is the right trail," Dug puffed through the enveloping snow, "I'd hate to see the wrong one!"

This, too, leveled out at last. They came to another sign saying RIGHT, but they couldn't see the fork; it had been hidden by the fall of snow. Where could they steer?

Dug solved the problem by going right at the sign. The sled hit it and crashed on. The others understood the logic, he hoped: they had to go along the path marked by the sign, which meant that the sign itself would be beside it. They might not be *on* the path, but it would be close to them.

Sure enough, the sled bumped, then dropped into a slight channel. It had found the path. Then the sides rose up, and they were cruising through a U-shaped valley. He had to steer with excruciating care, to keep them on course by banking on the turns. This was a really nervous workout! But was this the correct path? How could he be quite sure?

The valley curved, taking them around and around until they had completed a circle. But they were below the prior track. It was a corkscrew turn! The walls closed over the top, and they were plunging through darkness.

Dug heard water. Was there an underground river here? Then light came, and he saw that they had entered a cavern with a hole in the ceiling for a sunbeam. Ahead was a waterfall. The water came from the right side, and fell into the center of the cave, where it flowed on to the left. The sled bucked like a bronco as it traversed the slush by the river. They could still crash!

There was another sign. LEFT. But it was on the right side. "At least we're on the proper trail," Sherlock said, sounding relieved as Dug steered the sled directly toward the waterfall.

"How can you be sure!" Jenny demanded, seeing disaster looming.

"Because they wouldn't put another sign on a wrong trail; they'd just terminate it."

Then they plunged into the sheet of falling water. And through it. There was space behind it, descending. Sparks flashed as the runners scraped against bare rock. They skidded onto sand, and on down through a round hole just large enough to let them through. They sailed out into space and bright light.

And landed with a plunk on a monster pillow bush. Pillows popped, sending fluff flying wide. But they had stopped, safely. They were at the base of the chasm.

They climbed out and looked around. Behind them was the steep slope of the chasm wall, with its tiny hole up just too high for a standing man to reach from the floor. Ahead of them was a flat, open expanse. Beyond it was the far wall of the chasm, rising vertically to a ledge, and thence to another ledge. To either side was the length of the great valley, curving out of sight. It was actually a pleasant enough place. There was even a pie tree a short distance away.

Then they felt a shudder in the ground. It was followed by another. Whomp! Whomp!

"The Gap Dragon!" Jenny cried. "He's coming—and we can't escape him here!"

"If you have a plan," Sherlock said wryly, "it's about time to put it into effect."

"First I want to settle with that stupid cloud, what's-his-name, who couldn't put out enough snow to cover the slope," Dug said.

There was an angry rumble from above. Fracto was listening and reacting to the criticism.

"But it's the dragon we have to settle with first," Jenny said, alarmed. The whomping was getting louder.

"No, it's that wimpish cloud," Dug insisted. "If Fractal had the gumption God gave a turnip, he'd have laid snow all the way down to the floor so we could coast down properly, instead of having to shunt into a watery cave. But I guess that's what happens when you depend on airheads."

There was a louder rumble, but it was matched by the closer whomping. In a moment the Gap Dragon would round the turn and spy them. "Dug—" Sherlock said, looking pale around the gills, which was a good trick.

"I'm sorry," Dug said stoutly, "but I just can't let inadequacy pass. That pip-squeak cloud didn't do his job right, and we had to land in a bed of pillows instead of a bed of snow, the way it should have been. I don't know why the demons chose such a malingerer! They should have known Flacto would botch it."

"You keep getting the name wrong," Jenny shouted over the double noise of rumbling and whomping. "You're just going to make Fracto even madder!"

"So who cares if Fatso gets mad?" Dug yelled. "It's about time someone called a wimp a wimp! He couldn't work up a decent blow down here. He's just a stupid washout."

The mist along the slope pulled itself into a furiously swirling cloud. Jags of lightning shot out from it. The baleful face of Fracto formed, staring down.

Jenny screamed. "The Gap Dragon!"

"No, that's Crapto, the least of clouds. You can tell by his vacuous expression."

"I mean down on the ground. There!" She pointed.

Dug looked. Indeed it was the dragon. A serpentine, six-legged creature, with a long mouthful of teeth, puffing steam.

Dug stood his ground. "Don't worry," he shouted. "Framto wouldn't dare wet on the Gap Dragon, so the poopy cloud can't get at us."

Sherlock opened his mouth as if about to address an idiot. Then there was a little flash above his head, that wasn't lightning. He had caught on to what Dug was doing. "Yeah," he agreed. "Clouds are notorious cowards."

Fracto exploded. Pieces of cloud flew everywhere, each with the same furious face of the original. Toothpick-sized jags of lightning flew out from them, sticking into the ground. One mini-jag struck the charging dragon on the trail.

The dragon whirled, unhurt but stung by the barb. He sent a sizzling stream of steam at the main remaining body of the cloud. Unfortunately the hot vapor only gave the thing a jolt of extra energy. The central blob expanded rapidly, incorporating the surrounding cloudlets. More lightning flashed. Suddenly Fracto was formidable.

"Aw, it's all flash and no snow," Dug called. "The thing's too hot to make snow anyway." ·

The boiling cloud turned gray. Then snow began to fly. In a moment there was a blizzard, obscuring the dragon.

Dug grabbed the hands of the others. Silently he led them back to Roberta Sled, still amidst the pillow bush. They grabbed pillows to protect themselves from the sudden cold.

They heard the dragon casting about, searching for them. But the blizzard made visibility almost zero. As long as they were silent, they could not be found except by accident.

Sherlock squeezed Dug's hand appreciatively. The ploy had worked, and was hiding them from the dragon.

But Dug knew that this was only part of it. Before long the cloud would storm himself out, and the snow would melt, and the dragon would be waiting for them. So they had to act while the storm remained. In silence. Which meant that he couldn't explain the rest of his plan to the others; he would have to show them by action.

He tied pillows to his body by knotting their corners together. He got rope from his pack and strung it out so the others could hang on to it, not losing him. Then he set out across the floor of the Gap. He knew which way to go, because the sled pointed that way. If he veered a bit to the side, it didn't matter; he would find the wall soon enough.

He heard the dragon moving, still searching. There was a hiss as steam seared out to melt the snow, but more kept falling, as Fracto proved himself. The swirling snow blotted out both vision and smell. Dug angled his walk to steer well clear of the creature. Any little mistake could bring the steam, and then the dragon, and it would be over. If this weren't a fantasy game, he would have been almost too frightened to act. As it was, he was nervous enough.

Suddenly the wall loomed ahead. Good! He got down and silently scooped up a double handful of snow. He formed it into a ball, then rolled the ball, picking up more snow. When the ball was as large as he could conveniently handle, he rolled it to the base of the wall and left it there. Then he started another.

The others caught on. They made snowballs of their own, and rolled them big and added them to the first one. The pile grew rapidly, and expanded into a ramp, which they quietly packed firm. Then they rolled balls up it, to make it higher, wedging them into place and filling in the crevices with more snow.

By the time the storm began to ease, the ramp extended all the way up to the first ledge in the wall, well, above their heads. They rolled balls up to that ledge, forming a second, smaller ramp extending from that ledge to a higher one. Dug wasn't sure that the second ledge led where they needed to go, but there was no way to find out except to get there and see.

The snow stopped falling. The mist cleared up.

There was a snort. The dragon spied them!

"Get up to the ledge!" Dug cried.

They scrambled, leaving their last snowballs behind.

The dragon whomped toward them. But now there was a thick layer of snow on the ground, interfering with his navigation. He spun to the side and rolled tail over snoot. That gave the three of them time to make it to the ledge.

The dragon righted himself and blew out a thick stream of steam. The snow shrank nervously away from it. The dragon walked slowly toward the wall, melting snow before him. It was impressive.

Then Sherlock realized something. "The ramp! He can use it too!"

Oops! "We must knock it away, quickly," Dug said.

He and Sherlock sat on the edge of the ledge and kicked at the ramp, while Jenny hauled in the loose rope and coiled it. But the ramp was packed solid now, and gave way reluctantly. "We built too well," Sherlock said.

The dragon reached the base of the ramp. His steam melted the packed snow. He paused, considering. He was not all that stupid, it turned out. He aimed his steam upward, and started mounting the ramp.

Dug got out his club and whammed at the snow. But this too was ineffective, because he didn't dare swing hard enough to do real damage, for fear of hitting Sherlock. "Stand back," he cried. "I'll bash this out."

Sherlock got out of the way. Dug braced himself and swung a huge swing. The club bashed into the snow, caught—and jerked out of his hands.

"Oh, no!" Dug cried, diving for it. He got his hands on it, but overbalanced, falling onto the ramp himself. He scrambled to get back, but couldn't; instead he toppled off the ramp. He grabbed at it, but succeeded only in breaking his fall somewhat. He landed on his feet beside the ramp, holding the club.

Now he was in for it! One moment of carelessness had dumped him into the worst possible situation. He was pretty sure he couldn't fight the dragon; it would steam him before he got close enough to do any damage.

But maybe the dragon was too dull to realize what had happened. Maybe the creature would keep climbing the ramp and—

And what? Gobble up the other two people?

"Hey, steamsnoot!" Dug cried, waving his weapon.

The dragon spied him. He pondered again. Then he got smoothly off the ramp and advanced on Dug. He was not so dull as not to realize that the morsel on the ground was easier to nab than the two on the ledge.

Dug ran. In a moment he heard the dragon whomping after him. But again the snow interfered, and the dragon got fouled up in his own torso. It seemed that it required a delicate balance to whomp, and the snow prevented this. That gave Dug slightly more of a chance than otherwise.

Dug ran in a circle, pursued by the dragon, who had to melt a path ahead of him. Even so, he wasn't exactly slow. Dug looped back to the ramp and charged up it.

But the dragon whipped back on his tail, much faster. He had a cleared area where he had been. As Dug tried to cross to the ledge, the dragon whomped. His foresection sailed right up and came down across the ramp. His weight and mass knocked out a section of it.

Dug slid to a stop, almost falling on the dragon's back. The monster was already bringing his head sinuously back, ready to chomp him. Could he smite that snoot with his club? He lifted it in both hands—and the dragon sent a waft of steam and almost boiled him where he stood. Had he not still been protected by pillows, he could have been finished right then. Dug had to reverse and run back off the ramp.

Now the ramp was out, and he was trapped on the floor of the chasm. The dragon was getting steadily more savvy.

Well, could he fight after all? It seemed ridiculous to have the club and never even try to use it. If he timed the blasts of steam, so as to dodge them, then struck from the side—

He stood his ground as the dragon closed on him. He watched for the steam. The dragon inhaled, started to exhale, and Dug threw himself to the side.

But his foot slipped in the slushy snow, and he fell on his face. The blast of steam passed just over his back. The snow melted around him.

Dug scrambled up. He plunged to the side, trying to get into position for a strike. But the dragon's snoot was tracking him, and the dragon's torso was inhaling. Could he strike before the dragon's breath reversed and cooked him?

He tried. But the dragon's head dodged to the side and fired another hiss of steam at Dug's feet. Dug leaped clear, and the steam melted the snow where he had stood. He landed on his back in the snow, his club waving helplessly. Some hero he was turning out to be!

As he scrambled back to his feet, he saw that there was a hole in the ground where the snow had melted. It was just about big enough for a man to fall into. He was lucky he hadn't stepped there when it was covered by the snow.

He tried once more to bring his weapon into play. But this time the dragon's tail whipped around and stung his hand. He dropped the club and retreated, his hand smarting. He was having one close call after another!

It was no good trying to fight the dragon. He just wasn't cut out for it. He really didn't know how to use the club and was as likely to hurt himself as the enemy. He was probably better off without it. But the dragon was better coordinated than he was; he couldn't outmaneuver him. What could he do to escape?

Dug turned around and ran directly away from the dragon. But the dragon whomped after him with distressing vigor. Dug tried to dodge again, and slipped again. He sat up—and there was the dragon's snoot, right before his face.

The dragon's mouth slowly opened. Dug realized that he was done for. He had blundered all the way, made a thorough ass of himself, and now would be dispatched. He was disgusted. Why hadn't he used his brain to figure out some effective strategy, instead of just scrambling aimlessly through the snow?

His brain. Suddenly, in this seemingly hopeless situation, it was perking onto high. This was the game. There was always a way through. Maybe several ways. That hole in the ground—he might have crawled into that and escaped the dragon. Of course there might have been danger down there, like biting insects, ferocious rats, or goblins. Maybe it was an escape he could have used if he had chosen Goody Goblin as Companion; Goody would have related to the other goblins and gotten him through. If he had taken Horace Centaur as Companion, he might have ridden away from the dragon; he doubted that whomping could match the speed of a gallop. If he had stayed with Grundy, the golem might have talked with the plants down here and gotten information where there was a secret passage through the wall or something. Marrow Bones the walking skeleton might have—well, he wasn't sure what Marrow might have done but there was surely something. But he wasn't with any of those; he was with Jenny Elf, whose little cat had been unable to find a way out, and in any event, he was now stuck here alone. So there might be many ways out, but he had managed to avoid them all and make his situation worse. Because after provoking Fracto into hiding them with the blizzard, he had stopped using his mind and just slogged ahead physically.

He saw now that the dragon knew it was the game. Those near misses with the steam had been intentional. Maybe getting confused by the blizzard had been an act too. In real life he would have been chomped immediately. The dragon had been giving him a chance to get away, if he only had the wit to figure it out. Now the dragon was pausing, giving him one more chance. He had to take it.

He reached into his pocket and found the Germ of an Idea. He didn't need to put it to his forehead. He knew what to do with it, in this punnish realm. "Dragon, beware!" he cried. "I've got a germ. If you chomp me, you'll get it."

The dragon hesitated. So it did understand his words! And it was cautious about a germ. Few predators cared to eat diseased prey. Probably the dragon knew it wasn't that kind of germ, but by the law of the pun he had to accept it. Dug had finally used his brain and found a way.

"Go ahead," he said, playing it for what it was worth as he got up. "Chomp me. Gobble up the germ. Maybe it won't hurt you." For sure it wouldn't hurt the dragon!

The dragon closed his mouth, considering. Then a thought percolated through. He aimed his snoot and inhaled. He was going to cook the prey, getting rid of the germ that way.

But now Dug was on his feet. He put them into gear and ran for the wall.

A jet of steam singed the snow beside him. Another close miss. "Thanks, dragon-breath!" Dug muttered. But he knew the dragon wouldn't miss too many more times; there were limits even to the game. He had to make good his escape now, or it would surely be never.

He touched the germ to his forehead as he ran. The idea came to him. "Jenny!" he called. "Let down the rope for me! Anchor it."

Jenny threw down one end of the rope, while Sherlock tied the other end to a crag. Dug reached it, grabbed it, and hauled up his legs just as another bolt of steam splashed against the wall where they had been. He handed himself up the rope, walking the wall with his feet. Rappelling, it was called, or something. And the dragon was letting him do it. Because it was an approved way to escape. Obviously in real life the dragon could have dispatched him instantly, but the game required that the Player be given every chance. It had surely been the same with the roc in the tall hassle tree forest. And the censor-ship. All he had to do was to learn to play the game right.

He made it to the ledge and heaved himself over. Just in time; his arms were starting to cramp from the unaccustomed exertion. No matter that this was just a game, and he wasn't really here, and his real body was sitting mesmerized by the stupid screen. He was into the spirit and sensation of it, and he felt what he was supposed to feel. Which at the moment was mostly joy, because now he understood what he needed to, to get wherever he was going. He had made the sensible decision to part company with Nada Naga, getting rid of a foolish distraction. Now he had made the decision to play the game right. After almost losing track and getting skunked.

He stood on the ledge and peered down at the dragon. The dragon peered up at him. Then the dragon winked.

But one thing nagged Dug's mind. He had been clumsy, even after making allowances. He had fallen almost right under the dragon's snoot. At that point he had made what should have been a fatal mistake, and paid the price for it. Com Pewter had shown no mercy on him when he lost the riddle contest. Why had the dragon been so much more generous?

He reviewed it in his mind, suspecting that there was some key element he had missed. Key elements were important here. They could apply to more than one situation, as had been the case with the germ. He wanted to fathom this one.

He had fallen down while trying to bash out the ramp, so the dragon could not reach the ledge. So then he was on the ground, and the dragon was mounting the ramp. The dragon was about to gobble up the two people trapped on the ledge. So Dug had cried out, attracting the dragon's attention to himself.

And there it was. He had, in the heat of the moment, acted selflessly. He had put himself in peril, to save his companions. No matter that the dragon wasn't really after them, because one was the Companion and the other was just a fellow traveler. Dug had done a generous thing. He must have earned a bonus point, and because of it the dragon had let him go, after a reasonable show.

Now he understood. So now he winked back at the dragon.

After which he turned around. "Let's see where we can go from here," he said. "I'm sure there's some way up. What does Sammy say?"

The little cat bounded up the snow steps the two had made, to the higher ledge. He knew where to go—now that they were past the dragon. The Companion could help, but the Player had to handle the main challenge. Okay.

And what would be the next challenge? He could find out. "Jenny, what will we find south of the Gap Chasm?" he asked the elf girl as they followed the upper ledge to a hole in the cliff that now appeared.

"I'm not sure of the details, but I know there's quick sand and slow sand there," she said. "And the Gnobody Gnomes, and the Cow Boys and the Knock-Kneed Knights."

"Now, why do I have the feeling that those are not ordinary gnomes, or young men who herd cows?" Dug inquired rhetorically.

"The Cow Boys are bull-headed," she agreed. "And the Knights are empty. And there's also Com Pewter somewhere in there."

Pewter! This was the one he had been waiting for. The rematch. Jenny Elf didn't realize that he had already encountered the evil machine, and had a score to settle. He should have known that his path would lead him there, because he could not win the game without nullifying whatever had balked him before.

So now he knew his next major challenge. This time he intended to be prepared. "Pewter," he murmured, "I'm going to kick your metal butt!"

Then he focused on their climb out of the chasm, because he had learned better than to ignore the details of the moment. Sammy Cat was leading the way, but there could still be complications. They were now in a wormlike tunnel wending upward, festooned with spider webbing. But the worm would have had to be the size of the diggle. Well, maybe it had been a diggle, who forgot to phase out when traveling, so left a hole in the ground. Just so long as it led them back to ground level.

Meanwhile, he would keep an eye out for anything that might enable him to handle Pewter. So that he could continue playing the game, and remain in Xanth.

12
MERCI

Kim walked east along the Gap Chasm. The snow was already melting; it seemed that the evil cloud could blow up a snowstorm, but couldn't actually cool the land. That was just as well; Fracto had caused too much misery already.

"I guess we'd better fill you in on what we were up to before we met," Kim said to Nada Naga. "Jenny and I encountered the ogres of the Ogre Fen, then ran afoul of Fracto and got washed into the Water Wing, where Cyrus rescued us. On the way out I found Bubbles." She patted the dog. "Cyrus is looking for a wife."

Nada glanced sidelong at Cyrus. "So I gathered. He wouldn't happen to be a prince, would he?"

"No, I'm just a regular merman," Cyrus said. "Why?"

"I have been looking for a husband," she said candidly. "But I would prefer to have a prince."

"I would not do for you anyway, because I must marry either a mermaid or a fish. I would prefer the mermaid."

"I am not surprised. The naga sometimes must marry either full human folk, or full serpent folk, but we prefer our own kind. However, we also marry to cement liaisons with other species. But this is done only between princes and princesses."

"But your brother Naldo married Mela Merwoman," Kim said. "She wasn't a princess, was she?"

"My brother Prince Naldo has an eye for the ladies," she replied evenly. "He happened to catch a glimpse of Mela's panties, and decided to marry her. Mela fills her panties very well, considering her age."

"She's young?" Cyrus asked.

"No, old. But she retains her youthful proportions, which are generous. My brother noticed." She shrugged. "Males have never been much for following the rules. Our father was annoyed, until he met the merwoman. Then he concluded that this was a warranted exception to our policy."

"Sounds like sexism to me," Kim muttered.

"Her proportions are surely not more generous than your own," Cyrus said diplomatically.

"Oh, I believe they are! You have to understand that merwomen are not quite the same as mermaids; they are better endowed. I think it is because the sea is colder than the lakes and rivers. Perhaps the salt has something to do with it." She glanced again at him. "Have you ever swum in salt, Cyrus?"

"Never. But I shall be happy to give it a try."

"I understand that the merfolk of the sea and the merfolk of the lakes are incompatible, for that reason," Nada said. "But that is only hearsay."

Kim heard something. "Is that a storm, down inside the Gap Chasm?" she asked.

The others paused to listen. "That sounds like Fracto," Nada said. "Do you think that Dug was crazy enough to aggravate that cloud again?"

"Well, I was crazy enough to do it before," Kim said. "Dug's like me, in some respects."

"Oh? Do you like him?"

"Yes, I guess I do," Kim said shyly.

"Why didn't you say something?"

"Well, where I come from, a girl doesn't."

"You are not where you come from," Nada pointed out.

Kim shrugged. "Still, he's from Mundania too. He's handsome, while I—" She didn't care to finish.

"I suppose he is," Nada said. "I hadn't noticed. He does seem to be interested in—" She hesitated. "Mature women."

"Oh, was he getting fresh with you?" Kim asked, morbidly curious.

"He tried to glimpse my panties, and almost got put out of the game. After that he was more careful."

"So that explains it," Kim said. "I thought he was remarkably polite, for a teenage boy."

"He became polite. He seems clever enough, when one allows for his immaturity."

"*All* Mundane boys are immature. That's why they need girls to mature them."

Nada smiled. "They're not so different that those of Xanth." She peered into the chasm. "I think that's another snowstorm. I wonder what's going on down there?"

A small light flashed over Kim's head, melting the last of the snow in her vicinity. "A blinding blizzard! Would that hide them from the dragon?"

"I think it might," Nada agreed.

"Then Dug must've deliberately insulted Fracto, to create that diversion," Kim said, delighted. "So they could get through safely."

"You *do* like him," Nada said.

"But he has no interest in me, so it doesn't matter. Let's get on and win this game."

Bubbles was happy to lead the way, her tail curling up in a perfect semicircle. The path was clear, and there were no bad creatures in the way. But Kim knew that there would be another challenge before too long. She hoped she would be ready for it.

As they went, they had to discard items of clothing, because of the returning warmth. It was hard to imagine that this had so recently been a snowscape.

Bubbles barked. Kim looked around, because there was always something when the dog gave warning.

Specks appeared in the sky. They danced around, growing larger. They did not seem to be birds or insects; their outlines were squared off, and their motions too bobbing. "What are those?" Kim asked.

Nada looked. "Kites, I think. They like to fly about the Gap, because of updrafts there."

"Oh, I used to love to fly kites!" Kim exclaimed. "Are these magic?"

"Everything is magic in Xanth," Nada said.

"There's a string," Cyrus said. He strode forward, reaching for it.

"I wouldn't," Nada said warningly.

But he was already grabbing the string. He hauled on it, bringing the kite down. It was a huge cubic thing, brightly colored.

The kite suddenly plunged, looming close. It swept into Cyrus, knocking him down. Then, free, it sailed back up out of reach.

Kim dashed over to help him. "Are you all right?" she asked worriedly.

Cyrus sat up, shaking his head. Three little birds were flying around it, cheeping. "Just dizzy, I think," he said dizzily. "What happened?"

"You grabbed the string of a box kite," Nada explained. "It boxed you."

Kim helped him stand. He was unsteady, but the little birds evidently decided he was all right, and flew away. "No more kites," he said.

"No more kites," Kim agreed.

Nada looked around. "That's odd."

"What's odd?" Kim asked, concerned. She saw that Bubbles seemed perplexed, too.

"We seem to be a good deal farther along than I would have thought. This looks like the terrain beyond Gap Village, and maybe beyond the goblin village too."

Kim realized that the terrain had changed during their distraction by the kite. They were still north of the Gap, proceeding east, but the lay of the land was different.

"Could this be a device of the game to move us more rapidly to the next challenge?"

"It must be," Nada agreed. "Professor Grossclout has demonic powers."

"Well, he *is* a demon," Kim agreed.

As they proceeded, Kim saw that not only had the scene changed, it differed in type. Instead of idle stones by the wayside, there were crystals. In fact, they soon became fancier, with pretty colors. They looked like diamonds, rubies, sapphires, emeralds, opals, amethysts, garnets, and all manner of other gems. Many were small, but some were large, and a few were huge.

Kim gazed at them in wonder. "Oh, I've always loved pretty stones," she said. "But the best I could afford was smoky quartz, which is to real gems as glop is to gold. I've never even imagined such a display!"

"I think they're hiquigems," Nada said. "Impossible to use."

"High-que gems?" Kim asked. "Are they dangerous?"

"No, they are harmless. But you really can't touch them."

Bubbles was sniffing at a nearby gem. Kim squatted, reaching for the lovely red spinel the size of an apple. "I won't get shocked, or anything?"

"Nothing like that. But you are wasting your time."

Kim's fingers closed around the beautiful gem. She picked it up with an oooh of appreciation, admiring its facets.

Then something happened. "Oh, I dropped it!" she exclaimed, chagrined. Indeed, something red fell to the ground. But it didn't look like a gem. It looked like a blob of red gelatin. It landed silently.

Then, as her eyes focused on it, she saw that she had been mistaken. It was the same gem she had picked up, undamaged. But how could she have dropped it? It had somehow seemed to flow through her fingers, a weird sensation.

She picked it up again, cautiously. Again it fell. But this time she saw it happen. The thing lost form, became a big drop of red liquid, slid between her fingers, landed on the ground—and reformed into the gem.

Cyrus tried to pick up a diamond. It, too, slipped through his grip and turned up on the ground, unchanged. He stared, bemused.

"Hiquigems," Nada repeated. "They don't allow folk to move them."

"It's like a dream," Kim said, as impressed by the willful magic of the gems as by their number, size, and beauty. "They seem so real, yet they might as well be illusion."

"Much of Xanth is illusion," Nada said. "The rest is puns and dragons."

"Pun the magic dragon," Kim murmured under her breath, smiling.

They walked on through the glorious display. Slanting sunlight struck the myriad facets of the gems and refracted even more colorfully up, so that they walked through air as pretty as the ground. Apparently this was just a passing diversion, not a challenge. Unless she was supposed to find a way to take one of the gems. Could there be one among them that was takable, that would help her in the future? She decided to let it be; she preferred to leave these magic stones alone.

They left the gems behind. They rounded a turn—and there before them was the broad expanse of the sea. The path went right down to it—but so did the chasm. So the only way to cross the chasm was to cross the sea, and this time they didn't have a boat. Had this trek been for nothing?

"Maybe we can make a boat," Kim said. "It isn't far, to cross to the other side of the chasm."

"Perhaps we can swim across," Cyrus said. "I don't see any monsters."

"This is salt water," Nada reminder him. "See, there is saltwater taffy growing by the shore."

"All the more reason to try it." He walked boldly to the beach and dipped his toe. "Yow!"

"I warned you," Nada said. "You're a freshwater merman."

Cyrus stepped back, chagrined. "That brine is awful! What self-respecting creature would touch that, let alone swim in it?"

There was a cheery cry from the sea. "Ooo-ooo!" It was a melodious female voice, with the accent on the first syllable. "Are you land folk lost?"

They peered out to sea. There was the head of a young woman. She was swimming.

"We are trying to get to the other side of the Gap Chasm," Kim called back. "But we don't know if it's safe to swim, and one of us doesn't like the salt water."

The woman swam rapidly closer. "It's perfect salt water," she said indignantly. "I have spent all my life in it." To illustrate her point, she dived under, showing her flukes.

Cyrus stared. "That's a mermaid!" he cried.

"Merwoman," Nada clarified. "Look at her décolletage."

Indeed, Kim saw that the creature was superbly endowed. In fact, she had a set of breasts best described as monumental, yet perfectly contoured. The kind Kim herself would never dare dream of having.

Cyrus' attention was no less fixed than Kim's own. "What a creature!" he breathed.

Another little light flashed over Kim's head. "There's your wife, maybe," she said.

"What's that?" the woman called from the sea.

"I'm Kim Human, and this is Nada Naga," Kim called back. "Are you married?"

"No. Bachelor mermen don't grow on shoe trees, you know. My mother had to make legs and trek endlessly on land to find a suitable husband."

Another light flashed. "Your mother—was she by chance Mela Merwoman?"

"No. There was no chance about it. She was Melantha from the day the storkfish delivered her, as sure as water quenches fire. I'm her daughter Merci."

"Why did she need a husband?" Cyrus said. "Didn't she have your father?"

Merci's lovely brow clouded. "A stupid dragon toasted him when I was away at a school of fish, just ten years ago when I was a merchild. Mother fretted a bit, then finally took the plunge, as it were, and went landward to nab her man. It was all so complicated. It wasn't as if she was choosy. All she wanted was the nicest, handsomest, most manly bachelor prince available. She finally landed Prince Naldo Naga. Since then she's been so busy entertaining him that I hardly see her. They seem to believe in long honeymoons. It's pretty lonely. Now I am dangerously close to twenty-one, hardly a mergirl any more and nary a merman in sight."

Indeed, she was hardly a girl! "There's one in sight now," Kim said. "Merci, meet Cyrus Merman."

Merci turned her beautiful dark eyes on Cyrus. "Really? Let's see you in tails."

"I can't change here," Cyrus said. "I'm a freshwater creature."

"Oh, sure," Merci retorted. "How do I know you're not a regular ordinary sneaky man, trying to trick me into legs so you can catch me away from water and make me do something nymphly with you? I'm tired of you louts who think it's all right to tell a girl anything, just to get your germy hands on her innocent torso."

Nada made an appreciative moue. "I like this creature," she murmured.

"So do I," Kim replied.

"Not as much as I do," Cyrus said. Then, to Merci: "Find me some fresh water, and I'll be glad to show you some germ-free tail."

"There's a freshwater spring a little way up the beach," Merci said.

So they walked up the beach, away from the chasm, and Bubbles found the spring. She lapped some of its water. It was hot, but bearable. Cyrus dipped his toe and pronounced it fit. "Turn your backs, ladies," he said to Kim and Nada. "I must strip, so I don't ruin my clothing."

They dutifully turned their backs. In three quarters of a moment and half an instant there was a splash. They turned again, and Cyrus was basking in the spring.

"But I can't see your tail from here," Merci called.

"Then come over here," he called back.

Merci swam to the very edge of the sea. She changed, and stood, resplendent with a fine set of legs. Bubbles went down to intercept her with a woof. Merci walked up across the beach to the spring and peered down. "You *are* a merman!" she said, delighted.

"Get your tail in here," he invited. "The water's fine."

"Don't be silly. I'm allergic to fresh water. The only way I can handle it at all is in this form." She gestured at her legs with her hands.

He eyed her appraisingly. "Actually, you are not wholly unattractive in that form, though it can not of course compare with your natural one." Evidently it was not a violation of merfolk propriety to view a merwoman in legs or a merman in tail.

"I like this creature," Merci murmured.

"Maybe he can make legs again, so you can get acquainted on land," Kim suggested.

"I'm not sure that would be decorous," Merci said.

"Certainly it wouldn't," Cyrus agreed. "However, we can make it decorous by donning human clothing. Perhaps Kim and Nada will be so kind as to fetch you a skirt, while I return to my trousers."

So they took Merci to a nearby fabric plant and wrapped a length of seersucker around her body, fashioning a serviceable dress. They found lady slipper flowers and put a delicate pair of slippers on her dainty feet. Nada brushed her somewhat matted hair and set a passion flower in it. Now she looked just like a perfectly lovely human woman.

They returned to the spring, where Cyrus was dry and back in clothing. He looked like a perfectly handsome human man. "Oh, you are surely the creature I wish to marry," he said. "Except—"

"And you are surely the creature I'd like to wed," Merci agreed. "Except—"

"Except that you can't stand each other's water," Nada said. "What irony!"

"Suppose we had merchildren?" Cyrus said. "They might be intolerant of both kinds of water!"

"I fear our love is doomed," Merci said sadly.

Kim knew the feeling. She reacted against it. "There must be some compromise," she said. "Couldn't you, uh, get together in human form, and return to your lake and sea betweentimes?"

"That would be uncouth," Cyrus said. "Legs are so clumsy and unaesthetic."

"Tails are the only way to party," Merci agreed.

They certainly seemed to be well matched. "There must be some way," Kim said. "We just have to find it."

"It would be nice," Cyrus said. "Merci is exactly what I have been looking for except for the incompatibility of medium." He glanced at her wrapped torso again. "In fact, perhaps even more than I was looking for. Freshwater mermaids are somewhat more slender."

"That's fine, if you like that type," Merci remarked.

"I find I like your type."

"Well, we'll figure it out," Kim said. "Maybe there's a spell. But at the moment, maybe you can help us, Merci. We need to find a way to cross safely to the south side of the Gap Chasm."

"You might swim, if you don't mind fifty-degree water and a loan shark or two."

Kim had tried swimming in eighty-degree water once, and found it too cool for comfort. "I think swimming is out. Anyway, Cyrus can't touch sea water. Is there a tunnel or something?"

Merci pondered. "There is a tunnel under the Gap. But it is not safe."

"It must be safer than shark-infested water!" Kim said.

"It is a goblin tunnel," Merci explained.

"Ouch!" Nada said. "I don't relish goblins. I can chomp one or several, but they tend to come in hordes. We had better avoid that."

Kim looked around again, knowing she would see nothing useful. "I wonder whether there is enough dry wood to make a raft."

"I suppose you could build a raft," Merci agreed. "It should only take a few days."

Kim sighed. "Maybe it will have to be the tunnel. And knowing the way the game works, we'll have to prepare to fight off the goblins."

"Game?" Merci asked.

"She's from Mundania," Nada explained. "She's here as part of a game the demons organized. I'm her Companion, here to guide and protect her."

"Oh. Well, I will show you the nearest entrance to the tunnel. But I don't know how you can deal with the goblins. Once when I made legs to walk to land to fetch some flowers, goblins tried to catch me so they could do something horrible to me. Since then I have been very cautious about going on land, and I don't like goblins at all."

The merwoman led the way to a thicket of bushes some distance back from the Gap, where the land was not too far above sea level. There beneath their cover of foliage was a hole in the ground. Bubbles sniffed it.

"It's dry?" Kim asked. "Though it goes under the water?"

"It's dry," Merci agreed. "Though I understand there are portals in the bulkheads to flood it, if necessary. I can't think why the goblins would want to make it that way."

"This is naga work," Nada said, examining the bricked rim of the hole. "I recognize the type. Naga must have made this, and later lost it to the goblins. We have been slowly losing ground to them for centuries."

"In fish school they taught me that the goblins once roamed freely on the ground," Merci said. "But that now there are relatively few there. Most are under-ground."

"That is true," Nada said. "The harpies and humans warred with them, and drove them out of much territory. But they are in Goblin Mountain, and there's always the Goblinate of the Golden Horde, the worst tribe of them all. We don't know much about the ones deep belowground, but suspect there are many." She turned to Kim. "Hold my apparel; I will investigate this."

Then Nada turned serpent and slithered out of her collapsing clothing. Kim picked up the outfit and folded it. The serpent slithered into the hole and disappeared.

"They must go on," Merci said to Cyrus. "But must you go with them?"

"There seems to be little point in my remaining here," he said sadly. "I can not enter your sea realm, any more than you can enter my lake realm. I fear our love is doomed before it starts. I must go on, to see whether I can find a fresh mermaid."

"I suppose you must," she agreed. "Perhaps we shall kiss before we part."

"Perhaps we shall," he agreed, perking up slightly.

"It will be a remarkable experience," she said dreamily.

"And a poignant memory."

Kim had another notion. "Hey, what about a wetsuit?" she asked.

"We do not wish to get our clothing wet," Cyrus said gently. "It is not as durable as skin and scales."

"No, I mean a bodysuit for diving. We have them in Mundania. We use them to keep the water out and the heat in, so we can swim in cold water. If one of you wore a wetsuit, could you swim in the water of the other?"

"I suppose," Merci agreed. "It would not be very comfortable, but it might enable us to visit each other's homes."

"But it would not be very nice for summoning the stork," Cyrus said.

"Which is an occasion which should not be ruined."

"I fear it would be little better than doing it in human form."

"Ugh!" she agreed. "I suppose it could be tolerated in an emergency."

"True. Human beings have to tolerate it, knowing nothing better."

Kim was getting to feel like an inferior species. Imagine having to, as they put it, summon the stork while wearing ungainly legs!

Fortunately Nada returned at this point. She formed her human head on her snake's body. "It is clear, though there is the smell of goblins about it. I think we can get through if we move rapidly and are lucky."

"But how will we see, in that darkness?" Kim asked.

"There is glow fungus on the walls. It seems dark compared to daylight, but is light compared to night. You will be able to see well enough."

"Let's go, then," Kim said. "Why don't you come too, Merci? You can return to the sea from the other side, if you want."

"I suppose I could," the merwoman agreed. She did not seem at all eager to separate from Cyrus, and he seemed to return the uneagerness.

Kim climbed down into the hole, Bubbles scrambling along with her, and the two merfolk climbed down after her. The interior was not dank, as she had feared, but a bit like a subway tunnel with tiled walls. As her eyes adjusted, she saw the glow on the wall.

The tunnel curved away. They followed it in a downward spiral. Now Bubbles was happy to lead the way, her tail curving high. The dog was never so happy as when she was escorting people somewhere. The glow seemed to get brighter as they went, though she knew this was just the continued adaptation of her eyes.

She lost count of the circles they completed. This was a good deep tunnel! But finally it straightened out and headed in what she trusted was the right direction. From it debouched side tunnels every so often, going she knew not where. Maybe this had once been a subterranean naga city. She wondered what that community had been like. Then the main tunnel narrowed, and the offshoots stopped.

Bubbles barked.

Nada, slithering along in her naga form, abruptly lifted her head. "I smell fresh goblin!" she said, alarmed. "They were not here before."

"Maybe they make regular checks," Kim said. "Is there anywhere we can hide?"

"No. We are directly below the Gap now, and below the water of the sea inlet within it. This is the narrowest section."

"Then we'd better go back and take an offshoot," Kim said. "Maybe there's a room or something to hide in, there."

"But they are coming from the rear," Nada said.

"Then we'd better run forward!"

"They are coming from that direction too."

Kim recognized a game challenge when she encountered it. They were pinned underground between converging hordes of goblins. How could they get out of this fix?

Her concentration was interrupted by the approach of the goblins. "Look, fresh meat!" one cried from in front.

"You have it wrong, zilchpuss," one cried from the rear. "First we entertain ourselves wickedly with the damsels. *Then* we dump them in the pot."

"You're both wrong," another cried. "First we boil them until they turn blood red. Then we use them for entertainment. Then we eat them. Don't you know anything about protocol?"

Bubbles growled.

This was getting more serious by the instant! Not only were they going to be cooked, some of them were going to get tortured as well. Kim hadn't realized that such things happened in Xanth, but she hadn't reckoned with the goblins.

There had to be a way out! But what was it? All she saw on the walls were indented handholds, no tools or weapons.

Her desperate gaze crossed the low ceiling. She saw a circular indentation. A portal! They could let in the water of the sea!

But how would they breathe? The merfolk could breathe water—but one of them would be caught in the wrong kind of water. So there was mischief, no matter what.

Bubbles woofed. She was sniffing a circular indentation in the floor, right below the one in the ceiling. "What's that?" Kim asked. Wild hope flared. "A secret escape?"

"It is marked for fresh water," Nada said, peering at the inscription on it. "The upper one is for salt water. Apparently my people had uses for each, perhaps when they cleaned the tunnel."

No escape. Both portals sealed off water. Kim's heart sank to about the level of her stomach, and her stomach sank to her belly.

Meanwhile the goblins were advancing like the jaws of a vise, or perhaps more accurately like the pincers of a garbage scoop. They had clubs and spears, but weren't waving them threateningly, not wishing to damage the merchandise before having their fun with it.

Then Kim thought of a way, maybe. This was a sealed tunnel, which meant that the air was likely to be trapped in it. That just might be their salvation.

"Open the ports!" she cried. "Both of them! Let the water in!"

"But—" Cyrus and Merci said, almost together.

"You open the top one, Merci. That's sea water; it won't hurt you. You open the bottom one, Cyrus; that's fresh water. It won't hurt you. Then just hang on, staying in your type of water. We're going to wash these goblins right out of our hair!"

"But how will we breathe?" Nada asked.

"There'll be air in the top half of the tunnel. Just keep your head up. And hang on; we have to stay right here in the center."

The two merfolk applied themselves to the hatches. They turned the plates, unscrewing them. Kim grabbed one of the handholds set in the wall with one hand, and caught Bubbles' collar with the other. Nada curled her tail into another handhold.

Cyrus' portal opened. Water blasted in at high pressure, deflected by the cover, which seemed to be anchored from below by the screw in its center. He hung on to that cover, holding it steady so that the water sprayed out in a rough circle.

Merci's portal opened. Water blasted in from above, similarly deflected. She hung on to that anchored cover, so that her water also made a circle.

For good or ill, Kim's plan was now in effect.

The surging waters merged on either side, coursing down the tunnel. The water was cool but not unbearably cold. The currents swept into the goblins, fore and aft, shoving them back. They were too surprised even to swear effectively. Suddenly they were fighting for their footing—and their lives, because they were not anchored.

The waters quickly filled the tunnel, pushing violently outward. But a level of air remained trapped at the top, having nowhere to go. Kim held Bubbles up so she could breathe it, while breathing it herself. Nada's face was close to hers, and she did the same. The best place to be was in the center, where there was no unified current, just the chaotic backsurge.

Soon the goblins were gone. They had been swept out in both directions, helplessly. Where they went Kim didn't care; they hardly deserved any good breaks.

"Close hatches!" Kim cried.

The merfolk turned the disks the other way, screwing them back into their niches. It was hard work, but they had leverage. They got them closed, and the spraying water was cut off. The roar of it subsided, and the currents calmed.

Nada's human head glanced around. "That was well wrought, Kim," she said. "You won the challenge. I didn't think you would figure it out in time."

"It was a close call," Kim admitted. "If Bubbles hadn't called my attention to the second portal, I don't think I would have seen the answer." She kissed the dog's wet ear, and Bubbles wagged her tail as well as she could in the water.

"Now, let me see," Nada said. "I can slosh through water and hold on better in human form. We're all females here except Cyrus, and he's a merman, who has no concern about nakedness as long as he is in his natural form."

"True," Cyrus agreed. "I do not wish to offend, but my interest in creatures without tails is small."

"So I will change." Nada became human, a splendid figure of a bare woman. "In any event, it is all right, because I'm not wearing panties at the moment. Now I believe I can find the way out, by following the old naga signals." She started half walking, half swimming along the flooded tunnel.

Cyrus looked at Merci. "Now, there's what I call an interesting creature," he said. "From head to tail."

Merci returned his look with similar candor. "I feel the same."

Then the little light flashed over Kim's head. "You're both in the same water—and not having trouble!"

Both merfolk were startled. "How can that be?" Cyrus asked. "I can't stand salt."

"And I can't stand fresh," Merci said. "This water is brackish, which makes it uncomfortable, but I can stand it."

"I agree," he said. "I can stand brackish water, though it is not my delight."

"The salt and fresh water mixed," Kim said. "So it's all brackish now. Half and half. Now the twain can meet."

"The twain can meet," Merci said, approaching Cyrus. "Maybe we can make it, in this water." She put her arms around him.

"Maybe we can," he agreed, kissing her. Several little red hearts appeared, floating around them. Their tails twined together.

Nada turned back. "Don't make it here! Wait for the nuptials."

The kiss broke and the hearts faded. "Of course," Merci said, blushing.

"Certainly," Cyrus agreed, embarrassed. "The proprieties must be observed."

"Too much was already being observed," Nada remarked.

Kim was privately slightly vexed. She knew that part of the propriety related to her: they considered her at age sixteen to be a borderline case, and were careful to honor the Adult Conspiracy. She had been curious about just how merfolk did make it. Still, it was nice that the merfolk had discovered how to relate to each other.

She set her face forward and followed Nada. There was no sign of the goblins, who must have been washed right out of the tunnels, perhaps to some lower level where they were trying to figure out what happened.

The water slowly sank, so that it was waist deep, then knee deep. The tunnel widened, and more cross-tunnels appeared, all similarly flooded. There was a sound of falling water, suggesting that there was indeed a drain somewhere. The tunnel would be dry again in due course. They needed to get out of it before that happened, because it was only the water that kept the goblins out.

Nada led them to another spiral, this one going up. The water was left behind. That was a relief for Bubbles, who definitely preferred land to water. The two merfolk had to change to legs and don clothing from Kim's pack, while the others turned their backs. Finally they climbed out through a hole.

They were on the south side of the Gap Chasm. And there on the beach was a small wooden boat. "Merci could have brought that across to us, if we had only known it was there," Kim said, chagrined.

"Why, so I could have," Merci agreed, surprised. "I have known about that boat for ages."

Kim almost inquired why Merci hadn't told her about the boat, but she knew the answer: she hadn't asked. This was the game, where the Player had to figure things out. Kim had inquired about a passage, and Merci had answered. Kim had not asked about a boat. A raft, yes, but not a boat. She had missed the obvious.

"Well, Nada and Bubbles and I have to be on our way," Kim said. "I guess you'll want to stay here, Cyrus, with Merci. When you want to get together with her, all you have to do is find a place where a river meets the sea and the water mixes, or maybe there's a freshwater spring under the sea where there can be a similar effect. I'm sure you'll figure it out."

"I am sure we will," Cyrus agreed. "I thank you, Kim Mundane, for bringing me here. You have indeed solved my problem."

"And mine," Merci agreed. She turned to Cyrus. "I know where there is a freshwater spring by the shore. I would love to show you more tail."

"I am eager to see it," he said. They kissed again, then waved farewell and walked eagerly down along the beach, arms around waists.

"So the adventure resumes," Kim said, with mixed feelings. She was glad for the merfolk, but also envious of their happiness. She knew that she faced a horrendous trek though the jungle, where she might encounter anything at all. It was the nature of the game.

13
VIRUS

D ug blinked in the bright light as they emerged from the vole hole. Sure enough, there was solid jungle all around.

He turned to Jenny. "Now this is the game," he said. "And I understand we're somewhere near the lair of Com Pewter, the evil machine. And that I have to settle with him before I can get much farther. So do you know of a fairly direct, safe path there? I want to get this over with."

Sammy jumped down and scampered along a faint path that seemed to appear only after the cat found it. "Wait for me!" Jenny cried, chasing after him.

"There's a path," Sherlock agreed. "But are you ready for the machine? I understand those things can really mess up folk who don't know how to handle them."

"For sure! Maybe I need to think about this a little more."

"Sammy, stop!" Jenny cried. "He's changed his mind!"

The cat stopped, losing interest in the path. The others caught up to him. The path where the cat had been was clear, but ahead there seemed to be nothing but brambles, briers, and branches.

"Maybe a slightly indirect route," Dug said, smiling. "Maybe passing a place where there is something I need."

Sammy resumed motion. This time his pace was slower, so that they could keep up, and it curved more. But the oddity of the path remained: there didn't seem to be any until the cat found it.

They came to a large field filled with weird plants. "There's something here you need?" Sherlock inquired with a lifted eyebrow.

"There's sure to be," Dug said. "So I'll just start looking for it."

"If you tell Sammy exactly what it is, he'll find it for you," Jenny said.

"I don't know exactly what it is but I hope to know it when I see it," Dug said. "Why don't the two of you get some rest while I look? This may take a while."

Both Jenny and Sherlock looked perplexed, but Sammy didn't. In fact, Sammy elected to join him in the search.

Dug stepped into the field. He saw that the assorted plants were in rows, and each had a little sign identifying it. That ought to help!

The first plant he looked at had a number of light cones, each looking suitable for ice cream. Or, as it was in Xanth, eye scream. Sure enough, it was labeled CONEFLOWER. But that wasn't what he needed.

As he squatted to look at the next, he developed an itch in an awkward place. He straightened up and faced away from the others, so as to be able to scratch it inconspicuously, but the itch had gone. So he squatted again—and the itch returned. The closer he leaned toward the plant, the worse it got, making him fidget something awful. Then he saw the sign, and understood: COCKLEBUR.

As he moved toward the next, which seemed to be a clump of grass, something chafed in his trouserleg. He looked down and saw a number of long arrow-shaped thorns in it. He pulled these out, carefully, and resumed motion—only to have more strike him. He looked at the sign. No wonder! This was ARROW-GRASS.

Then his clothing seemed to get tight around the joints. Suspecting the next plant, he squinted to see its sign from a distance. Sure enough, it said BINDWEED. Next to it was a KNOTWEED, which he avoided.

Now he came to a nicer section, passing BUTTERWEED, MILKWEED, and CANDYTUFT. Those would do with a meal, if there weren't enough from other sources.

Then he encountered a more awkward section, spying LOVEGRASS, VIRGIN'S BOWER, BRIDAL WREATH, and MATRIMONY VINE. Near those was a TWINFLOWER. Obviously this was what a woman needed if she wanted to reproduce more rapidly. Just send such a flower to the stork depot, to let the stork know how many to deliver.

The next section was animalistic. There was a CATTAIL, KITTENTAIL, PUSSYTOES, DRAGONHEAD, HOUND'S TONGUE, and SQUIRREL-TAIL. Then full creatures: BEE PLANT, BUTTERFLY WEED, CHICK-WEED, DUCKWEED, GOAT GRASS, MONKEY FLOWER, and OYSTER PLANT. But none of them were what he needed.

Then there were assorted sewing plants: PINCUSHION, NEEDLE AND THREAD, THIMBLE BERRY, LEATHER FLOWER, and HEMLOCK. That last was evidently what women wearing long skirts used to prevent the hems from unraveling so that they stepped on them. There was a warning: it shouldn't be taken internally, lest it lock up the innards.

The next section had an emaciated SKELETON WEED, a bright SHOOTING STAR, a WALLFLOWER, and a PAINTBRUSH slopping a new color on it.

Then came some seed plants: STICKSEED, TICKSEED, and BUGSEED. Sammy was inspecting the last closely. "Yes," Dug murmured, harvesting some of its seeds. "That may be what I want." He put the seeds in his pocket and went on, because he did not want to draw attention to the nature of exactly what he wanted.

Then he came to an ugly section: CHEATGRASS, POVERTY WEED, SNEEZEWEED, TUMBLEGRASS, and CHOKE CHERRY. He managed to sneak past those without suffering too many afflictions.

But what followed was worse: a patch of STINKWEED. He had had enough trouble with the stink horn to know the danger of this, so he intelligently moved right on to the SMARTWEED and then wisely to SAGEBRUSH.

The last plant in the row was labeled CRYPTOGRAMMA. This was very puzzling; he just couldn't figure it out, so he left it alone. It was also called ROCK BRAKE, but he couldn't tell whether it stopped big rolling stones or broke them up into pebbles.

He walked back along the second row. There were endless wonders there, but he paid them less attention, because he already had what he had come for. Then he saw a group of MONIAS: old, middle-aged, young, and new. This might be even better! So he took a New Monia flower and set it in a buttonhole.

He returned to the others. "Did you find what you wanted?" Sherlock inquired.

Dug coughed. "I think so."

"You okay, man? Sounds as if you have some congestion."

"I'll be all right," Dug said, trying not to hack. He hadn't realized that the flower would take effect so quickly. But of course things could be instant, in this magic land. He would just have to suffer through.

Sherlock and Jenny had fixed a good meal, but Dug did not have much appetite. He felt feverish and weak, and his breathing was getting difficult. But he pretended to be normal. He had a reason.

They finished eating and moved on, following the leisurely paths Sammy found. Dug had to struggle to keep moving. "Listen, there's something wrong," Sherlock said. "Ever since you looked through that garden patch, you've been stumbling as if you're sick. What happened in there?"

"Nothing I can tell you," Dug said hoarsely. "Just let me be."

Sherlock exchanged one long glance and two short ones with Jenny, and let it drop. The long glance bounced on the ground and shattered when it was dropped, but the short ones survived intact.

But when Dug staggered, stumbled, and fell, Jenny took action. "You're my responsibility," she said. "Because I'm your Companion. I will get in trouble for not guiding you well if you lose because you are too ill to continue. We must find a healing spring. That will make you well."

Dug was now too sick to protest effectively. He knew that what she said was true. But he also knew that he had to persevere, or he would lose again to Pewter. He could not tell them why, lest the evil machine learn of his words through some spy, and be prepared to foil his ploy.

Sherlock made a travois from wood and vine, softening it with pillows. He lifted Dug onto it, and hauled him along that way. Jenny had Sammy find the nearest spring. She wasn't able to clarify its particular type: it seemed that to the cat, one spring was much like another. She was able only to establish that it not be a regular ordinary water source. It had to be a magic spring.

As it turned out, there was one not too far away. They reached it, but were cautious. Dug heard them discussing it, though he was now too tired to join the dialogue.

"We have to be sure it's a healing spring," Jenny said. "Because there are different kinds, such as love springs and hate springs. It will be worse than nothing if we dose him with the wrong kind of elixir."

"But how can we tell, without trying it?" Sherlock asked. "We don't want to taste a love spring or a hate spring either."

"We certainly don't!" she agreed. "No offense to you. Because a love spring isn't just romantic; it leads immediately to a violent summoning of the stork. That would be a violation of the Adult Conspiracy, because I'm still a child."

"We don't want to violate any conspiracy," Sherlock agreed. "But inaction isn't any good either; we have to test the water somehow. Could we just sniff a little, so all we get is a mere suggestion?"

"Maybe that will be all right," she agreed doubtfully. "Let me try it first. Then if I start getting romantic, or whatever, you run away."

"Those springs must be potent," Sherlock remarked.

"Exactly."

So Jenny got down and sniffed the spring. "Oh, I feel young!" she exclaimed.

"Well, you *are* young. What kind of spring is it?"

"Not a love spring," she decided. "I don't love you or hate you. But I do feel changed."

"So maybe you've been healed of whatever was bothering you," he said reasonably. "This must be the one we want."

"Maybe. I'm not quite sure. There's something odd about it. You better sniff it too, and see what you think."

Sherlock got down and sniffed. "Wow! I feel two years younger!"

"You look a bit younger too," she agreed. "Is it healing you?"

"No. I have a sore toe, and it's still sore."

"Maybe you should dip your toe, and see if it heals."

"Good idea!" Sherlock removed his shoe and dipped his sore toe. The skin turned fresh but did not actually heal.

Then they paused while an insect flew down to taste the water. But the insect turned into a grub.

"It must be a transforming spring," Jenny said. "It changed into another kind of bug."

"No, it reverted to its earlier form," Sherlock said. "Insects hatch from grubs. It's their youthful stage—" He broke off, realization coming.

"A youth spring!" Jenny cried. "This must be the Fountain of Youth! Nobody knows where it is, and we stumbled on it by accident!"

"Sammy didn't stumble on it," he reminded her. "He was looking for a magic spring."

"That's right. And what a spring he found! But it isn't the one we want. Dug's only a year older than I am, really; he doesn't want to be any younger."

"You're fifteen?" Sherlock asked. "I thought you were a child."

"I am a child, by game definition. But outside the game I'm sneaking up on adult status, and actually I know the secret of the Conspiracy. Maybe I look younger to you, because I'm an elf; I'm smaller than a human girl my age would be."

"That must be it," he agreed. "Well, none of us need this elixir, so we'd better move on. It's an irony, though; a lot of people would give their fortunes to drink from this."

"People are funny," she agreed.

Dug wanted to tell them to mark the place carefully, so they could find the spring again, because the knowledge would be invaluable. But his breath was so short he couldn't speak.

They resumed their search, following the cat to another spring. Dug caught a glimpse of it before Sherlock laid the travois flat on the ground. The spring was round, with a quilted surface, as if the waves lacked the energy to ripple properly. This time when Jenny sniffed, she turned over and lay down on the water. "It must be an ether spring, putting you to sleep!" Sherlock said, horrified.

"No it isn't," she replied. "It's a bed spring. Oh, I could just lie here forever and sleep." Indeed, she was floating on the soft water. It was one big water bed.

"Don't do that!" He bent down and picked her up. He carried her away from the spring, until she recovered enough to stay away.

"I guess you're right," Jenny said sadly. "This is not the time to rest. But it sure was the most comfortable bed I ever felt."

So they moved on again. Dug faded out, feeling delirious, so didn't know how long it took to reach it. But it was definitely later in the day.

Jenny sniffed it. Faint stars appeared in her eyes. "Oh, guest stars," she said, smiling. "I love them." Then she turned to look at Sherlock. "In fact, I love—"

"Get away from there!" Sherlock cried. "That's a love spring!"

"Much better than a hate spring," she replied dreamily.

"Get away!" he repeated firmly.

"Anything you say, you handsome creature." She moved languorously away. "Wouldn't you like to carry me again?"

"Not this time! You just breathe the air away from the spring for a while until it wears off."

Reluctantly the elf girl did so. Dug had never had reason to question the black man's decency, but if he had, this scene would have resolved it. He was getting just enough of a whiff of the spring to understand that it would be extraordinarily easy to take advantage of a situation.

So they set off for yet another spring, as the day waned. Dug hoped the next one wasn't a hate spring, because then Jenny and Sherlock might come to hate him, and leave him to expire alone.

As the sun set, they came to it. Jenny sniffed. "I think this is it!" she said, excited.

"You're not trying to trick me into tasting a love spring?" Sherlock asked.

"Dip your sore toe."

He did. "Hey—it healed!"

They brought some of the water to Dug. With the first drop on his lips he began to feel better. He swallowed, and felt better yet. He inhaled the vapor, and his lungs began to clear. This was definitely the healing elixir.

But his chest did not heal quite all the way. He knew why: he was still wearing the New Monia flower, and it was still sending illness into his lungs. He could have been better long ago, if he had just thrown that flower away. But he refused. He had to wear it just as if it were harmless.

"I'm better," he announced. "But I'd better take some of this elixir along, just in case of relapse." He dipped a small bottle in the spring, filled it, and corked it. It was amazing how sick he had felt, though he knew this was all pretense; an effect of the game couldn't touch him in real life. It certainly had seemed real, though.

It was now dusk. They foraged for food and camping materials, and set up for the night. There was no regular camping place here; evidently they had wandered from the normal route of the game. But if anything happened, they could heal quickly, because of the spring.

Dug thought he had been resting while the others worked, but now he discovered how tired he was. He sank into blissful sleep.

In the morning they resumed their trek, heading for Com Pewter's lair. At first they had to pick their way through thick jungle. Dug wondered why, since it seemed to thin in a nearby valley. Then he saw a dragon feeding on something, and realized that the easiest route was not necessarily the best. Sammy Cat was leading them the safe way—which was where the dragons weren't foraging. His encounter with the Gap Dragon had been more than sufficient to teach him respect—and that had been merely a steamer, not a firebreather.

They heard a companion. There ahead was a clearing, and in the clearing was a giant spinning object. "What's that thing doing here?" Dug demanded.

"I think that's the Big Top," Jenny said. "It's part of another story. I don't think we had better mess with it."

Dug was learning to take such warnings seriously. "We leave it alone," he agreed.

Now they were able to use some of the paths; Sammy Cat seemed to feel these ones were safe. They came to another area of commotion. It seemed to be an enclosed field, with many animals confined. "The stock market," Jenny explained. "It's full of charging bulls and bears. It's not safe for ordinary folk to enter. People get trampled there all the time, and wiped out."

Dug nodded. Literal bulls and bears. It figured. The Mundane version was scary enough, he understood; he didn't need to mess with this one.

They also bypassed a big shopping centaur. Dug didn't even ask.

At last they approached the region of the evil machine. Dug remembered how easy it had been to reach it, before, using the shortcut. But now they were in much better control. He would not be blindly stampeded into Pewter's cave.

This time he was able to appreciate how cunningly this particular trap was laid. The shortcut to success had indeed been a shortcut, for an innocent who didn't ask where it went or whose success it meant. It had amounted to an enchanted path, safe from other hazards, lulling him into false security. Then the invisible giant had come, scaring him into the one seemingly safe place—which was the worst place.

Dug felt his lung congesting. He quietly took another drop of healing elixir, and felt better. The New Monia flower remained bright and firm, the color of diseased lung tissue with spots of congestion; it was still trying to do its job. That was the way he wanted it. But he was really glad that Jenny had insisted on finding the healing spring; that made all the difference. Now, if his devious and punnish plan jest, uh, just worked . . .

He had a spot decision to make. Should he be wary of the giant, and sneak in to confront Pewter by surprise? Or pretend to be spooked in the usual fashion, so that the evil machine did not realize what Player it was at first? He decided on the latter course; that would be easier, and would surprise Pewter just as much. Perhaps more, because it would seem that this was a new victim being driven in. A surprised machine was more likely to make a mistake, and that was what Dug wanted. Pewter was dangerous, but the game required that he could be beaten, and surprising him was surely the best strategy.

In fact, Dug had a different Companion now, and a fellow traveler. If Pewter saw them first, he would be sure that this was a different Player. He would probably figure that it was Kim, and so would be prepared to freak her out, rattling her and making her fail to think of whatever her winning strategy might be.

"Um, friends," Dug murmured. "Before we go on, there's something I must explain. I met up with Pewter before, and got skunked. I got kicked out of the game, and had to start over, with different paths and challenges. That's why I'm being so careful now. He's got a slick routine to drive folk into his cave, and then he changes reality to whatever he wants it to be. Now, Sherlock, this isn't your responsibility, so maybe you should wait here until I settle with him, one way or the other. But I think you're stuck for it, Jenny, being my Companion."

"Yes," Jenny said. "It's my job to warn you to stay away from Pewter. But I know you can't do that, because you have to beat him to cancel out what happened before. So I'll try to help you. But once we're there, I won't be able to do anything, because he'll just change my script. You're the only one who can stop him, and I don't know how you can do that. Sammy won't be able to help against him, either."

"Right. It's always the Player who has to handle the real crunch. If it's a game challenge. My illness wasn't supposed to be part of the game, so you and Sherlock got me out of it." He paused. "By the way, if I didn't say thank you before, I'll say it now. I really appreciate what both of you did for me during my illness, and I'll try to repay you some way."

"I just did what I'm supposed to," Jenny demurred.

"You'd have done the same for me, if I got sick," Sherlock said.

"I know that. But a False Companion might have just let me be, washing out. And there are plenty of folk who would have figured it was no skin off their noses. So both of you really helped me, and I hope I can turn in a good performance report on Jenny, or whatever it is, and I hope we'll find the ideal place for the Black Wave."

"Let's get on with the action," Sherlock said gruffly. Dug could see that the man wasn't much for compliments, and he liked that.

"Okay. So Jenny and I will head in just as if we are surprised by all of this, and let the invisible giant drive us into the cave. One thing you can do for me, Jenny, if you will: you lead the way into the cave, so that Pewter sees you first. I want him to think it's Kim, until the last moment."

"You do have a plan," she said appreciatively.

"I do. It may not work, but I'll give it the old college try." He turned to Sherlock. "If I lose, I won't come out of that cave. But if Jenny calls the Demon Game Master, and explains how you got stranded here because of the Player, maybe he'll tell you where to go. A place for your Wave, I mean. It's worth a shot."

"Don't worry about that," Sherlock said. "I'm coming in with you. I want to see this dread machine."

Somehow Dug wasn't surprised. Sherlock hadn't backed off from anything yet. "Okay. If you want to follow Jenny in, it'll really surprise the machine. Then I'll appear, and try to polish him off with my sneak play."

"It's sure got me fooled," Sherlock said. "You've just been really sick, and you still don't seem all the way recovered despite that healing water, yet you're eager to get back into the fray."

"Maybe I'm just a crazy teenager," Dug said, smiling.

"Crazy like a fox, maybe."

"Foxes aren't crazy," Jenny protested. "They're pretty smart. Like wolves." She looked momentarily pensive.

No one commented. They walked out into the path leading by the cave.

Soon there was a shuddering of the ground. Trees crashed in the distance. "Hey, there's a meteor crashing!" Sherlock said.

"No, that's just the giant. I think he won't actually step on us. Remember to spook when he gets close."

There was another crash, and a giant footprint appeared. "No problem!" Sherlock said.

They spooked. They ran down the path, away from the approaching giant steps. The mouth of the cave appeared, and they scooted into it just ahead of the last footprint. So far so good.

Jenny ran ahead, toward the dim light of the interior chamber. Sherlock followed. "Good thing we found this cave," he called. "That monster almost squished us."

"It's Com Pewter's cave!" Jenny cried. "Quick, we must get out of it!"

There was a pause. Then she spoke again. "No, we must go on inside."

Dug, hanging back, smiled. Pewter had written a change on his screen.

"I don't like the look of this," Sherlock said. Then: "But maybe it's okay."

Dug moved quietly toward Pewter's chamber, where the two were now standing.

"But Sherlock's not the Player!" Jenny protested. "He's just a fellow traveler."

Dug saw a big question mark on the screen. Pewter had been caught by surprise! He had assumed that Jenny was escorting a Player, and that Sherlock was that player. Exactly as Dug had hoped. The evil machine's circuits had to be in turmoil. Now was his chance.

He strode boldly forward. "No, I am the Player," he said. "I have come to stop your clock, you crock of refuse."

The screen flickered. DUG MUNDANE! ERROR!

"No error, capacitor face. I fought my way back, just so I could settle your metallic hash."

YOU COULD NOT HAVE. NOT WITH YOUR COMPANION.

"Well, I did! And I changed Companions along the way. Which you didn't anticipate, did you, screen-for-brains?"

CHANGE PROGRAM. ADAPT FOR SMART-POSTERIOR MUNDANE TEEN. RECOMPILE. The screen went black while the recompilation proceeded.

Dug didn't give it the chance to complete its operation. "And here's how I'm going to do it, you nutty and bolty contraption. On my return route I picked up the Germ of an Idea and here it is." He brought out the bit of fluff and dropped it on the machine.

REJECTED! the screen printed desperately.

"And a bugseed," Dug continued relentlessly. "That'll put a bug in your program, for sure."

REJECTED! The screen was flickering.

"And here's the piece of resistance," Dug said. "Pardon my French." He lifted the flower from his buttonhole. "My third offering to you, which you can't refuse, because you've already rejected my first two." He held the flower above the screen. "A New Monia posy. That will give you a virus, for sure." He dropped it.

A VIRUS! NONONONOOOO . . .

"Tough turnips," Dug said cruelly. "He who lives by the pun, dies by the pun. You've been infected, wirebrain. In other words, YOU LOSE."

The screen went crazy. Characters and symbols flowed across it in weird patterns. Then the words GENERAL SYSTEM FAILURE appeared. Then the letters fell from the words and collected in a pile at the bottom of the screen. The screen faded into black.

"Let's get out of here," Dug said, satisfied. "This pile of junk has nothing for us."

They walked out through the passage. Sammy was happy to show the way. "What kind of logic was that?" Sherlock inquired. "What's this rule about not rejecting three things?"

"Computers are logical but not sensible," Dug said smugly. "In Pewter's state of confusion, it seemed to make sense. But I probably could have taken him out anyway with the New Monia, just by throwing it at him. Because a virus is a virus, and that one was good and potent. You saw what it did to me."

"That flower!" Jenny exclaimed. "I should have realized!"

"That's why I made it seem like just a decoration," Dug said. "I figured if you didn't catch on, Pewter wouldn't either—until I told him. In Mundania a living virus and a computer virus are two different things, but in Xanth they have to be the same. So I punned him to death."

"That was brilliant!" Sherlock said.

Dug smiled. "Elementary."

The giant was nowhere to be seen. Of course that didn't mean anything. But he wasn't heard, either, so they proceeded along the path unmolested.

"I think you're going to do well in this game," Jenny said.

"Maybe, maybe not. I just make it a point to learn from my mistakes. My first mistake was having eyes only for Nada Naga. My second was not taking puns seriously. So I dumped Nada, and now I'm playing the game to win. But the truth is, I'm just in it for the challenge and the fun now. I think this is a great, if foolish, adventure."

"Well, your next challenge should be the Good Magician's castle," Jenny said.

"One thing nagging me," Sherlock said. "Maybe nothing."

"Nothing's nothing here," Dug said. "What's your point?"

"You mentioned Nada Naga. I can see why you found her distracting. So did I. But there was something funny about her."

"Well, she's a princess," Jenny said. "They tend to be sort of reserved. Except for Princess Electra, who wears blue jeans."

"It's not that. She's a lovely creature, and a good lady. But there was

something about her. When you said how a False Companion would just have
let you be sick, something nagged at me. I finally figured it out. Nada would
have let you go."

"No she wouldn't," Dug said. "I'll never forget how she fought to help me
douse the censor-ship!"

"The what?"

"That was in my first game session. The one I wiped out on with Pewter.
But that was my doing; Nada was in my corner all the way, except when I tried
to sneak a peek at her panties, and even then she welcomed me back. I know
she's human under the princessly mantle."

"Certainly she is," Jenny agreed. "She's a good person. She was willing to
marry Prince Dolph, despite not loving him, because he loved her and her family needed the liaison with the human folk. Then she got in trouble with the
gourd realm, really by accident, so now she's serving her time with the demons,
in this game. Same as I am. But she always does her best, and she's always nice."

"I'm sure she is," Sherlock said doggedly. "I could see that myself. Maybe
that's why I picked up on the wrongness. It was as if she felt guilty for something. Something relating to you, Dug. I saw it when she looked at you, when
you weren't looking at her."

"She has no cause to feel guilty about me," Dug said. "I was the one who
tried to sneak a peek at her body. She had warned me not to, but I—" He
shrugged. "I was young and foolish. She never did anything wrong."

"Of course she didn't," Jenny agreed. "She would never do anything wrong.
The very notion would tear her up." Then her eyes widened. "Oh, no!" she
breathed.

"Right." Sherlock took a breath. "So how would she react if she maybe got
selected as a False Companion, the second time around?"

Dug was stunned. "It could be different each time, couldn't it! She could
be True the first time, and False the second time. Still, it's hard to believe that
she could—"

"She wouldn't exactly have a choice. She had to play by the rules of the
game."

"I remember now," Jenny said. "She was the one who suggested that you
exchange Companions. Could it be because she didn't want to be False to you,
Dug?"

Dug's mind was spinning. Suddenly little things were clicking into place.
Why had Com Pewter been so sure that he couldn't fight his way back, with
his Companion? Maybe because the evil machine had known she was False,
just waiting for the perfect opportunity to wash him out. Why had Nada been

reserved in little ways, when she had been more open before? Her attitude *had* subtly changed, as if she were possessed of some secret sadness. Exactly as would be the case if she were required to turn traitor to the one she had before been pledged to help.

The more he pondered it, the more certain he became that it was true. Nada was a False Companion. She had not tried to torpedo him, because he wasn't far enough along to make it really count. Too soon, and he would just come back in another game and take another Companion, or take her again, when she wasn't False. So she would wait, hoping that he would wash out on his own. But if he didn't, and was about to win the prize, then she would arrange to betray him, making him forfeit his victory.

Now that he knew this, he could anticipate that betrayal, and reject her advice at the critical time. If she said the left fork had the prize, he could take the right fork. The key was in judging just when she was going to pull her act of betrayal. Forewarned was forearmed, but it would still be tricky.

Still, it hurt to know that she was now his secret enemy. He had given up on trying to see her panties, but had hoped to win her favor. Now that was impossible. "Brother!" he muttered. "She's like another virus, lurking to destroy the one she's with."

"Good thing you switched Companions, eh?" Sherlock said.

"I didn't switch for that reason," Dug said. "I didn't realize—" Then he got the point. "Kim! Now she's got the False Companion! She's in trouble!"

"It means she'll lose," Sherlock agreed.

"Unless she can play again, and get back into it. But by that time I may have won the prize. It's not fair."

"So?" Sherlock inquired.

Dug came to his decision. "So I'm going to find her and warn her, or take back my False Companion! I'm not going to let her take the fall for me."

"You'll have trouble finding her. You'll likely have to go off the game routes."

"I know. It'll be rough. Not right to put you through that. So I guess this is where we part company. I'm sorry we didn't find any good places for your folk to settle. But maybe you can go down to the Good Magician's castle and ask him. Jenny can tell you how to get there, I'm sure."

"Forget it," Sherlock said. "I'm not leaving you yet. I just wanted to be sure you'd say what I thought you'd say."

"But this is no longer the game, really," Dug protested. "If I mess up, I'm just out of it. But if you get in trouble, your people will suffer. You've got more at risk than I do."

"More to gain, too. How do we know where I'll find a good place? It may be in the middle of some area you never were slated to cross. I might as well take a look at it. And a party of three can travel better than a party of two."

"Especially when one gets sick," Dug agreed, relieved. "Glad to have you along, then." He turned to Jenny. "Where do you think they went, and where can we best intercept them?"

"Sammy will know," she said.

The cat jumped down. "Wait for me!" Jenny cried, dashing after him.

They were on their way.

14
FOUNDRY

Kim was sweaty-hot, stinging-scratched, and worn-out fatigued. This might be a game, not quite real, but it felt distressingly real right now. Bubbles Dog did not seem much better off, though she didn't complain. "Oh, we'll just have to rest," Kim said.

She found a spreading tree with wide ridged roots radiating out. She sat down, leaning back against the trunk, and pulled the dog into her. "What did I get you into, Bubbles?" she asked rhetorically. "You're old; you don't want to struggle through wilderness like this! Maybe I should have left you in that floating bubble."

Bubbles whined, her tail dropping low.

Kim hugged her. "No, I couldn't have done that! You needed someone to adopt you, and I guess I needed a pet. I never had a dog before. I'm glad I found you."

A huge serpent appeared. Its head changed, becoming human. "Oh, there you are," Nada said. "I thought I'd lost you."

"We're just so tired," Kim confessed. "This perpetual jungle! Are you sure there isn't some easier route to the Good Magician's castle?"

Nada's face was unreadable. "There may be. But there are complications. The direct route would require us to cross the Kiss-Mee River, and though it has now been restored to its original friendly contours, that can be awkward."

Kim thought about swimming through Kiss-Mee water. There could indeed be complications! Would they be kissing water, fish, or each other? If she were still traveling with Dug she might have risked it. "Better avoid that," she agreed.

"So I have been trying to find a path north of Lake Kiss-Mee," Nada said. "But I am unfamiliar with this region, so it is difficult."

Kim was beginning to miss Jenny Elf and her cat Sammy, who could find things. He would have found them a safe, walkable path. As it was, they just had to struggle through. Still, it seemed harder than it had to be.

Then she spied something through the trees. It was a cloud in the sky, but not a rainy one. It might even be smoke. Was it true in Xanth, as in Mundania, that where there was smoke there was fire? And where there was fire, could there be civilization? Travelable paths? Anything seemed better than this endless jungle!

Kim hauled herself back to her feet. "Let's investigate that smoke," she said.

"I'm not sure that is wise," Nada demurred.

"Why not?"

"It may be a smoker dragon."

Ouch! Kim hadn't thought of that. Then her impulsive nature got the better of her. "But it might *not* be a dragon," she said. "Let's go see, carefully."

Nada shrugged, which was impressive in her natural form, and slithered out in the direction of the smoke. Kim and Bubbles followed.

Before long it was apparent that the smoke was coming from the chimney of a little house in the wood. "If that house is made of candy, I'm going to be a mite suspicious," Kim muttered.

It turned out to be a normal house, with wooden walls and a thatched roof. Still, that did not guarantee that its occupant was friendly. But Kim was so tired that she did the easy thing: she hoped for the best. She approached the door and knocked, while Nada waited nearby in serpent form.

The door opened. A woman stood there. She was absolutely repulsive. She opened her warty face. "Yes?" she said in a voice like gravel in a gearbox.

Kim glanced down at Bubbles. The dog hadn't barked. That suggested that this woman was not a menace. She might even be a decent person, under all that piled-on ugliness. "I'm—I'm a traveler, looking for an easy route to the Good Magician's castle," Kim said hesitantly. "I wondered if—"

"Why, you poor girl," the woman graveled. "You look so tired and hungry! You must come in and have a bit to eat!"

Kim glanced again at Bubbles. Still no objection. She decided to trust the dog's judgment. "Thank you," she said. "I'm Kim. This is Bubbles. May she come in too?"

"Of course, dear, if she's housebroken."

Kim realized that she didn't know about that. "I—" she started doubtfully.

"Oh, that's all right; I'll clean it up if there's a problem. I'm Ma Anathe. I love to have visitors, but I receive so few."

They entered the house. It was larger inside than outside, which was possible in a magic land. It was neatly arranged, and clean.

"Let me serve you some gruel," Anathe grated, as if rocks were caught in a grinder. "It is simple, but all I have."

"I'm sure it will do," Kim said doubtfully. She took her place at the wooden table.

Anathe set a wooden bowl of gruel before her, and another down on the floor for Bubbles. The dog lapped hers appreciatively, once again reassuring Kim. So she took the wooden spoon and tried a cautious sip—and it was good. It definitely was not gruel and unusual punishment.

"Now, about your trip to the Good Magician's castle," Anathe graveled. She seemed to have only those two tones: grate and gravel. "You must get on the enchanted path—"

"I can't," Kim said apologetically. "I'm—I'm a Player in a game, and I have to take my chances."

"Oh, so that's why you are so far into nowhere!" the woman grated. "That's why you are visiting old Anathe Ma! You're desperate."

Kim considered her response. Some diplomacy was in order. "It is true. But if I had known how nice you are, I would have visited anyway."

"That's sweet of you to say," Anathe said sourly. "I don't know much about this game, but I know better than to interfere with demons. If they say you can't use the enchanted paths, then you had best avoid them. That means you will have trouble crossing Kiss Mee."

"Yes," Kim agreed. The gruel was making her sleepy. She saw that it had the same effect on Bubbles, who was going into a dognap.

"Unfortunately that will route you past the foundry," Anathe continued. "The centaurs may be difficult. They don't like strangers there."

She continued to talk, but Kim was just too tired and sleepy to listen. She put her head on the table and slept.

She woke to the sound of Nada Naga's human voice. "What have you done with her? I warn you, if you have hurt her—you're not one of the game challenges, so you have no call to—"

"Hush, woman!" Anathe grated. "Your friend is just sleeping. How could you let her get so tired? And her poor dog, too—that animal is too old for prolonged adventure."

Kim was about to raise her head, to reassure Nada. But something made her wait. She had not chosen Nada as her Companion; Dug had. She had gone along when he offered to trade, but she had never been quite sure this was legitimate. So while Nada certainly seemed to be a nice person and a competent Companion, Kim had just the slightest guilty tinge of doubt about her. Would Nada do the same job for her as she would have for Dug? So she was curious how Nada would react when Kim seemed to be in trouble.

"Did you give them a magic potion?" Nada demanded. "The demons won't like it if—"

"No potion!" Anathe graveled. "Just good, simple gruel, with a tiny drop of healing elixir. It was all I had. They were both ready to collapse when they came here. I couldn't let them go on like that. If you're supposed to be helping them, you should be ashamed."

Nada strolled across the chamber to the table. "Kim! Are you all right?"

Now Kim lifted her head. She felt somewhat refreshed. It had indeed been good gruel. "I'm all right. I was just so tired, I must have fallen asleep."

"Are you sure?" Nada herself looked unsure.

"Yes. Anathe is very nice. Her gruel is very good." Kim reached down to pat Bubbles, who was now also awake. The dog wagged her tail.

Nada did a visible reassessment. Then she turned to Anathe. "I think I owe you an apology. I assumed—"

"Don't bother," the woman grated. "I understand. Everyone thinks that I must be as evil as I look. It is why I live alone."

"Appearances can be deceptive," Nada agreed awkwardly.

"Yes. Few would believe you are a serpent woman."

Now Nada was startled. "How did you know that?"

Anathema smiled. The effect was horrendous. "There are old pine needles in your hair, but none on your clothing, so you weren't rolling on the ground. You must have been in another shape. A werewolf would have walked over the fallen needles, but a serpent would be right down in them. I knew that a lovely young woman like you would not be guarding a person unless she was sure of her power. I have heard about the naga folk. You must have been in serpent form, and just changed."

"True." Nada brought out a comb and ran it through her lustrous gray-brown hair. Several needles fell out, as well as some bits of thread. "There are those who see me in serpent form and are horrified."

"At least you can change your form."

Nada nodded. "You have no magic to compensate?"

"My talent is making good gruel."

There didn't seem to be much help there. "Well, thank you," Nada said. "We must be on our way."

"Yes. I was just telling Kim the route. You must try to get past the foundry without aggravating the centaurs."

"We shall try," Nada said.

"But how can we repay you for the gruel?" Kim asked, standing.

"The pleasure of your brief company was enough," Anathe graveled. She bent down to pat Bubbles' head, and the dog wagged her tail. Then, in a murmur only Kim could hear: "Be watchful, girl; I fear something is afoot."

They left, and resumed their travel west. There was a path from the house, which made it much easier. Kim continued to feel better, as if the gruel had a developing effect as it was digested. Bubbles, too, was more alert.

Then Kim realized something. The dog had accepted Ma Anathe's pat. She had shied away from all others before, except for Kim herself. Bubbles had been right that the woman was not evil, and the dog even liked her, in her non-demonstrative fashion. That was most interesting. Especially since Bubbles was just as cautious about Nada as she was about anyone else.

And Anathe Ma had warned her about something. Kim might have dismissed it, but she trusted the dog's instinct. Anybody Bubbles trusted enough to receive a pat from had to be taken seriously. But what should she be watchful for? She didn't know, and probably Anathe had not known either; it was just intuition. But it aligned with Kim's own. Something was subtly not right.

All she could do was follow the advice: to be watchful. That she would.

The path wound along through the forest as if it had not a care in the world. Sometimes it made a straight rigid backbone, while at other times it practiced sinuous curves. It flirted with a big tangle tree, but stayed just out of reach. Once it set a couple of muddy puddles for unwary feet.

Bubbles hesitated, looking nervous. Kim was learning the signs; the dog was shy about most people, especially strangers, and barked when there was danger. She ignored most objects, but distrusted those that were unusual. So there must be something unusual here.

She saw a patch of flowers beside the path. But they were strange, even for Xanth. They were grotesquely ugly, and they smelled worse. Yet she recognized them as roses. They had the general configuration of roses, but somehow gave the opposite impression. Perhaps that was because they were the color of barf with the smell of puke. Beyond them were regular roses, pretty and sweet-smelling; only one circular patch was ugly.

Kim paused. Could this be a garden cultivated by Anathe? But the woman did not have an ugly house or personality, and her gruel had been good; why should she have ugly roses? There must be some other explanation.

Then she saw a single small chip of wood in the middle of the ugly patch. It looked like a fragment of the heart of pine, the kind her dad had used to start a fire in the fireplace, because it had so much clotted sap that it burned like a torch.

Suddenly it clicked. "Reverse wood!" she cried. She stooped to pick it up.

"Be careful!" Nada exclaimed. "That could be dangerous!"

"Not to me," Kim replied. "I'm a Mundane. I have no magic. As far as I know, reverse wood reverses magic, not mundane things."

Nada looked doubtful, but did not protest. Kim picked up the chip, and sure enough, it did not hurt her or change her perception. But the roses that had been in its vicinity were already changing, becoming as lovely as the ones beyond the range of the chip. They were magic blue roses, with chocolate perfume; the magic had been reversed by the wood.

She held the chip down for Bubbles to sniff. The dog evinced no fear of it; apparently it had been the reversed roses that had bothered her. She was evidently Mundane, like Kim, so that chip didn't affect her directly.

That sent Kim into a brief spell of wondering. If Bubbles was of Mundane origin, how had she gotten into that floating bubble? Mundania did not have any magical trash disposal. Well, maybe sometime she would learn the answer.

Kim tucked the chip into a pocket. She was sure it would come in handy, in due course. After all, this was the game; things didn't happen just by accident. Maybe a dragon would try to toast her with fire, and the wood would turn it to cool water. The chip was surely the key to an upcoming challenge.

There was a dim sound ahead, but it grew brighter as they approached it. It sounded like metal being pounded.

They came to a cabin formed from knotted trees. "That's an ogre den," Nada said, alarmed.

Kim had had more than enough experience with ogres. She looked for a way to bypass the cabin. But again the jungle closed in thickly, making it impossible to deviate from the path. They would have to chance it. "Maybe those ogres aren't looking for trouble," she said with faint hope.

"Peaceful ogres? That's an oxymoron!"

But Bubbles wasn't barking, and that was a positive sign. As Anathe had shown, not all ugly folk were bad. Anyway, the way she was being channeled here suggested that it was another challenge. So she would just have to handle it. Watchfully.

The sound turned out to be an ogre pounding centaur shoes. These were not like people shoes; they were U-shaped bits of metal. Sparks flew up with each blow, and the metal turned red-hot. There was no forge; the ogre's blows were so hard that the heat came directly from them.

Kim wanted to try to sneak past without the ogre noticing, but knew that the game would never let her get away with that. Sure enough, in a moment the ogre looked up and saw her. "See she!" he roared.

But Bubbles didn't bark, so Kim stood her ground. In a moment an ogress came from the house. Or was she an ogress? There was something exceedingly odd about her, and in a moment Kim realized what it was: she wasn't ugly. She was at worst ordinary. No fangs. No hairy nose. Just a reasonably homely countenance. Kim had heard of only one un-ugly ogress in Xanth, but this one wasn't she. Was it possible that there were two of them? What was ogredom coming to!

The ogress looked at Kim. Simultaneously, Bubbles growled. That meant trouble.

The ogress did not seem threatening. She smiled and stepped toward them. But Bubbles whined and hid behind Kim.

Was this the danger Anathe had warned her about? Was the pretty ogress smiling to cover some sinister plot? What could it be? The woman was making no threatening gestures.

Nada Naga stepped in front of Kim. "Stop there, ogress," she said firmly.

But the ogress didn't stop. She just kept smiling and advancing. Nada, annoyed, strode forward to intercept her. "What are you up to?" Nada demanded.

"I just want to touch you," the ogress said, extending her hand.

"Why?" Nada asked, with understandable mistrust.

"I just have to do it," the woman said. Then she lunged forward, and her hand touched Nada.

Immediately Nada changed. Not to serpent form; she became ugly. In fact, she was as hideous as Ma Anathe. The ogre woman, in contrast, became radiantly beautiful.

"Oh, ugh!" Nada cried, realizing what had happened. She changed to serpent form, but that didn't help; she was an ugly reptile.

Kim now had some understanding of the threat. But she didn't care. "Hey, change her back!" she cried, advancing on the ogress.

"I can't," the ogress wailed. "I want to, but I can't. It's my curse."

"What do you mean, you can't?" Kim demanded. "If you can enchant a person, you can break the enchantment, can't you?"

"No I can't. It is my talent to make others ugly. To take their beauty for myself. I have to do it; I can't stop myself. And it ruins me, because no ogre will marry a pretty ogress. Father has been trying to get me married off for years, but every time I start to get suitably ugly, some pretty girl comes along and ruins it." She broke into tears, which was a decidedly unogrish thing to do.

Kim's mind was chugging along with a high compression ratio. Was this the challenge? If so, there was a way to handle it. Suddenly she knew what that way was.

"Take this," she said, bringing out the chip of reverse wood. "Touch her again."

The beautiful ogress took the chip, confused. She poked a lovely finger at the serpent, as if afraid it would get bitten off. Nada, realizing that Kim was onto something, remained still, and allowed herself to be touched.

Suddenly the serpent was beautiful, and the ogress was mediocre. The effect had been reversed!

"Oh!" the ogress exclaimed, delighted. "What fine magic! What is it?"

"It is reverse wood," Kim explained. "It reverses the effect of your magic."

"You mean that with it, the ones I touch will become pretty while I turn ugly? Oh, this will change my whole life! I must have it. What do you want for it?"

"Oh, I just found it by the path," Kim said. "You can have it. But I can tell you something you might like to do. There is a woman in a house to the east who is very ugly. She—"

"Yes, Anathe Ma! I have always envied her ugliness."

"Touch her with the chip, and her ugliness will be yours."

"Oh, I will!" the ogress cried. "Father, I must run. But when I return, I'll be truly ogrish!" She ran off down the path. Before long the ogress would be phenomenally ugly, and a kind old woman would be beautiful. It seemed fitting.

Kim picked up Nada's clothes and put them in her pack. Nada continued in serpent form, as there was a male in view.

They paused by the laboring ogre. He ignored them. Bubbles did not seem unduly distressed, so Kim figured he was not a threat to them. She had the feeling that there was more here to be gleaned. This work must be connected to the foundry, and she would have to pass the foundry.

The ogre was doing impressive work. His centaur shoes were minor works of metallic art, and were surely a great help for those centaurs who required them. But what was there here that might help her handle the foundry?

The ogre pounded. A hot fragment of metal tore free and spun into the ground almost by Kim's feet. She stepped back, not wanting to be burned— then reconsidered, and stepped back to where she was. She picked up two sticks and used them to pick up the cooling metal. It was almost in the shape of a crude key.

A key. Could be. Just as the chip of reverse wood had helped solve a problem, this might help solve another. When she encountered that problem. She had the answer; now all she needed was the question. Maybe.

She found a heavy leaf, and set the key in that. Then she folded the leaf around it, and put that in her pocket where the reverse wood chip had been. "Thank you, ogre," she said.

"Girl some welcome," he grunted, continuing his labors.

Kim walked on, satisfied. She had the feeling that she was making progress in the game.

But had she taken care of the thing Anathe had warned her about? She wasn't sure.

Once they were beyond the ill-kempt view of the ogre shoemaker, Nada returned to human form. She was completely lovely again. There was no doubt of this, because she was bare. Every charm practically scintillated. Kim gave her back her clothing, stifling another surge of jealousy. Oh, to look like that! "I think I found a way to thank Anathe for her kindness," she said. "Now she will look as nice as she is."

"I'm just glad you had the reverse wood chip," Nada said. "I have no desire to be an unbeautiful beast."

Neither did Kim. But magic wasn't going to make her beautiful. She would always be a distinctly ordinary girl. In and out of the game.

They moved on. There was a sign ahead: FOUNDRY. "I hope this is the last challenge before we reach the Good Magician's castle," Kim said. "I like Xanth, but I'm getting tired of constantly exercising my brain and body."

"It has been wearing for me too," Nada said. "No offense."

"How did you get to be a Companion?" Kim asked. She had read the Xanth books, but couldn't remember that detail. "Did you volunteer?"

"No, I committed an indiscretion in the realm of the gourd, and was required to pay for it in this manner. Jenny is serving her year for the Good Magician, having done a favor for a friend."

"Well, at least you get to stay in Xanth. Dug and I have to leave, when our games are over."

"But you can return to play again."

"Yes. But it's not quite the same. I wish I could live here all the time."

"All Mundanes do."

They crested a hill, and there in the next valley was the foundry: a huge building surrounded by centaurs. Many of them were lying down; others were standing, but seemed uncomfortable.

They approached the nearest centaur cautiously. "If I may inquire," Kim inquired, "what is going on here?"

"We are all foundering," the centaur replied, pained. "Is that not evident?"

"I guess it is," Kim said. "I suppose this is because of the foundry?"

"This, too, should be evident."

"But why did you come here, if it is so dangerous for you?"

"We came to attend CentaurVention, of course. But a random cursor passed, and dropped a cursory curse, rendering our Vention Center into this awful foundry. Now we are unable to get away, because of our tender feet."

"There's an ogre making centaur shoes to the east," Kim said. "Would those shoes help you to walk?"

"Certainly. But none of us can hotfoot it over there, and in any event, there probably are far too few shoes for us. What we need to do is nullify the cursor's curse. Then the foundry will be gone, and we will not need shoes."

"I am sorry to learn of your distress," Kim said. "But I am not sure what I can do about it. It's really not my problem."

"Have no concern. When you attempt to pass the foundry, as you must to proceed along your route, you too will founder. Then it will be your problem also."

Kim considered that. This definitely sounded like a challenge. She would have to rise to it. "What do you think I can do about it?"

"Since you have not yet foundered, you might be able to find the natural antagonist to the foundry, which of course is the lostwet."

"Of course," Kim agreed. Puns were serious business in Xanth. "The lostwet would cancel out the found-dry."

"Precisely. Then we would all be free of our founder."

Kim decided to test the extent of this challenge. "On the other hand, I might avoid the whole thing by going back the way I came, and seeking another route south."

"You would have to cut cross-country through the impenetrable jungle," he pointed out. "I suspect you would find that very tiring. Then you would encounter the Big Top, the Gnobody Gnomes, and Com Pewter. I suspect you would rather accept a ride from one of us, bypassing all those hazards."

Kim saw the way of it. "I suspect I would," she agreed. "Where do you suppose I might find the lostwet?"

"There is a lost wax trail to the south which ought to lead there."

"Lost wax?"

"It was lost in the process of casting the foundry curse."

She should have known. "I shall follow that trail," Kim agreed.

They turned south. Bubbles soon sniffed out the smell of wax. It looked as if a huge vat of melted wax had spilled and flowed and cooled and solidified, forming the path. This would be known as the lost wax process. Now it had hardened so that it was easy to walk on.

At the end of the trail of wax was a small lake. The wax seemed to have flowed out across the surface of the lake, cooling, and finally formed a thin wax seal over it. The seal was very strong, so that they were able to walk out on it without falling in the lake. It was transparent, so that they could see right down to the bottom of the lake.

This seemed to be a flat expanse. At the near end was a smooth slope, while at the far end was a portal, similar to the ones she had used to let the water into the naga tunnel. In the center of the portal was a small keyhole.

Kim brought out the key she had saved from the ogre's work. It was now cool and firm. Could this be the key to that lock? This was the game; it was bound to be the proper key. So she would have to put the key in that lock, and open that portal. Beneath it should be the lostwet.

But how was she going to get the key there? She could see the keyhole, but the transparent wax was so hard that she couldn't scratch it, let alone poke a hole in it. She was being tantalized by a goal so near yet so far. "Do you know anything about this?" she asked Nada.

"I knew there was a challenge here, but not its nature," Nada confessed. "I don't know anything about wax."

It figured. The Companion's job was to get the Player safely to the challenges, but not to solve them. So Nada had braced Anathe when it seemed that the woman was interfering with Kim, but was no help in fathoming this riddle.

"Do you have any idea, Bubbles?" Kim asked.

The dog wagged her tail and started sniffing the waxed surface. Kim wasn't sure that Bubbles had really understood her question, but the dog obviously wanted to be helpful.

In a moment Bubbles stopped. She had found something. Kim checked, and saw a tiny hole in the wax. Maybe she could get her finger into it and pull the wax up, making an access to the water.

But her finger wouldn't fit; the hole was too small. And anyway, the wax was so strong that she would need a keyhole saw to cut through it, and of course Xanth didn't have such machines. So what good was the hole?

Then she considered the key again. It was just small enough to fit through that hole. But if she put it through there, she would just lose it in the lake, being unable to retrieve it. That seemed even more pointless than her other options.

But this was the game. There had to be a way. She just had to figure it out.

Kim strained her brain, but could not squeeze out any useful notion. The key was here, the lock was there, and never the twain could meet, it seemed. Unless—

The light of an idea flashed over her head again, but dimly, because she wasn't sure she had the right clue. It was only half a flash, really. She had played with a puzzle in a book once, in which a string passed through small holes, and something had to be transferred from one loop to another, when it was too big to fit through the holes. The trick had been to manipulate the string, passing it around the object and through the holes, until the puzzle could be solved. Here she had a key, and a keyhole, and a small hole leading to the wrong place; was there a way to get the key to the keyhole indirectly? She didn't have any string, and string wouldn't do the job anyway, but maybe the principle applied.

She lay down on the wax and peered through it, studying the situation. Now she saw that there were a number of bugs running around on the bottom of the lake. They looked like ticks, the kind that had to be kept off people and dogs, but these had to be water bugs, or at least capable of living in water. There were letters of the alphabet on their backs, identifying them. They didn't seem to be doing anything, just moving back and forth in semicircular paths, as if they were pendulums. All of them faced the same way, as if they had fled from the locked portal. When they moved, they didn't turn left or right; they skittered sideways, maintaining their orientation. Every time they reached the end of a semicircle, they clicked. Click-click. That struck Kim as odd behavior, even for such odd creatures.

Pendulums. Clicks. As in big clocks. Making ticks and tocks. So they *were* ticks, Xanth-style. Kim had read how the Good Magician Humfrey in his youthful days had lived on a tick farm, growing ticks for clocks, and had a real problem when the ticks mutated and made mischief. She remembered how aggravating the cri-tic had been. Could it be that some of those errant ticks never had been run down, and here they were? Just waiting to accomplish something?

The other half of her idea flashed. Maybe she could get them to move the key for her! To take it to the lock she couldn't reach. If only she could figure out how to do it.

She held the key in her hand. Suppose she dropped it through the hole, and simply asked the ticks to move it for her? But why would they bother, even if they understood what she wanted? She had to have some way to encourage them. And there had to be a way, because this was the game.

If they were ticks, where were the tocks? All the bugs were the same; there didn't seem to be any tocks. Where did the tocks come from? She hadn't read of any tock farm. Actually, in a clock, a tock was just the other side of a tick. So were tocks really ticks turned over? If so, there were really tocks as well as ticks.

This was crazy, but maybe it made punnish sense: ticks might not help her, but tocks might. If she could just get them to turn over. The ticks were all facing away from the portal and its keyhole, but tocks might face toward it. So maybe they could take the key the right way.

What could she lose? Kim put the key to the hole in the wax. It dropped through and plinked on the floor of the pool.

Immediately the ticks changed their behavior. They stopped swinging aimlessly, and started advancing on the key. But Kim realized that they would push it the wrong way, away from the lock. She needed tocks to push it the right way.

"Tick-tock!" she cried. But the ticks ignored her.

She realized that nobody would respond to a general call. If someone called "People-smeople!" she would ignore him too. But if someone called her by name or description, she would react.

"Fran-tic!" she called. No tick responded. "Fantas-tic!" Still nothing. "Gigan-tic!" The ticks continued toward the key, and the first one was beginning to push the key off toward a trench Kim now saw some distance beyond. If it fell in there, it would never be recovered!

She was getting nowhere, and she couldn't remember any more of the ticks she had read about. Then she realized that she had it backward: Humfrey had dealt with all those ticks. She had to address those ticks that had escaped his notice.

She strained her brain. She saw a tick that was somewhat dusky, as if spoiled. Its letter was N. "Necro-tic!" she cried.

The tick paused. She had identified it!

"Necro-toc!" she said. And the tick turned around and faced the other way. She had done it!

"Necro-toc, push the key!" she called.

The tock skittered sideways and reached the key. It made little clocks, rather than clicks, as it moved. It braced its head against the key and pushed. The key moved toward the lock. Kim had found out how to do it. She would get a lick at the lock.

But other ticks were coming to push the other way. One got placed squarely before the key, and it came to a halt. Then a second tick lined up before the first, and the key began to slide back.

Kim saw that one of the ticks seemed a bit doubtful. Its letter was A. "Agnos-tic" she cried, and it paused.

"Agnos-toc. Push the other way!"

The tick turned around and pushed from the other direction. Now it was two to one, and the key resumed motion toward the lock. It was getting close. "Go, go, go!" Kim whispered fervently, urging her team on.

But another tick crowded into the space left by the Agnos-toc, and pushed the other way. So it was two to two, and the key stopped moving again. Then a third tick arrived, making it three to two, and the key started moving away again.

The third tick was not very active itself, but it seemed to stir the other two up, and they pushed harder. Its letter was C. Suddenly Kim recognized it.

"Cataly-tic!" she cried, and it paused. "Cataly-toc!" It turned around. "Push the key." It pushed.

Now the Necro and Agnos tocks were revitalized, becoming very active. The key moved so rapidly that the other ticks could not catch it, and at last it reached the keyhole of the lock. They pushed it in, and then pushed it around so that it turned. There was a loud clock! sound, and the C fell away, leaving the (c)lock. The lock opened.

The water swirled into it. Kim realized that it was like the lock of a canal, handling water. The water would be held there until it was moved on to the next lock.

As the water drained from the pool, the thin wax covering it lost its support. It collapsed, and the three of them had to scramble to get off it before getting dunked.

The ticks and tocks and fragments of wax swirled into the lock along with the water. Soon there was just a dry depression there. They walked down into it. It seemed to be nothing but a fairly level region. Where was the lostwet?

Bubbles paused to sniff something. Kim looked. It was a blinking little square or oblong, so small Kim would not have seen it if the dog had not called her attention to it.

She picked it up. It seemed to have no mass; it was just a tiny manifestation she could balance on the tip of her finger. What could it be?

Then she understood. "It's a cursor!" she cried. "We had to get rid of the water—to get the wet lost—in order to get it. It's the cursor that made the foundry and then got lost in the wet. With this we should be able to reverse the damage it did."

Both Nada and Bubbles looked doubtful, but neither argued. Kim marched out of the lost pool and back onto the lost wax trail, balancing the blinking thing on her finger. They followed.

She reached the place where the centaurs had foundered. "I got it! I got it!" Kim cried, brandishing her blinking finger.

Heads turned to look at her. The male centaurs frowned. The females blushed. What was the matter with them? Centaurs were notoriously unflappable.

Then Kim realized what was wrong. She seemed to be making a signal with her finger. It might not have the same meaning in Xanth as it did in Mundania, but it could hardly be considered polite.

She straightened out her other fingers. "I have the cursor," she explained. "The one to nullify the curse, I think."

"Of course," the nearest centaur replied. "Put it on the foundry."

Kim walked on to the foundry. As she got closer, her feet started to hurt. Her shoes felt too tight. She wanted to get the weight off. But she knew what it was: she was foundering. All she had to do was nullify the curse, and it would go away. So she gritted her teeth and walked on.

The pain got worse, until it felt as if she were walking on acid-soaked pincushions. She couldn't stand it any more. She had to stop.

But now she was close to the foundry. She held up her finger. "Take this!" she cried, jabbing it toward the building. The cursor flew off and struck the foundry wall.

There was a flash. Kim blinked with the brightness of it. As her eyes cleared, she saw that the building had changed. Now it was the Centaur Vention Center. She had done it!

The centaurs got up and trotted in. "Now we shall give you and your Companion your ride to the Good Magician's castle."

"Thank you," Kim said, gratified. She knew she had managed to win another challenge.

15
TALENTS

Dug ran after Jenny, who was running after Sammy, while Sherlock followed them all. Jenny knew enough to hold on to Sammy when telling him to find something, but she kept forgetting. She was, after all, a child, Dug remembered; he had to make allowances. Certainly her little cat's talent was useful.

The trouble was that the paths the little cat took were not necessarily suitable for people. They soon got tangled in brambles, burrs, and thistles. "Stop, Sammy!" Jenny cried. "We can't keep up with you!"

The cat stopped. Jenny picked him up. She was about to ask him to pick out an easy and safe path for them to follow, when she paused.

Dug and Sherlock were pausing too. They had blundered into an odd section of the forest. It wasn't that the trees were different, just that their arrangement was odd. Instead of being randomly scattered, they were growing in lines and curves, as if part of some huge ornamental garden. A garden cultivated by a giant, perhaps.

"I think we should quietly move away from here," Sherlock murmured.

Dug agreed. He did not like the look of this. He turned back the way they had come.

But there was a commotion back there. Something was following them. "Oops," Jenny said. "I think maybe we're somewhere we shouldn't be."

"My sentiment exactly," Dug said, reversing course. He led the way to the side, trying to avoid the thing behind by going at right angles to its motion. But he came up against a massive hedge of woven trees. There was no way through it, and the thorns on the trunks made it impossible to climb up and over. "In fact, I think maybe we're in another challenge." It was the last thing he wanted. He didn't care about the game at the moment; he just wanted to intercept Kim so he could warn her that she had a False Companion who would betray her at the key moment. The longer it took to catch up to her, the greater the risk of her betrayal.

He walked beside the dread hedge, seeking somewhere to hide. But the hedge curved around, herding him toward the center of the tree garden. Meanwhile the thing closed in from behind. There seemed to be no escape.

"All right, already," Dug said. "I'll face it!" It had not been fear of bodily harm that had driven him to hide, but fear of delay. He wanted to skip the game for now, until he could warn Kim, and maybe exchange Companions back so that the liability would be his instead of hers. It was the right thing to do.

They stood and waited for the thing. And Dug was surprised again. Because it wasn't a monster, it was a pair of horses with riders. And a foal. A halfway handsome man rode the stallion, and a lovely woman rode the mare. The man wore a sword. But the oddest thing was the metal. Each horse had heavy chains wrapped around its body. What was going on here?

The man spied them. He waved. "Hi there, friends," he said in a friendly fashion. "What are you doing in the Garden of Talents? I thought it was closed to the public."

Appearances could be extremely deceptive, in Xanth. But Dug saw nothing to be gained by being too defensive. This just possibly barely might be a chance encounter. So he told the truth. "I am Dug. I am playing in a game. This is Jenny Elf, my Companion, and this is Sherlock, who is looking for a place for his Black Wave to settle in peace. We strayed in here unintentionally, and wish only to leave it behind."

"The game?" the man asked, his brow wrinkling.

"The demons are running it," Jenny explained.

The woman took an interest. "Then it must be fun." She turned to the man. "Let's learn more of this, Jordan."

The man was amenable. "Okay." He jumped down from his horse, while the woman floated down. He strode forward. "I'm Jordan the Barbarian. My talent is to heal quickly. This is my wife, Renee. Or Threnody, if you like that better. She's half demon. These are our friends the ghost horses: Pook, Peek, and Puck." The stallion, mare, and foal nodded their heads in turn when named, showing that they understood human dialogue.

"Oh, I know of you," Jenny said. "I learned about it in centaur school. You came from more than four hundred years ago, in Xanth's history, and met Threnody—"

"In the year 677," Threnody said. "We had a small misunderstanding, but later we got together again."

"In 1074," Jordan said. He counted on his fingers. "Eighteen years ago. We've been happily exploring the wilderness ever since. And whatever." He pinched Threnody's well-rounded bottom.

"There's a certain charming naturalness about barbarians," Threnody said, smiling as she kicked his shin. "They're so ill-mannered."

"And a certain sexy mystery about demon women," Jordan agreed. He tried to pinch her again, but this time his hand seemed to pass through her body as if it were smoke.

It occurred to Dug that the two were well matched. Jordan liked a woman who was mysterious and sexy and had certain demonly qualities, and Threnody/Renee liked a man who had few human restraints. She probably didn't give him any trouble about seeing her panties, but she could prevent him from handling her flesh when she chose.

"The demons are running the game," Jenny said. "It's for two Mundanes: a girl who won a prize, and—well, I'm not sure how Dug got in."

"Pirated copy, probably," Dug said. "I should've asked. My friend who wanted my girlfriend got it."

"Pirates, eh?" Jordan said, interested. "They're like barbarians."

"I'm from Mundania," Dug said. "I'm just visiting Xanth, playing the game. But right now I don't want to play it, I want to intercept the other player, Kim, so I can—"

"Wipe her out!" Jordan said, pleased.

"Not exactly. I really don't care about the prize. But—"

"But you like the girl," Threnody said. "So you want to catch her and make like a barbarian." She pinched Jordan's bottom.

"Uh, not exactly that, either," Dug said, privately intrigued by the byplay between the two. "I maybe did something that's going to wipe her out, and I have to warn her before it happens. So it's fair."

"Fair?" Jordan asked blankly.

Threnody nudged him. "You know about fairness. It's in the *Barbarian Handbook*. Page 432, Footnote F."

He looked sheepish. "I guess I didn't read that far. Barbarians aren't much for books."

"I quote: 'If all else fails, try fairness. Fair women can be very appealing.' "

He brightened. "Oh. Sure. All I need now is a fair—"

He broke off, because she had just drawn a knife and cut off his mouth. Jordan looked surprised. Then he fetched out a big handkerchief, mopped the blood, and gave her a reproving glance. Already his mouth was healing. New lips were growing to replace the lost ones. Well, he had said that his talent was fast healing. He had meant it literally.

"Anyway," Dug continued, refusing to act as shaken as he was by this incidental demonstration, "I just want to get on away from here and on my way. But the big thorny hedge is stopping me. Do you know any way past it?"

"I could phase through it," Threnody said. "I can become demonically insubstantial when I choose. But I don't suppose that will help you much."

"That hedge usually doesn't bother us," Jordan said. He lisped a bit, because his mouth had not yet grown back to full size and flexibility. "But probably you can't get by it. You see, it grows only when it wants to catch someone, and then it grows in a circle, so they can't get out. You have to find a magic talent to get out."

"That's a game challenge!" Dug said. "How could you have encountered it, if you're not part of the game?"

"Threnody told me we might have a bit part to play in a game," Jordan admitted. "I guess this is it. Maybe it will relieve the boredom of being stuck with one woman."

Threnody lifted her knife, but this time he caught her hand, then kissed her with his new-formed lips. Dug doubted that Jordan was really bored.

"Well, then, can you tell me how I find a magic talent? I'm Mundane; I don't have any magic of my own."

"Sure. There's a box of talents in the center. You can't miss it. Only there's a catch."

"There's always a catch," Dug agreed wearily.

"You have to pick out talents blindly. You have to use a talent at least once before you can put it back and take another."

That didn't seem like much of a catch, so Dug knew it couldn't be the whole story. "What's the catch to the catch?"

"Hey, you're thinking like a barbarian!" Jordan said with approval. His mouth was now almost the way it had been before. "Never trust any civilized person. The catch is you don't know what talent you've got, so you'll have trouble using it."

"But it will take forever to guess, without a hint," Dug protested.

"There's a hint," Threnody said. "It's a list of fifty talents. You can check them off as you identify them. If you use up all fifty, there'll be a new list. If you get one that will enable you to escape the garden early, you won't need to return it; it will fade out in a day or so anyway."

So that was it. If he were lucky, and quick to fathom his luck, he could be on his way rapidly. Otherwise he might be stuck for hours. Or days.

Dug turned and walked to the center of the glade. Sammy jumped down to show him the way. The others followed.

"May I pet Puck?" Jenny asked, approaching the ghost foal. "He's so cute."

The chained foal approached her, agreeing to be petted. "Why are they wearing those chains?" Sherlock asked.

"That's the way ghost horses are," Jordan said. "Without their chains they'd fade out. It's the chains that hold them in this realm."

"Wouldn't it be kinder to unwrap them and let them go?" Jenny asked.

"Then what would we ride?" Jordan asked sensibly.

Sherlock and Jenny didn't argue. They evidently realized that there was not too much point in discussing gentle social concerns with a barbarian.

Dug came into the central glade. There was the spellbox. It was circular, with a flat top. Behind it was a billboard, titled 50 SPELLS.

There did not seem to be any opening in the top. But Dug was getting used to the ways of magic. He touched the top with his hand, and sure enough, his hand passed right through it, disappearing beyond, as if the top were a sheet of liquid paint. His questing fingers caught something. He drew his hand back, hauling out the thing—and his hand was empty. But he felt subtly changed.

The others were watching him. "Do you have a talent?" Jenny asked.

"I have something," he said. "I suppose it's a talent. But I don't know which one."

"You can read the list, and try them in order," Sherlock suggested.

Dug read the list:

1. Change Color of Anything.
2. Change One Food to Another.
3. Null Taste.
4. Alter Smells.
5. Make Objects Adhere.

The talents seemed straightforward and harmless. "Okay, how does a person make his magic work?" he asked.

"I have to get injured before mine works," Jordan said. "Then it's automatic."

"I just will myself smoky," Threnody said. "And solid again. It's slow, but it happens. It's not really a talent; I simply partake of some human and some demon nature."

"I just hum," Jenny said. "Anyone who isn't paying attention enters my dream."

Dug hadn't realized that Jenny had a magic talent of her own; he had assumed that it tied in with her cat. "Okay, I'll will something to change color." He looked around. "That stone there: turn pink."

He concentrated, trying to turn the stone pink. Nothing happened. "No luck," he said. "So it's not that."

"Are you sure?" Jenny asked. "Maybe you have to call it 'anything.' "

"Okay." He addressed the stone. "I dub thee 'anything.' Now turn pink."

Again, nothing happened. "So I'll try the next." He fished in his pocket and found a few nuts left over from his last snack: two M's, one N, one O, and three P's. He lifted the P-nut. "Change to a marshmallow," he ordered it.

Nothing happened. "Maybe it's a marshmallow in the shape of a P-nut," Sherlock suggested.

Dug tasted it. "No, it's still peanut-flavored." He glanced at the list. "So now I'll null its taste." He concentrated, then tasted it again. It remained P-flavored. So he tried the next: "Make it smell like a rose." With no success. "Then make it adhere to my finger." He touched his finger to it, but there was no adhesion.

He sighed. "This is apt to be tedious." He read the next five talents:

6. Change Water to Vapor or Ice, and Back.
7. Make Raw Food Cooked.
8. Sense When Someone Is About to Die.
9. Call Up Small Intense Gusts of Wind.
10. See Through Objects.

"We have any water?" Dug asked.

Jordan had a flask. He poured a bit out, and Dug tried to vaporize or freeze it, but without success. Then he tried to cook the P-nut, with no luck.

#8 brought him up short. "How do I tell when someone's about to die, if no one *is* about to die?"

"I can slay someone for you," Jordan offered cheerfully, drawing his sword.

Dug would have laughed, but he had the eerie feeling that the man wasn't joking. "No thanks! That talent wouldn't help me get out of here anyway, so I'm just going to assume this isn't that. I'll try the next, and see if I can call up a small, intense gust of wind."

"That's not magic," Sherlock said. "I can do it naturally." He bent over.

"That won't be necessary," Dug said quickly, though he was strongly tempted to laugh. Jordan didn't worry about temptation; he burst out with a rich ho-ho-ho!

"That's another way of doing it," Sherlock agreed.

Pook, the ghost horse, didn't bother to laugh. He simply let fly with his own loud gust of wind.

"Thanks, folks," Dug said. "But I'm the one who has to break the, uh, make the wind." He concentrated, but no other wind stirred.

Next he tried to see through objects. He couldn't. "Just as well," Jenny said. "You might have looked through Threnody's or my clothing and seen our panties."

Dug hadn't thought of that. He bit his tongue so as not to laugh, knowing that they took such things more seriously than he did. "Right. Close call."

He addressed the next five talents:

11. Make Others Mute.
12. Extinguish Fires.
13. Heal Cuts & Abrasions.
14. Resist Bad Dreams.
15. Reverse Someone's Sex.

"Okay, in order," Dug said. "Do I have a volunteer to become mute?"

"Sure, try me," Sherlock said.

Dug concentrated. "Sherlock, become mute!" he intoned. "Did it work?"

"No."

Dug went on to the next. "We'll have to set a fire, to see if I can quench it magically."

Jordan went to Pook and fetched two small stones. He squatted by some dry grass and knocked the stones together. A fat spark flew out, igniting the grass. There was a little fire.

Dug focused on the fire, but he couldn't put it out. So Jordan brought out some marshmallows and began toasting them on the end of a stick.

"Now, can I heal a cut?" Dug asked. "I don't think we should cut anyone to test this! Anyway, we have some healing elixir, which would do the job. Let's skip this one for now."

"No, we can test it," Jordan said. He took his knife and passed the tip across Threnody's arm, scratching it. "Heal this."

Dug focused on the scratch, but nothing happened. "I think that's not it."

Jenny brought out the healing elixir and dripped a drop on the scratch. The scratch disappeared.

But the next one was worse. "How can I find out whether I can resist bad dreams, if I'm not asleep? And if I were asleep, and dreaming, suppose only good dreams came? It could take a month before I had a bad dream to resist."

"Maybe you could try a bad daydream," Jenny suggested.

"Mare Imbri would never deliver one of those," Threnody objected.

"Who is Mare Imbri?" Dug asked.

"She's the day mare who brings good daydreams," Jenny explained. "She brought Kim the daydream of floating bubbles, and Kim got Bubbles Dog from one of them."

Live and learn. "Well, I'll try to imagine a bad daydream, and see if I can resist it," Dug said. He concentrated, imagining falling into an endless hole. That notion had always scared him, and it still did. "I don't seem to have any special resistance," he said.

But there was no easing the difficulty of the progression. "I don't want to change someone's sex!" Dug said.

"You could change one of us, then change him back," Threnody suggested.

"Who volunteers for that?" Dug asked. He glanced at Sherlock. "You want to be a woman for a minute?"

The man shook his head no. He pointed to his throat.

"That's what I thought," Dug said. "It could be a one-way trip. So I'll just skip this one, for now." Then something registered. "Why did you point to your throat, Sherlock?"

The man didn't answer. He just pointed again.

"He can't speak!" Jenny cried. "The mute talent worked!"

"No it didn't," Dug said. "He said it didn't."

Sherlock pointed to Jordan. "Jordan said it," Threnody said.

"Well, I thought it didn't," Jordan said. Threnody gave him a disgusted look.

Dug looked at Sherlock. "The magic really did make you mute?"

Sherlock nodded vehemently.

"Well, at least that identifies it. But it's not the one I need. Let's see if I can unmute you." He concentrated. "Sherlock, speak again."

There was no result. It was a one-way talent.

"It should wear off in a few hours," Threnody said.

Sherlock grimaced, not completely pleased.

"Gee, I'm sorry," Dug said. "I guess I'd better not experiment on real people any more."

"I can make you feel better," Threnody said. "I'll give you a gourd-style apology for your inconvenience. She approached Sherlock, took hold of him, and gave him a demonically passionate kiss.

Dug could have sworn that the man's feet left the ground for a few seconds. His eyes rolled back in his head, and a dreamy smile washed across his face. He looked as if he had been anesthetized. Certainly he felt better.

"Renee has that effect," Jordan remarked nonchalantly. "A demoness can make a man deliriously happy, if she chooses. I happen to know."

It was evidently true. Sherlock seemed to be beyond caring about any little inconvenience such as not being able to speak. In fact, he looked as if he would have been speechless even if he weren't already mute.

Dug returned to business. "So I don't need this talent, because it won't get me by the thorntree hedge. All it proves is that the magic does work, and that I have a whole lot of talents to check through." He looked around. "Where do I ditch this mute magic?"

"You just reach back into the spellbox," Threnody said. "It will let go, so you can take another."

"But won't I risk getting the same talents back?"

"No, new talents float to the surface; used ones sink to the bottom. Just don't reach too deep."

Dug reached in, and he did feel something leave him. He caught a new something, and brought it out.

He read the next five talents:

16. Can Merge with Others.
17. Can Re-create Any Sound Heard.
18. Can Create Heat.
19. Can Cause Objects to Levitate.
20. Can Adjust Weight of Things.

"Nuh-uh! I'm not trying to merge with anyone!"

Threnody sighed. "And I was so looking forward to it."

Dug didn't comment, because again he suspected that she wasn't joking. She was opposite to Nada Naga in everything other than beauty.

He tried to re-create sound, but couldn't. He tried to heat something, and couldn't. He tried to make something float, and couldn't. He tried to make a stone become heavier, and failed again.

So he tried the next five:

21. Immunity to Poison.
22. Can Ease Pain in Others.
23. Can Breathe Anywhere.
24. Can Change the Magic of Water.
25. Can Make Trees Fall.

Dug refused to try the first. He wasn't sure how to test the second, until Threnody touched her knife to Jordan's arm, making it bleed. Dug tried to make the barbarian's pain stop, but couldn't. Fortunately it soon stopped itself, as Jordan quickly healed. Dug couldn't test the breathing, because he couldn't find a vacuum or a deep lake to try. Similarly he had no magic water to change from Hate to Love or Lethe. He wasn't going to mess with the vial of healing elixir they had, just in case it got spoiled. And the trees ignored his attempt to fell them magically.

He ground on through the remaining talents of the list. Nothing matched. "But how can that be?" he asked plaintively. "It's got to be one of them!"

"Maybe one of the ones you skipped," Jenny said.

"Or one of the first fifteen," Threnody suggested. "You didn't test them, this time; you picked up where you left off after the first talent."

She was right. Of course he had to test all the talents each time. Which made the job even more tedious.

Resigned, he tried #1, Changing Color. And it worked: he turned the rock pink.

"Two down," he said. "Only forty-eight to go." He was coming to appreciate how long it could take to test fifty times, for fifty different talents each time. Magic was becoming a lot more tedious than he would have thought.

"Maybe Sammy can help," Jenny said.

"I really don't see how—" Dug started. But the little cat was already bounding to the spellbox. "Wait for me!!" Dug cried, grabbing for Sammy before he fell through the porous lid.

But the cat didn't fall through the lid. For him it was solid. He sniffed the surface, looking for something, then seemed to find it.

Could it be? Dug reached into the box by the cat's nose, and caught the first spell he found there. He brought it out.

Was this the one he needed? But what *did* he need?

He skimmed through the list. Attract Animals. Mimic People's Appearance. Create Light. Darkness. Communicate with Anyone. Repel Dragons. Slow Time. Calm Tangle Trees. Reverse Emotions. Make Fire.

Would that last one enable him to burn down the thorntree hedge? He tried to make fire, but didn't get as much as a curl of smoke.

Make Earth Tremors. Blow Hurricane Force.

Maybe one of those would shake down the hedge, or blow it away. But he was unable to evoke either.

Create Pain. Sniff Danger. Control Animals. Make Others Sleep. Make

Invisible Shield. Make Things Invulnerable. Reverse People's Actions. Generate Hatred. Mimic Person's Talent.

"I just don't see how any of these can get me out of here, really," Dug said, frustrated.

Sammy jumped off the spellbox and ran to Threnody, who picked him up.

Dug was learning to pick up on insignificant details. What did that cat have in mind?

Suddenly it clicked. "Mimic Someone's Talents!" he cried. "Threnody can become smoky. If I can make things turn smoky-diffuse, we can get through." He approached the woman. "Give me your talent, please."

"I thought you'd never ask," she said with a dusky smile. She held her hand out to him, cupping it in the air.

He took whatever it was she held. Then he turned to face the thorntree hedge. "Become diffuse," he ordered it.

Then he walked to it and tried to put his hand through it. "Ouch!" He had skewered his extremity on a thorn, but that wasn't the whole reason for his pain. The magic hadn't worked.

Then he reconsidered. That thorn had gone right through his palm and out the other side. It had hurt, but not as much as it should have. His hand was not bleeding.

He touched the hedge again, more cautiously, and this time his hand passed through it with faint resistance, as if the hedge were made of thin gelatin. Or viscous fluid. The magic was working! Threnody's ability to turn smoky was slow, so his was slow too, but in time it did get there.

He turned back to the others. "I have made the hedge pervious," he said. "Thanks to Sammy's hint, and your talent, Threnody. Thank you both."

Threnody stroked Sammy's back. "We were getting bored," she said.

It figured. They knew he would get the talent eventually, but they didn't want to wait three more days. So they had helped him. Was this cheating? At the moment he hardly cared; he just wanted to get on with the journey, hoping to intercept Kim before her disaster struck.

"Let's go," he said. He walked through the hedge, which was now fully smoky. Jenny and Sherlock followed, and Sammy jumped down to join them. Jenny paused to wave goodbye to Jordan and Threnody, then hurried on.

Beyond was the thick jungle. It was quickly evident that they were not about to make swift progress through it. There was also the smell of dragon smoke, which boded ill for their safety.

But Dug had another notion. "If this talent of Threnody's is safe to use on people, I can make us smoky, and we can move right on through, the way a demon would."

He tried it on himself. Jenny watched, while Sherlock gathered small, thin vines and began weaving them into some sort of pattern. Slowly Dug diffused, until he was able to walk through a tree. "Good enough," he said faintly. "Let me do the rest of you, and we'll be on our way."

Then a breeze came up, and blew him away. He saved himself only by scrambling into another tree, where the wind couldn't catch him. "I'm having a second thought," he confessed.

"Maybe if you did Sherlock and me," Jenny suggested, "and not Sammy. Then he could scamper to intercept—" She paused, realizing that the cat was about to take off. "To do something. And haul us along by a rope. Because we wouldn't weigh much. That should be pretty fast."

"Brilliant!" Dug cried airily. "If you weren't a child, I'd kiss you!"

"I'm only a year younger than you," she said, looking hurt.

Dug realized that the matter of age could be as sensitive to an elf as to a human. Jenny looked little, because she was an elf, but she wasn't. She was a child by game definition only. "Okay, I'll kiss you," he said.

He pulled himself from the tree as the wind died down, and walked over to her. He leaned down to kiss her. But his face passed right through hers. *I wish there were a boy of my kind here.* Then he drew back again, tried again, and did it right, just barely brushing her lips with his own, so that they didn't overlap.

Then he wondered why he should have been wishing for a boy of his kind here. There had been a romantic implication. That was hardly his idea of romance! In any event, there were other human beings in Xanth.

Oh—that had been Jenny's thought, not his own. He had picked it up when his brain overlapped hers. She was an elf of a different fantasy world, unlike the elves of Xanth. Her prospects for romance here were nil, unless she wanted to cross species boundaries. That sort of thing seemed to be more common in Xanth than in Mundania, but still, it was only natural to want the company of her own kind.

Xanth seemed like a land of puns and silliness, but under the surface there were the same real concerns that the people he knew back home felt. This was a solid reminder.

But he couldn't stop now to think through the philosophical ramifications. He had to move swiftly to intercept Kim, so he could warn her of the danger she was in.

"Let me change you," he said to Jenny, who had not seemed to notice his pause for thought. Perhaps she had paused for her own thoughts. "Then I'll change Sherlock, and we'll be on our way."

He focused on her, and she slowly turned diffuse. He tested by touching her hand every so often; when her hand seemed solid to him, he knew she was as diffuse as he was. "Don't let the wind get you," he warned her.

Then he addressed Sherlock. Soon the black man was as smoky as the other two.

Belatedly Dug remembered something. "We should have made a bag, or net, or something to hold us, so Sammy can haul us. A solid framework, not a phased-out one, so—"

Sherlock pointed to his tangle of vines. He had started work on that even before Jenny made the suggestion, anticipating the need. Because the vines were small, the net was light; it would be possible for the cat to pull it.

But there was a problem. They were too diffuse to handle the vines. Their hands passed through the vines without contact.

Dug pondered. "I wonder just how versatile this talent of Threnody's is?" he asked. "If I can make just our hands more solid, or part of the vine smoky—"

The second idea seemed better. He concentrated on the tail end of the net, making that smoky. He tested it by picking up the end, while his hands passed through the lead harness. Then he worked his way forward, changing it partway. It was possible!

They put their legs through holes in the pattern, and strung it around themselves. It spread out enough so that all three of them could hang on without crowding.

Then Dug made the harness end smoky, and Jenny called Sammy, and Dug put the harness on the cat. Once it was secure, he made it solid again, so that Sammy would not simply walk through it when he got going. But the vines connecting to the rest of them were phased out, making them almost weightless. As long as the phasing was in parts of the same vines, they were tight; it was when one thing was phased out and another wasn't that they passed through each other.

"I think we're ready," Dug said.

Jenny spoke. "Sammy, go find Kim."

The cat took off. The net followed, hauling them abruptly forward. They were on their way.

Their separation ended. They were jammed together. The world might seem insubstantial, but they were fully solid to each other. Dug lifted his arms to try to hold the other two off, but it was impossible. "Okay, so we travel together," he said, putting his arms around Jenny Elf, who was right in front of him. Sherlock, beside them both, put his arms around both of them. Now they made a compact, stable mass.

Sammy, under no restraints, chose his own route. He scampered between two close-growing trees. The three of them passed through the trees. He squeezed under a root. They went through it. He found a cat-sized tunnel through a mass of thorns. They went through every thorn. But without getting stuck.

There was indeed a dragon. The thing loomed up, belching clouds of smoke. Sammy zipped under its tail. The dragon whipped around, trying to catch the cat, but was too slow. Instead its talons swiped through the netful of people, without effect. But Dug flinched and Jenny stifled a scream. The dragon, frustrated, blew out a hot blast of turbulent smoke. It surrounded them, making the world dark, but didn't make them choke. In a moment they were out of it, unscathed.

"I could get to like this kind of traveling," Dug said, making an effort at bravado.

Jenny nodded. She was looking a bit motion-sick. Sherlock had done the sensible thing: his eyes were closed. Dug, seeing that, closed his own. Then he just seemed to be floating through faintly rushing water.

As they moved along, Dug thought of something. "Threnody's talent—that was making herself smoky," he said. "But I was not only doing that, I was making other people and things smoky. Can demons do that?"

"I don't think so," Jenny said, surprised.

Dug decided not to question this further, because his conclusion might turn out to be dangerous to their progress. Possibly he had inadvertently wiggled through a small hole in the game program.

After a time they stopped. Dug opened his eyes. They were on a trail—and two centaurs were bearing down on them at a gallop. What now?

"I see Kim!" Jenny cried. "And Nada!"

Now Dug saw. They were riding the centaurs. He tried to untangle himself from Sherlock, Jenny, and the net, so he could signal them to stop and talk.

Kim was looking one way, Nada the other. Nada saw them; Dug saw the shock of recognition in her eyes. She turned her face away, saying something. The two centaurs galloped faster.

The cat, perhaps concerned about getting trampled, bolted into the brush. The centaurs galloped on past, their hooves throwing up divots of dirt. "Wait!" Dug cried. "I have to talk to you!"

It was too late. The centaurs were already well along the path, and nobody was looking back.

"She's False, all right," Dug said. "She saw us—and made them speed up, so they'd be by before Kim saw us. We'll never catch them now."

"But we know where they're going," Jenny said. "The Good Magician's castle."

"But the cat's tired," Sherlock said. "Going to be hard to catch them now."

Dug looked at him. "Your muteness has worn off! The magic's fading."

"And that means that your ability to diffuse us is about to fade, too," Sherlock said. "Better make us solid while you still can, or we'll be stuck in ghost form."

"Good point!" Dug got to work changing them back to solidity. But he did so with a heavy heart. They were going to have to walk to the Good Magician's castle, and chances were that by the time they got there, Kim and Nada would be gone. And with Nada warned what he was up to, she was likely to betray Kim before he could catch her.

"I'm afraid there's going to be trouble," Dug said heavily. Jenny and Sherlock nodded agreement.

16
GOURD

K im was glad to be traveling so rapidly, after the slow slogging she had done before. But much as she liked horses, and therefore also centaurs, she would be glad when this ride was done. She didn't have the hang of it; she kept bouncing, and her thighs were getting sore. So she was annoyed when the two centaurs accelerated. "What's the matter?" she asked.

"Nada saw something, and warned us to get past it swiftly," the centaur replied, turning his head. "It looked like a tangle of bodies."

Kim didn't know what that could have been, but was glad not to have encountered it. Still, she would rather have made the decision herself. Nada was maybe just a little bit pushy, forgetting that Kim was the Player. Maybe it came of being a princess. Kim had agreed to exchange Companions only because Dug had wanted to; she really had preferred Jenny Elf. "Well, I guess we're past it now," she said. "So let's slow down again, okay?"

They slowed, and her thighs took less of a pounding. That was a relief. She was able to focus on her own thoughts again. She was making good progress toward her game objective. But she wished she could have associated longer with Dug, in the foolish hope that maybe, by some ill chance, she might have made a small impression on him. She knew he was probably as shallow as the average boy was at that age, and that she shouldn't take much note of the fact that he was handsome. But there it was. If she saw him again, she would try to arrange to stay together longer. Somehow. For what little it might be worth. Maybe another snowstorm would come, and they'd be jammed together again in a tent. Maybe he'd become aware of her, as Cyrus and Merci had become aware of each other. Maybe they would kiss before they parted.

Meanwhile, it was nice having Bubbles for company. She was holding the dog before her, which was sometimes tricky, because Bubbles weighed more than half as much as Kim. The dog could not have enjoyed the bumping any more than Kim did, but she did not complain. In fact, Bubbles was a very quiet, polite dog, undemonstrative. But Kim was learning to read her little signs, the angle of her half-floppy ears, the curl of her tail, her general manner, and the dog's attitude was coming through with increasing clarity. Bubbles just wanted to be with Kim, and to help her in whatever she was doing. Nothing else. It was straightforward, and easy enough to accept.

At one point a shadow crossed the foliage, moving toward them. In a moment Kim saw a small flying dragon. It cocked its head, eying them. Both centaurs unslung their bows and whipped arrows from their quivers, nocking them and orienting on the dragon in smooth, continuous, synchronous motions. The dragon veered away, losing interest. The two arrows went back into their quivers and the two bows were slung back across the centaurs' shoulders, again together. Nobody much, it seemed, fooled with a pair of male centaurs, even if it wasn't an enchanted path.

Kim wondered whether it was mostly bluff. But later her centaur fetched his bow again, nocked his arrow, and loosed it without pause. It transfixed a small ugly creature resembling a lizard with wings. The other centaur never drew an arrow, being unconcerned.

"But that little thing couldn't have hurt us," Kim protested.

"It is a basilisk," the centaur explained. "It was about to look at us."

Kim felt a chill. A basilisk. A winged lizard whose gaze could kill. One swift arrow had stopped it—and the other centaur had been so confident of his companion's marksmanship that he hadn't bothered to react.

No, there was no bluffing in centaurs. They were simply competent, and secure in that knowledge.

In due course the centaurs slowed. "This is the Good Magician's castle," her mount said. "You will have to undertake three challenges to enter it, after which the Good Magician will speak with you. Decent fortune."

"Thanks," she said as she slid to the ground. Centaurs weren't much for overstatement.

Nada dismounted with a certain princessly flair. Then the centaurs were off, not even resting. They had done their job, and were heading home, taking no note of fatigue.

Kim and Nada and Bubbles stood and gazed at the castle. It had a moat, and there was a water monster in it, but the creature was yawning; it didn't expect them to be so foolish as to try to swim across. The drawbridge was down, so that they could cross that way.

Except that there was a giant plum before the bridge, and the fruit had split apart to reveal its huge pit, and the pit had opened, and in the pit was a small bull. The bull looked aggressive. They could not reach the bridge without crossing through the region of the pit, and the bull made it evident that it was inclined to fold, spindle, or mutilate anyone who tried that.

"That's a bull pit," Kim said, catching on to a possible pun. Then she did a double take. "Or a pit bull. Or maybe a bully pulpit. Or bull pen. Or something. I'm getting myself confused. But that's what we have to get past."

"I can assume large serpent form and hiss it off," Nada suggested.

"I don't think that's fair, when it's a challenge, as it obviously is," Kim said. "I have to figure out a way to handle it myself." That was true, but it wasn't the whole story. Kim didn't want to accept Nada's help on it; she wanted to prevail by herself.

"As you wish," Nada said, shrugging.

Kim looked around. There was always a way, both in the game and in the normal castle challenges. But all she saw was what looked like a big pillbox. It was probably a military one, because on the side was written FIGHT.

Bubbles walked over to sniff the box. She was mildly curious about everything, with her curiosity being satisfied by a sniff. But this did show one thing: the box wasn't dangerous. Kim followed, lifted the lid, and peered in. There were hundreds of pills, bouncing frantically around. What did this mean?

After a moment she realized that the pills were fighting. Each one was trying to bash any other it encountered, perhaps trying to crack it and pulverize it. That must be why the box said FIGHT on the outside: it was full of fighting pills. But how did this relate to what she had to accomplish?

Well, maybe she could find out. She reached in and swooped out a fighting pill.

The thing was a handful! It banged back and forth in her hand, and expanded in size if not in ferocity. It didn't hurt her, because as it grew it became softer. She hung on, first to its body, then to an end, and finally to a corner as it got to be almost as big as the dog. It was no longer a pill, it was a pillow! And it was still fighting, buffeting her arm, the side of the pillbox, and anything else it could reach. What a scrapper! She didn't dare let it go, because then it would surely be whamming her worse.

Something percolated through her mind. Fighting pillow. Fighting pills. Pillow fight. Pill fight.

The familiar light flashed above her head. She could indeed use these pills.

She swooped her free hand into the pillbox and caught as many fighting pills as she could. It was a struggle to hang on to them. She ran across to the pit bull. "Take this!" she cried, throwing the fighting pillow at him. "And this!" She threw the expanding handful of fighting pills.

The big pillow and small pillows attacked the pit bull with enthusiasm. Wham, wham, wham, WHAM! They needed no anchor; they were able to do their whamming without support. The bull, confused, tried to fight back. He managed to gore the big pillow. Feathers started flying out, adding confusion to the scene. But as the large pillow lost its stuffing, the smaller ones grew to size, their buffeting becoming harder as they did. The bull was entirely distracted.

"Let's go!" Kim cried. She and Bubbles and Nada ran across the plum pit region, and the pit bull didn't even notice them. They left the action behind and got on the drawbridge.

And stopped. For there in the middle of the bridge was a stool, and on the stool perched a pigeon. The stool was covered with bird droppings. In fact, it *was* a bird dropping—an amalgamation of droppings that had mounded into that shape. It stank.

As soon as the pigeon saw them, it flew up above the bridge and dropped another dropping. And another. In fact, droppings fairly rained down around the stool. "Nyaa, nyaa!" it squawked. "I'll bomb you with stools, and your smell will make the castle shut you out. You can't get by me." It dropped another dropping, in the shape of a small stool.

"I can't pass under that dirty bird," Nada said, wrinkling her nose. "It wouldn't be princessly. It thinks it's a harpy." Bubbles, though no princess, seemed no more eager.

"A stool pigeon!" Kim exclaimed, disgusted. She didn't want to get soiled either.

So what was the cleanest way to get past this obnoxious creature? She looked around, but saw nothing but dung on the bridge. She looked out across the moat, but there was only the moat monster, looking on with amusement. She looked back the way they had come, but saw only the pit bull, still fighting pillows. One pillow, instead of whamming the bull, seemed to be trying to press the bull down, without much effect.

A pillow pressing down. A down pillow.

Kim ran back, grabbed the pillow, and zipped away before the bull could round on her. She threw the pillow at the pigeon.

Sure enough, the pillow landed on the bird and held it down on the giant stool. The pigeon couldn't fly up to bomb them. "Yuck!" the stooled pigeon squawked.

They picked their way through the mess and to the far side of the moat. But the end of the bridge was blocked by a pile of melons. One large melon was bossing the others. "Honey, move over here," she said, and the addressed melon moved over, displacing the other melons, which rolled around before settling down. "Honey, get up on the bridge." The other melon rolled up on the bridge.

Kim stood and watched, trying to fathom the pun. Those looked like a particular type of melon—

"Honeydew!" Kim exclaimed. "Telling the others what to do. And they're so busy doing it that we can't get by the pile of them."

Now she knew the problem. But what was the solution?

Kim looked around again, but this time saw nothing to help. In fact, there was no longer a retreat across the bridge, because the pigeon had succeeded in pecking the down pillow apart, and the down was dropping into the moat. The pit bull had succeeded in goring the remaining pillows, and they too were expiring. So whatever there was that could help, had to be right here.

Bubbles was cautiously sniffing the nearest melons. That didn't necessarily mean anything, but sometimes Kim got notions from watching what the dog did. Could there be anything here for her?

She peered at the constantly shifting pile of melons. They were of different types. Buried almost out of sight was one whose name she couldn't quite remember. But it was suggestive. So she cudgeled her brain and forced it out: cantaloupe. It was a ripe cantaloupe.

And that, perhaps, was her answer. If she could manage to play it right. It was an excruciating pun, but of course she would never have entered this game if she had wanted to avoid that sort of thing.

"Honeydew, there's a cantaloupe in your pile," she said boldly.

The honeydew paused in her stream of directives. "Yes, I know. I'm trying to get rid of it, so I can elope with my honey."

"You think it means can't elope," Kim said. "But it doesn't. It means an incantation of elopement. It's In the Pile, a Cantation of Elope. It's been trying to help you all this time, and you've been refusing to listen."

The honeydew was speechless for a moment. But she recovered quickly. "Then let's elope!" she cried. "Honey, do it now!" And she rolled away from the bridge and around the castle. All the other melons followed her.

"That may be quite a ceremony," Kim murmured appreciatively. "You might say a melon-choly occasion."

Now the way was open. Kim had navigated the last of the three punny challenges. She marched ahead and up to the main gate of the castle.

The door was closed. She lifted a knuckle and knocked.

In a moment the door opened. There stood a pretty young woman of about eighteen, whose hair matched her brown shoes and whose eyes matched her pink dress. Kim was a bit startled by the eyes. "May I help you?" the girl asked softly.

"Um, yes. I'm Kim. I'm playing the game, and I've come to see the Good Magician Humfrey, so I can find out where to find the prize."

"Of course," the girl said, smiling. "Is anyone with you?"

Kim was slightly annoyed. "Of course. Can't you see them?"

"No." The girl looked apologetic. "I'm sorry; I should have told you. I am Wira, the Good Magician's son Hugo's girlfriend. I am blind."

Suddenly Kim felt about two feet high. She had made a pushy, smart re-mark about sight! She felt herself blushing. "I, uh, they're, uh, Nada Naga, who is my Companion, and Bubbles, my dog."

"Oh, a real dog?" Wira asked. "We don't see many of those here. Our cas-tle dog Canis Major is away right now. May I pet her?"

"I, uh, she doesn't like strangers much," Kim said, feeling worse.

But Bubbles was already stepping forward, wagging her tail. Wira stooped to pet her on the head, and the dog accepted the pet.

Kim was amazed. This was only the second time she had seen Bubbles take to a stranger. "You must have a way with animals," she said.

"It's my talent," Wira said. "I am sensitive to things, and can tell how they are. Animals like me." She straightened up. "But I must not delay you. I will take you to Ivy."

"Princess Ivy? I'd love to meet her. But my business is with the Good Ma-gician."

"Ivy has taken over his appointment book," Wira explained. "It is too hard for the several wives to keep track, since they're always in and out. Ivy will know when he is scheduled to see you."

Oh. Once again Kim had embarrassed herself with an ignorant remark. She shut her mouth and followed Wira, and Bubbles and Nada followed her.

They came to a chamber with a desk and book. There was a young woman, marking items with a pencil. She looked up. "Yes?"

"You're Princess Ivy!" Kim exclaimed, forgetting herself again. "What are you doing as a clerk?"

Ivy smiled. "You must be a Player."

"She is," Nada said from behind her. "Hello, Ivy."

"Nada Naga!" Ivy exclaimed, delighted. She jumped up with unprincessly haste and went to embrace Nada. "I haven't seen you in months!"

"I'm serving my time for sipping red whine in the gourd realm," Nada explained. "This is Kim, the Player I am Companioning."

"She needs to see the Good Magician," Wira added.

"Oh, of course. Let me see." Ivy went back to the book. "Yes, that's an hour from now. That will give you time to clean up and have a bite to eat."

"I'll take them to MareAnn," Wira said.

"MareAnn?" Kim asked.

"She's the Good Magician's Wife of the Month," Wira explained as she set off down the hall without hesitation. She evidently knew her way around the castle, so was not inhibited by her lack of sight. "She was his first love, but his fifth and a halfth wife, because she wouldn't marry him early. She can summon equines."

"Oh. Yes," Kim said, remembering. She had read about that, just as she had read about Wira. Now she remembered that Wira had been put to sleep by her family, because she wasn't much use to them. Fortunately she had met the Good Magician's family in the dream realm, and they had rescued her. Somehow what she had read didn't register readily here in real-seeming life. The people she was meeting were far more impressive than those she remembered from books.

MareAnn was in the kitchen, baking animal cookies in the shape of horses. Cookies might grow on plants by the banks of the With-A-Cookee River, but elsewhere it seemed easier just to bake them instead of making the long trip to fetch them from the river. MareAnn was a pleasant older woman who seemed not at all out of the ordinary. Yet Kim had a vision of her as she was in her youth, with lovely brown hair and eyes matching the manes and tails of the unicorns she could summon then, with marvelously formed legs because of all the equine-back riding she did. She had met and loved Humfrey when they both were in their teens, in fact when they were even younger than Kim was now, sixteen. But MareAnn had been determinedly innocent, so the unicorns wouldn't leave her, and refused to marry Humfrey though she loved him. It had been such sweet sorrow. Kim saw her riding, her hair flung out behind, a tear on her cheek, as she left Humfrey to be King of Xanth. Humfrey had married a demoness instead, but it was always MareAnn he loved.

Kim snapped out of it, aware that others were looking at her. "Oh—I guess I was daydreaming," she said, embarrassed again.

"Of course," MareAnn said. "Mare Imbri is here. She brought you a daydream. She tells me she also brought you the dream of the disposal bubbles."

Kim almost thought she saw the outline of a small black mare behind the woman. "Yes. It was the strangest thing, turning real at the end. That's how I got Bubbles, my dog." She petted Bubbles. "Just now she showed me how it was when you were young. You were so beautiful and nice!" Then she realized that she had committed yet another gaffe. "I mean, not that you aren't now—"

"My dear, I am happier now than I was then," MareAnn said. "Even though I can no longer summon unicorns. The other equines still do come to me, though." She petted Mare Imbri, who perked her ears forward. The horse *was* there, though invisible.

Then Mare Imbri glanced elsewhere, and abruptly bolted through the wall and away. Someone else had a daydream coming. Kim felt a twinge of envy for that person.

There was a garden behind the castle with toiletrees that helped them get cleaned up and back in order. They returned to find the cookies on the table, along with a coiled chain. "What's this?" Kim asked doubtfully.

"A food chain, of course," MareAnn said. "A ghost horse brought it in. Just break off any link you want."

She should have known. She dimly remembered that ghost horses wore chains wrapped around their bodies, which they could rattle to distract and frighten living folk. It hadn't occurred to her that such chains might be edible.

They broke off links and chewed on them, and the food was good. Each link was a different texture and flavor. Some were like vegetables, some like breads, and some like meat. As a general rule, the vegetables were at the lower end of the chain, and the meats at the upper end. Kim broke off a link at the very top and gave it to Bubbles, who found it quite intriguing.

After the meal it was time for the appointment with the Good Magician. Wira showed them the way up the winding stone stairs to the gloomy cubbyhole the Magician called his own. Kim realized that it made sense for the blind girl to do this, because the lack of light did not concern her. She could find the Good Magician in complete darkness.

And there he was, almost hidden behind a monstrous tome. "What do you want?" he demanded grumpily, evidently irritated about being disturbed.

"This is Kim, the game Player, Father Humfrey," Wira said. "She has an appointment."

"Oh." He glanced at Wira and the barest hint of a flicker of the corner of a smile brushed by his glum mouth. Kim realized that he really liked the girl, though he labored gnomefully not to show it.

"I have a Question," Kim said. "But I don't think I can pay for it. I mean, you require a year's service for an Answer, but I'm Mundane, and can't stay in Xanth that long."

"It is part of your Companion's service," Humfrey said. "It has been factored in. Ask and be done with it."

Just like that! But suddenly Kim realized that this too was a challenge. The obvious question was where the game prize was to be found. But she had lost much of her interest in that, about the time she met Dug. Now she wished she could ask about something that didn't concern the game. But of course that was out of bounds.

Or was it? She didn't *have* to go for the win, did she? Why not play the game her way, and if she lost, at least she had expressed herself. She pondered a good two-thirds of a moment, then asked: "How can I get what I most desire?"

Humfrey turned the pages of his tome. "D," he muttered as he did so. "Demagogue, demon, depraved, descent, desire. Ardent, bestial, confused, decayed, foolish . . . most. Ape, baboon, canary . . . human. Player, game. Female. Young. Kim." His forehead added a wrinkle. "Now, that is interesting." He glanced up at Kim. "Your greatest desire changed recently."

That was one comprehensive reference tome! "I suppose it did, sir," she confessed meekly.

"No matter. Go to the realm of the gourd. You will find it there."

Bubbles wagged her tail.

"The gourd?" Kim asked somewhat blankly.

"That is the realm of dreams, accessible by a certain variety of gourd," Nada said. "I can find one for you."

Kim had known that. Her blankness was because she could not see how the realm of dreams could possibly help her do anything but dream, when what she wanted was a better reality. *The Book of Answers* must have slipped a cog, or whatever it did. Maybe that was because this was a computer game, and only so much could be programmed into it. The game would naturally assume that her most ardent desire was for the game prize. It was foolish to expect the game to know or care anything about her real life or feelings.

"Thank you, sir," she said, trying not to show her disappointment. "I will visit the realm of the gourd."

Humfrey's nose was already buried in the tome. He had tuned her out.

As they went back down the stone steps, Wira spoke. "The Good Magician's Answers may seem cryptic or unsatisfactory at first, but they are always correct. I am sure your greatest desire will be found in the realm of dreams. Mine was."

"Thank you," Kim said. But her doubt remained.

"Magician Grey Murphy brought in three fresh gourds yesterday," Wira said. "We have them in the guest room."

"You knew yesterday that someone would need gourds?" Kim asked. She was not impressed so much as resigned. Obviously the Good Magician had a standard Answer lined up for game Players, and that was to direct them to the next stage of the game. Kim had now explored much of Xanth, except for the gourd. It made sense that she explore that too. How could the game know that though her body would continue going through the motions of the quest, her heart had been foolishly diverted? Only an idiot would go to Xanth for anything but laughs. Unfortunately she was that idiot.

Wira showed them to the guest room. Sure enough, there were three gourds lying on mattresses. "You must hold hands as you look into the gourds," Wira explained. "Otherwise you will not find yourselves in the same region."

"How did you get into the gourd world, being blind?" Kim asked.

"There are other ways. When I was put to sleep, I was in a coffin, and its magic let my soul drift from my body and join the souls of the others of that realm."

So when Wira was put to sleep, it had been a lot like dying. Kim could think of similar cases in Mundania.

She looked at Nada. "You really don't have to join us in this," she said. "I know what the dream world is like."

"I insist," Nada said with a peculiar expression. Had Kim not been distracted by her own private concerns, she might have wondered what was on the Naga princess' mind.

They lay down on the mattresses and held hands. Kim was in the middle; her left hand held Nada's right, and her right hand held Bubbles' left forepaw. Then Wira turned Kim's gourd around so that the peephole was toward her. Though she was blind, she seemed to know exactly what she was doing. Kim realized that it made sense to have Wira here, because it was impossible for her to be accidentally caught by the gourd.

Kim looked into the peephole—and abruptly found herself standing in a gloomy field near an even gloomier cemetery. Oh, no! This must be the section of the dream realm reserved for the walking skeletons. She could handle it, but she would have preferred to be in a candy garden or the pasture of the night mares.

In a moment minus an instant Bubbles appeared beside her. "Oh, Bubbles!" Kim cried gladly. "I never thought to ask whether you wanted to come here. But I'm glad you're with me." She petted the dog, who licked her hand.

Then Nada Naga appeared. "Oh, the graveyard shift," she said. "That is not my favorite."

"Mine neither," Kim agreed. "But maybe we don't have to deal with the skeletons. This is just our starting point. The prize may be somewhere else."

"Defended by a challenge," Nada agreed. "The most rigorous one." There was something about the way she said it that made Kim a trace uneasy, but she couldn't fathom why. Nada had been a proper Companion throughout, though somewhat reserved. That was to be expected of a princess.

"Well, then, let's look elsewhere," Kim said. It seemed to her that the Good Magician's Answer, all-purpose as it might be, was not a great help, because she knew that the realm of dreams was as big in its fashion as all the rest of Xanth. The prize could be anywhere at all. But of course this was the game, so there would surely be a hint for her to pick up on.

But as they started to walk away from the cemetery, a skeleton spied them. "Hi-yo!" it called, hailing them. "Are you looking for something?"

Kim realized that if her route lay through the cemetery, the game would not let her avoid it. So she turned back with resignation. "I am a Mundane playing the game. I am looking for the prize."

The skeleton seemed somewhat taken aback. Its general configuration indicated that it was male. "Oh, I had understood you sought what you most desired," he said.

Kim was startled. "That is what I asked for," she admitted. "But how did you know that?"

"Oops, I slipped," he said. "I was not supposed to tell you what I knew, only to guide you to the challenge. I am painfully sorry."

The light flashed over Kim's head. "You are Marrow Bones!" she exclaimed.

The skeleton was chagrined. "How did you know that?"

Kim had to smile. "I saw you as one of the prospective Companions, and I suspect you folk have to work at other chores if you're not chosen. So you must be working here, in your bailiwick, as it were."

"You are correct, of course," he agreed. "But I was supposed to assume another identity for the role. I hope you will excuse this irregularity."

"I am happy to," Kim said, feeling better. "I feel as if I know you, having read about you before."

"That is nice," Marrow said uncertainly. "I do know Princess Nada Naga, of course, ever since we met when she was a child of eight."

"I was actually fourteen," Nada said. "I had to pretend to be eight. Prince Dolph was really disappointed when he found out."

"I think it worked out for the best," Marrow said. "Electra seems a better match for him, no offense."

"No offense at all," Nada agreed. "I never was able to relate very well to younger men."

The skeleton turned to the dog. "But I do not believe I know this one."

"This is Bubbles," Kim said. "She's my dog." But as she spoke, she felt a wash of regret. She really liked the dog, and it was going to hurt to have to leave her behind when she finished the game and returned to Mundania. She realized that the dog was just another game character who would revert to her normal life once this chore was done. Still, she wished it could be otherwise. She trusted Bubbles in a way she did not quite trust Nada.

"Well, I'm afraid our show will not be very effective, since you recognized me," Marrow said. "It is supposed to be a challenge of fear, but fear does not work well when the basis of it is known. I am not quite sure what to do."

"No problem," Kim said. "I'm not eager to rush on with it. Let's sit and chat for a while first."

"But this is not game protocol," Nada protested.

"To bleep with protocol," Kim said. "If I can't have my heart's desire, I might as well enjoy the adventure." She plumped down on the nearest gravestone. Bubbles lay down by her feet. "Marrow, just how did your kind come about? I'm sure you did not evolve as skeletons from the outset."

Marrow sat on another gravestone. "It is a somewhat degenerative story. I am not sure you would relish it."

"Try me and see." Kim was enjoying the prospect of messing up the all-knowing game a bit. Maybe she would even ferret out a hole in the program.

"Very well. Long ago, before the Night Stallion tamed the magic of the gourd realm, human beings who looked through the peepholes of the hypno-gourds would be trapped, not knowing the secret of breaking the spell, which is simply to have a friend break the contact of the eye with the peephole. Thus many of them were forever trapped here. They would remain alive in the dream realm, no matter how wasted their physical bodies became, so long as their eye socket oriented on the peephole. But their dream bodies would waste away, re-flecting the condition of their physical bodies. So in time the gourd realm be-came inhabited by zombielike figures, and finally by walking skeletons. Each was horrified by his or her appearance, and the appearance of others. I have to say that they were somewhat enamored of their flesh, especially those portions of it that distinguished their male and female attributes. That was not the worst of it; the gourds are living vegetables, and when a particular gourd sprouted and dissolved, the person trapped by it would be released. At this state, however, this meant death. So the folk within the gourd faded out at that point. This was all they had to look forward to: captivity, emaciation, skeletonization, and finally disappearance.

"But one day a male skeleton and a female skeleton held a dialogue, and fell in love despite their grotesque appearances. Their minds were compatible, and it was their minds they loved. But when they came to love each other, they found each other's body less repulsive. They experimented, and discovered the skeleton key, and made a skeleton child. It was not easy, because they had to borrow bones from their own bodies, and this made it harder for them to function. Nevertheless, their accomplishment was phenomenal, because for the first time they were able to reproduce their kind—as animated skeletons. They had found love and familyhood within the gourd. They hastened to tell other skeletons of this, and others managed to make their own offspring. They did not tell the little skels that they would soon fade out of existence; that knowledge was too cruel. Instead they took pleasure in the innocence of the little ones, making a facsimile of heaven within hell. They adapted their histories to the gourd setting, and developed new myths to replace the old. They tried to explain everything in terms of the dream reality, so as to spare their children knowledge of the terrible truth.

"But they had accomplished more than they knew. Two things happened. First, the little skels did not fade out when their parents did; they did not derive from Xanth or fleshly creatures, and so did not cease to exist when gourds rotted. For the gourds are merely apertures; they convey the minds of their captives to the dream realm, much as an eye conveys the image to the mind. The folk of the dream realm are not in the gourds themselves any more than the images are stored within the eyeballs. So a new species had been created within the dream realm. Second, the little skels grew. They did not do it by eating, for they lacked digestive systems and neither imbibed nor excreted, if you will excuse the vulgar terms. Instead they found stray bones scattered around and added them to themselves, becoming larger. When the surviving parents realized this, they were generous with their own bones, knowing that these bones would only be lost when their possessors faded out. So there was suddenly a large supply, and the skels prospered and grew more rapidly. In time there came the first generation of dream realm adults: folk who had never known the outer realm, and to whom it was merely a repulsive alternate world peopled by flesh-clad parodies of skels. They became proud of their own heritage, and their own offspring believed that this was the way it had always been. They were no longer limited to human skeletons; there were now assorted animal skels, existing the same way. All of us learned how to disassemble and reassemble our bones, so as to form strings of them or other shapes. This was convenient when we needed to navigate high cliffs or other hazards. We came to regard ourselves as the most versatile of creatures, with some justice.

"Then the Night Stallion came, and organized the dream realm, and sent out the night mares with dreams crafted to punish those sleeping folk who deserved it. It turned out to be a considerable market; it was amazing how many living folk had guilty consciences which earned them bad dreams. As the dream business prospered, fancier dreams were crafted, and the call went out for specialists to craft them. Some gourd folk became carpenters, and some artists, and some sculptors, making the settings and scenery. Some became organizers and directors, coordinating the efforts of others. Some became writers, scripting the scenes. And some became actors in the scenes. The realm of the gourd had assumed meaning."

Marrow Bones paused. He shook his skull. "So it remains, for most of my kind. But accidents of fate and magic caused me to get lost within the gourd, until I was rescued by Esk Ogre from the dread outer realm. I discovered that the fleshly folk, though repulsive, were not as horrible as we had believed, and in time I came to accept them as they were, flesh and all. In fact, I came to prefer existence outside of the gourd; it was a different and often fascinating world. Later Grace'l Ossein was expelled from the gourd, because she had interfered with a bad dream she believed was wrong, and I came to know her, and she came to know this realm. Now we are both satisfied to live externally, and we have two offspring, Picka Bone and Joy'nt Bone, in whom we delight. They are content to exist in this realm, too."

"That's fascinating," Kim said. "But I understand that you skeletons don't have souls. How can you exist out here without them?"

"This is a problem," Marrow agreed. "We are trying to acquire souls for ourselves and our children, but souls do not grow on trees." He tilted his head, indicating that this was to be considered a humorous remark. "Supposedly it is possible for mortal folk to share their souls, giving half away, and they then regenerate. But so far we have found none willing to do this. We fear that in time those of us who exist in the outer realm will fade, much as our distant human ancestors did within the gourd." He shrugged, and his bones rattled. "However, this is by no means your concern. You must try to win your game, and I must try to prevent you from doing this, abiding by the rules of the game."

"Yes, I suppose that is true," Kim said. "I wish there were a better way." She sighed. "Well, let's get on with it. What's next?"

17
ASS

Dug stared down the road. He knew there was no chance to catch Kim now; the centaurs were simply too fast. But he was not about to give up. Guilt drove him on. "We'll just have to walk toward the Good Magician's castle, and hope to catch her before anything happens," he said.

"Nada's really a nice person," Jenny said. "I'm sure she's very unhappy about having to be False."

"Nevertheless, she is now the enemy," Dug said. "What I want to do is catch up to Kim, tell her the danger, and trade back. Then you can help Kim win her prize, and I'll—well, I don't know what I'll do, but at least I won't feel like such a heel."

"But you didn't know about Nada when you traded," Jenny said. "It isn't your fault she's False."

"Doesn't matter. It's not right to let Kim get washed out, when it was supposed to be me. I feel guilty."

"I like your attitude," Sherlock said.

"So do I," Jenny said.

"It's just a routine attitude everyone should have. What I need now is to find the fastest way to the castle. Which I guess is simply hotfooting it south."

Dug's pack was sitting a bit uncomfortably, after the wild ride in smoky condition. He took it off, and discovered to his surprise that it was a pretty golden color. It wasn't gold, just gold-colored as if it had been painted. "Look at this," he said, surprised.

"It changed color!" Jenny said. "It's pretty."

"But how did it happen?" Dug asked. "I was wearing it, so I didn't see it happen. Did either of you?"

They both shook their heads no. It was a minor mystery. However, Dug didn't trust mysteries. Not in this treacherous game. Little things could signal important developments.

He opened the pack and took out a somewhat squished sandwich—and it too was painted gold. Yet he was sure it hadn't been, a moment ago. He touched a spare shirt—and saw it change color. "I'm doing it!" he exclaimed. "Everything I touch turns to gold!"

"Uh-oh," Sherlock said. "I heard about King Midas. That's one mean curse."

"But the stuff isn't solid gold," Dug said. "Just gold-plated. See, this shirt's still flexible, it's just changed color. And the sandwich's still soft; the wrapper's golden, is all."

"It still does seem like a curse," Jenny said. "Maybe you shouldn't touch anyone else until you know how to stop it."

"I'd love to stop it," Dug said. He concentrated on not changing color, and touched another item in the pack. But it turned golden anyway. He walked to the side of the path and touched the leaf of a tree. It too turned golden.

He realized that this could not be random. He had not done anything special in the last few minutes, so didn't think he had invoked any magic. He hadn't picked up a stink horn, for example. So why should this spell be on him?

He stared at the golden pack. Gold-plated pack, actually. It had been gilded. It was gilt.

Gilt. That sounded like guilt. And one thing he was feeling now was guilt. He had said so.

He groaned. "I'm being victimized by a pun," he said. "Gilt by association."

"But we don't feel guilty," Jenny said.

"Gilt. G I L T. If you associate with me, and I touch you, you'll be gilded. Gold-colored. Gilt. Gilty. Someone's made it literal."

"Then you should be able to stop it," Jenny said.

"Maybe now I can." Dug stood and faced the forest. "I deny any gilt by association," he declaimed. Then he touched another item in his pack. It did not change. "Ha. I neutralized the pun."

"Curses," someone muttered. "Foiled again."

The three of them passed a glance around. None of them had spoken.

There was a swirl of air, like a small whirlwind. It became smoky, then solid, taking the shape of a well-proportioned woman, scantily clad.

"Metria!" Jenny exclaimed. "What are you doing here?"

Dug remembered that there had been a lady demon among the choices available for Companion. This would be her.

"Two things," the demoness said. "I'm investigating your chaos."

"My what?" Dug asked.

"Confusion, disorder, misapprehension, ferment, jumble litter—"

"Foul-up?" Dug asked.

"Whatever," she agreed crossly. "What are you doing with the wrong Companion?"

"We traded," Dug said. "I decided that Jenny Elf was better for me than Nada Naga."

"But the challenges were pitched for Nada!"

Dug wondered whether that was good or bad. "You mean that she could have helped me through better—or that she couldn't?"

"Oh, I don't know. Just that Grossclout had it figured one way, and you were playing it another. Using the cat to find your way through. Zilch only knows how the other player's been doing with the serpent woman."

"So is there a rule against it?" Dug asked.

"Not exactly. Nobody thought anybody'd be fool enough to pull a stunt like that."

"So what's the problem?"

The demoness fidgeted. "It's just not steak."

"Not what?"

"Encounter, converge, intersect, unite, connect, join—"

"Meet?" Dug could handle puns when he had to.

"Whatever. It's just not meet to change things around like that. Now I have to recomplicate things."

"You mean I'm doing okay, so you're going to mess me up?" Dug was bemused. He wasn't even trying for the prize. He just wanted to undo the mischief he had inadvertently caused.

"Approximately," the demoness agreed.

"Wait half a moment," Jenny said. "Metria, did Professor Grossclout tell you specifically to interfere with Dug's progress?"

"What's it to you, waif?"

"I'm Dug's Companion. It's my job to steer him past unnecessary confusions and complications, so that he won't think he's in some other game where that sort of thing is supposed to be standard. You strike me as exactly that kind of mischief. What exactly did Grossclout say to you?"

The demoness fidgeted. "He said to investigate, and use my judgment."

"He meant to judge whether Dug was in some unwarranted trouble, because of the mixup," Jenny said. "He's not, so all you have to do is go back and report that all swell."

"All what?"

"Bulge, grow, increase, billow, bloat, inflate—"

"Hey!" Dug protested.

"I mean surfs, seas, waters—"

"Wells?" Metria offered.

"Yes. Only the other way around: swell."

"Oh, you mean that everything is satisfactory."

"That's what I mean," Jenny said evenly. "In your own imitable fashion. So you can now buzz off and tell him that. No more turning his guilt literal, or whatever else your demonly fancy conceives. He is not for you to play with, Metria."

Dug saw that Jenny was trying to do her job. Obviously the demoness would only interfere with whatever he was trying to accomplish. He liked the elf's attitude.

Metria pondered. She glanced at Dug, then at Sherlock. Her garment flashed translucent, not quite showing her panties. Assuming she was wearing any. "But these are such interesting men. I think I'll stay and investigate some more."

"But you have to go back and report to Grossclout," Jenny reminded her.

"I have to use my judgment. My judgment is that I should hang around a bit more." For an instant she assumed the form of a woman being suspended by the neck until dead.

"But you aren't supposed to interfere with my legitimate Companioning."

"But Nada Naga's supposed to be his Companion," Metria pointed out. "You're not his legitimate Companion. You're Kim's."

Jenny turned to Dug. "This is likely to be trouble," she said. "Fortunately her attention span is not great. If you ignore her, she'll go away after a while."

Metria smiled. "Yes, ignore me, Dug Mundane." She stepped into him, her clothing disappearing.

Dug expected her to be smoky, but she was completely solid. He realized belatedly that she was not half demon, the way Threnody was, but full demon. She could change instantly.

Metria squeezed against him. Not only was she nude, she was voluptuous. She reached up and drew his head down for a kiss. "You should have chosen me to be your Companion," she murmured. "I could have made your life deliriously exciting."

He realized that it was true. He had taken one look at beautiful Nada and chosen her, but now he saw that the demoness could make herself just as shapely, and she had no princessly attitude to counter it. He probably should have chosen her. He might not have gotten far in the game, but he would have enjoyed the distraction. He was now appreciating first-hand (first-mouth) what Sherlock had when he had gotten kissed by a demoness.

"Still could," she added, sliding her bare front across his clothed front as she inhaled. He realized that it was no bluff. Innocent was not a term anyone would ever apply to this creature.

However, at the moment he had a different mission. He had to catch up to Kim and warn her about her False Companion. So he steeled himself to ward off the demoness' allure. "Forget it," he said. "Maybe some other time, you infernal creature."

Right away he realized that he had blundered. Metria's mouth curled into a frown, and then on into a fanged, tusked muzzle. It snapped at his nose, but was insubstantial as it closed. Dug was startled but unhurt.

Then the demoness faded into air. "I'll be back," her words came.

"Oh, mice!" Jenny swore. "I told you to ignore her, not to insult her. Now she'll be seriously mischievous."

"She was getting hard to ignore," Dug said defensively.

"All she was doing was getting in your way."

"She was hard to ignore," Sherlock said. "A child wouldn't understand."

Jenny shrugged, obviously not understanding what appeal there could be in a lusciously shaped bare demoness who wasn't wearing panties. Dug was glad for Sherlock's support.

They set off south. But soon they encountered a huge gray donkey. "Well, now," the creature said. "Are you the three folk the demoness said are looking for trouble?"

Already the mischief of a demoness scorned was manifesting. This was obviously no ordinary equine. In fact, he saw that it had a whole bundle of tails. Dug thought fast. This was really just another kind of challenge: how to turn mischief into something positive. "No, we are the three folk who are *in* trouble," he said. "We're looking for a way out of trouble. She must have misunderstood."

"Hee haw haw!" the donkey brayed. "That's for sure."

"In fact, what we need to get out of trouble is a ride," Dug said. "A fine animal like you could do us a big favor."

"Hee haw! I'm the Ass O' Nine Tails. I can give you a ride anywhere. But you'll have to listen to my tales."

Dug glanced at the other two. "Seems fair to me. Can you take us to the Good Magician's castle?"

"Hee haw! That I can. Hop on."

Dug congratulated himself, internally. He had succeeded in converting a menace into an asset. A genuine ass-et.

Jenny looked doubtful, but didn't protest. That meant that she had concluded that the giant ass was not dangerous to ride. So he helped her mount, and then climbed on behind her, and Sherlock climbed on behind him. There was generous room for all three, as well as Sammy Cat in front of Jenny.

The Ass started off. "Hee haw! I have nine tales, of course," he said. He flicked up the first of his tails. "First I will tell you about the Deadly Night Shade and the Kith of Death. It seemed that a certain shade of the night was lonely, having no kithing kin. So he decided that nobody else should have kithing cousins either. He became the deadliest night shade of all."

At first Dug found the tale interesting. But after a while it palled, because the Ass was great on de-tail but not on plot. He told how the shade killed one cousin after another, using his deadly kiss, until all the kith were dead. There it ended. There was no resolution and no justice, just continuous killing. Dug realized that the Ass's memory was a good deal better than his originality. Yet he realized that he had seen many similar stories on TV back in Mundania.

"Then there is the tale of Rubella and the Fool Moon," the Ass continued as soon as the first story expired in dullness. He told how Rubella kept fooling the moon, adding a measly pockmark on the moon's face each time. After an hour or so of the narration, the moon's whole face was pocked and cratered, but the moon was too foolish to learn how to stop Rubella. Again, there was no point; it was just one pock after another.

Then there was the tale of the Fait Accompli and the DeOgreant. Fait set out to weaken the ogres by eliminating their powerful smell. She used a special roll-on gunk to deogreize each ogre in turn, until no ogre had a strong smell. Unfortunately she accomplished nothing, because the ogres remained horribly strong and still crunched bones at a great rate. The bulk of the tale was concerned with a description of each of a hundred or so ogres Fait dealt with.

Then there was the tale of Michael Velli and the Crow Bar. Michael set out with devious cunning and no ethics to ruin the crows' favorite hangout: a bar where they could drink themselves silly on corn squeezings. He did this by informing each crow separately that the bar was closed. When, after another hour of narration, he had told each of about three hundred crows this, the bar was indeed closed for lack of patronage. Michael was very pleased with his connivance.

Dug wasn't. He was lulled to sleep by the dullness of the tales, while the huge Ass plodded on.

He woke amidst the tale of Mother Hen and her sons Vim and Vigor. Exactly what kind of a trial these cocky youngsters were to Ms. Hen he was never to learn, because he realized that they were approaching a castle. The party had arrived, thank goodness.

"The Good Magician's castle!" he exclaimed, waking Jenny, Sammy, and Sherlock, who it seemed had been just as bored as he with the endless tales. They slid down to the ground, flexing the dullness out of their legs.

"No, this is Castle Roogna," the Ass said, surprised, flicking several tails.

"So it is!" Jenny said, recognizing it. "There's the orchard and the zombie graveyard."

"But we were supposed to go to the Good Magician's castle," Dug protested.

"By no means," the Ass demurred. "I was going to Castle Roogna."

"But you agreed to take us to the Good Magician's castle!" Dug was adding annoyance to his confusion.

"Hee haw! You asked could I take you there, and I agreed I could. I did not say I would, and you did not ask me to. So I came here."

Dug realized that he had been had by the Ass. There had been no definite commitment. It had been, as it were, a handshake agreement, not worth the paper it was written on. And the Ass had told them such continuously dull tales that all three of them had fallen asleep and been unable to correct the route when it went wrong. Jenny Elf would have recognized the wrong direction, and acted to correct it. Certainly Sammy Cat could have found the way to the right castle, had he too not been lulled into sleep. But nobody could have remained awake for the whole of that barrage of asinine tales. Dug felt like a fool moon, and a real country rubella, being the victim of this fait accompli.

The Demoness Metria appeared. "Oh, too bad," she said silkily. "I see that your Companion has let you down, and allowed you to be delivered to the wrong castle. How unfortunate, when you could so readily have had a more competent Companion." She inhaled again, allowing her full blouse to turn translucent, not far from Dug's face.

"Hee haw haw!" the Ass brayed gustily.

Jenny looked as if she were about to speak a word not properly in the Juvenile Lexicon. Dug saved her the trouble by taking action he knew he would regret. He swung a fist at the demoness' face.

Naturally his hand passed right through Metria's head without resistance. Then she stepped into him and planted a too too solid kiss on his mouth. Then she faded into smoke and drifted away on the nearest vagrant breeze. She had had her revenge.

Dug realized that he had lost this challenge. Fortunately it had not been a game challenge, just the mischief of a jealous fantasy female. There was no point in belaboring it; he'd just have to get back on track and get where he was going. And hope he wasn't too late.

"What's the fastest way to the Good Magician's castle?" he asked.

"Be sensible, man," Sherlock said. "She's there already. You need to figure out where she's going from there."

"He's right," Jenny said. "And the best place to ask is Castle Roogna."

"You figure the king will know?"

"Oh, we shouldn't bother King Dor about this," Jenny said. "I was thinking—well, I can't say right now, but maybe it will work out."

Dug looked at her curiously. "You can't say what you expect to happen?"

She fidgeted. "It's a special situation. I'm doing my best, really I am."

Dug looked at Sherlock, who shrugged. There was no question that Jenny meant well, but was she competent? Dug couldn't see how this could concern the dread Adult Conspiracy she was so concerned about, and couldn't think of any other reason for her to be evasive. But if she did have a worthwhile notion, he needed it. "Okay. Lead the way."

Jenny gladly obliged. She led them by assorted fruit trees to the moat, where the huge horrendous moat monster eyed them. "Soufflé!" Jenny exclaimed. "What are you doing here?"

The monster hissed.

"Oh, you're here to baby-sit the twins? Where's Electra?"

The monster hissed again.

"Oh, she and Dolph are off visiting the Isle of View? What would they be doing there?"

"You know he can't tell you that!" Sherlock said.

Jenny was abashed. "That's right, he can't!" She faced the monster again. "This is Dug, who is a Player in the game, and this is Sherlock, of the Black Wave. They're friends."

Soufflé Serpent nodded and swam back across the moat. Jenny led the way over the drawbridge. Dug wondered whether she had made up the dialogue with the monster, who had perhaps recognized her by smell and accepted her.

Then he saw two little children, hardly more than babies, in pink bassinets at the edge of the moat. The monster was indeed watching them.

"But is that safe?" he asked. "That monster could gulp them down in an instant."

"As safe as anywhere," Jenny said. "Nobody will bother them with Soufflé on guard. They like him, and he likes them. He hasn't had much chance to play with royal children recently."

Dug could appreciate why not. "I gather that Electra is their mother? Who is she? I seem to remember you saying something about blue jeans on a princess."

"Princess Electra is Prince Dolph's wife. She was caught by a curse meant for a princess and slept for much of a thousand years until Prince Dolph kissed her awake. Now she *is* a princess, so maybe the curse knew what it was doing. The twins are Dawn and Eve. When they get old enough to talk, Dawn will be able to tell anything about any living thing, and Eve will be able to tell anything about any inanimate thing."

"Those are good talents," Dug said.

"Yes, they are Magician-class talents. Such magic runs in the royal line."

They came to the main door. It was open. Dug wondered at this easy access to the leading castle of the land. But with a moat monster on guard, maybe it made sense.

A young woman appeared. She had jade-green hair and aqua-green eyes. "Hi, Ivy," Jenny said.

"I'm Ida," the woman said.

"Oh, I keep confusing you two!" Jenny turned to the others. "This is Dug, who is in the game; I'm his Companion. This is Sherlock, who is a member of the Black Wave." Then, after a pause: "This is Princess Ida, Ivy's twin sister."

Dug was taken aback. He didn't know what to say to a princess. Fortunately Sherlock did. "Nice to meet you, Princess. We met Princess Nada Naga before."

Dug realized that he hadn't thought of Nada that way, despite being frustrated by her princessly liabilities. Why should he be abashed here, when he hadn't been with Nada?

"Oh, yes, she and Ivy are best friends," Ida said brightly. "I am here to learn the ways of princesses, because I didn't know I was one, until recently. What are you here for, Sherlock?"

"I'm looking for a place for my people to settle. I figure there's bound to be somewhere where we're needed."

"Oh, I'm sure there is," Ida agreed brightly. She turned to Dug. "I did not know that Castle Roogna was participating in the game. Why did you come here?"

"I was an ass," Dug said. "I mean, I let an ass fool me into going to the wrong place. Now I just have to believe that there is some way to do what I have to do."

"Oh, I'm sure there is," Ida said, exactly as she had with Sherlock. She seemed to be a very positive person.

"That's wonderful!" Jenny exclaimed.

Dug and Sherlock looked at her. "It's wonderful that the Princess is being polite to us?" Dug asked.

"Oh, princesses are always polite," Ida said. "She means that she's glad that both of you will succeed in your quests."

"No offense, Princess, but how can you know that?" Sherlock inquired.

"It is my talent," Ida explained. "The Idea. When I have an idea, it comes true. But it has to originate with someone who doesn't know my talent. Neither of you knew."

"You mean that just our telling you our hopes will make them come true?" Dug asked doubtfully.

"That's the way I hoped it would be," Jenny said. "Now we'll just have to see how these things happen."

Sherlock glanced at Dug. "This as weird to you as it is to me?"

"At least," Dug said. "I didn't even say what it is I have to do. It's not winning the game, it's warning Kim in time. And I still don't know how to reach her. But I guess there's a way."

"There is; I'm sure of it," Ida said. "But come in; I didn't mean to keep you standing here." She turned and led the way into the interior.

Dug wondered whether things were really as positive as others chose to believe. But this was a magic land, so maybe things were magically positive.

They came to a central chamber where a man was sitting. He stood as they entered. "Ah, these must be the folk I am looking for," he said, smiling.

"I'm sure they are," Princess Ida agreed.

Sherlock seized the moment. "If you're looking for neighbors—"

"As a matter of fact, we are," the man said. "We would like several hundred men, women, and children to colonize the fringe of Lake Ogre-Chobee and keep it civilized. We are too busy with our plays to take proper time with it. But most other Xanthians are too busy with their own pursuits to tackle a chore like that." He paused. "I'm Curtis Curse Friend, here on a recruiting mission."

"The Curse Fiends—uh, Friends are all right," Jenny murmured. "They have a long history."

The man glanced at her. "So do the elves. But I never before saw one your size."

"Do you care about the color of those men, women, and children?" Sherlock inquired cautiously.

"Of course. We prefer that they not be green, because they would get lost in the vegetation as well as getting confused with the chobees swimming in the lake."

"Well, we have several hundred black people up in the isthmus who are looking for a home. But it's quite a journey this far, what with the Gap Chasm and all, and I believe Lake Ogre-Chobee is farther south. It could take some time for them to get there."

"Do you care about cursing?"

Sherlock looked at him sidelong. "Do you curse without cause?"

"Only to protect ourselves, or to clear rubbish." Curtis paused. "I trust you realize that we are talking about explosive magical curses, not harpy talk."

"Right. No fowl language. We feel about curses the way we do about arrows: we don't want them hurled at us from ambush. We just want to mind our business and get along with our neighbors."

"We have a way for you to travel," Curtis said. "We have some magic bubble jars we traded for. Each bubble will hold one large person, or two small ones, and will float safely to the destination named for it. It would take about one day for a string of bubbles to cross Xanth."

Sherlock stuck out his hand. "I think we got a deal."

Curtis took it. "I was sure we would." He brought out a little bottle. "Oops, this one's almost empty; there's only enough for two bubbles left." He fished in his pocket for another.

"May I have that one?" Jenny asked. "I know someone who could use it."

Curtis shrugged and gave it to her. He brought out another for Sherlock. "This will make several hundred bubbles, if used carefully. Simply blow a bubble with this bubble-ring, and have a person step into it in the first minute before it sets. Then tell it where to go. Don't touch it from outside until it gets there. We'll have a man waiting at Lake Ogre-Chobee to pop the first one; after that you can handle them yourselves."

Sherlock turned to Dug. "It seems that my quest is done. I'll be going back to the isthmus with this bottle, as soon as I know you are okay."

"I will blow a bubble to carry you to the isthmus, as soon as you are ready," Curtis said.

"You might as well go now," Dug said. "You have been a great help to me, and you don't owe me anything."

"No, I want to see it through. If my solution was here, yours must be too. We just have to find it."

"Well, we might ask a magic mirror," Jenny suggested.

"I will fetch one," Ida said, hurrying off.

"That's one nice young woman, even if she is a princess," Curtis said. "I came here to explain my mission, hoping that the answer would be here, and she was very positive. I had this idea that maybe I'd find some colonists today, and she agreed. She must have known you were coming."

"*We* didn't know we were coming here," Dug said. "It was an accident." Then he remembered how the Demoness Metria had tricked them. "I think."

Ida returned with an ordinary mirror. "Ask this," she said to Dug. "You don't have to rhyme, but it helps."

Dug pondered rhymes. "Mirror, mirror, in my hand—where is Kim in this land?"

A picture formed: a green melon. That was all.

"She's in a melon?" Dug asked, perplexed.

"That's a gourd!" Jenny said. "She's gone to the hypnogourd. Oh, that's an adventure."

"I've heard references to some kind of gourd," Dug said. "But how can a person be in one?"

"It's a whole nother realm," Jenny explained. "You just look in the peep-hole, and you're there. I'll go with you, and Sammy will find Kim. But I warn you, this will be a weird adventure."

"Weirder than what I've seen already?" Dug asked disbelievingly. "Weirder than having a nine-tailed ass make an ass of me?"

"Much." She looked at Sherlock. "So I guess you don't need to wait any longer. We'll get gourds here, and that will be it."

"You sure?" Sherlock asked.

"Oh, yes. Obviously the prize is in the gourd realm, so she'll either win it or lose it, and her game will be over."

"Okay." Sherlock extended his hand, and Dug shook it. "It's been great knowing you, Dug, and if you're ever traveling around Lake Ogre-Chobee—"

"I'll drop by," Dug said, suddenly sorry to see the man go. "I just want to say—"

"I know." Sherlock wasn't any more for emotional display than Dug was.

"We do have gourds in a garden near the castle," Ida said. "We shall bring three in for you and Jenny and Sammy."

"Thanks," Dug said. His mouth felt dry.

18
PRIZE

K im looked around. The place she least wanted to enter was the boneyard, so this was surely where the prize was hidden. So she nerved herself and marched forward.

Bubbles stayed right with her, nervously close. The dog shared her apprehension about this place. Kim knew that there really wasn't anything to fear from bones; they were dead, so were no more dangerous than stones or chips of wood. Even with magic they shouldn't be fearsome, because they formed into characters like Marrow. In any event, this was the dream realm, where nothing was truly physical. A dream, in a fantasy land, in the game, which was all imaginary to begin with. Still she felt a superstitious chill. She was glad she had Bubbles and Nada for company.

Marrow had disappeared, but she knew he would turn up again, and in a guise intended to repel her. She braced herself for the show.

Meanwhile the landscape was bad enough. It was dark, and growing darker. A monstrous gibbous moon emerged from behind a cloud—and the moon was bone white, with bony pocks. In fact, it looked like one big bone. That very word, gibbous, had always made her flinch, though she knew that all it meant was rounded, more than half full. It had nothing to do with gibbons, which weren't bad animals anyway. But the moon was always gibbous when something awful was going to happen, such as a poor girl getting murdered or a vampire striking.

"Careful," Nada murmured.

Kim looked. She had almost walked into a pool, because she had been looking at the moon instead of where she was going. The water was dark and looked almost slimy, as if pus had oozed into it and turned it to jelly. Ugh! Where had she gotten a notion like that?

There was something under the water. Kim peered—and saw bones. And perhaps pieces of attached flesh. As she looked, they seemed to move. Double ugh! She averted her gaze and walked on.

They crested a hill and saw a sinister valley. In the most dismal depths of it squatted a truly ugly castle. The moon, by the alchemy of this region, was now setting behind that edifice, illuminating it so that every facet of its misshapen structure showed clearly. There was of course a moat, and high ramparts, and a portcullis, and turrets and embrasures. But somehow instead of seeming delightfully medieval, it seemed frightening.

As she got closer, Kim saw that it was worse than she had thought. The castle was not made out of wood or stone; it was made of bones. Big bones framed the front gate, and little bones filled in the crevices, and sharpened bones topped the walls. A rotting flag hung from a spire, showing a skull and crossbones. The portcullis was actually a giant skull with pointed fangs.

"Maybe the prize is not in there," Kim whispered.

But the moment she tried to turn away, she discovered that there were palisades encroaching from either side, channeling her in toward the castle. She looked directly back, and saw a foul fog swirling up over the crest of the hill, rendering visibility zero and harboring who knew what. If she tried to go back through that fog, she would probably stumble into the corpse-filled water. There was no place to go but forward. Of course.

The closer she got, the larger the castle seemed, until it loomed impossibly high. The big bones seemed to have been carved by a cleaver to fit their assignments, and the smaller ones seemed to have been chewed on. Some were split lengthwise. This was the kind of castle a brute ogre would fashion when in an ill mood.

The fluid of the moat looked even worse than the pond water. Even Bubbles shied away from it. Something stirred within its noisome depths, but Kim didn't care to see what it was. Instead she scrunched up most of her remaining nerve and set foot on the bone planks of the drawbridge. One of them rolled under her foot, causing her to lose her balance and almost pitch into the murky water.

She righted herself and took another step—and another bone rolled, trying to send her off to the side. So she got down on her hands and knees—and felt the slickness of the surface of the bones, as if they had only recently been stripped of their flesh. She gritted her teeth and moved forward—this time feeling a string or something. She looked, and saw it was a tendon, not quite separated from the joint. Triple ugh!

She made it across the moat, with Bubbles crawling along beside her. She stood on the bone pavement, which seemed to have been formed of hipbones embedded in bone fragments, and gazed at the awful entry. Would that giant fanged upper portcullis jaw crash down on her as she tried to enter? Surely it would; that was what it was for.

She heard something rumble behind her. She jumped and looked back. The drawbridge was lifting! Gross tendons were hauling it up until it was vertical, leaving no escape from the castle. Now she really couldn't change her mind.

"Everything about the place seems to be one-way," Nada noted. "The fog, the fencing, the bridge. You aren't allowed to change your mind."

"It's victory or defeat," Kim agreed. "And I guess victory is better."

"Of course it is," Nada said warmly. "What is the point in playing the game, if not to win the prize?"

What use to explain about human feelings to a princess? "I suppose so," Kim agreed. "But I sort of liked just being in Xanth."

"You will be able to return. And with the magic talent you win as the prize, you'll be able to play longer and better."

Kim realized that she was right. Since she couldn't have her true heart's desire, she might as well have the prize. "Yes. Let's get on with it."

She took a step toward the portcullis. Bubbles whined.

Kim stopped. As far as she knew, the dog had no magic. She wasn't like Jenny's cat Sammy, who could find anything. That didn't mean that Bubbles wasn't worthwhile, just that her reactions to magic effects might not be wholly accurate. Still, she generally had reason for her concerns. "What is it, Bubbles?" Kim inquired, putting a hand on the dog's back.

Bubbles looked up at the deadly fangs of the portcullis, and her tail dropped low.

Oh—naturally the dog did not want to enter the mouth of a monster!

Kim took another step. Bubbles yelped as if someone had trodden on her tail.

"Something's wrong here," Kim said. "You think that big mouth is going to close on us?" As she said it, she realized it was true: that was what a portcullis was. A gate that came crashing down to shut out intruders. Maybe down *on* them, if they moved slow. "It *is* going to come down on us! It's one more way to be wiped out." A wipeout here would be just as final as a wipeout in Xanth proper, even if this was the dream realm.

"It must be," Nada agreed. "Maybe there's another way into the castle."

They walked to the side, but the moat quickly closed in, squeezing the ground out until there was no break between the water and the bonewall. There was no other entry.

"So it has to be the portcullis," Kim said. "Maybe we can put a block on it, so the fangs can't come down on us."

But there was nothing to use as a block. "Maybe we can climb the wall to a window," Nada suggested. "I can climb in serpent form."

Kim tried to get a handhold on a projecting bone, but it was slippery, and there was no good bone to grab above it. Even if she could climb the wall, Kim knew she would grow faint before she reached any height, and probably fall off. And how could the dog ever climb it? So that was out.

She sighed. "I think we'll just have to go through the main entrance. I'll bet it has to be fast. And right together, three abreast. That portcullis has to take a moment to get started. So it should crash down behind us."

"It should," Nada agreed.

They lined up. "Ready, set, go!" Kim cried, and they took off.

They crossed the line of the gateway—and the portcullis came crashing down. Wham! the fangs plunged into the floor at their heels. The retreat was closed. But they had made it through unscathed.

Only then did Kim wonder what would have happened if they had not been in perfect alignment. Suppose the dog had lagged behind, and gotten trapped outside? Or, worse, chomped? Suppose the dog had run ahead, and triggered the drop too soon, so that it crunched the two people? This had been a very risky ploy!

Kim resolved to be more careful from now on. She looked ahead, and saw a dark hall leading into the center of the castle. Its walls were polished bones, tightly interwoven. She wasn't sure how bones could be woven, but these were. There was barely enough light for them to see.

Well, the hall must lead somewhere. Kim started to walk down it—and Bubbles whined.

Magic or no magic, she was coming to trust the dog's judgment. There was something fishy about this passage.

Kim looked around. There was a chink in a corner, and a bone fragment on the floor beneath it. In due course some skeleton crew would come by and use bone paste to fasten the chip back into place.

Bubbles went over to sniff the fragment. That didn't mean anything; the dog sniffed everything. It was her way of getting acquainted. But it reminded Kim that there was always a way through, in the game, and usually a hint about that way through. That fallen chip of bone was the only unusual thing here. Was it a hint?

Kim went to pick it up. It seemed quite ordinary. She tried to return it to its place in the wall, but it wouldn't stay. She didn't have any paste with which to fasten it there. She couldn't make the repair.

Then she thought of something else. This was Xanth, and one of the commonest forms of magic here was illusion. Things could seem to be what they were not. Or could not seem to be what they were. ·

Kim took the chip of bone and sent it sliding down the hall. The floor was smooth, because the bones were shored by plaster or cement. It was like sending a puck down a shuffleboard alley.

Then the chip disappeared. Kim smiled. "I think we've found what's wrong with this hall," she said.

She got down on her hands and knees again and crawled carefully forward. Bubbles joined her. When she came to the place where the chip had disappeared, she reached forward—and felt nothing. The floor was gone. There was a pit there. The floor looked continuous, but it was illusion, covering the trap.

Kim nudged up to the edge and felt deeper. There seemed to be no bottom to the pit. It would have been a bad fall, probably a wipeout.

But how was she going to get across it? Kim pondered. "I'm going to gamble," she said. She fished in her pack and found a spare pair of socks. She separated them, and rolled each one up into a ball. Then she tossed one ahead about four feet. It landed and rolled on along the hall, finally fetching up at the entrance to the next chamber. "So there is a continuation," she said, satisfied. "No more invisible pits. She tossed the second sock about three feet. It, too, landed and rolled.

But Kim couldn't reach across the pit; her questing fingers found nothing. So it couldn't be much under three feet. Still, three feet was jumpable.

"This is like the portcullis," she said. "We'll have to jump. But I think we can do it singly." She removed her pack and set it at the edge of the pit. "This is where the jump starts. I'll go first." She looked at the dog. "You wait." She hoped Bubbles would understand.

She walked to the front end of the hall. Then she ran down it, reached the pack, and leaped. She landed cleanly and slowed to a stop.

"Now you, Bubbles," she called.

The dog ran down the hall, leaped at the pack, and landed where Kim had. She was old and solid and barely made it, but her spirit was there.

"Now mark the place and toss over the pack," Kim said to Nada. "Then jump over yourself."

In this manner they traversed the hall and came to the central chamber of the castle. It was huge. Portals opened out around it in about nine directions, and more opened out from the balcony levels. In the center was a big ball of bright red string.

As they stepped into the chamber, the door to the passage slammed shut with a bone-rattling jar.

"I think I have this figured," Kim said. "Somewhere in this castle is the prize. I have to search to find it. And any door I pass through will be closed after me, so I can't go back. But maybe some of those chambers have several doors. So I'll mark my trail with string, so I'll know if I've passed that way before. If I find the prize before I lock myself into a dead-end chamber, I'll win."

"There must be dangers along the way, too," Nada said. "Judging by what we've seen so far."

"Yes. So this will be dicey. But winnable if I'm smart enough and lucky enough." Kim considered as she went carefully to fetch the string. "Bubbles, you're the most cautious about danger. You lead the way." She wasn't sure the dog would understand, but it was worth a try.

Bubbles sniffed around, then headed for one of the portals. She paused at the entrance to the chamber, waiting for Kim.

Kim tied the end of the string to a projecting bone and strung the line out behind as she went to join the dog. "Okay, Bubbles, you lead, but be careful."

The dog entered the chamber, but did not proceed to the center. She went to the side. As she did so, something came down from the high ceiling. It swung back and forth. It was a pendulum. A big sharp-edged bone on a long tendon, and it crossed the full chamber. But it shouldn't be hard to pass, if they timed it for when it was at one end of the chamber.

Then a second pendulum came down, with another knife bone. It swung opposite to the first, reaching the other end, so that there was no chance to pass; both ends were covered. However, when the two sharp bones were at the edges of their swings, it should be possible to run through the center.

And a third pendulum descended, timed to swing across the center while the other two were outside. But maybe they could pass a bit to the side, opposite that third, while the first and second were still out. And a fourth, going opposite to the third. Now everything was covered. The chamber was a criss-crossing pattern of swinging bones. There was no clearance at the edges; the blades almost touched the walls.

Nada shook her head. "I think we had better try another chamber."

Kim turned back—and saw that the door had quietly closed behind them. Again, they couldn't retreat.

"Maybe we could leap over them?" Kim asked. But then she realized that the swinging tendons were almost as dangerous as the sharp bones. They could catch a person, and tangle her, so that one of the other knives would swing back and cut her apart. The only safe course was to avoid the pendulums entirely.

Already Kim's eyes were glazing. No matter where she looked, a pendulum was passing or about to pass. There just seemed to be no way to cross safely.

Yet there had to be a way. If she could just figure it out. Some way to get through without blindly gambling.

Kim shut her eyes, closing out the bewildering array. There were only two sets of pendulums, swinging oppositely. While one set touched the edges, the other passed the middle. She judged that each single pendulum took two seconds to complete its swing from one side to the other, and that a person needed one second to get safely across the covered zone. With just two pendulums, that second would be available in the center or at the edge. But with the four, only half a second. Not safe.

She opened her eyes and studied the pattern again. This time she looked at one edge, and counted seconds. She discovered to her surprise that a blade came near one wall every second, not every half second. How could this be?

She sketched a diagram in the dust of the floor, and realized that she had made an error. Each single pendulum did take two seconds to swing across—and two more to swing back. That was a four-second cycle. So four pendulums reduced it to one-second cycles. She could make it! She had almost allowed herself to be dazzled by the crisscrossing blades, so that she was ready to give up when she didn't need to.

"Okay," she said. "We'll go through singly. It's going to be close but possible."

"But those blades—" Nada protested, alarmed.

"Are passing any given spot at one-second intervals, I think. So all we have to do is pick a spot, like maybe the center, and dash through there right after a pair of blades has passed. In fact, I think the thing to do is aim for the crossing blades. They'll be moving out of the way as we come, and the other two will just be starting in. So it should be clear for that second."

Nada still looked extremely doubtful.

"I'll go first," Kim said. "And this time I'll carry Bubbles, because I don't know how to explain to her how to time it, and I don't want to risk any confusion. Then you can pass, carrying the ball of string. Come on, Bubbles." She squatted, put her arms around the dog, heaved her up, and stood herself. Oh, Bubbles was heavy! And how did the game make her feel that weight, when this was all just animation on a screen? It didn't matter. She just had to be sure not to lose her timing.

Kim went up to the crisscrossing blades. She felt the breeze of their passing. She started counting, timing them. "One, two, one, two," as the first and second sets of pendulums passed the center. Then she retreated a step, nerved herself, and lumbered across, trying to time it to come just barely after "two."

She made it. She lowered the dog to the floor, feeling faint. She didn't like such nervous business!

Nada timed it similarly and came across. Whereupon the four pendulums slowed, stopped, and withdrew into the ceiling. "Just like 'The Pit and the Pendulum,'" Kim remarked. No explanation, no follow-up, they just quit when they got outsmarted.

They went to the next chamber. This one had a pit across its center, too wide to jump. There was a ladder-bridge formed of bones on the far side, that evidently could be lowered in the manner of a drawbridge. On the near side was a length of cord hanging from a ceiling beam. That was all.

Kim pondered the situation. She should be able to use the cord to snag the ladder and pull it down across the pit so they could cross. But the cord was firmly tied, and would not come loose. She might cut it—but she could not reach high enough to cut off enough to use for this purpose. She might grab hold of it and try to swing across the pit, but she was afraid it wasn't strong enough to hold her weight. That also prevented her from trying to climb it to the beam; it could break anywhere, ruining it. So what use was it?

Then her lightbulb flashed. She removed her pack, which was not heavy enough to break the cord, and tied it to the end. Then she swung the pack across the pit, getting the feel of it. It banged into the upright ladder. She swung it again, this time to one side, and it swung around behind the ladder, hooking it, and snagged. But the ladder did not fall.

Now she was in trouble. The cord was out of reach. How could she get hold of it?

Then she took her ball of string. She lofted that up over the near end of the cord and caught it. The string was not heavy, but it was strong enough to pull the cord down just within reach of her hand. Then she pulled on the cord until the snagged pack brought it crashing down across the pit. Now they could cross.

The next chamber was worse. The moment they tried to enter it, the ceiling started descending and the floor ascended. Both surfaces had knife-pointed bones sticking out. Pity the poor person who tried to scramble through there!

When they backed off, the floor and ceiling stopped moving, then retreated, ready to trap the next unwary person. Kim wondered why they didn't just keep going until they met halfway up and closed off the chamber.

Could that be a clue? Could it be that the way wasn't closed until the person was actually caught between those jaws?

She took her pack and set it on the edge of the chamber floor. The floor rose, and the ceiling dropped. Just before they crunched the pack, Kim pulled it away.

She ducked down and peered under the floor. It had been pushed up by a column of bones. She could see right by that column to the next chamber. There was her way through—*under* the floor!

Then the floor dropped, because there was nothing on it. The route disappeared.

She returned the pack to the floor. "Nada, take this off just before it gets crunched," Kim said. Then, as the floor rose, she ducked down and scrambled under it. "Come on, Bubbles!" she cried.

Nada seemed startled by the suddenness and daring of Kim's action, but she recovered in time to grab the pack.

"Now hurl it across to me," Kim said. "Before the floor subsides. I'll use it from this end to raise the floor for you."

The next chamber had a bone stair whose steps moved down when stepped on, so it was impossible to make progress. Kim finally managed to fool it by facing backward, so that it thought she was trying to walk down, and carried her back to what it thought was her starting place, the top.

In similar manner they wended their way through one chamber after another, avoiding any where the red string already crossed, until they were high in the castle. There seemed to be only one chamber remaining. Beyond it they could see a glowing golden chest. That had to be the prize!

But the intervening chamber had a sharply sloping floor, slippery slick. Anyone trying to cross it would be dumped into one of this castle's patented bottomless pits. What was the way through?

Kim gazed out the bone window. She saw that she was now three stories up, overlooking the lifted drawbridge. The landscape was just as gloomy as before. So why was she staring at it?

She analyzed her motive. She was foolishly hoping that the other Player, Dug, would show up. Because this was really the last chance, if she were to see him again. She had no idea where he lived in Mundania, so would be unable to locate him there, even if he had any slight interest in her.

Then she saw something on the horizon. Someone was coming along the dreary path! It was a small figure, chasing a smaller animal. That must be Jenny!

"Dug is coming," Kim said, excited.

"I can assume serpent form," Nada said. "I can grab onto a post with my teeth, and you can swing across on my tail."

"Sammy Cat must have found the way," Kim said. "Now they'll be here too."

"You must act quickly, before Dug gets your prize," Nada said.

But Kim dallied, watching the approaching trio. She saw the ugly fog roiling up behind them, herding them, and the palisades funneling them in toward the castle.

Then she did something absolutely foolish. She fished in her pack for a hankie and waved it out the window. Just as if she were a maiden in distress.

And Dug saw it! "Kim!" he cried faintly.

She thrilled to the sound. "Dug!" she called back.

"Wait right there! Don't do anything!"

What lovely words! "I'll wait," she cried gladly.

"What are you doing?" Nada demanded. "The prize is within your grasp, and you're letting him catch up?"

"Yes," Kim said dreamily. "I like him, and I won't get a chance to see him once the game is over. So if we can talk, if he's interested—"

"All he wants is to get the prize," Nada said.

"He can have it," Kim said. "I just want to exchange phone numbers before we leave the game. I was afraid he wouldn't get here in time."

As she watched, the little group below charged to the castle. The drawbridge was up, but that didn't stop them. Cat, elf, and young man plunged into the grimy moat and swam across. Apparently there wasn't a moat monster, or else Sammy knew that it was on the far side of the castle at the moment and couldn't get them. What an act of reckless daring!

"I was mistaken," Nada said grimly. "I believe he wants more than the prize. He wants me."

Now they were at the base of the wall. The cat still led the way, finding a section to climb, digging his little claws into the softening bones. There seemed to be handholds there that weren't closer to the drawbridge. In fact, it looked as if there were an inset ladder, making it much easier for them to climb the wall, avoiding all the hazards of the interior. Dug followed the other two, hauling himself along.

He tilted back his head, and saw her peering down. "Kim! Don't move from that spot! There's something I have to tell you!"

He wanted to tell her something. He was interested after all! "Oh, yes," she breathed. Then something registered. She turned back to face Nada. "What?"

"He chose me as his Companion because he liked my looks," Nada said grimly. "He wanted to see my body. But he was too sneaky about it, and almost got put out of the game."

"Yes, so he lost interest," Kim agreed. "But I'm not a princess, and—"

"By this time he will have learned that the Companions, too, are a challenge. A Player may do anything with a Companion he desires, if he is able to find the correct way. It is a matter of approach. If he treats his Companion with proper respect, he can earn her respect. He can force her cooperation, with the right words. So if he has found the appropriate manner to approach me—"

Kim suffered a sudden flare of jealousy. Dug could get at this beautiful, luscious princess? What the hell would he want with a nothing girl like Kim, then? "The prize—and you?" she said, appalled.

"I have no way to prevent it," Nada said seriously. "If he gets you to trade back Companions, and if he knows the key dialogue. So you must act swiftly, before he gets here. I will not be able to advise you, if you trade."

Kim, torn by doubt, gazed down again from the window. The cat was almost there, with Jenny not far behind, and Dug close behind her. "What do you want, Dug?" she asked.

"Nada!" he gasped. "I must trade her back from you, because—"

"Oh!" Kim cried, her lingering hope dashed. He was just another selfish, careless, horny teenage boy. She was tempted to throw her pack down on his head, but it wasn't handy. She turned away from the window. "Let's go for the prize, Nada!"

Nada immediately assumed serpent form and slithered from her clothing. She lunged at the bone beam above the tilting floor, and caught it with her teeth. Her body slid down across the floor, but in a moment she curled her tail up for Kim to grab.

Bubbles whined.

Kim hesitated. Was something wrong here? It occurred to her that she should have to solve the riddle of the chamber herself, rather than letting her Companion solve it for her. Yet she could appreciate why Nada did not want Dug to recover her as his Companion.

She glanced back, hearing something. The cat appeared in the window and jumped to the floor. Jenny Elf's head was next. "Wait, Kim!" Jenny cried.

Of course Jenny now served Dug, and would help him do whatever he wanted to do. Even if that meant getting herself traded back. Jenny could not be trusted while she was Dug's Companion.

Kim caught hold of Nada's tail, bracing herself for the sliding swing across the slanted floor. Would she be able to catch hold of the far edge and haul herself up to the golden chest?

Bubbles whined again, her tail curled all the way under her body. The dog was really upset. "Don't worry, Bubbles," Kim said. "I'm not leaving you. I'm just crossing to the prize." But now she wondered: what would happen to the dog, when Kim won and left the game?

Suddenly she was overwhelmed by realization. "Oh, Bubbles, I don't want to leave you!" she cried, dropping Nada's tail so that she could hug the dog. "But how can I take you with me? What will become of you?"

"You *can* take her," Jenny said. "There's a way."

"A way?" Hope flared.

"I have a jar of bubbles. Like the one you got her from. I can give it to you, if you take me back as your Companion."

· It was another ploy to make her trade! Furious, Kim caught Nada's tail again and stepped into the slanting chamber. She was starting to swing down—

Then Dug was there, tackling her around the waist before the serpent could take her weight. The elf had distracted her just long enough to get caught!

"Let me go!" Kim cried, struggling to twist out of his grasp so she could swing across. Half her body was hanging over the edge, while Dug's arms were wrapped around her thighs and waist. If she could just wriggle free—

But he hauled her back and into him, using his strength to make her captive. "Kim!" he cried. "I've got to tell you—"

"I don't want to listen!" she cried, letting go of the serpent's tail so she could flail at him with her hands. "I was willing to let you have the prize, but no, you had to—"

"I don't care about the prize!" he said, pinning her arms. In any other circumstances she would have been glad to have him hugging her this close. "You can have it! I know that's what you came for. All I want is to tell you—"

"That you want Princess Nada Naga for more than just guidance!" she finished for him. "Oh, I hate you!"

He looked surprised. "No, I only want to talk to you, to save you from—"

"Me?" Foolish hope flared again. "It's me you want?"

"Yes. To explain—"

"Oh!" she exclaimed, overcome with opposite emotion. Her feelings were swinging like a pendulum. "Really?"

"Really. I was afraid I wouldn't be able to catch you before—"

"Oh, yes!" she cried. She lifted her head and kissed him hard on the mouth. It was the most wonderful sensation. "I feel that way about you, too, Dug! My number is area code Tee zero zero, 555–4377. What's yours?"

He looked confused. "I—I mean, I had to tell you that Nada's a False Companion. She was about to drop you down the hole. You can trade back, and

Jenny will help you get the prize. It wasn't right to let you get torpedoed by what was meant for me."

She was stunned. "You—you came to warn me?"

He let her go. "Yes. I was afraid I wouldn't reach you in time. I'd never forgive myself if you lost your prize because of me."

She realized that it was true. There had been little things about Nada, and the way Bubbles had reacted—of course she was a False Companion! Dug had done the natural, decent thing, when he figured it out. He could nullify Nada, knowing her nature. But he wouldn't bother, because he wasn't even trying for the prize. Maybe he'd just experiment, to see how far the princess would go before he got washed out of the game.

And Kim had assumed that it was something else. She felt the great-grandmother of all blushes washing over her face, turning it glaring red. She covered her face with her hands. "Thank you," she said in as controlled a voice as she could manage. "I will—I will trade back Companions."

"Good," he said. He caught Nada's tail with one hand. "Let go, Princess, and I'll haul you in. Unless you prefer to drop down the hole you meant for Kim."

The serpent let go of the beam, and Dug did haul it in. Then he turned his back. "Change and get dressed. I don't care if you shove me in the hole; you are my Companion now, and you can't touch Kim."

Nada changed, becoming a naked woman, getting quickly into her clothing. Kim suppressed a surge of jealousy for her splendid proportions and complexion.

"Now I will help you," Jenny said. "I have found a bubble maker that can make two bubbles. You can use the first bubble to float safely across. Then you'll be able to use the last bubble to go home." She showed the jar.

"Why, that's a regular bubble mix," Kim said. "Children use them to blow soap bubbles."

"No, these are magic bubbles, big enough to hold people. Sherlock is using them to carry the Black Wave to Lake Ogre-Chobee, where they will settle as neighbors to the Curse Fiends—I mean, Curse Friends."

"I'm glad that worked out," Kim said. "Those must be the same type of bubbles I found Bubbles in." She patted the dog.

"Yes. They are used to carry people or things where they want to go. So they are just what you need now."

"No," Kim said firmly. "I must find my own way to the prize." For one thing, it gave her something to focus on, so that she could try to forget her chagrin at her misunderstanding of Dug's motive. "I thank you, Jenny, but I want to do this myself."

"That's good," Jenny agreed.

Kim studied the situation. The floor tilted so sharply that a fly would barely be able to cling to it. The space was too wide for her to jump. She saw a notch where the floor would fit if it were level; evidently it was hinged. Maybe the last Player had stepped on it and been dumped when it swung down.

She reached down and around, finding the edge of the tilting floor. Sure enough, her hand found its underside. She pulled—and the floor came up. She was swinging it back to its proper position! It was surprisingly light.

In a moment she had pulled it level and clicked it into place. But she knew she couldn't trust it. How could she make sure it would support her weight?

"Go across it, Dug," Nada said. "You can still win."

"You disgust me," Dug said. "First because you are False; you're still trying to make me get dumped. Second because I wouldn't take that prize anyway; it's Kim's to take. She deserves to win that prize."

He really was a decent person, Kim knew. If only—

She cut off the thought. She felt around the notch—and found a swinging bone that would lock the floor into place. Now it could be used.

She looked at Dug. "I don't need that prize either," she said. "If you would like it, you can have it."

"You can take it, Dug," Nada said. "She doesn't want it."

He shook his head. "You know, we don't have the right attitude about this game. We're supposed to be scrambling madly for the prize."

Kim had wanted the prize. But that desire had faded after she met Dug. Now that she had thoroughly embarrassed herself in that respect, what else was there but the prize? "I suppose somebody should take it," she said. She stepped out on the chamber floor, half expecting it to give way and drop her into the hole. But it remained firm.

Kim paused and looked back. Dug was standing there, watching her. Nada was facing away, her head hanging. Jenny was about to follow Kim. There was something wrong here, but Kim couldn't figure out what it was. There was an expectancy, a tension, as if all hell were about to break loose. What was going to happen, and who knew it?

She started to turn back toward the prize. Then Nada moved. The woman flung herself toward the notch, with its fastener-bone. But Sammy Cat leaped there first, covering it. And Dug tackled Nada much the way he had tackled Kim before. The serpent princess was brought up short of the bone. "Get on across!" Dug cried. "Before she—"

Kim jumped forward and picked up the prize box, just as Nada became a huge serpent. Kim opened the box as the serpent slithered out of Dug's grasp and toward her. Kim reached in to take the little globe inside as the serpent's head came up to knock the box from her hand.

Her hand glowed, painlessly. The globe had disappeared. The serpent saw the glow, and fell as if struck.

I am your Talent, a voice said in Kim's head. *I am the Talent of Erasure. When you return to Xanth, you will be able to Erase anything you choose. Try me now.*

Unsure how this applied, Kim reached out and stroked her hand across a section of the wall, as if erasing chalk on a blackboard. The wall disappeared behind her hand, showing the sky beyond the castle wall.

She stared. "Anything?" she asked.

Anything, living or inanimate. Use me wisely.

Wisely! She didn't want to use this at all! This was a destructive talent.

No, you may cancel my effect by reversing the stroke. Use the back of your hand.

Kim stroked her hand back across the open section, with her palm toward her, and the wall reappeared, except for one sliver her hand missed. Still, this power frightened her. She didn't want to be forever erasing innocent things!

Then she got smart. She willed the talent to turn off, then stroked her hand back across the wall. Nothing happened. She willed it on again, and touched the wall with one finger. A finger-sized hole appeared. She willed it off and stroked her backhand across the hole. Nothing happened. She willed it on and made the same reverse stroke. This time the hole filled in. She had it under control. This was a tool as well as a weapon, a talent of phenomenal power, when she learned to use it properly. But for now she didn't want to use it at all.

She returned her attention to the others. Nada had reverted to her normal form, that of a serpent with a human head, and was sobbing. "I didn't want to do it!" Nada said. "I didn't want to be False! But I had no choice."

"But why did you try to be False to me, when you were Dug's Companion?" Kim asked.

"Because he wanted you to win."

Kim looked at Dug, who nodded. But she wasn't satisfied. "There's got to be more of it than that. What aren't you telling us?"

To her surprise, Nada answered. "It really doesn't matter, now that the issue has been decided. I don't have to be False any more. I will tell you the whole truth."

"What's gone before was a half-truth?" Dug asked.

Nada smiled, becoming beautiful again. "Not even a quarter-truth, Dug. The Demon E(A/R)th was trying to take over this land from the Demon X(A/N)th. They made the decision in their normal fashion: they gambled. They set up the game, and chose characters. If X(A/N)th's Player won the prize, he won the wager. If E(A/R)th's Player won, he did. But Earth used a devious ploy: he sabotaged his own Player, and arranged for him to have a False Companion when he returned. Then he had the two Players exchange Companions. In this manner he thought to ensure that X(A/N)th's Player lost, even if E(A/R)th's Player did not reach the prize first. It would be at least a tie, requiring another game to settle the issue. When that ploy failed, because of the willfulness of Earth's Player, the False Demon made me act."

Kim was too surprised to speak. But Dug did. "What would have happened if the other Demon had won? If I had gotten the prize?"

"The magic of Xanth would have been lost, and it would have become just like Mundania." More tears squeezed from Nada's eyes. "Oh, I'm glad I didn't succeed! It was the most horrible thing! But I had to do everything I could to make you lose, Kim. I'm so mortified!"

Kim found her voice. "There was a whole lot more riding on this than I knew! Xanth without magic—" She couldn't finish.

"More than I knew, too," Dug agreed. "I just wanted to play fair." He looked at Kim. "Well, you better get on home with your prize. I guess you'll be a Sorceress next time you play."

"Yes, you must go," Jenny agreed. "The game is about to fade out, and we Companions will return to our normal pursuits."

"But what will become of Bubbles?" Kim asked. "I can't just leave her here!" She sat down and hugged the dog.

"Then take her with you," Jenny said.

"I can do that? I can take her to—to Mundania?"

"She's a Mundane dog."

"But in Mundania she'll die in a year or so," Kim said. "She's old. Here in Xanth she can live, because of the magic. I don't want to condemn her to death because of my own selfishness." Because she realized that that was the case: she wanted Bubbles with her.

"Save the second bubble in the bottle," Jenny said. "When you can't keep her in Mundania any more, send her back to Xanth. To one of the folk she likes."

"Like Ma Anathe," Nada said. "Or Wira."

Kim felt a great relief. "Oh, I'll do that! Oh, Bubbles, I can keep you with me!" Bubbles licked her face.

"I hope you can forgive me," Nada said to Dug. "I would much rather have been your Fair Companion, as I was the first time. If you will accept my apology—"

"What, a gourd-style apology?" he asked, smiling.

"Yes." She put her arms around him and kissed him passionately.

Kim, despairingly jealous, could only busy herself with her own business. She brought out the bottle. She found the little blower, and dipped it in the fluid. She brought it out, capped the bottle, and blew. A bubble formed. It expanded, until it became large enough for both girl and dog. She and Bubbles stepped into it. "Take us home," Kim said.

The bubble lifted. It floated to the castle wall, and through it. Kim had only an instant to look back, to see Jenny Elf waving goodbye. Then they were out floating over the landscape and leaving the bone castle behind.

The scene faded, and the chamber in the Good Magician's castle appeared. There lay Bubbles, Nada, and Kim herself, looking into the peepholes of the gourds. The bubble settled over the girl and dog, and the two of them merged with their other forms. When the bubble lifted, only Nada remained there.

They floated out the window and high into the air. Xanth spread out below them, then was lost under a screen of clouds. There was a shudder.

The scene changed again. Kim blinked. She was sitting in her room, before her computer screen, which had gone blank. She was out of the game. Back in reality.

It had all been the game. Now she had to face the mundane grind of schoolwork and dullness. Who would believe the adventure she had had? They would say it was just a game. As if her feelings didn't count. She felt an overwhelming grief.

Something nuzzled her hand. She looked down. There was Bubbles!

Kim got down and hugged the dog again. "Oh, Bubbles, I asked for what I most desired—and I got it! It was you, to keep!" Somehow the magic had reached out of the game, and given her this.

Yet that was not quite true. There had been another thing she wanted. But what was the point in brooding about that? In or out of the game, she remained just a plain girl.

The phone rang. Startled, Kim answered it.

"Now, don't hang up on me, Kim," a familiar voice said. "It's Dug. I know I made a real ass of myself. I've been good at that, recently. But I figured I might as well go whole-hog, or whatever pun fits. I'm really sorry about what happened—I mean, when you said—and I never picked up on—"

Kim felt the flush coming to her face again. "That's all right, Dug. I shouldn't have—"

"I mean, I've always been stupid about girls, which is why I'm out a girlfriend now. But I was really out to lunch on that one. So I called to apologize, and—"

"There is no need," Kim said. "I was the one who made the mistake." Her face was burning.

"And when you kissed me, I almost freaked out."

Would he never give over! "I—I—" Kim said, trying to find some way to get away from her shame.

"But you know, I'd be a fool to judge by one kiss," Dug continued relentlessly. "So if you can forgive me for being a blockhead, I'd like to try for more. Like maybe a gourd-style apology. That is, I mean—well, how about a date? So we can start really getting to know each other, you know, to be sure it's not just a fluke. I mean, I don't know anything about you, really, except that you sure can kiss, better than Nada does, and you're real! And—oh, come on, Kim, give me a chance! I can be an okay guy, once you get my attention, and you sure did that. Is it a date?"

"Yes," Kim breathed, realizing that she had after all gotten all of what she most desired. Dog *and* boy. The Good Magician *had* known!

Author's Note

This novel was phrased as a game because I had the notion for the Xanth Game of Companions, but lacked expertise to fashion a computer game. I'm a writer, not a programmer. So I did it my way, showing how the game works, and LEGEND is making the game. You may have noticed that after a while the setting of the game seemed real to the players. The first step was refocusing the eyes to get a three-dimensional effect. This is not magic; it's something that can be done by a Mundane outfit called STARE-E-O, making a flat picture become three-dimensional without colored glasses or anything, just the effort of refocusing the eyes. Impressed by this, I incorporated it into the game. The second step, of believing in magic—well, that's more difficult, but perhaps some players will be able to manage it, and reap the rewards thereof. There is hope for anyone who found this novel becoming real while reading it.

Real people seldom enter Xanth. Jenny Elf and her cat Sammy came to Xanth three novels ago, when the Mundane Jenny was hit and almost killed by a drunken driver. The real Jenny continues to improve, slowly, learning to sit without support and to stand briefly in her wheelchair. She has been in a special school, but hopes to return to regular school in due course. She is using a computer. Now a real animal has arrived: Bubbles Dog. Bubbles was originally adopted by a neighbor, who named her, while we had her sister Tipsy and her cousin Lucky. We wound up keeping her, and we didn't feel right about changing her name, though we weren't keen on it. Tipsy died of cancer in 1988, and Lucky of old age in 1991. We did not want to leave Bubbles alone outside, so we tried letting her into the house—and she turned out to be a perfect house dog. So at age twelve she changed her status and became closer to us, and we really liked her constant company. But larger dogs don't live as long as small ones, and she was over seventy pounds; we knew she would not live much longer. Indeed, just before her thirteenth birthday, while I was writing this novel, she died. The shock was considerable, because we had come to know and like her so well. She was a mongrel, but a really nice dog, and she had fitted so well into our lives. So I brought her into Xanth, where she can live the life she could not continue with us. In effect, I put her in the bubble, where Kim could find her. I don't need to tell you what Bubbles was like, because you know her from the novel.

Just before I started this novel, our horse Blue died, almost thirty-four. That was another shock, because we had had her fourteen years and she was the model for Mare Imbri. So it seemed fitting that Mare Imbri conduct Bubbles to Xanth in the form of a daydream that turned real. They were together in life; they are together in Xanth. Our house and our pasture seem empty now, but in our fond thoughts our friends remain. No, we're not looking for more pets. After a quarter century of having them, and being tied home because of them, we are now ready to relax and travel a bit. Then we'll see.

Between the last Xanth novel and this one another interesting thing happened. Jenny Elf had an iris flower named after her. You see, I had a letter from Thom Ericson, who breeds irises, inquiring whether it would be all right. So now Jenny Elf exists outside of Xanth, too, in the form of her unique flower. I asked Thom whether he had another flower, and the result was another: the Janet Hines Iris. You see, Janet Hines is a reader of mine who is in a sadder state than Jenny. She was not hit by a drunken driver, but by a devastating disease which slowly deprived her of her mobility and her sight. Now she is paralyzed, and can not talk, so she communicates by blinking her eyes, though she is blind. Like Jenny, she retains her mind, but not much use of her body. In 1991, I visited Janet and talked to her. She could respond only by blinking and smiling. But she was glad to know about the iris, and she likes to listen to my novels. I have loyal fans. She, too, is now learning to use a computer to facilitate communication.

I learned to my chagrin that I had gotten the name of a character wrong: Dana Demoness, Humfrey's first wife. How can that be, when she is a fictional character? Because the one who corrected me was Asia Lynn, who had suggested her. So next time she shows up in Xanth, she will make a point of correcting it: she is really Dara Demoness.

The talent of erasure Kim won was suggested a couple of novels ago by Stephanie Erb. I don't know when or whether Kim will show up in a future novel, but if she does, that's going to be some talent. She'll be able to erase the lock on a door, so she can get in, or erase part of a river so she can walk across dry, or erase an attacking monster. Kim herself, winning a prize in a talent contest, was suggested by Dawn Baker. But Kim's romance with Dug was her own idea.

I have half a slew of pun and notion credits, so will jam them into this paragraph in roughly the order they appeared in the novel, though sometimes I collect several under one name: self-popping popcorn, caramel corn—Jane Goulon; vocal cords—Vickie Brockmeier; electricitree—Joshua Ping; Stu-Pid— Stuart E. Greenberg; another demon trying to take over Xanth, deadly night shade, Miss Fire, guest stars—G. Beardwell; censor-ship—Mark Lord; Fairy Nuff—Carolyn Baxter; Ice Queen Clone—Adam Maule; strawberries and bull-frog—Cliff Hicks; lipstick—Jackson Chin; winged unicorns from *Spell* love spring breeding—L. K. Law; maidenhead with a hymen—Richard K. Reeves; Kiss-Mee made Kill-Mee by pulling the S's straight—David H. Zaback; fabric plant—Dawn Baker; Bec on Call—Rebecca Worrell; Curse Fiend history, skeleton history—Erin Schram; dream becomes reality, and vice versa—Dawn Baker; Black Wave—Princilla Claiborne; Black Smith—Randolph A. Crawford; humble pie—Rich Montgomery; useful bubbles—Derek Adams; pun-gent— Jon Morrison; roc-ettes—David Karty; money talks—Alyson Victoria Dewsnap; Germ of an Idea—Rose Platt; Lake Champagne—Mat Cannington, Alicia Littich, Heather Miller; box kite—Rhys-Michael Silverlocke; hiquigems—Verna; odd plants from coneflower to rock brake—John E. Ericson, PhD (Posthole Digger), who claims that all of them grow in Western Colorado; Com Pewter catches a virus—Najan Mughal; ogre girl's talent of ugly—Tamara Lynn Bailey; reverse wood to modify talent—Jonathan Carter; the three ticks: Necro, Agnos, and Cataly—Cindy Shipley; fifty talents—Matt Evans; pit bull, pillow fight, down pillow—Jeremy Lucash; stool pigeon, toiletrees—Dramon K. Hayes; honeydew—Tamara Lynn Bailey; cantaloupe—Jeremy Lucash, Aaron Wikkgrink, Travis Kincher; food chain—William S. Fisher; gilt by association— Gerald Lim; Ass O' Nine Tails—Mickey Bagala, Justin Studebaker, David Haley; Fool Moon—Rich Montgomery; DeOgreant—anonymous; Crow Bar—Dan McDonald; Mother Hen—Richard K. Reeves.

There were more puns and talents offered, but I was unable to use all of them in this novel. Some related to characters who didn't show up here. I will try to use them next time. I should also say that if certain regions seem to resemble counterparts in the Mundane state of Florida, such as Tallahassee (the tall hassle grove)—well, you probably just imagined it.

And to forestall the barrage of questions I may otherwise receive: yes, this Xanth novel has a new publisher. That doesn't mean that the prior Xanths are inferior, just that in the dreary world of Mundania these things happen.

My old 800 number was turned into a porno contact, to my dismay, but readers are welcome to check my web site at www.hipiers.com.

HARPY
THYME

1
GLOHA

Gloha flapped her feather wings until she was high above the harpy hutch. The Land of Xanth spread obligingly out below her, so that she could see all the way to its medium-far corners. There was Lake Ogre-Chobee, with its ogre tribe on the shore and its toothy reptilian swimmers. There was the great Gap Chasm with its horrendous six-legged Gap Dragon. There was all the monster-infested jungle between them. She loved all of it.

But she couldn't pause to appreciate the sights. She had important business. She had to go see the Good Magician so she could ask him a Question. With luck and a year's Service, she might have his Answer. Then maybe she would have her heaving little heart's desire.

She leveled off and flew swiftly toward the Good Magician's castle. She knew exactly where it was, but had never thought she would one day have to go there. That was because she had just somehow assumed that her life would work out well on its own, after the frustrations of childhood worked their way out of her system the moment she turned eighteen and became party to the Adult Conspiracy. Unfortunately, when she actually became party, she realized that she needed a male of her kind—and she knew of none. She was the only person of her new species in Xanth. That had become a problem.

So now she was off to the Good Magician Humfrey, and after doing her year of Service for his Answer, she would be able to settle down with the man of her dreams and live happily forever and ever after and torment their children unmercifully by not letting them know the secret of stork summoning. She was nineteen years old now, and would be twenty then, which would still leave her a faint bit of her youth for her true love to appreciate before they both became adult dullards the following year. She was not so vain as to assume that she would be different from all the other adults who had ever existed. It was too bad that life had to consist of the two problems of childhood and adulthood, with only that brief window of romance wedged in between, but that was the way it was. She knew; she had observed. She was mostly humanoid, and that was the way humanoids were.

She reached the region of the castle, and paused in her flight. There was a mean-looking vapor hovering over it. That looked uncomfortably like Cumulo Fracto Nimbus, the worst of clouds. But what would he be doing here? He wouldn't dare harass the Good Magician.

Reassured by that thought, she resumed flight. But the closer she got, the larger the cloud loomed, and the uglier it looked. Soon she realized that this wasn't merely the magic of perspective, that changed things according to their distance; that cloud was looming uglier on purpose. It *was* Fracto!

She flew lower, to pass under the mean-spirited blob. But Fracto extended his vapors downward to intercept her. She tried to go around, but he sent boiling fog out to the sides to cut her off. His big amorphous mouth formed a gassy O. HO HO HO! it gusted.

This was a real nuisance. Gloha had never liked Fracto, and this encounter was making her emotion ripen into active detestation. Of all times for the blowhard to be in her way! He must know where she was headed, so was getting his flatulent jollies from interfering with her. Somehow he always seemed to know when something important was happening, like a picnic, and he always came to spoil it.

How was she going to get through to the Good Magician's castle? She realized now that the evil cloud would stay here as long as she did, just so he could ruin her mission. She hovered in the air, and waved her fine little fist at the big ugly cloud. "Oh, you make me so angry, I could utter a bad word!" she exclaimed.

HO HO HO! A twisty gust reached out to blow her skirt up over her head so that way too much of her lithe little legs was exposed.

"Now stop that!" she cried, quickly pushing the skirt down. She realized belatedly that she should have worn slacks on this trip. But she had wanted to look dainty and feminine, because she would probably meet one of the Good Magician's five and a half wives. After she got through the challenges that would bar entry to the castle, of course. The Good Magician always had three challenges, to discourage those who weren't really serious about their quests for information. He didn't like to be bothered frivolously.

Then something clicked in her pretty little head. The challenges! This must be the first one! The disreputable cloud must owe the Good Magician a debt, and so was doing him a Service. It wasn't coincidence at all. She had to figure out how to get past Fracto.

That put an entirely different complexion on it. Her own comely little complexion relaxed. All she had to do was figure out how to get past this messy old cloud, and she would be a third of the way through. There was always a way; she just had to find it.

Could she insult Fracto, and make him blow himself out? That was the way Grundy Golem would do it. But Grundy had a mouth that was the envy of harpies; he could spew out insults faster than they could. Gloha was half harpy, because her father was Hardy Harpy, so she should be able to spew out a stinking stream of invective. But somehow she had never cared to acquire that ability. Her mother was Glory Goblin, who was beautiful and good, and Gloha just preferred to emulate her. If her brother Harglo were here, *he* could have let out an oath that burned a hole in the cloud. But this was a challenge she had to handle by herself.

So steaming Fracto was out. Avoiding him seemed to be out too, because he was hovering right over the castle she had to reach, by no accident. What was left? Outsmarting him? She just knew she was smarter than a creature whose brain was swirling vapor, but how could she prove it? This seemed to be a situation in which intellect didn't count for much. All he had to do was sit there and wet on her if she tried to get through.

Well, maybe she would just have to get wet. It wasn't as if she were made of spun sugar, whatever impression she preferred to give others.

Gloha set her firm little face in an earnest little expression and flew directly toward where she hoped the castle was, on a level course.

Fracto puffed up like a mottled wart. He opened his sodden maw and breathed out a sickly gust of wind. It surrounded her, coating her true little tresses with smog and her winsome little wings with dirty ice. Foul air clogged her nice little nose and fuzzed her open little eyes. Suddenly she was flying blind, and losing altitude. She was in danger of crashing!

Gloha sneezed. The force of it shot her spinning back out of the foul air, and she was able to blink her eyes clear. She still had some altitude, and was able to pull out of her tailspin.

She brought out her handsome little hankie and wiped her face. Fracto's ugly puss was laughing and spitting out broken bits of wind and cloud that drifted in stenchy colors. It seemed that she couldn't just try harder; the awful cloud had too much ill wind.

Well, if she couldn't fly there, she would walk there. She was a goblin girl with harpy wings, and though she had spent most of her time with winged monsters, she was at home on the ground too. Fracto couldn't stop her from using her fast little feet.

She glided down to the ground before the evil cloud could work up another foul gust to blow her away. She had hoped to find an enchanted path going there, but saw none. So her lovely little lady slippers touched down in an isolated glade, and she began to walk. There was an ordinary path that would serve; she had noted its direction as she descended, and was sure it would take her there. She would simply have to watch out for hostile monsters and other ilk, because they would be able to harass her on an unenchanted path.

Fracto was furious. He huffed and he puffed and he blew up such a storm that in two and a half moments snow was pelting down. In the remaining half moment it was piling up so thickly that all trace of the path was gone.

Oops. How was she to find her way now? She knew she would get lost in the trackless snow. She couldn't even make her own tracks, because the snow was covering them up just about as fast as she made them. In addition, it was cold; her tight little tootsies were freezing.

She would have to take shelter until the storm blew over. Maybe she could find a blanket bush and hide under the blankets, and the snow would cover her so that Fracto wouldn't know where she was, and would drift away. At least she would be warm while she waited.

But she saw no blanket bushes, and no pillow bushes. This glade was singularly bereft of useful plants. There was only a big snowball at the edge of the glade. She certainly didn't need that!

But as her teeth began to chatter in an unladylike manner, her mind squeezed out an odd thought. What was a giant snowball doing here? The snow had just started, and it was covering the ground with a level layer. It couldn't form itself into a snowball. Was there an invisible giant doing it? But there was no depression where the snow would have been taken from, and there was no smell of giant. "That snowball—that's no ball," she muttered, making temporary tracks toward it.

Then she realized that she had made a pun. "That snowball" had become "That's no ball," spoken the same way. And that gave her the cue.

She marched up to the ball and touched it. Her hands passed through its seeming surface. She stepped forward, and found herself within the entrance to a tunnel. It looked like a snowball from outside, but it was warm and dry inside. This was the way past Fracto's storm. All she had had to do was figure out the secret, and she was on her way. Her mild little mind had prevailed over the cloud's fury, and she had mastered (or maybe mistressed) the first challenge.

But there would be two more, and they wouldn't be any easier than the first. She had gotten through as much by luck as by wit, and might have used up her supply of both. Should she give up her quest?

But then she would never find her Perfect Mate and True Love, and would have to endure unhappily forever and ever alone, which was a fate worse than marriage. She wasn't ready to face that dreary prospect. After all, she had so much to offer the right man, she hoped. She glanced down at her fancy little figure, just to be sure.

So she proceeded resolutely down the passage. She would at least make an efficient little effort, and if she failed, then she would go somewhere and cry.

The passage opened out into a good-sized lighted cave. Along the sides were darkened alcoves, and at the far end was a monster. Uh-oh—she suspected that the next challenge was upon her. Instead of a cantankerous cloud, she would have to get by an aggressive animal.

But there had to be a way to do it without getting eaten. She merely had to figure out that way again. Somehow. Maybe if she proceeded very carefully it would happen.

So she took a tour of the chamber, looking in the alcoves. This turned out to be a slightly baffling tour.

The first alcove held a fat bird with a beautiful fan-shaped tail. Gloha cudgeled her balky little brain and managed to remember news of a bird like this, perhaps confined to Mundania: it was a turkey. She looked at it, and it looked at her, and that was it. The bird wasn't confined, but didn't seem inclined to depart its alcove. It was just there.

"You certainly are a beautiful bird," Gloha said politely. The turkey gobbled appreciatively.

She moved on to the next alcove. There was a rather unprepossessing young human man. Because he was human, he was about twice as tall as she was; goblins were twice as tall as elves and half as tall as humans. She wasn't sure how either other species could stand being so pitifully small or so dangerously large, but it wouldn't be polite to call attention to such failings, so she didn't. "I say, can you talk?" she asked the youth, who seemed to be no older than she was, though it was hard to tell with humans.

"Sure," the youth replied.

"What is your name? Mine is Gloha."

"Sam."

He did not seem to be much for conversation. "What are you doing here, Sam, if I may ask?"

"I'm part of your challenge."

That was certainly direct! "And what is your role in this challenge?"

"I'm a flunky."

"A flunky? I don't think I know that position."

He didn't respond. She realized that he merely answered questions, and as briefly as possible. Naturally the challenge creatures didn't volunteer much information.

"What does a flunky do?" she asked. Then she was afraid he would just say that he flunked. But Sam did give a meaningful response, fortunately.

"He does stupid errands for other folk."

"What errand will you do for me?"

"None."

So much for that. That time she might almost have preferred a less straight answer. She moved on.

The next alcove held a tub of dirty water. That didn't seem to be of much interest, so she went to the following one.

That alcove held a large four-footed animal, like a unicorn without a horn, with long ears. "Hello, creature," she said.

"Hee-haw!" it brayed back.

That gave her the clue. It was a Mundane donkey.

The next alcove held a sort of springlike metal thing sitting on a step. There were several steps, but it wasn't using them. But when she came to stand before it, it leaned over and its top end toppled to land on the next step below. The rest of it followed smoothly, making a turn from the upper pile of itself to the lower pile, until all of it was down. Immediately it bent again, and started sinuously transferring itself to the next step. When it reached the bottom of the little stairway, it stopped. That was all.

The next alcove held a vaguely humanoid creature with a most versatile tail. It jumped from bar to bar, swinging with its hands, feet, or tail. It moved very cleverly, never missing a bar, never falling. It chittered at her from its furry face. She pondered, and realized that this was another odd creature: a monkey.

So it went: each alcove held a creature or thing. They were all part of her challenge. But how did they relate? She could see nothing similar about them; this was like a little zoo with assorted displays.

At the far end was the monster. It stood taller than she was, on all fours, with a huge powerful foresection and a rather small hind section. It was in no alcove; it was in the exit from the chamber. She realized that she had to get by it, but the moment she approached it, it rose up and snarled with such ferocity that she had to step quickly back. It wasn't confined or chained, but it didn't pursue her.

She realized that this was the one she would have to deal with. So she stiffened her knocking little knees and came to stand just beyond the monster's snarl range. "If I may inquire," she said in her most timidly civil little voice, "what are you?"

The monster eyed her appraisingly. He licked his formidable chops. "Hi. I am the Yena," she said.

Gloha blinked. She had thought the monster was male. She looked again, trying not to blush because of the impolite nature of the act, and saw that it was indeed male. She must have misheard. "The Yena?"

"That's what I said, goblin girl," she replied.

Gloha looked yet again. The monster was female. How could she have thought otherwise? "Thank you," she said faintly.

"You're welcome, you tasty little tart," he said.

Gloha found herself getting confused and embarrassed. Once she had passed the magical age of eighteen she had sought information about the secrets hidden by the dread Adult Conspiracy, and had been somewhat disappointed when she learned their nature; she had almost wished she hadn't bothered. But she had gotten it straight, she thought. Now she wasn't sure. How could she be sure, when the creature's unmentionable region kept changing? When it might not be exactly the way a male goblin's region would be, not that she had ever seen such a region anyway? Of course the creature's voice was changing too, being now gruff and then dulcet. What a confusing (not to mention embarrassing) situation!

"You—you must be part of my challenge," she said after a moment. "I—I'm supposed to get past you, so I can go on to the next."

"And if you fail to find the key, I will get to crunch up your bonnie little bones," the Yena agreed.

Gloha had been afraid of that. But now, irrelevantly, she realized that there was something odd about the creature's mane. It was severely knotted. In fact it seemed to be twisted with balls of metal.

She pondered, and decided that it was better to inquire than to ignore. "Your mane—" she started after a pale little pause. "Would you tell me why it has metal in it?"

The Yena smiled, showing his distressingly big sharp teeth. "Ah, you are admiring my locks," she said.

"Um, yes. They are—unusual."

"Indeed," he agreed. "I'd give anything to be able to comb them out. But each one is locked in place."

Gloha picked up on a subtlety. There was something the Yena wanted. "Anything?" she asked hesitantly.

He considered. "Well, anything within my power, of course. I'm not exactly a wealthy monster."

"Even—even letting a minor little morsel get through without being eaten?"

She peered closely at Gloha. "You're catching on, morsel," he agreed. "But of course you would have to deliver."

Gloha realized that she had found only half the key to this riddle. She had to find a way to comb out the Yena's locks. But what could that be? They were solidly metal, and surely would not respond to her cute little comb.

Yet somewhere in this chamber must be the answer. Because that was the way it was, with challenges. Everyone knew that. What everyone didn't know was how to get safely through a particular challenge. That tended to discourage querents from bothering the Good Magician—which was of course the point. Humfrey didn't like to be bothered by folk who weren't serious. His time seemed to be impossibly precious, so he prevented it from being wasted.

She gazed around the chamber. What would comb out a metal lock? Surely not a donkey or a turkey. The flunky? She didn't see how; the metal would still be too hard to abolish. The same went for the monkey, and how that murky water could help was beyond her. Water made iron rust, which would be worse than ever, because it would make the locks impossible to work.

Something began to percolate through her meticulous little mind. These things here—there *was* something similar about them. They were all keys! Donkey, monkey—even the mur-key water. And a key should do for a lock, to unlock it. One of these keys must unlock Yena's locks.

But which one? And how would it work? She couldn't bring the donkey to comb Yena's locks; it just wouldn't work. There was something she still hadn't figured out. She didn't want to make a mistake, because that would get her eaten, which she probably wouldn't enjoy.

She went back to look at Yena. Now she saw that each lock of the monster's mane was different. Some were big padlocks, others were little keyhole locks, some were several types together—combination locks—and one was weird. "What lock is that?" she inquired, pointing.

Yena craned her head about to look. "That is the Lock Ness," he said. "It is a monster."

Indeed it was. It was a huge tangle of serpentine cables of metal knotted into a lock that seemed impossible ever to unlock.

"I suppose that if you could unlock that one, the others would be easy," Gloha said.

"Surely so. But if anyone tried to unlock it and failed, making it even worse, I would be most annoyed. I'd probably have to pulverize that person."

Gloha had suspected as much. She returned to the alcove exhibits. One of these had to be the key to that awful lock—if she could only figure it out. If she guessed wrong, she was doomed.

She looked at the don-key. She just didn't see how its hooves could do anything as intricate as unlocking a lock. The same went for the tur-key's claws. The flun-key was a man, who might have the necessary dexterity, but he had no tools to work on that horrendous Lock Ness. In fact none of these creatures and things seemed like likely prospects.

Maybe she had not yet fathomed the proper pun. Which of these keys was punnishly designed to open such a lock? Not the don, tur, flun, mon, mur, or— what was that slinky spring that marched down the steps called? The question brought the answer: it was a slin-key. That was no good either.

Then another theatrical little thought percolated through her petite little perception. Slinky—that was the way the Yena would like to have his/her locks. All combed out and slinky smooth. And the slin-key was metal, showing that metal could be prettily flowing. So maybe it could lend its attributes to the metal lock mess—uh, ness—and make it similarly smooth.

She wasn't at all sure that her reasoning was right, but since everything else seemed wrong, she gathered up her cornered little courage and made her move. She reached into the alcove and picked up the slin-key. It flexed iridescently in her hands but did not protest. She carried it to the Yena. "I think maybe this slin-key will smooth out your Lock Ness," she said with an adorable little ad-lib.

The Yena swelled up hugely. "Oh you do, do you?" he inquired ominously. "Are you sure?" she added.

"I—I'm not s-sure," she confessed in a dainty little dither. "But it s-seems the best chance."

"Remember, I'll chomp you if it doesn't work."

"Y-yes, I realize that," she said, shaking. "But I must try it."

"Well then, what's keeping you?"

"N-n-nothing," she said with a successful little stutter. She lifted the slin-key and put it to the Lock Ness.

The tangled cables twisted like snakes. They slithered around and through each other, forming a pattern like that of the slin-key. Then they flowed down and became slinky smooth, exactly as she had hoped. After that, all the other locks smoothed out similarly, making the fearsome Yena look positively handsome or beautiful, as the case might be. The entire hide glistened like polished water, showing her real little reflection.

Gloha almost went into a sweet little swoon.

"Well, you did it," the Yena said, standing aside. "You may pass on to the next challenge."

Gloha stiffened her nice little knees and prepared to walk on. "I'm just glad I got the right key."

"Oh, there was no danger of getting the wrong one."

"No danger? You mean you were only bluffing about chomping me?"

"No, I wasn't bluffing about that. But any of the keys would have worked."

She was aghast. "Any? But then where's the challenge?"

"It was a challenge of courage, just as the first was a challenge of nature. You rose to it, so you pass."

"Courage? But I was terrified!"

"That's the nature of courage: to do what you have to do, without yielding to fear. Every sensible person feels fear on occasion, but only cowards let it govern them."

"I never realized!"

"Well, it wouldn't have been as good a challenge if you had," the Yena said sensibly.

"I wonder what the third challenge will test," Gloha said musingly.

"Understanding, of course." The Yena curled up and went into a snooze, his tail twitching contentedly across her fur.

Gloha walked down the passage. She hardly cared to admit it, but her understanding had already been strained to the limit of her broadened little brain. She wasn't at all sure she could evoke any more understanding than she had already. But what was there to do but go on?

The passage was getting warmer. In fact it was getting hot. Gloha would have removed her bright little blouse, but that would have been unseemly. Certainly she couldn't take off her snug little skirt. So she spread her wings a bit and waved them slightly, making a delicate little draft to cool herself. This was certainly a change from Fracto's blizzard outside!

The heat increased. The floor got so hot that her sunny little sandals started smoking. She had to practically dance to stop her feet from getting burned inside them. Even so, she was soon surrounded by smoke.

Then she spied a water fountain by the side of the hall. She skipped to it and touched its magic button. A fortunate little fountain of chill water spouted, and she put her longing little lips to it and drank deeply. That cooled her, and the smoke dissipated. What a relief!

She proceeded on down the hall, no longer bothered by the heat. Now she didn't have to jump and flap her wings to cool her feet, but she was so glad to be safely by that region that she jumped anyway, dancing along. This hall was large enough so that she could stay in the air longer than a regular jump, by flapping her wings. She couldn't actually fly here, but at least it made walking fun. This was more like a frolic. All too soon she knew it would get serious, so she enjoyed herself while she had the chance.

The passage widened into another chamber. In the center was a small plant. She couldn't make out its details, but appreciated its presence. Plants always improved places, especially if they had nice flowers.

She walked toward the plant. But something funny occurred. She seemed to be slowing, though she was walking at the same pace as before. She just was making slower progress.

Realizing that this could be a problem, she hurried. But though she ran, she still moved more slowly. She saw now that her lazy little limbs were not going at the rate she thought; she was running, but they were molasses slow. She jumped, and she rose slowly into the air, then slowly fell.

Something was definitely amiss! She felt fine, but she wasn't getting any-where. What could account for this?

What else but the challenge? It was upon her, and she had to figure it out. The Yena had said it would be a challenge of understanding. So she would have to understand.

She had a bright little bit of feminine intuition. She lifted her purse and let it go. It fell slowly toward the floor. So slowly it would take several times as long as it should to get there. She reached for it, but her hand moved almost as slowly as it did, making it hard to catch. Meanwhile she herself was still in the air from her slow jump.

She paused. She settled slowly to the floor and looked at the plant. Now she recognized it: thyme. The herb that affected time. That was why she was slowing: she was in its field of effect. She would have to figure out how to get around it.

That was indeed a challenge. She really did not know much about thyme, except that the closer a person got to it, the more powerful was its effect. So if its effect was to slow her down, she needed to get away from it, because by the time she reached it she would be moving at no speed at all.

But now she saw that there was no way out of the chamber except the pas-sage on the far side—beyond the plant. She would not be able to reach that passage without going closer to the plant than she was now. That would take, literally, almost forever.

There was certainly plenty to understand! How could she pass a plant she couldn't pass in her lifetime?

Well, the first thing she had to do was back off, so as to be able to operate at normal velocity. She was afraid she was even thinking slowly at the mo-ment. In fact, it might be a longer moment than it seemed.

She backed away. Slowly her feet moved, and her body nudged backward like a small river barge. But as it moved, it gained speed, and soon she was back to normal.

She stopped at the edge of the chamber. She knew it was pointless to go back up the passage she had come down, because that didn't lead to the Good Magician's castle. She had to go forward—past the plant. Somehow.

There had to be a way. That faith had gotten her through the first two challenges. There must be something here that she just had to understand. As before.

She looked around. Now she spied seven glass cups on the floor at the edge of the chamber. Each was on its own built-in pedestal, or maybe it was just a two-way container, the same either way up, so that it looked like an hourglass. They seemed to contain assorted seeds. Each was labeled. One said SEC, and the next said MIN, and the next HR. Farther along one said DY, and another WK. Then MNTH, and finally YR. What could they be?

She started to reach into the first cup, to take up some of the seeds and see what kind they were. But she hesitated, because she didn't yet understand the nature of either cups or seeds, and if understanding would enable her to get safely through, a lack of understanding might wash her out in a hurry. She should figure out the meanings of the labels before she took any action.

Another thought percolated through her meandering little mind. A thyme plant—hourglass cups—these must be the seeds of thyme! Of time. Some of them might enable her to pass the mother plant. If she just figured out the right ones, and how to use them.

Now the labels started making sense. SEC—that would stand for Second, the briefest measure of time. MIN would be Minute. And so on, through Hour, Day, Week, Month, and Year. The SEC seeds were tiny, while the others were respectively larger, until the Year seed was so big that just one of it filled the cup.

What would happen if she lifted out that huge Year seed? Since the thyme plant itself slowed her down, that would probably speed her up, and a year would pass in maybe an instant. That wouldn't do her much good. But if she took a Second, that would hardly be worth it, because even an ordinary second passed pretty quickly. Which kind of seed could she use, and how could she use it?

She decided that if she took some seeds and walked toward the thyme plant, they should cancel out the slow effect, and enable her to maintain her speed. So she could get through on something like a normal schedule. If the seeds worked the way she was guessing they did.

She returned to the SEC glass and picked up one seed. The chamber blinked, and the seed was gone. What had happened?

She thought about it, and decided that the blink had been time jumping forward one second. She was now one second ahead of herself, as it were.

She tried her purse-dropping trick again. But this time as she let it go, she scooped several secs from the cup.

There was a triple blink, and suddenly the purse was on the floor, much faster than it should have been. Now she was sure: to touch a seed of thyme was to feel its effect, which was opposite to that of the thyme plant.

But how could she use any of these seeds? She needed to get them to the slow vicinity of the plant before touching them. She couldn't keep dashing back to the cup for more.

"Silly me!" she exclaimed as a dim bulb flashed just over her honeyed little head. She picked up the SEC cup itself. Seconds were all she cared to use; they were more manageable, and she could use them in handfuls if she had to.

She carried the seconds glass as far as she could before the slowdown was bothersome. Then she picked out one sec. This time there was no blink; instead she speeded up for an instant. The seed had canceled out a moment of the thyme's slowdown. It was working!

She moved ahead, dipping out more secs. Her progress was somewhat jerky, being either fast or slow, but that was to be expected. She had to use two seeds at a time as she got near the plant, and then three. When she was closest to it, she had a small handful of secs at a time. She didn't want to use them all up before she completed her journey across the chamber! But once she was beyond it she was able to get by with fewer secs, and finally she made it to the far hall, and she still had some secs left. That was a relief.

She set down the cup and started down the hall. She had made it through the third challenge!

But as she turned a corner, she came up to a broad desk set to block it. A woman sat behind the desk, writing on a pad of paper.

Gloha stopped, surprised. "Who are you?" she inquired.

"I am the SB," the woman replied, pointing to a nameplate that said SB. "I'm here to handle the Sin Tax."

"Syntax? You must be a writer."

"Sin Tax," the woman repeated. "S-I-N-T-A-X. You must pay. I am the Sin Bursar. It's my business to see that you pay."

"But I haven't sinned!" Gloha protested innocently.

"You were smoking, drinking, gamboling, and having secs," SB said evenly. "Those are all taxable."

"Smoking? But my shoes were burning up! And it was just one drink of water I took to cool off. And then I was so happy to be cool again that I did dance a little, but I never thought—" She paused. "What was that last?"

"You had most of the seconds available. You used them up. Now you have to pay the tax."

Gloha realized that she was stuck for it. Ignorance was no excuse, whether a person stuck her finger in a beehive or used the contents of a seed cup. "How do I pay the tax?"

SB toted up the total on her pad. "That's four counts. You will have to perform four tasks. You will have to wash her, dry her, sock her, and box her."

"Washer, dryer, soccer, and boxer?" Gloha repeated, baffled. "I don't—" But she stopped herself before saying "understand." After all, she had to understand, in order to get through this challenge, which she now realized wasn't yet done. "Could you explain that a bit more?"

SB touched a button on her desk. A panel in the wall opened. Beyond it Gloha saw a strange yet rather nice creature. It had the head and front legs of a horse, and the hind section of a winged dragon. So it was a winged monster, and therefore a creature Gloha could relate to, as she was a winged monster herself.

"There is the Glyph. Clean her up and pack her for shipment," SB said, and returned to her writing.

Gloha entered the Glyph's pen. Now she saw that the poor creature was quite dirty. Her wing feathers were soiled, her fur was grimy, her scales did not glisten, and her hooves were caked with mud. The poor creature needed attention. Gloha would have been glad to help her even if it wasn't to pay the Sin Tax.

There was a trough and bucket beside the stall, and brushes too. Gloha dipped the bucket full of water, and approached the Glyph. The creature shied nervously away from her. "Hey, take it easy, Glyph!" Gloha said soothingly. "You don't have to be afraid of me. See, I'm a winged monster too." She spread her wings and pumped them a couple of times.

The Glyph settled down. Gloha washed her, getting the fur and scales and hooves clean so that they glistened and shone as they should. Then she brushed off the wings so that the feathers turned light and bright. She fetched towels and dried her. But she wasn't sure how to sock her. She wasn't about to hit this nice creature.

Then she saw a plant with odd dangly foliage. It looked like a blanket bush, only smaller. She brought it to the Glyph, and the plant immediately reached around the Glyph's feet and legs. Tendrils stretched material, in a moment and a half both legs had socks. The socks sank in, and seemed just like nice black fur decorating the legs from the knees down.

Now it was time to box her. Gloha saw wood panels to the side of the stall. She could use these to make a big enough box around the animal. She went to fetch the first panel. But as she put her hands on it, she paused. Something was nagging her.

She turned. The Glyph was looking at her. Their gazes met. She had reassured the animal, and now the Glyph trusted her. But Gloha didn't trust the situation.

She left the panel and returned to the hall. "Why does she need to be boxed?" she demanded.

SB looked up from her writing pad. "It's on the bill of lading. One boxed Glyph."

"That's not good enough. Why does she have to be boxed, when she's tame? Why can't she just be led to where she's going? It's cruel to put an animal in a box."

SB checked her pad. "She's going to be a sculpted figure on a fancy building. She has to be crated for shipping."

"I don't understand," Gloha said, using the word she had tried to avoid. But she was upset. It was too late to take it back anyway.

"Why don't you?"

"This Glyph is a fine sensitive animal. She's been badly treated before; she should never have been left so dirty. Boxing her will be more bad treatment. I will never understand why that should be."

"What never?" SB asked.

"No, never!"

"What never?" SB repeated.

Gloha hesitated. She knew she was throwing away her chance to pass the third challenge and get in to see the Good Magician. But she liked the Glyph, and couldn't bear to see the creature mistreated. Who wanted to be stuck on a building, anyway? "No, never," she said in a tone that was neither cut nor little.

"Then you must share her fate," SB said. "Go mount her."

"You mean ride her? I'm sure she's a fine steed. But what's the point, if she's not going anywhere?"

"Wherever she is going or not going, you will go or not go too. That's the rule. I'm here to enforce the rule."

A realistic little realization came to Gloha. "You're doing your Service for the Good Magician!"

"Of course. That's the rule."

"What was your Question, if I may ask?"

"I asked him how I could be a writer. He said I should work on my syntax. Only it turned out to be the Sin Tax. I'm confined to this desk for this boring job. But I must say it concentrates the imagination beautifully. I have written several chapters of my novel between taxes."

"So you're getting to be a writer after all," Gloha said. "While you're doing your Service."

"Yes. I think I'll have a chapter about a crossbreed winged goblin girl and her friendship for a crossbreed winged animal. Do you think my readers will like that?"

"I hope so. It seems interesting to me."

"Now go ride the Glyph." It was evident that SB's affability did not extend to neglecting her duty.

Gloha didn't argue. She was satisfied to share the Glyph's fate, if she couldn't improve the animal's lot. She went to the stall and climbed on the Glyph's back, between the wings. "I'm sorry I couldn't save you," she said, patting the neck under the now-beautiful mane. "But I just couldn't box you, no matter what."

The ceiling disappeared. Open sky appeared. The Glyph spread her giant wings and launched into the air. She was through the hole in the roof and into the sky almost before Gloha knew it.

"But—but you're free!" Gloha said, amazed.

The Glyph neighed happily. Gloha could have let go and flown herself, but preferred to stay with her new friend. Where were they going?

A castle came into sight below. The Glyph angled down toward it. There was a nice solid flat roof with a pile of hay on it. The Glyph landed on this.

"But where are we?" Gloha asked, not yet over her amazement.

"The Good Magician's castle, of course," a voice answered.

Gloha saw a pretty young woman standing by a stair leading up to the roof. "But I shouldn't be here," she protested. "I messed up on the third challenge."

"Oh, I don't think so," the woman said, coming forward. "I am Wira, the Good Magician's daughter-in-law. I came here to lead you to him."

"I'm Gloha," Gloha said, disgruntled. "I—I told the SB woman I didn't understand, and it was a challenge of understanding, so she said I would share the Glyph's fate, and—" She broke off, realizing that something else was odd.

Wira was petting the Glyph. The Glyph was nuzzling her face. It was evident that the two knew each other. Wira brought out a sugar cube and the Glyph ate it. Then Wira petted the animal again and stepped away. "Come on in," she said to Gloha.

"The challenge of understanding—it wasn't about riddles or directions," Gloha said. "It was about decency."

The girl smiled. "Of course."

Gloha joined her, and they walked to the stairs. The Glyph began eating the hay, contentedly.

2
SECOND SON

The interior of the castle was pleasant and surprisingly light, considering the thickness of its walls. Probably magic accounted for that; after all, Humfrey was the Magician of Information, so he would know how to have a nice residence.

Wira led her to the kitchen, where a woman was seated at a table, facing away from them. "Mother, put on your veil, if you haven't already," Wira said.

"That's all right, dear; I heard you coming," the woman said. She turned, and her face was covered by a full, thick veil. Tiny serpents framed the region of her face; they seemed to be in lieu of hair. The effect was fairly attractive; they were pretty little snakes.

"This is the Gorgon," Wira said to Gloha. Then, to the other: "This is Gloha, who just passed the challenges. She has come to see Father."

Gloha was amazed anew. She knew of the Gorgon, of course, but hadn't expected to meet her. The woman's mere glance could turn a person to stone; that was why she was veiled. She was Magician Humfrey's fifth but perhaps not quite final wife; it was a complicated situation.

But what was also confusing Gloha was an oddness about Wira. Suddenly she remembered: Wira was blind! She had moved around the castle with such assurance that Gloha hadn't been reminded. So Wira, alone of people, had no fear of the Gorgon's gaze, because it was mostly the sight of the Gorgon's face that petrified others. It was for Gloha's safety that Wira had reminded the Gorgon about the veil.

"So nice to meet you, dear," the Gorgon said politely. "The Good Magician is ready to see you now." She returned to her business, which seemed to be the slow petrifying of a wedge of cheese: Gorgonzola, of course. Gloha had heard that it was one of her specialties, because she merely had to stare at it long enough.

Now it occurred to Gloha that the cheese must be able to see, at least a little, in order to be affected by the Gorgon's stare. One never could tell what things could do. She knew that when King Dor was around, inanimate things were highly responsive. If a girl stepped over a stone, the stone might make a remark about her legs, and possibly even blab the color of her panties, to her great embarrassment. So maybe it did make sense that cheese could see.

Wira led the way to another winding stairway. It was so gloomy dark that Gloha hesitated for fear of misstepping.

"Oh, I'm sorry," Wira said contritely. "I forgot that you are sighted." She moved a hand, and the walls glowed, showing the stairs.

"Thank you," Gloha said. "I normally don't use stairs anyway; the harpy hive doesn't have them."

"Oh, it must be fun to fly," Wira said. "Of course I would never have been able to do it, even when I was young."

"When you were young?" The woman was twice Gloha's height, because she was full human, but she looked no older than Gloha herself.

"When I was a child, I mean. I'm technically forty-one, but I've been awake for only nineteen years, so the Good Magician used youth elixir to youthen me back to my subjective age. So I think of myself as nineteen, and I am, physically, but my youth was a long time ago."

"You slept for twenty-two years?" One amazement was piling on another.

"Yes. My family couldn't afford to keep me, because I wasn't very useful, so they had me put to sleep when I was sixteen. Then I met Hugo in the dream realm, and he was sixteen too, and we knew each other for ten years asleep. Then we all woke together, when Magician Humfrey returned here, and got our ages set and started living normally for the past three years. The Good Magician likes to keep his age at about a hundred, though he's really a hundred and sixty, the same as his half wife MareAnn."

"She's physically a hundred, too?"

Wira laughed. "Oh, no, she prefers to be somewhat younger. She says that now that she's lost her innocence, she might as well be of an age to get some fun from life. It seems that old women aren't as appealing as old men, and of course they can't afford to get worn or dirty. She won't say how old she is now."

"Life certainly seems complicated here," Gloha said, not sure she would be able to keep all these ages straight, even if some weren't known.

"Oh, no; life is pleasantly simple here," Wira demurred. "It's only the background that is complicated. Just forget it and you'll have no trouble."

That seemed like good advice.

They reached a small chamber buried somewhere in the deep interior of the castle. It was filled to overflowing with books, scrolls, and stoppered little bottles. In the midst of it was an ancient gnomelike little man hardly larger than Gloha herself.

"Good Magician, here is Gloha," Wira said. "To ask her Question."

The gnome pulled his gaze from his tome with such difficulty that Gloha almost thought she heard a tearing sound. "Go see my second son," he said grumpily. His gaze plopped back to the tome.

"But I haven't even asked my Question!" Gloha protested.

Wira nudged her. "It's better not to try to argue with him. He doesn't pay attention."

"But I came all this way, and went through all those challenges, and I want to get what I came for."

"Please, don't annoy him." Wira guided her away with such concern that Gloha had to go with her. "He's already grumpy enough."

But when they were safely away from the Magician, Gloha voiced her protest more firmly. "I don't think it's fair to make me go through all the challenges to get here and not even let me ask my Question. What's the matter with him?"

"The Good Magician always has good reason for whatever he does. We just don't always understand it. When Mela Merwoman, Okra Ogress, and Ida Human came two years ago with their Questions, he listened to them and refused to answer them. Mela was so annoyed she threatened to show him her panty and freak him out. But later they learned that their Answers would have been a lot less satisfying if he had given them then, because there were other things they had to do first."

"I don't understand."

"Well, for example, Mela wanted to know how to find a good husband. He told her to ask Nada Naga. That didn't make any sense to her, but when she asked Nada, Nada sent her to her brother Naldo, who was then Xanth's most eligible bachelor prince, and he married Mela. Because he saw her freak-out panties, which he wouldn't have seen if there hadn't been complications on the way."

"So she might have lost him, if the Good Magician had told her to go after him," Gloha said. "I see the point. And maybe my case is similar, because I'm looking for a good husband too. But my problem is worse, because I fear there is no male harpy-goblin crossbreed for me. Certainly the Magician's second son isn't one!" She paused, suffering another unpleasant thought. "In fact, he only has one son, doesn't he? Hugo, whom you married?"

Wira was surprised. "Oh! I hadn't thought of that. I'm sure he hasn't had

any more children since Hugo. One of the wives would have mentioned it."
Then she brightened. "But he does have five and a half wives, and maybe some
of them had children before he went to Hell. So Hugo may not be the first son."

"Suppose he's the second?"

"Then you can ask him. I can quickly find him for you."

"You can?"

"Like this." Wira paused, then whispered, "Hugo, dear."

There was a scrambling on the stairway. A disheveled young human man
appeared. "You called, dear?"

"Isn't love wonderful?" Wira asked Gloha. "I'm so glad I met him." Then,
to Hugo: "Father told Gloha to see his second son. Is that you?"

"I don't think so," Hugo said uncertainly. "Father had several children before me, I think. So I must be the third or fourth, but I'm not sure."

"Do you know where I can find a good husband?" Gloha asked. "Prefer-
ably a flying goblin about my age."

Hugo shook his head. "I don't think there are any other flying goblins. The
goblins and harpies were at war for a thousand years or so before your parents
got together, so I don't think any of them, you-know." He had to stop, because
he was starting to blush.

"He's so sweet," Wira murmured. "Sometimes I wonder whether he ever
really joined the Adult Conspiracy." She winked, to indicate that she wasn't quite
serious. Then, again to him: "Do you have any idea who would know about all
Humfrey's sons?"

"Maybe Lacuna. She recorded his whole history."

"Yes, that's a good idea," Wira agreed, and Hugo smiled with pleasure at
the compliment. Gloha had to agree: love *was* wonderful. If only she could
find it for herself.

Meanwhile they went downstairs to see if the Gorgon knew. "I should
think that would be the business of his prior wives," she remarked. "They will
all show up here, in due course." She considered briefly, and a wisp of smoke
rose from the spot on the cheese where her masked gaze rested too long. "I believe Dara had a son, however."

"Who?" Hugo asked.

"Dara Demoness. His first wife."

"Oh, you mean Dana Demoness," Wira said.

"No, I mean Dara. Do you think I don't know her name, after meeting her
in Hell?"

"But Humfrey calls her Dana."

"Humfrey never did pay much attention to details. She never bothered to correct him, for fear he'd be grumpy. Names aren't as important to demons as they are to us."

"I don't think I can wait five months to check with all the other wives," Gloha said. "I'm getting constantly older, and my young little youth is fleeting."

The Gorgon laughed. "Believe me, dear, your youth will last long enough if you keep your fine little figure."

"Do you really think so?" Gloha asked, beginning to hope.

"Assuredly. You can keep your youth for several years merely by hiding your blasé little birthdays from men. All smart women know this."

"And hide your intelligence, too," Wira added.

"I never knew about such things," Gloha said, impressed.

"Which is part of your charm, dear."

"Maybe you should go home," Wira suggested, "and I'll ask the wives as they appear. Then I'll send you a message when we learn who his second son was."

"Thank you," Gloha said gratefully. She realized that this was her best and only chance to pursue her quest.

The Gorgon served them a snack of funny punwheel cookies and candy-striped milk, to fortify Gloha for her flight home. The Gorgon seemed slightly uncomfortable; her ringlet snakes were panting. The castle was warm, and it looked hot under the thick veil.

"If I may ask—" Gloha inquired with a halting little hesitation.

"By all means, dear," the Gorgon said, wiping her brow. "We aren't as fussy about questions as the Good Magician is."

"Why don't you get some vanishing cream from the Good Magician to make your face invisible—"

"I did that once, but it was awkward going about faceless, so I still had to wear a veil."

"And then mask it with the illusion of your face?" Gloha finished. "So that you would look just like you, snakelets and all, but wouldn't stone anyone."

The Gorgon paused, her veil flexing into an attitude of astonishment. "Why, I believe that would do it, when I'm Xanthside," she said. "Then I could have the spells nullified when I returned to my job as a horror actress in the dream realm. Thank you, dear; I shall see Humfrey about it immediately." She got up and headed for the stairway.

"He's grumpy today," Wira called warningly.

"He wouldn't *dare* grump at me," the Gorgon replied. "Not until after he provides those spells."

Wira giggled, and Gloha joined her. If there was one person who wasn't intimidated by the Good Magician, it was the Gorgon, and not merely because she was his wife.

They finished the cookies and milk. Then Wira opened a window, and Gloha bid her adieu, spread her wings, and took off. "Do visit again sometime," Wira called after her. "There won't be any challenges if you don't come with a Question."

"Maybe I will," Gloha called back. It had been nice visiting with a young woman her own age.

Then she mounted up, up into the sky, flying for home. It was good to be airborne again!

But in a moment she suffered a change of mind. That was one of the privileges of being feminine. She had been for a while at the happy hive; it was time to visit her goblin relatives, which included her mother Glory Goblin. So she changed course and headed for the Gap Chasm where the Gap Goblins lived.

Soon she was there. That was just as well, because the day was getting tired and the sun seemed hardly able to keep itself in the sky; any moment it would singe the trees to the west and dunk itself in the ocean and go out, leaving Xanth in darkness. She glided over the gloomy deep chasm and down to the village perched at its brink. The goblins didn't worry about falling into the chasm; if one did, well, there were plenty more goblins who didn't. In a moment she was hugging her mother, who was still one of the prettiest of goblin women despite being an ancient thirty-seven years old.

Then Gloha explained about how she had gone to see the Good Magician Humfrey, and failed to get a good Answer to her Question. "But the Good Magician always knows what he's doing," Glory said. "I remember when your Aunt Goldy met the ogre who was doing his Service for his Answer. That was a funny thing—the ogre was so stupid that he had forgotten the Question by the time he reached the castle, but he did the Service anyway. His Service was to protect the half nymph Tandy, and by the time he was done with that, he married her and was happy, and that was his Answer. And along the way Goldy got her magic wand and found a husband of her own, all because of her association with the ogre."

"And she was the mother of Cousin Godiva Goblin," Gloha agreed, having heard the story before. "And grandmother of Gwenny Goblin, who's only three years younger than me, and has already had adventures galore and become the first lady goblin chief, and I'm not even married yet!" she finished in a wail.

"Well, you're special, dear," her mother reminded her.

"The only one of my kind! How can I ever find a suitable man?"

"Maybe Humfrey's second son will know."

"And maybe he won't! And maybe it will take five more months to find out who the second son is. And I'll be pushing t-twenty!" For now she was suffering a delicate little doubt about the efficacy of extending youth by hiding birthdays. Suppose it didn't work? She'd be sadly stuck.

Glory saw how serious the matter was. "Maybe your Aunt Goldy will have a notion. Why don't you go ask her?"

"Thanks. I will." Gloha spread her wings.

"I didn't mean right this instant! Don't you want to stay and see your Grandfather Gorbage?"

"Not if I can avoid it."

Glory nodded understandingly. Goblin men just weren't the most pleasant folk. However, she had a more persuasive point. "Are you sure you want to fly in the night? When the other winged monsters might not recognize you?"

Gloha folded her wings. "Maybe I *will* visit with you tonight," she decided. "It's the family way."

"How nice of you, dear." Mothers had a special talent for getting their way.

But in the morning, before her grandfather could show up, Gloha gobbled her breakfast and bid her mother a modestly tearful parting. There were forms to be followed, after all.

Gloha took off and flew north toward Goblin Mountain where her Aunt Goldy lived. It was nice to have an excuse to visit there, now that her cousin-once-removed Gwenny was chiefess. If only the other goblin tribes could be governed by women too! Then the whole of goblindom would be so much nicer. But anything like that was a long way away, if ever.

The sun had dried itself off and recovered enough strength to climb the eastern sky. Gloha had never been quite certain how it managed to find its way to the east after drowning in the water to the west, but assumed that there was some kind of magic to handle it, because the sun's course was fairly reliable. The clouds, which had gotten somewhat damp and drippy in the night, were drying off and turning white and fluffy again. There was no sign of Fracto, fortunately.

She passed the region of the flies, and the dragons, and the elves, until she spied Goblin Mountain. Or was it? She hadn't been there in months, and what she saw below was distinctly odd. "Odds goblins," she murmured. Instead of a structure resembling an enormous anthill with the pox, she saw a prettily tiered network of gardens with flowers. That *couldn't* be it.

Then she remembered: the male goblins no longer governed Goblin Mountain. A female was in charge. So flower gardens made sense.

Reassured, she dropped down toward it. As she got close, she saw more detail. The flowers grew in patches of color, and the color spelled P-E-A-C-E. That was Gwenny's work, all right.

She landed by a prettily manicured front gate. There was a goblin guard, neatly uniformed. He snapped to attention as she approached. "A courteous greeting, Lady Gloha," he said politely. "Whom do you wish to see?"

Gloha was taken aback. What was the matter with this goblin? He should have greeted her with an insult or a threat, or at least a sexist innuendo. That was the way male goblins were. It was expected. She didn't trust this.

Then the goblin flashed a surreptitious scowl. "Don't look so surprised, wingback. This isn't *my* idea. At least I got half a look up under your sexy little skirt as you came down."

Gloha smiled as she smoothed down her skirt. So this was just a veneer over normalcy. Goblin nature had not been repealed. "I want to see Goldy."

"Very good." He turned to his talk-tube. "Gloha to see Goldy, presently." Then he turned to Gloha. "Get your galoshes going, goody-gams."

Gloha nodded, appreciating the goblin-style compliment. She walked on into the tunnel. Soon she found Aunt Goldy's apartment. She knocked on the portal.

It opened. There stood the gobliness, even ancienter than Glory because she was ten years older. But she looked better than she had, probably because she now had more status than before. All females did. "Why, how nice to see you, dear," she said, giving Gloha a hug. "Do come in."

The apartment was nicely finished, with flowers and pleasant pictures all around. Gloha sat gracefully on a cushion, resting her gams, uh, limbs, and especially her wings. "I went to see the Good Magician about a husband, and he told me to see his second son. But I don't know who that is. Mother thought you might know."

Aunt Goldy pondered. "I remember when I traveled with the ogre—his girl Tandy—there was something about her. I never did quite figure it out. But maybe the ogre did. Maybe you should go ask him."

"Ask the ogre? You know ogres and goblins don't get along well."

"This one's different. He's half human. He's a decent creature, and not nearly as ugly or stupid as he should be. He figured out how to work the magic wand, after all, then gave it to me so I could win a goblin chief. He has a way with these things. Talk to him, and maybe he'll help you find that second son."

Gloha shook her bemused little brain. "This is pretty farfetched. Are you sure you aren't getting senile?"

"Not at all sure, dear," Goldy said cheerfully. "Maybe you should ask someone else." But she did seem oddly sure of herself. She surely knew or suspected something, but wasn't about to say exactly what it was lest she seem truly foolish.

At least Gloha could check with the ogre. Then maybe she could find Lacuna and ask her. Someone, somewhere, was bound to know. "What's the name of this ogre?"

"Smash. He's Esk's father, I believe."

"Oh, Esk! I know of him. Esk Ogre. He married Bria Brassie, and they have three children."

"They do? I knew only of one."

"The stork brought them two more, I think. Twins."

"How curious. There seems to have been a rash of twins recently. Maybe the storks are up to something."

"Maybe it's a conspiracy," Gloha said, smiling. "An Adult Conspiracy."

"That must be it," her aunt agreed.

Before she left, Gloha went to see her cousin-once-removed Gwenny, who at sixteen was more like a straight cousin. She was the chiefess of Goblin Mountain, but perhaps would have half a moment to spare.

Gwenny was at a meeting, negotiating a treaty with the naga folk, but her Companion Che Centaur came out to see Gloha. He was a winged monster too, and they were friends. They hugged each other. He was only eight years old, but already he was substantially larger than Gloha, because he was of a larger species. He was also more intelligent, because that was the nature of centaurs.

"I'll tell Gwenny you were here," he said. "I know she would want to see you, but this treaty is so important that she just can't break away. The goblins and naga have long been enemies, and now they will be friends, or at least allies. The details are critical. Prince Naldo Naga is attending, though he'd rather be playing water games with his buxom wife Mela Merwoman, so you can appreciate how important it is."

"Yes, of course." There it was again: married folk having fun. Mela had a daughter two years older than Gloha, yet Mela had no trouble finding her man. "But it's nice to see you, too."

"I understand you are looking for the Good Magician's second son."

"Yes. But I don't know who he is. Do you know?"

"No, but I'm sure the Muse of History would know."

"I don't want to struggle with Mount Parnassus to see her! Aunt Goldy thinks Smash Ogre may know something."

Che cocked his head. "That is possible. At worst, he won't know anything, and then you can ask the Muse."

Gloha thanked him and went her way. Each person had a different idea whom she should ask. Maybe one of those people really would know. Yet once she found the second son, she would still be at the mere beginning of her quest, because the Good Magician hadn't said that his second son had the Answer. Who knew what convolutions remained? She really wasn't very pleased with Humfrey's offhand dismissal of her Question. Who cared about all the other folk whose Good Magician Answers had turned out, in retrospect, to be good? She didn't even have his Answer, just a stupid referral.

She emerged from the mountain and took off before the goblin guard could make any more smart-faced remarks. But she couldn't stop him from getting another peek under her skirt before she got out of range. She really did have to change her outfit, the moment she got home. But first she would see the ogre, because his home in the jungle was closer than the harpy hutch.

She flew south, crossing the Gap Chasm again. She saw a dark cloud, and quickly flew lower before it could see her, in case it should be Fracto. Then she spied the ogre's twisted-ironwood-tree house and descended.

A really ancient woman of fifty or so met her at the door. This was Tandy, the ogre's wife.

"No, Smash is out searching for stones from which to squeeze juice for stone soup," Tandy reported. "He's half ogre, you know, and every so often he likes to exercise his ogre nature. You may have noticed how all small dragons have vacated the area for now. But perhaps I can help you with your concern."

"I'm looking for the Good Magician's second son. Do you know who that is?"

"No, but I know someone who might be able to point him out. That's my father Crombie. That's his talent: to point to anything."

Gloha considered. "That might do it. But isn't your father pretty old, considering how aged you are?"

Tandy smiled in a way that reminded Gloha oddly of Aunt Goldy, who was of that general generation. "Exceedingly old. I think he recently had his ninety-first birthday. But he was once a major character in Xanth; and old characters never die, they just fade away. We just have to talk to him before he fades too far."

"That makes sense," Gloha agreed. "Do you know where he is now?"

"Oh, yes. He lives down in the underworld with my mother Jewel the Nymph."

"She must be horribly old too."

"Yes and no. Nymphs are ageless, really, remaining young and sexy forever or until they turn mortal. Jewel turned mortal when she married Crombie and sent off to the stork for me. So if we figure she was an apparent age of twenty then, she would be an apparent age of seventy now. That's probably manageable."

"I suppose so," Gloha agreed doubtfully. "But I'm not sure I could find my way through the underworld."

"Unfortunately I'm only half nymph; I look my age. But I'm still spry enough to show you the way to my father's home."

"Oh, wonderful!" Gloha exclaimed with guileless little glee, clapping her happy little hands.

"First we have to get to Lake Ogre-Chobee," Tandy said, scribbling a note. "The entrance to the underworld is there. Fortunately that's not too far from here. I can't fly, of course, so it will be slow, but we'll get there."

Gloha hoped it wouldn't be *too* slow. She did want to get there before the five months it would take to check with Humfrey's other wives was done. But of course she didn't say that, because it might upset Tandy and make her even slower.

Tandy pinned the note to a chair. Gloha saw that it said "SMASH—visiting folks—back soon. TANDY." Then Tandy went out to her kitchen garden, where she dug out a plant.

"Oh—to eat along the way?" Gloha asked.

"No, this is a light bulb, to make my poor old body light. In my youth I rode a night mare, but I am beyond that now." Tandy tucked the bulb into a pocket, and indeed, she did seem to step lighter now.

"I don't suppose you also grow heavy bulbs," Gloha said.

"Oh, yes, I do. But Smash uses them, when he's feeling light-headed; they bring more gravity to his thoughts."

They set off through the jungle. Gloha was concerned about encountering land monsters here who might try to eat them, but then saw that Tandy's shirt said OGRE'S WIFE across the back. That probably protected her from most creatures. Who among them would care to risk the wrath of an ogre?

The light bulb did seem to make Tandy faster on her feet; she was quite spritely. She fairly bounded along, while Gloha flew low. They followed a path marked by saplings twisted into pretzel knots and boulders cracked open by powerful blows. An ogre path, obviously.

Then they heard something. It was a weird sort of squishy noise smelling of fresh mud. It seemed to be moving on a course that would intercept their path somewhere ahead. "What is that?" Gloha asked nervously.

"I'm sure I don't know," Tandy replied. "Let's go see."

Gloha had an opposite notion, but did not want to be negative, so she agreed. They hurried forward toward the place the noise would soon be. In a moment Gloha was flying ahead, outdistancing Tandy.

It turned out to be a mud slide. Rich brown mud was coursing through the forest. The only problem was that there was no slope from which it was sliding. It was moving along the level ground, or even uphill.

The mud slewed to a stop. "Ho!" someone called from beyond.

Gloha flew up to see who it was. There to her special amazement was an old, old man sitting on a huge dinner plate set on the mud. Behind him was a prettily decorated cabin with little white curtains in the windows.

Gloha hovered before the man, perplexed. He looked vaguely familiar. "Hello," she said with a timid little tremor. "Did you call?"

"Why, hello, winsome little winged goblin girl; you must be Gloha," he said. "Yes, I called; I thought you might be able to help us. I'm King Emeritus Trent." Then, perhaps assuming that she wouldn't recognize the name: "Ivy's grandfather."

"Oh!" Gloha said with a squeamish little squeak. "I thought you had faded away."

"Not quite," Trent said. "We four grandparents are going to visit Esk's grandparents for a fade-out party. But we seem to have lost our way."

"You four? Where are the others?"

Trent turned his face back. "Hey, Sorceress, lift the veil," he called. "We have a visitor: Gloha Goblin-Harpy."

Immediately the cabin vanished. There sat three other old folk on plates: two women and a man.

"Uh, hello," Gloha said again with a certain awed little awkwardness.

"My wife the Sorceress Iris," Trent said. One of the old women became a beautiful young woman with a shining silver crown and button-bursting bodice. Except that it was laced, not buttoned, so she was a lace-lashing lady.

"So nice to meet you, Gloha," the sorceress said dulcetly, with a grand nod of her head.

"My friend Bink, Ivy's other grandfather," Trent said. The other old man became a handsome medium-young man in halfway casual clothing. He nodded.

"And last and least, his wife Chameleon, in her stupid phase," Trent concluded.

The other woman did not change. Gloha saw now that she was old but amazingly lovely; she needed no magical enhancement, despite being in ordinary garb. For now Gloha remembered from her history lessons that the Sorceress Iris' talent was illusion; she could make anyone or anything look any way she wanted. But Chameleon didn't seem to need illusion. Gloha hadn't believed that anyone that old could look that good.

"We hope you can help us, Gloha," Chameleon said. "We seem to have lost our way."

That was so obvious that it needed no restatement. Then Gloha remembered the thing about Chameleon: she changed with the moon, becoming beautiful and stupid, then ugly and smart. So she couldn't be counted on to speak intelligently.

Something Trent had said registered. "You're going to see Esk's grandparents? Why, so are we! I'm with Tandy, who knows the way."

"What a fortunate coincidence," Queen Iris said. She sent a curiously significant side glance at Bink. "You and Tandy must join us and show us the route."

"Oh, I'm sure we'll be glad to," Gloha agreed. "Let me go tell Tandy!" She darted away before belatedly realizing that this might be impolite. After all, if she remembered her history lessons correctly, all of them had been kings of Xanth at one time or another. But it was too late to correct her lamentable little lapse, so she just flew on.

In a moment she found Tandy, who had continued walking. "There are four—they want to—same place we're going—it's a coincidence," she said breathlessly or perhaps witlessly.

Tandy questioned her on the several pieces of her statement, and managed to fathom the general little gist. "That *is* a coincidence," she agreed. "For such a party to get lost right where we were going—there must be magic involved."

"Oh, yes, the Sorceress Iris is spreading illusion all around," Gloha agreed.

They reached the mud slide. The cabin was back on top of it, hiding the three, but King Trent remained in his handsome younger form. "And to what do we owe the honor of your presence here in the wilderness?" he inquired of Tandy.

"Gloha is looking for the Good Magician's second son, and I thought my father Crombie might point out the direction," Tandy replied.

"Oh, Humfrey is involved in this," Trent said, as if that had great significance. "Well, if you will show us the route, we shall give you a ride on Swiftmud here." He indicated the bank of mud on which his plate sat.

"I *would* rather ride than walk," Tandy agreed. "And perhaps Gloha would rather ride than fly. We shall be happy to make the deal."

So Trent set out two more plates, and Tandy managed to scramble up to one without getting too muddy, while Gloha flew to the other. Then the cabin expanded to enclose them all including Trent, and they were in what looked like a luxurious palace chamber.

"But don't stray from your plate," Chameleon cautioned with a smile.

Gloha extended a cautious finger to the cushioned floor beside her, and felt mud. Everything was illusion except the mud and the plate. But it was pleasant in this seeming cabin. "If I may ask—" she started.

"We are not quite as young as we once were," Trent said. "So now we prefer to travel in comfort. I transformed a mud grub into Swiftmud, and Iris provided plates from her kitchen. This seems to be an adequate mode of travel. Except that Swiftmud is not particularly bright, and strayed from the assigned route when we weren't watching, and now we aren't entirely sure where we are. But we suspected that there would be a fortunate coincidence, and now it has occurred. Show us the way, Tandy, and we shall slide there forthwith."

Tandy looked around. "I think I'll need to be outside for that."

Abruptly the cabin wall contracted, and Trent and Tandy were outside, while Gloha remained inside. In a moment Swiftmud started to move again, sliding smoothly and probably swiftly along. Yes—Gloha saw trees whizzing by outside the curtained porthole. They were on their way.

"Have some anthony and tell us your story," Iris suggested, extending a smaller plate on which several brushes and combs were piled.

"Anthony?" Gloha asked blankly.

"Ant-honey," Iris said more carefully. "Honey from ants. Sometimes in my age I slur out the hyphen. Some like it better than bee-honey or sea-honey."

"Thank you." Gloha took a honey comb from the plate and took a naughty little nibble. It was very good.

The others took honey brushes and chewed on them. Then Gloha explained about her quest to find a good winged goblin man for a husband, and the frustration of her visit to the Good Magician's castle.

"Yes, Humfrey is like that, now more than ever," Iris said, licking spilled honey off her fingers. "Age hasn't sweetened him."

"But he always has reason," Bink said. "I remember when he said he couldn't fathom my talent."

"What *is* your talent?" Gloha asked. "I mean, I know you're a Magician, because my centaur history book said so, but I don't think it said what your talent is."

"Well, that's an odd thing," Bink replied. "I think I have a notion of its nature, but every time I try to tell someone about it, somehow I don't."

"I don't understand," Gloha said.

Iris and Chameleon smiled and looked away.

Bink sighed. "I suppose I could make a demonstration." He took a breath. "My talent is—"

The Swiftmud lurched to a halt, almost pitching them from their plates onto the icky surface of itself.

"Whose fault is that?" Trent's voice called from outside the cabin.

"Oh, it must be mine!" Gloha cried with a chaotic little chagrin.

"Nonsense," Trent said. "This is bigger than all of us."

The cabin vanished, so they could all see what was outside. Swiftmud perched at the edge of a huge cleft in the ground. Trent had halted it just in time to prevent them from plunging into the chasm and getting horribly muddied.

"It must be an extension of the Gap Chasm," Tandy said. "But I don't remember any such fault in this region."

"Probably the original forget spell hasn't yet worn off all the tributaries," Trent said. "But I must admit it came as a surprise. I'm not sure how we'll get past it."

"If we could identify it, we might know more about it," Tandy said. "All the offshoots of the Gap Chasm have names."

"Right," Trent agreed. "So we must answer my question: whose fault is this?"

Gloha realized that he hadn't been accusing her before. Still, she felt somehow guilty. She struggled with her minor little memory of geography and managed to evoke a name. "Could it be San Andrea's Fault?" she asked. "The one that cracks on into Mundania?"

"Yes, it must be San Andrea's fault," Iris agreed. "I never thought much of San Andrea anyway."

"The question is," Iris said tartly, "how are we going to proceed? This fault appears to extend right across our route. If we detour, after losing time by getting lost, we shall be late for our engagement. We don't want the others to fade out without us."

"I can fly across," Gloha said. "But I'm too small to carry anyone else. I might haul a rope across, though, if that would help."

"I don't think we have time to make a rope bridge that would hold Swiftmud's weight," Bink said. "I wish we had thought to get no-fault insurance. Then we wouldn't have encountered any fault."

"We never think of what we're going to need ahead of time," Chameleon said. "Otherwise you and I would never have adventured in the Gap Chasm the first time, Bink."

Bink smiled. "You were almost as lovely then as you are now, dear."

She returned the smile. "And lovelier than I will be next week."

"Save those reminiscences for the fade-out party," Iris snapped. "I'll make us all beautiful then. How do we get there in time?"

"We can proceed, but it may not be entirely comfortable," Trent said. "Swiftmud is a fairly versatile creature; he can slide along any surface without losing his grip. But we might prefer to walk."

"At our age?" Iris asked. "You forget you're ninety-six years old, and I'm not a great deal younger. If we try to walk any distance, we shall both fade out sooner than planned."

"Then we had better ride," Trent agreed. "But we shall need to use some of your magic glue."

"Glue?"

"For our bottoms."

"What are you thinking of!"

"So we won't fall off our plates when Swiftmud slides down the face of the fault."

Iris considered. Then she dug into her purse and brought out a tube of glue she had evidently harvested from a glue plant.

They took turns applying it to their plates, having to stand on an extra plate Iris provided from somewhere while doing it. Then they sat down again, and their legs and posteriors fastened firmly to each plate. Gloha was nervous about it, and decided not to use the glue. "Maybe I can help find the way through the fault."

"That seems sensible," Chameleon agreed. Gloha felt a thankful little flash of gratitude; not only was the woman lovely, she was nice. Gloha had been afraid that someone would find fault with her suggestion about the fault. After all, it was the nature of faults to be found.

Trent gave a command, and Swiftmud started forward. He slid to the edge of the fault, and over it, making a square angle turn down. One by one the plates made that awesome turn. The others remained on their plates, but Gloha couldn't; she had to fly free.

She looped around and hovered near Swiftmud as he slid at an even pace straight down the wall of the fault. The five passengers remained firmly glued to their plates, but they did not look inordinately comfortable. Gloha suspected that under the illusion their hair and perhaps other parts of their bodies were sagging somewhat. Then the cabin reappeared, hiding them. That made Gloha feel better, at least.

She flew down to investigate the depths of the fault. It narrowed steadily, until it disappeared in a dark crevice too small for Swiftmud to enter. But it was also too wide for the creature to cross, she thought, unless it was capable of making a U-turn across nothing. What now?

She flew to one side, and then to the other. She found a section with a U-shaped connection of stone. That should do. In fact it looked ideal.

She flew back to Swiftmud. "Follow me," she said.

Swiftmud obligingly followed her to the side. She landed on the U-stone. "Cross here," she said.

Swiftmud did. Then it proceeded up the other wall. In due course it returned to the surface, and got level again.

The cabin vanished. "Very good," Iris said. "Now we must go full speed ahead, to make up for lost time."

"As soon as we get unstuck from our plates," Chameleon said, trying to fidget without being able to move her shapely posterior.

"Of course." Iris produced a tube of unglue, and they became unglued.

Gloha settled back to her plate as Swiftmud accelerated. Now the scenery fairly whizzed by. Gloha's hair flowed back in the wind, and so did Chameleon's. The others seemed unaffected, perhaps because their appearances were now illusory, confirming her prior suspicion. Gloha was glad of that, because in their natural states they did look stomach-irkingly aged. She had not realized that it was possible for a person to be older than fifty or so, but understood that some folk just didn't have much choice in the matter.

Soon they reached the great wide broad expanse of Lake Ogre-Chobee. "We had better pause for refreshment," Iris said, "before getting into the labyrinth of the underworld."

So Trent guided Swiftmud around the edge of the lake, looking for a campsite with pie trees and pillow bushes. Instead they found a village whose houses were all black. Sure enough, a sign said BLACK VILLAGE.

"I don't remember a village here," Trent said.

"It must have formed within the decade since our last visit here," Iris said. "I can clothe us with the illusion of invisibility if you wish."

"Don't bother. Just make us young and anonymous for now. I'm sure the natives are friendly." Indeed, there was a sign a bit farther along saying FRIENDLY NATIVES.

All six of them became young, except for Gloha, who didn't change. She was impressed by Iris' powers of illusion.

Swiftmud proceeded slowly down the center street. Soon a man came out. He looked ordinary, except that he was black. "What can I do for you tourists?" he inquired in friendly fashion. He wore a nameplate saying "SHERLOCK: Safe—Courteous—Reliable."

"We were just looking for refreshment," Trent said. "We're on our way to the underworld."

"You have come to the right place," Sherlock said. "We settled here last year and are promoting tourism. We have all manner of refreshments and entertainments, including regular presentations at the Curse Friend Playhouse. Or you can simply sun yourselves on the Ogre-Chobee beach and feed the tame ogres and chobees."

"Tame ogres?" Iris asked dubiously.

"It happens," Tandy reminded her.

"Oh, yes," Sherlock agreed. "We have Okra the Ogre Tamer, who can make an ogre named Smithereen perform ogre feats of strength for just a smile. Nobody believes it until they see it. And the chobees will allow themselves to be petted, for just a few marsh mallows and maybe a toe or two." He smiled. "A bit of safe, courteous, reliable humor there."

"Just fetch us some fresh pies to take along," Iris said.

Sherlock turned his head. "Pie assortment, to go," he called. Then, to Trent: "And what do you have in trade?"

"Do you need any illusion?" Iris inquired.

"We prefer to have no illusions," Sherlock said. "We like things here as they are."

"Do you need to have any person or creature transformed to something else?" Trent asked.

Sherlock considered. "Actually there is someone we'd like to transform. But it's his nature that needs transforming, not his appearance."

"What is his nature?"

"He's always trying to organize things into a state so he can run it. We have no need of this, but he just won't stop. His name's Nator. We even call the way he acts natorial. It's really bothersome."

Trent pondered. "I seem to remember a type of creature that enjoys that sort of organization. There are a number of them, but none of them want to be the leader. So they are usually in a state of confusion or a state of frustration."

"Nator would love to solve their problems," Sherlock said. "But are they human?"

"Not really. Does it matter?"

Sherlock considered again. "Perhaps not." He turned his head again. "Hey, Nator! Would you like to be a goober?"

Another man came out. "What's a goober?"

"Creatures who exist in a state with no leader, because no one wants to do it."

"I'd certainly like to shape them up!" Nator said.

Trent gestured. Nator became a creature vaguely resembling a cross between a peanut and a pink jellybean with multiple legs and long antennae. The antennae quivered. Then the goober ran away.

"Wait!" Sherlock called. "We don't know whether you like it yet."

But then they saw a green jellybean emerge from the jungle to meet the pink one, and a purple one arriving from another direction.

"They are very quick to locate each other," Trent said. "I'm sure Nator will be all right. They are highly social creatures."

"And they won't mind his being natorial?"

"They should love it. He'll be goober natorial."

A young black woman arrived with an armful of fresh pies. "I hope these are all right," she said. "They are black berry, which is our favorite, and green berry, purple berry, gray berry, and blue berry. And one goose berry. Be careful of that one; it's very fresh."

"Those are fine," Trent said. "Fair exchange. Thank you."

They took the pies. Gloha got the goose berry. It honked as she took a bite, but she avoided its other effect by flying up. Geese were flying creatures, and their food tended to make others try to fly, except those who were already doing so. So the pie's freshness didn't bother her; she knew how to handle it.

They bid parting to Sherlock and the young woman, and Swiftmud resumed sliding. A number of the black folk had come out during the dialogue and exchange, and were looking curiously at the mud. Gloha didn't blame them; it was a most curious creature.

"We shall have to tell Dor about this new village," Trent remarked. "It does seem like a nice place to visit."

"This region has been cleaned up," Bink remarked. "It used to be primitive country, but now it is parklike."

"That must be the work of the Black Villagers," Chameleon said. "Now I remember: I did hear something about a Black Wave that arrived from Mundania, but I never heard where they settled. Now we know."

As they ate their pies, Swiftmud slid out across the surface of the lake, having no more trouble with it than with the vertical walls of the fault. Soon they were surrounded by flat water. Gloha was impressed, because she had never seen so much water in one place. Not when she was actually on it.

This was an interesting journey. But was it getting her any closer to the achievement of her desire? She still had no idea how to find the man of whatever dreams she might want to have, assuming he existed. If only the Good Magician had Answered her Question, instead of dismissing her without even listening. Instead of sending her on this wild goose pie chase for his second son, who might not exist either.

3
RECONCILIATIONS

They had hardly finished their pies before they reached the dome-city of the Curse Friends. Sherlock, curiously, had called them "Curse Friends"; maybe he had misspoken. Actually the city didn't show on the surface; there was only a whirlpool there. A big one.

Swiftmud floated right toward it. "We aren't going into *that*, are we?" Gloha asked with a feeble little fright.

"Oh, that's right, you haven't been here before," Tandy said. "This is the way to the underworld. One of the ways, anyway, but goblins lurk along the others. Don't be concerned."

Gloha tried her best to be unconcerned as Swiftmud got caught by the vortex and floated around it in a diminishing spiral. The central hole loomed up hugely. Then they tilted into it and whirled around and around, going down.

After that it was a blur. Gloha squeezed her expressive little eyes tight-shut closed.

There was a bump and splash, and the awful spinning stopped. Gloha's eyes peeked open just a tiny slit.

They were in a dark cavern, floating on a somber lake. Gloha pried loose her jammed little jaw. "What happened?" she asked doubtfully.

"We landed at the bottom of the vortex," Tandy answered. "From here it's mostly smooth sailing to my mother's apartment."

That was a relief. If Gloha had had any idea what this trip would be like, she would have hesitated to make it. But no one else seemed concerned, so she crammed her startled little stomach back into place and pretended to be satisfied.

After a somewhat timeless time, because there was no sun here to mark it, just a faint glow in the water and on the stone walls, they came to a landing. An unusual woman came out from a doorway. She wore a gown set with so many bright gems that it made the whole region three and a half times as bright. "Oh, you're here!" she exclaimed. "But who is this?"

"Mother, this is Gloha, who has come to see Crombie," Tandy said. "Gloha, this is Jewel the Nymph."

Indeed she looked like a nymph, being of exquisitely crafted figure. Except for one thing: she was old. Gloha had never heard of an old nymph.

"Jewel was timeless until she loved and married Crombie," Bink reminded her. There was a certain diffidence about the way he related to the nymph that Gloha would have found perplexing if she had thought of it, but at the moment she was meeting too many people to have time for extra thoughts. About the only one who was really clear in her mind was Magician Trent, because she remembered him best from her history lessons. "Then she began aging from her apparent age of twenty, just as mortals do. We still call her Jewel the Nymph, but she's really no longer a nymph, and she will join our fade-out party."

Oh. That did not seem horribly clear, but Gloha was in no mental shape to be confused, so she just smiled and accepted things as they seemed to be. Though she was halfway sure that things weren't exactly as they seemed to be. What was there about Bink's attitude toward Jewel that bothered her? Jewel was Tandy's mother; that was enough.

"You are barely in time," Jewel said. "Crombie has almost faded."

"We were delayed while traveling," Iris said somewhat sourly. Gloha felt guilty again, remembering that the last delay had happened when Bink tried to tell her about his talent. The fault had shown up right then, without warning. Of course that couldn't have been *her* fault, yet somehow it seemed so.

"Gloha must talk to my father before he fades any further," Tandy said. "She is still young; most of her life is ahead of her."

"How nice," Jewel said. She led the way to a bedroom chamber.

There, amidst piled blankets and cushions, was a horribly wizened ancient old man. Gloha wasn't sure just what fading out entailed, but if this was it, she didn't much like it. Crombie seemed to be on the far side of sleep, lying on his back, his eyes staring up at the ceiling without focusing. She remembered how Wira's eyes had never quite focused on things; his were somewhat like that.

But she had to talk to him, and hope he could help her. "Sir Mister Crombie, the Good Magician Humfrey told me to talk to his second son, but I don't know where he is or even who he is, and my Aunt Goldy thought maybe Smash Ogre would know, but he was out and Tandy thought maybe you would know or at least be able to point the direction." Then she took a breath.

The decrepit figure stirred, weakly. The withered old mouth opened. "Can't," he breathed.

Gloha didn't know what to say. This had become her almost only hope, and now it was dashed. So she burst into tears.

The figure stirred again. "Ask—else," it breathed.

A thought found its way through her misery. Ask something else? If he could point out anything—or almost anything—why not ask him where her ideal man was? If he could point the way to that one, she wouldn't need to talk to Humfrey's second son anyway.

"Where is my ideal man?" she asked.

One arm moved. It fell off the bed, but it was pointing a definite direction. Gloha made careful note; she had a kind of answer!

But she needed more. "Is there anything that can help me in my search?" she asked.

The arm moved again. This time it pointed at King Emeritus Trent.

"Magician Trent can help me?" Gloha asked, startled. "But he's—" She caught herself before uttering the trite little truth that he was far too anciently old to be able to do anything much more than make it through his share of the fade-out party, and might have trouble even with that. "He's otherwise committed," she concluded.

Trent himself seemed startled. "He must be pointing to something beyond me," he said.

"Such as the wall," Iris said with half a smile. "I'm sure that will be a great help to her."

"Something beyond the wall," Trent said with the other half of the smile. "Just as was the case when he pointed toward her ideal man."

"Perhaps he got the questions reversed, and meant that *you* are her ideal man," Iris said with a quarter of a new smile.

Trent laughed. "How nice it would be to think so! But I think she is looking for one about seventy-six years younger. Here, I'll get out of the way, and Crombie can point again." He eased himself down and to the side, sitting on a cushion near Crombie's head.

Gloha was relieved to get the chance to clear up the confusion. "Mister Crombie, sir, could you point again to whoever or whatever might be able to help me in my quest for my ideal man?"

The withered arm shuddered and moved again. The gnarled forefinger pointed up beyond the decrepit head. Directly at Trent again.

Gloha was both chagrined and intrigued. It did seem that Crombie's talent was working, because the man wasn't even looking and couldn't have known exactly where Trent had moved. But how could ancient aged old King Emeritus Trent help her? There had to be some confusion.

She had asked directions four times: for Humfrey's second son, for her ideal man, and for something to help her, twice. Crombie had been unable to point for the first, but had seemed pretty sure about the other two. The confusion was more likely to be in the first than in the last. Odd that he had failed there. Did it mean the second son was dead? Then why had Humfrey told her to ask him? Was she supposed to find his ghost? That didn't seem quite reasonable; ghosts seldom answered questions.

Then Gloha suffered another astonishing little intuition. But she would have to verify it, because there was something confusing about it. "I—could I talk to Crombie alone?" she asked timorously.

"Why not?" Jewel said. "We can organize for our party."

The others left the chamber. Gloha emboldened herself enough to take Crombie's weathered and almost crumbling hand. Some of her young little vitality seemed to cross over and mend his old gross senility. "We are alone, Mister Crombie," she said. "I promise not to repeat what you tell me, if you want it that way. Will you tell me why you couldn't tell me where Humfrey's second son is?"

The wrinkled ash-gray head rolled from side to side. The worn lips quivered. "No," he shuddered.

"I have a suspicion," Gloha continued relentlessly. "I think the Good Magician had a reason to send me to his second son, and I think you do know where he is."

"No," Crombie creaked again.

"I think that maybe, just possibly, perhaps *you* are that second son. That I found my way to you despite not knowing."

He rolled his head some more, but didn't say no again.

"What I don't understand is why you don't want it known. Maybe if you told me, I would understand."

He was still reluctant, but in the face of her accurate little assessment he managed to recover enough to tell her the story. He was the son of Humfrey and the Mundane woman Sofia, whom Humfrey had married because she was the finest living sock sorter. Humfrey had had a son with his first wife, the Demoness Dara, and a daughter with his third wife, Rose of Roogna. But Humfrey had been more interested in his work than in his family, and more interested in training Magician-level children like Trent and Iris than in his own child. So Crombie had been pretty well ignored and alienated.

"Oh, I'm so sorry to hear that!" Gloha said with more than a slight little surge of sympathy. "No wonder you weren't happy. But still I don't understand why you don't want to be known as his son."

So Crombie told her about his experience with the Demoness Metria: how he had met her when looking for a better mother, and how she had helped him fight off the spooks of the night bedroom, and stayed with him until he turned thirteen and became aware of the female of the species. Then she dissolved into smoke and drifted away. He realized that she had stayed with him only in order to get into Humfrey's castle and spy out his secrets. He had looked for a girlfriend, and thought he found one, but when he wanted to see her panties she had puffed into smoke and he realized that the demoness was having more fun with him. He knew it was Metria, because she had a thing with words: she seldom could remember precisely the right one, and had to hunt through her vocabulary for it. That made her unique among demons, and always gave her away. But more important, she was female, and her mischief was always of a female nature. So he had sworn off women forever.

"I can see why," Gloha said. "She shouldn't have teased you like that. Everyone knows that all any man wants of a young woman is to see her panties. That's how Mela Merwoman nabbed Prince Naldo Naga, and she wasn't even very young. That's how I'll nab my ideal man, if I ever find him. But why did that make you not want to be known as Humfrey's son?"

So he told her how he had grown up and left home and gone out on his own, becoming a soldier. He had been supremely embittered by the disinterest of his father, and of course his mother was a woman, so there was nothing there for him. Later he had discovered a nice nymph, and she was all right, because nymphs weren't women, they were innocent creatures. So he had married her, and been satisfied, though she had loved someone else.

Gloha got a giddy little glimmer of something that surely was none of her business. "Whom else did she love?"

"Bink. He drank love elixir without realizing it, and saw her, and loved her though he was already married. In time she came to love him back, but by then his love had been nulled by the Time of No Magic. So she was left hurting. But I liked her, and I brought her a love potion, and then she loved me too. Of course it still took a while for her other love for him to fade, if it ever did, because it was natural."

That explained Bink's odd attitude toward Jewel. He had once loved her, and she had once loved him. That was the sad memory of what might have been between them. How romantic!

"Didn't it bother you that her love for him was natural, while her love for you was magic?"

"No, I knew the situation. All I asked of her was that she be a good wife to me, and that she was."

So Crombie had made his own life, and that was all right. Fortunately his daughter Tandy was half nymph, so he could stand her. But he never saw reason to let his connection to the Good Magician be known. Humfrey had never given any indication of caring, after all.

Gloha got an intriguing little insight of another intuition. "But suppose Humfrey did show he cared about you?" she asked. "I mean, everyone knows that he'd rather grump than breathe, and would never admit to any human passion, but just suppose he let slip a hint that he remembered you and wanted to know how you were doing? Would that make it all right for you to be known as his second son?"

Crombie thought about it, and seemed to be trying to fight off the notion, but its allure was too much for his frail old resistance, and he finally had to admit that that might make it barely all right. But he knew that Humfrey would never let slip anything like that, so it didn't matter. Now he would fade out in peace with his friends, and all would be forgotten.

"But you said Trent and Iris were the ones who took your father's attention from you," Gloha said. "Why should you be friends with them?"

"They didn't know how it was," Crombie said, his voice growing stronger. "They think there was some other reason, such as the demoness. So they let it be, and haven't told anyone. And indeed, I worked for them for years, when Trent was king, and he was a good employer. No fault in him. So now I don't want to embarrass them by having it known."

"And your daughter Tandy doesn't know?"

"She doesn't know. Neither does Jewel. So let's leave it that way. After the fade-out party it won't matter."

"Well, that party may have to be postponed."

The decrepit figure developed some semblance of animation. "Postponed! I can't make it beyond the day!"

"But you pointed to Trent as the one to help me find my ideal man. So he'll have to help me look. So he won't be able to join your party now. Wouldn't you rather wait until he can?"

"You are making typically female mischief!" he exclaimed, his insecurely fastened bones rattling with the effort.

"Well, that's my nature," she said with a golden little grin. "I think Humfrey misses you, and wants to be recognized as your father, but can't do it if you don't agree. He can't even admit that he wants it, for fear of your rejection. So he sent me to see you, hoping I'd jog something loose. I'll bet that if you gave even one nod of agreement, he'd be here to make amends."

"Never!" Crombie said with what might well pass for emphasis.

"What, never?"

"Of course never! The Good Magician is incapable of admitting to making any mistake ever in his long life."

Gloha had a tiny little tinge of doubt. So she suppressed it before it could grow. "Well, we can test it. Nod your head." Gloha hoped she was right. It would make halfway sense of half the confusion she had been experiencing.

"I don't have the strength."

"Maybe I can help you sit up." She leaned over him.

"All right! I'll nod! Then will you leave me alone?"

"Of course," she said with sweet little sweetness.

She put her hands on his bony old shoulders and hauled, and he managed to lurch into sit-up position. Then he nodded his head once, and fell back exhausted.

There was a silence. Nothing happened. Gloha realized that she had misfigured it. "Well, I guess you're right," she said. "I'll go away and let you be."

"Thanks," he breathed. He seemed almost disappointed.

She got up and went out of the doorway. Good Magician Humfrey met her there. "Are you through?" he inquired grumpily.

"Yes, I must be," she agreed sadly. She went on by him, letting him go in alone.

Then she paused. Her mouth dropped into an open little O. The others laughed.

"You did it," Trent said, looking even younger than before. The Sorceress of Illusion was overdoing it a bit, making him seem to be in his twenties. He now wore a bright shirt and trousers, with shiny boots and even a bold sword in its sheath. He looked utterly dashing. "I was hoping you would. I think I owe you a favor."

"Oh, you don't have to—"

"Humfrey brought some Fountain of Youth elixir. He'll give some of it to Crombie so he can survive the postponement of the fade-away party, and he gave some to me. So now I am in shape to help you on your quest."

Gloha looked at him again. "You mean—?"

"This isn't illusion any more. This is my physical age. Of course I'll take some more elixir, with reverse wood, to neutralize the effect after this is done. Then we ancients of Xanth can fade out in style."

"Oh!" Gloha said, feeling maidenly faint.

"However," Iris said sharply, in that tone which suggested that there was a formidable caveat coming to the surface, "the rest of us should not be expected to twiddle our tired thumbs while you two enjoy yourselves gallivanting around the country, slaying dragons and such. What are we going to do—play tag with monsters?"

Trent considered for a good three quarters of a moment. "Maybe you could rest in the Brain Coral's pool."

Chameleon laughed, but Jewel was serious. "Why not?" Jewel asked with nymphly innocence.

Iris answered her. "The Brain Coral likes to collect things in its pool, but it doesn't like to let them go. So unless we want to give up our freedom immediately, it is best to remain well clear of it."

"That's not so," Jewel protested. "I have been there many times on my errands, placing gemstones for mortals to find. Sometimes when I've been tired, the Brain Coral has let me rest in its pool, and then released me much refreshed. It honors any deal it makes."

Trent reconsidered. "Perhaps my humor was ill advised. We may have misjudged the Brain Coral."

"If it actually lets people go," Bink said, "that might be worth considering. The Good Magician knows it as well as anyone does; he could say."

"Did someone speak my name?" the Good Magician asked, appearing in the doorway. Beside him stood Crombie, looking about ten years younger and forty years happier. "My son and I could not help overhearing."

"Your son?" Jewel asked, surprised.

"It's a long story," Crombie said. "What's this about the Brain Coral?"

"Jewel says that the Brain Coral will honor a deal," Bink said. "When I was young I regarded it as an enemy, but that was some time ago."

"The Brain Coral does what it feels proper," Humfrey said. "When you sought to free the Demon X (A/N)th and thereby bring on the Time of No Magic, it fought you, knowing better than you did. But when you are not bent on mortal folly, it is not your enemy."

"So if we made a deal to rest in its pool until Trent returns for our fade-out party, it would let us go at the right time."

"Assuredly," Humfrey agreed. "But it would ask a price for such a service."

Bink turned to the others. "Then maybe we do have something to do while we wait. I understand that a sleep in the Brain Coral's pool is like an instant; you go in and come out immediately, yet centuries may have passed."

"That will do," Iris agreed.

"But you can take time out from that sleep," Jewel said. "You can be conscious if you want to, and talk with other folk there. There are some really interesting creatures in storage, with fascinating histories."

"Then let's go and inquire," Trent said. "See if we can make a deal."

"You go," Jewel said. "I want to learn this long story about who is whose son."

"Gloha and I will go," Trent said. "It's our mission."

The others exchanged a shrug, not objecting. It did seem that the rapprochement between Magician Humfrey and Crombie had excited their greater interest.

"Now just where is the Brain Coral's pool?" Trent asked.

Crombie pointed a direction. It seemed to be downstream, so they went to Swiftmud, who was muddily snoozing on the dark underworld river.

"Sip the water there," Humfrey said. "That will enable you to communicate with it."

They set off through the caves. Now Gloha was able to admire the glowing colors of the walls and ceiling, and the convolutions of stone under the clear surface of the water. This was really a rather pretty place, in its somber way.

They came to a cavern that seemed to be half filled with water. But when Gloha peered down through the water she saw that it was much deeper than she had thought, so that she could not see the bottom. The sides were shallower, and there on slopes and ledges were all manner of things and creatures. All were still; none were swimming or showing signs of life. It was an eerie display.

"This must be the place," Trent said brightly. Gloha had not yet gotten used to his youth and vigor; she would hardly have recognized him if she hadn't known about the youthening. He was a handsome and self-assured man, not at all doddering. Youth elixir was wonderful stuff.

They dipped their hands and brought sips of the water to their mouths. It tasted faintly of medicine.

What do you want of me, King Trent?

"I am about to start a quest with Gloha Goblin-Harpy, and my friends need a place to park for the duration."

What do you offer in exchange?

Trent smiled. "What do you want?"

What is your quest?

"To find my ideal man," Gloha said. Then she had a halfway bright notion. "I don't suppose you have a nice winged goblin male in storage?"

No. I have a winged centaur filly, however.

Gloha shook her head. "I can't marry her."

But perhaps this is our avenue of exchange. I understand that there is now a winged centaur male.

"Che Centaur—Chex's foal," Gloha said. "The only one of his kind. But he's still very young. Just eight years old."

Cynthia is not too much older. It is time for her to emerge and learn the ways of contemporary Xanth. By the time she does, Che may be grown.

"Cynthia," Trent said. "That name seems familiar."

It should, Magician! You transformed her back in 1021.

"I did? I'm not sure I remember. I transformed so many in those wicked days. Was that about the time I transformed Justin Tree?"

About. She came to me, and has been here seventy-two years in suspension. Xanth has changed somewhat in that period. She will need time to adjust, and it will be better if another winged monster assists her, and if she is protected from harm until she is competent.

"I begin to get your gist," Trent said. "You want us to see to that chore, in exchange for parking our friends here."

"Oh, let's do it!" Gloha cried. "I'm sure she's a nice person."

Trent glanced at her obliquely. "It would be better to verify that before making the commitment."

She realized that it was barely possible that his extra seventy-five years or so of experience counted for something. "I suppose," she agreed cautiously.

Then enter the pool and listen to Cynthia's story.

Trent looked at Gloha, and Gloha looked at Trent. This was safe? But if it wasn't, the Good Magician would come to see what had happened. So they shrugged, almost together, and prepared to enter the pool.

But there was a complication. Their clothing. It wouldn't be good to get it soaked, but it also wouldn't be good for the two of them to be unclothed in each other's presence. The Adult Conspiracy had firm things to say about that, even when no children were involved. Trent was a mature male man, and Gloha a fully formed (if petite) approximately human crossbreed woman. It would not be appropriate for him to see her panties.

Don't be silly. Leave your clothing on. Just jump in.

They exchanged another glance and shrug. Then they held their noses and jumped off either side of Swiftmud.

Gloha was afraid she would choke, but she had no trouble. She didn't seem to be breathing, but felt no discomfort. She just slowly sank down into the depth, which no longer seemed unpleasant. She saw Trent descending nearby.

"This is an interesting experience," he remarked without opening his mouth.

"Very," Gloha agreed without opening hers. In addition, her clothing didn't seem to be wet; it neither clung to her nor floated out from her. It remained about the same as it was in the air.

"I think we must be communicating in thoughts rather than sound," Trent remarked. "But our ears think it is sound."

"That sounds right to me," she agreed with a small little smile.

They landed on a pleasant ledge set with pretty shells. There was a winged centaur filly, with brown hair and mane, white wings, and a blouse and jacket covering her human section of torso. That was unusual in a centaur, for that species was normally completely open about bodily appearance and function.

"Cynthia, I presume," Trent said.

"You remember, Magician Trent!" the filly replied.

"It isn't often I transform such a lovely person."

"You haven't changed at all! But I suppose some time has passed above."

"Some has," he agreed. "This is Gloha Goblin-Harpy, who would like to get to know you.'

Cynthia looked at Gloha for the first time. "Oh! You're a winged monster too!"

"Yes. And the only one of my kind, perhaps. I would like to know your story, if you care to tell it."

"I'm happy to tell it, if you care to listen. Make yourself comfortable."

They found nice boulders and sat on them. They were so light, down here under the pool, that even the rough stone was comfortable.

Cynthia began to talk. Gloha soon not only heard her voiceless voice, but saw her sightless scene, as the ambience of the Brain Coral's pool made the scene come alive.

Cynthia was in most respects a regular run-of-the-mill human maiden (though perhaps prettier than most, she was tempted to believe) whom the stork had delivered to a nice family in the North Village barely sixteen years before. Her magic talent was moderate but convenient: she interacted remarkably well with children. She used this magic to make others happy with her baby-sitting. When the children's parents were away, Cynthia was, as a centaur put it, "In Loco Parentis"; that was his way of saying that she was like a substitute parent. Or as the children put it, "Crazy see-see!" which was their way of saying that she was fun and apparent.

But all was not well in Xanth. The Storm King was not paying proper attention to the weather, so that on some days the local pillow bushes got so dry that their feather stuffing leaked out and floated away, while on other days it rained so heavily that the pillows got all sodden and squishy. Meanwhile there was news that Evil Magician Trent was making mischief, trying to shake up the current monarchy. Though Cynthia didn't care much for the way the Storm King was handling the kingdom, she was almost certain that a hostile takeover wasn't the way to improve things.

Cynthia went to the edge of a placid lake to admire her brown-haired and brown-eyed reflection, as was expected of pretty girls her age. She saw a grapevine growing near the water, so she approached it. Grapevines were gossipy plants, notorious for their news about things that shouldn't concern right-thinking folk, so naturally no one listened to them. But Cynthia happened to be alone, and no one would know, so she yielded to temptation and put her ear to a grape.

"The horrendous Evil Magician is nearing the North Village, terrifying the denizens," it gushed, splattering purple prose on her delicate shell-pink ear. "Who can stop this monstrous incursion before it is Too Late?"

Oh, this was bad news indeed! She was firmly against the Evil Magician invading her peaceful village with his nasty transformations. She would have to try to stop him. Unfortunately she had not the least idea how to do it. All she could think of was to intercept him and try to persuade him to leave this village alone. She was a resourceful maiden with a talent for dealing with children; she would think of something to stop his childish behavior. She hoped.

One day while she was picking rambling roses she saw him approaching. She knew it was him, because she happened to see him change a butterfly into a pink elephant. The elephant seemed none too pleased with the transformation; it trumpeted a brassy melody and galumped off, flapping its ears like wings. That was definitely a sign of magic. So she moved to intercept the man before he could pass her by.

Suddenly she was face-to-face with him. She opened her mouth to utter a paragraph of remonstration as her eyes met his. And stopped, stunned.

Not by his magic. By his attractive face and general good looks. She had assumed he would be ugly, or at least somewhat crude and rough around the edges. Maybe stooped, with a limp and a sneer. Instead he was somewhere in the vicinity of divine, being tall and upright and even-featured.

"A greeting, pretty maid," he said, accurately enough. "Have we met before?"

"I, uh, um, er, not exactly," she said, luxuriating in the warmth of his handsome gaze. The roses fell from her flaccid fingers and rambled rapidly away, as was their nature. Her wits landed amidst them.

He bent down to help her collect her scattered wits. "Then allow me to introduce myself," he said as he handed them back to her. "I am Magician Trent."

Cynthia wanted to crank up her persuasive powers and ask him to go away. Instead she said, "I'm Cynthia. How may I help you, Magician?"

He smiled roguishly, and she realized that her present leaned-over posture was giving him rather too much of a glimpse down her bodice. She was after all not all *that* far from the innocence of childhood, and could almost feel the censorious eyes of the Adult Conspiracy following his eyes to exactly the same place. She nearly dropped her wits again, this time down into her nice new cleavage. Fortunately she managed to straighten up without too much of a blush.

"I would appreciate it if you would give me directions to the nearest good river," he said.

Cynthia, being naturally sweet and innocent, clung to her recovered wits and sweetly and innocently misdirected him. If he followed her directions, he would wind up on the rail that rode strangers right out of town.

Magician Trent gazed at her. "Are you sure?" he inquired gently.

"Well, maybe I got it confused," she confessed, fearing that he was suspicious. So she gave him directions to the nearest love spring instead. If he drank from that, he would fall hopelessly in love with the next female creature he encountered, like maybe a warty hog.

"Are you sure?" he inquired again.

"Quite sure," she said, stifling her impulse to confess all and maybe kiss him for good measure.

"I am sorry for that," he said. "You see, I happen to know this region. You have just directed me to a hostile rail and to a too-friendly love spring. I fear I shall have to deal with you, for such betrayal irks me. But I shall not interfere with your youthful beauty." Then before she could attempt to protest, he gestured with one manly hand.

Cynthia knew she was in trouble. She tried to flee, but already her body was changing. Her squeezable torso unsqueezed, stretched, expanded, and distorted. She became grotesquely huge. Her (for want of a nicer term) rump pushed out behind monstrously and sprouted a long hair tail. From somewhere in the center of her body four new appendages grew. Two were legs, but they didn't have feet; they had heavy black horny terminations. The other two were behind, and were white, feathery, and grotesquely convoluted. Her body turned mostly brown and hairy, with knobby knees and a belly as big as a barrel. Only her scant surviving bit of human torso remained clothed; her nether section had burst out of her skirt and was now devastatingly naked. Oh, utter horrors! She had become a complete monster. And the Evil Magician had tortured her further by claiming not to interfere with her beauty!

Properly appalled, Cynthia cried out in despair and humiliation and ran off as fast as her four cowlike legs could carry her. She knew she could never return to her home like *this*. But where could she go? What could she do? No use to ask the Evil Magician who had transformed her; he would just say, "Frankly, my dear, I don't give a dam." As if anyone could give or take anything as massive and watery as a dam. She would just have to hide until she could make her way out of Xanth and never be heard from again.

She was getting breathless, so had to slow to a trot. But she kept going as far as she could, hoping to get far enough away so that no one would know of her. But she couldn't go forever; the day was getting late.

She found a barn. Maybe she could hide there for the night, then sneak off early in the morning when few people were up and about. Maybe she could find a burlap bag to put over her head so she could not be recognized. Because she could tell by the feel of her face that it had not been changed; the Magician had done her the ultimate indignity of leaving her most recognizable aspects untouched, so that everyone would know her shame. There just seemed to be no end to the exquisite refinement of his vengeance on her.

She went to the back door, opened it, and wedged her ungainly body in. She was thirsty; maybe she could find some water here. She was also tired; maybe she could find some hay to lie in. Assuming she could lie down, with this clumsy contraption of a body.

"Who's there?"

Oh! She had thought this barn was empty. Cynthia tried to back out, but her huge hairy rump banged into the doorpost, making a crash that could be heard throughout. She tried to turn around so she could flee headfirst, but there wasn't room in this narrow passage. She was stuck, as the farmer tramped toward her from elsewhere in the barn.

He appeared around a corner. "Speak up, or I'll jab you with my pitchfork," he said gruffly, squinting into the gloom of her corner.

"Oh please, sir, don't hurt me!' she pleaded. "I'm trying to get out of your barn!"

"Why, it's a girl," he said, surprised.

"No, it's a monster. Please just let me go and I'll never bother you again."

"You sure sound like a girl. Let me get a look at you."

"No, please! Don't look at me! I'm all hairy and awful." She tried to hide her face, though that wasn't the hairy part.

The farmer appeared before her. He stared. "Why, you're a centaur filly! What's your kind doing here?"

Cynthia paused. "A what?"

"A centaur. Don't you know your own kind? What do you want in my old barn?"

A centaur! Suddenly she realized it was so. The four furred legs with their hoofed feet. The hairy tail. The massive belly. The human head and upper torso. "I didn't realize," she said. "The Evil Magician transformed me into a centaur.

Except—what are these?" She spread the folded white feathery appendages on her backside. They promptly banged into the walls, and she had to stop.

"Why, those are wings," the farmer said. "You're a flying centaur!"

"So even the centaurs won't accept me," she said, realizing how completely the Magician had punished her. She would be an outcast from both human and centaur folk, because there was no other creature of this kind in all of Xanth.

"The Evil Magician did this to you? Why?"

"I tried to deceive him, because I didn't want him taking over our land. But he wasn't fooled, and he transformed me. I'll never be able to live it down."

The farmer nodded. "I guess I'd feel the same way. Very well, you can spend the night here. I've got a stall I'm not using. I'll bring you some food. There's water in the stall." He showed the way to the central part of the barn.

She found a bucket of fresh cool water, and used her hands to dip some out to drink. It was wonderfully refreshing. Then the farmer returned with some wry bread. The chunk was warped, with a twisted expression, but that was the nature of this variety. She bit eagerly into it, and it was very good.

"Oh, sir, how can I ever thank you?" she asked gratefully, belatedly remembering her manners.

"What are you good at?"

"I used to be good with children. I was apparent: children saw me as a parent, so I could baby-sit."

"Well, I have a little boy, but he's such a handful that no one wants to take care of him. His talent is making things go awry. I think it's because he ate too much wry bread. This is a wry farm; it's what we grow, so we use it."

"All children get into mischief," Cynthia said. "I'm used to that."

"I have to go into town tomorrow for supplies. The wife's away visiting her endless relatives. If you could watch him tomorrow—"

"I'd be glad to."

So she slept on the soft hay, getting the hang of her new body. The horse section had no trouble, but it took her a while to get her human portion comfortable, because it couldn't lie flat the way it had before. She finally propped it against a wall, resting her head against her braced forearms. In the morning she combed some of the tangles out of her hair and washed her face. She wished she could change her shirt, but it was the only one she had. She knew that centaurs normally went bare-breasted, but she couldn't bring herself to be so exposive.

The nice farmer brought her a bowl of wry pudding. Then he brought out the boy, who seemed to be about six years old, and toe-headed. That was not a concern; children normally grew out of the toes as they matured.

"This is Wryly," the farmer said. "Wryly, this is Cynthia Centaur, who will watch you while I'm gone."

"Gee, a centaur!" the boy said, pleased. "I'll ride her all around."

Cynthia hadn't thought of that. The notion did not especially appeal. "Maybe later," she said.

"See if you can manage him," the farmer said.

Cynthia tried her talent on the boy. But she realized almost immediately that something was wrong. Wryly didn't change; he looked just as mischievous as ever. But the farmer seemed to go into a trance. His jaw went slack and his eyes stared fixedly.

She waved a hand before his face. Nothing happened.

Cynthia worked herself into a worry. She put her hands on his shoulders and shook him. "Snap out of it!"

The farmer blinked once, then again to be certain he had the motion right. "Wh—where am I?"

"You're here in your barn, about to go into town," Cynthia reminded him.

He looked around in bafflement, then wandered off in the rough direction of his house. The boy, bored with such activities, reached into his pocket and pulled out what appeared to be the rest of his last night's supper of chicken and wrys. He chewed on that while pondering what new mischief he could get into.

Cynthia was not stupid as girls went, though she wasn't sure that was also true as filly centaurs went. She assessed the situation. When she had tried to use her talent on the lad, his father had gone into a daze. A dim bulb flashed over her head.

"Oh, no!" she exclaimed, laying a hand on her fair cheek. "My talent—it's gone trance-parent! I send parents into trances!"

She realized that the boy's mischievous talent had affected her. It had gone awry.

She ran after the farmer, who was slowly recovering his common sense. "I can't use my talent on your son," she said. "It just messes up. But I think I can watch him while you go into town. Then I'll have to be on my own way."

He nodded. He was used to this. "There's wrys pudding in the kitchen for lunch," he said. "I'll be back as soon as I can."

It turned out to be a real chore, keeping Wryly out of mischief, but somehow she managed without invoking her useless talent. She was able to clean up most of the pudding the boy had thrown before the farmer got back, and had found enough water to put out the fire before it burned up the barn. But it was definitely time to be on her way. The boy was too eager to live the life of Wryly, which could be the death of Cynthia.

"You know, if you're looking for a place to be out of circulation," the farmer said, "what about the Brain Coral's pool?"

"The what?"

He explained how deep in the underworld there was supposed to be this really intelligent coral that lived in a pool and collected things. "I hear it's not a bad creature," he concluded. "It just likes to keep things a while, and let them go later. Maybe you could stay there until folk have forgotten about you."

The notion appealed. So Cynthia went in search of the Brain Coral. But that was a separate adventure, along with how she learned to use her new wings to fly. The odd thing was that when that happened, she lost her baby-sitting talent. She realized, when she thought about it, that a creature could have only one magic talent, and hers was now flying. Maybe she would get back her old talent if she ever got back into full human form. Meanwhile, she had to confess, flying was rather fun, and really handy when there was a rushing river or nickelpede-infested chasm to cross.

"And now I guess a couple of years have passed, and you've been exiled to the Brain Coral's pool too, Evil Magician," she concluded brightly. "I guess I can't really blame you for transforming me, because I did try to deceive you. And you have transformed another girl, to another winged form, but this time you got caught. So it must be all even."

Trent exchanged a rather wary glance with Gloha. Cynthia had the wrong idea!

"It's not quite that way," Gloha said. "Maybe I can explain. I'm natural. That is, I'm the product of the first goblin/harpy romance in several centuries. I'm looking for a man of my kind, that is, a winged goblin; my brother Harglo doesn't count, and Magician Trent is helping me. We came to take you back to Xanth, if you want to go."

"Goblin/harpy romance? I never heard of that," Cynthia said. "I thought they were enemies."

"Well, it happened after you came here. They're still enemies, mostly. But that's changing, because there's a lady goblin chief now, my cousin Gwendolyn."

"But you must be as old as I am. There hasn't been time to—to notify the stork and grow up."

"I am nineteen," Gloha said.

Cynthia was amazed. "You mean it's been twenty years? I had no idea!"

"Even longer," Trent murmured.

"Impossible! You don't look any older than you were when you transformed me. You're still as evilly handsome as ever."

Trent looked somewhat helplessly at Gloha. Gloha realized that she was better equipped to handle this particular revelation. "Do you know how winged monsters never lie to each other?" she asked Cynthia.

"Yes, that's in the *Big Book of Rules*. I encountered a winged dragon in that part of my adventure I didn't cover, and he told me that winged monsters might fight among themselves, but that they had to unite against ground creatures, and they never deceived each other. He also told me that I was a winged monster, and that was a compliment, not an insult, because he thought I was luscious." She switched her tail thoughtfully. "I believed him, because he didn't chomp me. Maybe he just wasn't hungry at the time."

Gloha wasn't quite sure of the logic, but let it pass. "Then I'm telling you as one winged monster to another that seventy-two years have passed since your transformation."

Cynthia's pretty mouth dropped open in astonishment.

"And Evil Magician Trent was exiled to Mundania, and later returned and was king of Xanth, and now his daughter is queen of Xanth, and he's not called evil any more. He is now ninety-six, and just took youth elixir to restore his youth so he could help me in my quest. Xanth has changed a lot since you left it."

"And I apologize for transforming you," Trent said. "I will be glad to transform you back to your original form. But your family is gone, and your friends will be gone or very old. So I am afraid I have done you a greater evil than I ever intended, and I wish I could make it up to you."

Cynthia looked at Gloha. Gloha nodded. "It is the truth. Winged monster honor."

"I—I can't go back?" Cynthia asked plaintively. "Then what will become of me?"

Trent looked as if he were about to say, "Frankly, my dear," and go on about dams, but he stifled it.

"I—we thought you might prefer to remain a winged centaur," Gloha said.

"As the only one of my kind? I'd rather stay in the pool!"

"There is another now. A family of winged centaurs, in fact. Cheiron and Chex Centaur, and their foal Che. He—you—we thought maybe—"

"A male winged centaur!" Cynthia said. "How old is he?"

"Well, he's young yet, but—"

"How old?"

"Eight. But he gets older every year."

"You expect a sixteen-year-old girl to go with an eight-year-old boy?"

Gloha saw how foolish it was. "I guess it was a bad idea. I'm not interested in any eight-year-old goblin boy."

"There is an answer," Trent said.

Both girls looked at him.

"As you can see, the elixir of the Fountain of Youth can reduce a person's physical age. There is some available. So if you—"

"I don't want to be eight years old again."

"Then maybe if Che were made older—"

"He would still be a child in a grown body."

"Then I can transform you back to your original form," Trent said. "You are a pretty girl with an appealing age; I'm sure you'll be able to make your way in the human realm."

But Cynthia was having a second thought. "This centaur boy—what's he like?"

"Oh, he's very special," Gloha said. "All the winged monsters are sworn to protect him, because he is destined to change Xanth. We don't know exactly how, but already he has helped Gwenny Goblin be the first female goblin chief, and that's changing Xanth for the better. He is her official Companion, which means he's away from home a lot, and his folks—but of course they understand about that."

"His folks miss having a child at home," Cynthia said. "I can guess how that must be."

"Yes. Gwenny and Jenny Elf lived with them for two years, but then Gwenny had to be chief, so—"

"Maybe I will take that youth elixir," Cynthia said. "I have a whole lot to learn about Xanth, and I'll just stumble around and get in trouble on my own. But if I could stay with a family of my own kind for a few years—"

"Oh, I'm sure they'd welcome you!" Gloha said.

"Then maybe if you are willing to see me safely there, and get me that youth elixir—"

"Certainly," Trent said. "It is the least I can do to make up for what I did. Come with us now, and this is the way it will be."

"Agreed." Cynthia Centaur extended her dainty hand. Magician Trent took it.

Gloha thought she might be mistaken, but she had the innocent little impression that Cynthia was rather taken with Magician Trent, whom she had never known as an old man.

Then the three of them walked up out of the Brain Coral's pool. They were about to be on their way.

4
ESCAPE

In due course the four of them set out: Gloha, Trent, Cynthia, and Swiftmud, whom Trent had transformed into a lightning bug to help light their way. This wasn't ideal country for a creature of Swiftmud's natural size. The other human folk were comfortably ensconced in the Brain Coral's pool, awaiting that seemingly timeless interval when Trent would return for the fade-away party. Tandy had decided to wait with the elders, because this might be her last chance to visit her parents before they faded out. Gloha had promised to deliver a message to Smash Ogre, so he would know what was keeping Tandy, if he noticed.

They had Tandy's pass, which had been duly authenticated by the demons, goblins, water monsters, and such, because she was related to legitimate underworld denizens. In times past there had been strife between the various factions, but in recent decades they had settled into their own regions and left each other mostly alone. So there shouldn't be a problem; not too many folk wanted war to break out because of a silly border incident.

The passage was marked by green glow. As long as they stayed on that, they would be left alone. It was like an enchanted path, on the surface. There would be camping sites with food and potable water. Gloha had been a bit distressed by the description of the water, until Trent explained that this meant a clean drinking pot, not the other kind of pot.

The first checkpoint they came to was in demon country. There was a demon at a desk. He had a broad-brimmed blue hat and huge flat feet. "Whatcha business?" he demanded from the side of his mouth.

"We're going to the surface," Trent replied.

The demon surveyed them. There was barely room for his gaze to get out from under his visor. "Oh yeah, manface?"

Trent gave the correct answer according to the protocol: "Yeah."

"I haven't seen any of you before."

"We haven't seen you before either."

The demon considered that. "You wouldn't know me, because I'd have been in a different form." He puffed into a swirl of smoke to illustrate the point.

"But you'd have known *us*, if you'd seen us."

The demon re-formed, hat and all. "Right." He did not seem to be the smartest of his kind. "Pass, then. Just keep your noses clean."

"My nose isn't dirty," Gloha protested.

The demon merely looked at her as if she had said something stupid. That made her suspect she had.

They went on through the demon settlement. Demons didn't need houses, because they had no set mortal forms, and didn't need food, because they didn't eat, but they did have a culture of a sort. Gloha understood that there was even a Demon University where magic was taught, and of course the demons operated the Companions Game, which allowed selected Mundanes to visit Xanth if they didn't bother regular folk. But exactly what their culture was, no one could be sure. Maybe it was all pretense, to deceive observers. Demons sometimes amused themselves by fooling mortals. So when colored balloons floated by and popped into smoke that formed into faces with glistening tongues and teeth that then threatened to bite the heads off the travelers, Gloha knew to ignore them. When the path ahead became a writhing mass of serpent coils with dirty noses on each loop, Gloha walked on without hesitation, though conscious of the tease. When giant eyes opened on the floor, looking up and winking, she hesitated; she was still wearing her skirt. Suppose a demon announced the color of her panties?

"Oh, are you concerned about the footing on the stare-way?" Trent inquired. "That's readily taken care of." He picked up a handful of sand and threw it across the floor. The eyes blinked madly, turned red, teared, and finally had to close and fade out. "Now I'm sure the footing is better."

"It is, thank you," she replied with a smile.

There was a swirl of vapor. It formed into a rather pretty nude human female figure. "Why, I'd almost think that was Magician Trent, except for the age," the demoness said. "But it couldn't be, because Trent is mortal, and just about ready to kick the cask."

"The what?" Gloha asked.

"Basin, tub, pail, vessel, can, receptacle—"

"Bucket?" Trent offered helpfully.

"Whatever," the demoness said crossly. "What are you several mortal creatures doing here in the demon realm?"

"You must be Metria!" Gloha exclaimed. "I've heard of you!"

"Of course I'm Metria," the demoness replied. "I always have been and always will be, except when I'm not. How did you hear of me?"

"Crombie told me how he knew you when he was young. He said you wouldn't show him your panties."

"Well of course I wouldn't!" Metria said indignantly. "Do you think I'm a perverse?"

"You're a what?"

"Contrary, obstinate, balky, willfull, disagreeable, intractable—"

"I think you mean you're not abusive of family conventions," Trent said.

"Whatever," she agreed crossly. "Would *you* show a child your panty?"

"I would not," Trent said with a remarkably uncurved complexion.

"Or an antlery teenage male?"

"By no means."

"So there." A matching skirt and blouse outfit appeared on her body, and sure enough, no panty ever showed. "So who are you, really?"

"Why do you want to know?" he asked in return.

"I'm chronically curious. Why else?"

"I am Magician Trent."

"But I explained why you aren't him, didn't I?"

"I took youth elixir."

"But only the Good Magician Humfrey and some unicorns know where the Fountain of Youth is, and they'll never tell."

"Humfrey gave me some elixir."

"I don't believe it. He's too grumpy. Transform somebody."

Trent gestured. The demoness became a blue toad with green warts.

The toad puffed into smoke. "I didn't mean *me*!" the smoke protested. In a moment the nude human figure was back, without panties. "But I suppose I can take your identity on faith. Who are these winged monsters?"

"I am Gloha Harpy-Goblin."

"And I am Cynthia Centaur."

The demoness squinted at them. "I don't think I've seen many of your kind before. Just Che Centaur's family."

"Is it a nice family?" Cynthia asked.

"You don't know? That's interesting." The demoness faded out.

"She's somewhat of a nuisance," Trent remarked. "But there's nothing to be done about her. She seldom does actual harm, at least."

"I thought she had been locked into the Companions Game," Gloha said, remembering something she had once heard.

A puff of smoke reappeared. "I served my time and got out on parole." It disappeared.

Gloha made a mental note: one could never be quite certain that a demon wasn't still around.

They walked on out of the demon realm. There were no more odd events. Evidently the demons had gotten bored with them. That was a relief.

The fungus along the marked route turned brownish. The air became chill. Gloha closed her wings closely around her body, insulating it with the feathers. Cynthia suffered less, because she had more furry mass, but she did take a jacket out of her backpack and put it on over her shirt to protect her maidenly human torso. Evidently she had never adopted the centaur mode of undress after gaining some experience with the form, and had retained some of her clothing in case of need. Trent, already competently garbed, seemed to have no problem.

The air proceeded from chill to frigid. Patches of frost appeared. The three stepped up the pace so as to warm themselves by the vigor of their exertion. Gloha would have been concerned if she didn't see that the trail-marking fungus continued, though now dark and dormant.

They turned a corner, entered a moderately large chamber—and came fact-to-snoot with a dragon. The creature had antennae instead of eyes, which made sense down here, but in other respects seemed formidable enough. It had dragonly form and mass, metallic overlapping dark gray–green scales, stoutly taloned feet, one and a half squintillion teeth, and an attitude. It moved forward, inhaling, growling inwardly.

"Wait!" Trent cried, advancing to meet it. "We have a pass for this path."

Too late. The dragon exhaled. A surge of snowy vapor blew him back. Ice crystallized on his body. He fell back into the girls, completely iced.

"It's a snow dragon!" Gloha exclaimed, appalled as the two of them automatically caught him before he hit the floor and shattered. "I thought all of them were white and in the winter mountains."

"Don't worry about that," Cynthia said. "Just get him back to safety and get him thawed."

She was right. They dragged the ice man back the way they had come, away from the dragon. Cynthia did most of the work, being much larger than Gloha. When they were around the corner and in a section of the tunnel too small for the bulk of the dragon, they laid him carefully on the floor. "Is he—?" Gloha asked, appalled.

"Not if we act promptly," Cynthia said. "The ice is on the outside. If we chip it off immediately, he shouldn't freeze inside."

They chipped at his body, and chunks of ice fell to the floor with tinkling sounds. "But his face—we must clear that so he can breathe," Gloha said. "But we can't just pound off the ice; we'd chip off his nose and lips too."

"You're right. We need to apply fast, gentle warmth. I think this means I have a pretext to do what I would have liked to do a year—I mean, seventy-one or -two years ago."

Gloha was bemused. "You mean—?"

"Yes," she said with naughty determination. "I'm going to kiss him. It's in a decent cause, even if it's not completely nice."

Cynthia suited action to word. She reached down, put her hands on the Magician's shoulders, and hauled him up with the kind of strength a centaur could muster. He rose board-stiff, his feet still on the floor. Then she put her head down, aligned her face with his, and planted her lips very firmly on his for a wild wet kiss.

After a moment she lifted her head. "Hy hips are hrozen," she gasped.

In a quarter of a moment Gloha made sense of this. "Your lips are frozen," she repeated. "I'd better take over while you recover."

"Hyes." The layer of ice was flaking off Cynthia's face, but her lips remained attractively blue.

Gloha stood on tiptoe to reach the Magician's angled face, and planted her warm lips against his slightly thawed ones. She kissed him as firmly as she could. The cold struck through, but as her lips congealed she felt his softening. It was working! When she felt she had no more warmth in that region to give, she withdrew, and was gratified to see a thin trace of vapor issue from his mouth. He was starting to breathe again!

Meanwhile Cynthia had been breathing hard and smacking her lips together to get them warmed. She couldn't use her hands because they were holding Trent up for the kissing. "I think I can go another round now," she said bravely. She put her mouth to his mouth again.

Gloha's hands were free, and she used them to waggle her lips and flake the ice off them. Then she flexed them and breathed rapidly, using the warm air to complete the job. By the time her mouth had recovered, Cynthia's had iced up again.

But now Trent's mouth was clear of ice and his breath was pluming nicely. So Gloha tackled his right eye instead, which was frozen shut. She kissed it, and as the warmth loosened the ice, she licked it off. When it finally opened and blinked she knew it was thawed. But her mouth had congealed again, and her tongue wasn't speaking to her.

"Good idea," Cynthia said. "His mouth is done, and part of his tongue, but he needs his eyes too." She kissed the left eye.

His tongue? Gloha didn't inquire.

After that they worked on his nose, and his ears, and finally his face was done. Then they worked on the remainder of his body, taking turns hugging him close and chipping away the rest of the ice as it thawed. His clothing was hardly even wet; they had managed to get most of the ice off before it did more than melt around the edges.

Trent moved. "Hthank you, hladies," he said somewhat coldly. But the coldness was of the body, not of the heart. "There are whorse things than being khissed and hugged to lhife by two lhovely young lhadies."

Gloha and Cynthia exchanged a solid glance and a half. Then they exchanged a half-body flush. That was a significant achievement for each of them, because the centaur's clothing and fur normally concealed any such expression, and Gloha's skin was goblin dark. But in a moment steam was rising from both their faces.

"Don't waste that heat!" Trent cried. "I'm still cold." Indeed, he was shivering.

"In for a nickel, in for a dime," Cynthia said through her burning chagrin. She was referring to archaic Mundane coins reported to have the magic properties of getting things started or suddenly stopped.

They hauled the Magician up again and hugged him from either side, giving him the heat of their embarrassment. Soon enough he had been warmed. "I thank you both for saving my life," he said. "But perhaps we won't speak of this elsewhere. Others might not properly understand."

They emphatically agreed. It would be their secret. But even more secret was Gloha's private feeling. She had never actually kissed a man of any kind before, not directly on the mouth like that, and certainly had never done anything like licking off his face. Trent, rejuvenated as he was, had the body of a handsome young man. Now she realized that she had, on some suitably hidden level, rather liked the experience. She suspected that Cynthia had also, for she had admitted to being flustered by the Magician's aspect when she had first encountered him. She might be a centaur now, but she retained her origin and upper front section as a human maiden. So perhaps she had had her revenge on Trent, if that was what it was. This had perhaps given each of them a taste of what it would be like to get really friendly with males of their own kind.

"But now," Trent continued, evincing the quality of leadership that made him a man, not to mention a former Magician–King, "we need to deal with that dragon.

"Yes," they agreed together, evincing the quality of agreeability that made them innocent maidens, however much that innocence had been stained by the recent event.

"I can of course transform it into something harmless, being now warned about its nature. But I don't want to do mischief by acting hastily. I did enough of that when I was as young as I now look." He glanced significantly at Cynthia, who then demonstrated that she had not expended quite all of her color before. "Do you think it was a misunderstanding, and the dragon iced me before realizing that we had a pass?"

Gloha considered. "I think the dragon could have sent another cold draft down this tunnel, and frozen us all, if it had wanted to. So maybe it *was* a misunderstanding."

"Yes, that makes sense," Cynthia agreed. "Maybe we should give it another chance."

"But if it inhales, I'll transform it," Trent said grimly.

They advanced tentatively around the corner again. The dragon was there. "I say, old chap—we have a pass, you know," the Magician said.

The dragon nodded. Its snoot was not crafted for apology, but it was evidently making the effort.

"So if you will just let us pass without molestation, we'll just forget this little misunderstanding," Trent continued.

The dragon nodded again. So the three of them approached it. But Gloha noted that the Magician's hand was ready to gesture, just in case. She doubted that it was the gesture that did it; probably the motion was just to get his hand within transformation range of the target. But it was clear that Trent was not one to be caught twice the same way. He might look young, but he had the better part of a century's experience. Which might be the reason Crombie's magic had pointed him out to help on this quest: Gloha was a trifle short on experience, and this more than made up the difference.

The dragon did not try to frost them again, so Trent did not transform it. They passed it and entered a new network of tunnels. But the dormant green glow fungus still marked the trail, and the farther they got beyond the snow dragon's lair, the warmer the air got and the healthier the fungus became.

In fact the environment went from chill to warm to sweaty. Cynthia removed her jacket and packed it away, retaining the shirt. True centaurs were of course completely unself-conscious about their bodies, and showed things and did things openly that the Adult Conspiracy forbade to straight humans. But as a transformee Cynthia had more of the human foibles than did most centaurs, or she would not have been embarrassed about having to kiss the Magician back to life. Gloha, as a first-generation crossbreed, was uncertain exactly what social hang-ups she was expected to have, so followed the human ones until she had reason otherwise.

The air got downright hot. Both Cynthia and Gloha flapped their wings to keep their bodies cool, and Trent looked as if he would have liked to remove some clothing. If this got any worse, they would have to have a discussion about whether there were special cases where nudity was tolerable. Were they walking into the lair of a firedrake dragon?

No, it turned out to be a fire pit without a dragon. Dark liquid bubbled up from nether crevices, and formed burning pools. The marked path skirted it by digging a small ledge into the side of the wall. But there was room in the cavern for Gloha and Cynthia to fly, so they had no trouble. Trent was the one who had to navigate the inadequate trail.

"If only you could transform yourself, the way Dolph can," Gloha told him.

"Dolph?" Cynthia inquired.

"His grandson, Prince Dolph, who can change to any living form he wishes," Gloha explained. "He's the same age I am, but he's already married, and they have twins." She tried to keep the envy out of her voice, without a whole lot of success.

"So Magician Trent is a great-grandfather."

"Yes. But I don't think anyone we meet will believe that." They both laughed as they hovered. It was good to be flying again, however briefly. That was another thing that Cynthia had clearly learned to do before she retired to the Brain Coral's pool. Maybe that was why she had decided to remain in this form; it did have an ability that her original form had lacked. Gloha could not imagine life without flight; she would rather die than lose her wings.

Meanwhile the man was trying to stay on the tiny path, with diminishing success. There just wasn't enough room for his shoes. He was too likely to fall off it and roll down the steep slope of the wall right into the fire.

He paused. "How do you fly, Cynthia?" he called.

"You transformed me, and you don't know? I just flap my wings and take off."

"The reason I inquire is that I have heard that the other winged centaur family has the magic of making things light by flicking them with their tails. When they flick flies, the flies become too light to stay perched, and fly away.

When they flick themselves, they become light enough for their relatively small wings to lift. When they flick a person, that person becomes light enough to be carried. If you can do that with me, you can carry me across this hot cavern."

"No, I don't flick myself, except to tag flies, and that's not to make them light but to knock them off," Cynthia said. "I never get light, and can't make anything else light. I just fly."

"Perhaps we should verify this." He got down off the path and quickly retreated to the end of the cavern before his feet got too burningly hot from the stone.

Cynthia flicked him with her tail. He did not get light. Then he tried holding on to her as she tried to fly, but she couldn't get aloft. Her wings sent a powerful draft of air down, enough to lift her, but not enough to lift very much else. It was evident that her magic was different from that of the other winged centaurs. Her magic was in the power of the downdraft she made, to lift her up.

"That's interesting," Gloha remarked. "He transformed you, and must have given you the magic to fly, yet he didn't know how it worked."

"That is the case," Trent agreed. "I don't understand my talent, I just invoke it. But this leaves me with a problem; I just don't see how I can use that little walkway."

"Maybe if you flew alongside him, and pushed him against the wall," Gloha suggested. "So he couldn't fall."

They tried it, but it was problematical, because Cynthia needed room for her wings. She tried facing away from the wall, so that her rump could brace Trent, and that worked, but then she couldn't fly sideways to pace him across the cavern. Gloha was too small to help at all.

"Could you transform one of us into a form that would be able to help?" Gloha asked.

"Would you want to be transformed?" he countered. "You know, you could find your ideal man quite readily if I transformed you to a suitable form."

"Oh, no, I like the way I am!" she protested. "I don't want to change, I want to succeed in life *my* way. But for just a temporary time, I maybe could stand it."

A cloud of smoke appeared before her. A mouth opened on its vague surface. "You fool."

"I didn't ask you, Metria," Gloha retorted, beginning to understand how a person could become annoyed with the demoness.

"Then I won't tell you how to get him safely by," the smoke said, and dissipated.

"How about a vine?" Trent asked. "You could take root at one end, and Cynthia could hold the tip of the vine at the other end, and I could use it as a rail to hold."

"A plant?" Gloha asked, dismayed. She hadn't thought of that, and probably never would have.

"The rock's too hot," Cynthia pointed out. "The plant would wilt."

"A flame vine wouldn't."

"That's right," Cynthia agreed, surprised.

Both of them looked at Gloha. She really didn't care for the notion, but saw no polite way out. She was about to say a grudging yes, when a realization saved her. "You can't transform me when I'm out of your reach, right? But I have to be all the way across the cavern."

"No, you could be this side, and I could fly you to the other side," Cynthia said helpfully.

"Or you could carry her to the other side to take root," Trent said. "Make sure there is a suitable place first."

The centaur flew across. "Yes, there's even some nice warm dirt here," she reported. "It looks quite rich. Maybe bats have enhanced it."

"Bats!" Gloha exclaimed indignantly. But she realized that she was stuck for it. "All right," she murmured, hoping she wouldn't be heard.

No such luck. Trent reached toward her, and suddenly she was a thing of flames and tentacles and leaves. She felt very insecure, because her roots didn't have much purchase. She was, indeed, a flame vine. She wasn't actually burning; she was merely fire-colored, with the capacity to generate small flames at the tips of her leaves if she chose.

Then Cynthia picked her up and carried her across the cavern. It was pleasantly warm in the center, then cool again at the edge. The centaur set her down on a patch of what her roots tasted as volcanic soil. That was ideal. She sank her roots deep and proceeded to grow. She focused on one long vine, sending it along the wall above the path. Wherever she found a crevice she ran a tendril in, anchoring it. She put out regularly spaced leaves to take in the radiation of the fire along the cavern floor. It tasted almost as good as the soil. This was fun!

Soon she was all the way across, solidly anchored all the way. She didn't need Cynthia to hold her end; no one was going to pull her off that wall until she let go of it herself. For one thing, there were tasty minerals in that wall.

She waved a tendril at the Magician: get on with it!

He set out again along the path. He put a hand on her vine—and quickly removed it. He dug into his own pack and fetched out a pair of heavy gloves.

Then, wearing these, he tried again, and this time was able to maintain a grip on her hot vine.

Toward the center where the ledge got thinnest he had to hold on quite firmly, but she strengthened her tendril anchors and stayed firm. Then he reached the near side. "Thank you, Gloha," he said. "Now I will change you back. But first we must get you all together, because otherwise parts of you may be stuck to the wall."

Gloha saw the logic. Cynthia flew back and carefully pulled the long vine out as Gloha released her tendril grip, stage by stage. Cynthia collected the vine in a bundle and flew slowly back with it as more was released. Gloha hated to do it, because there was still plenty of nutritious mineral there, but she suspected that her winged goblin form would be annoyed if she didn't. Of course why anyone would want to be a goblin when she could be a flame vine—

Then she was herself again, complete with her blouse and skirt in place. She quailed at the thought of remaining a flame vine; obviously a winged goblin was better. Yet now she could appreciate the differing perspective of the plant. Each form of life found itself marvelously compatible, and distrusted all others. Perhaps she should try to remember that lesson of life, if she didn't get distracted by more important things.

They moved on, following the passage generally down. It didn't seem to be in any great hurry to reach the surface. Now they entered a region of stalag—stalac—those pointed pillarlike things that lived in caves.

"Stalagmites and stalactites," Trent said. "My, these are very thick—and look where the path goes!"

"How can you remember the difference?" Cynthia asked him. "I mean, between the ones that cling to the ceiling and the ones that grow up from the ground?"

The Magician laughed. "You have solved the riddle already! The ceiling-clinging ones are spelled with a *c* for *ceiling*, and the ground-growing ones with a *g* for *ground*. StalaCtite and stalaGmite. I think the other distinguishing letters, *t* and *m*, also indicate it; *t* is for *top*, but I forget what *m* is for."

The ball of smoke appeared. "Moron?" it inquired. He batted a hand through it, and it dissipated, leaving a dirty smell. It seemed that the demoness had not quite lost interest in them, and naturally she couldn't get the word.

"Mound," Cynthia suggested.

"Whatever," Gloha agreed, trying to look cross. But the effect was spoiled when they both giggled.

But they had a more serious problem to concern them. The C tites and G mites were so thickly spread that it was impossible to squeeze between them.

The fungus path went across the points, coating the upward- and downward-pointing tips. There was room between them for the girls to fly, but Trent was out of luck again.

"I am beginning to wonder what the advantage is to being human," he remarked.

"The problem is not in being human," Gloha said. "It is in being wingless. If you had wings, you'd be all right."

"Thank you," he said. She realized that there was more than one way her statement could be taken, and she felt another faint flush trying to form. Fortunately she hadn't enough left to embarrass her.

"Maybe I can clear a path through these," Cynthia said. She faced away from the wall of G mites, then let fly with a well-placed kick. The nearest mite broke off and toppled, crashing down between the others.

But almost immediately there was a shower of spearlike C tites from above. The three mortal creatures barely got out of the way in time to avoid getting skewered.

"I think we would never be able to clear that path," Trent said. "This cave protects its own."

"Maybe we can find another way," Gloha said. She flew up and between the needlelike tips of the upper and lower fields of stalacs and stalags (or whatever), careful not to touch any of them. But all she found beyond was a passage angling up to a medium-small river going merrily about its own business. There was no other exit; the passage continued along the river.

She flew back and reported. "I am beginning to wonder whether we are on the right trail," she concluded. "This one seems entirely too difficult for human folk to manage. It's hard to believe that Tandy traveled this way alone."

"I suspect she had her ogre husband along before," Trent said. "These hazards would not have dared to interfere with an ogre."

That seemed to make sense. But meanwhile what were they going to do? This cave seemed to be even less passable than the others.

"You say there's a river?" Cynthia asked. "Do you suppose it could be diverted?"

"It seemed pretty self-absorbed. Oh, you mean, to change its channel? I suppose that's possible; one bank was sandy. But that would just make it flow into this cave, and fill it up."

"Yes. Then maybe Trent could swim between the tites and mites without disturbing any of them."

Trent considered. "Do you know, you may be almost as smart as you are pretty. I think it could be done."

Cynthia's powers of coloration had evidently regenerated without impairment. She might once have been the Magician's enemy, but that was a long time ago. Now it was clear that she found him rather intriguing. Gloha found it easy to appreciate the feeling. Trent was handsome, intelligent, experienced, disciplined, and had one of the strongest magic talents in Xanth. There wasn't a lot more required of a man.

Gloha flew back to the river. She landed on its bank and used her fine little feet to scuff a channel in the sand. The water flowed eagerly through it, and plunged down into the cave. It widened the channel as it went, so that more water could follow. Soon the entire river was headed for this interesting new region, forming an expanding pool around the base of the G mites.

She flew back. "I have diverted the river, and it seems to be quite entertained," she reported.

"We suspected as much," Trent said dryly, which was a good trick because he was standing knee-deep in the pool.

The river disported itself mightily, and the level of the pool steadily rose. Gloha and Cynthia hovered over it. "Are you going to be all right?" Gloha asked the Magician.

"Oh, certainly; I can swim. You girls go ahead and wait on dry land; I'll be along in due course."

They did as bid, for hovering soon enough became tiring. "He's a brave man," Cynthia said as they flew.

"And a marvelous Magician," Gloha agreed. "It's hard to imagine that they ever called him evil."

"Oh, that was because he was trying to take over Xanth before the Storm King was ready to fade out. And he was transforming a lot of people. But I gather he was a good king, when he finally got the office.

"Yes, Xanth has prospered. Bink's son Dor and Trent's daughter Irene have done well too. I guess it shows that you never can tell how things will turn out."

"You never can tell," Cynthia agreed wistfully.

They landed on the dry part of the bank, then watched the water rise around the G mites. Every so often one of them flew back to check on the Magician, who was doing what he called treading water, though it looked exactly like swimming in place.

At last the water covered the tip-tops of the G mites, so that only the descending points of the C tites showed above it. Now the cave looked like a dragon's mouth half full of saliva. But Gloha wasn't entirely comfortable with that image, so let it go.

Trent came swimming along, having no trouble. Only at the end did one of his feet accidentally kick a hidden G mite. The pool shook, and several C tites dropped into the water with menacing splashes. But Trent had already gotten clear.

They moved on again. The river path deserted the river, having no loyalty, and wended its way up to another large cave. This one was dome-shaped, with a single massive stalagmite in the center. There was neither dragon nor fire here; the floor was bare. But there was also no exit. The glow-fungus path went to the center and stopped.

They looked all around, but the wall was solid. The only hole in it was the one through which they had entered. The circular wall was painted with pictures of assorted creatures: dragons, griffins, chimerae, sea serpents, sphinxes, and the like; nothing really unusual. Here and there were even some men with spears.

"Do you know, this must be an ancient cave," Trent said. "These are the creatures the early men of Xanth hunted. They painted pictures of them to be sure of the magic necessary to bring them down. Or perhaps it was opposite: they were working magic to protect themselves from such predators. Either way, this is a historic artifact."

"How could they hunt such creatures down here?" Gloha asked. "All we've seen are dragons."

"Perhaps they hunted all the others to extinction."

"Or perhaps the dragons hunted the humans to extinction," Cynthia said. "Because no men seem to live here now."

"You have a sobering point," he agreed.

"But how are we going to get out of here before *we're* extinct?" Gloha asked plaintively.

Trent grimaced. "That is a somewhat better question than I feel competent to address at the moment."

Then Cynthia noticed something. "The glow-fungus path doesn't stop here. It circles up the stalagmite!"

They looked, and found it was so. The fungus spiraled right up toward the distant ceiling. And there, at the very top, was a hole. The G mite poked a short way into it.

"And there's our exit," the Magician said. "And once again I feel inadequate to the need. I don't believe I can climb that smooth column, and this time there is no water to float me up."

"But this time you can use your talent," Cynthia said. "Simply transform me into something huge enough to lift you up there, then transform me back to this form."

"I can if you wish this," he agreed. "You have been most generous in your attitude toward me, considering our prior experience, and I have not wished to impose on you by transforming you again."

"Well, a lot has happened since then, and we're not on opposite sides any more," she said with a smile that might in some other circumstance have seemed ingratiating. "Now we have to work together to get through."

"We do, at that," he agreed. "Very well, I'll transform you to a roc, which should be strong enough to carry me there. But we shall need to calculate this carefully, for if I then transform you back before you are through the hole, you could fall."

And such a fall could kill her, Gloha realized. Then she realized that she had fallen into a mental trap: a flying centaur wouldn't fall, she would just fly away. But the hole looked way too small for such a creature to squeeze through, so there was still a problem. But she had an answer: "Then you transform her to a little bird, who can fly on up through the hole. *Then* back to centaur form, when she is safe."

"You, too, are uncommonly clever," Trent told her. Gloha discovered that she had not after all used up her own store of blush.

Then the Magician gestured, and the centaur became a truly monstrous bird. The roc took the suddenly tiny-seeming man in its ferociously huge beak, spread its giant pinions, and launched into the air. Now, there was an act of trust, Gloha realized: the bird could cut the man in half simply by closing its beak. It flew up, circling the stalagmite, until it reached the top. Then it flipped its head, opened its beak, and the man sailed up through the hole. He didn't fall out again, so he must have landed somewhere.

Now the roc flew as close to the hole in the ceiling as possible without colliding with the stalagmite. The tip of one wing brushed past the hole—and the big bird vanished. In its place was a tiny hummingbird.

Gloha had been halfway keeping pace, staying clear of the immense downdraft from the roc's wings. Now she flew up through the hole herself.

There were Trent and Cynthia, waiting for her. "See? It was routine," the centaur filly said nonchalantly as she let go of the man. He must have held her steady as he transformed her, or perhaps she had clung to him for balance as she adjusted.

Trent smiled obliquely. "Routine," he agreed.

But Gloha was seriously wondering how many more such tricky transitions they would be able to make. This did not strike her as a safe or easy route. It was more like trying to gain entry to the Good Magician's castle. But she didn't want to alarm the others, so she kept her meek little mouth shut. About that and whatever else she might conjecture about that wasn't her business.

They moved on again. This time the passage led to a snoozing goblin. "Ahem," Trent said.

The goblin rolled over on his mat. "Go away, dunderhead," he muttered without opening his eyes.

"I presume this is the goblin checkpoint," Trent said. "We want you to be sure you know that we have a safe conduct pass."

The goblins forced open an eye. Then suddenly both eyes wedged wide. "What are you creatures doing here?"

"We are on our way out of the underworld," Trent said evenly. "We are following the established exit route, for which we have a pass." He showed the pass.

"But that's impossible! We changed the route so nobody could get through."

Trent, Gloha, and Cynthia shared three halves of a glance. Suddenly something was making sense. Goblin mischief.

The Magician turned back to the goblin. "And why would you change the path?" he inquired with truly deceptive mildness.

"Because we don't honor any deals made by the crappy saps who ran this region before we got here, but we didn't want to say so outright before we got really well established. So we could claim that travelers just got lost or something, in case the demons snooped."

"And the regular path is easier to travel?"

"Of course it is, yokel. It just winds straight up past the checkpoints to the surface. But now we'll erase that, and eat any more travelers who come, pass or not."

"That could plunge the underworld into war, after decades of peace."

"Yeah," the goblin said zestfully. "So now get ready for the pot, because we're going to stew you three for supper. Better take off your packs and clothes; they don't boil well." He squinted at them. "One dumb human man, one stupid winged goblin girl—oh, we'll have fun with you before we cut off those wings!—and one idiotic winged centaur filly." Then the goblin did a double take. "A winged centaur! We *hate* winged centaurs! Ever since that little snoop came to Goblin Mountain and made it possible for a girl to be chief. What a pain! We real he-man goblins just had to get the Hades out of there and find a place to regroup. Oh, we'll pull out your feathers one by one, and make you hurt worse and worse, until you're just begging to be dumped into the boiling pot! What a treat we have coming!"

Gloha felt an awful chill, and she could tell that Cynthia was experiencing the same ugly draft. But the Magician seemed oddly unconcerned. Gloha was pretty sure that was misleading, she hoped.

"And this path now goes straight on up to the surface?" Trent inquired conversationally. "No more hazards?"

"Sure. But you won't be taking it, man-puss, because we're closing the gate. You might as well eat that pass before we feed it to you."

"And you are the only goblin guarding this path?"

"Right." The goblin paused. "Except for the other hundred that moved in while we were talking." He waved, and suddenly the passage beyond was crammed with goblins carrying spears and clubs. "You thought maybe you'd just run over me and be gone, meat-man? You're even dumber than you look."

Gloha felt a worse chill. Suddenly they were faced with bad faith—because of bad goblins who had fled the enlightened female chiefship of cousin-once-removed Gwenny and come here to establish their evil order. She knew the three could expect no mercy, because she knew what goblin men were like in their natural state. This was doom.

"I take it that you don't know who I am," Trent said, seeming unperturbed.

"Human scum, I am proud to tell you I have no idea who you are, and don't care to soil my mind learning. You'll taste just as good as anyone else, once we add the spices. Now get those clothes off before we hack them off."

"I am Magician Trent. Perhaps you have heard of me."

"Of course I never heard of you, crapbrain! And even if I had, I—" He paused. "Who?"

"The Magician of Transformation."

The goblin began to sidle away. "It don't mean nothing to me! You're probably lying anyway."

Trent strode forward, gesturing. The goblin became a large purple snake with venom dripping from its fangs. "Now go greet your comrades," Trent said.

But the snake did not flee. Instead it slithered toward the Magician. Gloha realized that the change of form did not stop it from being an enemy, any more than her change of form had stopped her from being a friend. Trent's magic could not change personality.

The purple snake became a pink elephant, the kind of monster that drunks dreamed of. But the passage was not large enough for it, so it filled the space completely, blocking off the other goblins. But it also blocked off the easy escape route to the single-G-mite chamber.

"We need another exit," the Magician said mildly. "Gloha, can you find your way through goblin tunnels?"

"Yes. But there will be enemy goblins in them. They'll attack us from ambush before you can transform them. They'll throw stones from beyond your range. I don't think we can get through them."

"What about some passage they won't use?"

"They can go anywhere we can, because you can't fly." She hated to bring that liability up to him again, but it was unfortunately true.

"Then find a passage you two can use and they can't. I'll keep them from following, if they make the attempt."

He was offering to sacrifice himself so that the two of them could escape. Gloha knew she wouldn't accept that, and she thought Cynthia wouldn't either. In fact she was pretty almost certainly sure Cynthia wouldn't. But there was no point in arguing about that right now. She peered down the passages that debouched from this region. Already she heard the sounds of goblins running through passages, closing in on this one by devious routes.

Then she spied a goblin sign. "I see a forbidden tunnel!" she cried. "This way!" She ran toward it.

"Why is it forbidden?" Cynthia asked as she trotted after her.

"I don't know. But it means that goblins won't use it, and that's what we want."

They entered the tunnel as goblins appeared in the one behind them. This one was well lighted by fungus and big enough for them all to use comfortably, which made Gloha wonder, because both the man and the centaur were twice the height of any goblin. Why should such a large tunnel be forbidden? If they were afraid to use it, why hadn't they blocked it off?

It led fairly directly to another large cavern whose base was filled with water. That was all; there was no offshoot passages. Just the quiet pool.

"The goblins are afraid of this?" Cynthia asked, perplexed.

"Yes," Gloha said. "I don't understand why. If there were any really bad monster here, they would have blocked off the tunnel, so that it couldn't come out after them. Instead they merely marked it forbidden. This is distinctly odd. But it doesn't mean that it's safe for us, or that it is any way out. Just that they won't be coming in here."

Cynthia peered across the dark water. "I think I see something."

They all peered. "It looks furry," Gloha said.

The thing came toward them. Indeed it was furry; in fact, it seemed to be a big ball of fur. But when it got close, it opened a furry mouth that seemed somewhat bigger than it was, and snapped with large furry teeth. Sparks flew as the teeth clashed together.

"This is not a place to swim," Trent said. "I gather the fur monster does not leave the water. That means that the goblins don't need to fear it coming after them. They just have to stay clear of its pool."

"Yes, that would explain the simple warning sign," Gloha agreed. "Goblins are lazy; they don't do anything they don't have to. If there's no need to block off a tunnel, they won't bother. So they just posted the warning and let it be."

"But this doesn't look like enough to back off a whole goblin tribe," Cynthia said. "The creature is hardly half as massive as I am. That's enough to gobble up any goblin that might fall in the water—"

"Or be thrown in," Trent suggested.

"But the tribe could gather and throw a barrage of spears at it from the edge," Gloha finished. "You're right; goblins are lazy, but in a case like this their meanness should make up for it. They should take pleasure in attacking it from the safety of the shore, just because it's there. There must be something more."

"And we had better find out what it is," Trent said, his mildness fading now that there was no one close by who needed deceiving. "Now I can transform this creature into something innocuous. But I don't know whether it's the only one, or what else may be lurking near. I am not comfortable with this."

The man was a master of understatement! "I suppose you could transform me into something that shouldn't fear the furball," Gloha said. "Like maybe an allegory. Then I could explore the depths of the pool to see if there's any exit from it. There doesn't seem to be any above or around it."

"Let's not act too quickly, if we don't have to," Trent said. "I have learned to be careful about what I don't understand. There is a mystery about this pool that the presence of a monster doesn't satisfactorily explain."

Cynthia leaned forward over the water and dipped the tip of a finger. Immediately the furball shot through the water and snapped at her hand. "Oh!" she cried, whipping it away.

"That thing is fast," Gloha said.

"It's not that. That water stings." She brought her finger to her mouth.

"Don't do that!" Trent snapped, startling her. "That water may be poison."

"Oh!" she repeated, staring at her hurting finger.

Gloha brought out a handkerchief. "There is a bit of healing elixir in this," she said. She used it to wipe off the finger, which she saw was already blistering. Poison indeed!

"Oh, thank you," Cynthia said. "That feels so much better."

"So now we know another reason why the goblins avoid this pool," Trent said. "It is poison water. The fur monster must be specially adapted to it. Still I'm not sure we have fathomed the whole of this unpleasant mystery—and I think we shall have to, if we want to pass through this pool to escape this region."

"How can we know there is any way out under the pool?" Gloha asked. "There might be underwater caves that don't go anywhere."

"I see no water dripping down from the dome above it. Yet the pool is not brackish or cloudy. It seems to be fresh water, such as it is. That suggests that there is a wellspring somewhere below the surface. If we find that inlet, it may be our outlet."

"I suppose," Gloha said dubiously. "We certainly don't seem to have any other way out."

"But we can't go through poisoned water," Cynthia protested.

"I wonder," Trent said thoughtfully. "It seems unlikely that it would be poisoned by contact with the local rock, because then other waters in the region should suffer a similar effect, and we have not noted this. That river we diverted was quite pure. I think the goblins would not have poisoned it, because that just makes it useless to them. That suggests that this pool is magically poisoned."

"Magically poisoned!" Gloha exclaimed. "You mean, like some pools are love springs, and some are hate springs, and some are youth springs, or healing springs, and so on—this one is a poison spring?"

"Something like that," he agreed. "If it did not wish to be molested by goblins, this device would be effective."

"It certainly would!" Gloha agreed. "But that stops *us* from molesting it too."

"But perhaps we can make a deal with it. Sometimes the inanimate has special desires."

"You mean things that aren't alive, like pools, want things?" Cynthia asked.

"My son-in-law Dor has the ability to talk with the inanimate. It is clear from his experience that inanimate things have concerns, just as animate ones do. We lack the ability to communicate as he does, unfortunately, but maybe we can handle it."

"We can talk to water?" Gloha asked, as doubtful as Cynthia. Stones might be considered individual entities, but water was just fluid.

"Perhaps. I suspect that the fur monster understands the pool, and perhaps it will tell us what the pool desires that we might provide."

Both girls looked at him, not trusting this.

"Suppose I transform one of you into a similar furball, also immune to the poison," he said. "I can do this, despite not really knowing its nature, because my talent takes care of the details. Then you could communicate with it, get some answers, and perhaps make a deal."

"You transformed Cynthia last time," Gloha said. "It's my turn." She hardly believed that this would work, but what other hope was there?

The Magician approached her and gestured. Suddenly she was a hairy furball. She rolled into the pool with a satisfying splash. The water felt wonderful.

The other furball charged aggressively across, its teeth leading the way. "Wait, furface!" she cried in its language, which wasn't exactly verbal but which came naturally to her. "I'm your kind. Let's talk."

"You're female!" the other said, amazed. "I'm male. Let's—"

"Talk first!" she insisted. She hadn't expected this particular complication.

"What about?" he demanded impatiently.

"About this pool. Is it magically poisoned?"

"Of course. Isn't it great? No one else bothers me. Of course I do get lonely. So let's—"

"Can the magic be nullified? So regular creatures could pass through it without getting dissolved?"

"Sure, if Aqui wants. But what's the point? Now let's—"

"That's the pool? Aqui?"

"Sure. And I'm Fur. We get along great, but we get bored with just each other's company, you know? So let's—"

Gloha realized that Fur had a one-track mind. She probably wouldn't get much help from him until she got his concern settled. Well, she was of age. It was more of a sacrifice than she had anticipated, but they did have to find a way out of the underworld. "Exactly what is it you want to do?" she asked guardedly.

"I want to play, of course. I haven't had a playmate in years. Neither has Aqui. We're getting bored with each other."

"Play? Just how do you mean?"

"You know. Racing around the pool. Splashing each other. Playing hide-and-peek down below. All that fun stuff."

Gloha realized that though she was of age, Fur wasn't. He was still a child, and wanted childish play. She could readily oblige him in that. "Catch me if you can!" she cried, and took off through the water at a zoom. She didn't know exactly how she did it, as she had no arms or legs or tail; she just moved.

"Great!" he responded, and zoomed after her.

She dived. Immediately she saw that there *was* an exit: water was flowing in from a hole well below the surface, and filtering out through a lattice on the opposite side. This was indeed fresh water, that surely was as fresh and pure as ever, the moment it left the magic ambience of the pool. Trent had been right about it. He seemed to be right about most things.

But she should make sure. So as Fur was about to catch up with her, she dodged to the side and shot into the spring.

"Hey, no fair!" he cried.

She paused in the current. "Why?"

"Because that doesn't go anywhere fun. Just straight up to the outside world. I don't want to go there."

"I'm sorry," she said apologetically. "I didn't realize." She shot back down with the current so swiftly that Fur wasn't able to tag her before she was past him. "Pokey Fur! Pokey Fur!" she cried.

"Am not! Am not!" he retorted. "Anyway, you're worse."

"How?"

"Because you're a gurl!" The term was neither written nor verbal, but he managed to misspell it anyway.

She paused as if stricken. "Oh, my, you're right! How can I ever live it down?"

He was immediately contrite. "Aw, I didn't mean it. You can't help it. I'm sorry."

"That's okay," she said generously. Then, seizing the moment: "If you two had a nice new playmate to stay here, would you let three funny creatures go by?"

"A playmate to stay? Gee, yes!"

"Then check with Aqui, while I check with my folks," she said. She realized that it was best to be positive and assertive when dealing with children and the inanimate.

"Okay." Fur zoomed somewhere down in the depths of the pool while she zoomed for the surface.

She went to the edge. "Transform me back," she cried.

But she saw the Magician hesitate. Then she realized why. He didn't know which fur monster she was. So she moved in a pattern across the water. G-L-O-H-A she spelled, then zoomed back.

This time there was no hesitation. The Magician gestured, and she was the winged goblin girl again.

"We can make a deal!" she gasped. "There's a river out! Right to the surface. But we need to give them a playmate to keep. I was thinking maybe you could transform an ant or something into another furball, and—"

"We may not need to do that," Trent said. "We have with us a creature who loves fresh water in what he wishes to be his natural form."

"We do?" she asked blankly.

"Swiftmud!" Cynthia exclaimed. "I had almost forgotten him."

"But he's not the same species," Gloha said.

Trent looked around. "We three are of different species, or even five or six species, depending how we count it, yet we get along. Swiftmud is quite a character in his natural form, when you get to know him. Let's inquire." He brought out the lightning bug, set it carefully on the floor, and suddenly the giant mud bank was there, taking up the tunnel behind them. "Swiftie, we have a lonely Aqui pool and a lonely kid furball," he said. "If you can get along with Aqui and Fur you may stay here, your service to us done."

Swiftmud promptly slid into the pool without making a splash. He seemed to have no trouble with the poison.

Fur appeared. The two would have sniffed noses, if either had a nose. Then they began frolicking in the water. Swiftmud, no longer constrained by having to stay on the surface carrying other folk, dived and swirled, became a cloud of dirty water, then formed back into a mud bank. Fur circled around him, then rolled over him and splashed back into the water on the other side. The ball was having a ball.

"I think we have our answer," the Magician said. "Of course we'll have to make our way by foot and wing when we reach the surface. But I had told Swiftmud that if he served us loyally, I would see that he found a compatible situation. He really does like fresh water. He'd take all of it if he could."

"How will we get through the lake and the underground river?" Cynthia asked. "Our wings won't be effective, and we won't be able to breathe."

"You two will have no trouble; I'll change you to fish. It is myself I am worried about."

"Maybe we could help you, if we were the right kind of fish," Gloha said. "Lungfish, maybe, for breathing."

"Lungfish," he agreed. "That would do it." He leaned down and touched his finger to the water. "It is safe now; Aqui is satisfied with the deal."

Gloha and Cynthia verified that the water was no longer poisonous. Then Trent transformed them both to lungfish and they flopped into the water.

Gloha discovered that she liked this form, too. Each form that she assumed had its own virtues, and there was much to be said for being a fish in water. Cynthia seemed similarly satisfied.

Then Trent dived into the pool. He swam down to the river hole, and into it, the two fish showing the way. Then Cynthia swam up to his face and put her mouth to his. It looked like a very solid kiss, and maybe Cynthia thought of it that way, but it was more. She used her lungs to breathe some fresh air into him. Her gills were enough for herself.

They swam on upstream. Gloha took her turn, planting her mouth on the man's mouth and giving him another lungful of air. She found it was fun thinking of it as a deep kiss. Of course she would never admit to enjoying such illicit contact with a male of another species, any more than Cynthia would. But its secret nature added to its appeal.

In this manner they continued until the light of day showed ahead, and the Magician reached the surface.

He clambered out, then reached over the water to transform them to their regular forms. They came out, shaking their wings dry. Their clothing would take longer.

They were by a small river that tunneled into a gully. Now they knew where it was going. Meanwhile they were back on the surface of Xanth. It was wonderful.

Xxxxxxx

I've lost my direction," Gloha said, dismayed, as they dried in the sun. They had agreed that technically they were of three different species, so need have no concern about each other's exposure; nevertheless, they studiously avoided looking. Gloha's sneak peeks indicated that Trent, at least, was honoring that tacit agreement. "I got all turned around on the way out of the underworld, and don't know which way Crombie pointed."

"It was southeast," Trent said. "Back toward Lake Ogre-Chobee."

"Oh—maybe that's why he pointed you out to help me," she said. "Because you would remember."

"That must be it," he agreed with part of a smile.

"Then this must be where we part company," Cynthia said, seeming not completely pleased. "Because I must go find the winged centaur family."

"Not yet," the Magician said. "I undertook to get you safely to a compatible situation. Since I know where that is, I believe I should complete that task before seeing to Gloha's more mysterious quest."

"Yes," Gloha said quickly. She liked Cynthia and wanted to be sure she was all right. Also, she was a bit wary of her quest, and not as eager to get on with it as she thought she should be. She wasn't quite sure she should travel alone with Trent, and this wasn't because she thought he would do anything untoward. Not at all. So this was an excellent pretext for delay.

"You are very kind," Cynthia said. She would have been clearly relieved, but her eyes were tearing a bit, so she was cloudily relieved.

"It is the least I can do, for someone who has kissed me as often and firmly as you have."

Cynthia seemed to be learning how to handle his teasing, because her flush progressed to no more than pale pink this time, and no farther down than her (temporarily) bare breasts. Gloha was glad the remark hadn't been directed at her, so she didn't have to flush similarly despite being as guilty of such kissing as Cynthia.

"The winged centaur family is north of the Gap Chasm," Gloha said. "The two of us could fly there, but that won't work for you, Magician."

"I regret being such a drag on this party," Trent said. "It reminds me of when I traveled with Bink and Chameleon, when they were young. I rather interfered with their progress too, for a while."

"Well, you were evil then, weren't you?" Cynthia inquired.

"So I was called. But I think I don't need to hold you folk back. I can transform one of you into a roc again, and you can carry me there." He glanced at the sky. "It's about noon now; I lost track of time below, but we can make better progress now and be there before the day is out."

Cynthia sent a wavering glance out. Gloha intercepted it and sent it back. Suddenly she realized that neither one of them was quite ready to end this segment of their journey. It wasn't exactly uncertainty about their respective futures, though that helped, and not exactly that the youthened Magician Trent was pleasant company, though that also helped. They just weren't yet ready to end this interlude, for reasons that were surely best left unfathomed.

"Let's just remain with our own forms for a while," Gloha said. "Cynthia needs practice in today's Xanth."

"As you wish," he agreed. "I merely did not wish to delay either of you. We can proceed north at my limited pace."

In due course their clothing was mostly dry, and they took turns dressing while the others tried not to peek too much. Their packs remained damp, but would probably survive.

They set off, following the stream, which moved generally north and northwest. Cynthia and Gloha remained on the ground, since they were the ones who had declined the chance to become big enough to carry the Magician through the air. There turned out to be interesting things down here, such as colored stones in the streambed and pretty flowers along the bank. Each of them picked a pink flower to put in her hair; then they picked two blue flowers for Trent's hair. "So no one will confuse you with a girl," Gloha explained, lightly kissing his left ear to make the flower stay in place.

"Or a winged monster," Cynthia added, kissing his right ear, for a similar reason.

"If I did not know better, I'd suspect one of you of flirting with me," he responded. "Unfortunately I can't tell which one."

"We'll never tell," they said together, not even bothering to blush.

The stream climbed a hill, then relaxed by filling in a pool. There by a ledgelike bank in the pool were three young female human heads. One was blond, with her long fair tresses artfully obliterating her right eye on their way down. One was red, with her hair spreading out across the ledge in front. The third was dark gray-brown, with hanks of hair swirling tantalizingly across her heaving bosom. All three had eyes as deep and blue as the very freshest water.

"Eeeek! People!" the blond screamed cutely, not sounding frightened.

Then, as Gloha and Cynthia crested the hill, the redhead clarified it. "Two half people. Female. I can tell by their pink flowers." She sounded disappointed.

"And one straight human man," the brunette said. "I can tell by his blue flowers." She sounded interested.

"And who are you?" Trent inquired in friendly fashion. But Gloha saw that he was casually moving to within transformation range. He was not the most trusting person, which was just as well.

"Merely three beautifully bored mermaids," the blonde said as the three lifted their tails behind them. "Ash, Cedar, and Mahogany. I'm Ash, of course. Who are you, who come to us with your ears kissed?"

"Trent, Gloha, and Cynthia," the Magician said. "I'm Trent."

"You are named for trees?" Gloha asked.

"For colors," Cedar said, making an appealing moue. "The local wood nymphs got all the water colors, so we had to take wood colors."

"We would love to give you a wonderful time, Trent man, but you seem to be already well attended," Mahogany said. "We see that your mouth has been rather soundly kissed, too. However, should you too be bored with overly familiar things—"

"We are just rapidly passing through," Cynthia said, just possibly not quite pleased by the presence of three more pretty crossbreeds.

"Still, diversions are seldom and slow," Ash said. "Can we not persuade you to dally a moment?" She gave Trent a wonderfully liquid look as she lowered her tail and lifted her marvelously full bare breasts from the water.

"Only if you have something interesting or useful to offer," Gloha said somewhat disparagingly. Her tone was sheer bluff, because she knew that never in her wildest fantasy dreams would she have a bosom as globular as that. Water folk were able to wear more flesh than air folk, because it helped them float and didn't help them fly. That was one of the unfairness of reality.

"Well, we do have one talent between the three of us," Cedar said, performing a similar maneuver with slightly better exposure. "As your brightly kissed eyes may see, if you wish." She inhaled.

"But do you have a magic talent?" Cynthia inquired, knowing that crossbreeds often did not, and if they did, it was likely to be related to their survival as crossbreeds. Such as flying, for the winged ones.

"Why, yes," Mahogany said, taking her turn at the maneuver and managing a truly double-barreled (as it were) display. All three of them were distressingly well endowed in that particular respect. "We read titles."

"Titles?" Trent asked. He had, perhaps diplomatically, stayed clear of much of the prior dialogue, though he had kept a firm eye on the proceedings. Most of the firmness had been elsewhere, however.

"Whatever title is written, we can read," Ash explained. "The three of us have to do it together, and we can't read any more than the title, but it can nevertheless be interesting."

Trent shook his head. "We are more interested in making progress toward our destination than in reading titles."

But now Gloha, perversely, was intrigued. "What kind of adventures are we in for?" she inquired.

Trent considered. "It's hard to know, since none of us happen to have a talent for seeing the future."

"But sometimes you can get a hint by checking the chapter title of the Muse of History's ongoing series on the history of Xanth, can't you? If we could glimpse the current chapter, it might save us some complications."

The Magician seemed bemused. "In theory, yes. But that presumes that she has already written the chapter. I suspect she waits until the action has been finished before describing it."

"But maybe she describes it, and then the action happens," Gloha said. "Doesn't an event have to be scripted before it can happen?"

He shrugged. "We can try." He faced the three mermaids, who inhaled in unison at that moment, perhaps coincidentally. "Can you read the title of the current chapter of the current volume of history?"

"We can try," one or more of them echoed with a winning smile. They swam together, linked hands, closed their eyes, and concentrated with perfect coordination. Their three flukes lifted and slapped the water as one.

In a moment they separated. They swam back to their ledge bank and resumed their former display. They fixed the Magician with three well-tempered gazes.

"Did you find the right volume?" he asked after a moment.

"Yes," Ash breathed fetchingly. Gloha sent half a glance of disgust to Cynthia.

"And did you read the right title?"

"Yes," Cedar agreed as the surface of the water formed a marvelously rounded decolletage. Cynthia's returning glance was tinged with envy.

"And will you tell us what it is?"

"That depends," Mahogany murmured as innocent little currents in the water managed to carry her decorative tresses away from her heaving bosom so that nothing obscured the view. Neither Gloha's nor Cynthia's glance was able to nudge those tresses back into place.

"And on what does it depend?" Trent asked, hardly seeming to be bothered by such irrelevancies as breathing or tresses.

"On how long you care to stay to hear it," Ash said, propping her chin on her right hand without interfering half a whit with the view of her left upper quarter.

"That certainly sounds like fun," the Magician said. "But I feel I should advise you that I am somewhat older than I may appear."

"We like mature males," Cedar said, her pupils alluringly large.

"In fact I am an old man, recently youthened by youth elixir."

Mahogany began to grow cautious. "How old?" The wayward currents were now carrying her hair back into place.

"Ninety-six."

All three heads descended into the water before the mermaids recovered equilibrium. They emerged with their lustrous hair somewhat matted and their expressions somewhat dissolved. "True?" Ash asked.

"True," Gloha and Cynthia said together.

The mermaids' torsos seemed to deflate. "The title is meaningless," Cedar said.

"How so?" Trent asked, seeming as oblivious of their deflation as he was of their prior inflation.

"It's just 'Xxxxxxx,' no words," Mahogany explained.

Trent shook his head. "I was afraid of this. It's like trying to inquire about Bink's talent. Something always interferes. The Muse evidently knew we would look at the title, so left it blank."

"We are so sorry you have to go so soon," Ash said.

"Yes, so sorry," Cedar agreed.

"Why couldn't you have been younger?" Mahogany asked rhetorically.

"I didn't realize I would be meeting three such intriguing females," Trent said, walking on past the pool.

"Just as well," Cynthia muttered.

Gloha could only agree.

They followed the stream onward. It wound around as if trying to lose them, but wasn't successful. Then a small mean dragon emerged from the brush. It eyed them hungrily, breathing rapidly to stoke up its fires.

"Dragon, allow me to show you something," the Magician said. He gestured at a small burr-weed that was about to stick a burr in his sock. It became a cacklebird. The bird, almost as astonished as it was dismayed, took flight without even remembering to cackle.

"Now your turn, if you wish," Trent said. He strode purposefully toward the dragon.

The dragon reversed course so suddenly it almost left its tail behind. In only part of a fraction of a moment, it was gone.

"But that dragon could have given you an awful hotfoot before you got within transformation range," Gloha said.

"The aspect of confidence can be deceptive," the Magician remarked mildly.

After a time the stream changed its mind about running in gullies or valleys and diverged up into a mountain pass. But there was a suitable path through the forest which seemed interested in getting somewhere. As evening thought about setting in they found a pleasant glade. "I think we should camp for the night here," Trent said. "Perhaps tomorrow we shall reach an enchanted path and make better progress."

Then they saw a crude shelter under a nut and bolt tree, with a fire by it. "Someone else is here," Gloha said, alarmed.

"It's a centaur!" Cynthia exclaimed, quickly touching up her hair.

It turned out to be two people: a male centaur and a female human. They were glad to share their accommodations in return for some pie from the pie tree Trent made by transformation. They ate pies by the fire and agreed to exchange stories.

"I am Braille," the centaur asserted. "I have a forbidden love."

"I am Jana," the young woman confided. "I am that love."

"You met at a love spring?" Gloha asked, surprised.

"No, we just happened to get to know each other, living nearby," Jana said. "His magic talent is transcribing documents, so that those who can't read can sense their meaning. He did some work for us, and I got to know him, and I realized that no man I know was half the creature of this centaur."

"Of course intellectually I knew this was folly," Braille said. "But emotionally I found no centaur to match the qualities of Jana. The situation is distinctly awkward." He glanced at Cynthia. "I gather you are in a similar situation."

Cynthia blushed halfway between pink and red. "Oh, this man and I are not a couple! We are merely traveling together."

"Same for me," Gloha said quickly. "I am looking for a male of my kind, and Magician Trent is helping me search. Cynthia is going to join a winged centaur family."

"You're a Magician?" Jana asked, awed. "What's your talent?"

"I transform living things," Trent said. "Didn't you see me change the weed into the pie tree?"

"Oh, I thought that was all of it," she said, embarrassed. "I mean, that you made pie trees, nothing else."

"By no means. I can, if you wish, transform you into a centaur filly, or Braille into a human man."

The two looked at each other. "But I'm not interested in a human man!" Jana protested. "I love your centaurly qualities."

"And I love your humanly aspects," Braille said.

"We are going to ask the Good Magician for a solution to our problem," Jana said.

That did seem best.

In the morning Jana got on Braille's back and they moved smartly west. Trent, Cynthia, and Gloha proceeded north. "You know," Cynthia remarked, "I could probably carry you, Magician, in similar manner, on the ground. That might speed our progress."

"I could transform a fly to a horse and require it to carry me," Trent replied. "I haven't felt the need, unless you are in a hurry. My rationale is that you need to learn the current ways of Xanth by slow experience, and I can protect you from most hazards as long as we travel together, so time is not of the essence. I must admit, however, that I am enjoying this experience myself, as a reminder of what ordinary life is like for the young. Once I am done with my missions, I will return to my wife and friends, resume my actual age, and we shall fade away as planned. Somehow I feel less urgency about that than I did before."

"I feel similarly little urgency about settling in with strangers," Cynthia agreed. "But of course this is just a diversion from Gloha's mission, so we shouldn't delay her."

"Let's face it," Gloha said. "I'm looking for a male of my own crossbreed species, when as far as I know there isn't one. That suggests that the faster I complete my mission, the sooner I will be disappointed. I'm not in any great rush for that."

"I could transform some other male into a male of your kind," the Magician said. "That may be why Crombie pointed to me. In which case—"

"No!" Gloha cried more sharply than her caring little concern warranted. "It wouldn't be the same. Just the way Braille and Jana didn't want each other transformed. Some other creature wouldn't have grown up as a product of the harpy and goblin cultures, and wouldn't understand what it feels like. I don't want an artificial man." Yet there was a tiny little trace of doubt, for she remembered how comfortable she had felt being a flame vine or a furball or a lungfish; the sentiments of the species had come with the form. Did she really have a case?

"So it seems that none of us have much motive to hurry," Trent said. "For reasons that are sufficient for ourselves. So we might as well proceed as we have been doing until we have reason to change."

"Yes," Cynthia said. "I feel easier about that."

"So do I," Gloha agreed.

They continued roughly north, because that was the way the best path insisted on going. When anything threatened them, Trent discourage it either by drawing his sword or by transforming it to something harmless.

Then they came to a several-way fork in the path. There was a sign:

DRAW WELL STEPPES PIER COM PEWTER

"I am getting thirsty," Trent said. "I would be happy to pause for fresh well water."

Cynthia and Gloha agreed. The Magician had conjured watermelons along the way, but they were ready for straight natural water.

They took that path. It led to a round stone structure whose top was a large flat panel. As they approached, a jointed stick unfolded before the panel and made rapid movements.

Trent put his hand on his sword. But the weird thing did not seem threatening. It was just doing its own thing, whatever that was. There was no sign of water.

Then Gloha realized what was happening. "It's drawing a picture!" she exclaimed.

Indeed, the thing was sketching a picture of the three of them: a human man, a winged centaur filly, and a winged goblin girl. It was an excellent group portrait done in black and white.

"It's a draw well," Cynthia said. "Just as represented."

The appendage caught the edge of the panel, and tore off a sheet of paper. It threw it aside, then commenced drawing Cynthia alone. Apparently it oriented on whoever moved or spoke, and drew a picture of that person. It didn't care what happened to its pictures; it was just interested in drawing them well.

Trent shook his head. "I would have settled for nice cold water."

The appendage ripped off the centaur picture and drew one of Trent drinking a beaded goblet of water. Gloha laughed. So naturally it drew one of her laughing. She salvaged that drawing as it got ripped off.

There was nothing to do but retrace their steps, as the path ended here. They returned to the fork and went along the STEPPES path. "Steppes are broad grassy plains with few trees, easy to travel across," Trent remarked.

But instead the path fed into an isolated mountain completely covered with stairs. Some of them were dainty small, others gigantic huge, and still others were ornate and decorated. "What's this?" Cynthia asked.

Again Gloha figured it out. "The steppes! Many steps."

"Xanth is made mostly of puns," Trent said. "We seem to have walked into a zone of them."

"I don't remember encountering this sort of thing in the North Village," Cynthia said.

Gloha glanced at her paper. She discovered to her surprise that it had changed. It was now a picture of a sleepy dull village.

"This is because the North Village has always been the staidest place in Xanth," Trent explained. "That is why we retired there. It is very conservative, with little humor and not a great amount of imagination. The wild effects are mostly elsewhere. Even Fracto finds it too boring for a storm."

"Fracto?" Cynthia asked.

"Xanth's meanest cloud," Gloha explained. "Wherever folk are having fun, Cumulo Fracto Nimbus goes to drown it out. You don't want to run afoul of him; he's not bright, but he's all wet."

Meanwhile the paper was a picture of a mean-spirited cloud gleefully raining out a picnic.

"I don't suppose that well knew what kind of adventure we're going to be having next," Gloha said.

The picture was of an assemblage of junk in a cave, with a piece of glass projecting from its center. Across the glass was printed the word CURSES.

Trent and Gloha laughed, while Cynthia looked blank. "That's Com Pewter," Trent told her. "Formerly Xanth's second worst scourge, until Lacuna tricked him into reprogramming as a nice machine. He has the power to change reality in his vicinity. But I really wasn't thinking of going there."

"So we'll have to try the pier next," Gloha said.

They returned down the path as the picture was of a lake with a dock.

They returned to the fork and took the path labeled PIER. This led to a small lake where there was indeed a dock. But there was something odd about it. It didn't actually enter the water; instead it was along the bank. It was made of boards, and the boards did not lie still; they moved. One would jump over the others, laying itself down at the head of the line; then another would jump, getting ahead of the first. In fact they were walking by themselves, making their way around the lake.

"That's the first time I've seen a board walk," Trent said wryly. They watched the boards walk until they came to a small river entering the lake. There was a rickety little bridge across it. The boards laid themselves down on this, starting across.

"Get off there!" someone cried. "Shoo! Shoo!"

It turned out to be an ugly greenish troll. Trent's hand hovered near his sword again. "We mean no harm," he said. "We are merely looking for a fair way northwest."

The troll's head turned. "I wasn't talking to you," he said. "It's these confounded walking boards. They think they can walk all over everything. I'm trying to protect the bridge from their traffic."

"They don't seem to be doing any harm," Cynthia said.

"Well, they don't actually harm it. But it's my job to keep this bridge clear. Suppose someone came to use it, and it was all cluttered with moving boards? This would make a very bad impression."

"Where does the bridge lead?" Gloha asked.

"Nowhere. It's just there. This is a useless sinecure. But what am I to do? I'm a troll. Trolls guard bridges, and this is mine."

"Perhaps we should introduce ourselves," Trent said. "I am Magician Trent, and these are Cynthia Centaur and Gloha Goblin-Harpy. We are on a quest or two to find compatible situations."

"I am Tristan Troll. I was banished to the sticks after betraying my village. But the sticks turned out to be boards, and now I'm bored stiff."

"Bored with boards," Cynthia said. "I can appreciate that."

"How did you betray your village?" Gloha asked.

"We had a raid on a human village, and I let a little human girl go instead of bringing her in to be boiled for dinner. I was supposed to have a really bad dream for that, but Grace'l Ossein, the walking skeleton, messed it up and got in trouble herself. It was a bad scene."

"Oh, you are that troll!" Trent said. "My grandson Dolph defended Grace'l in her trial. She was found to be too nice for bad dreams, and she married Marrow Bones."

"Who?" Cynthia asked.

"Another walking skeleton from the realm of bad dreams," Gloha said. "It's a long story. He's a nice person."

"But he must be a dead person!"

"As I said, it's a long story. This is a troll we know of; he's decent, for a troll."

"Things certainly have changed! In my days trolls were all horrible."

"They still are," Gloha said. "Except for Tristan."

"Who was punished for his unbad deed," Trent reminded her. "And the troll tribe was not wrong in doing so, by the standards of its culture."

"Why don't you just walk away from this boring job?" Gloha asked the troll.

"Several reasons. For one thing, the other trolls would catch me and bring me back, or give me an even worse assignment. For another, it isn't easy for a troll to find a job. Bridges are about it. I would expire of boredom if I didn't have something useful to do."

Gloha got a glancing little glimmer of a notion. If this path went nowhere, they would have to take the next one, and fulfill the well's prediction of an encounter with Com Pewter. Meanwhile here was a decent troll with a problem. This might not be coincidence. "What would you do if you had your choice?" she asked Tristan.

"I'd like to get into one of the forward-looking bridge jobs, like information processing," Tristan said. "A bridge to knowledge. But who would pay attention to the mind of a troll?"

"So it's your mind you wish to exercise, rather than your body."

"Who would remain with a troll's body, if he had a choice?" Tristan asked rhetorically. "But of course I'm stuck with the way I am. I'm surprised that you handsome folk are even talking to me."

"Well, we're sort of having an adventure, without being in a hurry to conclude it," Gloha said. "I think we just might be able to do something nice for you."

"Don't risk it!" he said, alarmed. "Favors can become expensive."

"But sometimes worthwhile even in their expense," Trent said, glancing briefly at the two females. "What was that glib little glimmer of a notion I saw flickering through your head, Gloha?"

"That maybe Tristan could work with Com Pewter. Pewter's supposed to be a clean machine now, and maybe he could use an assistant. Someone interested in his sort of business."

"And we are going to have to take Pewter's path after all," he agreed. "That machine may no longer be evil, but he could still be mischievous. We just might be able to trade favors with him."

"We'd have to do him a favor so he would take Tristan?"

Trent smiled. "Pewter would have to do *us* a favor if we gave him Tristan."

Gloha felt her mouth forming an orotund little O. "Oh," she said.

Trent turned back to the troll. "I am a transformer. I can render you into a different shape. Then we can take you to Com Pewter and inquire whether he can use an assistant. What form would you like to assume?"

"Oh, anything would do. Even a bug."

"Very well. I shall transform you into a humbug for now, and we can decide on a final form later." He reached toward the troll, and Tristan abruptly became a small bug.

"Now find a suitable place to ride on one of us," Trent said. "And don't fly away, because if we lose you, I will be unable to transform you again."

The bug considered. Then it hummed and flew up and perched on Gloha's hair. "Hhhummmm?" it inquired.

"That's all right," Gloha said. "I don't mind if you ride there, as long as you don't—" She hesitated, not wishing to speak of anything as dirty as bug excretion.

"Nnnummmm!" the bug hummed negatively. It wouldn't do anything like that on such nice hair.

They left the walking boards and returned once more to the fork. This time they took the path leading to Com Pewter.

It turned out to be an enchanted path, leading them almost immediately to the machine's den, though it was supposedly some distance.

But as they approached the entrance to the cave, there was a terrible shaking of the ground. "Eeek!" Cynthia screamed. "A ground quake!"

"No, I think it's the invisible giant," Trent said. "He works for the machine."

Sure enough, a monstrous footprint appeared in the ground nearby, squishing two trees and a boulder into two toothpicks and a grain of sand.

"We're going to get squished into mites!" Gloha cried, alarmed.

"I don't think so," Trent said. "His purpose is to herd clients into Pewter's cave, in case any should be hesitant. Fly up to the region of his head and tell him we're coming voluntarily."

"But I can't see his head!"

"You don't need to. Fly up until you smell his breath. His head will be in that vicinity."

Gloha flew up. So did Cynthia, who was just about as nervous about the ground near those footprints as Gloha was.

Way up above treetop range they encountered an awful wind. Not only did it blow them off course, it smelled like a wagonload of cabbage that had sickened and died before managing to rot. The humbug on Gloha's head coughed and choked.

"I think we've found his breath," Cynthia gasped, her hair blowing out sideways from her head as if trying to flee the odor. "I'm losing control." She glided erratically away. Fortunately she was able to recover somewhat as she got out of the wind; Gloha saw her gliding safely back down toward the forest.

Gloha nerved herself, held her neat little nose, and flew into the putrid breeze. She had a smaller nose than Cynthia did, so it didn't take in as much of the stench. When she banged into an invisible cable she grabbed onto it. This was a strand of the giant's hair. She worked her way down to an ear. "Hey, don't step on us!" she shouted. "We're coming to see Com Pewter anyway!"

"OOOOGAA!" the giant responded deafeningly.

"Pump down the volume!" Gloha screamed.

"What did you say?" the giant whispered.

"I said that we're coming to see Com Pewter anyway," she shouted. "So you shouldn't step on us."

"Okay." There was a stir as something huge moved. He was turning his head. "Say, you're a pretty little creature."

"Thank you," she gasped.

"But your nose is swollen."

"That's because I can barely breathe."

"Why is that? Are you ill?"

Gloha pondered perhaps five of her moments, but only a quarter of a giant moment. She decided to tell the truth. "It's your breath," she shouted. "It's awful."

"That's nothing. You should smell my cousin's breath. It can knock over an ogre at fifty paces."

"Well, I'll go away now, so I can recover," Gloha said. But then, so as not to be impolite, she introduced herself. "I'm Gloha Goblin-Harpy."

"I'm Greatbow," he replied. "Nice to meet you."

Gloha couldn't honestly express pleasure at encountering the giant, so she evaded the issue by asking a question. "Why is your cousin's breath so bad?"

"My cousin Graeboe? He's ailing. He has some sickness. He's even turned visible, which means he's not much longer for happy stomping."

"How horrible," Gloha said. "Well, I must be gone." She let herself drop, which wasn't at all difficult at this point. Only when she got down near the trees did her breathing begin to clear. Surely a person could not blame the giants for being as big in odor as they were in person, but the dialogue had been a strain. She had at least accomplished her purpose: the giant was no longer stomping. They should now be able to enter the cave safely.

Cynthia had reached the ground, and joined Trent at the mouth of the cave. "I'm so sorry I couldn't stay up there," Cynthia called as Gloha glided in. "I just couldn't—"

"I understand," Gloha said. "Maybe my experience with goblins and harpies gave me strength to endure it. Or maybe my smallness enabled me to take smaller breaths."

Trent and Cynthia exchanged a generous glance. "Or perhaps your spirit is larger than your body," Trent said. "Shall we tackle the next incidental challenge?"

Gloha felt a chill, though she had been in a sweat when bathed in the giant's breath. Just how safe was this venture? "I suppose, if there is no other path."

They entered the dark cave. There was just enough light for them to see the one route forward into the mountain. Com Pewter was supposed to be a nice machine now, but his record as an evil machine was much longer, and Gloha had, if not a doubt, certainly a qualm.

They came to a chamber with a collection of junk on the floor. One pane of glass was propped up in the center. WELCOME, USERS appeared on that surface.

Trent strode forward to stand over it. "I am Magician Trent; perhaps you know of me."

YOU CAN'T TRANSFORM INANIMATE CREATURES, the screen said, flickering worriedly.

Trent smiled. "I have not come to quarrel with you, Commie. The only viable path led here, so I thought I would pay you a call. If you don't attempt to change my reality unpleasantly, I won't transform this creature to a sphinx who will sit on you." He indicated Gloha.

AGREED. The screen brightened with surprise. YOU LOOK YOUNG, MAGICIAN.

"Youth elixir subtracted seventy years. I will return to my real age when this mission is done."

WHO ELSE IS WITH YOU?

"Gloha Goblin-Harpy, whom I am helping to find her ideal man. Cynthia Centaur, whom I transformed some time ago, and am now escorting to the single winged centaur family of Xanth. And Tristan Troll, whom I have transformed to a bug."

A BUG! the screen printed, alarmed. DON'T LET IT NEAR MY PROGRAM.

Trent nodded. "As I remember, you have been known to have a problem with a virus. I can appreciate your caution. But I come not to bury you but to do you a favor."

I DON'T BELIEVE IN FAVORS.

Gloha was impressed. It was evident that the machine was quite wary of the Magician, and there were surely very few people or creatures in Xanth who commanded such respect.

"Naturally I expect a return favor," Trent continued smoothly.

OH. NOW YOU ARE MAKING SENSE. WHAT DO YOU WANT?

"Nothing difficult. Merely a clear, pleasant, and safe path from here to the residence of Cheiron Centaur."

The screen dimmed a moment as Com Pewter pondered. THERE IS ONE TO WHICH I CAN DIRECT YOU. IT CROSSES THE GAP CHASM VIA THE INVISIBLE BRIDGE AND PAUSES AT THE RESIDENCE OF GRUNDY GOLEM. WILL THIS BE SATISFACTORY?

"Certainly. Grundy isn't much, but his wife Rapunzel is delightful."

WHAT RETURN FAVOR DO YOU OFFER?

"It happens that Tristan Troll is a thoughtful and decent creature, unlike many of his kind, who seeks employment as an information processor. It occurred to me that you could use an assistant."

I DON'T WANT A TROLL! THE LAST ONE I ENCOUNTERED TOOK MY WHEATSTONE BRIDGE.

"Well, perhaps if he had another form. Such as a cat—"

NO.

"Or perhaps a mouse."

The screen blinked. A MOUSE!

Trent shrugged. "Of course if you're not interested, he could be a spring chicken."

THE MOUSE WILL DO!

Gloha stifled a laugh. Spring chickens were notorious for aging rapidly and ceasing to be attractive. They were almost like harpies in that respect. But what would Pewter want with a mouse?

Trent reached toward Gloha. The humbug jumped from her head to his hand. Then it became a cute mouse. Trent set the mouse down before the screen. It ran around, and the path of its motion was traced by a line on the screen.

AH, YES, PERFECT: YES. NO.

"Now if you care to show us the path," Trent suggested.

WATCH THE MOUSE.

And the mouse ran to the wall—where there was an opening Gloha had not seen before. She could almost have sworn it hadn't been there a moment ago, but of course she was a nice girl who would never swear.

They entered the new passage. The mouse sat up and squeaked. Gloha squatted down. "Thank you, Tristan," she said. "I hope you are happy here." She extended one finger to stroke his head.

"Just exactly what does a mouse have to do with a funny machine?" Cynthia inquired as they moved on.

"I understand it is very useful in helping people relate to the machine, perhaps because they prefer to have a living interface," Trent said. "With a mouse, much more information can be processed in a simpler way. It's a special kind of magic that few in Xanth understand, but I knew that Pewter would. Of course there are those who don't like mice, with or without a machine. That won't bother Pewter; he'll be happy to have his mouse spook them, while remaining nominally nice."

Now Gloha understood better. Pewter surely wasn't happy having to be nice all the time. Now he could be nasty while seeming nice.

The tunnel led directly out of the mountain—and there before them was the great gulf of the Gap Chasm. "So soon?" Gloha asked, astonished, as they peered down on the top of a small cloud that happened to be slumming.

"Com Pewter changes reality in his vicinity," Trent reminded her. "He gave us a direct path."

"He certainly did!" She was almost disappointed, because she was rather enjoying this journey with Cynthia and wasn't eager for it to end quickly.

Trent followed the path to the brink and put one foot cautiously over the edge. "Yes, it's here," he said, and walked out into air.

"Eeeek!" Cynthia screamed, jamming a good four *e*'s into her ek.

"It's the invisible bridge," Gloha reminded her.

"I thought that was a joke."

"I believe it was built after your time," Trent said cheerily from midair.

Cynthia flew near him and reached out to touch the invisible structure. "It's there!" she exclaimed. "It's really there."

"All the same, I'll fly across," Gloha said. "The troll's bridge and invisible giant were bad enough; I don't need to trust an invisible bridge."

"Me too," Cynthia agreed. "I'm glad for my wings." Then, suffering a second thought, she added: "Thanks to you, Magician. I would no longer be comfortable as a human maiden, or even a regular centaur. What made you choose this form for me?"

"You were so pretty, I didn't want to spoil it. But I didn't want you joining the centaurs, who can be as difficult as straight human folk. It was a spur-of-the-moment compromise. He glanced up at her as she hovered close by. "I think it was a good decision, given the exigencies of the moment. I would not do such a thing today, but I believe you remain as pretty as you were then."

Cynthia blushed again. She flew on ahead, so as to hide her face. Gloha knew why: Cynthia still found the Magician insidiously attractive. Gloha understood the feeling, because she felt that attraction herself. She had been trying to deny it, but it would not be denied. But like Cynthia, she would not care to be transformed to a full human woman, even if the Magician were interested in her, or unmarried, or actually as young as he looked. She liked her own form too well. But it didn't stop her half-witted little heart from having naughty little notions.

Trent completed his crossing. Gloha was relieved; she knew the invisible bridge was sturdy, but it was still easy to imagine him plummeting into the chasm. Perhaps if she had gotten on the bridge herself, and kept her hands on the handrails, she would have had more confidence. That was another reason she never wanted to be without wings: the groundbound human form was so limited by mountains and chasms.

The way led north through the forest. Now that they had crossed the bridge, she knew it was an enchanted path, free from menace by dragons, griffins, basilisks, mean men, and other ilk. That was a relief; she hoped never to meet an ilk. But she had to admit that their small encounters along the other route had been interesting. Maybe they would have been less so if there hadn't been a Magician along to protect the innocent maidens. Yet they wouldn't have had to stay down on the ground if he hadn't been along, so wouldn't have needed protection. So her impressions were sort of mixed up.

Soon they came to a giant club stuck endwise in the ground, the thorny business end up. As they came close, it quivered, as if about to lift itself up and take a swing at them. The thing was so massive that a single blow would crush any of them.

"Does the enchantment still hold?" Gloha asked in a nervous whisper.

"It should," Trent said. "But sometimes there are flaws in the magic, and something gets through. It is best not to take any threat for granted."

"Let me fly by it first; I don't think it could move fast enough to hit me," she said. "If it comes out of the ground and chases me, then we'll know."

"I'll agree only if you fly along the path. The club may be dangerous to anything that strays off the path, and merely threaten whoever passes on it."

"That would make sense," Cynthia said. "It might make a feint, scaring someone off the path. Then it could smash that poor person, because the enchantment doesn't extend beyond the path. The enchantment can't protect someone from foolishness."

Trent nodded. "That's probably its ploy. So if we simply refuse to react, we'll be safe. Nevertheless, I think you had better test it. If it actually strikes in the pathway, I'll transform Cynthia into a giantess who can grab it by the handle and tame it."

Gloha flew swiftly by the club, while the Magician and centaur waited behind. The club quivered, working its way out of the ground, about to take off.

"Gloha!" someone cried.

Gloha spun around in the air, looking back. There was a tiny man standing on top of the club. "Grundy!" she called back. "What are you doing here?"

"I'm home. This is my clubhouse. Don't worry; it doesn't bother friends. I came out the moment it started to shake." He tapped his foot on the wood. "At ease, house. Gloha's okay." The club stopped moving.

"You had better introduce it to my friends, too," Gloha said, indicating Trent and Cynthia.

Grundy turned to look. "A winged centaur!" he exclaimed. "But she's too young to be Chex."

"Actually she's older than Chex," Gloha said. "Remember, Chex is only a year older than I am. She matured rapidly."

Grundy squinted. "Still, this one looks only about sixteen."

"She was delivered in the year 1005."

"She's eighty-eight years old? You're pulling my little leg, harpy-wings. Next you're going to tell me that young man beside her is ninety-six!"

"Right. He's Magician Trent."

"Sure, and let's see him transform something."

Trent squatted and pointed to an ant on the path. Suddenly it became a giant, a humongous creature the size of a unicorn. It looked around as if startled to see the world become so much smaller, vibrated its antennae, and made ready to chomp someone with its mandibles.

Trent transformed it to a pink bunny. The bunny hopped toward the forest.

"That's not nice," someone called. "Change it back to its natural form before it gets lost and hurt."

Trent went after the bunny and transformed it back into a small ant.

"That's Magician Trent, all right," Grundy agreed. "But what's he doing so young, and with you folk?"

"He's helping me find my ideal man," Gloha explained. "And the centaur is Cynthia, whom he transformed long ago; she's been in the Brain Coral's pool until now."

"So she's not really all that old!" Grundy said. "She was in suspended animation."

"Yes. Now we're taking her to join the winged centaur family."

The golem nodded. "But she's a bit old for Che."

"Magician Trent has some more youth elixir."

"Gotcha." Grundy looked around. "I heard my wife a moment ago—ah, there she is. Come on out, dear, and meet these folk."

The tiny woman came out of the tiny door in the clubhouse. Suddenly she was full human size, with a head of dark hair that reached to the ground and then some, turning brown, red, blond, and eventually white on the way, despite being braided and bound. She was lovely in a dress covered with ads for places and things.

Grundy jumped down to her extended hand. "My wife Rapunzel, wearing her address," he introduced. "I call her the hairy monster."

Rapunzel lifted him to her face, made as if to bite his tiny head off, and kissed his face instead—his whole face at once.

"One of these days she's going to be inhaling when she does that, and I'll be gone," Grundy said ruefully.

Rapunzel shook hands with them all. Then she reached to the clubhouse again. "Let me introduce our daughter, Surprise," she said.

A figure even smaller than Grundy came to the doorway and stepped into Rapunzel's hand, joining Grundy. "Here she is," he said proudly. "Delivered by surprise six months ago." He turned to the child. "Say hi to the nice folk, kid."

"Hi, nice folk," the girl said.

Gloha's jarred little jaw dropped. So did Cynthia's. "I thought you said she was six months old," Gloha said.

"That isn't what he said," Rapunzel said, smiling. "He said she was delivered six months ago."

"But she's talking!"

"Yes, she talks a lot," Rapunzel agreed. "She's five years old."

Even Trent looked startled at this. "How can she be that old, only half a year after being delivered?"

"It was a surprise," Grundy admitted. "So we named her—"

"That I think I understand," Trent said. "Still—"

"We think the stork got lost on the way," Rapunzel explained. "We had ordered her some time ago, and kept expecting her, but somehow she never arrived. Then, when we least expected it, there she was. The stork didn't speak to us; he just flew quickly away, as if greatly relieved."

Trent shook his head, acting for all of them. "I thought I had seen some unusual things in my day, but this does surprise me. Does she have a talent?"

Grundy and Rapunzel exchanged several fragments of a glance. "Not exactly," Grundy said, looking uncomfortable.

"Talent!" the tiny child exclaimed. Suddenly she was full human child sized, with a sweet smile and a headful of curly black hair. Rapunzel had to set her quickly on the ground, almost spilling Grundy in the process.

"Size changing!" Gloha exclaimed. "How nice. But of course it must run in the family."

"Not exactly," Rapunzel said with the same uncomfortable look Grundy had had a moment before. "We don't like to mention it, because—"

"Not mention a fine talent like that?" Gloha asked. "But why not?"

"Talent!" Surprise repeated. Suddenly her hair was growing. It curled down around her shoulders, turning dark brown. It extended to her waist, becoming light brown. Then it reached to her knees, becoming red. Finally it touched her feet, blond.

Rapunzel quickly gathered it up before it could drag in the dirt. She borrowed several pins from her own tresses to fasten it in place, while the child played idly with a pebble she found on the ground.

"Two?" Gloha asked. "I thought no one in Xanth had that!"

"Well, one may not be a—I mean, both these things take after her mother, sort of," Grundy said.

"But that's still amazing! Maybe she does have two talents."

"Talent!" Surprise said a third time, evidently picking it up from their discussion. She held up the pebble—and it became a dragon's tooth.

This time Trent's jaw dropped as far as the others' did. "Shape-changing of objects!" he said. "A third—" He cut himself off as both parents looked about to faint.

"This *is* a surprise," Gloha said. "How many—whatevers—does she have?"

"Just one, we think," Grundy said. "One at a time, that is. We never know ahead of time which one it will be."

"Or whether we've seen it before," Rapunzel added. "It's very unnerving."

Gloha appreciated the situation. "I can see why you named her Surprise."

"Surprise!" the child cried, and vanished.

This time the jaws of Grundy and Rapunzel dropped. "Oops," he said.

"This is a new one," she said.

"Is she invisible, or elsewhere?" he asked.

Rapunzel reached out to where the little girl had been standing. "Invisible," she said with relief.

"She never acted up in company before," Grundy said, looking wary.

"Perhaps we are a disruptive influence," Trent said diplomatically. "We have to move on anyway."

"Yes, we should reach the winged centaur family by nightfall," Gloha said. Actually they had no schedule, and weren't rushing it, but if they were inciting Surprise to mischief, they needed to depart quickly, before anything really bad happened.

"Nightfall!" the childish voice cried happily. Suddenly it was night. Not blackness, but actual night: the stars were shining down.

"Farewell," Trent said, somewhat hollowly. "We'll just shoot on out of here along the path. The stars give us enough light."

"Shoot! Star!"

One of the stars moved from its place in the sky. It came swiftly toward them, leaving a trail of light behind. "Did somebody say my name?" it demanded. "I'll plug him dead!" A bolt of thin lightning zapped out.

"All we needed," Trent muttered. "A shooting star."

"With an attitude," Gloha agreed.

"I think it's cute," Cynthia said.

The star paused, brightening. "You do? Well now." It shot back to its place, pleased.

Before long the region turned reddish-dawn-colored, and then the light of the day returned. They paused and looked back. They were still on the path, having felt its smooth surface underfoot, and nothing was threatening them. But behind was the black blob of night, covering the clubhouse and its neighborhood.

"That child will be a handful," Trent muttered. "That's at least five talents she's shown, and some border on Magician class. I wish we could help them, but I think they'll just have to work things out themselves."

"Yes," Gloha agreed. It hadn't occurred to her that a strong talent could be a problem. But that child had too much talent at too young an age; she had learned how to invoke it, erratically, but lacked the responsibility that went with such magic.

They followed the path north, and in a surprisingly short time came to a pleasant glade with a large thatch cottage in the shape of a stall. Before it was an anvil where horseshoes might be hammered. Com Pewter had been true to his part of the bargain, giving them a direct route to the centaur residence. It probably would have taken a lot longer, and been much more difficult, otherwise.

Trent paused, turning to Cynthia. "I think now is the time to use the Fountain of Youth elixir Magician Humfrey gave me."

Cynthia looked doubtful. "I don't want to deceive anyone, especially centaurs. I'm really not a child."

"You're really not sixteen, either," he pointed out. "In Xanth, appearance counts for most of reality. We are not going to deceive anyone. We'll simply adjust your age as appropriate to the situation."

Still she hesitated. "My body may be young, but my mind will still be almost seventeen. I wouldn't blame them for objecting to that."

"My mind is ninety-six," he said evenly. "Has that bothered you?"

"Oh, no! You have been marvelously knowledgeable and helpful."

"Were I really twenty-six, I doubt I would have acted always with propriety, especially when you uncovered your upper torso, or when you were kissing me back to warmth. There are advantages of age and experience."

"I suppose," she agreed uncertainly. "Too bad you weren't really that age. I might have given you man thoughts to match my woman thoughts."

Trent's lips pursed, but he managed to ignore the remark. He turned to Gloha. "We seem to have a difference here. What do you say?"

"I think you should youthen her, and let the centaurs decide. If they don't want her, she can stay with us."

"But I'll be nine years old!" Cynthia protested.

"Your mind will be sixteen."

"It's not the same."

Trent shrugged. "Then let's meet the family now, and use the elixir later, if it seems warranted."

"Yes," Cynthia said, relieved.

They went to the house. Trent knocked on the door, which was double, opening in the middle and hinged at the outsides, as with a barn. A woman's face appeared in the window panel, looking surprised. Then the door opened. A mature winged centaur filly stood there, magnificently bare-breasted. "I recognize Gloha," she said, "but not the man or the—oh, my!" For now she had seen Cynthia's wings.

"Chex, I am Magician Trent, youthened for the time being. I am accompanying Gloha on her quest to find her ideal man. This is Cynthia, whom I transformed to this form in my youth. She has been in the Brain Coral's pool since. She—"

"She wanted to meet the only other winged centaurs in Xanth!" Chex said. "Oh, I'm so sorry she isn't younger!" Then she put her hand to her mouth, embarrassed. "I shouldn't have said that. It's just that—"

"Why would you want her younger?" Trent inquired, as if merely curious.

"I had this foolish notion—our foal Che—it was a wild presumption, for which I apologize. I was just so startled to see another winged centaur."

Trent didn't even need to swap glances with Cynthia. "We have some youth elixir. She can readily become a decade younger, physically."

"But why? She's already been through her childhood. She would hardly want to do it again."

"She might, if she could be with her own kind."

Chex looked at Cynthia. "You were human, before you were transformed?"

"Yes," Cynthia said. "I was sixteen. I've been a centaur less than a year, in living time. I learned to fly. But I was the only one of my kind. The real centaurs—they—" She clouded up, evidently suffering an unpleasant memory.

Chex stepped quickly forward. She put an arm about Cynthia's shoulders. "I know the feeling. They reject crossbreeds. Even my own grandsire and grand-dam refused to associate with me, at first. If you would like to join us—"

"Yes!"

"Do you know centaur lore?"

"I'm afraid I really don't," Cynthia said, abashed.

"Would you be willing to learn it? It would take several years. You see, a human being of your age is the equivalent of a centaur of eight or nine, intellectually. Our foal Che is eight."

"I want very much to learn it."

"Che isn't here now; he's at Goblin Mountain. We—" Chex looked momentarily pensive. "We miss the children."

Cynthia looked at Trent. He held out the tiny vial of elixir. She took it, opened it, and gulped down its few drops of liquid.

Suddenly she was a physical eight year old. The dose had halved her age. In a unicorn that would have been full grown, but centaurs paralleled humans, and she was half grown. Her jacket hung baggily on her. "Oh!" she exclaimed faintly. "I didn't realize it would be so quick."

"First centaur lesson," Chex said. "You don't need clothing, unless the weather requires it. As you see, I have no concern about exposing my body." She helped the filly remove the material. In a moment Cynthia stood bare. Her formerly ample breasts had vanished, leaving her human section boylike, but they would grow again in due course. Her hair had dwindled into a ponytail.

"I think our business here is done," Trent said.

"I guess it is," Gloha agreed. She flew up to give Cynthia a parting hug, for the centaur child was now just about the height of a grown goblin girl. "Maybe we'll meet again soon."

"Oh, I hope so!" the young Cynthia agreed. "We have known each other for half of my life."

Gloha had to laugh through her tears. The statement was perhaps technically correct in a way that most others would not understand. Cynthia had lost half the age she had been during their acquaintance. Then they separated.

Cynthia looked at Trent. There was something in her demeanor that suggested that she had not entirely forgotten her adult feelings, but she did not speak. Gloha remembered Jana and Braille Centaur, for some irrelevant reason.

The Magician pretended to be oblivious. "Farewell, centaur filly," he said.

"Thank you—for whatever," she replied.

Chex led Cynthia into the house. The door closed. Gloha knew that this clean break was best. She turned resolutely away. There would be other times. Meanwhile she had her own quest to fulfill.

6
MARROW

They walked back the way they had come, away from the house. Gloha saw Cynthia's hoofprints and blinked back tears of nostalgia. It had been only an interim episode, but she liked the winged centaur filly and missed her already.

"This isn't the same path," Trent remarked.

"But it has to be, because we're retracing our steps."

"The scenery's different. We're no longer on Com Pewter's magically direct route. See, there's a volcano."

"A what?"

"A mountain that magically catches fire and dumps its ashes all around." He gestured, indicating the oddity.

She looked, and saw it. The thing was cone-shaped, with smoke issuing from its narrow tip. As she watched, it belched out a cloud, and the cloud spread out and settled across the landscape. Gray particles drifted down like snow. She put out a hand to catch one. Sure enough, it was a bit of ash. "Marvelous," she said.

"That depends on the volcano's attitude. If it doesn't like us passing too close, we'll have to find another path."

"But we don't want to leave the enchanted path. We wouldn't be safe then."

"We may not be safe now," he said. "This may no longer be an enchanted path."

That seemed odd to her. "Let's follow it anyway. If it gets dangerous, then we can look for another."

"I can't transform an inanimate threat," he reminded her. "I would be helpless against that mountain, if it got angry."

"Then we'll just have to hope it doesn't get angry," she said, hardly concerned. Imagine a mountain with a temper!

The mountain rumbled warningly. More smoke plumed from its top. But Gloha still couldn't take it seriously. Mountains were inanimate, after all; they couldn't have feelings. They couldn't resent anyone passing close to them. Maybe stones had personalities when King Dor talked to them, but a mountain was a feature of the landscape. So the rumble was coincidence.

"I think this is Mount Pin-A-Tuba," Trent said. "I heard of it once. When it gets mad, it breathes out so much ash and vapor that it shades the whole of Xanth so the sun can't get through, and the land cools."

"What a weird name for a mountain," she remarked.

The path was headed right to the base of the volcano. Trent was right: this wasn't the way they had come. Cynthia's hoofprints no longer showed. The way had magically changed. With magic, anything could happen, but this was slightly strange. She must have spent too much time in the air, so had never become properly familiar with the routes of the land. Of course she could fly away at any time, but Trent couldn't so it was easiest just to stay aground.

There was another rumble, and more smoke. This time the ground itself shook. It did seem as if the mountain were reacting like an irritable sphinx. Yet that had to be her imagination.

"I don't like this," Trent muttered.

"Could you transform a creature into something that could carry us swiftly past it?"

He looked around. "There don't seem to be any living creatures or plants within range." Indeed, the region was covered by a layer of gray ash, like off-color snow.

"Then maybe transform me into a roc bird, and I'll carry you over it."

"That would be even more dangerous. I believe that mountain dislikes big birds, and fires hot boulders at them with unpleasant accuracy."

There was a larger rumble. A boulder shot out of the mountain's mouth. It arced high through the sky, and landed with a thunk to the side. More and thicker smoke poured out, blotting out much of the sky. The ashfall became stronger. Ash was getting in her hair and coating her wings. She was increasingly uncomfortable.

"I guess you're right," she said. "We'd better go back and find another path."

"It may be too late for that." It was unusual to see him so gloomy.

"Let's hurry," she said, as yet another rumble built up inside the mountain, getting ready to come out.

They turned and started away from the volcano. But the rumble only built up power and vigor, and burst forth in a cloud of swirling black smoke. The day darkened, and ash descended so thickly it was hard to see and breathe.

They tried to run, but the ground shook so violently that it was hard to keep their footing. Gloha spread her wings to fly, but hot ash came down to burn them speck by speck and feather by feather, and gusts of hot wind threatened to blow her away. She quickly folded them again, so as to minimize exposure. She was stuck on the ground, for now.

Then a boulder crashed into the path ahead, gouging out a crater. "It's got our range," Trent said.

"Oh, I'm sorry I didn't listen to you before!" she cried with a certain dismal little dismay.

"I didn't think it would be this bad. We'll have to change our course erratically, so it can't catch us." He dodged off the path to the side, running through the thickening layer of ash. His forming tracks were almost immediately covered by newly falling ash.

Gloha followed. The swirling winds buffeted her, and the gloom and ash almost made her lose sight of him. Then he ducked back and caught her by the wrist. "I can transform you to something safe, at least," he said.

"But that won't help *you*!" she protested.

"Maybe I don't deserve help."

"What?" she demanded, appalled.

"Never mind. Just keep clear of falling boulders."

She didn't need to worry about that, as he was hauling her along, preventing her from getting lost in the terrible ash storm. "Why don't you deserve it?"

"Because I was reacting in a manner unbecoming for my age and marital status."

"What are you talking about?" Another shower of ash came down, but most of it missed them. The volcano couldn't catch them as long as they kept moving erratically. "You have behaved perfectly throughout."

"I wanted to transform Cynthia back into a human woman."

So he had not been impervious to her interest! Gloha, half human herself, though without a human parent, had understood enough of Cynthia's feelings to perhaps comprehend Trent's. More than enough! "Handsome and pretty people find each other attractive," she yelled over the ash wind. "It's what they do that counts."

"Not what they feel?"

She found she couldn't debate that. "Maybe there is some guilt. But you did the right thing. You maybe wronged her when you transformed her to a winged centaur, but you righted her when you didn't change her back. She'll be happy now, with her new kind. And I just know Che Centaur will like her, when he meets her. Maybe you are helping him to achieve his destiny, which is to change the history of Xanth."

"Perhaps," he said, seeming slightly more positive.

She had reassured him. But it was odd, because he had surely had many times her total experience with male/female interest, in his life that was five times as long as hers. He had been married twice, and had at least one child. He had to know volumes about love and passion. How could her limited perspective help him in any way?

There was a series of boomings behind them. Mount Pin-A-Tuba was sounding off almost musically. But it wasn't musical business; Gloha knew that it was spitting out more boulders and ash. If they didn't get out of its range quickly, one of those rocks might score.

"Well, now."

Gloha looked. There was a swirl of smoke that wasn't quite like that of the mountain. "Metria!"

"You mortals have a funny idea of entertainment," the demoness observed.

"We are not amused," Trent said. "We're trying to get out of range of the volcano."

"You can't," Metria said confidently. "You'd do better to get under cover."

"If I thought you knew of any close cover, I'd ask you," Trent said contemptuously. His urbane manner was deteriorating under the pressure of this threat that was beyond his ability to handle. For the first time, she was seeing him unguarded. For what obscure reason she couldn't fathom, she found she liked him better for it.

"I do too know of it," the demoness retorted, becoming smoky and getting her vapors riled.

"I don't believe it," he said. Gloha was appalled; why was he vexing the demoness right when they needed her help?

"Right in the next unclean," Metria said.

Suddenly Gloha caught on. The demoness meant to tease them, but Trent was making her give them the information. "The next what?" she asked.

"Dirty, smirch, sully, violate reputation, character assassination—"

"Defile?" Trent asked.

"Whatever," Metria said crossly, fading into the swirling ash.

"We must find that sully," Trent said. "I mean gully." He forged on, still hauling Gloha along. She felt his male man strength as she practically flew behind him, but his grip on her arm was not painful; he was being careful not to hurt her despite his aggravation. This, too, impressed her.

"But a gully will just fill up faster with ash," Gloha protested. "And boulders will roll down into it."

"Metria always speaks the truth, in her fashion," he replied. "There's shelter of some sort nearby. We just have to find it."

"I hope so," she agreed weakly.

They crossed a rise, but the depression beyond seemed to be filled only with more choking smoke and the sound of falling rocks.

Then she saw something. She blinked, trying to get her aching little eyes clear of ash dust. "I think I saw a house made of bones," she said.

"Must be the remains of an animal who perished here," Trent said.

"Must be. Maybe I'm hallucinating."

"Where did you see it?"

"Over there." She pointed blindly.

He leaned into the awful wind and tramped in that direction. Suddenly he stopped. "You're right! A bone house!"

"Please don't tease me," she begged. "I'm already miserable enough."

He moved forward again. Abruptly the bones loomed close. There really was such a house!

"Anybody home?" Trent called.

A door opened. A skeleton stood there. "Flesh folk!" it exclaimed.

"Marrow Bones," Trent said. "It must be you. I'm Magician Trent, and this is Gloha Goblin-Harpy. We need shelter."

"Then come in," Marrow said. He extended a bone-hand to help. In a moment they were both inside, and the tumult of the flying ash cut off as the door closed.

Gradually Gloha's eyes watered clear, and she got a good look at the interior of the house. It really was made of bones. They were so cunningly fitted together, and so securely bound with tendon, that the walls and roof were ash-tight. The demoness had been right: this was the cover they had needed.

"Thank you, Marrow," Trent said. "It is fortunate for us that your dwelling was here."

"What are you two fleshy creatures doing in a fleshless region like this?" the skeleton inquired.

"Gloha is on a quest to find her ideal man, and I'm helping her."

"That is nice of you." The skull angled, the eye sockets peering at him. "I must say you look younger than I expected. Aren't you Prince Dolph's grandfather?"

"I am. I am old, but under the influence of youth elixir at the moment. I appreciated the way you helped him on his quest to find the Good Magician, even if he succeeded only in getting himself betrothed to two girls at once."

"He was young," Marrow said. "The young can have maladjustments of emotion."

"So can the rejuvenated," Trent murmured.

"But he had excellent magic," the skeleton continued. "Similar in respect to yours, I believe."

"Yes. I am proud of my grandson, and of my granddaughter, the Sorceress Ivy."

"What are you doing here, Marrow?" Gloha asked. "I thought you had a family now."

"I do, I do," the skeleton agreed. "I married Grace'l Ossein, and we have two little bone-buckets, Joy'nt and Picka Bone. But I do not have a soul, and without it I shall shortly fade away, for I am a creature of the dream realm. So I agreed to participate in the demons' Game of Companions if they would give me some indication how I could acquire a soul. I was not selected to be a Companion, but for my service the Demon Professor Grossclout told me that though my head lacked even mush, I might acquire half a soul if I camped beside the volcano long enough. So while I waited here, I foraged for animal bones and made this house, because I didn't like being constantly pelted with pieces of ash. Do you happen to know how I might acquire half a soul?"

Trent considered. "I have heard of the Demon Grossclout. He's so arrogantly intelligent that not even many demons can stand him. But he always knows what he's talking about. I suspect he meant that you could get half a soul from some mortal passerby. I would offer you half of mine, as they normally regenerate if properly treated, but it is so old and withered that I fear the halves would fall apart and do neither of us any good."

"I suppose you could have half of mine," Gloha said doubtfully. "Does it hurt to lose half your soul?"

"It does not," Marrow said. "But I couldn't take yours. It would serve only briefly, because you are female. I need half a young, vital male soul, if it is to be healthy."

"Then we do not seem to be the ones you have been waiting for," Trent said. "Yet your presence here has helped us, and we appreciate it, and would like to repay the favor. Is there any way to do that?"

"I don't think so. Your kind and mine do not have a great deal in common. But I thank you for the offer."

"Maybe there is a way," Gloha said. "Maybe what the Demon Professor meant is that if you were here, and you helped someone, that person would then help you to find a soul somewhere else."

"This is possible," Marrow agreed, surprised. "Certainly this region seems inhospitable to souled folk."

"So maybe you should come with us, and along the way there will be a chance for your own quest," she said. "At least it's worth a try."

"Perhaps it is," the skeleton said. "If you do not object to my company."

"Any friend of my grandson's a friend of mine," Trent said.

"And you are a friend of Chex Centaur too, aren't you?" Gloha asked. "It seems to me I heard something like that."

"We have interacted compatibly on occasion," Marrow agreed with gaunt conservatism.

"Then let's travel together, at least until you find a suitable lead on getting half-souled." Gloha was a small little wee bit surprised at herself for making the offer, because she had never before associated with a walking skeleton. But she was still in the early pangs of loneliness after losing Cynthia Centaur as a companion, and she knew that Marrow had not merely been a companion for Prince Dolph, he had been a truly good and dedicated adult at a time when a nine-year-old boy really needed guidance. Gloha had encountered Prince Dolph often enough in the interim, being the same age, and had had the story from him. It should even be fun, because the skeletons had unusual powers that could be quite helpful at times, especially to an already groundbound companion.

"Is there any living thing here?" Trent inquired, combing the last ash out of his hair.

"Only a bone flea, which I have been unable to eject," Marrow said. "I try to let living things be, but I must confess that bone fleas make me nervous."

"How could a flea hurt you, when you have no flesh?" Gloha inquired.

"A bone flea eats bone," Marrow explained. "It tries to drill into the center, where my marrow-essence is, and gorge on that. Without my marrow, I would fade immediately away from this realm. I find the prospect uncomfortable."

"Then you won't mind if I transform that flea to something else?" Trent inquired.

"I should be most satisfied to see it transformed."

"Where is it?"

Marrow pointed a bone-finger to a slightly chewed section of the bone wall. There was a tiny creature chomping blithely away.

Trent moved his hand close to the flea. Suddenly there was a fair-sized pot pie bush, growing from a pot, bearing a steamingly ripe pie. "Oh, wonderful!" Gloha exclaimed, realizing how hungry she had become. "But it looks too hot for us to touch."

"I have utensils," Marrow said. He produced several long thin bone slivers. "I chopped these up to use to seal crevices, but they may also be serviceable for your purpose."

"Ah, chopsticks," Trent agreed. He took two and held them with the fingers of one hand.

"You can eat with those?" Gloha asked, perplexed.

"With a little practice, so can you," Trent said. "Marrow, if you will be so kind as to harvest that pot pie and set it on your table for us, we shall dine."

Marrow plucked the hot pot pie with his bare fingerbones and set it on his bone table. Trent drew up a bone chair, and Gloha, being much smaller and lighter, perched on the edge of the table, the other side of the pie.

"Thus," Trent said, demonstrating with his chopsticks. He poked into the pie and brought out a chunk of something that looked and smelled good, pinned between the two ends. He lifted it to his mouth.

Gloha took up two suitably sized bone slivers and tried to hold them the way he did. When she moved them, they flipped out of her less than gainly little grasp. She tried again, and began to get part of the hang of it. In due course, she was able to spear a chunk of vegetable.

So they shared the pie. Trent ate most of it, because he was far more massive, but Gloha had all she wanted.

It had gotten dark. Marrow started a bone fire with some otherwise useless bone fragments. Its light and warmth were small, but the need was similarly small. They were comfortable.

"I think we had best rest here the night," Trent said. "Perhaps by morning the volcano will have forgotten us."

"Why should it matter?" Marrow asked. "When I go out, I merely make myself resemble a clog of ashes, and it doesn't recognize me."

"Why didn't we think of that!" Gloha exclaimed.

"You have less space in your skull," Marrow said diplomatically. "All that living meat gets in the way of thought."

"That must be it," Trent agreed before Gloha could organize her reaction. "We living folk are at a disadvantage compared to you fantasy folk. I am surprised that you wish to join our number by acquiring a soul. Don't you know it will make you mortal?"

"Half a soul should not go that far," Marrow said. "A living person can regenerate a full soul from half a soul, but that will not be the case with my kind.

My half soul will merely endure, enabling me to reside permanently in exterior Xanth. That is all I want from it."

"You may discover that it provides you more than you want," Trent remarked.

"Then I shall politely decline what else it offers," Marrow said. "I need only permanence in this realm."

Trent's gaze crossed Gloha's gaze briefly, not really establishing a glance. She knew what he was thinking: the skeleton, never having had any part of a soul, did not understand the consequence of being souled. Perhaps it would not be possible to explain.

But something else occurred to her. "What about your family?" she asked. "Will they survive without souls?"

"By no means. But it is my hope that I will be able to share my half soul with them, so that each of us has a fragment, and then Grace'l, Joy'nt, and Picka Bone will endure with me satisfactorily ever after in Xanth proper."

Gloha nodded. It was a good answer.

Trent transformed the pot pie plant into a blanket bush, and each of them harvested a nice warm blanket. They lay down in separate corners. Gloha found the blanket on bones, cushioned by her sturdy wings, to be surprisingly comfortable, but something was lacking. She focused her minute little mind, which tried to hide its thought from her, and finally ran it down. She was dissatisfied because she was sleeping alone. She wished she could be snug beside a winged goblin man. So she tried to picture one. The odd thing was that he seemed to have the face and form of Magician Trent. She knew that was foolish, but didn't quite get around to changing the image. She relaxed, and slept so quickly that it was as if the morning came before the evening ended.

In the morning she got up, stretched her wings, and tried the knee-knob on the bone door. The door swung open on smooth joints, and she looked out across the ashy vista.

It was lovely in its fashion. All the irregularities of the landscape had been smoothed over. It was like a gently surging sea, frozen in place. The mountain itself was quiet, with only some scatters of white cloud drifting near its peak. It looked peaceful.

"I made you hats," Marrow said from within.

Gloha turned, startled. She had forgotten that he didn't sleep. "Thank you." She accepted the broad woven bone hat he proffered and put it on her head. It was decorated with ash on top, so that from above it should look like a piece of ash.

She stepped outside. The ash was knee-deep on her, so she spread her wings and flew above it. The mountain did not react, so either the hat was still effective, or Pin-A-Tuba was asleep. She found a suitable gully, landed, and caught up on a function or two that was best done privately. Then she flew back to the bone cabin.

Trent's tracks led around to the back of the house. She would not be so un-couth as to conjecture, of course, but it was possible that he was in quest of a similar gully.

She entered the bone house. There was a sugarplum bush. How thoughtful of the Magician! She plucked the sweetest plum and ate it for breakfast.

They set out, wearing their ash hats. Marrow looked funny in his, because of the incongruity of a skeleton wearing anything. The volcano did not seem to be too smart, because it didn't notice them. They crossed to the original path, and followed it on toward the mountain, because that was really about the only way to go.

Pin-A-Tuba blew a few resounding bass notes as they came close, and puffed up some smoke. But this was a mere turning over in its sleep; their ash hats concealed them well enough so that the mountain was not roused from its slumber. They skirted its base—the skirt was made of fallen ash, of course—and proceeded on south.

"Phew!" Gloha said. "I was afraid old Pun-A-Tub would catch on and dump more ash on us."

The ground shuddered. An awakening rumble traveled up the cone of the mountain. An irate column of smoke shot up.

"Oops," Gloha said. "It heard me."

"Let's move," Trent said.

They hurried along the path. But they were not far enough away from the mountain. The rumbling became horrendous, and a great ugly crack of a vent opened along the side of the cone. Roiling purple gas rose out of it and rolled down toward them.

"I think you living folk would do well to avoid that vapor," Marrow said politely. "On occasion I have seen it encompass creatures."

"Oh! What happened?" Gloha inquired.

"That is where I got the fresh bones for my house, after the vapor passed."

"Point made," Trent said, breaking into a run. But the path was bearing downhill, and the ball of gas was rolling faster than he could run. It would soon catch them.

Gloha spread her wings and flew. She could rise above the gas. But she knew that wouldn't do Trent much good.

"It will not harm me, of course," Marrow said, keeping the pace. "But if you have any emergency procedures, this would seem to be the time to invoke them."

"I'll have to transform you," Trent puffed to Gloha. "Then you can carry us both away from here."

"All right, if you wish," she said, flying down close to him, to get within his range. "What kind of creature do you—*squawk, squawk, squawk?*" she concluded from her big bird's beak. She had become a roc.

The gasball was almost upon them. She reached down with two feet and caught both man and skeleton. She closed her talons carefully, so that they formed a kind of round barred cage instead of transfixing or crushing anyone. Then she pumped her wings and heaved into the sky.

The ball rolled underneath her. The draft from her wings beat at it, battering it apart. It lost cohesion, and became a sinking pool of ugh-colored ick. Served it right, as far as she was concerned.

The mountain, balked, shot out a furious blast of ash. The fragments were so hot they glowed as they arced toward Gloha's wings. They would set her on fire if they caught her! But she was at the fringe of the volcano's immediate range, and was able to fly clear before the burning bits reached her. Now she truly appreciated the Magician's prior caution; indeed, no big bird was safe near that deadly cone.

She looked for a good place to land, but the terrain was too rough for a bird this size. She needed a reasonably level region clear of trees. So she flew on south—and in a surprisingly brief time she spied the yawning gape of the Gap Chasm. She realized two or maybe three things: she had reached it so rapidly because big strong rocs flew with much bigger wing-strokes than did little weak-winged goblin girls. It was yawning because this was still morning and it hadn't had time to wake properly up yet. And if she could travel this readily and swiftly, she might as well continue until they reached their starting point above Crombie's cave. Then they could head southeast, the direction he had indicated.

As she flew, she had a daydream. In it, she was turning the pages of a big book. The pages were filled with text, but she was unable to read it. Then she came to one that said "Chapter 5: Xxxxxxx." She recognized that title: it was her story! So she turned more pages, until in the middle of the following chapter the pages turned blank. The chapters were numbered through 12, but there was nothing written in the last six. Which meant, of course, that her story was as yet unfinished. Then there was the flick of an invisible tail, and Mare Imbri, the bringer of daydreams, galloped off to her next assignment.

Gloha was surprised to realize that almost half her story had been told, and she hadn't yet started the main part of her quest. It was high time to get on with it, so a little velocity here wouldn't hurt at all.

But where exactly was Crombie's cave? She had come to it mostly by water before, and underground. She had returned to the surface through a convoluted system of caves that left her with no idea where she had been. She didn't know how to identify its location from here.

Well, maybe she should return to the place where they had emerged. That should be somewhere in the right vicinity. Maybe Magician Trent or Marrow Bones would have a notion how to proceed from there.

She found that in this form she had a fine eye for details on the ground. She saw where Com Pewter's cave was, and the board walk, and the pool of the three mermaids. Well, maybe that was close enough, and would do for a landing place; there were no trees in the middle of the pool.

She glided down. She swooped low and slow over the pool, and let the two figures go. They dropped into the pool with two splashes. She knew that the mermaids would rescue Trent if he had any trouble, and the skeleton could simply sink to the bottom and walk out, as he didn't need to breathe.

She climbed again, and saw that it was as she had surmised: Trent was surrounded by the three lovelies. Then one of them went to rescue Marrow Bones—and changed her mind. Maybe she hadn't seen him clearly before. It must have been a shock to recognize his nature. Gloha somehow wasn't too sorry.

She descended again, and this time splashed into the water herself. It had a wonderfully cushioning effect, but wasn't as deep as she had thought; her feet touched bottom. Then she realized that it had been deep but was so no longer; her entry had splashed most of the water out. The three mermaids were stranded by the suddenly dry shoreline, their once-lovely hairdos matted, glaring in perfect harmony.

Gloha waded out. When she reached Trent, she returned to her natural form. "Sorry about that," she said with as much apology as she could muster.

"Quite all right," Ash said through gritted teeth. "It will fill again any week now. We shall surely flounder through in sufficient style."

"Perhaps sooner," Trent said. He gestured, and a stranded fish near him became a very large watermelon vine with a number of huge fruits. He poked a melon, and it burst, its water flowing into the pool.

"Oho!" Cedar exclaimed, catching on. She poked another fruit, adding its water to the pool.

Trent slogged on around the depression, turning fish and weeds into more watermelon plants. The others followed, poking the fruits. All this water, added to what was flowing back from the higher slopes, soon had the pool about half full again. There was enough for the mermaidens to swim in, and for Marrow and Gloha to wash in. Trent, thoroughly splashed by the bursting melons, was pretty well clean anyway.

"Thank you," Mahogany said. 'I suppose if you wanted to put your clothes out to dry and dally a bit in the water, Magician, we just might manage to forget exactly how old you claim to be." She smiled reasonably winningly from amidst her bedraggled dark tresses.

"I fear we have to move on," the Magician said. "But I thank you for the consideration."

The mermaids did not press the issue, evidently being not completely forgiving of the splash. The encounter was less than ideal. For that, Gloha was privately thankful.

They followed the stream down to where it entered the mountain. Then they looked for some way southeast from there. Beyond the river's gully was a mountain. There was a path that seemed to lead around the obstruction, but it did not look entirely healthy. There were bits of bone and feather strewn along it, and it smelled of dragon's breath. "I could become the roc bird again, and carry you over to the other side," Gloha suggested.

"We're not sure exactly where Crombie's residence is," Trent reminded her. "It might be under this very mountain. If we skip the mountain, we might already be beyond it, and the farther we went, the less likely we would be to fulfill your quest."

She nodded. "But I hope it has nothing to do with the dragon who maybe lives near this path."

"I'll transform the beast if necessary."

They set off afoot. Gloha couldn't have flown ahead to check, but the path wound under such a dense canopy of foliage that it was impossible to see from above. So she kept her wings ready, but remained low.

There was indeed a dragon. A big one. It was snoozing with its head across the path. Its dragon ears perked up at their approach, and wafts of smoke surged from its nostrils.

"A smoker," Trent said grimly. "We won't be able to get close enough to it for me to transform it."

Gloha understood why. The most feared dragons were fire breathers, but smokers could be devastating too in close quarters. Their smoke surrounded and suffocated the prey, and when it cleared, the dragon could chomp victims at leisure. Here under the close canopy the travelers would have no chance.

"We'll have to go back and look for another path," she said.

"I see no reason for that," Marrow said, striding forward.

"But the smoke—" she cried warningly.

He walked on, straight at the dragon. The dragon was as surprised as they were. It huffed and it puffed and it shot twin jets of smoke from its nostrils that looked almost thick enough to walk on. The smoke bathed the skeleton—who plowed on through it, unaffected.

"He doesn't breathe!" Gloha murmured, remembering. "He can't choke!"

"He has no eyes," Trent agreed. "He can't be blinded. And he's immune to any heat that isn't high enough to burn bone."

"But what can he do to stop the dragon from simply chomping him into bonemeal?"

"That I am not sure. But he seems confident."

The dragon's big eyes grew larger as he saw the skeleton emerge from the bath of smoke. He inhaled again, getting ready to send out a worse blast. But Marrow jumped forward and grabbed onto the dragon's nose!

"He'll get himself chomped to splinters!" Gloha cried, appalled. For the dragon's head was larger than Marrow's whole body.

"Maybe not," Trent said appraisingly. "He has changed his form."

"That's right—they can do that," she agreed. "They can disassemble their bones and put them together in strings or other combinations. He looks like one big clamp now."

Indeed, the long bones of what were Marrow's legs had become man-sized pincers, clamping the dragon's nose closed. The dragon tried to paw Marrow off, but immediately the clamp tightened painfully, forcing the creature to desist. The skull, perched at the top, looked around and spied them. "You may pass safely," Marrow called. "He can't breathe smoke through his mouth, only his nose."

"He's right," Trent said appreciatively. "That dragon is largely helpless. Certainly I can now approach near enough to transform it. But I think I don't need to."

They walked by, almost close enough to touch the dragon's huge nose. The creature looked as if he really wanted to chomp them, but that clamp tightened warningly and he had to relax.

"But won't he chomp you the moment you let go?" Gloha asked.

"It will take him a moment to get reoriented," the skull said. "In any event, I don't taste very good. There's no meat on me."

So they went on by. Once they were safely out of smoke range, they called, and heard a muffled whomp as the clamp let go and the dragon resumed stoking smoke. In a moment Marrow appeared, striding nonchalantly as if this were routine.

"This is a creature to be respected," Trent murmured, not referring to the dragon. Gloha could only agree.

The path continued on around the mountain. There were no other dragons or other dangerous creatures. This was not surprising, because no smaller predator would dare to encroach on the territory of the big one.

The path finally left the deep forest and debouched into a halfway open valley. A village nestled within it, and there seemed to be a fair amount of activity therein. From the far side a cloud of dust or smoke wafted up into the sky.

"What are they doing?" Gloha asked.

"I believe this is the Magic Dust Village," Marrow said. "They mine the magic dust and blow it into the air so that it will circulate throughout Xanth, enhancing the magic everywhere."

"The Magic Dust Village!" she exclaimed. "Of course! I have heard of it. The most magical place in Xanth."

"Why, that's right," Trent agreed. "I should have realized; this is indeed the area. I shall have to be extremely careful about performing transformations, because the extra potency of magic in this region can be dangerous."

They walked on down to the village. An elderly troll moved to intercept them. "As far as I know, the natives are friendly," Trent murmured. "They have members of many crossbreed humanoid species living and working in harmony, including goblins and trolls. But perhaps you, Gloha, should stay behind me until we are sure."

Gloha was glad to agree. They had encountered one friendly troll, but that was a rarity. Another would be pulling on their luck.

"Hail, man, goblin, skeleton!" the troll cried. "Do you come in peace?"

"We do, if left in peace," Trent agreed.

"Then I must warn you that our village is about to become inhospitable. You must move on, lest you be exposed to hazard."

"We have had a moderately arduous day's journey, and were looking forward to a relaxed night," Trent said. "We are also on a quest, and it is possible that the object of that quest is to be found here. Let us exchange introductions and see whether it is possible for us to do each other any good."

"By all means. I am Pa, the eldest troll of Magic Dust Village. I am too old to work well, so I walk around and warn away strangers."

"Glad to meet you, Pa Troll. I am Magician Trent, formerly the transformer king of Xanth. This is Marrow Bones, formerly of the dream realm, and this is Gloha Goblin-Harpy, whose quest we are supporting."

"Magician Trent!" Pa exclaimed. "Perhaps you are the one we are waiting for." He paused. "Wait—you are far too young. You must be an impostor."

"I have been temporarily youthened," Trent explained. "I will demonstrate." He pointed to a tiny flowering plant beside the path. It became a monstrous spreading acorn tree whose trunk obliterated that path, shoving them into the surrounding brush. "Oops—I forgot the intensity of magic! That was supposed to be a medium-small acorn tree."

Pa Troll touched the massive trunk. "So it's not illusion. I apologize for doubting you, Magician." He glanced at Gloha. "And a crossbreed harpy—this is most interesting. Come to the village, and we shall see. I am most excited." Indeed, he was quivering in a manner trolls normally reserved for the anticipation of some truly dastardly deed. Gloha didn't need Trent's additional caution to remain on guard.

Trent restored the tree to its original state, this time getting it right. They came to the village square. A throng of crossbreeds of every description quickly gathered there. Not merely trolls, but elves, fairies, ogres, a small giant or two, goblins, gnomes, centaurs, griffins, masked basilisks, and other creatures too numerous or confusing to mention. "Ho, you rabble of low degree!" Pa Troll cried. "Maybe we have our salvation, and maybe not. This is Magician Trent, in the company of a walking skeleton and a honey of a harpy crossbreed." He indicated the three.

There was a muted ooooh of appreciation. Gloha was surprised and discomfited to find most eyes focusing on her. She realized that there were no harpies here, oddly.

"You see, we have a problem," Pa Troll continued, now speaking to the three visitors. "We have been told to carry on until Harpy Time, but no harpy has appeared, and we have only a day or two left before disaster. So if you are not able to help us, the village and all Xanth will be in deep dung."

"Exactly what is the nature of your problem?" Trent inquired. "And how do you think a harpy could solve it?"

"First you must understand the nature of our village mission," Pa said. "This is the site where the magic rock wells up from the unknown depths of magic. We pound it into dust, and our roc bird flaps his wings to blow it high into the sky, where it spreads and circulates and sifts down across all of Xanth. Without this service we render, the Land of Xanth would slowly lose its magic and revert to—pardon the expression—mundane nature. This is why we all work together despite having in our number creatures who otherwise would prefer to quarrel with each other and eat strangers." He glanced at Gloha again and licked his thin troll lips in a reminiscent manner that made half a shiver scramble up her back. "We use little magic, preferring to do the job by hand and foot, because the use of magic is dangerous in this vicinity."

He took a breath. "But recently a new vent opened in a nearby mountain. From it issues not magic stone, but poisonous thick fluid that slowly courses down toward the village, destroying all life in its path. We can not remove or divert it, because the fumes of its surface are also lethal. Our only resort is to remain well away from it. But soon it will ooze into the village itself, and begin to pool here, and then we shall have to flee, our labor will no longer be accomplished. The magic of Xanth will begin to fade, and in time our entire land will be as dreary as the drear region beyond." There was another ooooh from the villagers. Gloha had to agree; the prospect was appalling.

"So we sent a representative to the Good Magician Humfrey, to inquire how we can prevent this disaster. She is now serving her year's Service with him. But we can't say that we are entirely satisfied with his response."

"Whom did you send?" Gloha asked, unable to restrain her irrelevant curiosity.

"A winged monster, of another type than yourself. A glyph."

"I met her!" Gloha cried with dear little delight. "A nice horse/dragon crossbreed. She was one of my challenges on the way in."

"I hope they are treating her well," Pa said in paternal fashion.

"Oh, yes. At first I thought they weren't, but that was part of the challenge. She's really quite happy there."

"What was your Answer?" Trent inquired, more relevantly. "To carry on until Harpy Time?"

"Precisely. I must say that the Good Magician's Answers leave something to be desired, considering their expense."

"But they are always accurate and relevant," Trent reminded him.

Pa glanced at Gloha, this time refraining from licking his lips. "Were you satisfied with your own Answer?"

"Well, no. Actually, he didn't give me an Answer, exactly, so I didn't have to do any Service."

"So you can no doubt appreciate our dissatisfaction."

"Yes, I think I can. And I have to say that I don't think I'm the harpy you're looking for. About my only harpy aspect is my wings; apart from that I mostly resemble a goblin, unlike my brother Harglo. I have no idea how to stop that poisonous flow, because it would affect me too."

"And it is not something I can transform," Trent said. "But why didn't you make a dam to stop its advance?"

"We did, but it oozes between the stones and dissolves them, seeping on along its destined course. The only way we can stop it is to plug its source—if any of us could only get close enough."

"Could a roc bird drop a boulder on it?"

"No. It issues from a fissure in the steep slope. It should be fairly easy to plug, if only any of us could approach it. But our every effort has led only to disaster."

Then something occurred to Gloha. "Marrow, you were immune to the dragon's choking smoke. Would you be able to approach a poison vent?"

"Why, I see no reason why not," the skeleton said.

"Then you are the ones we have waited for!" Pa Troll cried. "You signal the Harpy Time."

"Perhaps," Trent said. "However, it should be clarified that Marrow Bones is also on a quest. He needs half a soul, so that he can remain indefinitely here in Xanth proper. If anyone here cares to—"

It was amazing how quickly the crowd dissipated. It seemed that the dedication of none of the villagers extended quite that far. Even Pa Troll had somehow found elsewhere to be. The three of them were left standing in the center of an apparently deserted village.

"These creatures have too much human nature," Trent remarked sourly.

"Yet their need is genuine," Marrow said. "Xanth will profit. I will plug that vent." He set off in the direction Pa Troll had looked when he spoke of the encroaching poison.

Trent shook his head, watching the departing skeleton. "I could almost swear he already has at least half a soul."

"Certainly he doesn't seem to need more than he has," Gloha agreed. "I had a lesson in decency not too long ago. This reminds me of it."

"It may be that souls aren't what they used to be."

"Maybe I'd better see if I can help him." She spread her wings.

"Not too close," he warned. "If you smell anything at all, get away from wherever you are."

"I will," she assured him. She pumped her wings and lifted into the air.

It was good to be flying again, in her own form. Her limber little legs had gotten worn with all that walking, while she was afraid her wings would dissolve with disuse. So maybe her decision to try to help Marrow was as much selfish as unselfish.

In a moment she saw the poison flow. It was like a messy black river flowing from a nearby mountain right toward the village. Every so often it jogged, and she realized that those were the places they had put up rock dams that hadn't quite done the job. No plants grew near it; everything within smelling distance was barren. It seemed to be aiming for the village as if guided by some malignant will. She would have dismissed that notion, except for her memory of how the inanimate things reacted when King Dor talked to them. They tended to be shallow, but they did have opinions and feelings. And of course Marrow Bones was not alive, being animated by magic, and he had an objective and a code of behavior. Then there was Pin-A-Tuba, the angry volcano who tried to stop folk from approaching it closely. So why shouldn't a poisonous flow have an objective too?

In fact, she realized now, that poison was from Pin-A-Tuba! That was the volcano's other slope. They had circled around it without catching on that it could have nasty vents on both sides, or that these could issue either noxious gas or nasty fluid. So they hadn't finished with this evil mountain.

Meanwhile Marrow was walking up the ruined slope toward the vent. But Gloha saw that he wasn't going to be able to reach it, because there was a small cliff in the way. The black poison goo had no trouble dribbling slowly down it, but there was no way for a person to climb up it. However, there was an indirect route, clear only from above.

She flew down to tell Marrow. But he was walking right beside the poison flow, supremely unaffected. The moment she started to think of getting faintly close, her breath began to choke and her vision blurred and her wings got shaky and weak. She plunged away to the side, so she wasn't directly above the flow, and recovered her equilibrium. No, she couldn't go and tell him directly.

But maybe she could signal him from afar. She flew back and forth before him, waving her arms. "Marrow!" she called, sure he couldn't hear her from this distance.

But in a moment he noticed her. He waved a bony arm.

"Go that way!" she cried, zooming to the mountain's right side. "There's a path!"

But he couldn't understand. He moved on beside the flow.

Was there any other way to get through to him? She racked her blank little brain but dredged up nothing. So she just followed along, hoping to be able to help when there was a chance.

He finally trekked to the cliff and stood looking up. It was obvious that he couldn't climb it. He looked around.

Now was the time. She flew to the right again and hovered there, beckoning him. This time he caught on. He walked that way, away from the flow. She led him to the place where a ledge angled erratically up the steep slope. From there it moved back across to the top of the cliff, and the way was followable.

Marrow found it, and made his way up. He was carrying something, and she realized that it was a piece of stone he hoped to use as a plug. It seemed to be an old stalactite that some cave had discarded.

She watched from afar as he went all the way to the vent. He studied the situation, then lifted his stalactite and rammed it straight down into the center of the vent, where the poison started flowing. It went partway in. Then he lifted off his skull—Gloha did a double take at about that point—and used it to pound in the spike.

That was it. He replaced his skull and walked away. Gloha saw that the flow was clearing near the top. It remained below, but there was no more coming out of the vent. He had plugged it.

Gloha thought of something else. Marrow had been too close to the poison. He probably reeked of it now, so that it wouldn't be safe for anybody else to get near him. He would have to get clean before he returned to the village.

She flew back and forth, signaling him as she had before. Then she headed for the nearest stream that didn't originate on Mount Pin-A-Tuba. He followed. The foliage on either side of his route wilted as he passed. The stream was far enough away so that she was able to land beside it. But when Marrow approached, sure enough, he reeked of poison, and she had to fly away before she fainted. "Wash! Wash!" she cried, pointing at the water. Then, afraid he couldn't hear her, she made vigorous scrubbing motions along her body.

He caught on, and waded into the water. He disappeared in it. The plants downstream began to wilt. Gloha was sorry for them, but at least it showed that the water was carrying the poison away from his body. Before too long it should get so diluted that it wouldn't hurt anyone anymore.

She hovered at a safe distance until he emerged. He walked downstream, and when he got beyond the wilted region, there seemed to be no further wilting in his vicinity. So she risked a closer approach. There were no deadly fumes. Finally she landed before him. "You're clean," she announced.

"Thank you for advising me," he said. "It had not occurred to me that I might have become unsanitary, but when you signaled I realized that life in my vicinity was perishing."

"Yes. That poison is very strong."

They returned to the village. Trent had evidently been at work there, because there was now a large pile of fresh food from plants and creatures he must have transformed. The villagers were aware that the poison was no longer flowing. That meant that the existing stream should slowly dry up or sink into the ground, leaving the village clear. They would be able to continue their business.

"I have talked with the villagers, and ascertained that there are no winged goblins here, nor have they even seen any before you," Trent advised her. "As far as they know, you are unique."

"I'm afraid I am," she agreed. "But Crombie wouldn't have pointed a direction if there weren't an answer. It just means it isn't here."

"True. We can rest here the night, and continue southeast in the morning." He hesitated. "I wouldn't judge the villagers too harshly with respect to their unwillingness to yield half a soul. Many are female, making them imperfect for this purpose, or old. Others are simply frightened. There are a number of misconceptions about souls that are hard to eradicate."

"I know," Gloha agreed, remembering her own concern about losing half of hers.

"I would not care to take half a soul from someone who did not freely wish to give it," Marrow said.

"We'll keep looking," Gloha said.

They had a good meal, really a feast, and the villagers were very appreciative of the service Marrow had done for them. "You have benefited all Xanth," Pa Troll said, with an emphasis that hinted that maybe it was all Xanth who owed Marrow the half soul, not the local village.

There was a nice house for them to use for the night, left by a family that had moved out recently in anticipation of a complete evacuation. Gloha had the pleasure of a private room with a nice soft bed. She slept well, despite still wishing that she had a perfect man with warm feet to share it with. She realized that the Good Magician had been right about a harpy (or part harpy) helping to save the village at the last moment. Maybe his son was right about the direction of the solution to her own quest. Meanwhile, she did feel slightly useful.

7
MADNESS

I n the morning they resumed their travel to the southeast. However, Pa Troll had a warning for them: "The wind currents carry the magic dust everywhere, but they are thickest immediately downwind from the village. Usually this is to our southwest, but at the moment it is to our southeast. Your route may take you through the fringe of it. You would be well advised to avoid that direction, at least until the wind changes and some of the dust can clear."

Trent looked at Gloha. "This is good advice."

She knew it was. She had heard stories about the effects of magic madness. "But is it possible that my perfect man and Marrow's half-soul donor will be found within the Region of Madness?"

"It is possible," he agreed. "I suppose if such quests seem unlikely to succeed in normal Xanth, the abnormal should be tried. But I'm not sure you appreciate just how weird the Region of Madness is likely to be."

"Oh, pooh! It can't be worse than Mount Pun-A-Tub was."

"Which threat you also doubted, at first," he reminded her evenly.

She knew he was making sense, and that she was being an unreasonable teen crossbreed female. Somehow that didn't cause her to become more reasonable. It didn't help that she wished she could make an impression on him as an intriguing adult female, for no legitimate reason, and didn't know how. So her fouled-up little feelings just made things difficult. "Anyway, I'm curious to see just what's so weird about it."

His gaze remained straight, yet somehow she had the impression he was rolling his eyes. "As you wish."

Marrow Bones tilted his skull. His nonexistent eyes were rolling too.

They proceeded southeast. Downwind. There was no problem. The country consisted of rolling hills covered by forest and fields, with an occasional river wandering through. Trent was about to wade through the first river, but the skeleton stopped him. "Kick me," he said.

"Thank you," Trent said.

Gloha thought they were joking, though neither creature had been much for humor before. But Marrow bent over, and Trent delivered a fine kick to the skeleton's hipbone. Marrow flew apart. The bones landed in a pile—in the shape of a small boat. Trent pushed the boat into the water, where it floated despite not seeming to be watertight, then stepped into it and sat down. The craft then moved across the water under its own power. Trent got out on the far bank, then kicked the boat, and the bones flew apart and landed back in Marrow's natural form.

Gloha finally got her gape hinged. She had known that the walking skeletons could change the arrangement of their bones, but hadn't realize how neat and useful this could be. After all, Marrow had changed to clamp the dragon's nose. Trent's kicks had merely facilitated the effort. She flew across the river herself. They resumed walking.

"We seem to be skirting the Region of Madness," Trent remarked. "Perhaps the folk of the Magic Dust Village were operating at reduced efficiency the past few days as the poison flow approached, so the dust level is not high. But now they are likely to be back at full efficiency, and we are apt to encounter more of the effect."

"I believe you are correct," Marrow agreed, his skull turning. "There may be a waft of it approaching now."

"Well, I don't see any madness yet," Gloha remarked impertinently. She shouldn't have.

Gloha sucked and licked at the sticky ends of her fingers. She was too old for Aunt Grobigatail's honey flummery, but a taste of honey always whetted her appetite for more. She sighed, her joy mixed with a little bit of sadness. She was, at the age of eighteen, getting more than a bit long in the tooth, too old for sweet treats. But she was still too young for goblin garbage rituals. Now she was too bored doing her usual good job of baby-sitting her obnoxious little brother Harglo. He might be her sibling, but he wasn't her kind; he had the head and legs of a goblin, but the full-feathered body of a harpy complete with tail, and no hands. He was a stronger flyer than she was, and a stronger runner too, but couldn't do much delicate handling of things with just his wings. He made up for that by having an excellent command of harpy vocabulary; already at age nine he could make some foliage wilt when he swore, and he was still confined to non–Adult Conspiracy words.

But today she was free of him, having a day off while he took flying lessons (and probably illicit cussing lessons) from Aunt Fowlmouth. So she could relax and enjoy herself. So why wasn't she happy? She tasted her fingers again, but this time her scalding-hot salty tears caused her fingers to hurt like the singing stinging threads of sea wasps. The problem was that today she had time to appreciate just how much it hurt being a half-and-half crossbreed, never quite fitting in with either the goblins or the harpies. So now she was caught up in her self-pity party. She had stopped grooming herself; her wing feathers were droopy and creased, her hooded blue bio-luminescent eyes were dull, and her glorious blue-black glossy hair hung in salty honey-sticky twisted loops.

Harpies flew overhead, hooting and hurling a golden coprolite about. This was a gold-plated fossilized ball of dragon dung that they caught in their claws and tossed up again. Whoever could get out the longest and foulest string of cussing before the next harpy touched the flying ball was winner for the moment. Harglo loved that game, and longed for the day he could play it; Gloha had never even tried, as she could not even begin to understand the implications of its most basic terms without going into a terminal blush.

These were good days in Xanth, in the harpy caves and goblin dens, when things went medium to bad instead of bad to worse. But from time to thyme a demonic, shot-fowl (or maybe foul-shot) rogue-awful day sneaked in, and this seemed to be one of them. So instead of enjoying her rest from spite, her respite, she was having Xanth's most miserable little mood.

It had started with dawn, which had lifted its brooding mists to reveal a bleary red-eyed sun surrounded by bruised purple clouds whose only desire was to make an acid rain and wet on someone's head. Then had come the snarling, whining, grunting, screaming rush to the breakfast cave, aptly termed the mess hall, where her dozens of aunts fought for the juiciest dripping raw bleeding morsels. Gloha had found herself wedged between Aunt Hoary Harributtes and the Grand Harridan Queen-Chief of this branch of the family clan, each of whom could screech more piercingly than the other. Gloha managed to plead difficulty clinging to the perch, so she took her quivering chunk of whatever to a separate bench where she could sit in what was disparagingly termed human style. Then someone had accidentally dropped a splash of hot coffee down her back, never mind that harpies never dropped anything they had ever snatched up unless they meant to. Gloha had had to flee to her personal nest to change clothes and put salve on her burn.

She had tried to cheer herself by dressing up. She donned her festival outfit: mock-leather jerkin, thongs of molten golden color trimmed in a musical pattern with mellow golden bells, brazen Hell's Bells, and icy crystal stars. A really nice outfit always made her feel so good. But then her tutor, Magpie, had told her not to wear it, because harpies didn't wear clothing and she would be a laughingstock.

"But I'm a laughingstock anyway!" she protested.

"Nonsense. You just haven't found your place yet."

"What do you know about it?" Gloha flared rebelliously. "You aren't really a harpy at all! You're just an unlikely kindly demoness."

"But I have worked with quite a number of mortals," Magpie said with an evenness impossible to mortals. "Okra Ogress thought her life was hopeless, and now she's a Major Character. Rose of Roogna thought she'd never find a good husband, and then she married the Good Magician and had a lovely daughter. I could list others."

Gloha knew she could. At length. So she didn't ask. Instead she went into Routine #2: a terrible little tantrum. "Don't tell me what to do!" she screamed with a great deal of hair tossing and foot stomping. Her show frightened several nearby birds, who flew under the bed to hide, disturbing the snoozing monster there.

But Magpie had seen it all before, and was unmoved. In the end Gloha had to remove her finery and return to her dull ordinary state. Her dreary life continued unabated.

Gloha shook her heavy little head. She was back in the forest with Magician Trent and Marrow Bones. What had happened?

"I had supposed your life was happy," Trent said, surprised. "But I realize now that no one living among harpies could be satisfied."

"You saw my flashback?" Gloha asked, amazed.

"It appeared before us," Trent said.

"I am not expert in the ways of living folk," Marrow said. "But it seems to me that it was not nice of that harpy to spill hot black liquid down your back."

"You really did see it? In wild living color? Even when I threw my—"

"I averted my gaze when you changed clothing," the Magician said. "I thought you might consider that private."

She had been going to say "tantrum," but now she realized that she had more to be concerned about. She had relived an episode of her past life, and they had seen it unfold exactly as she had. Including her temporarily bared body. What madness was this?

Then she realized the rest of it. This was the Region of Madness, with the intense magic of the concentrated magic dust making even memories become visible. She hadn't realized that it would be like this. She wasn't at all sure she liked it. "Let's get quickly out of here," she suggested.

"What, when the fun is just beginning?" a voice demanded.

"Who is that?" Gloha asked, alarmed.

Smoke swirled. "Nothing to concern you, antiseptic goblin girl."

"What kind of goblin girl?"

"Unpolluted, sanitary, unadulterated, immaculate, faultless—"

"Innocent?" Trent suggested.

"Whatever," the smoke said crossly.

"What are you doing here, Metria?" Gloha asked a brief little bit crossly herself.

"I poke around wherever anything interesting is happening. Anyone fool enough to blunder into the Region of Madness is bound to be interesting."

"Well, my past life is about as uninteresting as anything can get, so you might as well go away."

"Oh, I don't know about that. Magpie always takes the interesting characters to work with."

"You know Magpie?"

"She's a demoness, isn't she? She knows when something's going to happen, and she's always there to nursemaid it through."

"Well, nothing's going to happen right now, so—"

"That's what you think. Here comes another waft of madness."

"I don't believe it," Gloha said. "You're just saying it to tease—"

. . . and long lonely hours had been spent conducting endless imagined conversations with her adversary, that harpy flying tiger, her Aunt Hoary.

"Chaos and coffee!" Hoary Harpy screeched as she used one soiled wing to sweep strands of slop, glop, and flop out of the mess hall and into the fire pits. She clutched a teaming mug of brew in one claw while standing on the other scrawny leg. She vaguely resembled a black-feathered desultory stork, her red eyes glowing like soiled coals in the dusky purple shadows of the messy hall. She swept long dirty strands of feathery black hair back from her stony alabaster brow and glowered at her niece.

Gloha's sensitive little stomach knotted and burned, her heart cramped, and her hair wanted to wriggle out of sight. How had she gotten into this dill pickiement?

"I said, what game are you playing?" a low whispery voice repeated, which was somehow worse than the usual screech.

With an icy start Gloha realized that the subject of her worries was now focusing her formidable annoyance at her. She blushed, which of course only made things worse, making her seem even more guilty that she probably was. "Auntie?"

"You politely requested this early morning interview, which showed how unharpyish you are," the harpy said. "You should have demanded it in the foulest vernacular. Now what in the name of idiocy do you want?"

Gloha somehow nerved herself enough to speak her muted little mind. "Auntie Hoary, I've been made sick and tired by living a dull and middle-of-the-road life amidst creatures who aren't exactly like me. We all know what happens when you stay in the middle of anything: you get run over. Auntie, I want to be an alchemist, a geo-alchemist on a wizard's team. I think a person without a dream becomes mired in our st—st—" She faltered, unable to get the ugly word out.

"Stinking!" Hoary screeched. "S-T-I-N-K-I-N-G! Where's your harpy vocabulary? Girl, you need to learn to swear, if you're going to get along. Now try it again."

Gloha made an effete little effort. "M-mired in our st-stinking pig pit," she managed to eke out. "Over and over I dream a bad dream brought by a night mare, that I can no longer fly—that I am a crippled broken-winged bird. Let me leave the nest—"

"What kind of nest?" Hoary screeched.

"The st-stinking nest, and go to seek—"

"What in the hell is the hurry?" Hoary demanded. "Leave the safety of the flock when you still don't know how to swear? You'd really break your wings then! The nest is best for chicks."

"But I'm eighteen, Auntie," Gloha reminded her.

"And have the vocabulary of a dirty bird half your age," Hoary pointed out, cleaning gore from her teeth with a dagger like claw. "If a monster came to eat you, you wouldn't even be able to give it a toothache with either your voice or your hygiene. You'd be one mouthwatering little morsel."

All too true. But Gloha, knowing that she'd never get up the courage to broach this subject again, tried to see it through. "Couldn't you let me fly with a proper escort to pay a professional visit to the castle of the Good Magician Humfrey, there to ask my one Question and give my year's Service for his Answer? Oh, please, Auntie Hoary! I would do anything if only I could—"

"Harpies never plead!" Hoary snapped, disgusted by this weakness. "Show me that you can let out one incendiary oath, and I'll let you go."

Gloha tried. "Darn!" she cried. "Help! Ship!"

Hoary sighed. "You're improving; at least you are taking aim at the words. But you're off by one letter in each case. That nullifies it. There's not even a stir of fire in the air. Now pay attention: this is the proper mode of harpy expression." She took a breath. "*%#@ƒ$!!"

Gloha managed to cover her ears just in time. Even so, she felt the heat of the terrible blast. The air shimmered and burned, and scorch marks appeared on the table. A fiery smell wafted outward.

As fresh air moved in, making it possible to breathe again, Hoary resumed normal screeching. "Now can you do that, chick?"

"M-maybe in time," Gloha said, knowing it was impossible.

"In harpy thyme, maybe," Hoary said with resignation. "Gloha, you are still wet behind the ear feathers. It would be folly to let you go out alone or in incompetent company. Do you even know where the Seeds of Destruction are kept? Can you do an aerial survey and map or organize things according to the harpy thyme line? We, the horrid harpies, the stinking untouchables, the ultimate fowl-mouths, we have that knowledge and keep the temple of hope for Xanth until the time we choose to assume the mantle of dominance for ourselves. Our time is not yet, but drawing nigh. Once we have the harpy thyme—"

She broke off, realizing that she was saying too much. "Anyway, you must at least learn to swear effectively before you can safely go out on your own. When you can do that, perhaps I will let you go."

That was it. The discussion was at an end. Aunt Hoary had made what was by harpy definition a reasonable and moderate requirement. But how would Gloha ever be able to learn to swear like that? Her mild little mouth couldn't even begin to form the awful configurations necessary.

Gloha blinked. She was back in the forest. The waft of madness had passed. "Now that's a sensible harridan," Metria said approvingly.

"You saw—heard Aunt Hoary Harpy?" Gloha asked, embarrassed.

"Saw her? I *was* her!" the demoness said. "Look at the foliage."

Gloha looked. The leaves nearby were wilted, and some even burned, as if blasted by a truly ferocious oath. "But how could that be?"

"Those aren't mere memories," Trent explained. "The rest of us get caught up in the parts. The magic governs us."

"Then we must get away from here before something awful happens," Gloha cried, appalled. "Some of my memories are not nice."

"I don't think we can escape until your memories are resolved," he replied. "Something is bothering you, and until that is brought out and alleviated, we shall be locked in."

"Oh, I never wanted to get into this," Gloha wailed.

"You were an arrogant little snit," Metria said. "You thought the madness wouldn't take you."

"I was wrong!" Gloha cried in anguish. "I'll flee it!" She started running, but already she saw a slight wavering of the landscape, as if its level of reality were shifting. The effect was coming right toward her. There was a rushing sound, as of swiftly flowing water. Oh, no!

Behind the kitchen herb garden Gloha could hear Chrysalis Crystal Creek before she could see it. Hugely swollen by the weird weather, with consecutive drenchpours, the creek waters had taken the bit in their wet teeth and were in a dangerous mood. They were surging at boulders, trying to rip them out of the soil, and rushing at any living thing that dared approach. Whatever they caught they were carrying away, tossing about, and finally pounding to quivering bits. This was no safe place for an antiseptic, uh, innocent winged goblin girl.

Almost blinded by her rampaging feelings and tears, Gloha half ran, half flew down the very muddy, irregular, treacherous path to the very edge of the stream. Nearby monsters woke and stirred, sniffing the air, aware of the lingering odor of juicy, tender, young winged girl. Slowly they rose and moved toward her, blocking off her escape.

Affrighted, Gloha spread her wings, about to take flight. But the violent water signaled the air, and the air stirred, whirling itself into a deadly cone that reached for Gloha's winsome little wings. She did not dare take flight now, lest her feathers be plucked, leaving her truly helpless. She had to stay grounded.

But now she saw something even worse: silvery, slithering, slinky nickelpedes, going for her tender little tootsies. Tendrils were reaching out of the ground, casting about to catch her feet and hold her there while they burrowed into the flesh. She had blundered into a truly awful trap. How was she ever to escape?

She tried to run along the only path she saw, not knowing where it led. But a tendril caught a foot, sending her into a headlong fall to the ground. Her knocked little knee twisted on the way down, making her scream with pain. "Help!" she cried. But the roar of the water drowned her out, and she knew that no one would hear or come to her rescue.

The tendrils found her body and curled over it, anchoring her so that they could drill into her succulent little shape. The nickelpedes scuttled to arrive in time to gouge out their coin-sized chunks before the plants shriveled her body too far. The hungry shadow of a larger monster loomed close.

Gloha screamed. This time it was no meek little mock effort. It was a double-throated piercing ululation at ultrasonic and ultraviolet levels containing a suggestion of the vocabulary Aunt Hoary had been trying to teach her. The tendrils, momentarily stunned, writhed back away from her. The nickel-pedes clicked their pincers, briefly disoriented. The looming monster hesitated a third of a moment, or perhaps nine tenths of an instant.

Then all three threats recovered and converged. But in that meager instant Gloha made an exhausted little effort to fight for what hopeless little hope remained to save her lost little life. She heaved herself somewhere else.

She fell down a long sandy shaft of dirt, wings over heels. She was aware of wild glowing molds, bugs, and many intriguing shades of dirt touching barely mentionable parts of her body along the way. Then she fetched up against the ragged cobweb-covered gape of a hidden hole. She plunged heedlessly into it and discovered a dark tunnel leading she knew-not and hesitated-to-inquire where. It just had to be less unsafe than what was behind.

The tunnel twisted around as if trying to dislodge her, but she followed it through every convolution, not daring to delay. Finally it gave up and let her into a faintly flowing small, forgotten, long-unused set of carved stone caves hiding under the harpy hutch caves. Against all odds, she had found a secret place that almost seemed to be safe. She stumbled under rocky crevices holding poisonous-looking twining clumps of vines glowing in brilliant vegetable green, ultraviolet, Luna white, and blood-red, growing among broken sculptures of gargoyles, through rotting logs, and across the faces of prehistoric rocky ruins. She crawled over a perilous, crumbling, narrow, rotting wooden bridge across a gaping dark chasm filled with a horrible deep menacing rustling. As she passed it, it gave way, and collapsed behind her into the depths. She listened, but never heard the sound of its landing below.

At long last the magic path ended in a pool of sinister mist. She didn't quite trust this, so she grasped a tough root growing from a crevice in a ruin. After several timid little tries she managed to haul herself through muck and mud up to a higher level. She was, she hoped, safe for a while.

"How I wish I could fly, fly, fly up to the stars once more," she breathed. But she was too tired to fly, even if she hadn't been caught in a deep dank gloomy cave unimaginably far below anywhere she cared to be. So she did the sensible thing and let herself collapse into sleep.

After a time she had no idea when she woke. the Demi-Luna moon's silvery beams were streaming in through a network of cracks in the cave's ceiling. She lay quietly beneath her spread cape, barely breathing as she sought answers to the questions that squeezed into her helpless little head at too rapid a pace.

"Where am I?" she murmured, momentarily disoriented.

"In a long-forgotten cave," came a whisper, perhaps from a stony face. Somehow this did not seem unusual. She was probably imagining it anyway.

"Am I alone?" she asked.

"Yes and no," came the cold whisper. The stone face didn't move, so that wasn't it. In any event she knew stone didn't speak. Whence came the windy voice, since there seemed to be no one else in the cave?

Maybe this was sleep, and this was a dream a night mare brought. So all she had to do was wake up. She pinched herself cruelly on the arm, but though it hurt, nothing else changed. Except that now she became aware of her feet. Something was nibbling on her tasty little toes.

She moved her head, looking about. She lay with her head in a nest of egg-shaped stones and her feet in a circulating pool of chill water. There were indeed cute little fish tasting her toes, though they weren't actually biting. Maybe they were just trying to alert her to her situation.

She sat up, wrapped her cape around her, and climbed to her feet. She shouldn't have. She screamed with pain. Her right knee was swollen as big as a globular little gourd, and it hurt twice as large. She quickly sat down again. She was hungry, she was thirsty, and she missed her mother Glory Goblin and her father Hardy Harpy and her tutor Magpie ever so much. Why had she ever come to a place like this?

She took sober little stock. Well, she could do something for the thirst. Carefully she lowered her face to the cold, crystal-pure pool of water and touched it with her lips. She sucked in several greedy little gulps, and her raging thirst eased.

Now, with her face close to the pool, she paid attention to the gold and scarlet shapes in it. They were three tame Coy fish she knew from her occasional swims on the surface. She recognized their distinctive patterns. They weren't trying to eat her; they just wanted company.

She reached down with one hand. "I won't hurt you," she said. "I'm in the same position you are. Come, let me tickle you, and I'll share my life-and-death struggle with you." They wiggled appreciatively, and played faint music on their scales.

Suddenly the presence of the fish unnerved her. They gave her hope, and that frightened her. Maybe she could give them a message to take to the harpies, to come and rescue her. So she couldn't just give up and peacefully expire.

"Go, friends, and tell my folk where I am," she said. "Especially Magpie, if you can find her." Because Magpie, as one of the few caring demonesses, would surely have the will and ability to help.

The fish played another little melody and scooted away.

Gloha lay down again, trying to return to sleep, as there wasn't much else to do except suffer. It took her only eight long minutes and two or three short ones to realize that sleep was unlikely to come. She just lay there, cold, hungry, wretched, and rigid on the bed of egg stones, wishing it were made of ruffled feathers, though she had never been exactly comfortable on those either. The stones glowed in pretty colors, but remained uncomfortable.

So she got up, putting her weight on her swollen knee very carefully so that the pain was almost bearable. She walked to the largest crack in the cave wall. She looked at each stony detail with a reasonably clear and open little orb or two. If this were harpy thyme for her, so be it. She would make it as pensively little pleasant as she could.

She made her way to the center of the ruins in the cave, hummed to herself, and thought about Magpie. If the fish found her, she would come. If not—

Gloha tapped a column. It rang with a somber note. She tapped another. Its note was different. She found several other notes. She organized them into a tune, and sang along with it, setting the golden motes to dancing in the shards of sunlight which now fell through the jagged cave cracks. The rays of light vibrated like the strings of a harp, changing color, touching different places on the sandstone slab. The effort warmed her body, and perhaps the stone too. Each ruined runic surface seemed to resonate to her music, becoming friendlier. The spirits of the stones whispered counterpoint to her song, and clustered around a breach in the wall she hadn't seen before. She went there, and lo, it was a window to another world that might be part of the surface of Xanth, or might lead to it. This could be her way home. If she could just somehow wedge her battered little body through the crack and follow the new chamber up and out.

Her awareness of the surroundings increased, and she heard the whispering voices of the stoned gathering of gargoyles. Now she knew their identity, and what had happened to them. "Some day your story will be known, O gargoyles," she said. Then their faint voices increased, becoming an incoherent babble, as if the air were being sucked out of the cave. The cavern began to shake, and stone fragments flaked off the ruins. The crevice before her yawned wider.

Afraid that the cavern was collapsing on her, Gloha screamed, and with a dreadful little determination jammed herself through the crack, out of the cave, and into the next. She fell down slippery shale and slid to the base of the scene.

Was she truly free, or was this but a tantalizing dream? She would soon enough find out. She half ran, half flew, taking as much weight off her bad knee as she could without rising up to bang into the rough ceiling. She followed the steep trail up and around—and it opened on the surface, in sight of the harpy caves. She ran out, and the scene changed. She tripped, almost falling, and turned around.

There were no ruins behind her, no caves. Just Xanthly forest. So had it all been a bad dream? She wasn't sure.

Gloha blinked, realizing that another wave of madness had passed, leaving her damp but no longer immersed. She had relived the time she got lost in the nether caves—the ones the harpies claimed didn't exist. She knew better, and perhaps some day she would be able to prove it.

"So there are ancient ruins with gargoyles," Trent remarked. "Someone should excavate them and restore them to their original grandeur."

"You could see to that," Gloha reminded him, "if you decided not to fade away yet."

He smiled. "There will be others after me. It would be no good for us old folk to remain too long, cluttering the later history of Xanth. That's one reason the Good Magician keeps the secret of the Fountain of Youth."

She thought of something else. "Why is it *my* madness that keeps being explored? Doesn't anyone else have any bad memories?"

"Not I," the Demoness Metria said. "I'm infernal. I have no soul, therefore no conscience. My past doesn't bother me, so I would not have any bad memories or dreams even if I cared."

"I have no soul either," Marrow said. "But I would like to have one. Then perhaps I could suffer sieges of madness too."

"Which leaves me," Trent said. "I suppose if I stood upwind of you, I would feel the next wave of madness first, and perhaps then it would be my bad memories that animated."

Gloha hastily moved downwind from him. "Be my guest, Magician!"

Metria formed her smoky features into a huge sneer. "Twenty-five years of kingship—that must be a horrible memory!"

"From 1042 to 1067, when Magician Dor assumed the throne," Trent agreed. "However, the twenty years before that I spent in Mundania. You might consider that a terrible memory."

"Ugh, yes," Gloha agreed.

"What is so bad about Mundania?" Marrow asked.

"Everybody knows it's the dreariest place imaginable," Gloha said. "Because it has no magic. No wonder Magician Trent was desperate to return to Xanth."

"Not necessarily," Trent demurred. "Mundania just needs understanding."

"Here comes another wave," Metria said with relish.

Gloha found herself on the bank of a river. A solid stone bridge with a wooden drawbridge crossed it, and a group of women were washing clothing nearby in the shallow edge of the water. A two-wheeled covered cart drawn by a single unicorn—no, a horse, because it had no horn—was just crossing the bridge.

She looked down at herself. She was a child of five or six, wingless, in a human skirt and jacket, sitting on the bank above the women.

She looked to the other side, and saw a man standing not far off. He was sort of thin-haired, looking almost bald, with a short reddish beard and brown eyes. He had a funny little stand with a board on it, and he was facing it and looking every so often at the women and the bridge. Then she realized that he was painting the scene. So she got up and started toward him, to see what his painting looked like.

"Child!" one of the women screamed. It was the girl's mother; she just knew that without remembering it. "Stay away from that man! He's mad!"

So Gloha had to reverse course. Regretfully she went toward the bridge. The cart had gone on, but now a single man was walking across it. He was oddly dressed, and seemed to be somewhat confused. But he was somehow familiar.

He was Magician Trent! Looking much the way he did now, in his youthened state. But she knew that this was the original young Trent—and this must be Mundania, because it certainly wasn't Xanth. She was sharing his madness vision of his past.

She tried to call to him, but could not. The child she animated just watched. He crossed the bridge, then looked around. He saw Gloha but seemed not to recognize her. This wasn't surprising, because she wasn't herself at the moment. Then his eye fixed on the painter. He left the road and walked across to approach the man.

Gloha wanted to listen to their conversation, but knew her Mundane mother would forbid her getting close. So she busied herself on the bank, chasing down a bug, going one way and another, just sort of coincidentally getting closer to the painter. Finally she sat on the bank, and managed to scoot a bit nearer yet.

But she was disappointed. Trent tried to talk to the painter, but the man seemed not to understand him at all. Gloha realized what the problem was: Trent was speaking Xanthian, which came naturally to all residents, while the painter was speaking Mundanian. With different languages they could not communicate with each other very well.

Finally Trent gave up and went on. Gloha wanted to follow, but couldn't; the girl just was not going that way. She wrenched herself, trying to prevail. To her surprise, it worked, maybe. Something happened.

Then she was in an orchard. The fruit trees were flowering beautifully. They seemed to have hardly any leaves, but were completely covered with flowers. The painter was out there, painting the scene. She was unable to approach him again, because the woman she occupied was just walking by, but at least she could tell that this was a different day and different place.

However, it was Trent she wanted to see, not the painter. She wrenched again, and this time found herself in another body, watching him. He was somewhat ragged now; time must have passed, and he had had a hard time foraging for food in this strange country. But now he had found work at a farmstead, doing menial work, and seemed to be learning the language. Food and shelter seemed to be part of the deal; he might have to sleep in the loft of the barn with the chickens, but right now he was being served a wooden bowl of gruel by a plain young woman who must be the farmer's daughter. There was something familiar about her—

"Metria!" Gloha tried to exclaim, but of course nothing came out. She was just another farm child snooping on others' business. She was also—oops— male. A farm boy. Part of his body was weird. So she wrenched out of there and went to watch the mad painter. Well, he wasn't mad, of course; she just thought of him that way because this was a scene in the wave of madness, and he was the first man she had seen here. Still, the way her body glanced glancingly at him suggested that this native considered the painter highly eccentric if not outright crazy. But his painting was nice enough; it was of a wheat field, with a city in the background, and there was a sort of soft rounded quality to the wheat plants. And—he was animated by Marrow Bones. He didn't look like Marrow, but there was just something about the way he moved and the shape of his skull that made her certain. So he was a significant character of some sort, and it behooved her to keep an eye on him until she discovered how this sequence played out.

She found that she could control her wrenches better with practice. Each one took her approximately where she wanted to go, but always forward in time. She could see the season advancing with each jump. She had started in early spring; now it was summer.

Trent's relationship with the farmer's daughter improved. She evidently liked him, but was shy because she wasn't pretty. She was lean and homely, but of good character. Something was definitely developing there.

Meanwhile the mad painter was everywhere. Each day he tramped out to establish his position, and then he just stood there and painted. On rainy days he did "still lifes"—tables with fruit and pottery. But most days he was out painting the town in all its aspects. Trees, flowers, fields, clouds, houses, the sea, boats, and people. All of them had his rounded, sometimes slightly fuzzy flair, but all were pretty and realistic in their mad way. It was amazing how much variety he could find in what had seemed to Gloha like a pretty dull Mundane town. He never seemed to do anything with the paintings; they just got stacked up and forgotten. No one else seemed to want them.

Trent married the farmer's daughter. Gloha was gradually learning how to understand the weird Mundane language and writing, seeing it through the eyes of those she occupied, so now she was able to understand the information on the wedding paper: this was a place called Arles in a region called France at a time called 1888. All of that was meaningless to Gloha, but since she was here now she might as well know it.

The mad painter kept right on painting as the season progressed. Sometimes he painted at night and slept in the day. Sometimes he went inside and painted piles of books, or a pair of shoes, or chairs, or people eating at tables. But mostly he painted fields and houses and people going among them. Often he made sketches, and then completed the painting later. As winter came he painted flowers in pots. He seemed to be satisfied only when he was actually in the process of painting; the rest of his life was blah. But he really was mad, because he got into a fight with another painter-friend, then cut off part of his own ear, and took it to a house where a number of women lived. Their profession was something Gloha was not competent to fathom; it seemed to relate to making men happy for short periods. They weren't bad women; in fact they understood the mad painter about as well as anyone did, and showed him some sympathy. They had him taken to a place where folk got repaired and bandaged so that he wouldn't bleed to death. That slowed down his painting.

Trent was doing better. He came to know the painter, perhaps because both of them were considered mad in their ways, and now they were able to talk. If Trent told the man of the wonders of his homeland, no one would believe it if the painter spoke of it elsewhere. Maybe he did, and that only increased his seeming madness, because in the spring the painter went to a special place for the mad folk. He kept on painting, and when he couldn't go out he painted pictures of himself and others there, or even invented figures. Gloha was startled to see him paint a picture of her, with her wings, though she had none here. Either Trent had told—no, he couldn't have, because this was before Gloha had ever existed!—or the mad painter somehow saw without seeing.

Trent's wife ordered a baby the Mundane way, which Gloha found so weird that she didn't watch. There was no stork; instead—never mind. In the Mundane year 1889 it arrived, a boy, and on occasion Gloha animated it. But she also wrenched out to watch the mad painter, who was really more interesting right now. He finally left the madhouse and went to another town where a Mundane healer called a doctor tried to take care of him. That didn't seem to help much, but the painter did like the healer's slender sweet daughter. Suddenly Gloha was animating the girl, who was exactly her age of nineteen, and the painter painted her in a garden, and as she was playing a music machine called a piano. Then, suddenly, he killed himself.

Gloha, shocked, returned to Trent's family. This was proceeding normally. She watched the little boy grow older. But this lacked flair; she had become distracted by the mad painter, and now that he was gone she just wanted to get out of this scene. So she jumped ahead as fast as she could, seeing the boy become a teenager, almost a man—and suddenly a bad illness came, and Trent's wife and son died.

"Oh!" Gloha cried. "That was awful!"

"Yes," Trent agreed. "She was the only woman I ever loved, and the only son. There was nothing to do but to return to Xanth, where I had more power. But that was a separate story."

"The mad painter—" she said.

"I liked him too. He was named—" He paused, working to remember it after all this time. "Go. Van Go. Something like that. I think people got interested in his paintings after he died. But they all thought him mad while he lived. He wasn't; he merely had strong artistic passions. He understood about Xanth; he was the only one who believed me. That's why I liked him." He sighed.

"And the girl he painted, near the end? Who played the music."

"The doctor's daughter, Marguerite. A nice girl. Like you."

"This is odd," Marrow said. "I have never been a mad Mundane painter before. If I were capable of such emotion, I would have considerable sympathy for the man."

"He warranted sympathy," Trent agreed. "Had he lived in Xanth, magic could have helped him. He might have been successful and happy here. Instead he had to face life in Mundania."

"And he couldn't face it," Marrow said.

"I don't know how anyone faces drear Mundania," Metria said. "No magic—my kind doesn't even exist there." She hesitated. "Yet there was a certain ambiguity of feeling."

"A certain what?" Gloha asked.

"Doubt, uncertainty, indefiniteness, vagueness, equivocation—"

"I believe she had the right word the first time," Marrow said.

"Whatever," the demoness agreed crossly.

Trent glanced at her. "You animated my wife for a summarized period of fifteen years," he said. "I must say that if you did not feel emotion, you emulated it well enough to fool me."

"I felt it," Metria said, looking unusually pensive. "Understand, in real life I think you're an impossibly rejuvenated over-the-hill mortal human man, a fit object for endless scorn. But in that mad vision, I—she—" Something very like a tear glistened in her eye. "She did love you, didn't she?"

Gloha understood how that could be.

"And I loved her, and my son," Trent agreed. "Others called her unlovely, but in her spirit she was beautiful, and I think as time passed that came to be reflected in her physical aspect. She did not understand me as the painter did, but she treated me well from the outset, and taught me the language and ways of that land, and when we came to love each other, I learned responsibility in a way I had never known before. She made me what I was when I returned to Xanth."

"And you made her lovely," Metria said. "And she got you a fine son. Then that evil magic came—"

"A plague," he agreed. "An illness that swept across that land of France, and other lands, taking its toll of folk each time. I don't know why it spared me. I sold the farm we had inherited to finance an expedition to Xanth, which I happened to know how to reach, and recruited soldiers of fortune, trained them, prepared them to face magic, and then had the irony of achieving the kingship of Xanth without conquering it. But I would never have returned, if I had not lost those I loved." There seemed to be a tear in his own eye. The mad scene had shaken him. That, too, Gloha understood.

Meanwhile, she was also amazed. She was learning aspects of the Magician's history she had never suspected. "Didn't you love Queen Iris?" she asked.

"No. That was a marriage of convenience. We both understood the necessity."

"And your daughter, the Sorceress Irene?"

"Her, yes. And my grandchildren. Which is why I am ready to fade out of the picture and leave Xanth to them. My day is past."

Still Metria was unusually hesitant. Now she assumed the form of the woman she had animated in the vision, of mature age, with her hair tied back in a bun. She was not laughing at them or dissolving into smoke. She just gazed at Trent without speaking again.

"Please don't tease me with that form," Trent said mildly. But Gloha remembered how deceptive his mildness could be. His true emotion was not far from expression.

"I—I know it is the madness," Metria said. "But I never felt feeling before. Would you—"

The Magician evidently didn't trust this. "Would I what?"

The demoness actually fidgeted. "Would you—kiss me?"

Trent stared at her, then exchanged glances with Marrow and Gloha, who were just about as surprised. Then Gloha looked at Marrow, and decided. "Go ahead. I don't think she's teasing you."

"Agreed," the skeleton said.

"This *is* madness," Trent murmured. Then he took the image of his first wife in his arms and kissed her. It turned out to be a long and feeling kiss.

"Thank you," Metria said when he released her. There was definitely a tear on her face. "I wish it could have been real." Then she slowly faded out.

Magician Trent stood where he was, thinking his own thoughts. Then he spoke in a whisper. "Thank you, Demoness, even if it was only a game to you."

"I think she meant it," Gloha said. "The madness touched her."

"As it touched all of us," Marrow agreed. "More than ever now, I want a soul."

"Nevertheless, I think we had better get out of this region," Trent said, shaking off the mood. "I understand that the madness can strike in many ways, and many are not pleasant."

The others were glad to agree. They started walking at a swift pace, with Gloha flying ahead every so often to spy out the path. But several more waves of madness caught them anyway, though not as intense as the first ones; they were getting out of the worst of it.

During one siege Gloha returned to her harpy home and resumed her normal life—but somehow after her experience in the secret cave, that life was less satisfying than ever. In another siege the focus was on Marrow Bones, who got spooked in the boneyard by a rampaging monster—Gloha recognized Smash Ogre—and fled, only to get lost on the Lost Path. He was finally found by Esk Ogre, son of the ogre who had spooked him. Fortunately Esk was only quarter ogre, so they got along well enough. They even found another lost denizen of the gourd, Bria Brassie, who was so pleased to be found that she married Esk and set about living happily ever after. But Marrow never returned to the original boneyard, which was why he was now looking for half a soul. In that sequence Trent animated Esk's image and Gloha animated Bria's image. At one point Bria inadvertently embarrassed Esk, so she apologized in the gourd realm manner, by kissing him passionately. That was probably what led to their later marriage. But this time it was Trent and Gloha kissing. Oh well, Gloha thought as the madness faded; it wasn't as if it were the first time she had infringed on matters best left to the Adult Conspiracy.

In another siege Gloha was farmed out to harpy relatives on the Gold Coast. There she caught a rare illness. They were afraid it was the purple-hulled pink eye, whose cure would have required her to be dipped into a snakepit filled with a mixture of poultry poop and peanut hulls. Fortunately Magpie learned that it was something else, and all that was required was a foul-tasting potion. What a relief, even if the potion did taste like the contents of that snakepit. Marrow played the doctor who had made the misdiagnosis, and Metria returned to play Magpie. That was an easy role for another demoness to assume.

At last they won free of it, and came to the shore of Lake Ogre-Chobee. There were ordinary houses and gardens, not the creations of memory or horror. The madness was over. Gloha was glad they had passed through only the fringe, where it came in waves rather than solidly; more of a dose would have been troublesome indeed. Now all they had to face were the Curse Fiends.

"Let's go say hello to the neighbors," Gloha said. "Just to be sure they're real." Trent and Marrow nodded.

8
PLAY

They approached the first house. It was a neat cottage set amidst a yard with clusters of pretty mushrooms, with a little box on a post outside. On the box was neatly printed the words RICHARD C. WHITE.

"What's that?" Gloha asked.

Trent's lips pursed. "We may not be clear of the madness after all," he murmured. "That is a Mundane mailbox. See, the man's name is on it. They commonly use two or three names there."

"They keep men in little boxes in Mundania?" Marrow inquired.

Trent smiled. "No. Only letters, which are delivered each day."

"Delivered?" Gloha asked. "You mean the storks carry letters there?"

"No, there is a somewhat more cumbersome mechanism which varies from place to place and time to time. My concern is not about that, but because of the Mundane nature of it. My madness memories concerned Mundania."

"Do you remember a house like this?"

"No. So perhaps the similarity is mere coincidence."

The door of the house opened and a man emerged. He seemed to be in his mid-forties. "Hello," he called. "Are you folks lost?"

"We hope not," Trent answered. "We have just passed through a Region of Madness, and we hope this is not more of the same. Are you Richard White?"

"Yes. And I understand about the madness. I came through it myself, last year, on the way here. It was an awful experience, yet tinged with longing. I had my house built right at the edge, so I could return through it if I ever decide to. Usually the madness stays within bounds, though it has spread somewhat the past few days." He paused. "But I'm being insensitive. You folk are surely tired and confused after your experience. Come in and relax. Did you pass through the worst of it?"

"Only the fringe," Trent said. "Fortunately. I am Magician Trent, and this is Gloha Goblin-Harpy, and this is Marrow Bones. None of us are hostile folk." They followed Richard into the house.

"I have read of you, Magician Trent," Richard said. "But I thought you had faded out. And, if I may say so, you look remarkably young."

"I have been temporarily youthened for this adventure," Trent explained. "When it is done, I will fade out."

Richard brought out a bowl of oddly thin slices of something. Gloha wasn't sure what they were for. Trent took one, smiling. "I believe these are potato chips, a Mundane delicacy in some regions." He put one to his mouth, and it crackled as he chewed it. "You are recently from Mundania?" he asked Richard.

"Yes, I arrived about a year ago, though of course that may not relate well to Mundane time. The folk of the Black Wave and the Curse Friends helped me build my house. Now I put in septic tanks for them." He smiled at Gloha's blank expression. "Those are big containers I install underground. They take the refuse from the families' privies and turn it into soil for their plants."

"Oh, magic," Gloha said, understanding. "We could use some of those for the harpy dung heaps."

"Perhaps I shall be able to do business with them, when I catch up here," Richard said. "I like making Xanth cleaner and healthier, though it is really much better than Mundania."

Gloha finally got up courage to bite into a potato chip. It crunched for her too. "It's good!" she exclaimed, surprised.

"I am not yet fully acclimatized," Richard said. "I like it in Xanth, and I'm glad to be here, but there were some Mundane things I missed. So I tried to have them duplicated here. These aren't the best potato chips, but my technique is improving."

Marrow was looking at a picture on the wall. "Is that your home?"

Richard laughed. "No, that's my effort to show Jenny Elf's home in the World of Two Moons. I hope to meet her some day. We have something in common, in the way we—" But he broke off, evidently suffering a painful memory.

"You seem to know a lot about Xanth, for a Mundane," Trent remarked. "How did you come here?"

"I always liked Xanth," Richard said. "When things soured at home, I—

well, it's a story I'd prefer to leave in the Region of Madness. I'm just glad that I managed to find my way here, instead of getting lost."

"Few Mundanes are able to get here," Trent agreed. He looked around. We thank you for the food and dialogue. We have to go on about our quest now. Gloha and Marrow are looking for things we hope to find somewhere along this route."

"I understand. Some day perhaps I will travel, hoping to find a good companion." He showed them out.

"How did you get such pretty mushrooms?" Gloha asked, admiring the many clumps.

"I had some Mundane paper money with me when I arrived," Richard explained. "I knew it was useless here, so I buried it in jars for safekeeping, in case I should ever go back to visit my sister. But my hiding place turned out to be no good, because the mushrooms sprouted over each jar."

"Leave them there," Gloha said. "It's Xanth's way of keeping you here."

"It must be," he agreed. He glanced in the direction they were going. "I've never been down that way. I've heard there's a giant there, and I don't want to run afoul of him."

"Giants aren't necessarily hostile," Trent said. "But we appreciate the warning. We'll be careful."

They walked on, refreshed, waving goodbye to the nice man. They found a convenient path around a small hill. There was a tree house: someone had cut a door and windows into an old beerbarrel tree and made it into a house. There was no longer any smell of beer, so the tree must have drained some time before. It was surrounded by fancy iris flowers. Nearby were assorted fruit trees, and one spreading nut, bolt, and washer tree.

A woman of about thirty-three was just fetching in some edible washers as their party passed. She had harvested those that were in reach, and was trying to get her fingers on one that was just beyond. She was standing on tiptoes, somewhat unsteadily.

"Let me help you," Marrow said, stepping close.

She turned and saw him. "Eeeeek!" she screamed, putting a good five *e*'s into it. "Death!"

Gloha hurried forward, understanding the confusion. "No, merely a friendly walking skeleton," she said quickly. "He means you no harm."

The woman took heart. "A sweet little goblin girl," she said. Then her eyes went beyond. "And a young man."

"I'm Gloha," Gloha said. She introduced the others, giving only their first names. "We're on a private quest."

"I'm Janet," the woman said. "Janet Hines. I haven't been here long. I'm sorry I screamed. I have been told there is a giant in the vicinity, so I'm a bit nervous."

Marrow reached up and brought down the washer. He handed it to Janet. "In the realm of bad dreams, where I originated, it was my job to frighten folk," he said. "I apologize for coming upon you so suddenly."

"No, that's all right," Janet said. "I have heard of your kind. I shouldn't have reacted. Thank you for helping."

"How did you come here?" Gloha asked.

"It is a dull story. I wouldn't want to bore you."

"We recently emerged from the Region of Madness," Trent said. "We are relieved to find ourselves among ordinary folk."

"Well, it started when I was fourteen, in Mundania," Janet said. "I got sick. I was a pretty girl, some said, but this wasting disease—"

"You are still a handsome woman," Trent said, accurately enough. Gloha wasn't sure that anyone over the age of twenty could actually be pretty, but he hadn't used that word.

"It took away my ability to move, and blinded me, so that all I could do was listen, and blink my eyes to respond. But my mother read books to me, and wrote letters for me. I even had a nice new iris named after me—and I found it growing here, so I knew this was where I belonged, when I left Mundania."

That explained the irises. "But what do you do, most of the time?" Gloha asked.

"I've just been learning how to use my body again. It was a shock when I began to see, and I still don't see very well, but it's a little better each day. I had to get used to all the sights. At first I had to crawl out to pick up fruits and nuts and bolts that dropped from the trees, but later I learned to walk again. I think I'm almost normal now."

"But don't you get lonely, living alone?" Gloha asked, and was sorry the moment she said it, realizing that it wasn't a proper question.

"I do miss my mother, who took care of me all those years," Janet admitted. "But I don't think I can go back. I'm a little afraid to meet any other people. I haven't had the courage to go far from this house I found."

"How long were you ill?" Trent asked.

"Nineteen years," she said sadly.

"Then you never had an adult life," Gloha said. "No friends, no—" She stopped herself, realizing that she was going wrong again.

"I had friends," Janet said. "They came in and read to me. But I suppose it was rather limited."

"Maybe you should take a walk around the hill," Gloha said. "There's a nice man there you might like to meet. He's from Mundania too."

"Oh? I didn't realize. Perhaps I will."

They left Janet and went on to the southeast. But soon they came up against the shore of the lake.

"But are the Curse Fiends directly on the line Crombie pointed?" Trent inquired. "My impression is that it transects the lake, but not the center where the fiends live. Perhaps we can avoid them. They are not known for their friendliness to strangers."

"Oh, pooh!" a voice exclaimed. "I was hoping you wouldn't realize that you didn't have to brace the Curse Fiends. It would have been so much more interesting."

Trent exchanged a three-way glance with Gloha and Marrow: the demoness had just confirmed his suspicion.

"In that case we might as well walk around the lake," Gloha said, relieved. "Which end does the line cross?"

"The south end, I think. So we can walk south around it."

"Curses, foiled again," Metria's voice came.

Gloha wondered about that. She was afraid that there was something they were about to encounter that the demoness would find interesting, so Metria was trying to make them think the opposite. But that was only a suspicion, and in any event, they had to circle the lake one way or the other, or make a boat. Walking around seemed less likely to trigger an encounter with the Curse Fiends.

However, they encountered something else: an ant engagement. There seemed to be an ant war on, for an army of combatAnts were laying siege to a giAnt hill. Each ant was huge, and most looked formidable. "I think we had best detour around this," Trent murmured. "It seems that the warnings about the presence of a giant were well taken; we just didn't understand what kind. I could transform those ants that come close, but they could overwhelm us if they charged in from all sides."

An Antenna quivered. The head turned toward them. "That looks like a defendAnt," Marrow remarked. "See the Antagonistic mandibles."

"Let's get out of here," Gloha said. "We don't have an Antidote to getting chomped up."

They retreated. But then they heard the ant's Anthem, carrying to the distAnt wings of the formation. They were summoning their throng for an Anticipated attack. The sound was triumphAnt.

"I think we had better hurry," Marrow said. "They may see us as cliAnts."

"I think we need an inherAnt defense," Trent said. "They are already surrounding us."

Gloha saw that they were. "I'm not conversAnt with their tactics," she said. "What's relevAnt? A roc bird? If you transform me, so I can carry you away—"

"No. They have Antiaircraft artillery." He pointed to where several antis had great long snoots suitable for blowing rocks out with great force. "It is importAnt to select the right creature."

"Then what?" she asked, becoming alarmed.

"An Antelope," he said, reaching toward her. Suddenly she was a huge four-legged creature with big Antlers. Trent and Marrow got on her back.

The ants stopped closing in. Gloha wondered why, because she did not seem to be a really unusual creature. "You are now the Antithesis of the ants," Trent explained. "The equivalAnt of something they can't handle. Just walk on by them."

Gloha, nervously, did so. Soon she saw that the ants gave way before her. Magician Trent had known what type of creature to use.

Only one ant remained close. She saw that it had a clipboard, on whose paper it was making a note. "Merely an accountAnt," Trent said. "Tallying the ones that got away, I suspect."

Good riddance, she thought.

Once they were safely past the ant activity, Trent transformed her back to her natural form. They continued skirting the lake.

A cloud passed. It peered down at them. Then it huffed and puffed, making itself bigger and darker.

"That's Fracto!" Gloha cried. "What ill luck!"

A nebulous mouth formed on the cloud. "Ho ho ho!" it breathed, its breath forming new cloudlets.

"We'd better find a dry place to camp," Trent said. "I think we won't be getting much farther today."

They hurried on, looking for a place. The cloud continued to build, eager to catch them in the open.

"You think you've gotten past the Curse Fiends without trouble," a smoke-filled voice said. "But you haven't. Look there." A dusky arm appeared, pointing.

"Oh, no!" Gloha muttered. "Metria's back."

"But there is something there," Marrow said.

Ahead of them was a huge building. It seemed to be made of stone and brick below, with a dome-shaped roof above. It was right across the general re-

gion of their line to the southeast. A prominent sign before it said THUNDER-
DOME. But there was no thunder; all was quiet, except for Fracto's rising
winds.

"Could there be a winged goblin male in there?" Marrow inquired.

"I doubt it," Trent replied. "As far as I know, there are still no such males.
But we shall have to investigate."

"At least maybe it will be dry inside," Gloha said. The cloud was just about
ready to rain on them. Then a nagging thought nagged her. "Do you think
Fracto's trying to drive us into that building, because he knows there's something nasty in there?"

"Close," Metria said, her top half appearing. "It's Curse Fiend property.
They had it built recently, hoping to catch something in it."

The building nevertheless seemed to be deserted. "Halooo!" Trent called.
"Anybody home?" There was no reply.

They entered, as the door was open. They passed through a cavelike labyrinth
of passages and emerged in a great central chamber that seemed to take up most
of the building, extending right up to the dome. There were tiers of benches all
around, making the chamber resemble a monstrous covered bowl.

And there, lying curled on the floor, was a giant, asleep. So the rumors had
been true after all.

"How did he get in here?" Gloha asked. "He's way too big for the passage
we used."

"He must have lifted up the lid and stepped in," Marrow conjectured. "Perhaps he was looking for a dry place to sleep."

"As we are," Trent agreed. "Let's hope he is friendly."

"I suppose we had better find out," Gloha said. "Maybe we should wake
him, and if he tries to eat us, you can transform him into something harmless."

"Agreed," Trent said.

They advanced cautiously on the sleeping creature. They stood by his ear.
The air near him was foul, and Gloha realized that it was his putrid breath. But
maybe they could stay clear of the giant, once they ascertained his nature.

"Giant," she said carefully into the ear. "Please wake up and tell us whether
you are friendly to regular folk."

The giant snorted. The air grew even worse. His eyes opened. He turned
his head on the ground and peered at them. "Oh, hello," he said, his breath
nearly knocking them over both by its physical force and its stench. "I am Graeboe Giant."

"Graeboe!" Gloha gasped. "I met your brother!"

"I don't have a brother," he protested.

"Greatbow," she said, trying her brave little best not to choke impolitely. "He said you were ailing."

"Ah, my cousin! Yes, I have an unconscionable malady, and can no longer maintain my invisibility. I did not realize you were here, or I would not have intruded upon you. My apology. I shall depart, for I know my presence is uncomfortable for normal folk."

"No, we intruded on you," she protested. "You were here first. We should be the ones to go."

"As you wish," he said. "Stand back, please, for I shall now lift my head."

They retreated as the giant lifted his head and propped it with a hand. He was too big to sit up in the building. It was obvious that Graeboe was not unfriendly. But his breath—!

Marrow met them at the edge of the passage out. "I have just checked the exterior," he announced. "It is raining canines and felines, and lightning is striking every available target. I think it will not be convenient to depart these premises for the nonce."

"But there's a foul-smelling giant in there," Gloha said.

"Perhaps we can do something about that," Trent said. "Metria?"

"Why should I help you deal with the stink?" the demoness inquired, appearing. "I enjoy seeing you mortals sweat."

"Because we shall be unable to remain here unless we can breathe," he responded evenly. "So we shall have to go elsewhere, and you will not have the dubious pleasure of snooping on our otherwise surely interesting dialogue with the giant."

"You can't go elsewhere. Its raining bovines and equines."

"Dogs and cats," Gloha said.

"Whatever. You're stuck here."

"Not if I transform Gloha to a creature that likes water, such as a gargoyle."

Metria considered. "Um. You could do that. Very well, what do you want?"

"A sprig of parsley."

She vanished, and reappeared a moment later with the sprig. "I wouldn't let you manage me like this, if you hadn't kissed me," she said.

"Surely true," he agreed, taking the parsley. "I wouldn't have asked you, if I hadn't kissed you."

Metria looked stunned. That, too, Gloha was coming to understand. Trent had that effect on women who came to know him. Even demon women, it seemed.

He walked to Graeboe. "Here is a sprig of parsley. It has the magic property of purifying breath. If you will eat it, it may solve a problem."

"I didn't know that!" Graeboe exclaimed, pleased. He moved a huge hand and tried to take the sprig, but it was much too small.

"I shall stick it under your fingernail," Trent said. He fitted the sprig into the massive crevice. The giant lifted his hand and sucked the sprig from the finger.

The air cleared. "Thank you," Graeboe said. "Even I can smell the difference."

"Well, it wasn't really your fault," Gloha said. "You can't be blamed for your illness."

"It is kind of you to say that," the giant said. Now his breath smelled like new-mown hay. "I really don't like being objectionable, so I have tried to stay away from other creatures."

"Exactly what is your ailment?" Marrow asked.

"I am not entirely clear about that," Graeboe said. "It came on me gradually. I went to ask the Good Magician, but he refused to talk to me, understandably. He merely sent word that help would come if I remained in this region long enough."

Gloha took note; that was the word Marrow had received.

"What are the symptoms of your malady, apart from the breath?" Trent asked.

"Increasing general weakness and susceptibility to illnesses. I sleep much more than I used to, yet remain tired. I fear I will not be able to remain in Xanth much longer."

"Oh? Where will you go?" Gloha asked before she thought.

The giant smiled sadly. "To fertilize the trees, I think, lovely little lass. At least I shall then be able to do something some good." He glanced around. "I can hear thunder outside. This dome seems to attract it. I think you will not want to go out soon. I have food; do you care to share it?"

"Yes," Gloha said. She liked the giant, now that she could breathe freely near him. Possibly his compliment had something to do with it.

Graeboe brought out a snack from his purse: a gross of pickle pies and a keg of green wine. They accepted tiny portions, which were all they could eat, and settled down on the floor beside him.

It remained light in the dome, though it was dark outside. "Perhaps we could play a game, or something, to pass the time," Gloha suggested politely.

Graeboe brightened. "Do you like angry word puzzles?"

"I love them," Gloha said.

So they drew lines in the dust and alternated filling them in with words, and it was fun. The giant was ill and weak and somewhat homely, but not stupid; he had a good vocabulary and a fair sense of humor. Gloha realized that just because a person was different did not mean he was necessarily unpleasant. Then they settled down to sleep, hoping that the storm would be through by morning. Trent spied a flea and transformed it into a pillow bush, so they had plenty of pillows, including a huge pile of them for the giant's head.

Gloha woke to the sound of a general stirring or rustling, as of an enormous throng of people getting ready to witness some rare event, or maybe just a flock of birds cleaning bugs from a spreading acorn tree. She opened her eyes—and saw that her first impression was the correct one. The tiered benches of the bowl chamber were filling with people.

Startled, she looked at her companions. Magician Trent and the Giant Graeboe were still asleep, but Marrow, who didn't need sleep, was alert. "What's happening?" she whispered to the skeleton.

"The Curse Fiends are assembling," he replied.

"Oh, they must be getting ready to put on a play. We must depart before we get in their way."

"Adipose chance," a ball of smoke said.

"What kind of chance, Metria?"

The smoke expanded into the nether portion of an extremely well endowed woman. "Corpulent, obese, fleshy, potbellied, rotund, blubbery—"

"Fat?"

The top half of the figure formed. "Whatever," the face said crossly as the overall figure slimmed down. "They have latched down the dome and magically sealed the premises, so we can't get out."

"They can trap a demon?" Gloha asked, surprised.

"I don't quite understand about that," Metria said, disgruntled. "I've been having weird effects, since associating with you folk." Her eye fell on Trent. "Since the Madness."

Gloha got another glimmer. She remembered how intrigued Cynthia had become with the handsome Magician, and had felt the attraction herself. Metria had played the part of the one woman Trent had loved, and it had affected her. Maybe she didn't really want to depart just yet. But of course she wouldn't admit to having anything that could be seriously mistaken for human feeling. So containing magic that ordinarily might not restrain her now had greater force. At least it was a pretext to stay near Trent.

But that was an incidental concern. Gloha addressed the major one. "What do they want of us?"

"I suspect we shall discover that in one and a half moments," Marrow said. "One of them is approaching."

Sure enough, in one and a half moments the man reached them. Trent and Graeboe woke to the sound of his footsteps. Neither spoke, evidently realizing that they needed more information before reacting.

"Who is responsible for this intrusion of our premises?" the man demanded.

Metria huffed into harridan form. "Listen, oinkface—" she started.

Gloha realized that this would never do. "Cumulo Fracto Nimbus," she said quickly, realizing why the nasty cloud had chosen to harass them. "He blew up a storm last night, and we had to hurry to cover. This building seemed to be unoccupied, so we camped here for the night. We'll be glad to get on our way—"

"Chubby chance," he said sourly. "You have intruded on our demesnes, and must pay the penalty."

Gloha felt like huffing into harridan form herself. "Penalty? Just because we came in out of the rain?"

"Perhaps we should exchange introductions," Marrow said diplomatically.

"Certainly. I am Contumelo Curse Friend, Playmaster for the Thunderdome."

"I am Gloha Goblin-Harpy, and these are Marrow Bones, the Demoness Metria, Graeboe Giant, and Magician Trent."

She had thought that the last name would faze the man, but it didn't. Maybe the Curse Fiends were too insular to be aware of who was who in the rest of Xanth. "Well, strangers, you have usurped our stage for a play, disrupting our scheduled event. You must therefore provide us with equal measure before departing the premises."

Gloha looked around, but none of the others seemed inclined to argue this case. They were leaving it to her. Probably Marrow was too polite to argue with anyone, and Trent was biding his time in case he should have to transform someone. "What kind of measure?"

"A play, of course. The people have made the arduous journey across the lake to come to our new theater, and they must be entertained. If you ilk hadn't occupied our stage, preventing our scheduled company from setting up its props—"

"Ilk?" Metria said. She was all too ready to argue, but would probably just get them all into more trouble. "I'll show you ilk, you o'erweening wretch!" She began to huff into a truly awful configuration.

"What kind of wretch?" Contumelo inquired.

The smoky shape paused in mid-huff. "Pompous, insolent, swaggering, presumptuous, haughty, o'erbearing—"

"Arrogant?"

"Whatever," the half shape agreed crossly. "Oh, now look what you've done! I've forgotten what I was huffing into."

"Perhaps a frog," Contumelo suggested, almost smiling.

"Thank you." A huge green frog formed. "Hey, wait half a moment!" the frog exclaimed. "That wasn't it. I have three quarters of a mind to—"

"Really? I would have taken it for half a wit."

The frog seemed about to explode into a mushroom-shaped cloud.

"What kind of play did you have in mind?" Gloha asked quickly.

"Something we just might find useful in our repertoire," Contumelo replied. "Of course we would have to rewrite any abysmal effort that such poor players as you might essay, but after you strut and fret your hour upon the stage you will be heard no more. Sometimes we glean inspiration from the unlikeliest sources." A sneer hovered somewhere in his vicinity without quite getting established.

Even Marrow was beginning to look annoyed, which was an unusual effect considering the bony blankness of his countenance. Graeboe, who had been completely amiable hitherto, was starting to frown. Only Trent continued to look mild—which might be the worst sign of all.

"So if we put on a play for you—something that maybe makes you laugh— then you'll let us go in peace?" Gloha asked, hoping to avert what was threatening to be an ugly scene.

"Your mere attempt will surely make us laugh. What we require is something useful, as I just informed you."

Gloha sent a somewhat disheveled gaze across the others. "Then maybe we should try to do that," she said uncertainly.

Now Trent spoke. "We shall need props and scenery."

"You should have thought of that before you intruded, bumpkin," Contumelo said.

Trent started to gesture toward the man, but Graeboe spoke. "I think some folk are not aware of the impression they make on others. It was some time before I realized why folk were avoiding me, as my illness developed."

The Magician glanced at him and nodded. Gloha relaxed; Contumelo had just been spared a transformation he surely wouldn't have liked. "Perhaps we can provide our own props," Trent said.

"I should hope so," the Curse Fiend said. "We shall give you half an hour to prepare. Then we shall expect you to perform. Of course all five of you must have significant parts; we don't tolerate slackards." He spun neatly about on heel and toe and stalked away.

"Half an hour!" Gloha exclaimed. She would have snorted, but she didn't have the nose for it. "How can they expect us to get a play ready when we have no chance to make up scenery, to write a play, to rehearse—when we've never done anything like this before?"

"They don't," Marrow said. "They expect us to fail, and be their laughing-stock."

"Yes, I remember now," Metria said. "They hired the Black Wave to complete this stadium, and they like to lure strangers in and make them perform. Then they punish the strangers when they don't do well enough. It's how they relieve the dullness of their routine lives."

"And Fracto is in on it!" Gloha said, realizing.

"Of course."

"How do they punish the failures?" Marrow asked.

"They hit them with one of their massed curses. It so dazes the victims that they can barely wander away, and it may be a long time before they are able to function normally again."

Trent frowned. "I think the Curse Fiends are about due for a reckoning."

"Yet it is no worse than what dragons or goblins do to those they catch," Graeboe pointed out. He glanced at Gloha. "Present company excepted."

Trent nodded again. "Your tolerance becomes you. Yet if we are unable to put on a play that satisfies them, given what I deem to be unfairly short notice, I shall not sit still for a curse. I shall have to take action."

"Such as turning one of them into a sphinx who will then tromp the rest of them to pulp," Metria said enthusiastically.

"Oh, no, that would not be kind," Graeboe protested. "We must simply avoid the issue by putting on a suitable play."

"I never saw a giant as peaceful as you," the demoness said, not meaning it as a compliment.

"That is because the other giants are invisible; you have seen none of them," he pointed out reasonably enough. "Most of us do not wish to cause small folk any inconvenience. That is why we do not tread on their villages or fields. We wish only to exist in mutual harmony."

The more Gloha learned about the giants, the more respect she had for them. However, there was no time for incidental dialogue. "What kind of play can we do in a hurry? That puts all five of us into significant roles? I have no idea."

"Something simple, I think," Trent said. "Perhaps we should adapt a well-known fable or story. There should be one that provides suitable roles for all of us."

"For a giant?" Graeboe asked, interested.

"Jack and the Beanstalk!" Gloha cried. "Except that it's a mean giant."

"Well, perhaps I could portray such a giant, as long as it is only in a play."

"But there's no demoness in that story," Metria protested.

"Then maybe Aladdin and the Magic Lamp," Gloha said. "You could be the genie. Trent could play Aladdin."

"Or the Genie in the Bottle," the demoness agreed with relish. "With a female genie. Every time he uncorks the bottle, she smokes out and kisses him." She formed into smoke with a huge pair of lips.

"But there's no giant in those ones," Graeboe said.

"And no goblin girls in any of them," Gloha added.

"And no walking skeletons," Marrow said.

Trent scratched his head. "Can anyone think of a tale that includes a giant, a demon, a man, a skeleton, and a winged goblin?"

None of them could. "I suppose I could be some other kind of girl," Gloha said. "A fairy, perhaps, or even a human girl, if I pretended my wings were a white cloak."

"Or a princess," Graeboe said. "Many tales have princesses. And the demoness could assume some other form, such as a frog, for the Frog Prince."

"Say, yes," Metria agreed. "Maybe the Frog Princess, who marries the Little Prince." She looked at Trent again.

"But what form can I assume?" Marrow asked somewhat plaintively.

"Death," Graeboe suggested.

"Say, yes," Gloha agreed. "The same role your kind plays in dreams."

"In the Frog Prince?"

"We keep running into that problem," Gloha said. "No single tale works."

"But a medley might," Graeboe said.

"A medley?"

"A mixture of tales," Trent explained. "We can put them together, so as to have all the characters we need."

"But what about the scenery?" Gloha asked. "The costumes and things?"

"We'll just have to play ourselves, as it were," Graeboe said. "I'm dressed as a giant, you're dressed as a girl, Marrow's a skeleton, and Trent is a man. Metria can assume any form. We'd better concentrate on the story line."

"And the scenery," Marrow said. "That will be difficult to make in the small time remaining."

"I can transform local bugs into things like wallflowers and paintbrush flowers," Trent said. "We can make scenes from them."

Contumelo approached. "You have five minutes to curtain call," he said with evident satisfaction.

"We had better get organized," Trent said. "I suggest that we separate into committees. Metria and I can devise scenery, and Gloha and Graeboe can organize the plot."

"But what of me?" Marrow asked.

"You are perhaps our most objective member. You can coordinate the two committees, and make the announcements."

"But they won't pay attention to a skeleton!"

"Yes they will, if you're in costume." Trent spied a bug on the ground, and reached toward it. Suddenly it was hat tree. "Pick a suitable hat and wear it for announcements."

Marrow selected a tall stovepipe hat and donned it. Suddenly he looked very official.

Gloha flew up to perch on Graeboe's lifted hand, so she could talk to him conveniently. "We must assemble several tales into one in a hurry," she said. "I hope your imagination is bigger than mine right now."

"My head is larger, at any rate." He considered briefly. "Perhaps if we start with Jack and the Beanstalk, to get the man and giant, and then bring in a captive princess—"

"Yes! He wants to eat her—"

Graeboe winced. "Oh, I hope not. That wouldn't be nice."

"But this is only a play. The giant has to be mean, or it won't be exciting."

"But in the real tale, the giant valued precious things, like a hen to lay golden eggs, and a magic harp—"

"How about a magic harpy?" she asked, laughing. "And the giant doesn't want to kill her, he wants to marry her, but of course she'd rather be eaten, so—"

Marrow approached. "What scenery and props will be needed?"

"A magic bean to grow into a beanstalk," Gloha said. "A land up on a cloud. A castle for the giant—"

"That's enough to start," the skeleton said, and went to the other committee.

In a moment he was back. "Perhaps if I knew the story, I could narrate the interstices."

"Wonderful idea," she agreed. She described what they were working out.

Two more minutes of hectic coordination brought them to curtain time. Trent had transformed bugs to various things: several large wallflowers, a giant bedbug, pillow and blanket bushes, a big box elder tree with red, black, and yellow slats, and assorted other things stored within that box. They were perched around Graeboe's curled body, which actually took up most of the stage.

Gloha's confused little cranium was spinning. Could they possibly make this work?

"Are you ready to perform?" Contumelo inquired with grim relish.

Marrow stepped up, donning his tall hat. "Indeed. Please get out of our way, functionary."

Gloha would have laughed at the expression on the Curse Fiend's face, if she hadn't been so nervous about whether their scatterbrained assemblage would work. She retreated to hide in the box elder until her turn came to be on-stage. In a round theater like this there really was no way to go offstage, but the box served well enough.

A hush descended across the audience, which now pretty well filled the theater. Gloha was surprised by the number of Curse Fiends there were. Then she saw that a number of faces were black; the Black Wavers were attending too. They looked more friendly.

Marrow Bones stepped to the center of the arena. "Greetings, or should I say, curses to you," he said grandly, doffing his impressive hat for a moment. There was a murmur; Gloha wasn't sure whether it was of approval, mystery, or outrage. "We, the Haphazard Players, are pleased to present *The Princess and the Giant*."

He turned, making a grand sweep of one bony arm. "Once upon a thyme—" And a thyme plant appeared beside him. Gloha was startled, until she realized that it wasn't real; Metria had assumed the form. She saw with satisfaction that the audience was surprised too.

Marrow waited for the reaction to fade out. Then he resumed. "There was a handsome young man named Jack."

Trent walked out from the box and stood in the center of the stage, which was defined by the giant's curled body. He looked exactly as described.

"Jack was poor but honest," Marrow said. "His family had fallen on hard thymes—" Here "Jack" tripped over the thyme plant. There was a squeak from the depths of the audience; someone almost thought the joke was funny, but had managed to stifle the laugh.

"So Jack had to take the family bovine to town to sell for coins to live on," Marrow continued. Suddenly the thyme plant was a holy cow, seemingly none the worse for the huge holes through her body. Metria had changed form again.

Jack took hold of the cow's ear and led her in a circle around the field, which was that portion of the arena outside the giant's body. "Mooooo!" she complained loudly.

"But on the way to town Jack encountered a suspicious character," Marrow continued. He removed his announcer hat, put on a sleazy hat, and stepped up to meet Jack. This time there was a laugh; it was from Contumelo, who just couldn't resist the description of Marrow as suspicious.

"And where are you going, my fine innocent young mark?" the sleaze inquired.

"I am taking our family cow to town to sell for coins so we can eat," Jack replied innocently.

"Ah, I have something better than coins," the sleaze said. "I have this magic bean, which I will sell you for your holy cow, because I like your attitude."

"Gee, that's nice of you," Jack said naively.

The play took them through the exchange, and Jack went home to the box carrying the bean, which had appeared when the cow disappeared. He entered the box. "Mother, dearest, see what a good bargain I have made," he called from the box.

"A magic bean?" Gloha screeched in her best emulation of harpy mode, speaking for the unseen mother. "You %#¢*!! idiot!" She was rather proud of that word; it wasn't of full harpy cuss-quality, but it was within hailing distance of nasty. She took the bean and threw it back out onto the main stage.

"Jack's mother was not entirely pleased," the narrator said with fine understatement. "She threw the seed out the window, and Jack had to go to bed without his supper. However, it really was a magic bean, and in the night it sprouted and grew somewhat."

The bean sprouted on the stage, and grew rapidly into a giant green vine. That was Metria again, changing her shape. The vine grew up high, becoming as large as a tree, though somewhat more diffuse.

"In fact it grew right up to the clouds," Marrow said. The vine fogged, becoming a cloud that obscured the stage, giant and all. "And in the morning, when Jack saw that, he decided to see what he might find up in that cloud. So he climbed the beanstalk, and emerged on top of the cloud."

The cloud onstage cleared in one section, and there was Jack, just standing up, as if he had come up from below. He put up his hand to shade his eyes, as if looking around.

"And there on the cloud was a giant castle," Marrow narrated. More of the cloud thinned, to reveal an impromptu castle with walls made from wallflowers and a main turret formed by the box elder. Most of the structure was perched on Graeboe, as if he were the foundation. It was really fairly impressive, considering.

"So Jack went to the castle to see what he could find," Marrow said. Jack walked to it and pulled open a swinging wallflower to show the interior.

"Fortunately the giant was sleeping at the moment." And there was Graeboe's face before him, stretched out across several bedbug beds, snoring hugely.

Jack tiptoed around the sleeping face, and there on a pile of twenty feather quilts on the giant's hand sat Gloha, looking despondent.

"There in the giant castle he found the giant's captive, a princess," the narrator continued. "She was tied to her bed, and not at all happy about it."

"Who are you?" Jack asked.

"I am a captive princess," Gloha replied. "As you can tell by my fancy feather robe." She moved her wings a trifle.

"What's a nice princess like you doing in a place like this?"

"The giant wants to marry me, and of course I would rather be chopped up into little quivering pieces," she replied. "So he has tied me to this fiendishly uncomfortable bed." She gestured at the pile of quilts.

"But those look very soft," Jack protested.

"They are. But under them he put a bean. I might have tolerated half a pea, with an effort, but a whole magic bean was just too much. See, I'm all black-and-blue."

There was a snigger from the audience, because of course Gloha's natural body was goblin dark.

"But I outsmarted him, I think," she continued. "I managed to bounce around enough so that the bean rolled out, and fell to the ground below this cloud. So now I can sleep more comfortably. But of course I still groan every so often, so that the mean giant will think I'm still being tortured."

"So that was the bean I traded my holy cow for!" Jack exclaimed.

"Shhh! You'll wake the giant."

Indeed, the giant's face stirred and snorted. Both Jack and Princess were desperately quiet, and after a moment the snoring resumed.

"I must rescue you from this face, uh, fate," Jack said gallantly. "Let me untie you and take you home with me."

"Oh, you can't untie me," the princess said. "This is a magic cord." She lifted her wrist, showing the cord looped loosely around it. "Only the giant can untie it, and of course he won't, unless I agree to marry him."

"Then how can I rescue you?" Jack asked, perplexed.

"You must get the frog to help you."

"The frog?"

"The frog can fetch out a precious golden bottle that contains the only thing that the giant fears," she explained. "That's why he threw it in the cistern, thinking that nobody would ever find it there. But the frog knows."

Marrow stepped out again. "So Jack went to the rear of the castle," he announced while Jack did that, walking around to Graeboe's rear. "Where the frog lived in a deep cistern."

And there was a huge green frog: Metria in another role. "Croak?" the frog inquired.

"I need a precious golden bottle that lies in the bottom of the cistern," Jack said. "Because it contains the only thing that the giant fears. Can you fetch it out for me?"

"Certainly I can, manface," the frog agreed.

There was a pause. "Well?" Jack asked after a bit.

"Well, what?"

"Will you fetch out the bottle for me?"

"Oh, you asked only whether I could, not whether I would. Certainly I will, peasant man."

There was another pause. "Well?"

"You asked whether I would. You did not say whether you wished this."

Jack began to get impatient. "Listen, frogface—" Then he thought the better of it. "Yes, I wish this."

"That is good to know, mammal creature."

There was a pause. "Well, why don't you?" Jack asked.

"You did not say please."

"*Please* fetch out the bottle for me."

"What's in it for me, toothmouth?"

"Oh, you mean you want something in return?"

"Do I look like a charity outfit? Of course I want something in return!"

"What do you want?"

·"I want you to take me to your leader."

"Huh?"

"You're not the brightest character, are you?" the frog observed.

Jack, evidently somewhat nettled, nevertheless managed to remain mild. "Why do you want to go to my leader? I mean, I should think you'd prefer to remain in your nice chill puddle or something."

"You're a peasant, right? So your leader is a prince or king, right? I need to be kissed by one of those."

"Kissed by a prince? Why?"

"Because I am not an ordinary frog. I am an enchanted princess, doomed to remain a frog until kissed by a prince or king. If you were a prince, I'd have you kiss me. Since you're just a peasant, you're no good to me. But if you take me to your prince, he can kiss me. Then the enchantment will be broken, and I will return to my glorious natural form and can go home to my fabulous kingdom, okay?"

"Oh. I see. Okay, I'll take you with me. But it may be a while before I reach the king's castle."

"I'll wait," the frog said. Then she dived down to the bottom of the cistern and fetched up the golden bottle from where it sat at the edge of the stage.

Jack took it. Then he headed back to the castle.

"Hey, wait for me!" the frog cried. But he was already out of hearing.

He brought the bottle to the princess. "Now what?" he asked her. "I don't see anything in there."

"I don't know what's in it," she said. "Only that whatever it is, is what the giant fears."

There was a thumping at the wall-door. "Croak!"

"What's that?" the princess asked, alarmed.

"Oh, that's just the stupid frog wanting to come in."

"Why does it want to come in?"

"Because I told it I'd take it with me, so it could kiss a prince some day."

"Well, then, you made a deal, and you must honor it," the princess said sternly. "Let the frog in. Besides, it will wake the giant otherwise, with all that thumping." Indeed, one of the giant's eyelids quivered.

So Jack went out and let the frog in. It hopped up on the twenty-quilt bed. "Oh, this is comfy," it said. "But there's a discontinuity. There must have been a pea underneath, not long ago."

"There was a nasty old magic bean," the princess said. "How did you know?"

"I'm a princess. My skin is very sensitive. I felt the ripple left by that erstwhile bean."

"Oh, that explains it. Now what do we do with the bottle?"

"The peasant must take it to where the giant is sleeping, and open it. It contains a bad dream that will frighten him. He fears nothing in the world, but the dream realm is something else."

"So Jack took the bottle to the sleeping giant," the narrator said, as Jack did so. "He opened the bottle, and out poured a menacing vapor."

Indeed, the vapor swirled and thickened, then thinned to reveal—the narrator, in a pointed horror-hat. He did the "Danse Macabre," rattling his bones. "I am Death," the white skull said. "I have come to take you away with me, Giant!"

"Who?" the giant inquired blankly.

"Death. I was locked in that bottle, but now the deadlock has been unlocked and I am free to resume my business. When I take a dryad from her tree I leave only deadwood behind. Now I have come for you. So make yourself ready for your dead end."

"Oooh!" the giant groaned. Then he burst into tears. "Oh, I'm glad my mother the Queen of Giants can't see me now, bless her royal bones! All I wanted to do was make her happy by not marrying below my station, and now I'm going away with Death instead. Oh, woe is me!"

"He's a prince?" the princess and the frog asked together.

"So it seems," Jack said. "But don't worry. Death is reducing him to a quivering nonentity, and we shall soon be rid of him."

"Not so fast, Mack," the frog said.

"That's Jack."

"Not so fast, Jack. I want him to kiss me first."

"And I'm sorry we made him cry," the princess said. "I didn't know he was royal. Hey, Prince Giant! Would it make you feel better if I agreed to marry you after all?"

The giant woke. "Oh, yes," he agreed, immediately cheering up.

"But first kiss me," the frog said.

"Wait," the princess said. "If he kisses you, and you return to princessly format, he might want to marry you instead of me."

"Are you kidding?" the frog demanded. "I've got a princely boyfriend back home. My father doesn't like him, so he enchanted me to keep me from marrying my boyfriend. He figured my boyfriend would never find me and kiss me back to femininity before I got old and unattractive. Now we'll elope before my father catches on, and it'll be too late for any more enchantment."

"But I wanted to marry the princess," Jack protested.

Both princess and frog burst out laughing. "You? A peasant? Marry a princess? Just what fantasy world do you live in, Mack?" the frog asked.

"Well, I should have something for my trouble," Jack said, out of sorts.

"Oh, take a bag of money and get out of here," the giant said, tossing down a tiny bag that was nevertheless all Jack could carry.

Death doffed his hat, and the narrator donned his hat. "And so the giant kissed the frog," he said, as the giant did so, and the frog puffed into an extremely voluptuous princess with a remarkably low decolletage. "And then freed the other princess, and she kissed the giant," as Gloha flew up to perch on Graeboe's lower lip so as to kiss his upper lip. "And they married and lived happily almost ever after. Jack took his bag of gold home to his mother, who was fairly pleased, considering that it wasn't a bigger bag, and so were the village peasant girls, who suddenly discovered qualities in Jack they had somehow overlooked when he was poor. And Death, freed from imprisonment in the bottle, resumed business as usual, as many of you will discover in due course." He bowed to the audience. "We trust you have enjoyed our presentation," he concluded with a lipless grin.

The cynical Curse Fiends tried to retain their aloofness. Then it cracked. One of the members of the Black contingent started applauding, and then a few more. Gloha saw that the first one was Sherlock, whom she had met when riding on Swiftmud with Magician Trent's party. Others around him joined in, and finally some of the Curse Fiends. Not a majority, but a fair minority. She wondered whether Sherlock supported her because he recognized her and Trent, or because her goblin skin was as dark as his, or because he simply liked the play. She hoped it was the last reason.

Contumelo grimaced. "The applause meter said your effort qualifies, barely. We should be able to rewrite your play and make it into something presentable to ignorant children. You are free to go now."

"About time, curseface," the Frog Princess said.

Then Graeboe slowly heaved himself to a hunched sitting position, lifted up the edge of the dome, stood, and stepped out of the building. Gloha, Trent, and Marrow exited the arena in more conventional manner. Metria popped out of sight with a rude noise, leaving only a foul waft of smoke behind to annoy the Curse Fiends.

They saw the giant standing outside. He looked lonely. "What's the matter?" Gloha called to him.

"Well, I don't have anywhere to go," he replied. "Geographically or in life."

"Would you like to come along with us?" Gloha asked before she thought.

"Why, yes," he agreed. "I enjoyed our brief association, and would like to extend it. Perhaps I can be of some further service to you, before I expire."

"Fool!" Metria's voice came from the air beside her. "Your soft girlish human heart is going to get you into trouble sometime."

Gloha wasn't sure how they were going to manage with a sick giant along, but Graeboe was a nice person, so she didn't really regret her impulse. And it was possible that he would be able to help them out in some way, such as if they had to cross a mighty river, chasm, or desert.

Trent and Marrow didn't comment.

9
NYMPHO

They walked on along the invisible line Crombie had pointed out, southeast of Lake Ogre-Chobee. There were routine problems like rivers, dragons, cliffs, and unfriendly B's, but they were able to handle these with the giant's big hand and a little imagination.

Then as they were looking for a suitable place to camp for the night, where there was room for the giant to sleep, Gloha spied a creature flying in. For half an instant she was afraid it was a dragon or griffon, but then she saw that it was a crossbreed. It wasn't exactly a harpy, because the body was wrong, but it wasn't a griffon either. "Hey!" she called.

Startled, the creature hesitated. Then it flew away.

"Wait!" Gloha cried, flying after it. "I'm not an enemy! I'm a crossbreed. A winged monster. Like you."

The other creature paused, allowing Gloha to catch up. It turned out to be female. "Oh, so you are," she said. "I was afraid you were a man with a bow and arrow or something."

Gloha hovered near her. "No, I'm a unique creature. I think maybe you are too. What are you?"

"I'm half girl, half griffon. My name's Amanda." She blushed faintly. She seemed to be somewhat younger than Gloha. Her shoulder-length yellow hair was tied back with a blue ribbon that matched the hue of her wings. "My parents met at a love spring. They don't speak of it often."

Gloha appreciated that. "I'm Gloha Goblin-Harpy."

They shook hands, hovering.

"I'm looking for my species," Amanda said. "But I haven't found any others quite like me. I don't know what I should call myself."

"You look like a girlfon to me," Gloha said.

"A girlfon! That's perfect. Well, I had better get on home before Mom misses me."

"Bye," Gloha called as the girlfon flew away. She was somewhat sorry that it hadn't turned out to be a male winged goblin. Still, if there were a love spring nearby, there might be such a goblin. That could be why Crombie's finger had pointed this way. So maybe this was an encouraging sign.

She returned to their campsite. "It wasn't the one I was looking for," she said regretfully.

"Perhaps next time," Graeboe said. He was now sitting carefully beside their campsite. "You're such a nice girl, there must be a boy for you somewhere."

"Thank you," she said, flattered.

Trent had meanwhile transformed a small plant into a big tent caterpillar. The tent had room for himself, Gloha, Marrow, Metria, and the giant's face. The rest of Graeboe was covered by several other tents. Cushions from a transformed pillow bush served for their beds and Graeboe's head.

They feasted on berry pies, because pie plants were the easiest way for transformations to provide food. There were also pods of milk from milkweeds, and chocolate from a chocolate plant. Metria and Marrow did not need to eat, so contented themselves with exploring the surrounding region. Graeboe, oddly, did not eat any more than Trent did.

"Are you sure it's enough?" Gloha asked him, concerned.

"My illness diminishes my hunger," the giant replied. "Have no concern."

"But I *am* concerned. You can't do giantly things if you don't eat like a giant."

"True. I am weak and worsening. I know I am not the best of company. I appreciate your willingness to have me with your party. This gives me some valued solace."

"Don't you know anything about your malady? Maybe you could find a cure, if you had a name for it."

"I know only that it is a disease of the blood. My body does not make blood quite the way it should. As a result, I have less and less of it, and that makes me weaker each day. I would have trouble keeping up, were you folk not so much smaller than I am."

"Maybe Magician Trent could transform you to some other form, that doesn't need as much blood," she suggested.

"That would not help," Trent said. "That form would have the same illness. I can change folk's forms, but can't heal them."

"Maybe if we found a bloodroot—"

"No," Graeboe said gently. "My body can use only the blood it makes itself. It comes from my bones. But please do not dismay yourself on my account; I have no wish to cause you any discomfort, lovely little creature."

Gloha was flattered again. She wasn't at all sure she deserved the good opinion the giant had of her. Probably he was merely thankful for someone to talk to. "The Good Magician must have had reason to send you to this region, just as he indirectly sent me here. Maybe there are answers for both of us, just a little farther along."

"It is nice to think so," he agreed wanly.

Then Marrow and Metria returned. "What's this?" the demoness exclaimed. "Making out in a tent?"

"What passes for your mind is in a rut," Trent informed her. "Graeboe and Gloha have merely been talking."

"Then we were doing better than you," Metria retorted.

Gloha knew that this was supposed to arouse her curiosity and force her to inquire. She stifled it as long as she could, but it was too much for her to contain. "What were you doing?" she asked.

The demoness looked at her triumphantly. "I thought you'd never ask! We were summoning the stork."

Gloha, Trent, and Graeboe choked, almost together. "But—" Gloha managed to speak.

"She kissed me," Marrow explained. "That is not quite the same."

"It's close enough," Metria said stoutly.

"Walking skeletons do not summon the stork," Marrow said. "We assemble our little ones from spare bones. But in any event, I would not choose to summon or construct with a demoness. I am a married skeleton."

"Oh, pooh!" Metria said. "What's so special about marriage? The stork listens regardless."

"You are a demoness," Trent reminded her. "You have no soul, and therefore no conscience. You can't love. You have no basis for understanding."

"But I'd like to understand," Metria said, frustrated.

"Why?" Gloha asked, curious.

"In the Madness Region I was Trent's wife, for a time," the demoness said. "There was something there. It seemed interesting. I don't like missing out on anything interesting. I want to know what love is."

Graeboe shook his head slightly; any greater motion would have knocked down the tent. "I would like to know what love is too. Possession of a soul does not guarantee love."

"That's right," Gloha agreed. "I have never known stork-variety love."

"Because you're the only one of your type," Metria said. "When you find a winged goblin man, you'll get into stork language quickly enough."

"To answer your question," Trent said, "marriage is, to those with souls, a sacred contract. The parties to it agree to love only each other, and to summon the stork with no other people. It is possible to summon the stork outside of marriage, but this is generally frowned on. You, as a demoness, can assume any form you wish. You can go through the motions, of summoning the stork, simply by showing some naive man your panties and encouraging him to proceed. But that isn't marriage or love."

"Maybe if I married someone, I'd find out about love," she said.

"I doubt it. You could go through the ceremony, but it wouldn't mean anything to you. The only demoness I know of who was able to love was Dara, who married Magician Humfrey a long time ago. But she had a soul. As soon as she lost her soul, she reverted to form and left him in the lurch."

"But she came back," Metria said.

"A hundred and thirty-six years later," he reminded her. "Because she was bored. She doesn't actually love him now. She merely emulates the mood. However, you might ask her what it was like when she did love him."

"I have. She said I would never understand."

"So there you are. Maybe you should give it up, Metria, and let us proceed on our various quests without your kibitzing."

"No, I want to know what love is. You're my closest approach. Maybe if I watch you close enough, I'll learn."

"Not by trying to seduce married skeletons," he said.

Metria pondered briefly. Then her clothing began to fuzz away.

"Or married Magicians," Trent added, closing his eyes.

"Curses! Foiled again," the demoness muttered, dissolving into smoke.

Gloha closed her own eyes. She had a certain sympathy with Metria's frustration. It was not too far from her own.

In the morning they moved on. Gloha wasn't sure whether it was her imagination, but she had the impression that Graeboe Giant was weaker. It took him some time to get to his feet, and then he seemed unsteady. But it might simply be that he was always a bit fuzzy in the morning. So she flew up to inquire.

"Graeboe, are you all right?" she asked as she landed on his shoulder near his face. "I mean, apart from your malady?"

"Please do not concern yourself, pretty thing," he replied.

"Now stop that!" she said with an annoyed little irritation. "You did it last night. You think that because I'm so small, I must be childlike, and you're patronizing me. I *am* concerned."

"Oh, no, Gloha," he protested. "I don't see you as a child at all. You're a lovely person, in body and mind. I merely do not wish to burden you with any problem of mine."

"Well, tell me anyway," she said, mollified.

He sighed. "I am weaker each day. I think I shall be able to keep on my feet only a few more days. When I fear I will not be able to get up again, I shall make my way to some desolate wilderness and there expire, as I have said."

"But you're supposed to find help here, and it must be us who can help you, somehow. You can't just give up."

"Perhaps so," he agreed, not debating the matter.

"It *must* be so," she said firmly. She walked along his shoulder, came to his giant ear, spread her wings, and flew up to kiss his earlobe. Then she flew back down to ground level.

They proceeded southeast in their assorted fashions. Graeboe took huge slow steps, setting his feet down carefully so as not to crush any houses or trees. Metria smoked out at one place and smoked in again at another. Gloha made short flights. Trent and Marrow simply walked. No more monsters bothered them, perhaps having caught on that a party including a giant and a Magician made poor prospects for prey.

Then they came to the Faun & Nymph Retreat. They could tell, because there was a sign by the path saying that. It turned out to be a small mountain by a lake, where the fauns and nymphs cavorted happily all day long. The fauns were human in form except for their cute little horns and goat's feet, while the nymphs were completely human except for their attitude: when chased, they screamed fetchingly, kicked their feet, and flung their hair about. When caught, they—

Gloha looked around, nervous that children might be in the vicinity. Fortunately there were none, so no violation of the Adult Conspiracy to Keep Children Ignorant of Interesting Things was occurring. She understood that Princess Ida had grown up in this general vicinity, but she had been too innocent to know that she wasn't supposed to see such activity. Because what they were doing was stork summoning, constantly. The odd thing was that the storks seldom if ever responded to these constant signals. Maybe they knew that fauns and nymphs could not raise children, because they didn't have families. They were unable to remember anything overnight, so no enduring relationships existed.

"I wonder where new fauns and nymphs come from?" Gloha said musingly as they watched the activity of the Retreat. "I mean, if the storks don't come here—"

"They are immortal, I believe," Trent replied. "At least until some few of them become mortal. Remember, Jewel the Nymph didn't begin to age until she fell in love and married."

"Jewel was always a special nymph," Gloha said. "She put the gemstones in the ground for prospectors to find. She had a soul. I think she was able to remember things even before she married."

"Yes, she was special. She may have been on the way to womanhood, which was why she was capable of love. Now that she's retiring, a new nymph from this region is being trained to do the job, and no doubt she is starting to remember things too. But here they have no need for memory. It may be that any who leave the Retreat start to assume normal human qualities."

Marrow was tilting his skull, looking here and there. Metria noticed this. "You are interested in peeking at stork summoning?" she inquired snidely.

"No, I think for them that is mere entertainment," the skeleton replied. "What concerns me is the apparent imbalance in the numbers."

Now the others were curious. "Imbalance?" Gloha asked. "It looks to me as if they are doing it in the usual ratio: one faun to one nymph at a time."

"But see how many fauns are left over," Marrow said. "In fact lines of fauns are forming near each nymph. I had understood that the numbers were supposed to be approximately equal. That seems not to be the case."

He was right. There were about three times as many fauns as nymphs. As a result, the nymphs were considerably busier than the fauns. That did not seem to bother the nymphs, but the fauns seemed to be somewhat unfaunly out of sorts. It was evident that each would really have preferred to have one or more nymphs to himself.

"Perhaps we should inquire," Trent said with a third of a smile.

So Gloha stepped up to the nearest faun. "Why aren't there as many nymphs as fauns here?"

He looked at her. "A tiny winged clothed nymph!" he exclaimed. "I didn't know you existed. Come play with me!" He reached for her.

Marrow extended a bone-arm to block the faun. "This is not a nymph," he said. "Merely a foreign visitor. Answer her question."

"Oh." The faun stifled his disappointment. "I don't know why there aren't enough nymphs. There just aren't, is all." He ran off in pursuit of a nymph who was momentarily free.

"That, of course, is the problem," Trent remarked. "They don't remember. Something must have happened to a number of the nymphs."

"A dragon ate them?" Gloha asked, horrified.

"Dragons and other predators are impartial about the sex of their prey," Trent said thoughtfully. "They should take out about as many fauns as nymphs. There must be some other explanation."

"Men, maybe," Metria said. "Human men really like nymphs, I understand, while human women don't care as much for fauns."

"True," Trent agreed. "But human men are discouraged from raiding this Retreat."

"Oh?" Gloha asked. "How? I don't see any discouragement."

"Do you see that bed in the center of the Retreat?" Trent asked her.

"Yes, but no one's on it."

"It's what's under it that counts. Snortimer is there, I believe."

"Who?"

"Snortimer. My granddaughter Ivy's monster under the bed. He took the place of Stanley Steamer Dragon, protecting the fauns and nymphs. He can't leave the bed by day, of course, but any intruding men soon try to lie on it with a nymph or two, and that's when Snortimer grabs their ankles and scares them away."

"But adults don't believe in monsters under the bed," Gloha protested.

"They do when Snortimer grabs them," he replied. "This region is special, as the presence of the fauns and nymphs suggests. They have no trouble believing in him, being childlike. With so many believing in him, he has much more power than his kind usually does. Also, Ivy Enhanced him before she left, so he's unusual. I understand he does an excellent job."

"I find this hard to believe," Gloha said, shaking her head.

"Naturally, because you're an adult. Only children and old folk about to fade out recognize the validity of monsters under beds."

"I recognize it," Marrow said.

"So do I," Metria said.

"You folk are from the dream and demon realms; you don't count."

"I recognize it," Graeboe said, squatting down to join the conversation.

"Giants don't count either," Trent said with a good two-thirds of a smile. "Only normal run-of-the-mill close-to-human folk count in this respect. And I think you, Gloha, will be able to believe, if you make the effort, because you aren't exactly of that description."

Gloha made the effort. "Maybe, around the edges, I can believe," she said.

"But we must proceed to more serious concerns," Trent continued. "This Retreat is on the line we are following, which suggests that this could be where we shall find the solutions to one or more of our problems. We should explore it carefully before going beyond. I believe there are mainly the Ever Glades farther in the direction we are going, which we would prefer not to face if we don't have to."

Gloha had heard of the Ever Glades, which went on forever and ever. She hoped they would not have to go there. "I don't think I'm likely to find a suitable man here, and I don't think the fauns and nymphs have souls to share with anyone. I don't see anything to help Graeboe either." In fact she was feeling a tiny little tad discouraged.

"The ways of magic can be strange," Trent said. "We shall just have to explore this until we are certain that our answers aren't here."

He was making sense, which was the problem. Gloha wasn't eager to remain in this region of constant dubious activity. The male members of the party seemed to find it interesting, which also bothered her on some hidden level.

"Let's camp out of sight of the Retreat," Metria suggested.

At times Gloha could almost think of beginning to start to like the demoness. "Yes, let's," she agreed.

"As you wish," Trent said with the suggestion of a significant fraction of a smile.

So they camped by a stream that was hurrying to find the lake, and set up with tents and pies and such. There was still time in the day, so they explored the vicinity, especially along the invisible line that Crombie had pointed out. Graeboe stood and looked far in all directions, but spied nothing special. Metria puffed in and out to all intermediate directions, but also spied nothing special. Marrow walked fearlessly in all near directions, spooking stray plants and creatures, but he too spied nothing special. Trent lay back on a bedbug and pondered.

"What are you pondering?" Gloha inquired.

"I am trying to decide whether the mystery of the missing nymphs bears any relation to our several quests."

"How could it?" she asked listlessly.

"That is a mystery in itself. But suppose that whatever is causing the loss of nymphs also represents the solution to our problems? What do you suppose that might be?"

She focused her alert little attention on the question. "Something with half a soul to give Marrow, and a cure to give Graeboe, and an ideal man to give me."

"Something about that last bothers me," Trent said. "Suppose we do find a winged goblin male. How can you be sure that he will be your ideal partner?"

"Why," she said, flustered, "he would have to be, wouldn't he? The only other member of my crossbreed species."

"Yet I have encountered very few goblin males whom I would care to know."·

A goblin male. Gloha felt a pang of apprehension. The average goblin male was ugly, brutish, bad-tempered, violent, and somewhat stupid. Much like the average harpy female. Why should a winged one be any better? And why should she ever want to marry such a man?

"Oh," she said, distraught. "I've been seeking a fantasy!"

"Not necessarily," the Magician said. "It just may mean that the answer to your quest is not precisely what you have supposed. Perhaps it is not a winged goblin you seek, but self-discovery."

"I don't understand that at all!" she cried, and ran out of the tent. She knew that she couldn't actually run physically away from the truth, but she needed time to figure things out for herself.

She found herself walking toward the Retreat. But as she did she couldn't stop herself from mulling it over. What did she want? A nice, handsome, intelligent, thoughtful, considerate, loving, winged goblin man. And no goblin man was like that. Why should a winged one be any different? She was a fool to suppose that such an ideal man existed or could ever exist.

Yet Crombie had pointed out a direction. That suggested that there *was* such a man. How could that be reconciled?

She shook her perplexed little perception, wishing she could find an answer where she feared there was none. So Magician Trent thought she needed self-discovery. But she was satisfied with herself; it was her prospects that needed fixing. Didn't Trent know that? What good was self-discovery if she had to spend the rest of her lamentable little life alone? She'd much rather spend it with someone like Trent himself. He answered all of the description except for his size and lack of wings.

She spied something ahead, lying on the ground near the edge of the open region that was the Retreat. It looked like a piece of popcorn, but it was the wrong color. Popcorn was supposed to be buttery yellow, or caramel tan. This was bright red.

She came up to it and picked it up. It certainly looked like popped corn. She put it to her nose. It smelled like popcorn. She tasted it. It *was* popcorn.

She looked around. She spied another piece, right at the edge of the faun/nymph glade. This one was blue. She picked it up and ate it too. It was definitely popcorn, and very good. If she closed her eyes, she would not be able to tell what color it was; it tasted exactly like regular-colored popcorn, freshly made.

Now she stood at the edge of the Retreat. The fauns and nymphs were still at it, chasing each other down and striving enthusiastically to summon every stork in Xanth. Odd that they hadn't caught on that it wasn't working. But of course it took time for the stork to make a delivery, and these creatures remembered only the day they were in, so never learned better. That explained that, but didn't explain why so many nymphs were missing. Trent thought that mystery might be related to Gloha's quest for the ideal man. How could it? Maybe Trent's real age was making him senile, despite his greatly youthened body.

There were no more colored popcorns. Too bad; they had been delicious, as well as diverting her briefly from her private concerns.

She turned, about to go back to the camp. Then she saw another popcorn, this time a green one. And beyond it, a purple one. There was actually a trail of them; she had intersected it at an angle, so had seen only the last two.

She went to pick up and eat the green and purple pops, finding them as delicious as the first two. Then she followed the trail along the divergent path through the forest. How had these brightly colored morsels come here? Had someone been carrying a bag of them, and some had spilled out, leaving a trail? If so, she should catch up and tell that person to close up the hole before he lost the whole bagful.

She passed under a hugely spreading acorn tree, intent on the continuing trail. Suddenly a net dropped over her. She was so surprised she forgot even to scream. She just stood there stupidly wondering what had happened. Then she tried to spread her wings to fly away, but of course they were fouled in the net.

An ugly man dropped down beside her. He reached for her. His hands were huge and gnarled.

Now she remembered to scream. She inhaled, opening her mouth. "Ee—"

He clapped a hand over her mouth, stifling her scream before more than two *e*'s were out. Then he wrapped a bandanna around her face, covering her mouth so she couldn't get out any more of her scream. He picked her up, still swathed in the net, and carried her away.

Belatedly, Gloha realized how stupid she had been. She had wandered away from her companions, and foolishly followed a trail of popcorns, until she was well away from camp. Now she was the captive of some brutish man, and whatever was to become of her?

Meanwhile the man was tramping along a path of his own. It led to a dirty pond, and in the pond was a dusky island, and on the island was a battered old castle. The man got into a sodden boat, dumped her down, and paddled across to the castle. When he reached the island he hefted her up again, and carried her to the great dark wooden door. He hauled out a big metal key, put it in the keyhole, turned it, and then pulled the door open. He entered, then paused to close and lock the door behind him.

He carried her down a dark passage to a central chamber. She heard a faint whimpering. Then she saw where it came from: a small barred cell they were passing. There was a nymph in it, looking unnymphly unhappy. No wonder; nymphs lived to cavort in the open with the others of their kind. They couldn't stand being alone in a closed cell.

Now she realized that there were other cells along the way, containing other nymphs. She was beginning to understand where the nymphs had gone. They had followed trails of colored popcorn, and been netted and nymph-napped and brought here. Just as Gloha herself had been.

He set her down before an altar and drew off the net. Gloha immediately spread her wings and flew up out of his reach.

"Hey, you aren't supposed to do that," the man protested.

"You abducted me against my will and hauled me in here and you say I can't fly away from you?" she demanded, a taut little tinge of outrage coloring her fear.

"That doesn't matter. You're supposed to marry me."

Gloha had been opening her maidenly little mouth for a paragraph of protests, but his last two words sidetracked that. "*Marry* you?" she squeaked.

"Yes. Let's get on with it. Stand before the altar and say, 'I, so and so, hereby take you, Veleno, to be my husband, by the law of the Notar Republic.' I will say much the same, taking you as my wife. Then we'll go to the bedroom for the consummation." He glanced at her. "You're somewhat small, but I can live with that."

Gloha's mouthful got sidetracked again. "Just like that?" was all she could get out.

"It's very efficient," he agreed.

"I'm getting out of here," she said. She flew to the hall, and down it to the front door. But the door was still locked, and it was far too massive for her to open even if it had been unlocked. There seemed to be no windows on this level, and the stairs were closed off by other locked doors. She was trapped in the castle.

She looked at the cells along the hall. Most contained dejected nymphs. She knew better than to ask any of them about anything; they would have no memory of their abductions or of the layout of the castle. But she was getting the picture on her own, and it was so unpretty that her pretty little perspective could hardly compass it.

She flew back to the main chamber, because there was more room there. "You're a nymphomaniac!" she cried accusingly at Veleno. "You're obsessed with nymphs!"

"Well sure," he agreed. "That's all I can find here. But I never saw a winged nymph before. And you're smaller than the others, and you have clothing. Why is that?"

"Because I'm *not* a nymph," she said. "I'm a winged goblin-harpy crossbreed. I have better things to do than run around naked all day screaming, kicking my feet, and flinging my hair around."

"Oh? What things?"

"Like searching for my ideal man to marry."

"No problem. You'll marry me."

"Marry you! You insufferable—" Gloha discovered that she lacked the appropriate vocabulary. She really should have heeded her aunt's advice and learned to speak the burning word. So she settled for a succinct substitute. "No."

"No?" he asked, surprised. "Why not?"

"Because I don't know you, don't love you, and don't think you're anyone's ideal man, certainly not mine." Even without proper harpy vocabulary, that seemed to cover the situation.

Meanwhile he was picking up on her prior statement. "You're not a nymph!" he said, excited. "You can remember from day to day."

"I certainly can," she agreed angrily. "And I don't think I'll ever forget how you kidnapped me."

"So you're definitely the one I must marry."

This was getting to be a bit much for her. "Huh?" she inquired intelligently.

"I need to marry a girl who can remember she's married."

"Well, I'm not the one," she said with a certain firm little firmness. "Now let me go before my friends come to rescue me, or you'll be in trouble."

"You have friends?" he asked, surprised again.

"Of course I do!" she said indignantly. "Don't you?"

"No."

This put her offtrack yet again. "What, none?"

"No, none."

She couldn't believe it. "What, none?" she repeated.

"Well, once I had a pet poison toad, but I don't think he counts, because he hopped away once he got to know me."

She was beginning to realize that this was not an ordinary evil abductor. There were complications. "How did you come here to this castle?" she inquired. Maybe some background would help.

"That's a brief and dull story," he said. "Now why don't you come down here and marry me, so we can get on with the consummation."

"I'm not going to marry you, let alone consum—" But her nervous little nature would not allow her to say such a suggestive word. "Anyway, what makes you think you can just grab a girl and marry her?"

"That's what I've been doing. Each day I net a new nymph, and marry her, and consummate it, and next morning she doesn't remember. Then I have to start all over with another nymph. It's very frustrating."

"Well, let's hear your brief dull story," she said. If he was willing to be distracted from his disastrous ambition, she was willing to encourage him in that. "And be sure to include how you got this castle and why you call it a republic and why you're marrying anyone. Meanwhile I'll just stay well out of your reach, if you don't mind."

"I don't mind," he said. "It's nice to have some halfway intelligent dialogue for a change."

If all he had had to converse with was nymphs, whose minds were pretty much mindless, on the theory that no creature with a nymphly body needed a mind, then he might indeed miss the dialogue of a real person. Gloha settled down to the floor behind a chair, ready to fly instantly away if he tried to get near enough to grab her again. Meanwhile she listened to his history.

Once upon a thyme in the mists of antiquity—maybe thirty years ago—there lived an old crone. She was a weaver, and worked hard at her trade from morning till night to earn a living for herself and her innocent young daughter. She scarcely gave herself and her child a chance to rest. However, as busy and industrious as this crone was, she loved her daughter, and took time one day to give her good advice.

"Heather, my dear daughter, when the time of Rut comes over a young man, there is a failure on his part to act in a Timely and Responsive manner. Do you understand?"

"No, Mother dear," innocent Heather replied, exactly as a good girl should.

"No? Look, such a young man is so Hot to Trot that even the village sheep aren't safe. Do you understand now?"

"No, Mother dear," Heather said, embarrassed because she didn't like perplexing her mother.

"No? Well, do you have any notion of how to summon the stork?"

"No, Mother Dear," Heather said. "That's in the Adult Conspiracy, so naturally I never heard of the stork. Why are you telling me this?"

"Because once I was as ignorant as you, and that's how I came to summon the stork that brought you, Daughter dear. I don't want you to make the same mistakes."

"But how could you summon the stork, if you didn't know how, Mother dear?" Heather asked, doubly perplexed. "I can't do anything I don't know how to do."

"By the ogres and night mares of Xanth, Heather—just say No!!"

Heather was really impressed, because she had never heard a double exclamation point before. She took the lesson to heart, and saved up her very most positive No for the occasion when she should encounter a young man being Untimely and Unresponsive, or mistreating sheep.

However, as she became a teenager she became aware of certain social proprieties. She saw that her mother wore work clothes all the time, and labored with her hands, which were callused and gnarled, and she became ashamed of the old crone. So she did what any teen in such an insufferable situation did. She screamed at her mother, called her vile names like "Hag," "Witch," and "Harridan," in fact everything except the accurate term of "Crone," and to really make her point she ran away with Shadows, the village idiot. This man did not know the meaning of Timely or Responsive, and he was unconscionably mean to sheep, shearing them every spring, so this really broke the old crone's heart.

Naturally the idiot knew nothing of stork summoning either. So the two of them just had a good time. But by some curious coincidence a stork got the notion that this couple deserved a baby. This was obviously a confusion, because Heather, who had once had a figure reminiscent of a minute glass, seemed to be adding sand. She got fatter daily, and hardly seemed to be in shape to handle a baby. In any event she didn't know about the stork's notion. For a long while she pretended that she had no appetite, and she ate no food other than a few black and blue berries stolen from neighboring gardens, and some cookies. She said that these were nicer and tasted better than her mother's good soups and stews and homemade peasant bread. Shadows made her several gunky yellow banana slug stews, but they just caused her to toss her cookies. He resented this, because he didn't like seeing the cookies get wasted. That showed what an idiot he was, she reminded him frequently.

Finally there came a day when Heather was as displeased with Shadows as she had been with her cronish mother. As she lay in the dark one night, cold and hungry, her impatience with her situation boiled over in a chilly way.

"Well, I've done more than enough suffering for humanity in the last nine months. I want my mother, even if she is a crone. If that idiot Shadows doesn't like it, he can go jump in the Kiss-Mee Lake with some other damsel." Because she realized now that her health had started its reversal soon after the two of them had swum in Lake Kiss-Mee and in consequence done a whole lot of kissing. Maybe the water was also fattening.

So one fine morning a not-so-fine Heather left the idiot's sandy driftwood hut and walked home, leaving her accumulation of self-pity behind. She found her mother, the village midwife, and the stork standing at the front door, wringing their hands or whatever. They wept when they saw her.

"Why are you so sad to see me?" Heather asked as she pushed impatiently over to her dear little clean lavender-smelling bed. "Didn't you say I'd be back?"

It turned out that they weren't sad, they were glad, though their emotions seemed to be stuck in reverse. The stork was especially relieved, having feared it had come to the wrong address. It dumped a baby boy in the cradle and took off. In its haste it dropped a thyme seed that had been intended for another delivery. The seed landed in the garden, and from it grew a first plant which didn't do well, and a second plant, which in the course of sixty seconds became a minute plant, and in sixty minutes became an hour plant, and in a year it was an annual, and it continued to age with the obvious intention of finally maturing into a century plant. Since that would take some time, it had a brilliant crystal on top to mark its place in space-time. The crone ignored it, being too busy, thinking it didn't matter. She probably shouldn't have done that.

After seven days the village elders came to participate in the baby's naming ceremony. Heather named him Veleno, which she understood meant Poisoned Gift. The elders sprinkled Heather with rainbow rose water and declared that, in the light of recent events, she was no longer a child but an adult.

Immediately the weight of adult responsibility descended on her. She realized how she had summoned the stork during that time when she had done just a smidgen more than kissing. She was properly appalled, and resolved never to do that again. Heather joined her mother at the loom, never to leave it for the rest of her life, and concentrated on becoming a crone herself. From then on the little stone dwelling was known as "The House of Two Weavers."

Seven or eight years crawled by, and the baby boy managed to become a boy child. He was quiet, a loner, and he displayed his magic talent early. He changed plain white popcorn into rainbow-colored popcorn. This followed naturally from his mother's talent of changing plain white roses into rainbow-colored roses. She didn't use her talent much, because she seldom encountered a white rose, but at least she had the magic. No one ever found out what talent Veleno's father had, other than idiocy; Veleno never met the man.

Veleno's small world embraced his mother, grandmother, and the nearer region of his village. One day he woke from his midday summer nap under his favorite fringed umbrella tree, took a dip in the conservative gold-water pool to the right of the village, dressed himself in his cool white well-worn cotton clothes, and headed for home. But he found everybody in great disarray standing around the village fountain. They were screaming, tearing their hair, wringing their hands, and weeping bitterly.

"What's the matter?" he asked in a faltering whisper, fearing that something was amiss. After all, it wasn't comfortable to have one's hair torn, and was painful to put one's hands through the wringer, which tended to flatten them.

"A dreadful fiery dragon is approaching the village," a man with golden orange hair replied. His name was Menthol, but that had no significance and probably shouldn't have been mentioned. "It seems that nothing can stop it from massacring everyone here."

"But why are they so upset?" the boy asked, perplexed.

The man studied the boy for a moment. Then he nodded, as if coming to a private decision. "What is your name, little boy?"

"Veleno."

"What a nice name. What does it mean?"

"Poisoned Gift."

Menthol nodded again, as if he had just confirmed a suspicion. "Ah. Does an eight-year-young century plant grow in your yard, by any chance, helping your family keep thyme?"

"Yes."

"Well, Veleno, your mother doesn't want you right now. In fact she wants you to take a walk with me. Do everything I tell you to do, and I will give you a whole bowl full of boiled sweets."

"Great!" Veleno agreed.

So Menthol took Veleno by the hand and led him away. As it just coincidentally happened, Menthol was a child stealer. He recognized Veleno as a child marked by the demons for their eventual entertainment, so he brought him to the demons for a reward.

"And so the demons put me in this isolated castle," Veleno concluded. "And told me that I would have my every desire in life supplied except one: love. I can achieve that only by marrying a woman who will marry me and share her

love with me. What they didn't tell me was that the only human-seeming females in reach would be nymphs. They are incapable of love, and can't remember anything from one day to the next. But the demons did mention that
hidden among them might be one who could remember and love. So from the
time I grew old enough to join the Adult Conspiracy I have used my colored
popcorn to lure one nymph at a time away from the mountain. I have married
her and tried to summon the stork with her, hoping that she will remember in
the morning. But so far every nymph has forgotten, though she has been enthusiastically cooperative in making the effort to signal the stork. Thus our
marriage has been dissolved, and I have had to try again."

"But why do you keep them prisoner in the castle?" Gloha asked. "They
are naturally careless creatures, but they can not be happy in confinement."

"Because I can't tell one nymph from another. If I let them go after marrying them, I might catch the same one again, wasting my time. The only way I
can be sure each one is new is by holding the old ones out from the group."

It was starting to make sense. But Gloha still didn't like it. "Well, I'm not
going to marry you, and I shall be neither enthusiastic nor cooperative about—
about whatever. And I will never love you. No, not in the time it takes that century plant to mature. So you might as well let me go."

"Oh, no, I have to marry you, because you can remember. You are the one
who can love me, and with whom I can at last experience love. Then I will be
free of the demons' enchantment, and can live like a normal man."

Veleno did not seem to be paying very close attention to her declaration.
Was there some other way to discourage him? Gloha remembered something
about demons. "Are they watching this?"

"Oh, yes, of course. It's how they entertain themselves. But if I find love,
they'll know it immediately, and their amusement will be over. They'll dissolve this castle into smoke, and I will return with my bride to my village,
where we can live ever after as peasants scrounging a mean living from the reluctant soil."

"That's certainly a modest ambition," Gloha said. "And I wish you well
with it. But it isn't going to be with me. I am not going to marry you, and that's
that."

"Then I shall have to lock you in a chamber until you change your mind,"
Veleno said. "Because you may be my only chance for love, and I would be a
fool to let you escape."

Gloha realized that the man was not going to be reasonable about this. So
she flew away, seeking some other exit from the castle. She found a stairway
that wasn't closed off and flew upstairs, but all the windows were barred, and

most of the chambers were locked, with whimpering nude nymphs inside. Escape seemed to be hopeless.

Then she spied one dark passage she had missed in her prior haste. It was low and narrow, so she had to come to the floor and walk along it. It led to a winding stairway leading up. A secret exit to the roof?

She came to a small door. She tugged at its handle, and because it was small she was able to move it. Beyond was a closed little chamber with several barred windows. This must be the castle's highest turret, from which there was no exterior way down. The kind used to imprison reluctant damsels. But if she could get one of those windows open, or pry out a bar, she could leap from the window. She wouldn't fall to her death; she would merely fly away. The builders of this castle hadn't reckoned with a winged goblin girl.

She entered the chamber, crossed to the far window, and peered out. She was right: this was way high up in the sky, with glorious naked air all around. She took hold of a bar. It rattled—and there was a curious little click behind her. She turned nervously, and saw that the door had swung itself closed. Alarmed, she ran back to the door, to make sure it hadn't locked—and found that it had. It absolutely would not budge. She was trapped.

And she heard Veleno's footsteps climbing the stair. The nymphomaniac was coming for her, and he thought her to be a satisfactory substitute nymph.

What could she do? She did it. She put her frantic little face to the window and let out Xanth's most strident little scream.

10
GRAEBOE

Graeboe's giant ears perked. That was a faint distant scream! Could it be Gloha?

He peered in that direction, but all he saw was forested mountains. If Gloha was there, she would have to scream repeatedly before he would be able to find her.

He squatted, carefully, so that in his weakness he wouldn't lose his balance, fall over, and crush a fair section of forest and maybe a friend or two. He put his face near the tent. "I heard a scream."

The Demoness Metria popped into smoky solidity just under his nose. "You did? Where?"

"North of Nymph Mountain. All I saw was mountains and trees."

She faded out. In a moment she was back. "I have told Trent and Marrow. They'll hurry here. Can you carry them to that region?"

"Yes, I still have strength enough for that, I think."

"Meanwhile, stand up and show me exactly where it came from. Maybe I can investigate first."

Graeboe stood, unsteadily, breathing deeply to ease the dizziness he felt as his body straightened. He was a poor shadow of a giant! Then he pointed toward the mountains. "But it was faint, and I can't be sure it was Gloha," he cautioned her. "All maidenly screams sound alike to me."

"That's why I'm checking," she said, and with a *Zzzrrpp!* she was gone.

He slowly squatted again. Soon the Magician and the skeleton arrived. He repeated his news to them.

"Take us there," Trent said.

Graeboe opened his left hand and laid it palm-up on the ground. Trent and Marrow climbed on. Graeboe lifted them up to head height, then tramped delicately toward the mountains.

They had been at first perplexed, then alarmed at Gloha's disappearance. She had been right there, walking on the path to the Retreat, and then she hadn't returned. Trent had been the first one to be concerned, because it was his job to see that no harm came to the cute little creature. She might have taken a side path to address a call of nature, so they did not rush to seek her, but when time passed they realized that something was wrong. She was definitely gone.

She hadn't been caught by a tangle tree, because they had zeroed in all such threats in the vicinity, and Gloha knew better than to go near any. The same was true for dragons and other land monsters. Gloha didn't have to worry about winged monsters, being one herself. Graeboe had to smile at that; the girl was completely unconcerned about the term, not considering it to be anything other than a description. Trent was a human man, Graeboe was a human giant, Marrow Bones was a walking skeleton, Metria was a demoness, and Gloha was a winged monster. Such lack of affectation was one of her many endearing qualities. She was also pretty, nice, sensible, and caring. The man she finally found would be extremely fortunate.

He remembered how she had kissed him, in the play they had put on for the Curse Fiends. The notion of a tiny princess marrying a giant was ludicrous, but the play had been for entertainment rather than realism. For the finale she had walked up to his face and planted a delicious little kiss somewhere on his upper lip. There had been a laugh from the audience, but he had really liked that kiss.

In fact he really liked Gloha, and would be devastated if anything untoward happened to her. He would do everything he could to rescue her if she were in some dire strait. But first they had to find her. He tried to suppress the thought that it might be too late to help her. He had to hope that that scant little scream was hers, so that they could save her from whatever pit she had fallen into.

Metria reappeared, floating in front of him. "I assumed smoke form and drifted through the woods," she reported. "I found a few straight goblins, but no winged ones. I don't think she's there."

"We'll just have to hope she screams again," Trent said.

"If that really was her scream," the demoness said with demonly logic. "If the giant wasn't just imagining it."

"It is our best lead at the moment," Trent replied, seeming unconcerned. But Graeboe had come to realize that when the Magician seemed least affected, he was controlling his reactions. If someone assumed that this mild-mannered man was to be ignored or shoved aside, that person was likely to find himself transformed into a stink horn. The Magician was actually a very old man, youthened for this quest, and he had the experience and control of age. Graeboe respected him.

Graeboe came to stand beside the mountains. They were only a bit taller than he was, but they were more massive. He looked down at the carpet of forest covering them. It was quiet. Had he been mistaken about the direction of the scream? *Had* he imagined it? Could he have led Gloha's friends to the wrong place, while she was in some awful trouble elsewhere? He would never forgive himself, if—

The scream came again. This time they all heard it. It was from beyond the mountains, in the same direction they had been going.

"Score one for giantly imagination," Marrow remarked. The skeleton, too, was a good person, and Graeboe hoped he was successful in his quest for half a soul. Graeboe had a notion about that, because he knew of a soul that would before long become available. But right now was not the time to discuss that. Gloha was the immediate concern.

He looked for bare sections on the mountains, so he could climb over them. Slowly he stepped up, his head rising above the peaks so that he could see beyond them.

And there, in the valley beyond, was a castle. And from a window in its highest turret flew a colorful little pennant. It looked like Gloha's blouse.

Metria vanished so suddenly there was a pop. She was going to investigate. Meanwhile Graeboe told the man and skeleton what he had seen, and lifted them up high enough to see it themselves. His judgment about the scream had been vindicated. He was relieved, because now they could see about rescuing Gloha from her evident captivity.

Step by step he navigated the mountain range, treading over the peaks, and starting down the other side. The castle loomed larger and clearer. It was about as tall as Graeboe's shin, sitting on an islet in a muddy pond. A path led from it through a pass toward the Faun/Nymph Retreat. Graeboe began to get a glimmer of a suspicion.

Metria reappeared. "Gloha's captive, all right," she reported. "Along with a fraction of a squintillion sad nymphs. Seems this oafish man's a nymphomaniac; he's obsessed with nymphs, and keeps nymphnapping them for his one-night stands. Then he locks them into cells and goes for more. He thought Gloha was a nymph when he netted her."

Trent's expression became mildly grim. "Gloha is not a nymph, and he shall not hold her prisoner. I am not at all sure that he should be holding any nymphs captive either."

There was that dangerous mildness again. That nymphomaniac was surely in trouble. Graeboe wished he could speak with such deadly understatement. But he knew himself to be no more than an ordinary giant, even after allowing for his illness. If he were Trent's size, he would be of no consequence whatever.

"Perhaps we should rescue Gloha, then reason with the man about the nymphs," Marrow suggested.

"Yes. I want to take no chances with Gloha." Trent turned to Graeboe, which wasn't hard to do while standing on Graeboe's hand. "Are you able to lift off the roof of that turret, so she can fly out?"

"I will try," Graeboe agreed. He stepped toward the castle, kneeled beside it, reached forth, and put his thumb and forefinger on the conical tower roof. He lifted, but the roof was firmly secured. "I fear I lack the strength," he said with regret. "There was once a time when this would have been no problem. I might bash it back and forth to loosen it, but that might harm Gloha inside."

"Don't risk it," Trent said quickly. He turned to Metria, who was hovering nearby. "Can you form yourself into a key to unlock the door, so that Gloha can escape confinement and perhaps exit the castle by another route?"

"I thought you'd never ask!" She puffed out of sight.

But in a moment she was back, looking somewhat shamefaced for a demoness. "That's an enchanted castle! I can't touch any part of it."

"Can't touch it?" Trent asked, surprised.

"It's as if it's smoke to me," she said. "When I try to touch it, my hand and body pass right through it, as if I'm not real, though I am in solid form. I recognize it now as being demon-constructed. I can enter it and see what's happening, and talk with folk, but I can't actually touch the castle or any of its artifacts. It's frustrating."

Trent considered. "I could transform some creature into a monster that would attack the castle, but I have some cautions. The monster might harm the nymphs and Gloha too. And I would not have control over it. I deem this to be too risky, since the monster would be out of my reach when it entered the castle. I need to transform a friendly person or creature, to be assured that no inadvertent harm would be done."

"Perhaps I could enter the castle," Marrow said. "The barred windows would not stop me, if I could get my skull through, and I could climb the wall to reach such a window."

"The bars are set too close for your skull," Metria said. "I checked. And you may find the walls too slippery to climb. Enchanted castles aren't easy to handle, by no coincidence."

The skeleton nodded. "True. I fear that I too am defeated. If I could get inside it, someone might use one of my long bones to wedge the bars apart. But if Gloha can not get out, I can not get in."

"Then it must be up to me," Trent said. "I'm not surprised. Until this point Gloha has done as much to help me as I have to help her, but Crombie's pointings are always accurate. Now I shall do what I am here to do. She's a fine girl and certainly worth the effort. Graeboe, if you would be so kind as to set me on the roof of the main castle, I shall see about rescuing the princess."

Graeboe smiled. This endeavor did seem to be coming to resemble aspects of their Beanstalk play. He lifted Trent and Marrow to the castle roof and laid his hand flat so that Trent could dismount.

Marrow Bones also slid off. "But you don't need to risk yourself this way," Trent protested to the skeleton.

"Yes I do," Marrow replied.

Trent didn't argue. Graeboe withdrew his hand and watched from a reasonable distance. He would never say so, of course, but he was tired from carrying the two, small as they were, and needed to rest. What mischief this downward-spiraling ailment was!

Trent cast about on the roof, and found a tiny beetle-bug. He transformed this into a saw-fish. Marrow picked up the fish, for its serrated edges weren't as hard on his hands as they were on flesh. He carried it to the locked roof door. He put the fish's saw-toothed nose to the edge of the door frame, held it firmly, and let it saw through the frame and into the door itself. The fish sawed right around the locking mechanism, and when that fell out, the door could be opened. Then Trent transformed the fish back to a bug and returned it to the place he had found it. Graeboe found that interesting; the Magician was taking pains to do no unnecessary mischief, even to incidental bugs.

The two went into the castle. Graeboe traced their progress as they passed by the upper windows. They were in an unused wing, and there was another locked door between it and the main castle. So Marrow had to go back to fetch the beetle-bug, for transformation again, because it seemed that there were no bugs inside the castle. It appeared to be a sterile place.

"Hey, get a load of Veleno," Metria said in his ear, startling him. "He's headed up to the high turret with a costume."

Graeboe shifted position, trying to orient on the man. Night was looming, and lights were illuminating the castle. No one turned them on; they just did it, glowing in every room. In fact there seemed to be no servants or defenders in the castle. It was empty, except for Veleno and the captive nymphs. It seemed to run itself automatically. Since the demons had made it, according to Metria, they didn't bother with human servitors. There seemed to be a few pie trees growing in the central courtyard, which probably provided Veleno with his daily nourishment, and that was about it. It was a self-sufficient castle.

At least the lights made it easier to see what was going on inside, while Veleno couldn't see Graeboe outside, if he cared. The castle wasn't made of glass, but might as well have been in some sections, because of the view through the upper windows. Only the bottom story was completely opaque.

Veleno went on up to the turret chamber while Trent and Marrow were making their way past the second locked door. The man didn't seem to be aware of the intrusion. Maybe he had lived so long in this secure castle that it didn't occur to him that any invasion was possible. He came at last to the chamber. Graeboe put his ear down close so that he could overhear what was said.

"I have brought you a wedding dress in your size, so you can marry me in proper style," Veleno informed her.

"I told you before, I'm not marrying you," Gloha retorted. "My friends are about to rescue me from your fell clutches."

"No one can rescue you here. This castle is invincible to mortals. Now take this dress, put it on, and come down to the main chamber so that we can be married."

"What is it with you?" she demanded incredulously. "I just told you that I won't marry you. Aren't you listening?"

Veleno frowned. "You are a real girl, not a nymph," he said. "Therefore you can remember from day to day. That means that our marriage will not automatically dissolve tomorrow. At last I shall have fulfilled the requirement, and I shall know love, and be able to go home."

"You said all that before," she reminded him. "And I said before that I wouldn't do it. I am no nymph, and I'll never marry you. Now take back your stupid dress and let me go, and I'll just forget about this and go my way."

Graeboe shook his head. What a lovely little spirited creature she was! She wasn't taking any guff from her captor.

"If you don't come down and marry me," Veleno said evenly, "I shall bring you no food. Since you are real, you must eat. I think that when you get hungry enough, you will agree that it is better to be married and eat."

"You're trying to starve me into marrying you?" she demanded, aghast.

"Yes. Now are you ready?"

"No!"

"I regret this," Veleno said. "I had hoped to have a pleasant evening of consummation. But I suppose I can wait." He set down the dress between the bars of the door.

"Consummation!" Gloha cried. "Never!" She stamped her fine little foot for emphasis.

Graeboe sighed with admiration. Gloha did not buckle under pressure. And soon she would be rescued, so her resistance would indeed save her the grief of an unkind marriage.

Veleno went back down the stair. Metria appeared before him. "She'll never marry you, you clod of dragon dung," she said triumphantly.

"What are you, a rogue demoness?" he demanded. "Get out of my way." And he walked right through her.

Metria's face showed fury, but she stifled her retort. She couldn't affect Veleno or the castle, being unreal to them except in appearance. So she popped up to Gloha's chamber. "You told him," she said. "Good for you, goblin girl."

"I am getting hungry," Gloha confessed. "I haven't eaten anything since those colored popcorns."

"You'll be rescued soon. Trent and Marrow are making their way into the castle."

"Oh, that's such a relief to know," Gloha said. "I'm frightened of that man Veleno. I'm afraid he might—"

"Afraid of what?" the demoness asked.

"That he might try to—to consummate even without marriage."

"I hadn't thought of that," Metria said. "I suppose he might." She faded thoughtfully out.

Graeboe felt a surge of anger at the demoness. Instead of reassuring Gloha, she had made her feel worse. Demons had no human feelings, and it showed.

Meanwhile Marrow and Trent were sawing through the second door. But by the time they succeeded, Veleno was downstairs again, well out of hearing. Had he heard them, and come to investigate, Trent could have transformed him, making the rescue much easier.

Well, now they could go on in and up to the turret chamber, where Trent could transform Gloha into something small enough to get out of her cell. Then he could transform her back to her normal nice form, and she could fly away.

The two came to a third locked door, blocking a passage that ran beside an outer wall. Marrow turned back to fetch the bug again, but this time another door swung closed behind him, preventing him from getting there. The bars were too closely set to allow Marrow to get his skull through, just as Metria had said.

"Uh-oh," Trent murmured mildly.

Graeboe echoed the sentiment. In fact, the two of them were trapped, and couldn't get free because there was nothing to transform into a useful tool. The castle had outsmarted them, in its passive way.

"You could kick me, and I could assume another configuration," Marrow suggested.

"But your skull still would not be able to get out, and without it, the rest of your body could not function independently," Trent pointed out.

"True. I regret being inadequate to the occasion."

Metria appeared. "Now what picklement have you boys gotten yourselves into?" she demanded.

"We acted stupidly," Trent said mildly. "We are paying the price of our folly."

Metria reached up and tore two hanks of her hair out. "How can a mere stupid castle defeat us all?" she demanded rhetorically. "I'm just a soulless demoness, but I expected better of you, Magician." She let go of the torn hanks, and they dissolved into smoke and rejoined her body.

"You are right to be annoyed," Trent said, even more mildly.

Graeboe knew it was time for him to act. He leaned toward the just-formed cell. "Transform me, Magician," he said. "Make me be something small enough to get inside the castle, and large enough to be of some help."

Trent nodded. "I will render you into a mouse, so as to get in here, and then an elf so as to be able to search out a set of keys to unlock the doors."

Graeboe reached for the cell, his finger touching the bars outside. Magician Trent reached through and touched him, pinching his skin in tiny fashion. Then suddenly Graeboe was a mouse, dangling by one foot from Trent's pinched fingers.

Trent brought him inside before he could fall, and set him on the floor. Graeboe tried to walk, and discovered that he had to coordinate four feet instead of two. So he walked carefully on hands and feet, and that worked. He went somewhat awkwardly to the door that barred the way to the forward passage. He slipped through, then turned around to face the Magician. This was the first time he had been transformed, and it was a weird experience.

Worse, it was a depleting experience. Graeboe felt weaker than ever. He hadn't thought of this complication; how weak could he get, and still be able to function? He wouldn't be any help if he couldn't move around sensibly.

The Magician's huge hand came down. Was this the way that he, the giant, appeared to ordinary folk? That hand could squish him in an instant! Then Graeboe found himself in the body of an elf. He was even dressed like an elf.

That was just as well; he would not have wanted to appear naked. That was powerful magic the Magician had.

But he was also staggeringly weak. The second transformation had taken another dollop of energy from his meager supply. He had to grab onto the bars to keep from falling.

"Graeboe," Marrow said solicitously. "Are you in discomfort?"

"No, just very weak," Graeboe said weakly. "I—I fear I am not up to another transformation."

"I did not realize," Trent said. "I would not have transformed you, had I known it would hurt you. I apologize."

"Not hurt—just weakened," Graeboe gasped. "I will proceed in a moment."

"But I may have taken days away from your remaining life," Trent said. "That was not a kind thing to do."

"A few days hardly matter. Just so long as I am able to accomplish my purpose, and get you and Gloha free."

Trent and Marrow exchanged a glance, but did not remark on the situation further. "Rest," Trent suggested. "Recover some strength. Then Metria will show you where the castle keys are."

Graeboe rested, and after a bit he did feel slightly more stable, or at least acclimatized to his new form and state of energy depletion. "I am ready," he said.

Metria appeared. "Follow me," she said, and walked down the passage.

Graeboe tried, but with the first stride he fell against the wall. He pushed himself upright and took a tottering step before falling against the wall again.

"Oh for pity's sake," the demoness said, disgusted. "Can't you move any better than that? We'll be all night."

"He is weak from his ailment and the recent transformations," Trent called. "It behooves you to be more understanding."

"Why?" she asked, beginning to fuzz into smoke.

"Because it would make you emulate the attitude of a person with a soul, who is capable of love."

The smoke froze in mid-swirl. "Understanding would help me grasp love?" Then the smoke resumed swirling, and the demoness reappeared. "Say, I heard myself just then. I do need to practice understanding. Very well; I'll try. What do I do now?"

"Were I standing where you are," Trent said mildly, "I would try to help him to move, by lending what physical and verbal support I could."

She considered that. Then she walked across to the elf. "Let me help you," she said. "I'm sure you can accomplish your task with a little encouragement and support."

Graeboe remembered that he was the elf. He had halfway disassociated, listening to their dialogue. It was strange being so small! "Thank you," he agreed.

She put one arm out to support him. But she was normal human size, while he was elf size: one-quarter her height. So her hand barely reached down to his head.

"Hm," she said. Then she swirled into smoke again, and reappeared as an elf girl. He was surprised at how pretty she was in that form. But of course she could assume any form she chose, and her demonly vanity encouraged her to be attractively packaged. She reached out to put one arm around his waist and drew him in snug. "Come on, hold on to me," she said. "We've got to get moving—I mean, I'm sure you will be more comfortable that way."

He put his arm around her lovely slim and supple waist. This was certainly more comfortable, but perhaps not in quite the way she intended. They walked together, down the passage and around a corner, and when he faltered, she drew him in yet more snugly. He found his hand crossing a region it probably shouldn't.

"Oh, this isn't working," she said in a flash of impatience.

"I apologize," he said. "I did not mean to touch—"

"Oh, I don't care where you touch me," she snapped. "You're of age, aren't you? You can even see my panties, if you want to." Her clothing fogged out, leaving her nymphly naked except for a bright pink panty on which his hand now rested. "I mean this is too slow. I'll just carry you."

She smoked, and his hand fell right through her naughty panty and whatever flesh might be beneath it. Then she reformed in full human size, and his hand was resting on her shapely calf. She reached down to pick him up in her arms. Now his body was wedged against her large soft bosom. "Onward," she said, and marched swiftly down the passage.

Graeboe decided not to protest. The truth was that he had not had much experience with women, whether of the giant, human, or demon persuasion, and was somewhat at a loss about the protocol. So he let his weak head rest against her pleasantly soft bosom and let her take him where she chose. There were, he concluded, worse ways to travel, and this was probably the only occasion he would have to experience this mode before he died.

Metria carried him swiftly down to the ground floor, evidently having familiarized herself with the castle. She could walk firmly enough on its floors; she just couldn't affect it in any way. Since he was not part of the castle, she could affect him, and that was fortunate. He doubted that he could have walked this far alone.

Along the way they passed many cells, and in most of these were nymphs. "Oh please, kind folk, let us out!" the nymphs cried to them. "We know not how we came here, or what will become of us. We live only to cavort and be happy, but we are not happy here."

"We've got to free these poor creatures!" Graeboe said.

"Why?" the demoness asked.

She really didn't understand! "Because shallow as they may be, they do not deserve to be penned unhappily," he said carefully. "Every creature should be allowed to live its own life in its own way, so long as it does not interfere with the lives of others."

"Well, I'm looking for love, and this doesn't reference."

"Doesn't what?"

"Pertain, associate, connect, attach, belong, apply—"

"Relate?"

"Whatever," she agreed crossly.

"Yes, it does relate," he insisted. "Love is not simply the feeling of one person for one of the opposite sex. It is a generalized condition applying to the whole of existence. Only a person who is sensitive to the welfare of others in general is capable of truly loving any one other person."

"But isn't that a whole lot of trouble?"

"Sometimes it is. But that is a liability of the condition of being a person who can love and be loved."

"So if I cared what happens to those stupid nymphs, I could love a man?"

"I think the two are linked, yes. Because you are inhuman and lack love, you care neither about the plight of others nor about any particular man."

She was silent, evidently thinking it over.

They came to a small chamber just inside the main door where there was a hook, and on the hook hung a ring with a single key: the key to the castle. Veleno probably took it with him when he went out, or when he went to lock up a nymph, and kept it here betweentimes.

Metria set Graeboe down. He reached for the key, but it was too high. Metria reached for it, impatiently, but her hand passed right through it. "Oh, stink horns!" she swore. "I keep forgetting." Then she put her hands under Graeboe's shoulders and lifted him up so that he could get the key.

It was heavy, but not too much for him to handle. He got the key ring down. "Now we must go free Trent, Marrow, and Gloha," he said, pleased. "Thank you, Metria."

"Why bother thanking me?" she asked. "I'm only helping you because Trent told me to try to be understanding."

"Because I am a living, feeling creature, capable of love, and I appreciate being helped," he explained. "Especially in my extremities of diminished size and strength."

"You mean I have to act wimpish, if I want to learn love?" she asked indignantly.

He smiled. "No. Just have feelings, and show them on occasion."

"I have feelings. I get impatient with slow humans all the time, and I think it's funny when they mess up. And I love tantalizing them with my body." Her torso became wrapped in a bright, very tight red dress whose decolletage seemed to cover only the outer quadrants of her bulging breasts and whose short skirt had to struggle valiantly to keep her panties out of sight. She took a breath. "See? Your eyes are bugging."

Graeboe blinked, getting his eyes back into shape. "True. You craft a most impressive body. I compliment you on that."

She paused. "How would a feeling person react to that remark?"

"She would turn just the mere suggestion of a shade of pink, cast down her gaze demurely, and say 'Thank you' as if it were a matter of little importance. Inside, she would be pleased at the compliment. At least such is my judgment based on my limited observation of the gender."

The demoness turned a faint shade of pink, looked down demurely, and said "Thank you." Then she looked up again. "Like that?"

"Exactly. You learn very quickly."

She turned another faint shade of pink, looked down again, and repeated "Thank you."

Letter-perfect—and still without true feeling. Graeboe decided not to make an issue of the matter. "We had better get moving." He stepped out of the chamber, having recovered a bit of strength.

The nymphs in the nearest cells spied them. "Oh please let us out!" they chorused pitifully.

Graeboe hesitated. It would be unkind to leave them locked up, but if he took time to free them, the delay might prevent him from freeing his friends. He compromised. "I will return for you, as soon as I have accomplished my business," he told them.

"But you may never return!" they cried.

That was true. He sighed. And compromised. "I will free one of you, and she can look for another key to free the rest of you."

He went to the nearest cell and reached for the lock. Metria had to lift him up. He put the key in the keyhole and tried to turn it. It was too stiff for him. So Metria held him up against her extremely plush front with one arm across his body, and used her freed hand to brace his little hand, adding considerable power to his effort. The key turned and the lock clicked.

"Oh thank you, kind sir!" the nymph exclaimed. She pushed on the door, and it swung open. She stepped out in her pert nakedness, leaned forward, and kissed Graeboe on the forehead. He was still aloft, because Metria had not yet set him down.

"Is that a variant of a proper reaction?" the demoness inquired.

"Yes," Graeboe agreed, yanking his gaze from the nymphly assets. Small size was having unexpected benefits! "I did her a favor, so she thanked me in a nice way, though she is a soulless creature."

"Well, let's get moving," Metria said. She adjusted her grip so as to carry him as she had before, and started down the hall.

"Ho!" someone called. It was Veleno.

Metria paused, and the nymph screamed. "Eeek!" She kicked her feet and her hair flung about as she sought some hiding place—which turned out to be back in her cell.

"Well, I'm not waiting for this," Metria said. She strode right toward Veleno, whose eyes were glazing slightly as he took in her configuration and motion. Graeboe had a notion how the man felt. The effect would have been even stronger, had Graeboe himself not been covering the most eye-popping section of her body, by being carried against it.

"You can't escape," Veleno said, reaching out to grab the demoness.

There was a collision. Not with Metria. With Graeboe. The demoness, unable to interact with the things of the castle, passed right through Veleno's body and out the other side. Graeboe was left in Veleno's arms, because he was a real creature, and therefore solid to the castle. The demoness must have lost cohesion with respect to his body when it collided with the man's body.

The two looked at each other. "Ugh!" they said together. Veleno dropped Graeboe, who was able to land on his feet without too much of a jar. He discovered that his small size made him light, so that a fall that could have killed him in giant form didn't hurt him in elf form. He staggered to the side, where a nymph reached between the bars to catch him and help support him.

Veleno turned and stared after Metria, who was well worth staring after. "You're a demoness!" he exclaimed, disappointed.

"So?" she demanded, turning impressively so that her full display was functioning. "You're no prize yourself, nympho."

"If only you'd been mortal," he said. "You'd be ten times as good to marry as that freaky little winged goblin."

Metria turned a faint shade of pink. She cast down her demure gaze. "Thank you," she breathed, the top contours of her dress dipping slightly to facilitate the effort.

Veleno seemed about to lose his balance. That wasn't surprising, as Graeboe would have lost his own footing had the nymph not been steadying him.

"What's she got that we haven't got?" the nymph inquired, evidently not impressed in quite the same manner.

"Clothing," Graeboe answered. "It adds mystery, as well as support and, uh, uplift."

"Oh, pooh! We could don clothing if we wanted to."

"She can also doff her clothing when she wants to," he replied. "With no hands."

But their dialogue was merely incidental. The main interest was in the center of the hall.

"What are you doing carrying an elf in here?" Veleno demanded of Metria.

"What are you doing immuring nymphs?" she retorted.

"Doing what to nymphs?"

"Penning, committing, jailing, impounding, imprisoning—"

"Incarcerating?"

"Whatever," she agreed crossly.

"I'm looking for the one who will love me."

"Well, you're a dung beetle, and you'd better—" She paused. "To do what to you?"

"To love me."

"I thought you just wanted a body to maul." She adjusted her position, and inhaled more deeply. Her decolletage, overmatched, would have given up, had it had any common sense.

"That too," he agreed. "When I find love, I'll be free of all this." He gestured at the castle around them.

"Why don't you let the nymphs go, once you know they don't love you?"

"I told you that before."

"Not me you didn't."

He sighed. "Because I can't tell one from another. So I have to save all the used ones."

Metria shook herself, remembering something. Her dress was definitely supernatural; nothing less would have survived that motion. Then she walked back through Veleno, who seemed dazed. She picked Graeboe up again and headed down the passage.

"Hay, wait!" Veleno cried, trying to recover some notion of initiative. "You can't take that elf! He's got my key!"

"He sure has," she agreed, accelerating. Graeboe actually bounced against her bosom. Fortunately it was so soft that he suffered no harm.

"No you don't!" Veleno said, starting after them.

"Yes I do," Metria retorted, breaking into a full run. She came to a stairway, clambered up it, turned at the landing, and was ascending the second flight as Veleno reached the first.

He glanced up, and lost his stride. Graeboe realized that the man must have caught a glimpse of demonly panties from the angle, and been suitably stunned. Metria was really using her assets.

But in a moment they heard the pursuit resuming. Veleno could no longer see what he should not be seeing, so was able to remember what he was supposed to be doing. However, Metria now had a good lead, and she continued to move swiftly.

"I wish I could be a souled creature, just for an hour," she said. "Just long enough to find out what love is."

"I wish you could too, Metria," Graeboe said. "For whatever reason, you are really helping me, and I appreciate it. I wish there were some way to reward you."

"Me too. But I think I just have to learn love by myself."

"I think you do. Maybe you will find the way."

They came to the upper section. This was the level where Trent and Marrow were confined. But there was a problem: Metria in her haste had taken another route back, and they were in another passage. One that did not pass that cell. Metria cast about, trying to find the way, but there seemed to be none. Meanwhile Veleno was catching up.

"Free us! Oh free us!" the confined nymphs there chanted in unison. But the demoness ignored them, searching for the connection.

"Where the funk *is* it?" Metria demanded. "I didn't explore this floor carefully before. I could pop right over there, but only you can carry the key."

"Maybe this way leads on up to Gloha's cell," Graeboe said. "We can release her first, then see about the others."

Veleno came into sight. "Ha!" he cried. "Got you trapped!"

"Never, you creep," Metria cried. She kicked her feet, turning around, and her hair flung out in almost nymphly fashion as she oriented on the passage ahead and got up velocity. She found the circling stairway and zoomed up it, bounce by bounce. Graeboe just hung on to the key.

They reached the top. There was Gloha's cell. "We've got the key!" Graeboe gasped as Metria came to a sudden stop almost against the door.

"Oh, wonderful!" Gloha cried. "But who are you?"

Graeboe realized that she did not know about his transformation. "I am Graeboe Giant. Trent and Marrow were captured trying to rescue you, but I reached out to Trent and he transformed me to this form so I could get the keys."

"Graeboe!" she echoed, astonished. "How you've changed!" She peered at him more closely. "But you do have his features. I mean your features."

"Homely," he agreed without depreciation. 'It usually doesn't matter how an invisible giant looks."

Metria held him up while he put the key in the lock. Then she helped him turn it, as before. The lock clicked.

Graeboe pulled on the door, and Metria pulled on him, and it swung open. "Oh thank you, both of you!" Gloha cried, impulsively hugging Graeboe. She, as a goblin, was about twice his elf height, instead of Metria's quadruple. She just sort of leaned down and picked him up in her embrace. It was a delightful experience, because she, unlike Metria, was sincerely caring.

"Ha!" It was Veleno. He charged up to the cell and pushed the door shut. The demoness tried to block him off, but he ran right through her, as before.

"The key!" Graeboe cried, remembering, as Gloha set him down. "It's still in the lock!"

"Not any more," Veleno said with grim satisfaction. He turned the key, locking the door again, and drew it out.

"Let go of it!" Metria cried, trying to grab the key from him. But her hand passed through it and him. She was completely ineffective. "Oh, fudge!" she swore.

"What kind of confection?" Veleno inquired snidely.

"Oh, go fry an eyeball!"

He faced the cell. "Let me know when you are ready to marry me, goblin girl. I will check on you every few hours. I suspect you will grow hungry and thirsty before too long, as will your elf friend."

"Never!" Gloha cried as he departed.

Outraged, the demoness puffed into smoke and dissipated.

"Wait, Metria!" Graeboe cried desperately, thinking of something.

She reappeared inside the cell. "I can't do anything for you," she said. "I can't touch him or the key. So I guess I'd better go amuse myself elsewhere."

That was what he had been afraid of. "Metria, you have really made progress in learning human emotion. Now perhaps you can make more. You can do the generous thing and get help for us."

"Why should I bother?" she asked.

"Because it's the kind of thing a feeling person would do. You do have some feelings, as you explained before. Maybe you can get the one you want, if you just keep acting the way a person who had such feeling would."

She considered. "All right. I'll give it one more shot. What do you want this time?"

"Pop over to Gloha's relatives and tell them where she is, and how she is about to be married against her will. Then lead them here."

Metria considered further. "That *would* be a feeling thing to do, wouldn't it?" she mused.

"Very feeling," Gloha agreed, catching on to the ploy. "Maybe tell the winged centaurs too. And the giants."

"You're asking for a lot!" the demoness said, bridling.

"Yes. Only a really generous and feeling person would consider it," Graeboe said.

"Oh, all *right*!" Metria agreed crossly. She vanished.

There was a silence. Then Gloha turned shy. "Are you really Graeboe?" she asked. "Not just an elf in his image?"

"I really am. I confess it is strange being this size, but it is what seemed necessary." He looked around. "Do you mind if I sit down? I am very weak."

"I'd offer you a cushion, if I had one," she said. "I'm afraid the stone floor will have to do."

"Thank you." He sat, leaning against the wall. "I'm sorry I didn't succeed in rescuing you."

"But it was nice of you to try."

"I should have remembered to take the key out," he said, angry at himself. "What a stupid mistake."

"No more so than my getting myself caught like this," she said. "You really didn't have to risk yourself like that."

"Yes I did."

She smiled. "I think your decency is as big as you are. In your natural size, I mean."

"No, it wasn't that. I'd have done it anyway."

"Why?"

"I—" Suddenly he realized why, and knew he couldn't say it. What was the point, when they existed on two different scales, and he was so soon to die anyway? "It was just the right thing to do."

"No, I was foolish, and should pay for it. It's not right to get you and Trent and Marrow in trouble because of me." She paused, angling her head in thought. "Maybe I should agree to marry him, if he'll let the rest of you and the nymphs go."

"No!" he cried, stricken.

She looked at him in surprise at his vehemence. Then she changed the subject. "What is it like to be a giant?"

"Big," he said succinctly.

She laughed again. He thrilled when she did that. "How true! But I mean, what do you do? How did your breed come to be? To be so big, and invisible too?"

"That's not much of a story," he said, fidgeting.

"Are you uncomfortable about it? I'm sorry; I shouldn't pry. I was just curious."

"Oh, it isn't that," he protested. "I'll be happy to tell you our history. I'm fidgeting because I'm very weak and the stone is very hard."

"Oh, yes, it is, isn't it?" she agreed. "But maybe I can do something about that. Let me hold you."

He thought he had misheard. "I—think I don't understand."

"I am larger than you now, and softer. I can handle the stone. Let me hold you, and shield you from its hardness."

"Oh, that wouldn't be right," he protested.

"Why not?"

"Because I—" Again he had to stifle it. Because he would so very much like to be so close to her.

She cocked her head again. "Are you going to give me a reason, Graeboe?"

"No."

"Then come on," she said. "You have been a friend to me when you didn't have to be, and I will be a friend to you. It is little enough, considering our situation."

He found that he wasn't able to demur when she phrased it that way. He tried to get to his feet, but had difficulty.

"Oh, you really are weak," she said solicitously. "I keep forgetting. It carried right through from your other size. Here, I'll get you." She got readily to her feet, stepped across the cell to him, sat beside him, reached across, and heaved him onto her lap in a sitting posture. She put her arms around him, holding him steady. His head came up just to her petite bosom. "Is that better?"

"I feel like a child," he said.

She laughed once more, rocking him with the expression. "That's the way I usually feel, when dealing with regular human folk. It's about time I made somebody else feel that way." She settled back against the wall. "Now tell me about the giants."

Centuries ago, the ancestors of the giants were ordinary human folk. They lived in a village in central Xanth, and harvested not-holes from the local pining trees, which they traded to other villages for other goods. Wherever there was an unwanted hole, one of their special not-holes would eliminate it, without the necessity for any rebuilding. So there was a fairly steady demand, and the village got by, trading the holes for what else they needed.

But there were problems. There were a number of monsters in the vicinity, such as dragons, griffins, river serpents, ogres, and trolls. Any villager who wasn't careful was apt to discover himself in the stomach of a monster. This made them feel rather insecure. They wished that they didn't have to worry about monsters. Meanwhile, their numbers diminished, because the monsters were eating them faster than they could grow new children. At this rate, the day would come when no village was left.

Then one of them heard that a Magician, or at least a person with a very strong magic talent, was in need of assistance. It occurred to them that they might be able to make a deal with the Magician. If they helped him, maybe he would help them. So they sent a representative to negotiate. It turned out that the Magician's talent was making things very large. Huge, in fact. And suddenly they realized that if they were large, they wouldn't have to worry about dragons and whatnot; they would be big enough to throw the dragons away. This notion had considerable appeal. So they made the deal: they would build the mountain the Magician wanted, if he would make them too big for any dragon to devour.

They packed up their things and traveled to the Magician's place of residence. He touched the first man, and the man began to grow, enormously. He grew right out of his clothing, which was embarrassing; in fact his bare bottom was blushing. "Do not be concerned," the Magician said. "Your bodies will not show."

"They will show across the length and depth of Xanth!" a woman protested. "We must have giant clothing!"

"Just watch, and you will see," the Magician said, unperturbed.

"That's what's bothering us!" the woman said, covering the curious eyes of her children. "We are seeing too much. Those aren't exactly moons in the sky."

But as the man grew further, something weird happened. He began to become less visible. His body seemed to be thinning, in the manner of a demon turning to smoke. "He's fading away!" someone cried. "He's not mooning us anymore."

"No, he is merely becoming visually diffuse," the Magician said. "There is only so much to see in an ordinary person. When his body expands, that sight gets spread across a wider surface. Finally it expands so much that he can't be seen at all. But he is still solidly there."

They watched, amazed, as the first man became a virtual shadow of himself, a faintening outline, and finally nothing. But when they went up to where he had stood, they discovered his monstrous bare feet. He was indeed still there.

"We didn't agree to this!" someone said.

"Consider this sensibly," the Magician responded. "As big as you will be, you will have little if any need for clothing for warmth, because of an aspect of magic called the square cube ratio, and if you do need it, you can make it of suitable size. Meanwhile no one will stare at you or be concerned when you walk near, because no one will see you. Thus you have the ultimate privacy along with your size. This combination should work very well for you."

They considered, and the more they thought about it, the more sense it made. So they decided that it would be all right to be invisible, and they would communicate with each other by calling back and forth. They would make do.

So the Magician made the rest of them large. There was much blushing as they burst out of their clothes, and some glances of admiration before they faded out, and finally all of them, even the children, were huge and invisible. They could see perfectly well; they just couldn't be seen.

"You are fortunate that you aren't in Mundania," the Magician said. "Because there your invisibility would make it impossible for you to see, and you would be blind with the light passing right through your eyes and never stopping to give you the picture. But here in Xanth you don't have to be concerned about such confusions."

Then they got to work, and with their enormous bare hands they scraped up a big mound of earth and rock for the Magician, forming his mountain. When he was satisfied, they linked hands and walked away, seeking a region where they could dwell without stepping on anyone, because they were peaceful folk who did not like to make trouble. They found an isolated region, and there they settled. They found that indeed they did not need clothing, unless they wanted to become visible. When they did wear clothing, it tended to fade after a while, becoming invisible too, so there didn't seem to be much point in it. Anyway, they found they liked being invisible; it had a number of advantages.

After a time some giants left the community to find separate employment. Some just wandered around seeking good works to do, taking care where to set their feet so as to do no harm. Sometimes one would find that a storm had blown a big tree down on a normal person's house; he would quietly lift that tree away, so as to free the people trapped beneath, and the people would think that the wind had done it. Graeboe's cousin Greatbow found employment with Com Pewter, scaring folk into the evil machine's cave. But Greatbow himself was careful never to actually step on anyone or to do irreparable damage to the forest.

Another cousin, Girard, was so softhearted that he tried to water trees in a drought and to help injured animals. He took do-gooding to an extreme that became a fault. When he tried to help a little human boy, he wound up getting a bad dream that had been intended for the boy, and in that dream saw Gina Giantess, with whom he fell instantly in love. But she was only a figment crafted for the dream, making fulfillment of his love impossible. But finally he was able to find her anyway, in the dream realm of the hypnogourd.

Graeboe himself had not even gotten around to seeking love. His malady had come upon him, and slowly wasted him, so that his breath turned too bad for other giants to stand, he lost his invisibility (apparently there was, after all, a bit of magic involved in that), and he became increasingly weak. Yet the Good Magician seemed to think that there was an answer for him, and he had sought that answer. Now he realized that there was no answer, or he had lost it along the way. So he was satisfied to try to do what bit of good he could before he expired.

"Oh, but that's very sad," Gloha said, trying to comfort him. "You're such a nice person. You really deserve to live beyond your youth. Just how old are you?"

Graeboe counted on his fingers. "Just about coming onto my majority," he said. "I was found on a cabbage patch forty-eight years ago."

"But that's old!" she exclaimed, amazed.

"Not for a giant. Ordinarily we live to be two hundred or so. So I'm not yet a quarter through my scheduled life. In your terms I would be about—" He concentrated, trying to do long division on his fingers, but it wasn't working very well.

"About nineteen?" she asked.

"Yes, I think so," he agreed. "That sounds right. If I were to stay in this body, and live out my term, I would not live any longer than you would. But of course that's academic."

"There must be some way to save you," she said.

"I am more concerned with saving you," he said. "It would be intolerable to let Veleno have his way with you."

"Yes, you are here now because you tried to help me," she agreed. "Well, you rest for a while, Graeboe, and I shall see if I can think of any way to help any of us."

"Maybe Metria will get help."

"Maybe she will." She held him and rocked him, and he found himself fading into sleep. Her embrace was wonderfully comforting.

Graeboe expected to die without revealing it, but he could no longer hide the foolish truth from himself: He was by nature a giant, and she was a goblin-harpy crossbreed, but he loved her. All he could do was hope that Gloha escaped this prison and found her desire. Meanwhile he could not imagine a nicer way to fade out than this, being rocked in her arms.

11
METRIA

Gloha held Graeboe while he slept. She felt so guilty for foolishly getting herself caught here, and thus leading her friends into captivity too. Trent had accompanied her to protect her, and he had tried to, but there were limits, and she had stretched them too far. Marrow had come along to see if perhaps his own quest for half a soul might be found, and he had been helpful, and now was also a prisoner. But Graeboe was the worst, because he had nothing to gain from them, yet had tried his best to help, and now had no chance to pursue his quest for life. It was interesting that in giant terms he was just about her own age. That was way too young to die!

There was a tramping on the stairs. Veleno appeared, carrying a lamp, for it was now dark. "Are you ready yet?" he inquired.

"Never," she said quietly, so as not to disturb Graeboe's sleep. The poor giant had enough trouble, without having his rest disturbed, and she was glad to do this much for him.

"You will change your mind eventually," he said. "I'll wait."

"And if I don't?"

"You're mortal. You'll expire."

"You wouldn't dare!" she exclaimed, too vehemently, for Graeboe stirred. She increased her rocking, hoping he would not awaken.

"Of course I would dare," he said. "I don't expect you to call my bluff. The hungrier and thirstier you get, the more reasonable my proposal will seem. And I think that goes double for your mortal friends. You won't want them to suffer unduly on your behalf."

Gloha stiffened. He was right. How could she do this to Trent and Graeboe? Graeboe might be about to die anyway, but Trent wasn't. She just couldn't let them pay such a horrible price for her defiance.

Yet the idea of being married to this gross man Veleno, who was twice her height and not remotely like the one she was looking for, forever ending what foolish dreams she might have had—that was too appalling to contemplate. If she had to marry a human man, it should be someone more like Magician Trent. That particular foolishness had considerable appeal. But she did know better.

What was she to do? She couldn't stand either alternative. So all that was left was for her to hope that the Demoness Metria succeeded in summoning help. So that she and her friends could be rescued from this fell man with his fell castle.

Veleno waited a moment, and when she didn't answer again, he turned and tramped back down the stairs. He was sure that time was on his side. Maybe—perish the thought!—he was right. Unless Metria—

A swirl of smoke appeared. "Well, I'm back," the demoness said.

"Did you summon help?"

"Not exactly. I consented them."

"You whatted them?"

"Whatted?"

"What did you do to them?"

"Oh. Agree, enlighten, apprise, acquaint, inform, notify—"

"You advised them?"

"Whatever," the demoness agreed crossly.

Gloha contained her temper, still trying not to disturb Graeboe. "Whom did you advise?"

"Oh, everyone. Your goblins, harpies, winged centaurs, giants—"

"Giants?"

"Graeboe's a giant, isn't he? When he's himself?"

Gloha glanced down at the elf she held. "Yes. If the invisible giants come, they can just lift off the roof and free us all. Good thinking, Metria."

The demoness turned faint pink, averted her gaze, and said, "Thank you."

Startled at this display of modesty, Gloha lost her chain of thought. However, it didn't fall far, and she was able to recover it. "So is anyone going to come to help? Did you tell them where we are?"

"Oh, sure. And I even told Smash Ogre that Tandy will be delayed returning, because you forgot to. He said that was okay for now. The others'll be here the day after tomorrow, maybe."

"The day after tomorrow!" Gloha exclaimed, then quickly rocked to lull Graeboe back to sleep. "We could starve of thirst by then!"

"Starve of what?"

"Never mind. I don't think Graeboe can last that long without food and water. We're going to have to do something sooner."

"Such as what?"

Gloha stifled her groan. "Such as marrying Veleno."

"What, me marry him?"

"No, me. I'm the one he wants to marry. I hate the notion, but I see no alternative."

But the demoness had caught hold of an idea that intrigued her. "I wonder if I could marry him?"

"No way. You're a demoness. You can't love, remember? His enchantment won't be broken until someone loves him."

"And you can love him?"

Gloha stiffened again. "Oh, you're right. I may be capable of love, but not with him. I can't stand him. So even if I married him, I wouldn't break the enchantment. It would be a wasted effort." That realization was actually a relief.

"Suppose I married him, and pretended to love him. If I fooled him, would that do it?"

That was a difficult question. "I don't think you could fool him, Metria."

The demoness bridled. "I can fool just about anyone, when I try. Anyone except Grossclout."

"Who?"

"The Demon Professor Grossclout. He's so smart he thinks everyone else's head is filled with mush. He proves it all the time. I tried to fool him with Woe Betide, but he saw right through her."

"Who?"

Metria disappeared. In her place stood the most darling, sweet, cute, innocent, huge-eyed forlorn little waif of a girl imaginable, dressed in rags. "Hi," she piped. "I'm Woe Betide. Buy a match?" She offered a tiny twig of wood.

Gloha was impressed. "That would fool me," she agreed.

The waif's face clouded tragically. "It didn't fool Grossclout. Nothing fools him. He's a terror."

Graeboe woke. "Who's that?" he asked, startled.

The ragamuffin turned her great sad orbs on him. "I'm just downtrodden Woe Betide, the poor little match girl. Everybody gaits on me."

"Everybody what's on you?" he asked.

"Paces, struts, tracks, hobbles, shambles—"

"Steps?" he asked.

"Treads?" Gloha asked at almost the same time.

"Whatever," the waif said crossly.

Graeboe laughed weakly. "Hello, Metria."

Woe Betide puffed into smoke. "What gave me away?" the demoness inquired, re-forming in her full buxom edition.

"It was just a lucky guess," he said.

Metria sent him a suspicious glance, but didn't argue the case.

Gloha remained intrigued by the prior subject. "I wonder if you *could* feel Veleno?" she asked. "Not that it would be ethical."

"Who cares whether it's ethical, so long as it works?" the demoness asked.

"Fool Veleno?" Graeboe asked.

"He wants to marry someone who will love him," Gloha explained. "Metria might marry him and pretend to love him."

"Why?"

"To get the rest of us free."

"Why?" he asked again.

"Because it would be a caring thing to do," Metria said shortly. "So I could learn to rapture."

"To what?" Gloha asked.

"Adoration, esteem, amour, passion, stork—"

"Oh, love," Gloha said.

"Oh, whatever," the demoness agreed crossly.

"I think I understand," Graeboe said. "Veleno wants to marry and love, and Metria wants to do something caring, so she might help us by making him think he had found love, so that he would release all the others."

"Might, schmight!" Metria said. "We'd make a deal: he releases them, or he gets no nookie."

Gloha wasn't familiar with the word, but decided not to inquire lest the correct word be troublesome. "I don't think it would be ethical," she repeated. "Therefore we can't do it, tempting as it is."

"You haven't said why ethics matters," Metria said.

"It matters to feeling folk," Graeboe said.

"Oh, why do you have to put it that way!" the demoness exclaimed, more than crossly.

"It's just very hard to explain feeling things to one who doesn't feel," Gloha said, somewhat at a loss.

"Let me get this straight: it's all right for him to capture folk and starve them to make them do what he wants, but it's not all right for them to fool him into letting his victims go?"

"Oh, my," Gloha said, taken aback. "Put that way—"

"Veleno is being unethical," Graeboe said. "But that does not give us leave to be unethical too. We prefer to be governed by the best standard, not the worst."

"Yes," Gloha agreed, appreciating his clarification.

"Okay, let's get practical. Suppose I tell him I'm a demoness and can't really love him, but I'll pretend to for a couple of days, so he can break his geis, and—"

"Break his what?" Graeboe asked.

"I got the right word," Metria said crossly. "Geis, pronounced *gaysh*, plural geasa, as in girl. No, that's not quite it; forget the plural. It's a magical obligation. He has to find love, so he can get out of here. That's his geis."

"A geis," Gloha said musingly. "That's interesting. I wonder if anyone else has such an obligation?"

"Oh, many do. You should hear about the geis of the gargoyle. But that's a whole nother story. So anyway, he wants something, you want something, I want something; why can't we make a deal?"

"Perhaps, if the terms are clearly understood and honored, it would be ethical," Graeboe agreed.

Gloha was moved to something like wonder. "You would do this, Metria, just to get the feeling of doing something generous?"

"Sure. You people seem to have all kinds of feelings I don't understand, and they make you do funny things. You seem to get a lot of fun out of love. I want to try it, once, just so I know what it is."

"But there is no guarantee that doing something nice for us will enable you to love," Gloha said.

The demoness shrugged. "There's no guarantee it won't."

Gloha thought about the ugly alternatives she faced. If this could free her of those . . .

"Perhaps it is worth trying," Graeboe said. "So long as you do speak truly, and do follow through."

"The follow-through is easy. Any demoness can make any man deliriously happy, if she chooses."

"I wouldn't say that," he demurred.

"Oh wouldn't you? How about when you were bouncing on my bosom? Didn't you like that? And what about sleeping on *her* bosom? Don't you like that even better?"

Both Gloha and Graeboe stiffened. He scrambled off her lap. "I—" he started, while Gloha tried not to flush.

"And you have to tell the truth, right? So tell me it isn't so. I could assume goblin girl form too, you know."

He was silent. Gloha managed to come to his rescue. "Real folk can make real folk happy," she said. "But that's not the same as a demoness doing it."

Metria fogged out, and reappeared as Woe Betide. "Maybe someone your size," she said to Graeboe. "Suppose I do a strip mine?" She began to dance, pulling off her innocent bonnet.

"What kind of—?" Graeboe began.

"Never mind!" Gloha said. "We'll grant that a demoness can—can do what you said, when she wants to. How can we be sure you'll tell Veleno the truth? So we aren't ethically compromised?"

"Suppose I do it right here? So you can listen?"

Gloha exchanged exactly one glance with Graeboe. "That seems fair," she agreed.

"Done! When he comes here to torment you again, I'll make the deal."

Gloha was hardly sure how she felt. If this was ethical, and it worked . . .

The demoness popped out, leaving them alone in the cell. Graeboe found a place to sit down against the wall.

"You don't have to go there," Gloha said.

"I think I do. I never wished to cause you any embarrassment."

"And you didn't. It was the demoness who did that."

"Still, I will not contribute to any problem for you, in any way I can prevent."

Something that had been hovering around the periphery of her thoughts came into focus. "You like me, don't you?"

"Well, that isn't relevant to our situation. Anyone would have tried to help you."

"No, I mean you—" She hesitated. "You *really* like me."

He brightened. "I—do. But I have no wish to cause you any distress, or to interfere in any way—"

"Yes, that's what you said. And you are such a good man. If only you weren't—"

"A giant," he finished wanly.

"No." For she was just now coming to understand something Magician Trent had said, about knowing her own mind. "If only you weren't dying. I think I could—could like you the same way. To be a friend to you as you have been a friend to me. But even if I get away from this castle, you can't get away from your fate. You'll never be a happy giant again, going your way, marrying a nice giantess, and living happily ever after."

Graeboe seemed to reconsider something, and to come to a painful conclusion. "Friends, yes," he agreed. "That is true. I am sorry I did not think far enough ahead to realize that it was not only pointless to make new friends at this time, it was cruel. To those friends. I was so hungry for company that I did not question it in the way I should have. I have done all of you a disservice."

She considered. "I see your logic, Graeboe, but not your feeling. I think I would not want never to have known you or Magician Trent, whatever happens. All this time I have been looking for a winged goblin, when I should have been looking for truly good friends. Friends like you."

"No, I am not truly good. I am ordinary in all but body, and even that is fading."

"And so am I. Ordinary, I mean, in spirit." She shook her head. "At least I have learned to look beyond the body. Much good may it do me."

They lapsed into silence. Gloha hoped that Trent and Marrow weren't feeling too despondent. Her guilt for their fate remained. If only she hadn't stupidly followed that popcorn! She had sidetracked their whole quest and gotten them all in trouble. Now their only hope was a demoness whose only reason for helping was infernal curiosity.

She heard the tramping of feet on the stairs. Was Veleno returning so soon? Or *was* it soon? It was hard to tell, in the dark. Maybe she had snoozed in the interim.

This time the man had brought a tray with food. "Are you ready to marry me?" he asked.

"No, but maybe someone else is," Gloha said.

"The nymphs don't count. None of them remember that they married me. You will remember."

"There is another who will remember. Who is willing, as I am not."

He showed interest. "Who?"

"Metria."

"Who?"

"The demoness."

"Oh. Demons count even less than nymphs do, because they can't interact with me or the castle."

Metria appeared. She was exquisitely garbed, showing less of her voluptuous body than usual. Her dress was of silk and gauze, and she wore a sparkling necklace, and a tiara in her glossy hair. "I have learned something about this castle of the Notar Republic," she said. "No demon can interact with you within it, but any demon can outside it. And anyone who marries you can interact with you in the castle, because it will then accept that person as its mistress."

"Why, that's true," Veleno said, surprised. "I had forgotten. I thought it didn't matter, because no demoness had any interest. Are you saying that you do?"

"Yes. I will marry you. For a price."

"A price?"

"Let all the captives go. All the nymphs, and the mortal folk, and the walking skeleton too."

"I told you before: I can't let the nymphs go until I find the right one."

Metria considered. "Well, when you're sure that I'm the right one."

"The moment I find love, none of them will matter. They'll all be freed automatically, and your friends too."

"Automatically?" Gloha asked.

"When this castle dissolves."

"Oh, the geis," Metria said. "Yes, that's right. So we don't have to worry about that. Still, we must bargain. I want you to feed everyone who needs it now. These two here, and Trent in the other cell."

"If you marry me tonight, they shall eat tonight."

"Deal. Let's do it."

Gloha cleared her throat.

"But there's something else I have to tell you," Metria added. "You know I'm a demoness. I can't really love anyone. But I can pretend to, and make it so good it will fool you. Maybe it will fool the castle too."

It was Veleno's turn to consider. "It seems worth a try. If it doesn't work, the castle won't dissolve, all the captives will remain, and the goblin girl will have to marry me next."

"Hey, I'm not agreeing to that!" Gloha protested.

"You don't need to. I'll simply start starving you and your friends again, until you change your mind."

"Your logic is inescapable," Gloha said cuttingly.

"So let's get with it," Metria said.

"Come down to the nuptial chamber."

"First feed my friends."

He sighed. "Very well. I have a tray here. I will fetch another."

Metria reconsidered. "I don't want a stupid simple chamber wedding. I want a full-scale bash."

"But that will take time."

"I can wait if you can." Metria's dress shifted, becoming a fancy wedding gown. "Don't you want to do it right, for once?"

"That would mean having witnesses and all that inconvenience."

"There can be witnesses. Let my friends attend. The nymphs too."

"But I'd have to let them out of their cells."

"So the castle's still tight, isn't it?"

"One's a Magician. He could change one of the others into a monster to devour me."

"He has a point," Graeboe said. "He has no reason to trust us."

"Make them take oaths of nonhostility," Metria said. "In this castle, all oaths are binding, even if the people who make them aren't honest."

"You *have* learned about it," Veleno said.

"Sure. The Notar Republic isn't really the castle, it's a situation. Anything it oversees has to be true. Wherever the castle is, that's a piece of the Republic, and its law governs. So the oaths will do it."

Veleno looked at Gloha and Graeboe. "Will you make the oath of non-hostility? That means you can't do anything hostile to me, such as trying to act against my interest. Such as trying to escape."

Gloha felt a chill. "Oh, I don't like this," she murmured.

"You don't have to swear to marry him," Graeboe pointed out. "Just not to hurt him."

It occurred to her that the freedom of the castle would be a lot more comfortable than confinement to this chamber. For one thing, she needed to get to the privy room. "All right."

"Then swear, and I'll give you the freedom of the castle," Veleno said.

Gloha closed her eyes, nerved herself, and spoke. "I hereby swear the oath of nonhostility to the proprietor of this castle." At that point she felt several loops of a silken cord settle around her and draw gently tight. She opened her eyes, surprised, but there was nothing to see. She realized that these were the ties of the binding oath; it bound her invisibly, but securely.

Graeboe took the oath. Then Veleno unlocked the door. He handed Gloha the key. "Let your other friends out—but only after they make the oath. I'll go see about more food, and arrangements for the wedding."

Surprised again, Gloha took the key. "You have this tray," she said to Graeboe. "I'll have the next. After I release Trent and Marrow."

"And I'll make sure of those wedding arrangements," Metria said with enthusiasm. "Oh, I'll make Xanth's most beautiful bride." She vanished.

Gloha followed Veleno down the stairs. Things had happened so swiftly she felt dizzy. But at least now there was a chance for things to work out better.

"That way," Veleno said, pointing to a side passage. He continued straight ahead.

She followed the passage, and came to the cell. "You got free!" Trent cried gladly.

"Not exactly. Metria is marrying Veleno, so he is giving us the freedom of the castle, provided we swear an oath of nonhostility. We can't try to harm him or to escape, until it is clear that the marriage is valid. Graeboe and I made the oath, and you must make it now."

"I am not ready to make that oath," Trent said mildly.

"Then I can't unlock your cell."

"This is interesting. Have you learned honor?"

"I thought I always had it. But it doesn't matter. When I made the oath, invisible bindings bound me, and I must honor it. It's a geis."

"An obligation of honor," he agreed. "If Metria's marriage doesn't work, what becomes of you?"

"Then I am back where I started. I haven't agreed to marry him, but I would get locked up and starved until I did agree. And so would you and Graeboe."

"Yet you honor your agreement, despite this risk?"

"Yes. Now are you going to make the oath? You will be fed anyway, but I can't let you out without that oath." She hesitated. "Please, Magician, I don't want to leave you confined." In fact she didn't want to leave him at all. She remembered how he had confessed his desire to transform Cynthia Centaur back to human form, for a reason he didn't need to state, considering Cynthia's interest in him. Gloha couldn't help wondering how it would be to be transformed to human woman form, at least for a night with him. Of course the Magician had no notion of her interest, and she would not tell him. She just—wished.

"I don't need to make the oath," Trent said. "Neither does Marrow."

"Yes you do. Because otherwise I can't let you out." The binding oath held her firmly, though she really wanted to free him so she wouldn't have to leave him here and go about her remaining business alone.

He smiled. "Let me explain. You meant well, but you came within transformation range just now. I could have changed you to a flea, and picked up the key ring as it fell to the floor. Then we would have been free without the oath."

"Oh!" Gloha said, stepping hastily back. She knew it was true. "Why didn't you?"

"Because part of what I learned during my exile from Xanth was honor. I have never since that time played false to any person or creature. It would not have been honorable to use your naivete to trick you into violating your oath. So though I am not entirely at ease with the compromise you made with the master of this castle, I must adhere to the deal you made, and may offer no hostility to him. My continued incarceration thus becomes pointless." He pushed on the door, and it swung open.

Gloha gaped. "How did that get unlocked?"

Marrow held up a crooked bone. "Skeleton key," he explained. "I have learned how to adapt. I wish I had thought of this before Graeboe got caught, but my hollow head isn't always efficient with thoughts. Once I did think of it, it seemed best to wait until we knew the full situation of the castle."

"You mean you could have gotten out without making the oath—if I hadn't made it?" Gloha asked, appalled.

"True," Trent said. "But it was your decision to make, as this is your quest we are on."

She shook her head. She could only hope that Metria's decision to marry Veleno worked out. Otherwise the demoness might have made more mischief than she knew.

They went downstairs. Gloha located the castle privy, then checked the rest of the main floor layout. It seemed to be a well-designed castle, but very quiet, because there were no servants. There in the castle dining room Veleno had laid out several more pies from his courtyard pie trees. The fare here was limited, but that couldn't be helped. They were hungry.

"I'll take mine up to eat with Graeboe," Gloha said. She would rather have remained with Trent, but the giant needed her company more. She laid the key ring on the table where Veleno would find it, and started off.

"I shall wait here for Veleno to reappear," Trent said, sitting down to attack his pie.

"I shall release the nymphs," Marrow said. "They don't need oaths either; they are harmless." He picked up the key ring. "And they surely appreciate weddings."

Gloha wasn't sure about that. Each nymph had been married to Veleno for one evening, and then suffered what must have been by Notar Republic rules an automatic annulment when she didn't remember it next morning. But she agreed that it wasn't right to leave them locked up.

Gloha followed the route to the highest chamber. Graeboe had hardly started eating his pie. It wasn't that he wasn't hungry, but that he was too weak. That was what she had been afraid of.

"Come on. I'll help you." She sat on the floor beside him. She didn't ask him if he wanted help, because then he would have remembered his pride. She just used the spoon that she had picked up with her pie. She fed him one mouthful after another. Betweentimes she ate bites of her own pie.

"Thank you," he said, seeming to recover somewhat. "I regret putting you to this trouble."

"I wish I could feed you something to make you strong again," she said wistfully.

"I am glad just to have known you."

"Thank you." She leaned down and kissed him on the ear.

When he had eaten as much as he could, she finished off her pie and his, then lifted him and carried him carefully down to the main floor. She wanted to be able to keep track of him, though she had no idea what she could do if he got worse.

Meanwhile, things were changing. Every chamber was lighted. Nymphs were all over the place, helping with the wedding preparations. Marrow Bones was directing the construction of benches for a number of folk to sit on. Metria was fogging in and out, giving spot instructions on decor. The demoness could not do anything physical herself, but seemed to enjoy directing all the others. The nymphs did not seem to find it unusual for a demoness and a skeleton to be supervising things. Since their memory did not extend back to yesterday, they probably thought that this was the way it always had been. Trent must have transformed one of the plants of the courtyard garden to a fabric tree, because nymphs were tearing brightly colored lengths of cloth and hanging them up as decorations. The castle was becoming festive, in strange contrast to its normal atmosphere.

Two more figures appeared. "Magpie!" Gloha exclaimed, stepping up to hug her old tutor. "What are you doing here?"

"Why, I came for the wedding, dear. And so did Dara."

Gloha looked at the other woman. She was elegantly formed and garbed, looking much like a queen. "You're Dara Demoness? Humfrey's first wife? I've heard so much about you," she said insincerely.

Dara smiled. "Not all of us are like Metria, as you should know from knowing Magpie."

Metria appeared, trailing smoke. "I heard that! You lost your soul, and *pzoop*! you were gone. That's just like me."

"But I reformed," Dara said evenly. "Now I act as if I have a soul, though I don't. That won't be a problem for you, I suspect."

"No problem at all," Metria agreed. "I'm only going to stay long enough to find out what love is. Then I'll be out of here."

"Oh, I don't think so, dear," Magpie said.

"Well, what do you know?" Metria demanded. "You've spent too much time being a servant to mortals. It was bad enough with that Princess Thorn—"

"Princess who?" Dara inquired.

"Prickle, spur, barb, spine, spike, nettle, cactus, blood-red, flower—"

"Rose?"

"Whatever," Metria agreed crossly. "Princess Rose. But then you got into lesser ones, even goblins and ogres like that Gumbo."

"Okra," Magpie said. "Okra Ogress."

"Whatever. You've lost your perspective."

"I doubt it," Magpie said, unperturbed. "I wouldn't miss this occasion for anything."

"Well, you might as well make yourself useful, then. The wedding's in only a time and a couple of moments."

"I shall be glad to," Magpie said. "The job might as well be done right." She vanished, to reappear elsewhere in the room just in time to prevent three nymphs from hanging a festoon upside down.

"And who is your young man?" Dara inquired, glancing at Graeboe.

Gloha realized that she was still carrying the elf. Hastily she set him down. "This is Graeboe Giant. He's not my—"

"A giant?" Dara said, surprised. She looked more closely. "Why, so he is. Is the Magician Trent in the vicinity, by any chance?"

"Yes, he transformed Graeboe. It's complicated."

"It certainly is. But it will soon simplify dramatically. I wish you every happiness together." She moved off to untangle several nymphs who had gotten themselves wrapped in material; shapely arms and legs were waving at odd angles and screams were starting to emerge.

Gloha turned to Graeboe, embarrassed. "She just assumed we were—"

"She just came on the scene," he said. "She doesn't know."

Another figure appeared before them. This was a portly elder demon with a frighteningly certain face. "Of course she knows," he said. "Are your heads full of mush? You would have seen the outcome yourselves if you had any wit at all."

Gloha made a wild guess. "Hello, Professor Grossclout," she said politely. "I am surprised to see you here too."

"I couldn't avoid it," Grossclout said. "I have to officiate." He glanced sourly around. "I must say, Metria holds the dubious distinction of being the worst of all the nitwitted, inattentive, mushminded students ever to disgrace my classes."

Metria reappeared. "I love you too, Professor." She kissed him on the cheek with a resounding smack.

"Stop that, you wretched creature!" he exclaimed, seeming almost ready to detonate.

"It's really nice of you to take the trouble," she said, unconcerned by his ferocity.

"I came only to make absolutely certain that you go through with it, you irresponsible inamorata."

"Irresponsible what?"

"Flame, lover, beloved, sweetheart, mistress, paramour, concubine—"

"Fiancée?" she asked.

"Whatever," he agreed crossly.

Metria colored faintly pink and averted her gaze. "Thank you," she said modestly.

He poked a chubby finger at her nose. "You are about to get what is coming to you, you infernal nuisance."

"Just so long as I learn love. That's something you never taught in your classes, Professor."

"I taught the love of knowledge, but you were incapable of learning it." He paused, reconsidering. "But indubitably you will learn something now," he added, obscurely gratified.

Metria vanished. Grossclout shook his head. "She is the most annoying female," he grumbled. "She definitely does not think like a scholar."

"But she is trying to do something decent," Gloha said.

"For the wrong reason." He focused disconcertingly on Gloha. "Whereas your case is far more positive. You deserve the joy you are about to achieve."

"Joy?" Gloha asked blankly. But the Demon Professor was already turning away.

"I really don't understand demons," Graeboe said.

"Metria says that he's the only one who can't be fooled," Gloha replied. "But if he thinks I face my prospects with joy, he's way out of touch."

Grossclout marched to the podium in front of the benches. "Take your seats, please," he said in a voice so fraught with authority that the timbers of the castle trembled. "The ceremony is about to commence."

Immediately the nymphs scrambled to perch cutely on the benches. Magpie appeared before Gloha. "You and Graeboe must sit at the front, as friends of the bride."

"We aren't exactly friends," Gloha said.

"All the better, dear. This way." She guided them to the place.

"All the better?" Graeboe whispered after they were seated.

"I don't understand this at all," Gloha confessed.

Magpie reappeared. "Oh, I'm sorry—I forgot. You are the maid of honor, Gloha."

"Me!" Gloha exclaimed, horrified. "I don't know anything about—"

"We demons can't interact with the castle directly, and in any event there needs to be a mortal contribution to the ceremony. It's important."

"But Veleno has been marrying a nymph every day, without any such fanfare."

"Yes. And none of those marriages lasted. This one will."

"It will?" Gloha asked, beginning to hope.

"If it is done correctly. Come."

So Gloha got up to follow Magpie, whose judgment she trusted. The demoness could not interact with Veleno or the things of the castle, but could touch Gloha. Quickly she fashioned a suitable maid-of-honor dress, complete with a dainty little hennin—a long conical hat with a bit of material descending from it. She guided Gloha to a mirror.

There stood a pretty goblin girl whose wings blended nicely with the gown. "Oh, I wish I could always look like this," Gloha breathed.

"You always do, to others," Magpie assured her. "They think of you as an angelic little angel. Now you must get out there for the ceremony."

"But I don't know what to do," she protested.

"Just be there to witness the ceremony, and to take the bouquet during the placing of the ring."

"That's all?"

"That's enough." Magpie urged her onward.

The ceremony was already under way. There was music from somewhere, not exactly an organ; it turned out to be Marrow Bones, playing notes on his rib cage. The notes were surprisingly accurate; she recognized the Wedding March.

And there was Metria, in a splendiferously stunning gown and veil, marching down the center aisle with a phenomenal bouquet of flowers, She almost floated, which she certainly could do if she wished to. The nude nymphs went "Ooooo!" almost in unison, wishing they could dress like that.

Veleno waited at the front. He was almost handsome in his dark formal suit.

They came together—and there was Professor Grossclout, speaking words so solemn and full of import that Gloha was to wish ever after that she could remember what they were.

There was a pause. "The ring."

Trent stepped forward from the other side. He too was handsomely suited. He presented a little box. Gloha realized that the ring must also be of castle substance, so could not be handled by demons. So Trent was playing the part of best man. Gloha wondered if that wasn't taking nonhostility to an extreme. Yet why not? If the marriage actually worked, they would all be free without violence or deceit.

Veleno took out the ring. Metria looked for a place to put her bouquet. Gloha quickly stepped up to take it. But as she did, it puffed into smoke. Oh— it wasn't real; the demoness had formed it out of her own substance to add to the effect. Still, to maintain appearances someone had needed to take it at this stage of the ceremony.

Now came the critical part. Veleno lifted the ring, and Metria lifted her left hand. Would the ring fit on her, or would it pass right through her substance the way all the other things of the castle did?

The ring stayed. Metria held her hand up triumphantly, showing it off. She had become real to the castle.

"Man and wife," Gloha heard the Professor intone.

Then Veleno took her in his arms and kissed her. His hands did not pass through her, and neither did his lips. She was real to him too.

Satisfied, Professor Grossclout grandly faded out. So did Magpie and Dara, more petitely. They had done what they had come to do.

The scene dissolved into the wedding feast. The nymphs did not need to eat, but they nibbled at the assorted pies anyway. Gloha, Trent, and Graeboe had already eaten, but they also nibbled. Meanwhile the groom and bride disappeared into the nuptial chamber for the consummation, where Metria would make Veleno deliriously happy for an hour or so. Gloha knew it didn't mean anything; what counted was whether the bride remained solid and with her memory intact on the following morning. Until then, nobody could be released. That was the deal.

Meanwhile it was left to the rest of them to clean up. They all pitched in, restoring the castle to its previous condition, with one exception: they left the decorations. Why not be festive another day?

At last it was done. The nymphs retired to their cells to sleep, feeling most comfortable there. In the morning they would remember none of this. But their cells would no longer be locked, so they would be able to come out and deport or disport themselves as they wished. There weren't any fauns here, but perhaps the nymphs could run around and scream a little anyway.

Trent, Marrow, Graeboe, and Gloha sat at the kitchen table, unwinding. Soon they too would return to their cells to sleep, this time taking pillows with them to make it comfortable. Everything depended on the morrow. "Do you think it will take?" Trent asked.

"Oh, I hope so!" Gloha said fervently. "The demons seemed to think it would."

"I understand that the Professor Demon is never wrong," Marrow remarked.

"It is odd that he came to handle the service himself," Graeboe said. "Considering that he has no respect for Metria."

"His attitude does seem odd," Marrow agreed. "It was almost as if he thought she wouldn't like being married."

"He said that she was going to get what was coming to her," Gloha said, remembering. "And when I said that we weren't exactly Metria's friends, Magpie said it was all the better."

Trent shook his head. "Strange. I think we have not yet grasped the full import of this occasion."

They sat in silence for a while and a half, not getting up the gumption to retire after their arduous day.

Metria appeared, wearing a gauzy nightdress which showed the pink halter and panty beneath. "Oh, are you folk still up?" she asked, surprised.

"By inertia," Trent said. "Why are you here?"

"I made Veleno so deliriously happy that he pooped out. It will take him several moments to recover for the next bout. So I sneaked down to fetch a nice pie."

"But you don't need to eat, Metria," Gloha said.

"Not for me. For him. He'll be hungry, after all that effort."

Even Marrow seemed to be taken aback by this. "You are trying to do something nice for him that isn't what is strictly prescribed by the deal?"

"Well—yes," the demoness said defensively. "Can't a wife do something for her husband if she wants to?"

"It's almost as if you care," Graeboe remarked.

Metria looked nonplussed. "That must be an illusion."

Trent squinted at her, evidently thinking of something. "Say something mean about him," he suggested mildly.

Metria opened her mouth. "I—don't care to."

"If I didn't know better, I'd suspect you of having part of a soul," Trent said.

"That's nonsense! I'm just trying to make him deliriously happy for a few hours. It's a matter of professional pride."

"Since when do you have that kind of pride?" Gloha asked.

"Since—I got married," the demoness replied, surprised.

"That ceremony—it must have done more than marry you," Gloha said. "When I took the oath of nonhostility I felt invisible bonds close on me, binding me to what I swore. Did you feel that?"

"Why, yes," Metria said, similarly surprised. "I was so concerned with doing it exactly right that I didn't pay much attention. It did make me start relating to the castle, so I could pretend to summon the stork with him."

"Pretend?" Graeboe asked.

"We demons never summon storks unless we want to," Metria explained. "We just go through the motions, deluding mortals, but it isn't real. Who in her right mind would want to mess with a baby?"

"I would," Gloha said. "If I had the right—the right family."

Trent pursed his lips in the very mildest of expressions. "And you don't have the right family, Metria?"

"I didn't say that! Veleno's not a bad man, just isolated. There's nothing wrong with him that a good loving woman can't fix."

"And are you that woman?"

"Of course not!" Then she looked pained. "But—there's something. I don't know."

"Is it wonderful yet painful, leaving you so confused you hardly know what you feel?" Graeboe asked.

"That's it exactly!" the demoness agreed. "How did you know?"

"I think you are experiencing the first confused pangs of love," he said.

"I am? But—but that's what I was looking for!"

"And it isn't what you expected?" Gloha asked, interested.

"No. I don't know what I expected, but not this. It—I don't know if I like it."

"Love doesn't necessarily care whether you like it," Trent said sadly. "It can bring you enormous grief. But you would never trade it for any other experience. Metria, I believe that your wedding ceremony brought you half of Veleno's soul. Now you are able to experience the full range of human emotions and commitments."

"Not half of them?" Gloha asked.

"Half a soul is still a soul," he said. "It normally regenerates, becoming complete. You have a considerable experience ahead of you."

"But I didn't want a soul," Metria protested. "I just wanted to see what love is like."

"I think Professor Grossclout knew that," Graeboe said. "He knew you would be getting more than you wanted. He came to make sure it happened."

"Grossclout!" Metria exclaimed. "That infernal spook! He wanted to get back at me for never taking his classes seriously."

"I'd say he found a way," Trent said.

"What am I going to do with a soul?" she expostulated.

"You whatted?" Gloha asked.

"Shouted, yelled, howled, bellowed, proclaimed, argued earnestly—"

"Exclaimed?"

"Whatever," she agreed crossly. "Say, wait—I didn't say the word!"

"I still didn't understand it," Gloha said.

"Well, anyway," the demoness said tragically. "Where will I go, what will I do?"

"Frankly, my dear," Trent started, with three-fifths of a smile, "I don't—"

"Suffer," Graeboe said instead. "You'll suffer, Metria."

"Well, I'll have none of it. I'm going to—" She paused, distracted.

"You're going to what?" Marrow asked.

She sighed. "I'm going to get that pie for him." She puffed out.

Trent shook his head. "I think I wouldn't care to cross Professor Gross-clout," he remarked.

"If that is his penalty for being crossed, I would gladly do it," Marrow said. "I want half a soul."

Gloha saw Graeboe look thoughtful, but he didn't comment. "Well, we had better sleep if we're going to," she said, standing.

Graeboe tried to stand, but didn't make it. "Perhaps I will remain here," he said.

He was trying to be gracious about his weakness, and not bother anyone else with it. Gloha didn't want to embarrass him by offering to carry him again. "Maybe I'll stay here too," she said.

"I should think it would be more comfortable in your private cell," Marrow said.

"Well, it might, but—" she started.

"So I shall be glad to carry Graeboe there," the skeleton finished. "He carried me before."

"That is kind of you," Graeboe agreed. The skeleton picked him up and walked away.

"I'll fetch pillows," Gloha said quickly.

But when she had several pillows, she realized that they were too big for her to carry. She would have to make the long trip to the highest cell with one pillow at a time. That promised to be tedious. It would also use up more of the time she had hoped to have for sleeping.

Metria reappeared. "Got a problem?" she inquired.

"None you need to concern yourself about," Gloha said shortly.

"Yes I do. You are a nice person who never did anyone any harm, and you deserve assistance. I'll carry those up."

Gloha was taken aback. Then she remembered the soul. The demoness had become a caring person. "Thank you, Metria."

"It's weird, having to be concerned how others feel," Metria remarked as she carried the pillows. "But this business of love—I'm so afraid I'll do something wrong, or that he'll do something wrong, though I know these concerns are foolish. Sometimes I'm happy and sometimes I'm terrified. I'm just so mixed up. I wish—"

After a moment Gloha realized that the demoness wanted to be asked. This was definitely not the old Metria. "What do you wish?"

"I wish I had a—someone to—to listen—to understand—to advise—I don't know what. This is all so new."

"You wish you had a friend," Gloha said in a burst of realization that brightened the passage.

"That must be it. But there isn't—demons don't have friends."

"Maybe they do if they want them," Gloha said.

"Who would ever want to be friends with a demon?" Metria asked plaintively.

Gloha saw that the demoness' problem was her problem too. She had gotten Metria into this, and it had saved Gloha from a horrible fate. Maybe the demoness had done it for her own selfish reason, without knowing the full consequence, but Gloha owed her a considerable favor. "I would, maybe," she said.

Metria paused on an upper landing. "Would what?" she asked cautiously.

"I would be your friend."

The demoness froze. "Oh, I couldn't ask," she said. "I—oh, thank you. I feel so much better now." She was smiling, but tears were flowing from her eyes.

"I haven't experienced love myself, exactly," Gloha said, touched. "But I think your feelings are normal."

"I hope they get untangled soon."

They reached the high chamber. Marrow and Graeboe were there, talking, but they stopped as the others arrived.

Metria set down the pillows. "I have to get back," she said. "But—"

"Pop in, anytime," Gloha said.

The demoness nodded, and faded out.

"I will depart now," Marrow said, and did so.

Gloha arranged the pillows to make Graeboe comfortable. He seemed thoughtful as well as weak, but she decided not to ask what he and Marrow had been talking about. In a moment he was asleep, and in another, so was she.

Something was strange. The floor seemed to be sagging. That was impossible, of course, but Gloha couldn't just dismiss it. She sat up, looking around.

Dawn was brightening. Beyond the barred window a pink cloud was losing its color. The window looked slightly skew. She got up, knowing that it was merely an effect of the magic of perspective, but unable to restrain her curiosity. She touched a bar—and it felt not quite hard. Not soft, certainly, but not metallic. More like wood.

She looked up—and saw a dip in the ceiling. Imagination? She spread her wings and flew up to touch it. And it was slightly soft. And it gave a bit where her finger poked it. It *was* sagging!

Something was definitely amiss. She dropped to the floor. "Graeboe—I think we'd better get out of here."

He woke. "I think not."

"Not?"

"I don't think I can get up. I think my time is coming."

Something seemed to tear inside her. "No, Graeboe!" she cried. "Not yet. You haven't found your—your answer."

"I found enough. You must pry open the bars and fly out."

"Pry open the—! I can't do that!"

"The castle is dissolving. It means that Veleno has found someone who remembers her wedding the following morning. The enchantment is dissipating. You must escape before you are caught in the collapse.

Gloha realized that he had correctly understood the situation. That explained the sagging of the castle. The bars would no longer be strong enough to hold her, and that was the fastest exit. She went to them and wedged them apart as if they were strands of rubber. Looking out the window and down, she saw the entire castle leaning lopsidedly as its foundations lost their solidity.

She hurried back to Graeboe. "I'll take you too," she said.

"Gloha, it isn't worth your effort. I will be gone before the morning is done anyway. This is as good a way as any. But if you would—" He paused, somewhat as Metria had.

"What do you wish?" she asked, her heart hurting.

"If you would kiss me before you go—"

"I'm not going!" she cried. "Not without you." She got down, about to pick him up. But as she did so, she realized that the flight down, carrying him, would be perilous; she wasn't that strong a flyer. So she didn't gamble. She put her face down and kissed him on his little mouth.

Something went through her, like a gentle shock. Then the floor tilted, and she had to act. She hauled Graeboe up in her arms, scrambled to the window, and jammed through. It was slanting crazily, and the bars stretched readily. She lunged out, fell, spread her wings, and flew as hard as she could.

But it wasn't enough. Graeboe's weight bore her down, and she was falling too fast to land safely. She struggled to fly harder, but was able only to slow her descent. They were going to crash.

"Drop me!" Graeboe cried.

"No!" she cried back, hanging on to him more tightly.

The ground rushed up. Gloha closed her eyes.

She struck something soft and springy. She bounced.

She opened her eyes. She had landed on a big resilient cushion. It had enabled her to light harmlessly. But how had it come there?

The cushion opened a mouth as Gloha landed the second time. "Don't look so surprised," it said. "What are friends for, anyway?"

"Metria!" she cried gladly.

The cushion faded, leaving them on the ground. "Must see about Magician Trent," the lingering words came.

"Why did she save us?" Graeboe asked as she set him down on a nearby hummock.

"We're friends. We agreed to be, on the way up to the room last night. She needs a friend." Gloha looked up at the melting castle. "And it seems I needed one too."

"Ah. Because she is new to conscience and love. It must be difficult for her."

"It is. She has to sort it out all at once. But she must be succeeding, because the enchantment is ending. I'll help her all I can. After all, she saved me from something I very much didn't want." She glanced at the ground. "Twice."

"Which perhaps leads into my second question. Why didn't you drop me and save yourself, when it was apparent that you couldn't save us both?"

"I just couldn't!"

He did not pursue the matter. They watched the castle fold in on itself as its substance lost cohesion. Meanwhile the front door opened and nymphs ran out across the drawbridge, their hair streaming behind them. They had been freed, and were going home, where they would surely be welcomed. But where were Trent and Marrow?

Then those two emerged as well. They were the ones who had gotten the nymphs out.

"What about Veleno?" Gloha asked.

Metria appeared. "Are you kidding? I got him out first, of course. He's waiting over there."

They looked where she gestured. Veleno was lying on the ground, which accounted for why Gloha had overlooked him before. He had a dreamy smile on his face.

Gloha walked across to him. "Are you all right?"

"Never better," he replied. "I had to ask her to let me be for a while; there's only so much delirious happiness a man can stand all at once, when he's not used to it."

"I guess you did meet the demons' requirement," Gloha said. "You found a woman to love you."

"Metria's no mere woman. She's something else." He closed his eyes, and the dreamy smile returned. Evidently he was satisfied.

The castle continued to settle, as if on a very hot surface. Smoke rose from it, fuzzing into the sky. It collapsed into a mound, and the mound shrank into a pile, and the pile bubbled into a molehill. Finally the last of it steamed away, leaving only a bare island in a dirty pool.

"Well, that's it, dear," Metria said to Veleno. "I was going to bug out after this point, but somehow I no longer want to. Let's go home to your village."

"Weren't you helping these folk to fulfill their own quests?" he asked.

"In my fashion. But now they're free, so they can go on about their business."

"That's true," Gloha said. "Metria has done her part, and helped us a great deal. We can handle things on our own now."

"All right," Veleno said. "We might as well go."

But now Metria demurred. "Maybe I should see them through to the completion of their quests. We can wait, after all; that village doesn't even know we're coming."

"Or care," Veleno agreed. "Maybe we should go somewhere else. I really don't care, as long as you're there."

"You must be ready for some more delirious delight," the demoness said, advancing on him.

"Well—"

"Perhaps we should find some food, and resume our journey," Trent said briskly.

"But Graeboe can't travel," Gloha said.

"We can surely help," Metria said.

"But why should you take the trouble?" Gloha asked her.

Metria approached her. "Please," she said quietly. "I have a husband, but I'm new at all this, and I have only one friend. I'm not ready to face it all alone."

"Oh," Gloha agreed quickly. "Of course."

"We may have another concern," Marrow said, his skull facing the sky.

There were large creatures flying rapidly toward them.

12
LOVE

Gloha recognized them. "The flying centaurs!" she cried happily. In a moment four centaurs landed. Two were adult, and two were juvenile. Gloha flew up to make introductions. "Hello, Cheiron and Chex and Che and Cynthia," she said. "And Gwenny Goblin—why did you come here?"

"Metria said you needed help," the goblin girl chief said, jumping down from Cheiron's back to give Gloha a hug. "So we arranged for a contingent of goblins to come here to rescue you. Naturally I had to come myself to make sure they behave."

"And naturally I had to come with her, as her Companion," Che said.

"And naturally we wouldn't let them go into an unknown and possibly dangerous situation alone," Chex said.

"But the situation has been resolved," Gloha said. "Metria married my captor, and got half a soul, and the castle dissolved down to nothing. So we don't need rescue any more."

"That's too bad," Gwenny said.

"Too bad?" Gloha asked, surprised.

"Because the goblin forces will be arriving at any moment, and they'll be in a fighting mood."

"Oh." Gloha appreciated the problem. Goblin girls were always lovely, sweet, and nice, but goblin men were not like that. If there wasn't some enemy for them to fight, they were all too apt to find something else to fight, such as their friends.

"I wonder how the harpies will react," Metria remarked.

"They're coming too?" Gloha asked, alarmed.

"I tried to notify interested parties," the demoness said.

"It's a good thing the giants didn't hear of this," Graeboe said with a weak laugh.

"Of course they heard," Metria said. "You were in trouble too, weren't you? They said they'd gather a big force and tramp right over here."

Gloha was aghast. "Who else did you tell?"

"Nobody except the skeletons of the gourd."

Gloha was relieved. "At least they can't come out here. They're locked in the dream realm."

"Not if Trojan deems the matter important enough to give them a pass to the waking realm," Marrow said.

Trojan was the horse of a different color, who ruled the dream realm. He was a no-nonsense creature. "No danger of that," Gloha said, relieved.

There was the sound of marching. It grew louder. Not only that; it seemed to be coming from several directions. What was going on?

Gloha and the winged centaurs flew up to investigate from a suitable height. "Oh, no!" Gloha breathed.

For there were four groups converging. From the north came a rabble of goblins armed with clubs, spears, and stones. From the south came a screech of harpies armed with dungballs and explosive eggs. From the east came a crunch of giants; they were invisible, but their footprints could be seen advancing by giant steps. From the west came "a skeleton stiff!" Metria said, smoking into view at the same altitude.

"A skeleton what?" Gloha asked.

"Remains, cadaver, stink, decompose, body—"

"Corpse?"

"Whatev—no, that's not quite it. Band, force, squad, unit, team, crew, troop—"

"Corps?"

"—ver," the demoness agreed crossly.

"And they're all going to meet by the dirty pond," Cynthia said. She was flying beside Che Centaur, and they did make a nice couple, though both were still children. Gloha was glad to see that aspect of her adventure working out well.

"We'll just have to explain," Gloha said.

"That will not be easy," Chex said. "The goblins will obey Gwenny, grudgingly, but the others won't. They will want to have a big battle."

"And they are more or less natural enemies," Gloha said. "It was difficult to stop the goblins and harpies from going to war when my parents got together. I almost wish our captivity had lasted a little longer."

"Maybe Trent will know how to handle it," Cynthia said. "He was king for a while, wasn't he?"

"Yes," Gloha agreed. "He must have faced difficult situations before."

They flew down to rejoin the ground party. "There are goblins, harpies, giants, and skeletons converging," Gloha reported to Trent. "We need to stop them from quarreling."

The Magician nodded. "A distraction would be good. Perhaps some temporary quest to take their attention."

"Yes! But what?"

He glanced over to Graeboe. "I fear you are about to expire. What is your last wish?"

A horrible chill shuddered through Gloha. "Expire? Now?"

"I would like to be taken to some isolated region and transformed to my natural form," Graeboe said. "And I would like Marrow Bones to have my soul."

"Oh, I would not take your soul!" the skeleton protested.

"I would not care to have it be wasted, when it expected a longer life," Graeboe said. "I can not think of a worthier creature to have it."

"But you can't die!" Gloha cried. "You were supposed to be saved!"

"That appears to have been a vain hope," Graeboe said sadly. "I want Marrow to have my soul."

"Perhaps half of it," Trent said.

The sound of tramping was loud. At any moment the converging forces would appear. "I do not wish to intrude on a sensitive moment," Marrow said, "but I think that dealing with the assorted contingents should have priority."

"This is my notion," Trent said. Then, inexplicably, he addressed Graeboe again. "Did the Good Magician say anything else, except that help would come if you waited in this vicinity?"

"No, not that I recall," Graeboe said. "Just that I might be transported."

"Transported?" Gloha asked.

"Shipped, hauled, delivered, moved, carried, conveyed—" Metria said helpfully.

"Surely to the place suitable to my expiration," Graeboe agreed. "I must have misunderstood the message."

"That's easy to do, with Humfrey's words," Marrow said. "I may have similarly misunderstood Professor Grossclout's admonition to tarry near the volcano."

"I am not sure of that, in either case," Trent said. "Humfrey's Answers are always relevant, when understood. So are Grossclout's. Your fates may be linked, along with Gloha's."

Now the giant steps were so close the ground was quaking, and the harpy flight was appearing on the horizon. Why wasn't Trent paying attention?"

"That word," Trend said. "Could it have been 'transplanted'?"

"Why, yes, I believe it was," Graeboe agreed, surprised. "I misremembered it. But that must be merely another way to suggest that I would be moved to another locale."

"And you, Marrow," Trent said. "Was there anything else, however seemingly irrelevant, that Grossclout told you?"

The skeleton tapped his skull. "Only that it would be a fair trade. Since I have nothing to trade for a soul, that does not seem to relate."

The goblin army appeared to the north, and the skeleton crew to the west. The timing seemed perfect: all four groups would arrive together.

Trent turned back to Graeboe. "If you were to trade half your soul for something, what would that be?"

"I am not seeking to trade my soul," Graeboe objected. "I seek only to give it to a worthy person."

"Speaking hypothetically: what would be worth it?"

Graeboe made a wan smile. "My life, of course. But—"

"What kind of a transplant would give you life?"

"New blood. Since that is not possible—"

"Where does your blood come from?"

Graeboe shook his head. "I don't understand."

"I do," Cheiron Centaur said. "The blood comes from the bones, at least in part. He would need a bone transplant."

The others laughed at the impossibility of that. Except for Trent. "Or perhaps a marrow transplant?"

"Well, yes, of course," Cheiron agreed. "The center part of the bone. I thought that was understood."

The skeleton's jawbone dropped. "You mean I could trade some of my marrow, to give him life? I would gladly do that, regardless of the soul."

"But Graeboe's a giant," Gloha said. "Marrow doesn't have enough in his whole body to provide more than one finger's worth."

"Not when Graeboe is in his present form," Trent pointed out.

The others stared at him. "That's right!" Marrow said. "He is small at the moment."

"Oh, Graeboe, you can be saved!" Gloha said. "Once you get better, you can be as you once were, an invisible giant." Yet somehow her joy in that realization was tempered.

"Thus perhaps we see the nature of the trade," Trent concluded. "Marrow for half a soul, and both achieve their objects."

Now the contingents from the four directions arrived. They drew up and flew down to a stop, forming a perfect square bounded by goblins, giants, harpies, and skeletons. The giants were indicated only by their imprints, but those were huge.

"I shall be happy to make that trade," Marrow said.

"And so shall I," Graeboe agreed, amazed.

"There is just one problem," Trent said. "As I recall, a marrow exchange has to be facilitated by bloodroot and a trans-plant. Does anyone know where such a plant grows?"

There were blank looks all around. No one knew.

"I think we have a search to make," Trent said. "Fortunately, we have a competent search party assembled, capable of checking land, air, and underground. In one of those regions there should be a plant." He looked around. "But we need to locate it before the day is out, because I think Graeboe will not survive until tomorrow."

"What does the plant look like?" Gloha asked.

"It is fairly small, with vinelike branches," Cheiron said. "Its leaves are green, and it has coiled projections terminating in spikes." He took a stick and made a sketch in the dirt. "Approximately this configuration." Then he drew an enlarged flower. "You can most readily identify it by its distinctive blossom."

"Let's see which contingent can find such a flower first," Trent said.

The word went out to the four groups. Immediately they scattered, seeking the trans-plant. The possible strife had been averted.

Cynthia looked thoughtful. "I dimly remember something about such a plant," she said. "Of course that was when I was a child, seventy years—" She caught herself. "Seven years ago. It may be gone now."

"Where did you hear it was?" Che inquired.

She turned a surprisingly competent little-girl smile on him. Che of course knew her origin and original age, but seemed to like her very well regardless. That was perhaps not surprising, for not only was she the only other winged centaur child in Xanth, who was most eager to get along well, she had more than a suggestion of her former and later prettiness. "I'd rather not say. Because if I'm wrong it will make me look even duller than I am. I think I'll just go look."

"Not alone," Chex said severely. "Not at your age, in this region."

"Oh," Cynthia said, momentarily discommoded. "Yes, of course. It's probably not there anyway."

"I will go with you," Chex said. "And you don't look dull." She was of course speaking literally. Cynthia's mind might be dull compared to that of a normal centaur, but her appearance was bright.

"Oh," Cynthia repeated, more cheerfully. "Yes." The two of them took off.

Gloha realized that Che wasn't going, because he was staying with Gwenny, whose companion he was. He never separated from her. It was clear that the two were as close as any two could be, but that this was friendship and not romance. It was a significant distinction. Cheiron stayed also, to give Gwenny a ride, because she couldn't fly. Thus Gwenny was directing the goblins from the back of a winged centaur, and no one seemed to find that remarkable.

Soon the only ones remaining by the pond were Gloha, Graeboe, Marrow, Trent, Metria, and Veleno—and the last two disappeared into the forest, theoretically to search, but probably to have privacy for another dose of delirious happiness. Gloha remained amazed how that had worked out, and a bit jealous. The demoness and the nymphomaniac had turned out to be right for each other, while Gloha had found nothing right for her. If only it had been someone like Magician Trent who had captured her in the castle, but younger and single—but her foolish little fancy was going offtrack again.

"Perhaps we should eat and rest now," Trent said. "Because when that plant is located, we shall likely have some traveling to do."

"Could it be brought here?" Gloha asked. "It would be better if Graeboe didn't have to travel."

"The bloodroot, yes. We need only a sprig of that. But I believe that the trans-plant itself can't be transplanted," he said. "Just as I can't transform myself. Some magic relates to oneself, and some to others. So we shall have to find a way to move Graeboe comfortably. Perhaps I can transform a volunteer into a form suitable for such service."

"Transform me!" Gloha said immediately.

"Please, no," Graeboe said. "I would not have you trouble yourself further on my behalf."

"But I want to help you. I can't stand the thought of you—" She couldn't finish.

"I have been already too much of a burden," he said. "You have been more than kind to me already."

"Perhaps we should accomplish the exchange," Marrow said. "Then there need be no further concern about burdens, for Graeboe will be healthy and able to be transformed to any form he wishes."

"Exactly," Gloha said. "He can be an invisible giant again. And I can help that happen by being transformed to a suitable carrying form."

"I think it will be better to get some other volunteer," Trent said.

"Why? When I want to help?"

"It's just an opinion," he said mildly.

Gloha decided not to argue further. She and Marrow went foraging for nuts and fruits and a blanket for Graeboe, because he seemed to be getting cold. Trent transformed a weed into a flame vine that provided heat. They ate a belated breakfast and rested. Gloha discovered that she was tired; the events of the morning had taken mental as well as physical toll. So she settled down on a cushion beside Graeboe and tried to relax. She knew she wouldn't really be able to rest until there was news of the trans-plant.

She woke some time later, somewhat refreshed. It seemed to be near noon. Graeboe was asleep beside her, wrapped in his blanket, still looking cold. Others were talking some distance away.

Metria popped in before her. "Mixed reports," she said. "The goblins are scouring the ground and underground. The harpies are checking the mountains and treetops. The giants and skeletons are checking far crannies together. They've found plenty of bloodroot. In fact, here's a sprig." She showed a blood-red root. "But there seems to be no trans-plant growing anywhere to be found."

Gloha didn't want to hear that, so she inquired about a detail. "The giants and skeletons are working together?"

"Yes. The giants can travel far, but aren't much for detail work like peeking into beerbarrel tree knotholes. So they are carrying handfuls of skeletons, and the skeletons do the peeking." The demoness smiled. "Some ordinary folk have freaked out when they peeked into houses."

Gloha could appreciate why. "I hope somebody finds it. It would be really mean of the Good Magician to tell him he'd find help, if it can't be."

"Yes, Humfrey always amused me before. Now I would be sorry to learn of such a deception."

"Well, you have a soul now." Gloha sat up. "I guess I haven't been much of a friend to you. I've been distracted."

"It's a funny thing," Metria said. "Once you said you would be my friend, I got much more confidence, and it was easier to adjust. I didn't need your advice."

"That's the way friendship works sometimes." She looked at Graeboe. "If only I could be more of a friend to him."

"You've done all you could, haven't you?"

"I haven't saved his life. I try to find ways to help, but I can't do what really counts."

The demoness looked unusually thoughtful, as if her recent experience had given her some insight. "I'm sure you'll find a way."

Then two centaurs appeared in the sky. Chex and Cynthia. "It was there!" Cynthia exclaimed, her pigtails bobbing. "Right where I'd heard it might be."

Gloha leaped up. "You found the trans-plant? Oh, wonderful!"

"Don't be overjoyed just yet," Chex said. "It is by no means easy to reach."

"We'll reach it anyway," Gloha said. "We have to. Where is it?"

"In a crevice on Mount Pin-A-Tuba. That's not a nice mountain."

Sudden dread surged through Gloha. "I know. Oh, this is awful. How will we ever get to it without being buried in burning ashes?"

Magician Trent strode up to join them. He accepted Metria's sprig of blood-root and tucked it into a pocket. "I think the creatures who came to help us will have some real action after all. We shall have to lay siege to the mountain."

"But that won't get us safely into its crevice!" Gloha protested.

"It will if the distraction is sufficient."

Gloha saw the logic. The evil mountain wouldn't be able to keep track of every single goblin and harpy. If they were careful, and escaped its notice long enough, the ploy might work.

The retreat sounded, and the various parties began returning to the rendezvous. As they did, they got briefed. There were hollers and screeches as the goblins and harpies learned that violent action would be required, but abrupt silence when they found out the nature of the enemy. This was more of a challenge than they really cared for. But neither group could back down in the presence of the other. The skeletons were not as concerned, being less vulnerable to hot rocks. The giants were neutral; they could normally get away from something like that in two or three giant steps, but they knew that they could be hurt by flying boulders, and the closer they got to the mountain the worse it would be.

"Now we shall have to get moving," Trent said.

"But the siege hasn't even started," Gloha said.

"Precisely. We must seek a devious route that will take longer, so that the mountain never suspects the real object. The siege will be in place by the time Pin-A-Tuba might realize that an insignificant party is approaching—and then it may assume that this is merely a distraction from the real object. This is chancy, I agree, but seems to be the best course."

"What is the real object?" Gloha asked. "I mean, the one that we hope the mountain will think is the real object?"

"The harpies discovered a marvelous lake on the other side of the volcano from the trans-plant. They call it Miracle Lake. The apparent object will be to capture and exploit that lake."

"Why would anybody want a lake beside a mean-spirited volcano?"

"There are boats on that lake, floating at anchor. Barnacles grow on the bottoms of those boats. The surfaces of those barnacles are so highly glossy as to be reflective. They can be harvested and assembled into full-sized mirrors. Thus they are mirror-barnacles, or miracles for short."

"But mirrors can be made from glass or polished stone," she said. "Why go to the trouble of fashioning them from shiny barnacles?"

"They are magic barnacles. They make magic mirrors."

"Oh!" Gloha exclaimed, suddenly understanding. "I never knew where magic mirrors came from."

"There may be other origins," Trent said. "But I suspect that we have stumbled upon one of Magician Humfrey's secret sources. Certainly the mountain will zealously guard its treasure. So I think this is as good a diversion as any."

"I should think so," she agreed, impressed. "I wouldn't mind having one of those mirrors myself."

He smiled. "You have other business, I think."

"Oh, of course! I wasn't suggesting—" Then she realized that he was teasing her. His ways were sometimes so subtle that she had trouble interpreting them. That was part of what she liked about him. He was just so—so manly.

He turned to other business. "Metria and Veleno are now scouting out a possible route to the trans-plant. They seem to work well together."

"But Veleno can't go near that mountain."

"He can in his present form."

"His—?"

"I transformed him. He is a parrot legal, one of the few creatures the volcano tolerates near its cone. Perhaps because they are very good at arguing their cases."

"Arguing cases?" she asked blankly.

"Parrots are talkative birds, and these ones like to perform legal tasks, though they are neither secretary-birds nor lawyer-birds. They are merely paralegals. They argue Pin-A-Tuba's case that he has a right to sound off in as great a volume as he chooses, though he blows phenomenal amounts of gas and ash into the sky. So he doesn't object to their presence. Veleno is flying through the region, while Metria makes spot detail checks on the terrain. I think they'll get the job done."

"But why should Veleno help us? He was holding us captive, and he almost wanted to—to make me be his—"

"He was doing what he thought he had to, to achieve freedom from his enchantment," Trent said. "You caused Metria to marry him. He is grateful, and perhaps suffering some tinge of guilt. He believes that the guilt will not entirely dissipate until he has helped you achieve your quest, just as you helped him achieve his."

Gloha shook her head. "I suppose it does make sense. But why couldn't Metria explore the whole region herself?"

"Because she's a demoness, and the volcano doesn't much like demons. It seems that they used to play pranks on him, such as dropping stink bombs into his mouth. So whenever a demon materializes close by, Pin-A-Tuba lets fly with vigor and blasts it out of there. Metria can remain close only so long as she never materializes."

"But then she can't communicate with anyone, can she?"

"She can communicate with Veleno, because she has half his soul. So Veleno is indeed proving to be useful to our cause."

Gloha shook her head again. It was amazing how things could turn out.

Metria appeared. "We have a route," she reported. "I didn't have time to investigate every nuance, but I think it's good. It won't be fun, but it should get you there."

"Where's Veleno?"

"He paused to argue a case with another parrot legal who didn't recognize him. He'll be along soon."

Indeed, in only four moments the parrot winged in. He had bright purple plumage with orange stripes. Metria held out her hand, and he landed on it. She brought him in and kissed him on the beak. "I have been beakissed," he exclaimed, fluttering his wings. "There is no precedent."

"Are you ready for your next form?" Trent inquired.

"Proceed with your case, counselor," the parrot said.

The Magician put his hand close, and the parrot became a glob of goo. "Eeek!" Metria screamed in almost nymphly fashion, trying to hold the goo in her hands. But it slipped through her fingers and landed with a splat on the ground.

Metria turned to face Trent. "What did you do to my love?" she demanded. "He's all icky!"

"No he isn't," Trent said mildly. "He's merely not yet quite firm. He will shape up in a moment."

Sure enough, in exactly one moment the blob shaped itself into what appeared to be a reclining chair. Metria touched the surface. "Oh, he's like centaur hide," she said appreciatively.

"Precisely. He is ready to carry Graeboe to the trans-plant."

"But what kind of creature is he?" Gloha asked.

"A slowmud. A smaller cousin of Swiftmud. Large enough to carry one elf. He can hear and understand us, but can respond only with bubbles: white for yes, black for no, and shades of gray for other responses."

"Carry an elf?" Gloha asked. "You mean—?"

"Graeboe lacks the strength to make this trip," Trent reminded her. "We are fortunate that he was able to rest and recuperate enough to survive beyond noon."

That was certainly true. Graeboe remained asleep, or—

Gloha hastily checked him. His eyes were open, but his forehead was cool. "Oh, Graeboe, you're fading!" she said.

He gave her a reassuring smile, but it was a weak one.

"We need to reach that plant before the day is out," Trent said quietly. "Does your route permit that, Metria?"

"Yes, if you move right along," the demoness said. "I'll lead the way. I won't be able to solidify near the mountain, but Veleno will receive my communications."

"You had better lead invisibly from the start," Trent said. "So that we can work out the miscues before we get within range of the mountain."

"Gotcha," She smoked out.

He turned to Gloha. "I think it will be best if you move Graeboe to the chair."

Gloha agreed. She got down and slid her arms under the elf form and the blanket. She heaved him up, wincing as she saw him wince. She set him carefully in the chair, which adjusted to accommodate the body. The surface of the slowmud was plush and did seem to be about as comfortable as it could be. Trent had chosen the transformation well.

"Lead on, Metria," Trent said.

The demoness did not appear. But Veleno started to move. He just slid smoothly along the ground, in the manner the larger Swiftmud had, evidently responding to Metria's hidden touch or silent word. Shared souls were wonderful.

"But we can't get there from here," Gloha said, hurrying after the slowmud, which was getting to respectable velocity. "It's beyond the Faun & Nymph Retreat, Lake Ogre-Chobee, and the Region of Madness. It took us days to come this far. How can we do it in hours?"

"Maybe we can go into ogre-drive," Trent said, unconcerned as they moved onto a slight hill. "Or take giant steps."

"But we're not—"

The hill rose into the air. "Eek!" Gloha cried, exactly like a nymph. She kicked her feet, flung her hair about, spread her wings, and flew up, alarmed.

Trent and Marrow sat down beside the chair. "On the other hand, let's just relax," Trent said. The group rose up beyond the tops of the trees.

Chex and Cynthia flew over to join Gloha. "I see you are on your way to the nasty mountain," the elder centaur said. "We can't go there, so we'll return home now. But please stop by when your quest is done."

"Yes, please do," Cynthia said. "I really enjoyed traveling with you and Magician Trent." There was just the suggestion of a flush as she mentioned the name, as if she had some unchildish memory. "I would hate to lose touch."

"I, uh, of course," Gloha said, somewhat discombobulated if not actually disconcerted, because she understood Cynthia's memory all too well. Also, she was confused by the mysterious flying hill.

"I'm so glad I was able to help," Cynthia said.

"Yes. Thank you."

The centaurs flew away, looking somewhat like dam and filly, or more properly dam and future filly-in-law.

Then Gloha saw a giant footprint form in a field. Oh—an invisible giant was carrying them! One whose breath didn't smell. Now she realized that the hill the others rode on was in the general shape of a hand with a tarpaulin spread across it. Somehow she hadn't gotten the word about this detail.

She flew to the hand and landed. There was no sense wearing herself out with a long flight.

Then she remembered Trent's pun: take giant steps. On the other hand. Figures of speech to be taken literally. Darn the man!

In a surprisingly short time their flying island sank down to the land. In the distance was the peak of a smoking mountain. She saw other islands floating in, and realized that the armies of goblins, skeletons, and harpies were being similarly transported. "The giants can't approach the volcano for the same reason the demons can't," Trent remarked. "It seems that once an absentminded giant trod on one of Pin-A-Tuba's ash gardens, and now none of them are welcome. A boulder of hot rock can make an uncomfortable burn. But the giants are contributing to the effort in this manner before going home." He patted the tarp. "And we certainly appreciate the transportation." The flesh beneath gave a twitch of appreciation. Gloha knew why the giant did not speak; it would give away the operation if the mountain overheard.

They dismounted from the hand, and the tarp slid off and became limp. The hand had departed.

They were at the edge of a dry plain spread with what looked like dishes. Veleno, answering an invisible directive, slid briskly into it. Trent and Marrow paced it on either side. Gloha was left perplexed again.

Unable to subdue her curiosity, she went to inspect the closest of the dishes. It turned out to contain what looked like vanilla ice cream. What was that doing way out here in nowhere? She checked another. It contained several brownies, smelling very chocolaty. A third dish contained butterscotch pudding. Others had pie, cake, tarts, sweets, fruits, sugared nuts, and assorted other desserts.

Suddenly it registered. This wasn't a desert plain—it was a dessert plain! Filled with plain desserts. In fact it must be the region of Just Desserts she had heard about but never expected to visit.

Well, there was no sense in letting all this wonderful food go to waste. She picked up a dish with a mouth-watering slice of meringue pie. She was about to eat it when Marrow's skull turned to face her. "That may not be wise," the skeleton said. "Fumes from the volcano may have tainted these desserts."

Good point. She threw the pie away. But it looped around and came back to her hand. "Boo!" it said.

Astonished, she threw it away again, harder. It skated just above the ground in a big loop, and came right back to her. "Boo!" Couldn't she get rid of it?

"Boo-meringue pie, I believe," Marrow observed.

Oh. The kind that always came back to a person. So she held on to it for now; she'd find a way to get rid of it soon, she was sure.

She flew ahead to see what other wonders might be along this route. Beyond the desserts was a low valley. In it were hoods. Just assorted pointed or rounded headdresses, sitting there for anyone to take. She picked one up that was about right for her and put it on her head.

Immediately it closed on her forehead and ears with such force it was painful. She tried to take it off, but it clung, curling around her mouth, trying to suffocate her. Choking, she fell to the ground.

Then the hood climbed off her face. She gasped in a breath, not moving for the moment. The hood crawled to her hand and wrapped itself around the dish of pie. Then it rolled away with the pie.

Gloha sat up, staring after it. That was a robbing hood! A criminal type. And she, unsuspecting, had let it waylay her. What a fool she had been to trust a hood.

She got up, dusted herself off, and set forth again. She hoped the others had not seen her stupidity with the hood.

Beyond the hooded valley was a field with a single tree. The tree had branches with spinning needlelike spikes, leaves that radiated X rays, and tendrils that squirted jets of water or made horrible sucking sounds. The very sight of it made Gloha shiver with horror. That was a dentis tree! The most feared of all trees. Her teeth ached with the mere thought of getting within range of that monster.

The party caught up as she hovered, not daring to proceed. "No need to be concerned about that," Trent said reassuringly. "That's a dentis tree."

"I kn-know," she agreed, her teeth chattering.

"Such a tree can be very useful, when there's a toothache, I understand," Marrow said. "It doesn't bother folk with healthy teeth."

Veleno proceeded right past the tree. Gloha nerved herself and followed. She was relieved when the tree did not grab her.

Now the route descended into a broad, deep cleft. This was good, because it concealed them from the view of the mountain. But there was something odd about it. "I don't like it," she said.

"Like it it," a voice replied with an annoying inflection.

"Who said that?" she asked, not quite pleased.

"Said that that," the voice said with a sneer.

"Are you making fun of me?" she demanded.

"Fun of me me," it agreed ironically.

"Pay it no mind," Trent advised. "It's obviously a sar-chasm."

"Sar chasm chasm," the voice agreed tauntingly.

Gloha nodded, not trusting herself to speak again, because the chasm had a way of reversing and demeaning the import of whatever she said.

There was a remote clamor. It sounded like goblins and harpies hurling insults at each other. That was good news; it meant that the siege was starting. That should distract Mount Pin-A-Tuba from the real mission.

But soon there was another sound: that of distant thunder. Trent cocked his head. "Uh-oh," he said mildly.

"Could that be Fracto?" Marrow inquired.

"It surely could," Gloha said. "He always shows up at the worst times."

"Malign beings do seem to congregate," Trent agreed. "The evil cloud may have a pact with the evil mountain. Our siege alerted it."

"Well, as long as Fracto doesn't realize what we're up to."

The cloud moved in with dismaying speed. The sky darkened. Thunder crashed, and lightning jags taunted the land. The rain started.

"I think this chasm won't be suitable much longer," Trent said.

"Maybe if we hurry, we'll get out of it soon," Marrow said.

They hurried. Veleno fairly whizzed along. The rain came down more thickly, and the runoff from higher slopes poured into the chasm in assorted waterfalls. The base began to fill with water.

"Maybe we had better get out of this chasm," Gloha suggested. "I mean by getting straight out now, not trying to get out the far end of it."

"Metria is showing the route," Trent said. "She should know whether it is safe to leave the chasm now." He glanced at Veleno.

A black bubble came from a nozzle at the slowmud's front. That meant No. It wasn't safe to leave.

So they continued, as rapidly as they could. But the rainfall increased. Water sluiced into the chasm, and the runoff poured more thickly into it. Evidently this was one of the mountain's natural drainage clefts, excellent for travel during dry weather, but a disaster in a storm. Metria could not have known that Fracto would get into the act. The level not only rose in the chasm, it developed a turbulent flow. They had either to get out of the chasm, or fight that flow. It was getting more difficult.

"Still not safe to leave this depression?" Trent inquired mildly.

Another black bubble.

"I'll see for myself," Gloha said impatiently. She spread her wings and hauled herself into the air despite the buffeting of the winds. She got her head up above the level of the brink and peered out.

It was a hellish scene. The chasm was winding through a landscape of jagged rocks surrounded by ash. Steam rose from hot spots, and sinister smoke issued from mean-looking vents. There seemed to be no clear path through it except the chasm. Metria had signaled truly.

"Not safe," Gloha said shortly as she dropped back to the bottom. "We have to continue here."

"We shall have to float," Trent decided. "Slowmud can do it, and Marrow can form a boat for me, as he did before. But each can support only one person. We have one extra."

"Me," Gloha said. "I will have to go back, so that the rest of you can make it."

"No," Trent said firmly. "You must be along. It is your quest."

"But Graeboe has to be along, and so does Marrow. You don't mean that you will go back?"

"I fear for your safety if I am not with you. I may need to transform you if there is an emergency."

"Then transform me now, into a form that can handle this."

"I don't think that's wise."

"But we have to do *something*!" she cried despairingly.

"See if you can hang on to the slowmud," he said. "You can float without putting your weight on it."

She hadn't thought of that. Maybe it would work.

Trent kicked Marrow in the hipbone, and the skeleton flew apart and formed into the small boat. There was even a line of small bones extending across so that the slowmud could grab on. That way they wouldn't get separated in the rapids.

Trent found a long piece of driftwood he was able to beat into a crude paddle-pole. He got in the boat and jammed the pole down through the surging water as an anchor. Gloha saw now that the bone boat had flipper-bones below that served to propel the craft.

Meanwhile Veleno stopped trying to glide through the shallows and set out to float on the deeps. It did seem to work better, except that the swirling current tended to turn him around. Gloha grabbed on behind, and the current hauled her back, so that she served as a stabilizer. Then the slowmud was able to forge forward.

They moved slowly on up the river. Gloha hoped it would end soon, so that they could get back on land, but it seemed interminable. The rain kept pouring down, preventing the river from drying up. Fracto probably didn't realize that they were there, or he would have made it much worse. This was just the fringe of his effort to wash out the goblins and harpies elsewhere.

A dark ugly shape flapped over the chasm. Gloha saw its silhouette against the bleary sky. It looked like a vulture, only worse. It peered down with its beady eyes. It plopped a smelly poop into the water. That enabled Gloha to recognize it: the thing was a vulgar. Probably one of the mountain's mean-spirited creatures. What would happen if it spied them, and told Pin-A-Tuba?

Then two smaller ugly shapes appeared. "There's one!" the first screeched.

Harpies! Part of the siege force. Gloha had seldom been happier to see her winged relatives.

"Well, let's tear it to quivering bits!" the second harpy screeched enthusiastically.

The two dived for the vulgar. All three shapes disappeared beyond the chasm brink. There was a medley of screeching, and a grimy feather drifted down. The harpies had saved the little party from discovery.

They followed the chasm river around a turn, and came to a filling pool. Here it was slightly quieter, though the storm was still pounding overhead. They pulled over to the side, where it was shallow enough for them to get some temporary footing and rest briefly.

Trent looked back. "Trouble," he said mildly.

Gloha looked around, expecting some new threat. But there didn't seem to be anything. "What is it?" She noticed that the sar-chasm effect was gone; there was no longer a mean-spirited echo.

"Graeboe is leaving us."

"What?" But she knew what he meant. She pulled herself around to the side and looked at the elf-giant.

His pallor was worse. He was conscious, but looked as if he expected not to be so at any moment. The violence of the river travel had depleted his scant remaining strength.

Gloha was stricken. What good was this trip if the rigors of travel wiped Graeboe out before the trans-plant could heal him? "What can we do?" she asked plaintively.

"We can do nothing," he said gravely. "You can do much."

"I don't understand!"

"Tell him the truth."

"I haven't lied to him, or to anyone."

"Except to yourself, perhaps."

The Magician could be so irritating at times! What was he talking about? "What haven't I been truthful about?" she demanded. "How is it hurting Graeboe?"

"Your feeling."

"My feeling? I want him to be cured, so he can live and be a giant."

"Then tell him that."

Gloha shook her head, unkindly bemused. Graeboe was dying, and she was supposed to wish him a happy gianthood? Yet she had to say something.

"I can't tell him the truth," she said with difficulty. "It would only hurt him, and diminish me. And you."

"I doubt it," he said with that infuriating mildness.

"Then *you* hear it first!" she snapped. "I am—am fascinated by you, and if I had my choice I would become a human woman and do everything with you that you had in mind for Cynthia." There: it was out, for whatever mischief it was worth.

He seemed unfazed. "I think not."

"Because you're not interested," she agreed dully.

"Oh, but I am."

"So you can just go on being amused by—" She paused. "What?"

"You are lovely, innocent, caring, faithful, and sincere. You are the kind of woman any man could love. You are a rare prize. And I could readily transform you to a fully human woman."

She stared at him. "You—you return my interest?"

"I do. I am as fascinated with you as you are with me, and for similar reason. You are to your gender what you see me to be in mine. We could have a wonderful time together."

Gloha shook her heady little head. "Forgive me, Magician, but I am having trouble believing this."

"Believe it. But understand the whole of it: it would not endure. Because my perspectives are not yours, my friends are not yours, and I am a Magician while you are not. I exist in a different realm, and that would surely alienate us from each other after the first flush of fulfillment faded. You will never be able to match me in magic, and if you join me you will sacrifice the heritage you have. You would come to resent your inability to fly, and you would be ashamed that you gave up the quality that made you unique: the unification in your person of the goblins and the harpies. And so it would be a mistaken affair without a future—even if I were not old and already married. This is not your true desire, or mine."

She reeled under his harsh and appallingly adult logic. Suddenly she saw her dream for what it was: an utterly foolish fancy. She had known it, but never quite accepted it. Now she could no longer deny it. She could not give up her heritage for any temporary tryst, no matter how handsome, intelligent, or magical the man. And he could not give up his, though he had gone so far as to confess being attracted to both Cynthia and Gloha herself. He was, physically, a young, healthy man; he noticed and responded to pretty women. The difference between them was that he had experience enough to appreciate the truth, and the discipline to be governed by his head rather than his passion.

"Thank you, Magician," she said at last. "You have marvelously clarified my mind." She wiped away her tears, but more replaced them immediately.

"Now you must do the same for Graeboe, before he dies."

"I should set him straight, the way you set me straight? I don't think I could be so cruel."

"The truth is seldom cruel. I think you owe it to him."

"Because he—he thinks he feels about me the way I thought I felt about you?"

"Yes. But there is a difference."

"Yes. He's dying. I'm not."

"So there is very little time."

He was relentless! But what else could she do? She did owe a dying man the truth. She returned to Graeboe.

She reached out of the water and took his hand under the blanket. It was as cold as hers, but his wasn't wet. The blanket seemed to have a water-repellent quality, so was protecting him from a soaking. "Graeboe, I wish you could hang on just enough longer so that you can be cured, and live your life as an invisible giant."

"Thank you," he breathed. "I wish you fulfillment in your quest." He closed his eyes. "If you will, ask Marrow Bones to come near."

She saw that he was about to die. Something burst inside her. "Oh, it's not true!" she cried. "I don't want you to be a giant!"

Slowly his eyes opened. He was faintly startled.

"I don't want you to be any other creature," she said, amazed at herself. "I just want you to be mine. I love you, Graeboe, and I wish I could m-marry you, and to h-hell with my quest!" She fetched his hand in to her face and kissed it. "Oh, Graeboe, it's impossible, and I'm so selfish, and you're such a good man, and I have no right, but please, please don't die. Even if it can't be anything between us, because I know I could never endure as a giantess any more than as a straight human woman, I want you to be healthy and happy."

"But I am not handsome or really smart, and I have no magic talent. A wonderful creature like you can do so much better."

"You're just a really decent guy, who needs me, as Trent does not," she agreed. "And that's all I ever wanted. My heart knew. Except—"

His hand warmed. "I'd rather be a winged goblin with you, than a giant without you," he said. "I love you too, Gloha, but did not want to impose."

"A winged goblin!" she exclaimed. That had never occurred to her. "Of course that's possible. You can be anything, when Trent transforms you. Oh, Graeboe, *you* are the one I want. I knew you liked me, but I never thought you'd be willing to give up your natural form, so I diverted myself with another notion. Just hang on, and *be* the fulfillment of my quest."

He smiled. "I think perhaps I can do that now."

She leaned over him and kissed his little face. "You must, Graeboe. I would be desolate without you."

"I did not want to live, without you."

And so he had been fading, having no reason to fight to survive. Magician Trent had known. Now the rest of the truth was out. She had been unblinded.

Graeboe closed his eyes again, but this time he seemed to be headed for a restorative sleep instead of a final fade-out. He should be able to survive until they reached the trans-plant.

They resumed their float up the river. The rain was still coming down, and total gloom covered the landscape, but now things seemed brighter.

Finally the chasm narrowed and gave out. They emerged on a slanting plain of hardened volcanic rock; the covering of ash had been washed off. What had been the chasm was now a mere indentation. Trent kicked Marrow back to his normal configuration, and they followed the indent around a curving surface until a new and jagged terrain appeared. There were ridges and spikes interspersed with a cracked-glaze pattern of crevices.

A hulking knuckle-walking brute came around a pile of stones. "Huh?" it exclaimed, spying them. Then it lifted its snout and sounded a howl. "Awooooo!"

The mountain took note. The rock shuddered. Steam issued from the little crevices. Boiling red lava appeared, flowing in pursuit of the steam.

"We may have a problem," Trent said mildly.

"Pin-A-Tuba knows we're here," Gloha agreed. "It's focusing on us. We'll never get through."

"Metria," Trent said. "Materialize."

The Demoness appeared. "You realize this means more mischief," she said.

"If you are willing to act as a decoy, we may be able to proceed."

She pursed her lips. "Follow the path up to that crack in the cone," she said, pointing. "I'll do what I can."

Then Metria fogged into smoke, and re-formed as a monstrous toad. "Come and get me, you numbskull!" the toad croaked. Gloha hoped that the mountain was not smart enough to realize that it had to be a fake; frogs, not toads, croaked. But maybe it didn't matter; the mountain would know she was a demoness, and go after her regardless.

The toad hopped, landing with a plop. "Can't catch me, firesnoot!" she called.

The lava fairly boiled out of the cracks, hissing as the rain struck it. It formed pools, then began to flow after the toad. Scattered bits of wood and brush burst into fire as the lava touched them in passing. The several runnels formed into one big one, gaining speed. They seemed to have forgotten about the main party, but there was so much lava that it spread out across much of the surface as it flowed.

Trent led the way quickly to the nearest ridge, so that they could avoid the burning rock flow. It surrounded their elevation like a shallow lake. There was nothing to do except follow the ridge on up.

The crest became higher and sharper. The lava still prevented them from returning to more level terrain, so they had to stay high. The ridge turned pointed, until the two sides met in a knifelike cut.

Veleno had no trouble. The slowmud simply slid across one side of the ridge, sticking to it like a snail. Graeboe rode along, firmly fastened in place. Gloha was able to fly just above the ridge, though the rain and gusts of wind made this nervous business. Marrow straddled the crest, having no flesh to be cut. That left Trent.

But Marrow solved that problem. With a kick he assumed the configuration of a platform across the top, braced by arm and leg bones on either side. Trent sat on this platform, and the skeleton skidded smartly along, carrying him. Gloha was even able to join them, so that she didn't have to fight the foggy winds.

Then another vulgar flapped by. "Awk!" it exclaimed, spying them. Then it headed directly for the mountain's cone.

"We had better hurry," Trent said mildly.

They hurried. The skeleton platform clattered along the ridge, and the slowmud kept the pace. The ridge seemed to lead toward the crack in the cone that Metria had pointed out, but it turned away at the last moment. They were stuck at the end of a long island, with molten rock flowing between them and the cone. There was a crevice that might be used as a path up the side of the cone, but they couldn't reach it.

Mount Pin-A-Tuba got the word. The cone rumbled. Then a torrent of ash spewed out the top. It was trying to catch them with its ash, but they were too close. The worst of the ash and hot stones were flying too far out.

Gloha could fly across, though she feared for her wings in the moderate rain of hot ash. But none of the others could. "Transform me into a roc bird. I'll carry you across."

"No. The volcano could orient on a target of that size, and drop fireballs on your wings. We need to stay small."

"I can help," Marrow's head said from the platform. "Kick me into a ladder. Then cross on me."

"Good notion. But how will I stand on this ridge without your support?"

The slowmud blew a white bubble. Then it slid up until its muddy snout crossed the razor edge. The mud caked up on either side of the ridge, dulling the edge.

"Thank you," Trent said. He got off the platform carefully and sat astride the ridge, his midsection protected by the hard rounded mud. Gloha hovered nervously near.

Then Trent hauled the bone platform up, held it over his right foot, and gave it a good kick. It flew apart, and formed into a double line of bones, connected by crossbones. In fact it was a rope ladder without rope.

There was a skeletal hand at each end. Trent lifted the bundled ladder and put it on the end of the ridge. The fingers felt around the rock until they found good fingerholds, and the hand clenched tightly. Then Trent held the other end up for Gloha. She took the bone-hand and flew across to the base of the cone. The bone rope strung out behind her. It was heavy, but for this short hop she could handle it. She landed on the crevice and bent down to set the hand there. The fingers got a good grip, and the bone ladder drew itself tight.

The slowmud slid up onto the ladder and started across. Progress was slow because there wasn't much surface for the mud to cling to, but it was getting there, and bringing Graeboe along.

Mount Pin-A-Tuba realized what was happening. He sounded an enraged honk. "Oompah!" So much ash shot out of the cone, so fast and high, that it didn't come down; it stayed up in the high air and cooled Xanth a degree. But he couldn't stop the crossing.

Veleno and Graeboe made it across. Then Trent started. He went on hands and knees, gripping the rungs of the ladder as if he were climbing.

But now Cumulo Fracto Nimbus, the evil storm cloud, came to the volcano's rescue. He huffed and puffed, trying to blow the man down. When that didn't work, he formed a terrible funnel. The funnel seemed to be sucking up everything it touched, and it had a lot of power. Trouble indeed!

Trent saw it. "Metria!" he called.

The demoness appeared. "You realize that my appearance here will just draw Pin-A-Tuba's attention to—" She saw the funnel. "Point taken. I'll handle this." She changed into the biggest stink horn Gloha had ever seen; it fairly festered with contained stench.

The funnel swept in, casting somewhat blindly about for the man on the ladder. The screaming sound of the winds around it drowned out almost all else. The stink horn moved to intercept the mouth of the funnel. In a quarter of a moment the horn was sucked in and up.

There was a pause. Then the funnel exploded with the foul-smelling noise typical of stink horns. "BBBRRRRRRUMMPPPOOPOOH!" The noise dissipated into a miasmic fog that saturated the region. It was all Gloha could do to keep from choking as the stench reached them. The demoness had certainly found the way to get rid of the evil cloud's mouth!

Not only that. Fracto himself had been so disrupted by the taste of the fetor weed that he was unable to continue raining. His fragments drifted away, and a beam of sunshine ventured down, though it wrinkled its rays at the lingering reek. Even the molten lava below was revolted; it blistered and solidified. Nobody could stand a stink horn.

The volcano continued to erupt impotently. Trent completed his crossing, then hauled in the ladder after him. They were all on the crevice-path now, and not far from their destination. To keep them safe, Gloha flew up with Marrow's ladder end and helped him catch hold higher on the path. Then the others used the ladder as a guardrail so they weren't in danger of falling off the steep slope.

But now the mountain used its last weapon. High above them black goo issued from a fissure. It slid slowly down the cone toward them.

Gloha, alarmed, flew up to investigate. But Marrow's skull, which was in the middle of the bone ladder, called out a warning. "That may be poison!"

She halted just outside its range. She caught the barest whiff: the same stuff they had encountered at the Magic Dust Village. This was the worst menace yet!

She flew back down. "We can't handle that. We must flee before it reaches us."

"I think not," Trent said.

"But it will kill us all except Marrow and Metria, and they aren't even a couple."

"It won't kill the trans-plant, because that's one of the mountain's precious possessions. If we join the plant, we should be safe."

Could it be? Gloha wasn't sure just how logical the volcano might be. It might wipe out the plant to be sure of getting the intruders. But she realized that Graeboe would die if they retreated now. So they had to gamble on the plant, perhaps in more than one respect.

"Let's hurry," she said.

Again they hurried, working their way up as the poison blob worked its way down. The first nauseating whiffs of gas drifted down, making them cough. Gloha worried about Graeboe; any little thing could wipe him out, and this wasn't little.

But as they got closer to the opening in the cone that the crevice was leading to, the terrible odor faded. Gloha looked up. The deadly glob was detouring, sliding away from the cave. Trent was right: the mountain wouldn't destroy its treasure.

They came into the open grotto. There in the recess grew the trans-plant, exactly as it had been described. It hardly looked unusual, but her excitement made it almost seem to glow.

"Now let's get this operation done," Trent said briskly, "before the mountain thinks of some other device to balk us."

Veleno carried Graeboe to one side of the plant. Marrow Bones resumed his regular form and went to the other side. Trent set the bloodroot sprig down between them.

Gloha thought that there would be some procedure or invocation, but the plant simply wrapped tendrils around Marrow's left leg bone, and others around Graeboe's right arm, while still others picked up the bloodroot. Then it lifted needle stickers, drilled one into the bone, and the other into one of the elf's veins. Gloha winced, watching, but knew better than to protest.

It took longer to get into the skeleton's hard bone than into the elf's soft arm. But the plant did another thing. It brought a large yellow flower around until it was leaning over Graeboe's body. It looked like a sunflower, but of course couldn't be, because this wasn't the right type of plant.

There was a glow from the flower. It bathed Graeboe. He writhed, but did not seem to be in actual pain. His flesh did not change, but Gloha was sure that something significant was happening.

"My understanding is limited," Trent said. "But I think that the patient's defective marrow has to be killed, so that the new marrow can takes its place. That must be the radiation that accomplishes that. Graeboe will die very soon if the transplant is not accomplished. The marrow of the donor is liquefied and mixed with the blood of the bloodroot, and that mix is put into the body of the recipient, and finds its own way into the bone. Something like that. We simply have to trust that the process is effective."

"Oh, I hope it is!" Gloha breathed. She couldn't bear to watch any more, so she turned her gaze outward. And froze.

A squadron of vulgars was flying toward the cave. They would be able to come right in and attack the party.

Trent followed her gaze. "We shall have to defend ourselves," he said mildly. "I think I shall this time have to transform you, Gloha."

She realized that he had declined to do so on the way in because she hadn't yet done the thing required to give Graeboe the will to live: declaring her love for him. She had had to remain in her natural form until then, so that he would be assured it was her. But now she was free to defend the group. "Yes, transform me," she agreed.

"Be careful to look at none of us," he said. "Never turn your gaze into the cave."

"Why not?"

But even as he spoke, he was transforming her. She found herself in a lizard body. A lizard? What good would this do? She almost turned to direct a questioning glance at him, but caught herself. So instead she gazed out at the swiftly approaching dirty birds.

The first bird met her gaze—and abruptly plummeted from the sky. What had happened?

The second looked at her—and dropped out too.

Then she realized what it was. Trent had transformed her into a basilisk! Her very gaze could kill.

She glared around, and vulgars dropped like burning stones. Soon none were left. She was more deadly than a fire-breathing dragon.

Suddenly she was herself again. "A little of that goes a long way," Trent remarked.

Now it was safe to look at the others. Nervous in retrospect about the damage she could have done, she was relieved.

More time must have passed than she had realized. The trans-plant was withdrawing its needles. She went to Graeboe. "How do you feel?" she asked anxiously.

He looked surprised. "Better. I feel the new marrow taking hold, revitalizing my blood. I think it will be a while before I am completely restored, but surely it is happening." He paused, glancing at the skeleton. "There is something I must do now. Help me up."

She put her arm around his shoulders and helped him stand. He did seem stronger, though still weak. Some magic was not instantaneous, but that did not lessen its value. He walked unsteadily across to Marrow. "You have given me life. Take half my soul." He extended his hand.

The skeleton reached down to clasp the flesh-hand in his bone-hand. "Now I will accept it," he said.

The hands touched. There was a glow. Gloha, in contact with Graeboe, felt an eerie thinning or separation, not painful, just uneasy. It was his soul fissioning.

Then their hands separated. Graeboe tottered, weakened again, and Gloha quickly supported him. Marrow fell back against the wall. "Oh!" he said in wonder.

Metria appeared. "Now you know what I feel like."

"I believe I do," Marrow said. "It is wonderful yet frightening."

"Exactly," the demoness agreed. She stepped in to kiss him on the fleshless mouth. "But you do get used to it, gradually. Especially if you have a friend."

"He has friends," Gloha said. Graeboe nodded agreement.

Trent turned to the slowmud. "You have been most helpful," he said. "I think that any inconvenience you may have caused us has been ameliorated." Then Veleno was standing in his natural form.

"Yes!" Gloha agreed. "You risked your life to bring Graeboe here. I shall always be grateful." And she emulated Metria, flying up to plant a kiss on his surprised face.

"Now I think we had better get out of here before Pin-A-Tuba fields another ploy to dispatch us," Trent said. He went to the edge of the grotto and looked down. "I think we can't depart the way we came; the poison goo is all around."

"You could change me to a roc bird," Gloha said. "So I can carry the rest of you out."

"No, the volcano is alert for that. He's putting out hot rocks to set fire to feathers."

Gloha looked out. Pin-A-Tuba was sending a barrage of burning ashes into the air, furious that the party had won its way to the trans-plant. Lava and poison were strewn all across the ground. Their prospects for escape did look bleak.

Graeboe joined her. "I think I could make it out," he said. "In my natural form, invisible. I could step on the clean ridges, and be away before the volcano knows what is happening."

"Then by all means go," Gloha said. "The rest of us will follow when we are able."

"No. If I am able to do it, then we all are; I will carry you. You should be invisible too, if I curl my fingers around you."

"But you aren't invisible any more," Marrow reminded him. "And you are weakened by losing half your soul. I should not have taken it yet."

"I should be invisible when healthy. I am weak now, but healthy. And if I carry you, my soul will be reunited for that time. It might be a harrowing ride for you, but I believe I could do it. My natural body is familiar to me, and I should be able to keep my balance and step well."

Gloha looked at Trent. "Do you think—?"

The Magician nodded. "If he believes he can do it, he probably can. But it would be better to wait for him to recover more of his strength."

"I think not," Marrow said. "I believe I hear the scritching of nickelpedes."

"Nickelpedes!" Gloha cried in horror. "We can't stay here if they're coming. There'll be too many for Trent to transform, and they'll gouge out nickel-sized chunks of our flesh."

"Yes. I shall try to toss out as many as I can, but I fear a swarm."

Indeed, now they all could hear the scritching coming from deep inside the cave. As the mountain's creatures, the nickelpedes would not bother the trans-plant, but they would soon strip the flesh from any fleshly creatures they could get at. Gloha could become a basilisk again, but wouldn't be very effective against the antennae of creatures who were more interested in chomping than in looking. Pin-A-Tuba had found something they could not readily nullify.

Graeboe stood at the brink of the cave and extended his right hand toward Gloha. "All of you take hold of my fingers," he said. "Then transform me, Magician. I will try to hold you gently."

The offer would have been laughable if they had not understood what was about to happen, because the elf had the smallest hands of any of them. Gloha extended her hand to touch his tiny little finger; Marrow touched his next finger, Veleno his middle finger, Metria his forefinger, and Trent his thumb.

Suddenly Graeboe was gone. But the hand was there, incomparably larger—and invisible. Only their touches on the massive fingers gave them assurance.

Immediately they were scrambling up. Gloha had no trouble; she spread her wings and half flew to the top of the finger she was on. Marrow wrapped his skeletal arms around his finger. But Veleno and Trent were having problems. The nickelpedes were bursting into view, a swarming tide of them, pincers leading.

Metria fogged out. She reappeared behind Veleno in the form of an ogress. "Get up there, my love," she said, boosting him head over heels into the hand. Gloha saw him roll across the invisible surface and come to rest, bemused. "And you, Magician," she added, heaving Trent up similarly. Then she puffed into smoke just as the first nickelpede snapped at her feet.

The hand closed, carefully. They all tumbled together in the palm, held by loosely clenching fingers.

The hand lifted. Gloha righted herself and peered out between or through the invisible fingers. They were swinging way up through the air and the burning ashes, but they were protected by the giant's flesh.

Now the giant was tramping away from the mountain. Gloha saw a ridge squish flat, and a cleft fill in as if pressed by a phenomenal weight. Their speed was remarkable, for Graeboe was taking giant steps and not dawdling.

There was a sound behind: "OOMPAH!" Mount Pin-A-Tuba was venting his absolute rage at their escape. Such a torrent of material shot out of his cone that it was likely to cool Xanth another degree before it settled out. There were fiery boulders too, arcing down to fall all around them. But they were already getting safely out of range. They had made it!

The pace slowed. The giant stopped at a nice glade and brought his hand down so they could dismount. Then Trent faced the region where Graeboe stood. "What form would you like to assume now?" he called.

"I—" the giant's voice came. "I'm falling!"

Trent leaped for the hand. Then a naked winged goblin man was there, falling forward. Trent caught him. Had he not made the transformation, the giant might have fallen on the rest of them.

"Graeboe!" Gloha cried. "What's the matter?"

Then she saw for herself. His body was covered with terrible burns. He had been shielding them from that barrage, taking the burns without complaint. But he had been weak from his recent malady, and this had added intolerably to his burden.

Gloha whipped out her handkerchief. It had a bit of healing elixir in it. She needed all of it now. She dabbed it on Graeboe's burns and blisters, and they healed. When she ran out of dabs of elixir, she kissed the spots instead, and this seemed to work almost as well. "Oh my darling," she breathed as she worked. "You never said! You were getting all burned, protecting us—"

Trent had been holding Graeboe up, but Gloha's ministrations were rapidly restoring him, so Trent moved clear. Suddenly she realized that the ex-giant was not wearing anything. She moved to shield him from embarrassment— and suddenly was in his arms. They kissed.

After her head stopped spinning, Gloha drew back. "Of course you can be a giant if you really prefer. I never sought to—"

"I am getting healthier by the moment," Graeboe said. "Either get me some clothing, or take off yours."

The others laughed. Metria appeared with some clothing she had scrounged from somewhere. Soon Graeboe was decent.

But Gloha's trace of guilt remained. "You never asked me to become a giantess for you. I don't think it's right to make you change for me. So if you have any second or third thoughts—"

"Hold the tableau," the demoness said, and vanished.

"What's she up to?" Trent asked.

"Something nice, I'm sure," Veleno said. "She's a wonderful woman."

Gloha decided not to debate that, so she changed the subject. "I think I know what Graeboe and I will be doing," she said. "Also Veleno and Metria. Marrow will go home with his half soul to his family and share it with them. So all our quests have been accomplished. But what of you, Magician Trent? Are you going to fade out now?"

Trent looked thoughtful. "I must say I had forgotten how exhilarating youthful adventure could be. I believe I'll keep my youth for a while longer, and tell my wife to try it too. I think it is not yet time to fade out."

"I'm glad to hear that," Gloha said. She was understating the case, but didn't think it appropriate to say more.

Then the demoness reappeared. She handed Graeboe a mirror.

"What's this for?" he asked.

"It's a magic mirror the goblins liberated from a storehouse by Miracle Lake," Metria explained with a hint of the old mischief. "They said you should have it as a wedding present, and I think it's ideal. It will tell you anything your beloved seeks to hide. She'll have no secrets from you. You won't even need to ask her; just ask the mirror. Any private feelings, any doubts, any misgivings will be mercilessly revealed."

Graeboe nodded, unconcerned. "It's for you, my love," he said, handing it to Gloha. "Have a harpy time."

Author's Note

I don't do routine Author's Notes; nevertheless, this one is routine, so those who aren't interested in lists of credits might as well skip to the last page.

Gloha's quest for a husband, and the talent of Surprise, were suggested by Jeremy Brinkman. Lock Ness was from Michael Cowan. The Sin Tax was defined by Susan Bates. The Sock Her plant was hit by Patrick Geary. Joseph Slezak Washed Her, Dried Her, and Boxed Her. The Glyph's original home was with Sharon Stegemeyer. Susanna Alvarez figured out that the Gorgon's face could be made invisible with a face mask illusion. Chris Anthony (no known relation to me) provided the Light and Heavy Bulbs, Com Pewter's Mouse, and the Shooting Star. Swiftmud flowed from the Southwest Florida Water Management District. Robert Christensen got the Ant Honey. Whose Fault was it? Lee Mendham's fault. Cynthia Carman daydreamed Cynthia Centaur's history when she was sick; Mare Imbri really gets around. The Stare-way was suggested years ago—and I can't remember the originator's name. Also belated credit to another suggestor of contact lenses for Gwenny Goblin, whom I should have credited before: Deana Livingston. The Three Mermaids were drawn by Julie Brady on one of the most decorative envelopes I have received, with their fascinating fronts on the front and their beautiful backs on the back, so I named them and put them into the story. Braille, who transcribes documents, was made by Rich Cormier. Jana's love for the centaur was described by Dana Bates, who is no known relation to Dana Demoness; how could she be, since the demoness is really Dara? The Draw Well was by Michael Portney. Alyson Dewsnap walked the Steppes. Misty Malmstrom walked the Board Walk. Robert Smith named Graeboe. Missy DeAngelis was the Spring Chicken. The Ant puns were by Dan the Man Watson, except for the AccountAnt by Mark E. Stringer. Roger Brannon turned objects to other objects. Barbara Hay Hummel described Gloha's harpy past and Veleno's past; we remember her from the days of Rose of Roogna and Okra Ogress. Panther Ginnett had the Death puns. Cathy Hudson presented Richard C. White, who longed for Xanth and finally reached it. There's more of a story there than I care to tell.

Janet Hines was mentioned in the Note for *Demons Don't Dream*, when she had an iris named after her. She had been paralyzed and blinded by an unkind ailment, but still liked Xanth. She died while I was writing this novel. So I took her to Xanth, as I did with our dog Bubbles in the last novel, and gave her back her motion and her sight, so she could have a better life there among her irises. I don't undertake to do this for other readers, but it seemed appropriate in this case.

Amanda Dickason drew the Girlfon. Julia Lalor described the Nymphomaniac. Stephanie Erb, who gave Kim the talent of erasure in the last novel, this time came up with the Notar Republic and the Parrot Legal. The Not-Holes were from L. Charles Gattuso. Shirwyn Dalgliesh suggested the consequence when Metria married. Jeff Snavely donated Marrow's marrow. Bridget Colvin crafted the Miracle mirror-barnacles. Dakota Hain tasted the Dessert desert, and E. Jeremy Parish ate the Boo-Meringue Pie. Matthew Brennan was the Hood. Jeffrey Ku drilled the Dentis Tree, and Brad Bell uttered the Sar-chasm.

There was half a slew of puns and suggestions left over, some going back to prior novels they weren't used in. My apologies to those folk who have been waiting forever minus a moment; I'll try to catch up on them in the next novel, *Geis of the Gargoyle*. The story lines take their devious turns, and avoid some notions I expect to use. There are a lot of puns, but the welfare of the story always comes first. (That ugly creature who just exploded with laughter is a critic; he thinks this is the first funny statement in the book.)

Jenny Elf did not appear in this novel—she's entitled to some time off, you know—but her namesake in Mundania continues to improve. But there can be snags. For example, when she was at Cumbersome Horsepital (no, it's not really called that; I got the name from *Letters to Jenny*, which has more of our relationship) to sharpen her computer skills, she was outside when another patient had a seizure. Jenny's attendant hurried to help, forgetting that Jenny's wheelchair was on a slope. Jenny, strapped in, went rolling off the path and over a bank and cracked her head on the ground. Several stitches, but no internal damage. Her main complaint was when they hauled her off for treatment

without her makeup. She was sweet sixteen at the time, and makeup is important. Who says life in a wheelchair is dull?

My only adventure in this period was when I attended MagiCon, the World
Science Fiction Convention in Orlando, Florida. I wasn't going to go, but my
wife said she was tired of the dull home routine, so we went. My daughters
were there, of course; they've been Con freaks since I made the mistake of taking them to NecronomiCon in Tampa a decade before, and now have attended
more Cons than I have. I've never been to a World Con before. My attendance
was unannounced; I had given no commitments in advance, because I wanted
to do what I wanted to do, instead of what I was programmed to do, for once.
It was interesting, and I met a number of figures in the field, including one who
said I'd called him a Nazi. What bothered me was that he seemed to believe his
charge, and insisted on it in the presence of two publishers. I have been
charged with many things over the years, and I don't mean just bad writing,
but this was the first time anyone had the nerve to do it to my face with witnesses. So I am pursing it as a matter of slander, and we'll see. All my other
contacts were positive. My autographing session Sunday morning took almost
an hour and a half; the word had leaked out and my fans were appearing. Barbara Hambly called hello from the next autographing table, and I got to meet
Hal Clement, whose *Needle* and *Mission of Gravity* were part of my formative
years in the genre. I regret that I didn't get to meet the Guest of Honor, Jack
Vance, whom I regard as the finest fantasy writer extant. But that's the way of
big conventions: there are so many things happening all at once that the things
you want to do are squeezed out by the incidentals. So it was fun, once, but I
won't rush to do it again. We picked up literature on the 1995 WorldCon in
Glasgow, Scotland; we might attend that. I was born in England some time
ago, but have never been back; it's about time.

Thus my quiet life in the months of AwGhost, SapTimber, and OctOgre
1992.